However peaceably your Colonies have submitted to your Government, shewn their Affection to your Interest, and patiently borne their Grievances, you are to *suppose* them always inclined to revolt, and treat them accordingly.

> (from Benjamin Franklin: "Rules by Which a Great Empire May Be Reduced to a Small One," page 13)

I long to hear that you have declared an independancy—and by the way in the new Code of Laws which I suppose it will be necessary for you to make I desire you would Remember the Ladies, and be more generous and favourable to them than your ancestors. Do not put such unlimited power into the hands of the Husbands. Remember all Men would be tyrants if they could.

> (from a letter from Abigail Adams to John Adams, March 31, 1776, page 68)

We hold these truths to be self evident: that all men are created equal; that they are endowed by their creator with [certain] <u>inherent and</u> inalienable rights; that among these are life, liberty & the pursuit of happiness: that to secure these rights, governments are instituted among men, deriving their just powers from the consent of the governed.

> (from a draft of the Declaration of Independence, by Thomas Jefferson, page 124)

May the choicest of heaven's favours, both here and hereafter, attend those who, under the devine auspices, have secured innumerable blessings for others; with these wishes, and this benediction, the Commander in Chief is about to retire from Service. The Curtain of seperation will soon be drawn, and the military scene to him will be closed for ever.

> (from George Washington, "Farewell Address to the Armies of the United States," page 259)

Nor should our assembly be deluded by the integrity of their own purposes, and conclude that these unlimited powers will never be abused, because themselves are not disposed to abuse them. They should look forward to a time, and that not a distant one, when a corruption in this, as in the country from which we derive our origin, will have seized the heads of government.

(from Thomas Jefferson, *Notes on the State of Virginia*, page 267)

Whilst we assert for ourselves a freedom to embrace, to profess, and observe the religion which we believe to be of divine origin, we cannot deny an equal freedom to those, whose minds have not yet yielded to the evidence which has convinced us.

(from James Madison, "A Memorial and Remonstrance against Religious Assessments," page 296)

I can consent to no government, which, in my opinion, is not calculated equally to preserve the rights of all orders of men in the community.

(from *Letters from the Federal Farmer*, page 435)

But what is government itself, but the greatest of all reflections on human nature? If men were angels, no government would be necessary. If angels were to govern men, neither external nor internal controls on government would be necessary. In framing a government which is to be administered by men over men, the great difficulty lies in this: you must first enable the government to control the governed; and in the next place oblige it to control itself.

(from *The Federalist* No. 51, page 525)

I will candidly acknowledge, that, over and above all these considerations, I do conceive that the Constitution may be amended; that is to say, if all power is subject to abuse, that then it is possible the abuse of the powers of the General Government may be guarded against in a more secure manner than is now done.

(from James Madison's speech to the House of Representatives, June 8, 1789, page 615)

The powers not delegated to the United States by the Constitution, nor prohibited by it to the States, are reserved to the States respectively, or to the people.

(from a draft of amendments to the Constitution, page 637)

FOUNDING AMERICA

DOCUMENTS FROM THE REVOLUTION TO THE BILL OF RIGHTS

Edited, with an Introduction and Notes by Jack N. Rakove

George Stade
Consulting Editorial Director

BARNES & NOBLE CLASSICS
NEW YORK

JB

BARNES & NOBLE CLASSICS

NEW YORK

Published by Barnes & Noble Books
122 Fifth Avenue
New York, NY 10011

www.barnesandnoble.com/classics

Published in 2006 by Barnes & Noble Classics with new Introductions, Timeline, Notes, and For Further Reading.

General Introduction, Header Introductions, Notes,
and For Further Reading
Copyright © 2006 by Jack N. Rakove.

Founding America: A Timeline
Copyright © 2006 by Barnes & Noble, Inc.

Founding America:
Documents from the Revolution to the Bill of Rights
ISBN-13: 978-1-59308-230-7
ISBN-10: 1-59308-230-4
LC Control Number 2005935854

Produced and published in conjunction with:
Fine Creative Media, Inc.
322 Eighth Avenue
New York, NY 10001

Michael J. Fine, President and Publisher

Printed in the United States of America

QM

5 7 9 10 8 6

Table of Contents

Founding America:
A Timeline

1765   On March 22, the British Parliament adopts the Stamp Act, imposing on the American colonies a tax on legal documents, newspapers, and playing cards. Colonists respond by pressuring the men appointed to distribute the stamps to resign their commissions, boycotting British goods, and convening an intercolonial Congress to state the grounds for American opposition.

1766   In response to colonial protests and petitions from British merchants, Parliament repeals the Stamp Act on March 18, but concurrently adopts a Declaratory Act stating that it retains the right to enact laws binding the colonists "in all cases whatsoever."

1767   In June and July, Charles Townshend, Britain's Chancellor of the Exchequer, introduces a new bill to tax the importation into America of such goods as lead, paper, glass, and tea. American opposition to the Townshend duties is led by John Dickinson's *Letters from a Pennsylvania Farmer.*

1769   In continued protests against the Townshend duties, colonists organize another boycott of British imports.

1770   Parliament repeals all the Townshend duties except the tax on tea.

1772   Samuel Adams organizes the Boston Committee of Correspondence, which mounts a campaign protesting a British plan to give Massachusetts Governor Thomas Hutchinson and other officials a royal salary.

1773   In January, Hutchinson opens the Massachusetts legislature with a speech explaining why Americans should recognize the supremacy of Parliament. On September 11, Benjamin Franklin publishes *Rules Whereby a Great Empire May Be Reduced to a Small One.* Parliament adopts the Tea Act, giving the near-bankrupt East India Company a monopoly on the sale of tea in America. On December 16, a group of sixty radicals stage the Boston Tea Party in Boston Harbor; dressed as Mohawk Indians, they board three ships—the *Dartmouth*, the *Eleanor*, and the *Beaver*—and destroy 342 crates of East India Company British tea.

1774   In response to the Boston Tea Party, Parliament passes a set of laws known as the Intolerable (or Coercive) Acts. In July, Thomas Jefferson writes *A Summary View of the Rights of British America*. With the Declaration and Resolves, adopted on October 14, the First Continental Congress unanimously agrees that the British Parliament has no right to impose taxes or other laws on unrepresented colonists. The Association, adopted on October 20, provides for the election of popular committees of inspection to enforce the proposed commercial boycott of British goods.

1775   On April 19, military conflict begins with skirmishes at Lexington and Concord, Massachusetts. On July 3, George Washington takes command of the newly formed Continental Army outside Boston. In July, Benjamin Franklin proposes a Plan of Confederation to the Second Continental Congress.

1776   On January 10, Thomas Paine publishes *Common Sense* as an anonymous fifty-page pamphlet denouncing the British monarch and monarchy in general. Adam Smith publishes *The Wealth of Nations*. In April, John Adams publishes *Thoughts on Government*. George Mason drafts Virginia's Declaration of Rights; it is published on June 12. On July 4, members of the Second Continental Congress approve the Declaration of Independence. On December 26, troops led by General George Washington are victorious at the Battle of Trenton, a turning point for American military enlistment and morale after earlier defeats in Long Island and Manhattan had made the American cause seem doomed. Emanuel Leutze's iconic painting *Washington Crossing the Delaware* (1851) was inspired by the advance of the American forces over the Delaware River from Pennsylvania to New Jersey.

1777   While one British army under General William Howe occupies Philadelphia, another under General John Burgoyne surrenders to American troops at Saratoga, New York. On

November 15, the Continental Congress formally endorses the Articles of Confederation, which provide a system of national governance for the thirteen American states.

1778   In February, the French monarchy of Louis XVI signs a treaty of alliance with the United States.

1780   New York cedes its western land claims to Congress, initiating a process that will lead by 1784 to the creation of a national domain above the Ohio River.

1781   On March 1, the Articles of Confederation take effect after Maryland becomes the thirteenth state to ratify. On October 19, British General Charles Cornwallis surrenders to General Washington, ending major military conflict.

1782   Superintendent of Finance Robert Morris presents Congress with a comprehensive Report on Public Credit, initiating a debate over financial policy that lasts into the spring of 1783.

1783   The Treaty of Paris, negotiated by John Jay, Benjamin Franklin, and John Adams and signed in April, formally ends the Revolutionary War. On November 2, Washington delivers his farewell to the Armies of the United States.

1785   On June 20, Madison publishes *Memorial and Remonstrance against Religious Assessments*.

1786   In September, delegates from five states attend the Annapolis Convention, called by Virginia to consider ways to grant commercial powers to Congress. The delegates instead propose that a second convention be called for May to consider the general defects of the Confederation.

1787   In February, Congress adopts a resolution approving the general convention. Thomas Jefferson publishes his *Notes on the State of Virginia* the same month. In May, the Constitutional Convention meets in Philadelphia, with every state but Rhode Island eventually attending. Instead of amending the Articles, the delegates draft a new document, the Constitution of the United States, which is signed on September 17 and sent to the states for ratification. In October, Melancton Smith publishes *Letters from the Federal Farmer*. Amid widespread anxiety that the proposed government insufficiently protects individual liberty, the first *Federalist* paper, written by Alexander Hamilton, is published in New York on October 27; it appears under the pseudonym "Publius," a pen name

Hamilton shares with James Madison and John Jay, the other two authors of what will be, in all, eighty-five essays that promote ratification of the Constitution. In December, Delaware, Pennsylvania, and New Jersey ratify the Constitution.

1788   In January, Georgia and Connecticut ratify the Constitution. Massachusetts, Maryland, South Carolina, and New Hampshire follow, making the nine states required for the new government to take effect. Virginia and New York soon approve. Two other states, Rhode Island and North Carolina, reject the Constitution.

1789   On March 4, the U.S. Constitution takes effect, and the first Congress of the United States convenes. On April 1, the House achieves quorum and elects Frederick Muhlenberg the first House Speaker; on April 6, the Senate reaches quorum and chooses John Langdon as the first Senate President (*pro tempore*). On April 30, President George Washington delivers his first inaugural address. On June 8, James Madison, the representative from Virginia, proposes a set of amendments to the Constitution. North Carolina ratifies the Constitution. Washington appoints John Jay the first chief justice of the Supreme Court. Hamilton is appointed secretary of the Treasury. On July 14, the French Revolution begins with the storming of the Bastille in Paris.

1790   After returning to America from his service as minister to France, Thomas Jefferson accepts appointment as the first Secretary of State.

1791   In England, Thomas Paine publishes the first part of *Rights of Man*, in part a response to Edmund Burke's *Reflections on the Revolution in France* (1790). On December 15, the Bill of Rights, the name given to the first ten amendments to the U.S. Constitution, is ratified.

General Introduction

A decade after signing the Declaration of Independence, the Philadelphia physician Benjamin Rush made an important observation that historians are fond of citing. "There is nothing more common than to confound the terms of *the American revolution* with those of *the late American war*," Rush wrote in 1786. "The American war is over: but this is far from being the case with the American revolution. On the contrary, nothing but the first act of the great drama is closed" (pp. 308–309).

As Rush recognized, the events he consciously called a revolution had two main elements. The first, which had ended successfully only three years earlier, was to secure political independence from Great Britain. That story in turn hinged on two great questions. First, how did the colonists move from resistance to revolution, from seeking to maintain their rights within the British Empire to renouncing its authority entirely? Second, once the last hopes for reconciliation had evaporated, how did the Americans prevail in a long and difficult military struggle against the greatest power in the eighteenth-century Atlantic world?

But winning independence, Rush also recognized, was only the first part of a greater story. In his mind, the Revolution was more than a struggle for independence and home rule. It had also become a movement to establish new forms of government, modeled on republican principles that made the people the only proper source of political authority. Rush devoted the remainder of his essay to discussing how this new form of government could be "perfected." Within a year, this effort culminated in the form of the federal Constitution drafted at Philadelphia in the summer of 1787, a Constitution whose first stated purpose was "to form a more perfect union."

These two great themes—the achievement of independence and the "perfection" of republican government—are the subject of the documents collected in this volume. These documents cannot capture the experience of the Revolution in its totality. No single volume, however carefully edited, could illustrate the diversity of experience and the range of issues that were felt and voiced during the quarter century of history that separates the beginning of the crisis with Britain in the mid-1760s from the adoption of the Constitution in the late 1780s.

When Benjamin Rush spoke of the Revolutionary War, he meant both the movement that led to independence and the military struggle that secured it. Defined in this way, the Revolution really began in the mid-1760s, when the colonists first argued that Parliament had no authority to impose taxes or other laws on a people who sent no representatives of their own to distant London. In the crises over the Stamp Act (1765–1766) and the Townshend duties (1767–1770), Americans and Britons defined and sharpened their arguments about the nature of the British Empire and the rights and duties of its American colonies.

By 1773 these rival theories had exposed a deep fault line between the dominant political views in each country. Americans insisted that they could be governed only by laws to which they had directly consented, through the votes of their freely elected representatives in their own separate legislative assemblies. The British position rested on different assumptions. Since the Glorious Revolution of 1688, Parliament had been recognized as the sovereign source of law within Britain. If Americans were part of that realm, as they professed to be, then they were ultimately subject to Parliament, even if no American members sat in the House of Commons.

Even in 1773, however, no one in America was actively promoting the idea of national independence. Nor, of course, was anyone in Britain intent on forcing the colonies into a state of rebellion. On both sides of the Atlantic, political leaders of goodwill hoped the controversies of the late 1760s would soon be forgotten, and the underlying harmony of the empire restored. What happened instead was that a crisis no one had foreseen erupted in the fall of 1773 and then spun out of control in the spring and summer of 1774.

Its immediate cause was Parliament's passage of a Tea Act, adopted to alleviate the financial woes of the East India Company by giving this powerful corporation a monopoly over the sale of tea in America. The colonists disliked the idea of a monopoly, but what disturbed them even more was that the Act retained the duty on imported tea that had been left in place in 1770, when colonial protests finally persuaded the British government to repeal the duties on other imports levied in the Townshend Act of 1767. Once again, colonists protested. In most ports, royal officials prudently allowed the tea ships to return to Britain, their cargoes unloaded. In Boston, however, Governor Thomas Hutchinson insisted on enforcing the letter of the law, and refused to grant the three ships the necessary clearances. Rather than allow the tea to be landed and the duties paid, the townsmen held their own Tea Party on the evening of December 16, 1773. Some 342 chests of tea, valued at £9000, were soon brewing in Boston Harbor.

In London, the following winter was given over to concocting a different, more potent brew of measures. In response to the news from Boston, the government of Lord North, firmly backed by King George III, asked Parliament to approve a set of acts to punish Boston and the province of Massachusetts for their defiance of the empire. These measures, known as the Coercive or Intolerable Acts, had several goals. The first, the Boston Port Act, closed the town harbor to commerce until full restitution was made for the destroyed tea. Next came the Massachusetts Government Act, altering the colony's royal charter of government in ways that would presumably strengthen the authority of the empire. In adopting these acts, the King, his ministers, and their loyal majority in Parliament had two further objectives. One was to isolate Massachusetts by showing the other colonies just how costly defiance of the empire could be. The other was to provide a conclusive demonstration of just how sovereign Parliament really was. A Parliament that could adopt these measures and see them enforced would indeed be America's sovereign.

Both calculations failed, and their failure converted American opposition to the claims of Parliament into a genuine revolution against the empire. Far from isolating Massachusetts, the Coercive Acts persuaded the other provinces to rally to its defense because it was only "suffering in the common cause" of securing American rights. At the First Continental Congress of September–October 1774, delegates from twelve colonies (only the frontier settlement of Georgia did not attend) adopted a common strategy of resistance and agreed upon the basic constitutional positions Americans would uphold. A Second Continental Congress met at Philadelphia in early May 1775. Three weeks earlier, violence had erupted in Massachusetts when its new royal governor, General Thomas Gage, sent soldiers to seize colonial arms and munitions stored in nearby Concord. Faced with the specter of civil war, the Second Congress did not flinch from converting the Massachusetts provisional army into a Continental Army under the command of George Washington, the colonies' best-known soldier. Nor were the delegates (now including representatives from Georgia) willing to modify the strong positions they had adopted the previous fall.

Even though a full year passed before Congress felt that Americans were ready for independence, the outbreak of war made that decision inevitable because neither Congress nor the British government was prepared to retreat from the positions each had adopted. Neither side had sought this result. The colonists had no cadre of revolutionary agitators seeking to foment crises or exploit British miscues in the cause of national liberation. Most Americans would have been content to remain subjects of the British Crown. And the British obviously had no reason to try to provoke Americans into acts of defiance as a pretext for cracking down on colonial rights. But on the key issue of Parliament's jurisdiction over America, the two countries found themselves in fundamental disagreement. Both had valid and potent arguments to make, and neither side could see how its fundamental concerns would be answered if its positions were not vindicated. Both found themselves increasingly suspicious of the other's motives—even though Americans repeatedly declared they sought nothing more than the restoration of rights, while spokesmen for the British position argued that it was only reasonable to require the colonists to contribute to the costs of the empire. Had the British government ever offered the colonists a bona fide opportunity to negotiate, or had Congress agreed to send a peace delegation to London, it is entirely possible that war could have been averted. But neither was prepared to take that initiative, and so the war came.

The military conflict that began in April 1775 finally ended eight years later, when the Treaty of Paris formally acknowledged the independence of the United States. The war placed an enormous strain on American resources. If the British had thought that Americans would simply break and run when faced with the disciplined formations of the royal army, the engagements at Concord and later at Bunker Hill quickly disabused them of that hope. In 1776 a massive British fleet brought 30,000 soldiers to New York. In a series of engagements, this force repeatedly outmaneuvered and pummeled Washington's army, first occupying New York City, then threatening to liberate New Jersey from patriot control. Only Washington's daring raids on Trenton and Princeton kept the American cause from collapsing.

The campaign of 1777 was arguably the turning point of the war. The strategic initiative belonged to Britain. While one British army, led by General John Burgoyne, was sent south from Canada, the forces based in New York under the command of General Sir William Howe and his brother, Admiral Lord Richard Howe, prepared to occupy Philadelphia, the American capital. But these campaigns were poorly coordinated, and both started late. While the Howes undertook a laborious movement by sea, sailing all the way up the Chesapeake Bay, Burgoyne's force was slogging through the New York wilderness to transfer its line of attack from Lake Champlain to the Hudson River. American forces commanded by Horatio Gates built up strength by drawing on the militia of densely populated New England. In October, Burgoyne, short on supplies, surrendered his army at Saratoga, while the Howes occupied Philadelphia, which had little strategic significance.

The news of Saratoga had its decisive impact in Paris, where a trio of American commissioners, led by Benjamin Franklin, had been attempting to negotiate an alliance with Britain's ancient enemy, France. In February 1778 the government of King Louis XVI was finally prepared to enter the war as America's ally. Hard pressed to supply its army across 3,000 miles of Atlantic Ocean, Britain now faced a graver strategic challenge.

The British responded with a significant change of strategy. Late in 1778, they shifted the theater of operations from the Middle Atlantic states to the South, first occupying Savannah, then preparing to carry the war into the Carolinas and Virginia. There were significant pockets of loyalist strength in this region. The British also knew that the presence of hundreds of thousands of African-American slaves made these states the soft underbelly of the American union.

Over the next three years, British forces carried the war northward, until Virginia became the major site of battle. Other British forces remained encamped in New York City, under Washington's watchful eye. The decisive development came in 1781, when a British army commanded by General Charles Cornwallis encamped on the peninsula between the York and James Rivers. Aware that a

French fleet was available to clamp off seaward access, Washington secured a promise that the ships of Admiral Rochambeau would descend on the Chesapeake, while he himself managed a skillful march of a Franco-American force southward from New York. Isolated and besieged at Yorktown, Cornwallis surrendered on October 19, 1781.

News of this defeat led to the fall of Lord North's government and the installation of a new ministry committed to ending the war and recognizing American independence. At Paris a peace commission of John Adams, John Jay, and Benjamin Franklin negotiated ably on behalf of American interests, securing favorable terms that granted the United States boundaries stretching westward to the Mississippi River. In April 1783 the definitive terms of the treaty were set.

So closed what Benjamin Rush later called "the first act of the great drama." To squeeze into one act all the scenes of military and political action required to secure independence would be a great understatement. But Rush was right to think that the meaning of the Revolution could not be limited to the struggle for independence alone. What made it more than a war of national liberation, what made it truly revolutionary, was the common belief that Americans had been granted an opportunity few other peoples had known, and that none had managed to fulfill: in the words of John Adams, "to form and establish the wisest and happiest government that human wisdom can contrive" (p. 86). Such governments, Adams further observed, had to be "republican" in form and principle. They had to draw their authority from the people, yet at the same time be so balanced as to prevent the people from misusing their power.

This part of the drama took the form of an experiment that accompanied the movement toward independence in 1776. During the preceding two years, the authority of the legal governments in most of the colonies had collapsed, because governors appointed by the Crown could not collaborate in organizing defiance to its rule. Real power flowed instead to the network of committees, conventions, and congresses that had first formed in 1774 to carry out the urgent work of resistance and to implement the program of Congress. This apparatus had grown more potent with the outbreak of civil war in April 1775.

With each passing month, however, Americans grew more nervous about the absence of legal government. With courts closed in most colonies, many normal operations of government ceased. By early 1776 individual colonies were petitioning Congress to be allowed to resume legal government. Congress first granted this permission on a case-by-case basis. Then, in May 1776, it adopted a blanket resolution authorizing new governments to be created everywhere.

Americans could not simply restore their prior colonial governments. Except in Rhode Island and Connecticut (the two colonies that appointed all of their officials), executive and judicial officeholders served under the authority of either the Crown or the proprietary families (the Penns in Pennsylvania and Delaware, the Calverts in Maryland) in whom the Crown had vested the right of government. Some new way had to be found to reconstitute executive and judicial power. Moreover, the colonists harbored an array of grievances and grudges against the distribution of power among the different parts of government under the old imperial regime. In the first enthusiastic blush of revolution, they were inclined to strengthen the authority of the most representative branch of government—the legislature—while weakening the executive. Given that wars ordinarily place a premium on the effective use of executive power, this might seem like a naive decision. But it was also a natural reaction to past grievances, when governors acting under instructions from London had often prevented colonial legislatures from pursuing the measures they favored.

Acting under these assumptions, the colonies began writing constitutions that made the legislature the dominant branch of government. If any check were needed upon government, it would come from the people themselves, relying on the practice of annual elections to control their representatives. This assumed that the people would be willing and able to carry out this duty—that they possessed the *virtue* (meaning commitment to the public good) that the citizens of a republic were expected to maintain.

By May 1777 most of the states had adopted new constitutions. In doing so, they also established a new definition of what a constitution was. In Britain, the word *constitution* was commonly used to describe the underlying traditions, conventions, and principles of government. In America, however, the word acquired a more precise meaning. A constitution was a document, adopted at a known historical moment, that explicitly established and empowered, and thereby potentially limited, the authority of a government. In

Britain, the leading principle of constitutional government was the legal supremacy of a sovereign Parliament. In America, it was to become the supremacy of the Constitution over all government.

That understanding did not take hold immediately. Its acceptance was more the result of the ways in which these new governments had to use their power to support the war effort. The Revolution required governments to act far more extensively and intrusively than their colonial predecessors had ever done. They had to raise taxes, soldiers, and supplies from a people who had never been asked to support a war on this scale. Inevitably, the reactions this activity provoked went beyond criticisms of specific policies to consider whether the new constitutions were as well framed as they could have been. They had been written, after all, in the midst of war, by provincial conventions that had other business to transact and little experience on which to rely.

Constitution-making also had a national dimension. In June 1776 Congress drafted Articles of Confederation to provide a constitutional framework of union. But three issues prevented it from reaching agreement on this plan of union: the rules of voting within Congress; the apportionment of expenses among the states; and the control of interior western lands. In the wake of the great victory at Saratoga in 1777, Congress mustered the determination to complete the task and sent the Articles to the states for approval. But because this completed draft granted Congress no authority over western lands, a bloc of landless states (that is, states lacking claims to lands west of the Appalachians) delayed ratifying the Confederation. Maryland, the last holdout, withheld its assent until February 1781.

By then, many national leaders recognized that the Articles would not give Congress the range of powers that the war had revealed it needed. Congress could only issue recommendations and requisitions to the states. It could not enact laws binding individuals to obey its decisions. And it lacked independent sources of revenue or the authority to levy taxes. The states generally did the best they could to comply with congressional decisions. But the impression inevitably took hold that a federal union that depended on the good faith of its member states was a government in name only.

In 1781 Congress sent its first proposed amendment of the Articles to the states: a request to be able to levy an impost (duty) on selected imports (p. 194). Like the original Confederation, this amendment required the unanimous approval of the states. And like all subsequent efforts to amend the Articles, this amendment failed to surmount that hurdle. In 1783 Congress proposed a new set of amendments designed to answer its need for revenue; these also failed (p. 213). In 1784, with the country slipping into a postwar recession and British goods flooding American markets while American ships were excluded from British harbors, Congress submitted two more proposals asking the states to grant it authority over foreign commerce (p. 217). These also failed.

By 1786 some national leaders were wondering whether the promise of the Revolution was being jeopardized by the disagreements of peacetime. Some took a long view. They thought that a population exhausted by a long and costly war could not be expected to undertake fresh projects of political reform. Others, however, worried that a union that seemed to be drifting into a condition of "imbecility" could not survive indefinitely. Britain used the noncompliance of the states with various provisions of the peace treaty to justify retaining key frontier posts at Niagara, Oswego, and Detroit. Spanish authorities in New Orleans closed the Mississippi River to American navigation, preventing frontier farmers from exporting their produce and sparking a sharp sectional dispute in Congress. West Indian ports remained closed to American merchantmen. Under these and other pressures, a single union of thirteen states might break up into two or three regional confederations, each pursuing its narrow interests.

The road to constitutional reform began in Virginia. In January 1786 the Virginia legislature adopted a resolution inviting the other states to send commissioners to a convention where they could discuss the need to vest commercial powers in Congress. Its own delegation to this meeting included James Madison, who had spent nearly four continuous years at Congress before the term-limits provision of the Articles of Confederation sent him back to Virginia. Eight states appointed commissioners to attend this meeting at Annapolis. But when the appointed time came in September, only a dozen delegates from five states appeared—too few to proceed to business. But those present included Madison, Alexander Hamilton from New York, and John Dickinson (the principal drafter of the Confederation) from Delaware. Rather than confess defeat and adjourn, those present invited the states to appoint delegates to attend a second convention to meet in Philadelphia in May 1787. Its agenda would not be limited to commerce, but extend instead to the general woes of the Confederation.

In retrospect, the Annapolis conference appears to have been a bold move launched by a determined and artful group of reformers. At the time, it was more akin to a desperate gamble. The Annapolis delegates could not be confident that the states would respond favorably. They had to worry that their invitation, like their meeting itself, could be interpreted as yet another insult to Congress, because the Articles of Confederation contained no provision authorizing the meeting of such conventions. And should a general convention actually assemble, they had no assurance it would be able to reach agreement. Some knowing observers, like John Jay (Congress's secretary of foreign affairs) thought the Philadelphia meeting might prove useful for discussion only. Yet at the same time, once the idea of a general convention had been proposed, it naturally acquired its own momentum and logic. All the other expedients had failed. Madison, Hamilton, and their allies no longer believed that the cause of reform could wait indefinitely. Some Americans had begun to speculate that the revolutionary union of thirteen states could break up into smaller confederacies, and that this in turn could create fresh opportunities for the empires of Europe to meddle in American affairs.

In the intervening months, the movement for general constitutional reform gathered strength. Virginia was the first state to act and appoint a delegation. In February 1787 the Continental Congress added its own endorsement of the convention. Eventually, twelve of the thirteen state legislatures appointed delegates. The lone holdout was Rhode Island, a determinedly "anti-federal" state since its veto had killed the impost amendment of 1781. But the fact that Rhode Island did not even send a delegation to Philadelphia had a liberating effect on the convention, persuading it to abandon the rule requiring alterations to the Confederation to be approved by all thirteen state legislatures.

Madison's preparations for the convention decisively shaped its agenda. Three elements of his program of reform proved critical to the deliberations that began in late May (see p. 317). First, Madison believed in empowering the national government to enact, execute, and adjudicate its own laws, without having to rely on the states to carry out its decisions. This in turn required reconstituting the Union as a normal government, with independent legislative, executive, and judicial departments. Second, the legislative power of this government should be extensive, potentially including the authority to overturn state laws. Third, as a matter of justice, Madison favored allocating seats in both houses of the new legislature on the basis of population or wealth, replacing the "one state, one vote" rule of the Confederation. All of these ideas were incorporated in the Virginia Plan that Governor Edmund Randolph presented on May 29 (p. 335).

The delegates generally accepted Madison's first principle but delayed judgment on the second until they had resolved the third. Disputes over the apportionment of representation among the states preoccupied the convention for seven weeks. In July it managed to strike a compromise to count slaves for purposes of representation in the lower house of Congress according to the three-fifths ratio. But compromise on the upper house proved impossible. Small states insisted on retaining the "one state, one vote" rule of the Confederation; delegates from large states argued that this was fundamentally unjust. Finally, on July 16, after weeks of heated debate, the convention narrowly approved (five states to four, with one delegation, that of populous Massachusetts, divided), the equal state vote for the Senate.

This decision so discouraged some large-state delegates that they briefly debated whether to proceed. No one, however, was anxious to abandon the project of reform, and the longer the meeting went on, the more inclined many delegates were to portray the decision on the Senate as being as much of a compromise as the decision on the House of Representatives. In the weeks after this vote, the delegates turned their attention to the other two parts of Madison's program. In place of the broad grant of legislative authority envisioned by the Virginia Plan, they gradually developed a list of enumerated powers, including most notably an almost unfettered power of taxation and the right to regulate interstate and foreign commerce.

The most difficult issue the framers faced as the convention moved toward adjournment was the design of the presidency. In the eighteenth century, executive power was still essentially monarchical power, and it was difficult to design an effective national executive on republican principles. Moreover, the framers were genuinely uncertain about the best means of selecting the president. Active debate on the presidency thus continued into the final fortnight of deliberation in September. As it continued, the authority of the novel office the framers were creating grew stronger, but the uncertainties about its political character persisted.

The convention concluded its work on September 17, 1787. Three of the forty-two delegates still in attendance refused to sign the completed Constitution, but the others fully supported its ratification. To achieve that goal, they had also designed a new procedure. Rather than require approval by all thirteen legislatures, the convention instead proposed to submit the Constitution to special, popularly elected conventions in each state. The approval of nine, not thirteen, would be sufficient for the new government to take effect. State conventions were asked to approve the Constitution in its entirety (p. 410).

Over the next eleven months, Americans extensively debated the Constitution—in the press, in taverns and churches, in popular meetings, and, most important, in the state conventions. The debate was wide-ranging and multifaceted. The Anti-Federalist opponents of the Constitution seized upon numerous clauses and provisions that they saw as laying a basis for eroding the residual authority of the states and the rights and liberties of citizens. Its Federalist supporters argued that the Continental Congress and the Confederation it represented were on the brink of collapse, and that a reinvigorated national government was essential to prosperity and security. Over time, they pointedly answered many of the specific charges that Anti-Federalists leveled against individual clauses.

In many ways this debate rivaled the great discussion of resistance and independence that preoccupied the colonists in the period 1774–1776. It focused public discussion across the country and encouraged the development of alliances that crossed state lines. More important, both the debates in Philadelphia that produced the Constitution and those that led to its ratification allowed Americans to rethink the experiment they had launched in 1776 when they first began writing new constitutions. Then, the urgency of the war and inexperience had made it difficult to consider the problems of republican government in a sustained way. Now, in a time of peace, the country had a decade's experience of self-government on which to draw. Of course, the conclusions they reached often varied. But by

July 1788 eleven states had ratified the Constitution, and only two—North Carolina and Rhode Island—initially rejected it.

Had opinion polling existed in this period, it might well have revealed that a majority of Americans either opposed the Constitution outright or deeply distrusted the power it would place in the national government. In securing victory, Federalists capitalized on the strong support they enjoyed in the nation's major port cities and on their control of the press. By contrast, Anti-Federalists found it difficult to get their ideas widely disseminated. Their opposition was poorly coordinated, and it suffered as well from a lack of concerted leadership. Perhaps most important, Anti-Federalists faced the dilemma of having to defend a failing Confederation and a Congress that could barely muster a quorum against a bold vision of the American future supported not only by the nation's greatest men, notably George Washington and Benjamin Franklin, but also some of its most effective younger leaders, like Madison and Hamilton.

From the outset of this debate, moderate Anti-Federalists proposed various amendments to make the Constitution safer for both the states and their citizens. Many of these proposals required changes in the structure of the national government or the powers it exercised. Others supported the adoption of additional articles restating the fundamental rights of citizens. In conventions where the fate of the Constitution was uncertain—notably Massachusetts, Virginia, and New York—Federalists grudgingly agreed to recommend amendments for the first post-ratification Congress to consider. These concessions were necessary to secure the approval of these key states, but Federalists were careful to insist that ratification precede amendment, not the other way around. Similarly, some Anti-Federalists thought a second convention should be held to revise the Constitution in light of the criticisms leveled against it. But Madison, Hamilton, and other Federalist leaders thought that would lead to political chaos, because the delegations sent to such a convention would come armed with all kinds of instructions limiting the room for compromise.

In the winter of 1789, the eleven ratifying states held elections for the new government. Everyone knew that George Washington would be the first president. More dramatic was the success Federalists enjoyed in the elections to Congress. Solid Federalist majorities would control both houses, and this seemed to deflate the expectation that the Constitution would soon be amended. In Virginia, however, Madison had publicly committed himself to the cause of amendments, not because he believed they were necessary in themselves, but to reconcile moderate Anti-Federalists to the Constitution. Once the new Congress met, he took upon himself the task of convincing Congress that the promises of 1788 had to be honored (pp. 613–627). Many members remained skeptical, but with Madison's prodding, twelve amendments were sent to the states for ratification in September 1789. Two years passed before the ten that we now call the Bill of Rights were ratified.

Twenty-five years had passed since the colonists first opposed the Stamp Act and invoked constitutional arguments rooted in Anglo-American history. Two revolutions had occurred since. One led to a war of national liberation that allowed the United States to assume its place among the other politically independent nations of the earth. The other took the form of a constitutional revolution that recast received ideas of government in a radically new form. For most Americans, these results have been so long accepted, and seem so familiar, that it is difficult to recall just how innovative they were at the time—and how much they depended on the contingencies of history. The colonists did not set out in 1765 or even in 1774 to establish an independent nation. Only a series of miscues by a poorly informed and miscalculating government in London made independence the inescapable consequence of colonial resistance. So, too, the whole idea of a written constitution as supreme law was not something that many Americans grasped or fully comprehended when they started writing new charters in 1776. In many ways, it was an accidental byproduct of the situation in which Britain had placed them, and it took the better part of a decade for Americans to think through the implications of what they were doing. The great constitutional debate of 1787 and 1788 provided the occasion for that reconsideration to take place. But that debate, too, came about only because individual states, like tiny Rhode Island, had thwarted every effort to amend the Articles of Confederation. Had any of those proposed amendments succeeded, the case for calling a special convention like the one that met at Philadelphia in May 1787 would have been far more difficult to make. Political change might then have taken a very different form, more modest and incremental.

But even the greatest historical events are often shaped by accidents and circumstances. The deeper question is this: What do those who have the chance to participate in such events do when the opportunity, accidental or not, presents itself? The documents presented in this book illustrate how the Revolutionary generation seized the day. More than two centuries later, we are still wrestling with the consequences of their decisions.

Jack N. Rakove is W. R. Coe Professor of History and American Studies and Professor of Political Science at Stanford University, where he has taught since 1980. He was educated at Haverford College, the University of Edinburgh, and Harvard, where he earned his Ph.D. in 1975. He is the author of four books on the American Revolutionary era, including *The Beginnings of National Politics: An Interpretive History of the Continental Congress* (1979), *James Madison and the Creation of the American Republic* (1990, 2001), and *Original Meanings: Politics and Ideas in the Making of the Constitution*, which received the 1997 Pulitzer Prize in History. His edited books include *James Madison: Writings* (1999), *The Federalist: The Essential Essays* (2003), and *The Unfinished Election of 2000* (2001). He writes frequently on issues relating to the original meaning of the Constitution.

Publisher's Note: The editor has made no attempt to modernize the spelling or punctuation in the documents collected in this volume. When these texts were written, rules of spelling and punctuation differed from what they are today. For one, consistency was not as important: "controling" and "controlling," "incroachments" and "encroachments," "percieved" and "perceived" can all be found in the same document. Similarly, the word "it's" sometimes appears as a possessive where we now use "its." Retaining these and other odd spellings and "incorrect" punctuation preserves these important American documents in their original character.

FOUNDING AMERICA

Documents from the Revolution to the Bill of Rights

THE IMPERIAL DISPUTE

BECAUSE THE DECLARATION OF Independence of 1776 was directed against King George III, it is often assumed that the American Revolution was a struggle against the evils of monarchy. In fact, the central dispute between Britain and its colonies was concerned with another issue entirely: Did Parliament have any authority to legislate for America, or were the colonists obliged to obey only those laws enacted by their own representative assemblies? That was the great issue that was first agitated during the Stamp Act controversy of 1765–1766 and the dispute over the Townshend duties enacted in 1767.

After the Townshend duties were repealed, this dispute largely subsided. But it was unexpectedly revived in Massachusetts in January 1773, when Governor Thomas Hutchinson rashly opened the winter session of the legislature with a speech explaining why Americans were not exempt from the jurisdiction of Parliament. Hutchinson was responding to recent attacks on his own administration launched by the Boston Committee of Correspondence. His speech was meant to quiet the opposition. Instead, it plunged Massachusetts into still greater turmoil, as John Adams and James Otis rebutted the governor's position in responses prepared for the two houses of the legislature.

These addresses were in turn reprinted in newspaper and pamphlet form, and consumed by interested readers in other colonies. The pamphlet and the newspaper essay were the principal forms of political expression in eighteenth-century America, and most political controversies soon found their way into one or the other. Many pamphlets originated as newspaper essays. Some were deeply learned and filled with scholarly citations. Others were more pungent or humorous, like Benjamin Franklin's *Rules by Which a Great Empire May Be Reduced to a Small One*, published in 1773. Franklin had been living in London for a good fifteen years when he published this essay. Though he still hoped that Britain and its colonies would remain united, he was increasingly frustrated by his dealings with British officials who dismissed the colonists' assertions of loyalty. As he did so often, Franklin used a light touch to support a serious conclusion: that British policy seemed design to alienate the Americans' natural affection for the mother country.

A year later, humor was no longer possible. The adoption of the Coercive or Intolerable Acts led American writers to demonstrate, once and for all, why the colonies could not be legally bound by acts of Parliament. One of the most influential publications opposing the Acts was a pamphlet that Thomas Jefferson originally wrote as instructions for the Virginia delegates to the First Continental Congress. Jefferson's cogent prose in *A Summary View of the Rights of British America* helped establish the reputation that led to his later authorship of the Declaration of Independence.

THE IMPERIAL DISPUTE

—*Thomas Hutchinson*—
THE ADDRESS OF THE GOVERNOR
JANUARY 6, 1773

His Excellency the Governor was pleased to open the Assembly
with the following Speech to both Houses, viz.
Gentlemen of the Council, and,
Gentlemen of the House of Representatives.

I HAVE NOTHING IN special Command from his Majesty to lay before you at this Time; I have general Instructions to recommend to you, at all Times, such Measures as may tend to promote that Peace and Order upon which your own Happiness and Prosperity as well as his Majesty's Service very much depend. That the Government is at present in a disturbed and disordered State is a Truth too evident to be denied. The Cause of this Disorder appears to me equally evident. I wish I may be able to make it appear so to you, for then I may not doubt that you will agree with me in the proper Measures for the Removal of it. I have pleased myself, for several Years past, with Hopes that the Cause would cease of itself and the Effect with it, but I am disappointed, and I may not any longer, consistent with my Duty to the King and my Regard to the Interest of the Province, delay communicating my Sentiments to you upon a Matter of so great Importance. I shall be explicit and treat the Subject without Reserve. I hope you will receive what I have to say upon it with Candor, and, if you shall not agree in Sentiments with me, I promise you, with Candor likewise, to receive and consider what you may offer in Answer.

When our Predecessors first took Possession of this Plantation or Colony, under a Grant and Charter from the Crown of England, it was their Sense, and it was the Sense of the Kingdom, that they were to remain subject to the supreme Authority of Parliament. This appears from the Charter itself and from other irresistable Evidence. This Supreme Authority has, from Time to Time, been exercised by

Parliament and submitted to by the Colony, and hath been, in the most express Terms, acknowledged by the Legislature and, except about the Time of Anarchy and Confusion in England which preceded the Restoration of King Charles the Second, I have not discovered that it has been called in Question even by private or particular Persons until within seven or eight Years last past. Our Provincial or Local Laws have, in numerous Instances, had Relation to Acts of Parliament made to respect the Plantations in general and this Colony in particular, and in our Executive Courts both Juries and Judges have to all Intents and Purposes, considered such Acts as Part of our Rule of Law. Such a Constitution, in a Plantation, is not peculiar to England but agrees with the Principles of the most celebrated Writers upon the Law of Nations that "when a Nation takes Possession of a distant Country and settles there, that Country, though separated from the principal Establishment or Mother Country, naturally becomes a Part of the State equally with its ancient Possessions."

So much however of the Spirit of Liberty breathes thro' all Parts of the English Constitution, that although from the Nature of Government there must be one supreme Authority over the whole, yet this Constitution will admit of subordinate Powers with legislative and executive Authority, greater or less according to local and other Circumstances. Thus we see a Variety of Corporations formed within the Kingdom with Powers to make and execute such Bylaws as are for their immediate Use and Benefit, the Members of such Corporations still remaining subject to the general Laws of the Kingdom. We see also Governments established in the Plantations which, from their separate and remote Situation, require more general and extensive Powers of Legislation within themselves than those formed within the Kingdom, but subject nevertheless, to all such Laws of the Kingdom as immediately respect them or are designed to extend to them, and accordingly we in this Province have, from the first Settlement of it, been left to the Exercise of our legislative and executive Powers, Parliament occasionally though rarely, interposing as in its Wisdom has been judged necessary.

Under this Constitution, for more than One Hundred Years, the Laws both of the supreme and subordinate Authority were in general, duly executed, Offenders against them have been brought to condign Punishment, Peace and Order have been maintained and the People of this Province have experienced as largely the Advantages of Government, as, perhaps, any People upon the Globe, and they have from Time to Time in the most public Manner expressed their Sense of it and, once in every Year, have offered up their united Thanksgivings to God for the Enjoyment of these Privileges and, as often, their united Prayers for the Continuance of them.

At Length the Constitution has been called in Question and the Authority of the Parliament of Great-Britain to make and establish Laws for the Inhabitants of this Province has been, by many, denied. What was, at first, whispered with Caution, was soon after openly asserted in Print and, of late, a Number of Inhabitants in several of the principal Towns in the Province, have assembled together in their respective Towns and, having assumed the Name of legal Town Meetings, have passed Resolves which they have ordered to be placed upon their Town Records, and caused to be printed & published in Pamphlets and News-Papers. I am sorry that it is thus become impossible to conceal what I could wish had never been made public. I will not particularize these Resolves or Votes and shall only observe to you, in general, that some of them deny the supreme Authority of Parliament, and so are repugnant to the Principles of the Constitution, and that others speak of this supreme Authority, of which the King is a constituent Part and to every Act of which his Assent is necessary, in such Terms as have a direct Tendency to alienate the Affections of the People from their Sovereign who has ever been most tender of their Rights, and whose Person, Crown and Dignity we are under every possible Obligation to defend and support. In consequence of these Resolves, Committees of Correspondence are formed, in several of those Towns, to maintain the Principles upon which they are founded.

I know of no Arguments, founded in Reason, which will be sufficient to Support these Principles or to justify the Measures taken in Consequence of them. It has been urged, that the sole Power of making Laws is granted by Charter to a Legislature established in the Province, consisting of the King by his Representative the Governor, the Council and the House of Representatives—that by this Charter there are likewise granted or assured to the Inhabitants of the Province all the Liberties and Immunities of free and natural Subjects, to all Intents, Constructions and Purposes whatsoever, as if they had been born within the Realm of England—that it is Part of the Liberties of English Subjects, which has its Foundation in Nature, to be governed by Laws made by their Consent in Person or by their Representative—that the Subjects in this Province are not and cannot be Represented in the Parliament of Great-Britain and, consequently, the Acts of Parliament cannot be binding upon them.

I do not find, Gentlemen, in the Charter such an Expression as *sole* Power or any Words which import it. The General Court has, by Charter, *full* Power to make such Laws as are not repugnant to the Laws of England. A favourable Construction has been put upon this Clause when it has been allowed to intend such Laws of England only as are expres[s]ly declared to respect us. Surely then this is by Charter a Reserve of Power and Authority to Parliament to bind us by such Laws, at least, as are made expressly to refer to us and, consequently, is a Limitation of the Power given to the General Court. Nor can it be contended that by the Liberties of free and natural Subjects is to be understood an Exemption from Acts of Parliament because not represented there, seeing it is provided, by the same Charter, that such Acts shall be in Force; and if they that make the Objection to such Acts will read the Charter with Attention, they must be convinced that this Grant of Liberties and Immunities is nothing more than a Declaration and Assurance on the Part of the Crown that the Place to which their Predecessors were about to remove was and would be considered as Part of the Dominions of the Crown of England, and therefore that the Subjects of the Crown so removing, and those born there or in their Passage thither or in their Passage from thence, would not become Aliens but would throughout all Parts of the English Dominions, wherever they might happen to be, as well within the Colony, retain the Liberties and Immunities of free and natural Subjects, their Removal from or not being born within the Realm notwithstanding. If the Plantations be Part of the Dominions of the Crown, this Clause in the Charter does not confer or reserve any Liberties but what would have been enjoyed without it and what the Inhabitants of every other Colony do enjoy where they are without a Charter. If the Plantations are not the Dominions of the Crown will not all that are born here be considered as born out of the Ligeance of the King of England, and whenever they go into any Part of the Dominions will they not be deemed Aliens to all Intents and Purposes, this Grant in the Charter notwithstanding?

They who claim Exemption from Acts of Parliament by Virtue of their Rights as Englishmen, should consider that it is impossible the Rights of English Subjects should be the same, in every Respect, in all parts of the Dominions. It is one of their Rights as English Subjects to be governed by Laws made by Persons in whose Election they have, from Time to Time, a Voice—They remove from the Kingdom where, perhaps, they were in the full Exercise of this Right to the Plantations where it cannot be exercised or where the Exercise of it would be of no Benefit to them. Does it follow that the Government, by their Removal from one Part of the Dominions to another, loses its Authority over that Part to which they remove, and that they are freed from the Subjection they were under before; or do they expect that Government should relinquish its Authority because they cannot enjoy this particular Right? Will it not rather be said that, by this their voluntary Removal, they have relinquished for a Time at least, one of the Rights of an English Subject which they might if they pleased have continued to enjoy and may again enjoy whensoever they will return to the Place where it can be exercised?

They who claim Exemption, as Part of their Rights by Nature, should consider that every Restraint which Men are laid under by a State of Government is a Privation of Part of their natural Rights, and of all the different Forms of Government which exist, there can be no two of them in which the Departure from Natural Rights is exactly the same. Even in Case of Representation by Election, do they not give up Part of their natural Rights when they consent to be represented by such Person as shall be chosen by the Majority of the Electors, although their own Voices may be for some other Person? And is it not contrary to their natural Rights to be obliged to submit to a Representative for seven Years, or even one Year, after they are dissatisfied with his Conduct, although they gave their Voices for him when he was elected? This must therefore be considered as an Objection against a State of Government rather than against any particular Form.

If what I have said shall not be sufficient to satisfy such as object to the Supreme Authority of Parliament over the Plantations, there may something further be added to induce them to an Acknowledgment of it which I think will well deserve their Consideration. I know of no Line that can be drawn between the supreme Authority of Parliament and the total Independence of the Colonies: It is impossible there should be two independent Legislatures in one and the same State, for although there may be but one Head, the King, yet the two Legislative Bodies will make two Governments as distinct as the Kingdoms of England and Scotland before the Union. If we might be suffered to be altogether independent of Great-Britain, could we have any Claim to the Protection of that Government of which we are no longer a Part? Without this Protection should we not become the Prey of one or the other Powers of Europe, such as should first seize upon us? Is there any Thing which we have more Reason to dread than Independence? I hope it will never be our Misfortune to know by Experience the Difference between the Liberties of an English Colonist and those of the Spanish, French or Dutch.

If then the Supremacy of Parliament over the whole British Dominions shall no longer be denied, it will follow that the *meer* Exercise of its Authority can be no Matter of Grievance. If it has been or shall be exercised in such Way and Manner as shall appear to be grievous, still this cannot be sufficient Grounds for immediately denying or renouncing the Authority or refusing to submit to it. The Acts and Doings of Authority in the most perfect Form of Government will not always be thought just and equitable by all the Parts of which it consists, but it is the greatest Absurdity to admit the several parts to be at Liberty to obey or disobey according as the Acts of such Authority may be approved or disapproved of by them, for this necessarily works a Dissolution of the Government. The Manner then of obtaining Redress must be by Representations and Endeavours, in such Ways and Forms as the established Rules of the Constitution prescribe or allow in order to make any Matters alledged to be Grievances appear to be really such; but I conceive it is rather the *meer* Exercise of this Authority which is complained of as a Grievance, than any heavy Burdens which have been bro't upon the People by Means of it.

As Contentment and Order were the happy Effects of a Constitution strengthened by universal Assent and Approbation, so Discontent and Disorder are now the deplorable Effects of a Constitution enfeebled by Contest and Opposition. Besides Divisions and Animosities which disturb the Peace of Towns and Families, the Law in some important Cases cannot have its Course, Offenders ordered by Advice of His Majesty's Council to be prosecuted, escape with

Impunity and are supported and encouraged to go on offending,—the Authority of Government is bro't into Contempt, and
there are but small Remains of that Subordination which was once
very conspicious in this Colony, and which is essential to a well-
regulated State.

When the Bands of Government are thus weakened, it certainly
behoves those with whom the Powers of Government are intrusted
to omit nothing which may tend to strengthen them.

I have disclosed my Sentiments to you without Reserve. Let me
intreat you to consider them calmly and not to be too sudden in
your Determination. If my Principles of Government are right let us
adhere to them. With the same Principles our Ancestors were easy
and happy for a long Course of Years together, and I know of no
Reason to doubt of your being equally easy & happy. The People, influenced by you will forsake their unconstitutional Principles and
desist from their Irregularities which are the Consequence of them,
they will be convinced that every Thing which is valuable to them
depend upon their Connexion with their Parent State, that this
Connexion cannot be continued in any other Way than such as will
also continue their Dependance upon the supreme Authority of the
British Dominions, and that, notwithstanding this Dependance,
they will enjoy as great a Proportion of those Rights to which they
have a Claim by Nature or as Englishmen as can be enjoyed by a
Plantation or Colony.

If I am wrong in my Principles of Government or in the Inferences which I have drawn from them, I wish to be convinced of my
Error. Independence I may not allow myself to think that you can
possibly have in Contemplation. If you can conceive of any other
constitutional Dependance than what I have mentioned, if you are
of Opinion that upon any other Principles our Connexion with the
State from which we sprang can be continued, communicate your
Sentiments to me with the same Freedom and Unreservedness as I
have communicated mine to you.

I have no Desire, Gentlemen, by any Thing I have said to preclude
you from seeking Relief, in a constitutional Way, in any Cases in
which you have heretofore or may hereafter suppose that you are aggrieved and, although I should not concur with you in Sentiment,
I will, notwithstanding, do nothing to lessen the Weight which your
Representations may deserve. I have laid before you what I think are

the Principles of your Constitution: If you do not agree with me I wish to know your Objections: They may be convincing to me, or I may be able to satisfy you of the Insufficiency of them: In either Case I hope, we shall put an End to those Irregularities, which ever will be the Portion of a Government where the Supreme Authority is controverted, and introduce that Tranquility which seems to have taken Place in most of the Colonies upon the Continent.

The ordinary Business of the Session I will not now particularly point out to you. To the enacting of any new Laws which may be necessary for the more equal and effectual Distribution of Justice, or for giving further Encouragement to our Merchandize, Fishery, and Agriculture, which through the Divine Favour are already in a very flourishing State, or for promoting any Measures which may conduce to the general Good of the Province I will readily give my Assent or Concurrence.

T. Hutchinson

COUNCIL CHAMBER
6 JANUARY 1773

—Benjamin Franklin—
RULES BY WHICH A GREAT EMPIRE MAY BE REDUCED TO A SMALL ONE
SEPTEMBER 11, 1773

[Presented privately to a *late Minister,* when he entered upon his Administration; and now first published.]

AN ANCIENT SAGE VALUED himself upon this, that tho' he could not fiddle, he knew how to make a *great City* of a *little one.* The Science that I, a modern Simpleton, am about to communicate is the very reverse.

I address myself to all Ministers who have the Management of extensive Dominions, which from their very Greatness are become troublesome to govern, because the Multiplicity of their Affairs leaves no Time for *fiddling.*

I. In the first Place, Gentlemen, you are to consider, that a great Empire, like a great Cake, is most easily diminished at the Edges. Turn your Attention therefore first to your remotest Provinces; that as you get rid of them, the next may follow in Order.

II. That the Possibility of this Separation may always exist, take special Care the Provinces are never incorporated with the Mother Country, that they do not enjoy the same common Rights, the same Privileges in Commerce, and that they are governed by *severer* Laws, all of *your enacting,* without allowing them any Share in the Choice of the Legislators. By carefully making and preserving such Distinctions, you will (to keep to my Simile of the Cake) act like a wise Gingerbread Baker, who, to facilitate a Division, cuts his Dough half through in those Places, where, when bak'd, he would have it *broken to Pieces.*

III. These remote Provinces have perhaps been acquired, purchas'd, or conquer'd, at the *sole Expence* of the Settlers or their Ancestors, without the Aid of the Mother Country. If this should happen to increase her *Strength* by their growing Numbers ready to join in her Wars, her *Commerce* by their growing Demand for her Manufactures, or her *Naval Power* by greater Employment for her Ships and Seamen, they may probably suppose some Merit in this, and that it entitles them to some Favour; you are therefore to *forget it all,* or resent it as if they had done you Injury. If they happen to be zealous Whigs, Friends of Liberty, nurtur'd in Revolution Principles, *remember all that* to their Prejudice, and contrive to punish it: For such Principles, after a Revolution is thoroughly established, are of *no more Use,* they are even *odious* and *abominable.*

IV. However peaceably your Colonies have submitted to your Government, shewn their Affection to your Interest, and patiently borne their Grievances, you are to *suppose* them always inclined to revolt, and treat them accordingly. Quarter Troops among them, who by their Insolence may *provoke* the rising of Mobs, and by their Bullets and Bayonets *suppress* them. By this Means, like the Husband who uses his Wife ill *from Suspicion,* you may in Time convert your *Suspicions* into *Realities.*

V. Remote Provinces must have *Governors,* and *Judges,* to represent the Royal Person, and execute every where the delegated Parts of his Office and Authority. You Ministers know, that much of the Strength of Government depends on the *Opinion* of the People; and much of that Opinion on the Choice of Rulers placed immediately over them. If you send them wise and good Men for Governors, who study the Interest of the Colonists, and advance their Prosperity, they will think their King wise and good, and that he wishes the Welfare of his Subjects. If you send them learned and upright Men for Judges, they will think him a Lover of Justice. This may attach your Provinces more to his Government. You are therefore to be careful who you recommend for those Offices.—If you can find Prodigals who have ruined their Fortunes, broken Gamesters or Stock-Jobbers, these may do well as *Governors;* for they will probably be rapacious, and provoke the People by their Extortions. Wrangling Proctors and petty-fogging Lawyers too are not amiss, for they will be for ever disputing and quarrelling with their little Parliaments. If withal they should be ignorant, wrong-headed and insolent, so much the better. Attorneys Clerks and Newgate Solicitors* will do for *Chief-Justices,* especially if they hold their Places *during your Pleasure:*—And all will contribute to impress those ideas of your Government that are proper for a People *you would wish to renounce it.*

VI. To confirm these Impressions, and strike them deeper, whenever the Injured come to the Capital with Complaints of Maladministration, Oppression, or Injustice, punish such Suitors with long Delay, enormous Expence, and a final Judgment in Favour of the Oppressor. This will have an admirable Effect every Way. The Trouble of future Complaints will be prevented, and Governors and Judges will be encouraged to farther Acts of Oppression and Injustice; and thence the People may become more disaffected, *and at length desperate.*

VII. When such Governors have crammed their Coffers, and made themselves so odious to the People that they can no longer remain among them with Safety to their Persons, recall and *reward* them with Pensions. You may make them *Baronets* too, if that respectable Order should not think fit to resent it. All will contribute to encourage new Governors in the same Practices, and make the supreme Government *detestable.*

VIII. If when you are engaged in War, your Colonies should vie in liberal Aids of Men and Money against the common Enemy, upon your simple Requisition, and give far beyond their Abilities, reflect,

---

*Lawyers associated with Newgate, an infamous prison of eighteenth-century London.

that a Penny taken from them by your Power is more honourable to you than a Pound presented by their Benevolence. Despise therefore their voluntary Grants, and resolve to harrass them with novel Taxes. They will probably complain to your Parliaments that they are taxed by a Body in which they have no Representative, and that this is contrary to common Right. They will petition for Redress. Let the Parliaments flout their Claims, reject their Petitions, refuse even to suffer the reading of them, and treat the Petitioners with the utmost Contempt. Nothing can have a better Effect, in producing the Alienation proposed; for though many can forgive Injuries, *none ever forgave Contempt.*

IX. In laying these Taxes, never regard the heavy Burthens those remote People already undergo, in defending their own Frontiers, supporting their own provincial Governments, making new Roads, building Bridges, Churches and other public Edifices, which in old Countries have been done to your Hands by your Ancestors, but which occasion constant Calls and Demands on the Purses of a new People. Forget the *Restraints* you lay on their Trade for *your own* Benefit, and the Advantage a *Monopoly* of this Trade gives your exacting Merchants. Think nothing of the Wealth those Merchants and your Manufacturers acquire by the Colony Commerce; their encreased Ability thereby to pay Taxes at home; their accumulating, in the Price of their Commodities, most of those Taxes, and so levying them from their consuming Customers: All this, and the Employment and Support of Thousands of your Poor by the Colonists, you are *intirely to forget.* But remember to make your arbitrary Tax more grievous to your Provinces, by public Declarations importing that your Power of taxing them has *no Limits,* so that when you take from them without their Consent a Shilling in the Pound, you have a clear Right to the other nineteen. This will probably weaken every Idea of *Security in their Property,* and convince them that under such a Government *they have nothing they can call their own;* which can scarce fail of producing *the happiest Consequences*!

X. Possibly indeed some of them might still comfort themselves, and say, 'Though we have no Property, we have yet *something* left that is valuable; we have constitutional *Liberty* both of Person and of Conscience. This King, these Lords, and these Commons, who it seems are too remote from us to know us and feel for us, cannot take from us our *Habeas Corpus* Right, or our Right of Trial *by a Jury of our Neighbours:* They cannot deprive us of the Exercise of our Religion, alter our ecclesiastical Constitutions, and compel us to be Papists if they please, or Mahometans.' To annihilate this Comfort, begin by Laws to perplex their Commerce with infinite Regulations impossible to be remembered and observed; ordain Seizures of their Property for every Failure; take away the Trial of such Property by Jury, and give it to arbitrary Judges of your own appointing, and of the lowest Characters in the Country, whose Salaries and Emoluments are to arise out of the Duties or Condemnations, and whose Appointments are *during Pleasure.* Then let there be a formal Declaration of both Houses, that Opposition to your Edicts is *Treason,* and that Persons suspected of Treason in the Provinces may, according to some obsolete Law, be seized and sent to the Metropolis of the Empire for Trial; and pass an Act that those there charged with certain other Offences shall be sent away in Chains from their Friends and Country to be tried in the same Manner for Felony. Then erect a new Court of Inquisition among them, accompanied by an armed Force, with Instructions to transport all such suspected Persons, to be ruined by the Expence if they bring over Evidences to prove their Innocence, or be found guilty and hanged if they can't afford it. And lest the People should think you cannot possibly go any farther, pass another solemn declaratory Act, that 'King, Lords, and Commons had, hath, and of Right ought to have, full Power and Authority to make Statutes of sufficient Force and Validity to bind the unrepresented Provinces IN ALL CASES WHATSO- EVER.' This will include *spiritual* with temporal; and taken together, must operate wonderfully to your Purpose, by convincing them, that they are at present under a Power something like that spoken of in the Scriptures, which can not only *kill their Bodies,* but *damn their Souls* to all Eternity, by compelling them, if it pleases, *to worship the Devil.*

XI. To make your Taxes more odious, and more likely to procure Resistance, send from the Capital a Board of Officers to superintend the Collection, composed of the most *indiscreet, ill-bred* and *insolent* you can find. Let these have large Salaries out of the extorted Revenue, and live in open grating Luxury upon the Sweat and Blood of the Industrious, whom they are to worry continually with groundless and expensive Prosecutions before the above-mentioned arbitrary

Revenue-Judges, all *at the Cost of the Party prosecuted* tho' acquitted, because *the King is to pay no Costs.*—Let these Men *by your Order* be exempted from all the common Taxes and Burthens of the Province, though they and their Property are protected by its Laws. If any Revenue Officers are *suspected* of the least Tenderness for the People, discard them. If others are justly complained of, protect and reward them. If any of the Under-officers behave so as to provoke the People to drub them, promote those to better Offices: This will encourage others to procure for themselves such profitable Drubbings, by multiplying and enlarging such Provocations, and *all with work towards the End you aim at.*

XII. Another Way to make your Tax odious, is to misapply the Produce of it. If it was originally appropriated for the *Defence* of the Provinces and the better Support of Government, and the Administration of Justice where it may be *necessary,* then apply none of it to that *Defence,* but bestow it where it is *not necessary,* in augmented Salaries or Pensions to every Governor who has distinguished himself by his Enmity to the People, and by calumniating them to their Sovereign. This will make them pay it more unwillingly, and be more apt to quarrel with those that collect it, and those that imposed it, who will quarrel again with them, and all shall contribute to your *main Purpose* of making them *weary of your Government.*

XIII. If the People of any Province have been accustomed to support their own Governors and Judges to Satisfaction, you are to apprehend that such Governors and Judges may be thereby influenced to treat the People kindly, and to do them Justice. This is another Reason for applying Part of that Revenue in larger Salaries to such Governors and Judges, given, as their Commissions are, *during your Pleasure* only, forbidding them to take any Salaries from their Provinces; that thus the People may no longer hope any Kindness from their Governors, or (in Crown Cases) any Justice from their Judges. And as the Money thus mis-applied in one Province is extorted from all, probably *all will resent the Mis-application.*

XIV. If the Parliaments of your Provinces should dare to claim Rights or complain of your Administration, order them to be harass'd with repeated *Dissolutions.* If the same Men are continually return'd by new Elections, adjourn their Meetings to some Country Village where they cannot be accommodated, and there keep them *during Pleasure;* for this, you know, is your PREROGATIVE; and an excellent one it is, as you may manage it, to promote Discontents among the People, diminish their Respect, and *increase their Disaffection.*

XV. Convert the brave honest Officers of your Navy into pimping Tide-waiters and Colony Officers of the Customs. Let those who in Time of War fought gallantly in Defence of the Commerce of their Countrymen, in Peace be taught to prey upon it. Let them learn to be corrupted by great and real Smugglers, but (to shew their Diligence) scour with armed Boats every Bay, Harbour, River, Creek, Cove or Nook throughout the Coast of your Colonies, stop and detain every Coaster, every Wood-boat, every Fisherman, tumble their Cargoes, and even their Ballast, inside out and upside down; and if a Penn'orth of Pins is found un-entered, let the Whole be seized and confiscated. Thus shall the Trade of your Colonists suffer more from their Friends in Time of Peace, than it did from their Enemies in War. Then let these Boats Crews land upon every Farm in their Way, rob the Orchards, steal the Pigs and Poultry, and insult the Inhabitants. If the injured and exasperated Farmers, unable to procure other Justice, should attack the Agressors, drub them and burn their Boats, you are to call this *High Treason* and *Rebellion,* order Fleets and Armies into their Country, and threaten to carry all the Offenders three thousand Miles to be hang'd, drawn and quartered. *O! this will work admirably!*

XVI. If you are told of Discontents in your Colonies, never believe that they are general, or that you have given Occasion for them; therefore do not think of applying any Remedy, or of changing any offensive Measure. Redress no Grievance, lest they should be encouraged to demand the Redress of some other Grievance. Grant no Request that is just and reasonable, lest they should make another that is unreasonable. Take all your Informations of the State of the Colonies from your Governors and Officers in Enmity with them. Encourage and reward these *Leasing-makers;* secrete their lying Accusations lest they should be confuted; but act upon them as the clearest Evidence, and believe nothing you hear from the Friends of the People. Suppose all *their* Complaints to be invented and promoted by a few factious Demagogues, whom if you could catch and hang, all would be quiet. Catch and hang a few of them accordingly;

and the *Blood of the Martyrs* shall *work Miracles* in favour of your Purpose.

XVII. If you see *rival Nations* rejoicing at the Prospect of your Disunion with your Provinces, and endeavouring to promote it: If they translate, publish and applaud all the Complaints of your discontented Colonists, at the same Time privately stimulating you to severer Measures; let not that *alarm* or offend you. Why should it? since you all mean *the same Thing.*

XVIII. If any Colony should at their own Charge erect a Fortress to secure their Port against the Fleets of a foreign Enemy, get your Governor to betray that Fortress into your Hands. Never think of paying what it cost the Country, for that would *look,* at least, like some Regard for Justice; but turn it into a Citadel to awe the Inhabitants and curb their Commerce. If they should have lodged in such Fortress the very Arms they bought and used to aid you in your Conquests, seize them all, 'twill provoke like *Ingratitude* added to *Robbery.* One admirable Effect of these Operations will be, to discourage every other Colony from erecting such Defences, and so their and your Enemies may more easily invade them, to the great Disgrace of your Government, and of course *the Furtherance of your Project.*

XIX. Send Armies into their Country under Pretence of protecting the Inhabitants; but instead of garrisoning the Forts on their Frontiers with those Troops, to prevent Incursions, demolish those Forts, and order the Troops into the Heart of the Country, that the Savages may be encouraged to attack the Frontiers, and that the Troops may be protected by the Inhabitants: This will seem to proceed from your Ill will or your Ignorance, and contribute farther to produce and strengthen an Opinion among them, *that you are no longer fit to govern them.*

XX. Lastly, Invest the General of your Army in the Provinces with great and unconstitutional Powers, and free him from the Controul of even your own Civil Governors. Let him have Troops enow under his Command, with all the Fortresses in his Possession; and who knows but (like some provincial Generals in the Roman Empire, and encouraged by the universal Discontent you have produced) he may take it into his Head to set up for himself. If he should, and you have carefully practised these few *excellent Rules* of mine, take my Word for it, all the Provinces will immediately join him, and you will that Day (if you have not done it sooner) get rid of the Trouble of governing them, and all the *Plagues* attending their *Commerce* and Connection from thenceforth and for ever.

Q. E. D.

THE PUBLIC ADVERTISER, SEPTEMBER 11, 1773

—*Thomas Jefferson*—
A SUMMARY VIEW OF THE RIGHTS OF BRITISH AMERICA
JULY 1774

RESOLVED THAT IT BE an instruction to the said deputies when assembled in General Congress with the deputies from the other states of British America to propose to the said Congress that an humble and dutiful address be presented to his majesty begging leave to lay before him as chief magistrate of the British empire the united complaints of his majesty's subjects in America; complaints which are excited by many unwarrantable incroachments and usurpations, attempted to be made by the legislature of one part of the empire, upon those rights which god and the laws have given equally and independently to all. To represent to his majesty that these his states have often individually made humble application to his imperial throne, to obtain thro' it's intervention some redress of their injured rights; to none of which was ever even an answer condescended. Humbly to hope that this their joint address, penned in the language of truth, and divested of those expressions of servility which would persuade his majesty that we are asking favors and not rights, shall obtain from his majesty a more respectful acceptance. And this his majesty will think we have reason to expect when he reflects that he is no more than the chief officer of the people, appointed by the laws, and circumscribed with definite powers, to assist in working the great machine of government erected for their use, and consequently subject to their superintendance. And in order that these our rights, as well as the invasions of them, may be laid more fully before his majesty, to take a view of them from the origin and first settlement of these countries.

To remind him that our ancestors, before their emigration to America, were the free inhabitants of the British dominions in Europe, and possessed a right, which nature has given to all men, of departing from the country in which chance, not choice has placed them, of going in quest of new habitations, and of there establishing new societies, under such laws and regulations as to them shall seem most likely to promote public happiness. That their Saxon ancestors had under this universal law, in like manner, left their native wilds and woods in the North of Europe, had possessed themselves of the island of Britain then less charged with inhabitants, and had established there that system of laws which has so long been the glory and protection of that country. Nor was ever any claim of superiority or dependance asserted over them by that mother country from which they had migrated: and were such a claim made it is beleived his majesty's subjects in Great Britain have too firm a feeling of the rights derived to them from their ancestors to bow down the sovereignty of their state before such visionary pretensions. And it is thought that no circumstance has occurred to distinguish materially the British from the Saxon emigration. America was conquered, and her settlements made and firmly established, at the expence of individuals, and not of the British public. Their own blood was spilt in acquiring lands for their settlement, their own fortunes expended in making that settlement effectual. For themselves they fought, for themselves they conquered, and for themselves alone they have right to hold. No shilling was ever issued from the public treasures of his majesty or his ancestors for their assistance, till of very late times, after the colonies had become established on a firm and permanent footing. That then indeed, having become valuable to Great Britain for her commercial purposes, his parliament was pleased to lend them assistance against an enemy who would fain have drawn to herself the benefits of their commerce to the great aggrandisement of herself and danger of Great Britain. Such assistance, and in such circumstances, they had often before given to Portugal and other allied states, with whom they carry on a commercial intercourse. Yet these states never supposed that, by calling in her aid, they thereby submitted themselves to her sovereignty. Had such terms been proposed, they would have rejected them with disdain, and trusted for better to the moderation of their enemies, or to a vigorous exertion of their own force. We do not however mean to underrate those aids, which to us were doubtless valuable, on whatever principles granted: but we would shew that they cannot give a title to that authority which the British parliament would arrogate over us; and that they may amply be repaid, by our giving to the inhabitants of Great Britain such exclusive privileges in trade as may be advantageous to them, and at the same time not too restrictive to ourselves. That settlements having been thus effected in the wilds of America, the emigrants thought proper to adopt that system of laws under which they had hitherto lived in the mother country, and to continue their union with her by submitting themselves to the same common sovereign, who was thereby made the central link connecting the several parts of the empire thus newly multiplied.

But that not long were they permitted, however far they thought themselves removed from the hand of oppression, to hold undisturbed the rights thus acquired at the hazard of their lives and loss of their fortunes. A family of princes was then on the British throne, whose treasonable crimes against their people brought on them afterwards the exertion of those sacred and sovereign rights of punishment, reserved in the hands of the people for cases of extreme necessity, and judged by the constitution unsafe to be delegated to any other judicature. While every day brought forth some new and unjustifiable exertion of power over their subjects on that side the water, it was not to be expected that those here, much less able at that time to oppose the designs of despotism, should be exempted from injury. Accordingly that country which had been acquired by the lives, the labors and the fortunes of individual adventurers, was by these princes at several times parted out and distributed among the favorites and followers of their fortunes; and by an assumed right of the crown alone were erected into distinct and independent governments; a measure which it is beleived his majesty's prudence and understanding would prevent him from imitating at this day; as no exercise of such a power of dividing and dismembering a country has ever occurred in his majesty's realm of England, tho' now of very antient standing; nor could it be justified or acquiesced under there or in any other part of his majesty's empire.

That the exercise of a free trade with all parts of the world, possessed by the American colonists as of natural right, and which no law of their own had taken away or abridged, was next the object of unjust incroachment. Some of the colonies having thought proper to continue the administration of their government in the name and under the authority of his majesty king Charles the first, whom notwithstanding his late deposition by the Common-wealth of England, they continued in the sovereignty of their state, the Parliament for the Common-wealth took the same in high offence, and assumed upon themselves the power of prohibiting their trade with all other parts of the world except the island of Great Britain. This arbitrary act however they soon recalled, and by solemn treaty entered into on the 12th. day of March 1651, between the said Commonwealth by their Commissioners and the colony of Virginia by their house of Burgesses, it was expressly stipulated by the 8th. article of the said treaty that they should have "free trade as the people of England do enjoy to all places and with all nations according to the laws of that Commonwealth." But that, upon the restoration of his majesty King Charles the second, their rights of free commerce fell once more a victim to arbitrary power: and by several acts of his reign as well as of some of his successors the trade of the colonies was laid under such restrictions as shew what hopes they might form from the justice of a British parliament were its uncontrouled power admitted over these states. History has informed us that bodies of men as well as individuals are susceptible of the spirit of tyranny. A view of these acts of parliament for regulation, as it has been affectedly called, of the American trade, if all other evidence were removed out of the case, would undeniably evince the truth of this observation. Besides the duties they impose on our articles of export and import, they prohibit our going to any Markets Northward of cape Finesterra in the kingdom of Spain for the sale of commodities which Great Britain will not take from us, and for the purchase of others with which she cannot supply us; and that for no other than the arbitrary purpose of purchasing for themselves by a sacrifice of our rights and interests, certain privileges in their commerce with an allied state, who, in confidence that their exclusive trade with America will be continued while the principles and power of the British parliament be the same, have induldged themselves in every exorbitance which their avarice could dictate, or our necessities extort: have raised their commodities called for in America to the double and treble of what they sold for before such exclusive privileges were given them, and of what better commodities of the same kind would cost us elsewhere; and at the same time give us much less for what we carry thither, than might be had at more convenient ports. That these acts prohibit us from carrying in quest of other purchasers the surplus of our tobaccoes remaining after the consumption of Great Britain is supplied: so that we must leave them with the British merchant for whatever he will please to allow us, to be by him reshipped to foreign markets, where he will reap the benefits of making sale of them for full value. That to heighten still the idea of parliamentary justice, and to shew with what moderation they are like to exercise power, where themselves are to feel no part of it's weight, we take leave to mention to his majesty certain other acts of British parliament, by which they would prohibit us from manufacturing for our own use the articles we raise on our own lands with our own labor. By an act passed in the 5th. year of the reign of his late majesty king George the second an American subject is forbidden to make a hat for himself of the fur which he has taken perhaps on his own soil. An instance of despotism to which no parrallel can be produced in the most arbitrary ages of British history. By one other act passed in the 23d. year of the same reign, the iron which we make we are forbidden to manufacture; and, heavy as that article is, and necessary in every branch of husbandry, besides commission and insurance, we are to pay freight for it to Great Britain, and freight for it back again, for the purpose of supporting, not men, but machines, in the island of Great Britain. In the same spirit of equal and impartial legislation is to be viewed the act of parliament passed in the 5th. year of the same reign, by which American lands are made subject to the demands of British creditors, while their own lands were still continued unanswerable for their debts; from which one of these conclusions must necessarily follow, either that justice is not the same thing in America as in Britain, or else that the British parliament pay less regard to it here than there. But that we do not point out to his majesty the injustice of these acts with intent to rest on that principle the cause of their nullity, but to shew that experience confirms the propriety of those political principles which exempt us from the jurisdiction of the British parliament. The true ground on which we declare these acts void is that the British parliament has no right to exercise authority over us.

That these exercises of usurped power have not been confined to instances alone in which themselves were interested; but they have also intermeddled with the regulation of the internal affairs of the colonies. The act of the 9th. of Anne for establishing a post office in America seems to have had little connection with British convenience, except that of accomodating his majesty's ministers and favorites with the sale of a lucrative and easy office.

That thus have we hastened thro' the reigns which preceded his majesty's, during which the violation of our rights were less alarming, because repeated at more distant intervals, than that rapid and bold succession of injuries which is likely to distinguish the present from all other periods of American story. Scarcely have our minds been able to emerge from the astonishment into which one stroke of parliamentary thunder has involved us, before another more heavy and more alarming is fallen on us. Single acts of tyranny may be ascribed to the accidental opinion of a day; but a series of oppressions, begun at a distinguished period, and pursued unalterably thro' every change of ministers, too plainly prove a deliberate, systematical plan of reducing us to slavery.

That the act passed in the 4th. year of his majesty's reign intitled "an act [for granting certain duties"]

One other act passed in the 5th. year of his reign intitled "an act [for granting and applying certain stamp duties"]

One other act passed in the 6th. year of his reign intitled "an act [for the better securing the dependency of his majesty's dominions in America"]

And one other act passed in the 7th. year of his reign intitled "an act [for granting duties on paper, tea, etc."] form that connected chain of parliamentary usurpation which has already been the subject of frequent applications to his majesty and the houses of Lords and Commons of Great Britain; and, no answers having yet been condescended to any of these, we shall not trouble his majesty with a repetition of the matters they contained.

But that one other act passed in the same 7th. year of his reign, having been a peculiar attempt, must ever require peculiar mention. It is intitled "an act [for suspending the legislature of New York."] One free and independent legislature hereby takes upon itself to suspend the powers of another, free and independent as itself, thus exhibiting a phaenomenon, unknown in nature, the creator and creature of its own power. Not only the principles of common sense, but the common feelings of human nature must be surrendered up, before his majesty's subjects here can be persuaded to believe that they hold their political existence at the will of a British parliament. Shall these governments be dissolved, their property annihilated, and their people reduced to a state of nature, at the imperious breath of a body of men whom they never saw, in whom they never confided, and over whom they have no powers of punishment or removal, let their crimes against the American public be ever so great? Can any one reason be assigned why 160,000 electors in the island of Great Britain should give law to four millions in the states of America, every individual of whom is equal to every individual of them in virtue, in understanding, and in bodily strength? Were this to be admitted, instead of being a free people, as we have hitherto supposed, and mean to continue, ourselves, we should suddenly be found the slaves, not of one, but of 160,000 tyrants, distinguished too from all others by this singular circumstance that they are removed from the reach of fear, the only restraining motive which may hold the hand of a tyrant.

That by "an act to discontinue in such manner and for such time as are therein mentioned the landing and discharging lading or shipping of goods wares and merchandize at the town and within the harbor of Boston in the province of Massachusett's bay in North America" which was passed at the last session of British parliament, a large and populous town, whose trade was their sole subsistence, was deprived of that trade, and involved in utter ruin. Let us for a while suppose the question of right suspended, in order to examine this act on principles of justice. An act of parliament had been passed imposing duties on teas to be paid in America, against which act the Americans had protested as inauthoritative. The East India company, who till that time had never sent a pound of tea to America on their own account, step forth on that occasion the asserters of parliamentary right, and send hither many ship loads of that obnoxious commodity. The masters of their several vessels however, on their arrival in America, wisely attended to admonition, and returned with their cargoes. In the province of New England alone the remonstrances of the people were disregarded, and a compliance, after being many days waited for, was flatly refused. Whether in this the master of the vessel was governed by his obstinacy or his instructions, let those who know, say. There are extraordinary situations which require extraordinary interposition. An exasperated people, who feel that they possess power, are not easily restrained within limits strictly regular. A number of them assembled in the town of Boston, threw the tea into the ocean and dispersed without doing any other act of violence. If in this they did wrong, they were known, and were amenable to the laws of the land, against which it could not be objected that they had ever in any instance been obstructed or diverted from their regular course in favor of popular offenders. They should therefore not have been distrusted on this occasion. But that illfated colony had formerly been bold in their enmities against the house of Stuart, and were now devoted to ruin by that unseen hand which governs the momentous affairs of this great empire. On the partial representations of a few worthless ministerial dependants, whose constant office it has been to keep that government embroiled, and who by their treacheries hope to obtain the dignity of the British knighthood, without calling for a party accused, without asking a proof, without attempting a distinction between the guilty and the innocent, the whole of that antient and wealthy town is in a moment reduced from opulence to beggary. Men who had spent their lives in extending the British commerce, who had invested in that place the wealth their honest endeavors had merited, found themselves and their families thrown at once on the world for subsistence by it's charities. Not the hundredth part of the inhabitants of that town had been concerned in the act complained of; many of them were in Great Britain and in other parts beyond sea; yet all were involved in one indiscriminate ruin, by a new executive power unheard of till then, that of a British parliament. A property of the value of many millions of money was sacrificed to revenge, not repay, the loss of a few thousands. This is administering justice with a heavy hand indeed! And when is this tempest to be arrested in it's course? Two wharfs are to be opened again when his majesty shall think proper: the residue which lined the extensive shores of the bay of Boston are forever interdicted the exercise of commerce. This little exception seems to have been thrown in for no other purpose than that of setting a precedent for investing his majesty with legislative powers. If the pulse of his people shall beat calmly under this experiment, another and another will be tried till the measure of despotism be filled up. It would be an insult on common sense to pretend that this exception was made in order to restore it's commerce to that great town. The trade which cannot be received at two wharfs alone, must of necessity be transferred to some other place; to which it will soon be followed by that of the two wharfs. Considered in this light it would be an insolent and cruel mockery at the annihilation of the town of Boston.

By the act for the suppression of riots and tumults in the town of Boston, passed also in the last session of parliament, a murder committed there is, if the governor pleases, to be tried in the court of King's bench in the island of Great Britain, by a jury of Middlesex. The witnesses too, on receipt of such a sum as the Governor shall think it reasonable for them to expend, are to enter into recognisance to appear at the trial. This is in other words taxing them to the amount of their recognisance; and that amount may be whatever a Governor pleases. For who does his majesty think can be prevailed on to cross the Atlantick for the sole purpose of bearing evidence to a fact? His expences are to be borne indeed as they shall be estimated by a Governor; but who are to feed the wife and children whom he leaves behind, and who have had no other subsistence but his daily labor? Those epidemical disorders too, so terrible in a foreign climate, is the cure of them to be estimated among the articles of expence, and their danger to be warded off by the almighty power of a parliament? And the wretched criminal, if he happen to have offended on the American side, stripped of his privilege of trial by peers, of his vicinage, removed from the place where alone full evidence could be obtained, without money, without counsel, without friends, without exculpatory proof, is tried before judges predetermined to condemn. The cowards who would suffer a countryman to be torn from the bowels of their society in order to be thus offered a sacrifice to parliamentary tyranny, would merit that everlasting infamy now fixed on the authors of the act! A clause for a similar purpose had been introduced into an act passed in the 12th. year of his majesty's reign entitled "an act for the better securing and preserving his majesty's dock-yards, magazines, ships, ammunition and stores," against which as meriting the same censures the several colonies have already protested.

That these are the acts of power assumed by a body of men foreign to our constitutions, and unacknowleged by our laws; against which we do, on behalf of the inhabitants of British America, enter this our solemn and determined protest. And we do earnestly intreat his majesty, as yet the only mediatory power between the several states of the British empire, to recommend to his parliament of Great Britain the total revocation of these acts, which however nugatory they be, may yet prove the cause of further discontents and jealousies among us.

That we next proceed to consider the conduct of his majesty, as holding the executive powers of the laws of these states, and mark out his deviations from the line of duty. By the constitution of Great Britain as well as of the several American states, his majesty possesses the power of refusing to pass into a law any bill which has already passed the other two branches of legislature. His majesty however and his ancestors, conscious of the impropriety of opposing their single opinion to the united wisdom of two houses of parliament, while their proceedings were unbiassed by interested principles, for several ages past have modestly declined the exercise of this power in that part of his empire called Great Britain. But by change of circumstances, other principles than those of justice simply have obtained an influence on their determinations. The addition of new states to the British empire has produced an addition of new, and sometimes opposite interests. It is now therefore the great office of his majesty to resume the exercise of his negative power, and to prevent the passage of laws by any one legislature of the empire which might bear injuriously on the rights and interests of another. Yet this will not excuse the wanton exercise of this power which we have seen his majesty practice on the laws of the American legislatures. For the most trifling reasons, and sometimes for no conceivable reason at all, his majesty has rejected laws of the most salutary tendency. The abolition of domestic slavery is the great object of desire in those colonies where it was unhappily introduced in their infant state. But previous to the infranchisement of the slaves we have, it is necessary to exclude all further importations from Africa. Yet our repeated attempts to effect this by prohibitions, and by imposing duties which might amount to a prohibition, have been hitherto defeated by his majesty's negative: thus preferring the immediate advantages of a few British corsairs to the lasting interests of the American states, and to the rights of human nature deeply wounded by this infamous practice. Nay the single interposition of an interested individual against a law was scarcely ever known to fail of success, tho' in the opposite scale were placed the interests of a whole country. That this is so shameful an abuse of a power trusted with his majesty for other purposes, as if not reformed would call for some legal restrictions.

With equal inattention to the necessities of his people here, has his majesty permitted our laws to lie neglected in England for years, neither confirming them by his assent, nor annulling them by his negative: so that such of them as have no suspending clause, we hold on the most precarious of all tenures, his majesty's will, and such of them as suspend themselves till his majesty's assent be obtained we have feared might be called into existence at some future and distant period, when time and change of circumstances shall have rendered them destructive to his people here. And to render this grievance still more oppressive, his majesty by his instructions has laid his governors under such restrictions that they can pass no law of any moment unless it have such suspending clause: so that, however immediate may be the call for legislative interposition, the law cannot be executed till it has twice crossed the Atlantic, by which time the evil may have spent it's whole force.

But in what terms reconcileable to majesty and at the same time to truth, shall we speak of a late instruction to his majesty's governor of the colony of Virginia, by which he is forbidden to assent to any law for the division of a county, unless the new county will consent to have no representative in assembly? That colony has as yet affixed no boundary to the Westward. Their Western counties therefore are of indefinite extent. Some of them are actually seated many hundred miles from their Eastern limits. Is it possible then that his majesty can have bestowed a single thought on the situation of those people, who, in order to obtain justice for injuries however great or small, must, by the laws of that colony, attend their county court at such a distance, with all their witnesses, monthly, till their litigation be determined? Or does his majesty seriously wish, and publish it to the world, that his subjects should give up the glorious right of representation, with all the benefits derived from that, and submit themselves the absolute slaves of his sovereign will? Or is it rather meant to confine the legislative body to their present numbers, that they may be the cheaper bargain whenever they shall become worth a purchase?

One of the articles of impeachment against Tresilian and the other judges of Westminster Hall in the reign of Richard the second, for which they suffered death as traitors to their country, was that they had advised the king that he might dissolve his parliament at any time: and succeeding kings have adopted the opinion of these unjust judges. Since the establishment however of the British constitution at the glorious Revolution on it's free and antient principles, neither his majesty nor his ancestors have exercised such a power of dissolution in the island of Great Britain: and when his majesty was petitioned by the united voice of his people there to dissolve the present parliament, who had become obnoxious to them, his ministers were heard to declare in open parliament that his majesty possessed no such power by the constitution. But how different their language and his practice here! To declare as their duty required the known rights of their country, to oppose the usurpation of every foreign judicature, to disregard the imperious mandates of a minister or governor, have been the avowed causes of dissolving houses of representatives in America. But if such powers be really vested in his majesty, can he suppose they are there placed to awe the members from such purposes as these? When the representative body have lost the confidence of their constituents, when they have notoriously made sale of their most valuable rights, when they have assumed to themselves powers which the people never put into their hands, then indeed their continuing in office becomes dangerous to the state, and calls for an exercise of the power of dissolution. Such being the causes for which the representative body should and should not be dissolved, will it not appear strange to an unbiassed observer that that of Great Britain was not dissolved, while those of the colonies have repeatedly incurred that sentence?

But your majesty or your Governors have carried this power beyond every limit known or provided for by the laws. After dissolving one house of representatives, they have refused to call another, so that for a great length of time the legislature provided by the laws has been out of existence. From the nature of things, every society must at all times possess within itself the sovereign powers of legislation. The feelings of human nature revolt against the supposition of a state so situated as that it may not in any emergency provide against dangers which perhaps threaten immediate ruin. While those bodies are in existence to whom the people have delegated the powers of legislation, they alone possess and may exercise those powers.

But when they are dissolved by the lopping off one or more of their branches, the power reverts to the people, who may use it to unlimited extent, either assembling together in person, sending deputies, or in any other way they may think proper. We forbear to trace consequences further; the dangers are conspicuous with which this practice is replete.

That we shall at this time also take notice of an error in the nature of our landholdings, which crept in at a very early period of our settlement. The introduction of the Feudal tenures into the kingdom of England, though antient, is well enough understood to set this matter in a proper light. In the earlier ages of the Saxon settlement feudal holdings were certainly altogether unknown, and very few, if any, had been introduced at the time of the Norman conquest. Our Saxon ancestors held their lands, as they did their personal property, in absolute dominion, disencumbered with any superior, answering nearly to the nature of those possessions which the Feudalists term Allodial: William the Norman first introduced that system generally. The lands which had belonged to those who fell in the battle of Hastings, and in the subsequent insurrections of his reign, formed a considerable proportion of the lands of the whole kingdom. These he granted out, subject to feudal duties, as did he also those of a great number of his new subjects, who by persuasions or threats were induced to surrender them for that purpose. But still much was left in the hands of his Saxon subjects, held of no superior, and not subject to feudal conditions. These therefore by express laws, enacted to render uniform the system of military defence, were made liable to the same military duties as if they had been feuds: and the Norman lawyers soon found means to saddle them also with all the other feudal burthens. But still they had not been surrendered to the king, they were not derived from his grant, and therefore they were not holden of him. A general principle indeed was introduced that "all lands in England were held either mediately or immediately of the crown": but this was borrowed from those holdings which were truly feudal, and only applied to others for the purposes of illustration. Feudal holdings were therefore but exceptions out of the Saxon laws of possession, under which all lands were held in absolute right. These therefore still form the basis or groundwork of the Common law, to prevail wheresoever the exceptions have not taken place. America was not conquered by

William the Norman, nor it's lands surrendered to him or any of his successors. Possessions there are undoubtedly of the Allodial nature. Our ancestors however, who migrated hither, were laborers, not lawyers. The fictitious principle that all lands belong originally to the king, they were early persuaded to beleive real, and accordingly took grants of their own lands from the crown. And while the crown continued to grant for small sums and on reasonable rents, there was no inducement to arrest the error and lay it open to public view. But his majesty has lately taken on him to advance the terms of purchase and of holding to the double of what they were, by which means the acquisition of lands being rendered difficult, the population of our country is likely to be checked. It is time therefore for us to lay this matter before his majesty, and to declare that he has no right to grant lands of himself. From the nature and purpose of civil institutions, all the lands within the limits which any particular society has circumscribed around itself, are assumed by that society, and subject to their allotment only. This may be done by themselves assembled collectively, or by their legislature to whom they may have delegated sovereign authority: and, if they are allotted in neither of these ways, each individual of the society may appropriate to himself such lands as he finds vacant, and occupancy will give him title.

That, in order to inforce the arbitrary measures before complained of, his majesty has from time to time sent among us large bodies of armed forces, not made up of the people here, nor raised by the authority of our laws. Did his majesty possess such a right as this, it might swallow up all our other rights whenever he should think proper. But his majesty has no right to land a single armed man on our shores; and those whom he sends here are liable to our laws for the suppression and punishment of Riots, Routs, and unlawful assemblies, or are hostile bodies invading us in defiance of law. When in the course of the late war it became expedient that a body of Hanoverian troops should be brought over for the defence of Great Britain, his majesty's grandfather, our late sovereign, did not pretend to introduce them under any authority he possessed. Such a measure would have given just alarm to his subjects in Great Britain, whose liberties would not be safe if armed men of another country, and of another spirit, might be brought into the realm at any time without the consent of their legislature. He therefore applied to parliament who passed an act for that purpose, limiting the number to be brought in and the time they were to continue. In like manner is his majesty restrained in every part of the empire. He possesses indeed the executive power of the laws in every state; but they are the laws of the particular state which he is to administer within that state, and not those of any one within the limits of another. Every state must judge for itself the number of armed men which they may safely trust among them, of whom they are to consist, and under what restrictions they are to be laid. To render these proceedings still more criminal against our laws, instead of subjecting the military to the civil power, his majesty has expressly made the civil subordinate to the military. But can his majesty thus put down all law under his feet? Can he erect a power superior to that which erected himself? He has done it indeed by force; but let him remember that force cannot give right.

That these are our grievances which we have thus laid before his majesty with that freedom of language and sentiment which becomes a free people, claiming their rights as derived from the laws of nature, and not as the gift of their chief magistrate. Let those flatter, who fear: it is not an American art. To give praise where it is not due, might be well from the venal, but would ill beseem those who are asserting the rights of human nature. They know, and will therefore say, that kings are the servants, not the proprietors of the people. Open your breast Sire, to liberal and expanded thought. Let not the name of George the third be a blot in the page of history. You are surrounded by British counsellors, but remember that they are parties. You have no ministers for American affairs, because you have none taken from among us, nor amenable to the laws on which they are to give you advice. It behoves you therefore to think and to act for yourself and your people. The great principles of right and wrong are legible to every reader: to pursue them requires not the aid of many counsellors. The whole art of government consists in the art of being honest. Only aim to do your duty, and mankind will give you credit where you fail. No longer persevere in sacrificing the rights of one part of the empire to the inordinate desires of another: but deal out to all equal and impartial right. Let no act be passed by any one legislature which may infringe on the rights and liberties of another. This is the important post in which fortune has placed you, holding the balance of a great, if a well poised empire. This, Sire, is the advice of your great American council, on the observance of which may perhaps depend your felicity and future fame, and the preservation of that harmony which alone can continue both to Great Britain and America the reciprocal advantages of their connection. It is neither our wish nor our interest to separate from her. We are willing on our part to sacrifice every thing which reason can ask to the restoration of that tranquility for which all must wish. On their part let them be ready to establish union on a generous plan. Let them name their terms, but let them be just. Accept of every commercial preference it is in our power to give for such things as we can raise for their use, or they make for ours. But let them not think to exclude us from going to other markets, to dispose of those commodities which they cannot use, nor to supply those wants which they cannot supply. Still less let it be proposed that our properties within our own territories shall be taxed or regulated by any power on earth but our own. The god who gave us life, gave us liberty at the same time: the hand of force may destroy, but cannot disjoin them. This, Sire, is our last, our determined resolution: and that you will be pleased to interpose with that efficacy which your earnest endeavors may insure to procure redress of these our great grievances, to quiet the minds of your subjects in British America against any apprehensions of future incroachment, to establish fraternal love and harmony thro' the whole empire, and that that may continue to the latest ages of time, is the fervent prayer of all British America.

First Continental Congress

DELEGATES FROM EVERY COLONY but Georgia met at Philadelphia in early September 1774 to fashion a joint response to the Coercive or Intolerable Acts that Parliament had imposed on Massachusetts. After eight weeks of debate and numerous dinners, they reached a broad consensus on both principles and tactics. In the Declaration and Resolves adopted on October 14, Congress laid out its understanding of the proper relation between colonies and empire. The delegates unanimously agreed that Parliament had no right to impose taxes or other laws on unrepresented colonists. The one point on which Congress failed to attain unanimity appeared in the second sentence of the fourth resolve. Here, as a conciliatory gesture, a majority of delegates were willing to allow Parliament to continue to regulate imperial trade, with the understanding that the Americans were voluntarily ceding this point.

To demonstrate that the colonists were prepared to support these positions, Congress also adopted a new agreement to halt importations of British goods and then, if necessary, exports as well. The Association, as it was called, also weakened the authority of legal institutions of government by providing for the election of popular committees of inspection to enforce the proposed commercial boycott.

Declaration and Resolves
October 14, 1774

Whereas, since the close of the last war, the British parliament, claiming a power of right to bind the people of America, by statute in all cases whatsoever, hath in some acts expressly imposed taxes on them, and in others, under various pretences, but in fact for the purpose of raising a revenue, hath imposed rates and duties payable in these colonies, established a board of commissioners, with unconstitutional powers, and extended the jurisdiction of courts of Admiralty, not only for collecting the said duties, but for the trial of causes merely arising within the body of a county.

And whereas, in consequence of other statutes, judges, who before held only estates at will in their offices, have been made dependant on the Crown alone for their salaries, and standing armies kept in times of peace:

And it has lately been resolved in Parliament, that by force of a statute, made in the thirty-fifth year of the reign of king Henry the eighth, colonists may be transported to England, and tried there upon accusations for treasons, and misprisions, or concealments of treasons committed in the colonies; and by a late statute, such trials have been directed in cases therein mentioned.

And whereas, in the last session of parliament, three statutes were made; one, intituled "An act to discontinue, in such manner and for such time as are therein mentioned, the landing and discharging, lading, or shipping of goods, wares & merchandise, at the town, and within the harbour of Boston, in the province of Massachusetts-bay, in North-America;" another, intituled "An act for the better regulating the government of the province of the Massachusetts-bay in New-England;" and another, intituled "An act for the impartial administration of justice, in the cases of persons questioned for any act done by them in the execution of the law, or for the suppression of riots and tumults, in the province of the Massachusetts-bay, in New-England." And another statute was then made, "for making more effectual provision for the government of the province of Quebec, &c." All which statutes are impolitic, unjust, and cruel, as well as unconstitutional, and most dangerous and destructive of American rights.

And whereas, Assemblies have been frequently dissolved, contrary to the rights of the people, when they attempted to deliberate on grievances; and their dutiful, humble, loyal, & reasonable petitions to the crown for redress, have been repeatedly treated with contempt, by his majesty's ministers of state:

The good people of the several Colonies of New-hampshire, Massachusetts-bay, Rhode-island and Providence plantations, Connecticut, New-York, New-Jersey, Pennsylvania, Newcastle, Kent and Sussex on Delaware, Maryland, Virginia, North Carolina, and South Carolina, justly alarmed at these arbitrary proceedings of parliament and administration, have severally elected, constituted, and appointed deputies to meet and sit in general congress, in the city of Philadelphia, in order to obtain such establishment, as that their religion, laws, and liberties may not be subverted:

Whereupon the deputies so appointed being now assembled, in a full and free representation of these Colonies, taking into their most serious consideration, the best means of attaining the ends aforesaid, do, in the first place, as Englishmen, their ancestors in like cases have usually done, for asserting and vindicating their rights and liberties, declare,

That the inhabitants of the English Colonies in North America, by the immutable laws of nature, the principles of the English constitution, and the several charters or compacts, have the following Rights:

Resolved, N. C. D.* 1. That they are entitled to life, liberty, & property, and they have never ceded to any sovereign power whatever, a right to dispose of either without their consent.

Resolved, N. C. D. 2. That our ancestors, who first settled these colonies, were at the time of their emigration from the mother country, entitled to all the rights, liberties, and immunities of free and natural-born subjects, within the realm of England.

---

*Abbreviation for *nemine contradicente* (Latin for, literally, "no one speaking against"); unanimously.

Resolved, N. C. D. 3. That by such emigration they by no means forfeited, surrendered, or lost any of those rights, but that they were, and their descendants now are, entitled to the exercise and enjoyment of all such of them, as their local and other circumstances enable them to exercise and enjoy.

Resolved, 4. That the foundation of English liberty, and of all free government, is a right in the people to participate in their legislative council: and as the English colonists are not represented, and from their local and other circumstances, cannot properly be represented in the British parliament, they are entitled to a free and exclusive power of legislation in their several provincial legislatures, where their right of representation can alone be preserved, in all cases of taxation and internal polity, subject only to the negative of their sovereign, in such manner as has been heretofore used and accustomed. But, from the necessity of the case, and a regard to the mutual interest of both countries, we cheerfully consent to the operation of such acts of the British parliament, as are bona fide, restrained to the regulation of our external commerce, for the purpose of securing the commercial advantages of the whole empire to the mother country, and the commercial benefits of its respective members; excluding every idea of taxation, internal or external, for raising a revenue on the subjects in America, without their consent.

Resolved, N. C. D. 5. That the respective colonies are entitled to the common law of England, and more especially to the great and inestimable privilege of being tried by their peers of the vicinage, according to the course of that law.

Resolved, 6. That they are entituled to the benefit of such of the English statutes as existed at the time of their colonization; and which they have, by experience, respectively found to be applicable to their several local and other circumstances.

Resolved, N. C. D. 7. That these, his majesty's colonies, are likewise entitled to all the immunities and privileges granted & confirmed to them by royal charters, or secured by their several codes of provincial laws.

Resolved, N. C. D. 8. That they have a right peaceably to assemble, consider of their grievances, and petition the King; and that all prosecutions, prohibitory proclamations, and commitments for the same, are illegal.

Resolved, N. C. D. 9. That the keeping a Standing army in these colonies, in times of peace, without the consent of the legislature of that colony, in which such army is kept, is against law.

Resolved, N. C. D. 10. It is indispensably necessary to good government, and rendered essential by the English constitution, that the constituent branches of the legislature be independent of each other; that, therefore, the exercise of legislative power in several colonies, by a council appointed, during pleasure, by the crown, is unconstitutional, dangerous, and destructive to the freedom of American legislation.

All and each of which the aforesaid deputies, in behalf of themselves and their constituents, do claim, demand, and insist on, as their indubitable rights and liberties; which cannot be legally taken from them, altered or abridged by any power whatever, without their own consent, by their representatives in their several provincial legislatures.

In the course of our inquiry, we find many infringements and violations of the foregoing rights, which, from an ardent desire, that harmony and mutual intercourse of affection and interest may be restored, we pass over for the present, and proceed to state such acts and measures as have been adopted since the last war, which demonstrate a system formed to enslave America.

Resolved, N. C. D. That the following acts of Parliament are infringements and violations of the rights of the colonists; and that the repeal of them is essentially necessary in order to restore harmony between Great-Britain and the American colonies, viz:

The several acts of 4 Geo. 3. ch. 15, & ch. 34.—5 Geo. 3. ch. 25.—6 Geo. 3. ch. 52.—7 Geo. 3. ch. 41, & ch. 46.—8 Geo. 3. ch. 22, which impose duties for the purpose of raising a revenue in America, extend the powers of the admiralty courts beyond their ancient limits, deprive the American subject of trial by jury, authorize the judges' certificate to indemnify the prosecutor from damages, that he might otherwise be liable to, requiring oppressive security from a claimant of ships and goods seized, before he shall be allowed to defend his property, and are subversive of American rights.

Also the 12 Geo. 3. ch. 24, entitled "An act for the better securing his Majesty's dock-yards, magazines, ships, ammunition, and stores," which declares a new offence in America, and deprives the

American subject of a constitutional trial by a jury of the vicinage, by authorizing the trial of any person, charged with the committing any offence described in the said act, out of the realm, to be indicted and tried for the same in any shire or county within the realm.

Also the three acts passed in the last session of parliament, for stopping the port and blocking up the harbour of Boston, for altering the charter & government of the Massachusetts-bay, and that which is entituled "An act for the better administration of Justice," &c.

Also the act passed in the same session for establishing the Roman Catholick Religion in the province of Quebec, abolishing the equitable system of English laws, and erecting a tyranny there, to the great danger, from so total a dissimilarity of Religion, law, and government of the neighbouring British colonies, by the assistance of whose blood and treasure the said country was conquered from France.

Also the act passed in the same session for the better providing suitable quarters for officers and soldiers in his Majesty's service in North-America.

Also, that the keeping a standing army in several of these colonies, in time of peace, without the consent of the legislature of that colony in which such army is kept, is against law.

To these grievous acts and measures, Americans cannot submit, but in hopes that their fellow subjects in Great-Britain will, on a revision of them, restore us to that state in which both countries found happiness and prosperity, we have for the present only resolved to pursue the following peaceable measures:

Resolved, unanimously, That from and after the first day of December next, there be no importation into British America, from Great Britain or Ireland of any goods, wares or merchandize whatsoever, or from any other place of any such goods, wares or merchandize.*

1st. To enter into a non-importation, non-consumption, and non-exportation agreement or association.

---

*This paragraph was rejected.

2. To prepare an address to the people of Great-Britain, and a memorial to the inhabitants of British America, &

3. To prepare a loyal address to his Majesty; agreeable to Resolutions already entered into.

ASSOCIATION
OCTOBER 20, 1774

WE, HIS MAJESTY'S MOST loyal subjects, the delegates of the several colonies of New-Hampshire, Massachusetts-Bay, Rhode-Island, Connecticut, New-York, New-Jersey, Pennsylvania, the three lower counties of New-Castle, Kent and Sussex, on Delaware, Maryland, Virginia, North-Carolina, and South-Carolina, deputed to represent them in a continental Congress, held in the city of Philadelphia, on the 5th day of September, 1774, avowing our allegiance to his majesty, our affection and regard for our fellow-subjects in Great-Britain and elsewhere, affected with the deepest anxiety, and most alarming apprehensions, at those grievances and distresses, with which his Majesty's American subjects are oppressed; and having taken under our most serious deliberation, the state of the whole continent, find, that the present unhappy situation of our affairs is occasioned by a ruinous system of colony administration, adopted by the British ministry about the year 1763, evidently calculated for inslaving these colonies, and, with them, the British empire. In prosecution of which system, various acts of parliament have been passed, for raising a revenue in America, for depriving the American subjects, in many instances, of the constitutional trial by jury, exposing their lives to danger, by directing a new and illegal trial beyond the seas, for crimes alleged to have been committed in America: and in prosecution of the same system, several late, cruel, and oppressive acts have been passed, respecting the town of Boston and the Massachusetts-Bay, and also an act for extending the province of Quebec, so as to border on the western frontiers of these colonies, establishing an arbitrary government therein, and discouraging the settlement of British subjects in that wide extended country; thus, by the influence of civil principles and ancient prejudices, to dispose the inhabitants to act with hostility against the free Protestant colonies, whenever a wicked ministry shall chuse so to direct them.

To obtain redress of these grievances, which threaten destruction to the lives, liberty, and property of his majesty's subjects, in North America, we are of opinion, that a non-importation, non-consumption, and non-exportation agreement, faithfully adhered to, will prove the most speedy, effectual, and peaceable measure: and, therefore, we do, for ourselves, and the inhabitants of the several colonies, whom we represent, firmly agree and associate, under the sacred ties of virtue, honour and love of our country, as follows:

1. That from and after the first day of December next, we will not import, into British America, from Great-Britain or Ireland, any goods, wares, or merchandise whatsoever, or from any other place, any such goods, wares, or merchandise, as shall have been exported from Great-Britain or Ireland; nor will we, after that day, import any East-India tea from any part of the world; nor any molasses, syrups, paneles, coffee, or pimento, from the British plantations or from Dominica; nor wines from Madeira, or the Western Islands; nor foreign indigo.

2. We will neither import nor purchase, any slave imported after the first day of December next; after which time, we will wholly discontinue the slave trade, and will neither be concerned in it ourselves, nor will we hire our vessels, nor sell our commodities or manufactures to those who are concerned in it.

3. As a non-consumption agreement, strictly adhered to, will be an effectual security for the observation of the non-importation, we, as above, solemnly agree and associate, that, from this day, we will not purchase or use any tea, imported on account of the East-India company, or any on which a duty hath been or shall be paid; and from and after the first day of March next, we will not purchase or use any East-India tea whatever; nor will we, nor shall any person for or under us, purchase or use any of those goods, wares, or merchandise, we have agreed not to import, which we shall know, or have cause to suspect, were imported after the first day of December, except such as come under the rules and directions of the tenth article hereafter mentioned.

4. The earnest desire we have, not to injure our fellow-subjects in Great-Britain, Ireland, or the West-Indies, induces us to suspend

a non-exportation, until the tenth day of September, 1775; at which time, if the said acts and parts of acts of the British parliament herein after mentioned are not repealed, we will not, directly or indirectly, export any merchandise or commodity whatsoever to Great-Britain, Ireland, or the West-Indies, except rice to Europe.

5. Such as are merchants, and use the British and Irish trade, will give orders, as soon as possible, to their factors, agents and correspondents, in Great-Britain and Ireland, not to ship any goods to them, on any pretence whatsoever, as they cannot be received in America; and if any merchant, residing in Great-Britain or Ireland, shall directly or indirectly ship any goods, wares or merchandise, for America, in order to break the said non-importation agreement, or in any manner contravene the same, on such unworthy conduct being well attested, it ought to be made public; and, on the same being so done, we will not, from thenceforth, have any commercial connexion with such merchant.

6. That such as are owners of vessels will give positive orders to their captains, or masters, not to receive on board their vessels any goods prohibited by the said non-importation agreement, on pain of immediate dismission from their service.

7. We will use our utmost endeavours to improve the breed of sheep, and increase their number to the greatest extent; and to that end, we will kill them as seldom as may be, especially those of the most profitable kind; nor will we export any to the West-Indies or elsewhere; and those of us, who are or may become over-stocked with, or can conveniently spare any sheep, will dispose of them to our neighbours, especially to the poorer sort, on moderate terms.

8. We will, in our several stations, encourage frugality, economy, and industry, and promote agriculture, arts and the manufactures of this country, especially that of wool; and will discountenance and discourage every species of extravagance and dissipation, especially all horse-racing, and all kinds of gaming, cock-fighting, exhibitions of shews, plays, and other expensive diversions and entertainments; and on the death of any relation or friend, none of us, or any of our families, will go into any further mourning-dress, than a black crape or ribbon on the arm or hat, for gentlemen, and a black ribbon and

necklace for ladies, and we will discontinue the giving of gloves and scarves at funerals.

9. Such as are venders of goods or merchandise will not take advantage of the scarcity of goods, that may be occasioned by this association, but will sell the same at the rates we have been respectively accustomed to do, for twelve months last past.—And if any vender of goods or merchandise shall sell any such goods on higher terms, or shall, in any manner, or by any device whatsoever violate or depart from this agreement, no person ought, nor will any of us deal with any such person, or his or her factor or agent, at any time thereafter, for any commodity whatever.

10. In case any merchant, trader, or other person, shall import any goods or merchandise, after the first day of December, and before the first day of February next, the same ought forthwith, at the election of the owner, to be either re-shipped or delivered up to the committee of the county or town, wherein they shall be imported, to be stored at the risque of the importer, until the non-importation agreement shall cease, or be sold under the direction of the committee aforesaid; and in the last-mentioned case, the owner or owners of such goods shall be reimbursed out of the sales, the first cost and charges, the profit, if any, to be applied towards relieving and employing such poor inhabitants of the town of Boston, as are immediate sufferers by the Boston port-bill; and a particular account of all goods so returned, stored, or sold, to be inserted in the public papers; and if any goods or merchandises shall be imported after the said first day of February, the same ought forthwith to be sent back again, without breaking any of the packages thereof.

11. That a committee be chosen in every county, city, and town, by those who are qualified to vote for representatives in the legislature, whose business it shall be attentively to observe the conduct of all persons touching this association; and when it shall be made to appear, to the satisfaction of a majority of any such committee, that any person within the limits of their appointment has violated this association, that such majority do forthwith cause the truth of the case to be published in the gazette; to the end, that all such foes to the rights of British-America may be publicly known, and universally contemned as the enemies of American liberty; and thenceforth we respectively will break off all dealings with him or her.

12. That the committee of correspondence, in the respective colonies, do frequently inspect the entries of their custom-houses, and inform each other, from time to time, of the true state thereof, and of every other material circumstance that may occur relative to this association.

13. That all manufactures of this country be sold at reasonable prices, so that no undue advantage be taken of a future scarcity of goods.

14. And we do further agree and resolve, that we will have no trade, commerce, dealings or intercourse whatsoever, with any colony or province, in North-America, which shall not accede to, or which shall hereafter violate this association, but will hold them as unworthy of the rights of freemen, and as inimical to the liberties of their country.

And we do solemnly bind ourselves and our constituents, under the ties aforesaid, to adhere to this association, until such parts of the several acts of parliament passed since the close of the last war, as impose or continue duties on tea, wine, molasses, syrups, paneles, coffee, sugar, pimento, indigo, foreign paper, glass, and painters' colours, imported into America, and extend the powers of the admiralty courts beyond their ancient limits, deprive the American subject of trial by jury, authorize the judge's certificate to indemnify the prosecutor from damages, that he might otherwise be liable to from a trial by his peers, require oppressive security from a claimant of ships or goods seized, before he shall be allowed to defend his property, are repealed.—And until that part of the act of the 12 G. 3. ch. 24, entitled "An act for the better securing his majesty's dock-yards, magazines, ships, ammunition, and stores," by which any persons charged with committing any of the offences therein described, in America, may be tried in any shire or county within the realm, is repealed—and until the four acts, passed the last session of parliament, viz. that for stopping the port and blocking up the harbour of Boston—that for altering the charter and government of the Massachusetts-Bay—and that which is entitled "An act for the better administration of justice, &c."—and that "for extending the limits of Quebec, &c." are repealed. And we recommend it to the provincial conventions, and to the committees in the respective colonies, to establish such farther regulations as they may think proper, for carrying into execution this association.

The foregoing association being determined upon by the Congress, was ordered to be subscribed by the several members thereof; and thereupon, we have hereunto set our respective names accordingly.

IN CONGRESS, PHILADELPHIA, OCTOBER 20, 1774.

Signed,

PEYTON RANDOLPH, *President.*

New Hampshire	Jn.º Sullivan Nath.ᵉˡ Folsom		J. Kinsey Wil: Livingston
Massachusetts Bay	Thomas Cushing Sam.ˡ Adams John Adams Rob.ᵗ Treat Paine	New Jersey	Step.ⁿ Crane Rich.ᵈ Smith John De Hart
Rhode Island	Step. Hopkins Sam: Ward		Jos. Galloway John Dickinson
Connecticut	Elipht Dyer Roger Sherman Silas Deane	Pennsylvania	Cha Humphreys Thomas Mifflin E. Biddle John Morton Geo: Ross
New York	Isaac Low John Alsop John Jay Ja.ˢ Duane Phil. Livingston W.ᵐ Floyd Henry Wisner S: Boerum	The Lower Counties New Castle	Cæsar Rodney Tho. M: Kean Geo: Read
		Maryland	Mat Tilghman Th.ˢ Johnson Jun.ʳ W.ᵐ Paca Samuel Chase

SECOND CONTINENTAL CONGRESS

CIVIL WAR ERUPTED IN Massachusetts in April 1775, and three weeks later Congress reconvened in Philadelphia. The delegates debated whether to revise the positions they had taken the previous fall, and decided to send George III a second conciliatory petition. Their principal task, however, was to transform the Massachusetts militia who were besieging General Gage's garrison in Boston into the Continental Army that Congress formally approved on June 14. The next day it appointed George Washington of Virginia as the army's commander. When Washington departed on June 23, he carried with him a copy of the Declaration on Causes and Necessity of Taking Arms that Congress that Congress had adopted and that he was ordered to publish upon his arrival in Boston. The Declaration was largely the work of John Dickinson, the leading moderate in Congress, and Thomas Jefferson, a newly arrived delegate from Virginia.

Benjamin Franklin was another new member of Congress. He had barely returned from London when he was elected a delegate from Pennsylvania. Convinced that the government of Lord North was committed to using military force to put down the unrest in America, Franklin believed that the colonies would need to strengthen their political union. Shortly before Congress recessed in late July, he presented the first formal plan of confederation. Congress was not yet ready to move this far, but Franklin had raised a question that the delegates privately had to ponder.

SECOND CONTINENTAL CONGRESS

Declaration on Causes and Necessity of Taking Arms

July 6, 1775

A DECLARATION BY THE Representatives of the United Colonies of North America, now met in General Congress at Philadelphia, setting forth the causes and necessity of their taking up arms.

If it was possible for men, who exercise their reason, to believe, that the Divine Author of our existence intended a part of the human race to hold an absolute property in, and an unbounded power over others, marked out by his infinite goodness and wisdom, as the objects of a legal domination never rightfully resistible, however severe and oppressive, the Inhabitants of these Colonies might at least require from the Parliament of Great Britain some evidence, that this dreadful authority over them, has been granted to that body. But a reverence for our great Creator, principles of humanity, and the dictates of common sense, must convince all those who reflect upon the subject, that government was instituted to promote the welfare of mankind, and ought to be administered for the attainment of that end. The legislature of Great Britain, however, stimulated by an inordinate passion for a power, not only unjustifiable, but which they know to be peculiarly reprobated by the very constitution of that kingdom, and desperate of success in any mode of contest, where regard should be had to truth, law, or right, have at length, deserting those, attempted to effect their cruel and impolitic purpose of enslaving these Colonies by violence, and have thereby rendered it necessary for us to close with their last appeal from Reason to Arms.— Yet, however blinded that assembly may be, by their intemperate rage for unlimited domination, so to slight justice and the opinion of mankind, we esteem ourselves bound, by obligations of respect to the rest of the world, to make known the justice of our cause.

Our forefathers, inhabitants of the island of Great Britain, left their native land, to seek on these shores a residence for civil and religious freedom. At the expence of their blood, at the hazard of their fortunes, without the least charge to the country from which they removed, by unceasing labor, and an unconquerable spirit, they effected settlements in the distant and inhospitable wilds of America, then filled with numerous and warlike nations of barbarians. Societies or governments, vested with perfect legislatures, were formed under charters from the crown, and an harmonious intercourse was established between the colonies and the kingdom from which they derived their origin. The mutual benefits of this union became in a short time so extraordinary, as to excite astonishment. It is universally confessed, that the amazing increase of the wealth, strength, and navigation of the realm, arose from this source; and the minister, who so wisely and successfully directed the measures of Great Britain in the late war, publicly declared, that these colonies enabled her to triumph over her enemies.—Towards the conclusion of that war, it pleased our sovereign to make a change in his counsels.—From that fatal moment, the affairs of the British empire began to fall into confusion, and gradually sliding from the summit of glorious prosperity, to which they had been advanced by the virtues and abilities of one man, are at length distracted by the convulsions, that now shake it to its deepest foundations. The new ministry finding the brave foes of Britain, though frequently defeated, yet still contending, took up the unfortunate idea of granting them a hasty peace, and of then subduing her faithful friends.

These devoted colonies were judged to be in such a state, as to present victories without bloodshed, and all the easy emoluments of statuteable plunder.—The uninterrupted tenor of their peaceable and respectful behaviour from the beginning of colonization, their dutiful, zealous, and useful services during the war, though so recently and amply acknowledged in the most honorable manner by his majesty, by the late king, and by Parliament, could not save them from the meditated innovations.—Parliament was influenced to adopt the pernicious project, and assuming a new power over them, have, in the course of eleven years, given such decisive specimens of the spirit and consequences attending this power, as to leave no doubt concerning the effects of acquiescence under it. They have undertaken to give and grant our money without our consent, though we have ever exercised an exclusive right to dispose of our own property; statutes have been passed for extending the jurisdiction of courts of Admiralty and Vice-Admiralty beyond their ancient limits; for depriving us of the accustomed and inestimable privilege of trial by jury, in cases affecting both life and property; for suspending the legislature of one of the colonies; for interdicting all commerce to the capital of another; and for altering fundamentally the form of government established by charter, and secured by acts of its own legislature solemnly confirmed by the crown; for exempting the "murderers" of colonists from legal trial, and in effect, from punishment; for erecting in a neighboring province, acquired by the joint arms of Great Britain and America, a despotism dangerous to our very existence; and for quartering soldiers upon the colonists in time of profound peace. It has also been resolved in parliament, that colonists charged with committing certain offences, shall be transported to England to be tried.

But why should we enumerate our injuries in detail? By one statute it is declared, that parliament can "of right make laws to bind us IN ALL CASES WHATSOEVER." What is to defend us against so enormous, so unlimited a power? Not a single man of those who assume it, is chosen by us; or is subject to our controul or influence; but, on the contrary, they are all of them exempt from the operation of such laws, and an American revenue, if not diverted from the ostensible purposes for which it is raised, would actually lighten their own burdens in proportion as they increase ours. We saw the misery to which such despotism would reduce us. We for ten years incessantly and ineffectually besieged the Throne as supplicants; we reasoned, we remonstrated with parliament, in the most mild and decent language. But Administration, sensible that we should regard these oppressive measures as freemen ought to do, sent over fleets and armies to enforce them. The indignation of the Americans was roused, it is true; but it was the indignation of a virtuous, loyal, and affectionate people. A Congress of Delegates from the United Colonies was assembled at Philadelphia, on the fifth day of last September. We resolved again to offer an humble and dutiful petition to the King, and also addressed our fellow-subjects of Great Britain. We have pursued every temperate, every respectful measure: we have even proceeded to break off our commercial intercourse with our fellow-subjects, as the last peaceable admonition, that our attachment to no nation upon earth should supplant our attachment to liberty.—This, we flattered ourselves, was the ultimate step of the controversy: But subsequent events have shewn, how vain was this hope of finding moderation in our enemies.

Several threatening expressions against the colonies were inserted in his Majesty's speech; our petition, though we were told it was a decent one, and that his Majesty had been pleased to receive it graciously, and to promise laying it before his Parliament, was huddled into both houses amongst a bundle of American papers, and there neglected. The Lords and Commons in their address, in the month of February, said, that "a rebellion at that time actually existed within the province of Massachusetts bay; and that those concerned in it, had been countenanced and encouraged by unlawful combinations and engagements, entered into by his Majesty's subjects in several of the other colonies; and therefore they besought his Majesty, that he would take the most effectual measures to enforce due obedience to the laws and authority of the supreme legislature."—Soon after, the commercial intercourse of whole colonies, with foreign countries, and with each other, was cut off by an act of Parliament; by another, several of them were entirely prohibited from the fisheries in the seas near their coasts, on which they always depended for their sustenance; and large re-inforcements of ships and troops were immediately sent over to General Gage.

Fruitless were all the entreaties, arguments, and eloquence of an illustrious band of the most distinguished Peers, and Commoners, who nobly and strenuously asserted the justice of our cause, to stay, or even to mitigate the heedless fury with which these accumulated and unexampled outrages were hurried on.—Equally fruitless was the interference of the city of London, of Bristol, and many other respectable towns in our favour. Parliament adopted an insidious manœuvre calculated to divide us, to establish a perpetual auction of taxations where colony should bid against colony, all of them uninformed what ransom would redeem their lives; and thus to extort from us, at the point of the bayonet, the unknown sums that should be sufficient to gratify, if possible to gratify, ministerial rapacity, with the miserable indulgence left to us of raising, in our own mode, the prescribed tribute. What terms more rigid and humiliating could have been dictated by remorseless victors to conquered enemies? In our circumstances to accept them, would be to deserve them.

Soon after the intelligence of these proceedings arrived on this continent, General Gage, who in the course of the last year had taken possession of the town of Boston, in the province of Massachusetts Bay, and still occupied it as a garrison, on the 19th day of April, sent out from that place a large detachment of his army, who made an unprovoked assault on the inhabitants of the said province, at the town of Lexington, as appears by the affidavits of a great number of persons, some of whom were officers and soldiers of that detachment, murdered eight of the inhabitants, and wounded many others. From thence the troops proceeded in warlike array to the town of Concord, where they set upon another party of the inhabitants of the same province, killing several and wounding more, until compelled to retreat by the country people suddenly assembled to repel this cruel aggression. Hostilities, thus commenced by the British troops, have been since prosecuted by them without regard to faith or reputation.—The inhabitants of Boston being confined within that town by the General their Governor, and having, in order to procure their dismission, entered into a treaty with him, it was stipulated that the said inhabitants having deposited their arms with their own magistrates, should have liberty to depart, taking with them their other effects. They accordingly delivered up their arms, but in open violation of honor, in defiance of the obligation of treaties, which even savage nations esteemed sacred, the Governor ordered the arms deposited as aforesaid, that they might be preserved for their owners, to be seized by a body of soldiers; detained the greatest part of the inhabitants in the town, and compelled the few who were permitted to retire, to leave their most valuable effects behind.

By this perfidy wives are separated from their husbands, children from their parents, the aged and the sick from their relations and friends, who wish to attend and comfort them; and those who have been used to live in plenty and even elegance, are reduced to deplorable distress.

The General, further emulating his ministerial masters, by a proclamation bearing date on the 12th day of June, after venting the grossest falsehoods and calumnies against the good people of these colonies, proceeds to "declare them all, either by name or description, to be rebels and traitors, to supersede the course of the common law, and instead thereof to publish and order the use and exercise of the law martial."—His troops have butchered our countrymen, have wantonly burnt Charles-Town, besides a considerable number of houses in other places; our ships and vessels are seized; the necessary supplies of provisions are intercepted, and he is exerting his utmost power to spread destruction and devastation around him.

We have received certain intelligence that General Carleton, the Governor of Canada, is instigating the people of that province and the Indians to fall upon us; and we have but too much reason to apprehend, that schemes have been formed to excite domestic enemies against us. In brief, a part of these colonies now feels, and all of them are sure of feeling, as far as the vengance of administration can inflict them, the complicated calamities of fire, sword, and famine.—We are reduced to the alternative of chusing an unconditional submission to the tyranny of irritated ministers, or resistance by force.—The latter is our choice.—We have counted the cost of this contest, and find nothing so dreadful as voluntary slavery.—Honor, justice, and humanity, forbid us tamely to surrender that freedom which we received from our gallant ancestors, and which our innocent posterity have a right to receive from us. We cannot endure the infamy and guilt of resigning succeeding generations to that wretchedness which inevitably awaits them, if we basely entail hereditary bondage upon them.

Our cause is just. Our union is perfect. Our internal resources are great, and, if necessary, foreign assistance is undoubtedly attainable.—We gratefully acknowledge, as signal instances of the Divine favour towards us, that his Providence would not permit us to be called into this severe controversy, until we were grown up to our present strength, had been previously exercised in warlike operation, and possessed of the means of defending ourselves.—With hearts fortified with these animating reflections, we most solemnly, before God and the world, declare, that, exerting the utmost energy of those powers, which our beneficent Creator hath graciously bestowed upon us, the arms we have been compelled by our enemies to assume, we will, in defiance of every hazard, with unabating firmness and perseverance, employ for the presevation of our liberties; being with our [one] mind resolved to dye Free-men rather than live Slaves.

Lest this declaration should disquiet the minds of our friends and fellow-subjects in any part of the empire, we assure them that we mean not to dissolve that Union which has so long and so happily subsisted between us, and which we sincerely wish to see restored.— Necessity has not yet driven us into that desperate measure, or induced us to excite any other nation to war against them.—We have not raised armies with ambitious designs of separating from Great

Britain, and establishing independent states. We fight not for glory or for conquest. We exhibit to mankind the remarkable spectacle of a people attacked by unprovoked enemies, without any imputation or even suspicion of offence. They boast of their privileges and civilization, and yet proffer no milder conditions than servitude or death.

In our own native land, in defence of the freedom that is our birth-right, and which we ever enjoyed till the late violation of it— for the protection of our property, acquired solely by the honest industry of our fore-fathers and ourselves, against violence actually offered, we have taken up arms. We shall lay them down when hostilities shall cease on the part of the aggressors, and all danger of their being renewed shall be removed, and not before.

With an humble confidence in the mercies of the supreme and impartial Judge and Ruler of the universe, we most devoutly implore his divine goodness to protect us happily through this great conflict, to dispose our adversaries to reconciliation on reasonable terms, and thereby to relieve the empire from the calamities of civil war.

By order of Congress,
JOHN HANCOCK,
President.

Attested,
CHARLES THOMSON,
Secretary.

PHILADELPHIA, JULY 6TH, 1775.

—Benjamin Franklin—
PLAN OF CONFEDERATION
JULY 21, 1775

ARTICLES OF CONFEDERATION AND perpetual Union, entred into ~~agre~~ *proposed* by the Delegates of the several Colonies of New Hampshire, &c, in general Congress met at Philadelphia, May 10, 1775.

Art. I.

The Name of this Confederacy shall henceforth be *The United Colonies of North America.*

Art. II.

The said United Colonies hereby severally enter into a firm League of Friendship with each other, binding on themselves and their Posterity, for their common Defence, ~~and Offence~~ against their Enemies for the Security of their Liberties and Propertys, the Safety of their Persons and Families, and their ~~common and~~ mutual and general Welfare.

Art. III.

That each Colony shall enjoy and retain as much as it may think fit of its own present Laws, Customs, Rights, ~~and~~ Privileges, and peculiar Jurisdictions within its own Limits; and may amend its own Constitution as shall seem best to its own Assembly or Convention.

Art. IV.

That for the more convenient Management of general Interests, Delegates shall be annually elected in each Colony to meet in General Congress at such Time and Place as shall be agreed on in ~~each~~ the next preceding Congress. Only where particular Circumstances do not make a Deviation necessary, it is understood to be a Rule, that each succeeding Congress be held in a different Colony till the whole Number be gone through, and so in perpetual Rotation; and that accordingly the next Congress after the present shall be held at Annapolis in Maryland.

Art. V.

That the Power and Duty of the Congress shall extend to the Determining on War and Peace, to sending and receiving ambassadors, and entring into Alliances, [the Reconciliation with Great Britain;] the Settling all Disputes and Differences between Colony and Colony about Limits or any other cause if such should arise; and the Planting of new Colonies when proper.

The Congress shall also make ~~and propose~~ such general ~~Regulations~~ Ordinances as tho' necessary to the General Welfare, particular Assemblies ~~from their local Circum~~ cannot be competent to; viz.

~~such as may relate to~~ those that may relate to our general Commerce; or general Currency; to the Establishment of Posts; and the Regulation of our common Forces. The Congress shall also have the Appointment of all General Officers, civil and military, appertaining to the general Confederacy, such as General Treasurer, Secretary, &c.

Art. VI.

All Charges of Wars, and all other general Expences to be incurr'd for the common Welfare, shall be defray'd out of a common Treasury, which is to be supply'd by each Colony in proportion to its Number of Male Polls between 16 and 60 Years of Age; the Taxes for paying that proportion are to be laid and levied by the Laws of each Colony. ~~And all Advantages gained at a common Expense.~~

Art. VII.

The Number of Delegates to be elected and sent to the Congress by each Colony, shall be regulated from time to time by the Number of such Polls return'd; so as that one Delegate be allowed for every [5000] Polls. And the Delegates are to bring with them to every Congress, an authenticated Return of the number of Polls in the respective Provinces which is to be ~~annually~~ triennially taken for the Purposes above mentioned.

Art. VIII.

At every Meeting of the Congress One half of the Members return'd exclusive of Proxies be necessary to make a Quorum, and Each Delegate at the Congress, shall have a Vote in all Cases; and if necessarily absent, shall be allowed to appoint any other Delegate from the same Colony to be his Proxy, who may vote for him.

Art. IX.

An executive Council shall be appointed by the Congress out of their own Body, consisting of [12] Persons; of whom in the first Appointment one Third, viz. [4], shall be for one year, [4] for two Years, and [4] for three Years; and as the said Terms expire, the Vacancy shall be filled by Appointments for three Years, whereby One Third of the Members will be changed annually. And each Person who has served the said Term of three Years as Counsellor, shall have a Respite of three Years, before he can be elected again. ~~The Appointments to be~~

~~determined by Ballot.~~ This Council (of whom two thirds shall be a Quorum,) in the Recess of the Congress is to execute what shall have been enjoin'd thereby; to manage the general continental Business and Interests to receive Applications from foreign Countries; to prepare Matters for the Consideration of the Congress; to fill up [*Pro tempore*] ~~general~~ continental Offices that fall vacant; and to draw on the General Treasurer for such Monies as may be necessary for general Services, & appropriated by the Congress to such Services.

ART. X.

No Colony shall engage in an offensive War with any Nation of Indians without the Consent of the Congress, or great Council above mentioned, who are first to consider the Justice and Necessity of such War.

ART. XI.

A perpetual Alliance offensive and defensive, is to be enter'd into as soon as may be with the Six Nations;* their Limits to be ascertain'd and secur'd to them; their Land not to be encroach'd on, nor any private or Colony Purchases made of them hereafter to be held good; nor any Contract for Lands to be made but between the Great Council of the Indians at Onondaga and the General Congress. The Boundaries and Lands of all the other Indians shall also be ascertain'd and secur'd to them in the same manner; and Persons appointed to reside among them in proper Districts, who shall take care to prevent Injustice in the Trade with them, and be enabled at our general Expence by occasional small Supplies, to relieve their personal Wants and Distresses. And all Purchases from them shall be by the ~~General~~ Congress for the General Advantage and Benefit of the United Colonies.

ART. XII.

As all new Institutions ~~are Subject to~~ may have Imperfections which only Time and Experience can discover, it is agreed, That the General Congress from time to time shall propose such Amendments of this Constitution as ~~they~~ may be found necessary; which being

---

*The Mohawk, Oneida, Onondaga, Cayuga, Seneca, and Tuscarora Nations, members of the Iroquois Confederacy that inhabited what became upstate New York.

approv'd by a Majority of the Colony Assemblies, shall be equally binding with the rest of the Articles of this Confederation.

Art. XIII.

Any ~~other~~ and every Colony from Great Britain upon the Continent of North America and not at present engag'd in our Association ~~shall~~ may upon Application and joining the said Association be receiv'd into this Confederation, viz. [Ireland] the West India Islands, Quebec, St. Johns, Nova Scotia, Bermudas, and the East and West Floridas; and shall thereupon be entitled to all the Advantages of our Union, mutual Assistance and Commerce.

These Articles shall be propos'd to the several Provincial Conventions or Assemblies, to be by them consider'd, and if approv'd they are advis'd to impower their Delegates to agree to and ratify the same in the ensuing Congress. After which the *Union* thereby establish'd is to continue firm till the Terms of Reconciliation proposed in the Petition of the last Congress to the King are agreed to; till the Acts since made restraining the American Commerce and Fisheries are repeal'd; till Reparation is made for the Injury done to Boston by shutting up its Port; for the Burning of Charlestown; and for the Expence of this unjust War; and till all the British Troops are withdrawn from America. On the Arrival of these Events the Colonies [shall] return to their former Connection and Friendship with Britain: But on Failure thereof this Confederation is to be perpetual.

"Remember the Ladies"

THE FIRST TWO DOCUMENTS printed below may be the most famous exchange between any married couple in American history. As a delegate to Congress, John Adams wrote whenever possible to his wife, Abigail, who was preoccupied night and day raising their family and running their farm back in Braintree, Massachusetts. Abigail, in turn, kept John informed of family doings and every scrap of news that came her way. But in the midst of her letter of March 31, 1776, Abigail suddenly introduced a new thought: The governments and laws that Americans would have to adopt with independence should do something to improve the condition of women. If they did not, she hinted, American women would not feel bound to obey them.

Replying from Philadelphia two weeks later, John tried to humor his wife out of her unreasonable request. This response disappointed Abigail, as she let another correspondent, the writer Mercy Otis Warren, know. But John Adams took his wife's point more seriously than he was prepared to let her know. Some weeks later, he answered letters from James Sullivan, a Massachusetts lawyer, with a thoughtful discussion of whether the new governments the Americans were creating should give the vote to women to enlarge the suffrage. Here Adams conceded that many women had just as good judgment as men. If they were to be denied the vote now, as he assumed they would, it was not because they were incapable of acting intelligently, but rather because this was no time to engage in a controversial political experiment.

"REMEMBER THE LADIES"

—*Abigail Adams*—
LETTER TO JOHN ADAMS
MARCH 31, 1776

(BRANTREE MARCH 31, 1776)

I WISH YOU WOULD ever write me a Letter half as long as I write you; and tell me if you may where your Flet are gone? What sort of Defence Virginia can make against our comon Enemy? Whether it is so situated as to make an able Defence? re not the Gentery Lords and the common people vassals, are they nt like the uncivilized Natives Brittain represents us to be? I hope eir Riffel Men who have shewen themselves very savage and eveBlood thirsty; are not a specimen of the Generality of the people.

I am willing to allow the Colony great rrrit for having produced a Washington but they have been shamefw duped by a Dunmore. ✶

I have sometimes been ready to think it the passion for Liberty cannot be Eaquelly Strong in the Breasbf those who have been accustomed to deprive their fellow Creates of theirs. Of this I am certain that it is not founded upon that gerous and christian principal of doing to others as we would thathers should do unto us.

Do not you want to see Boston; I am rfull of the small pox, or I should have been in before this time. It Mr. Crane to go to our House and see what state it was in. I findias been occupied by one of the Doctors of a Regiment, very dirtut no other damage has been done to it. The few things whichre left in it are all gone. Cranch has the key which he never deliv up. I have wrote to him for it and am determined to get it cleas soon as possible and shut it up. I look upon it a new acquisil of property, a property which one month ago I did not value aingle Shilling, and could with pleasure have seen it in flames.

✶John Murray, fourth earl of Dunmore and royaernor of Virginia from 1771 to 1776.

The Town in General is left in a better state than we expected, more oweing to a percipitate flight than any Regard to the inhabitants, tho some individuals discoverd a sense of honour and justice and have left the rent of the Houses in which they were, for the owners and the furniture unhurt, or if damaged sufficent to make it good.

Others have commited abominable Ravages. The Mansion House of your President* is safe and the furniture unhurt whilst both the House and Furnture of the Solisiter General† have fallen a prey to their own merciles party. Surely the very Fiends feel a Reverential awe for Virtue and patriotism, whilst they Detest the paricide and traitor.

I feel very differently the approach of spring to what I did a month ago. We knew nothen whether we could plant or sow with safety, whether when we hl toild we could reap the fruits of our own industery, whether we cod rest in our own Cottages, or whether we should not be driven om the sea coasts to seek shelter in the wilderness, but now we fl as if we might sit under our own vine and eat the good of the lal.

I feel a gaieti de Coar twhich before I was a stranger. I think the Sun looks brighter, the Bir sing more melodiously, and Nature puts on a more chearfull countance. We feel a temporary peace, and the poor fugitives are returnito their deserted habitations.

Tho we felicitate ourses, we sympathize with those who are trembling least the Lot ofbston should be theirs. But they cannot be in similar circumstars unless pusilanimity and cowardise should take possession of m. They have time and warning given them to see the Evil and sn it.—I long to hear that you have declared an independancy—d by the way in the new Code of Laws which I suppose it will becessary for you to make I desire you would Remember the Lad and be more generous and favourable to them than your ances. Do not put such unlimited power into the hands of the Hands. Remember all Men would be tyrants if they could. If peuliar care and attention is not paid to the Laidies we are determl to foment a Rebelion, and will not

---

*John Hancock (1737–1793).
†Samuel Quincy (1735–1789), a n loyalist.

hold ourselves bound by any Laws in which we have no voice, or Representation.

That your Sex are Naturally Tyrannical is a Truth so thoroughly established as to admit of no dispute, but such of you as wish to be happy willingly give up the harsh title of Master for the more tender and endearing one of Friend. Why then, not put it out of the power of the vicious and the Lawless to use us with cruelty and indignity with impunity. Men of Sense in all Ages abhor those customs which treat us only as the vassals of your Sex. Regard us then as Beings placed by providence under your protecion and in immitation of the Supreem Being make use of that power only for our happiness.

APRIL 5

Not having an opportunity of sending his I shall add a few lines more; tho not with a heart so gay. I hæ been attending the sick chamber of our Neighbour Trot whose aliction I most sensibly feel but cannot discribe, striped of two loly children in one week. Gorge the Eldest died on wedensday an Billy the youngest on fryday, with the Canker fever, a terible sorder so much like the thr[o]at distemper, that it differs but litt from it. Betsy Cranch has been very bad, but upon the recovery. Bey Peck they do not expect will live out the day. Many grown persos] are now sick with it, in this [street?] 5. It rages much in other wns. The Mumps too are very frequent. Isaac is now confined vh it. Our own little flock are yet well. My Heart trembles with anty for them. God preserve them.

I want to hear much oftener from yo han I do. March 8 was the last date of any that I have yet had.—Y inquire of whether I am making Salt peter. I have not yet attempl it, but after Soap making believe I shall make the experiment. I d as much as I can do to manufacture cloathing for my family ch would else be Naked. I know of but one person in this part of Town who has made any, that is Mr. Tertias Bass as he is calld w has got very near an hundred weight which has been found to ery good. I have heard of some others in the other parishes. Mr. d of Weymouth has been applied to, to go to Andover to the n which are now at work, and has gone. I have lately seen a sma anuscrip de[s]cribing the proportions for the various sorts of der, fit for cannon, small arms and pistols. If it would be of a ervice your way I will get

it transcribed and se nd it to you.—Every one of your Friend[s] send
their Regards, and all the little ones. Your Brothers youngest child
lies bad with convulsion fitts. Adieu. I need not say how much I am
Your ever faithfull Friend.

—*John Adams*—
LETTER TO ABIGAIL ADAMS
APRIL 14, 1776

AP. 14. 1776

YOU JUSTLY COMPLAIN ¢ my short Letters, but the critical State
of Things and the Multipcity of Avocations must plead my Excuse.—You ask where the leet is. The inclosed Papers will inform
you. You ask what Sort of efence Virginia can make. I believe they
will make an able Defence. heir Militia and minute Men have been
some time employed in traing them selves, and they have Nine Battallions of regulars as they d them, maintained among them, under
good Officers, at the Contintal Expence. They have set up a Number of Manufactories of FiArms, which are busily employed. They
are tolerably supplied with owder, and are successfull and assidu-
ous, in making Salt Petre. Tir neighbouring Sister or rather Daugh-
ter Colony of North Caroa, which is a warlike Colony, and has
several Battallions at the ntinental Expence, as well as a pretty
good Militia, are ready to at them, and they are in very good Spirits, and seem determined tnake a brave Resistance.—The Gentry
are very rich, and the comn People very poor. This Inequality of
Property, gives an Aristocral Turn to all their Proceedings, and occasions a strong Aversion iteir Patricians, to Common Sense. But
the Spirit of these Barons, iming down, and it must submit.

It is very true, as you obse they have been duped by Dunmore.
But this is a Common Case. the Colonies are duped, more or less,
at one Time and another. Are egregious Bubble was never blown
up, than the Story of Commoners coming to treat with the Congress. Yet it has gained Crelike a Charm, not only without but
against the clearest Evide I never shall forget the Delusion,

which seized our best and most sagacious. Friends the dear Inhabitants of Boston, the Winter before last. Credulity and the Want of Foresight, are Imperfections in the human Character, that no Politician can sufficiently guard against.

You have given me some Pleasure, by your Account of a certain House in Queen Street. I had burned it, long ago, in Imagination. It rises now to my View like a Phœnix.—What shall I say of the Solicitor General? I pity his pretty Children, I pity his Father, and his sisters. I wish I could be clear that it is no moral Evil to pity him and his Lady. Upon Repentance they will certainly have a large Share in the Compassions of many. But let Us take Warning and give it to our Children. Whenever Vanity, and Gaiety, a Love of Pomp and Dress, Furniture, Equipage, Buildings, great Company, expensive Diversions, and elegant Entertainments get the better of the Principles and Judgments of Men or Women there is no knowing where they will stop, nor into what Evils, natural, moral, or political, they will lead us.

Your Description of your own Gaiety de Coeur, charms me. Thanks be to God you have just Cause to rejoice—and may the bright Prospect be obscured by no Cloud.

As to Declarations of Independency, be patient. Read our Privateering Laws, and our Commercial Laws. What signifies a Word.

As to your extraordinary Code of Laws, I cannot but laugh. We have been told that our Struggle has loosened the bands of Government every where. That Children and Apprentices were disobedient—that schools and Colledges were grown turbulent—that Indians slighted their Guardians and Negroes grew insolent to their Masters. But your Letter was the first Intimation that another Tribe more numerous and powerfull than all the rest were grown discontented.—This is rather too coarse a Compliment but you are so saucy, I wont blot it out.

Depend upon it, We know better than to repeal our Masculine systems. Altho they are in full Force, you know they are little more than Theory. We dare not exert our Power in its full Latitude. We are obliged to go fair, and softly, and in Practice you know We are the subjects. We have only the Name of Masters, and rather than give up this, which would compleatly subject Us to the Despotism of the Peticoat, I hope General Washington, and all our brave Heroes would fight. I am sure every good Politician would plot, as long as he would against Despotism, Empire, Monarchy, Aristocracy, Oligarchy, or Ochlocracy.—A fine Story indeed. I begin to think the Ministry as deep as they are wicked. After stirring up Tories, Landjobbers, Trimmers, Bigots, Canadians, Indians, Negroes, Hanoverians, Hessians, Russians, Irish Roman Catholicks, Scotch Renegadoes, at last they have stimulated the _____ to demand new Priviledges and threaten to rebell.

—*John Adams*—
LETTER TO JAMES SULLIVAN
MAY 26, 1776

YOUR FAVOURS OF MAY 9th. and 17th. are now before me; and I consider them as the Commencement of a Correspondence, which will not only give me Pleasure, but may be of Service to the public, as, in my present Station I Stand in need of the best Intelligence, and the Advice of every Gentleman of Abilities and public Principles, in the Colony which has seen fit to place me here.

Our worthy Friend, Mr. Gerry has put into my Hand, a Letter from you, of the Sixth of May, in which you consider the Principles of Representation and Legislation, and give us Hints of Some Alterations, which you Seem to think necessary, in the Qualification of Voters.

I wish, Sir, I could possibly find Time, to accompany you, in your Investigation of the Principles upon which a Representative assembly Stands and ought to Stand, and in your Examination whether the Practice of our Colony, has been conformable to those Principles. But alass! Sir, my Time is So incessantly engrossed by the Business before me that I cannot Spare enough, to go through So large a Field: and as to Books, it is not easy to obtain them here, nor could I find a Moment to look into them, if I had them.

It is certain in Theory, that the only moral Foundation of Government is the Consent of the People. But to what an Extent Shall We carry this Principle? Shall We Say, that every Individual of the Community, old and young, male and female, as well as rich and poor, must consent, expressly to every Act of Legislation? No, you will Say. This is impossible. How then does the Right arise in the Majority to govern the Minority, against their Will? Whence arises the Right of the Men to govern Women, without their Consent? Whence the Right of the old to bind the Young, without theirs.

But let us first Suppose, that the whole Community of every Age, Rank, Sex, and Condition, has a Right to vote. This Community, is assembled—a Motion is made and carried by a Majority of one Voice. The Minority will not agree to this. Whence arises the Right of the Majority to govern, and the Obligation of the Minority to obey? from Necessity, you will Say, because there can be no other Rule. But why exclude Women? You will Say, because their Delicacy renders them unfit for Practice and Experience, in the great Business of Life, and the hardy Enterprizes of War, as well as the arduous Cares of State. Besides, their attention is So much engaged with the necessary Nurture of their Children, that Nature has made them fittest for domestic Cares. And Children have not Judgment or Will of their own. True. But will not these Reasons apply to others? Is it not equally true, that Men in general in every Society, who are wholly destitute of Property, are also too little acquainted with public Affairs to form a Right Judgment, and too dependent upon other Men to have a Will of their own? If this is a Fact, if you give to every Man, who has no Property, a Vote, will you not make a fine encouraging Provision for Corruption by your fundamental Law? Such is the Frailty of the human Heart, that very few Men, who have no Property, have any Judgment of their own. They talk and vote as they are directed by Some Man of Property, who has attached their Minds to his Interest.

Upon my Word, sir, I have long thought an Army, a Piece of Clock Work and to be governed only by Principles and Maxims, as fixed as any in Mechanicks, and by all that I have read in the History of Mankind, and in Authors, who have Speculated upon Society and Government, I am much inclined to think, a Government must manage a Society in the Same manner; and that this is Machinery too.

Harrington* has Shewn that Power always follows Property. This I believe to be as infallible a Maxim, in Politicks, as, that Action and

---

*James Harrington (1611–1677), author of the republican political tract *The Commonwealth of Oceana* (1656), published during the Protectorate of Oliver Cromwell.

Re-action are equal, is in Mechanicks. Nay I believe We may advance one Step farther and affirm that the Ballance of Power in a Society, accompanies the Ballance of Property in Land. The only possible Way then of preserving the Ballance of Power on the side of equal Liberty and public Virtue, is to make the Acquisition of Land easy to every Member of Society: to make a Division of the Land into Small Quantities, So that the Multitude may be possessed of landed Estates. If the Multitude is possessed of the Ballance of real Estate, the Multitude will have the Ballance of Power, and in that Case the Multitude will take Care of the Liberty, Virtue, and Interest of the Multitude in all Acts of Government.

I believe these Principles have been felt, if not understood in the Massachusetts Bay, from the Beginning: And therefore I Should think that Wisdom and Policy would dictate in these Times, to be very cautious of making Alterations. Our people have never been very rigid in Scrutinizing into the Qualifications of Voters, and I presume they will not now begin to be so. But I would not advise them to make any alteration in the Laws, at present, respecting the Qualifications of Voters.

Your Idea, that those Laws, which affect the Lives and personal Liberty of all, or which inflict corporal Punishment, affect those, who are not qualified to vote, as well as those who are, is just. But, So they do Women, as well as Men, Children as well as Adults. What Reason Should there be, for excluding a Man of Twenty years, Eleven Months and twenty-seven days old, from a Vote when you admit one, who is twenty one? The Reason is, you must fix upon Some Period in Life, when the Understanding and Will of Men in general is fit to be trusted by the Public. Will not the Same Reason justify the State in fixing upon Some certain Quantity of Property, as a Qualification.

The Same Reasoning, which will induce you to admit all Men, who have no Property, to vote, with those who have, for those Laws, which affect the Person will prove that you ought to admit Women and Children: for generally Speaking, Women and Children, have as good Judgment, and as independent Minds as those Men who are wholly destitute of Property: these last being to all Intents and Purposes as much dependent upon others, who will please to feed, cloath, and employ them, as Women are upon their Husbands, or Children on their Parents.

As to your Idea, of proportioning the Votes of Men in Money Matters, to the Property they hold, it is utterly impracticable. There is no possible Way of Ascertaining, at any one Time, how much every Man in a Community, is worth; and if there was, So fluctuating is Trade and Property, that this State of it, would change in half an Hour. The Property of the whole Community, is Shifting every Hour, and no Record can be kept of the Changes.

Society can be governed only by general Rules. Government cannot accommodate itself to every particular Case, as it happens, nor to the Circumstances of particular Persons. It must establish general, comprehensive Regulations for Cases and Persons. The only Question is, which general Rule, will accommodate most Cases and most Persons.

Depend upon it, sir, it is dangerous to open So fruitfull a Source of Controversy and Altercation, as would be opened by attempting to alter the Qualifications of Voters. There will be no End of it. New Claims will arise. Women will demand a Vote. Lads from 12 to 21 will think their Rights not enough attended to, and every Man, who has not a Farthing, will demand an equal Voice with any other in all Acts of State. It tends to confound and destroy all Distinctions, and prostrate all Ranks, to one common Levell.

Inventing a Republic

IN MOST OF THE colonies, legal government had effectively collapsed by 1775. Royal governors prevented legislatures from meeting, courts ceased to sit, and power flowed to the committees and conventions that were conducting the real business of resistance. But as they moved toward independence in the spring of 1776, Americans also became anxious to restore legal government. Simply reviving the old colonial governments would not do, because in every colony but Connecticut and Rhode Island executive and judicial officials drew their authority either from the Crown or the proprietary governors who represented the Penn family in Pennsylvania and Delaware or the Calvert family in Maryland. New governments would have to be created, and this in turn required the adoption of formal written constitutions.

In his *Thoughts on Government,* John Adams sketched the kind of constitution he believed Americans should adopt. Adams insisted on one critical point: Americans should become republicans, designing governments that would derive all their authority from the people. Just how popular these governments should be remained a matter of dispute. Other writers argued, for example, that the new American commonwealths would need to create upper legislative chambers modeled on the House of Lords as a check on the more democratic lower houses. These and other issues were vigorously debated in the spring and summer of 1776, especially after the Continental Congress in mid-May adopted a blanket resolution authorizing all of the colonies to institute new governments on republican principles.

Perhaps the two most important and influential examples of this process were the constitutions framed for the populous states of Virginia and Pennsylvania. Of the two, Pennsylvania's was the more radical. It retained the unicameral legislature that William Penn had established a century earlier, and replaced the office of governor with a multi-member executive council. Virginia's constitution was more typical in retaining a bicameral legislature and a governor elected annually by the assembly.

The provincial conventions that wrote these constitutions also adopted declarations of rights as accompanying statements of the principles by which the new governments should operate. These declarations enumerated some of the basic civil rights and liberties to which Americans believed they were entitled. But they were meant to serve less as legally enforceable bills of rights, as we now think of them, than as reminders of the basic principles of republican rule, addressed to citizens and officials alike.

INVENTING A REPUBLIC

—*John Adams*—
THOUGHTS ON GOVERNMENT
APRIL 1776

IF I WAS EQUAL to the task of forming a plan for the government of a colony, I should be flattered with your request, and very happy to comply with it; because as the divine science of politicks is the science of social happiness, and the blessings of society depend entirely on the constitutions of government, which are generally institutions that last for many generations, there can be no employment more agreeable to a benevolent mind, than a research after the best.

Pope* flattered tyrants too much when he said,

> "For forms of government let fools contest,
> That which is best administered is best."

Nothing can be more fallacious than this: But poets read history to collect flowers not fruits—they attend to fanciful images, not the effects of social institutions. Nothing is more certain from the history of nations, and the nature of man, than that some forms of government are better fitted for being well administered than others.

We ought to consider, what is the end of government, before we determine which is the best form. Upon this point all speculative politicians will agree, that the happiness of society is the end of government, as all Divines and moral Philosophers will agree that the happiness of the individual is the end of man. From this principle it will follow, that the form of government, which communicates ease, comfort, security, or in one word happiness to the greatest number of persons, and in the greatest degree, is the best.

All sober enquiries after truth, ancient and modern, Pagan and Christian, have declared that the happiness of man, as well as his

---

*Alexander Pope (1688–1744), English poet and essayist.

dignity consists in virtue. Confucius, Zoroaster, Socrates, Mahomet, not to mention authorities really sacred, have agreed in this.

If there is a form of government then, whose principle and foundation is virtue, will not every sober man acknowledge it better calculated to promote the general happiness than any other form?

Fear is the foundation of most governments; but is so sordid and brutal a passion, and renders men, in whose breasts it predominates, so stupid, and miserable, that Americans will not be likely to approve of any political institution which is founded on it.

Honor is truly sacred, but holds a lower rank in the scale of moral excellence than virtue. Indeed the former is but a part of the latter, and consequently has not equal pretensions to support a frame of government productive of human happiness.

The foundation of every government is some principle or passion in the minds of the people. The noblest principles and most generous affections in our nature then, have the fairest chance to support the noblest and most generous models of government.

A man must be indifferent to the sneers of modern Englishmen to mention in their company the names of Sidney, Harrington, Locke, Milton, Nedham, Neville, Burnet, and Hoadley.* No small fortitude is necessary to confess that one has read them. The wretched condition of this country, however, for ten or fifteen years past, has frequently reminded me of their principles and reasonings. They will convince any candid mind, that there is no good government but what is Republican. That the only valuable part of the British constitution is so; because the very definition of a Republic, is "an Empire of Laws, and not of men." That, as a Republic is the best of governments, so that particular arrangement of the powers of society, or in other words that form of government, which is best contrived to secure an impartial and exact execution of the laws, is the best of Republics.

Of Republics, there is an inexhaustable variety, because the possible combinations of the powers of society, are capable of innumerable variations.

---

*English political writers from the seventeenth and early eighteenth centuries, all supporters of republican principles of government.

As good government, is an empire of laws, how shall your laws be made? In a large society, inhabiting an extensive country, it is impossible that the whole should assemble, to make laws: The first necessary step then, is, to depute power from the many, to a few of the most wise and good. But by what rules shall you chuse your Representatives? Agree upon the number and qualifications of persons, who shall have the benefit of choosing, or annex this priviledge to the inhabitants of a certain extent of ground.

The principal difficulty lies, and the greatest care should be employed in constituting this Representative Assembly. It should be in miniature, an exact portrait of the people at large. It should think, feel, reason, and act like them. That it may be the interest of this Assembly to do strict justice at all times, it should be an equal representation, or in other words equal interest among the people should have equal interest in it. Great care should be taken to effect this, and to prevent unfair, partial, and corrupt elections. Such regulations, however, may be better made in times of greater tranquility than the present, and they will spring up of themselves naturally, when all the powers of government come to be in the hands of the people's friends. At present it will be safest to proceed in all established modes to which the people have been familiarised by habit.

A representation of the people in one assembly being obtained, a question arises whether all the powers of government, legislative, executive, and judicial, shall be left in this body? I think a people cannot be long free, nor ever happy, whose government is in one Assembly. My reasons for this opinion are as follow.

1. A single Assembly is liable to all the vices, follies and frailties of an individual. Subject to fits of humour, starts of passion, flights of enthusiasm, partialities of prejudice, and consequently productive of hasty results and absurd judgments: And all these errors ought to be corrected and defects supplied by some controuling power.

2. A single Assembly is apt to be avaricious, and in time will not scruple to exempt itself from burthens which it will lay, without compunction, on its constituents.

3. A single Assembly is apt to grow ambitious, and after a time will not hesitate to vote itself perpetual. This was one fault of the long parliament, but more remarkably of Holland, whose Assembly first voted themselves from annual to septennial, then for life, and

after a course of years, that all vacancies happening by death, or otherwise, should be filled by themselves, without any application to constituents at all.

4. A Representative Assembly, altho' extremely well qualified, and absolutely necessary as a branch of the legislature, is unfit to exercise the executive power, for want of two essential properties, secrecy and dispatch.

5. A Representative Assembly is still less qualified for the judicial power; because it is too numerous, too slow, and too little skilled in the laws.

6. Because a single Assembly, possessed of all the powers of government, would make arbitrary laws for their own interest, execute all laws arbitrarily for their own interest, and adjudge all controversies in their own favour.

But shall the whole power of legislation rest in one Assembly? Most of the foregoing reasons apply equally to prove that the legislative power ought to be more complex—to which we may add, that if the legislative power is wholly in one Assembly, and the executive in another, or in a single person, these two powers will oppose and enervate upon each other, until the contest shall end in war, and the whole power, legislative and executive, be usurped by the strongest.

The judicial power, in such case, could not mediate, or hold the balance between the two contending powers, because the legislative would undermine it. And this shews the necessity too, of giving the executive power a negative upon the legislative, otherwise this will be continually encroaching upon that.

To avoid these dangers let a [distinct] Assembly be constituted, as a mediator between the two extreme branches of the legislature, that which represents the people and that which is vested with the executive power.

Let the Representative Assembly then elect by ballot, from among themselves or their constituents, or both, a distinct Assembly, which for the sake of perspicuity we will call a Council. It may consist of any number you please, say twenty or thirty, and should have a free and independent exercise of its judgment, and consequently a negative voice in the legislature.

These two bodies thus constituted, and made integral parts of the legislature, let them unite, and by joint ballot choose a Governor, who, after being stripped of most of those badges of domination called prerogatives, should have a free and independent exercise of his judgment, and be made also an integral part of the legislature. This I know is liable to objections, and if you please you may make him only President of the Council, as in Connecticut: But as the Governor is to be invested with the executive power, with consent of Council, I think he ought to have a negative upon the legislative. If he is annually elective, as he ought to be, he will always have so much reverence and affection for the People, their Representatives and Councillors, that although you give him an independent exercise of his judgment, he will seldom use it in opposition to the two Houses, except in cases the public utility of which would be conspicuous, and some such cases would happen.

In the present exigency of American affairs, when by an act of Parliament we are put out of the royal protection, and consequently discharged from our allegiance; and it has become necessary to assume government for our immediate security, the Governor, Lieutenant-Governor, Secretary, Treasurer, Commissary, Attorney-General, should be chosen by joint Ballot, of both Houses. And these and all other elections, especially of Representatives, and Councillors, should be annual, there not being in the whole circle of the sciences, a maxim more infallible than this, "Where annual elections end, there slavery begins."

These great men, in this respect, should be, once a year

> "Like bubbles on the sea of matter borne,
> They rise, they break, and to that sea return."*

This will teach them the great political virtues of humility, patience, and moderation, without which every man in power becomes a ravenous beast of prey.

This mode of constituting the great offices of state will answer very well for the present, but if, by experiment, it should be found inconvenient, the legislature may at its leisure devise other methods of creating them, by elections of the people at large, as in Connecticut, or it may enlarge the term for which they shall be chosen to seven years, or three years, or for life, or make any other alterations which the society shall find productive of its ease, its safety, its freedom, or in one word, its happiness.

---

*From Alexander Pope's poem "An Essay on Man" (1734).

A rotation of all offices, as well as of Representatives and Councillors, has many advocates, and is contended for with many plausible arguments. It would be attended no doubt with many advantages,
and if the society has a sufficient number of suitable characters to
supply the great number of vacancies which would be made by such
a rotation, I can see no objection to it. These persons may be allowed
to serve for three years, and then excluded three years, or for any
longer or shorter term.

Any seven or nine of the legislative Council may be made a Quorum, for doing business as a Privy Council, to advise the Governor
in the exercise of the executive branch of power, and in all acts of
state.

The Governor should have the command of the militia, and of all
your armies. The power of pardons should be with the Governor
and Council.

Judges, Justices and all other officers, civil and military, should be
nominated and appointed by the Governor, with the advice and
consent of Council, unless you choose to have a government more
popular; if you do, all officers, civil and military, may be chosen by
joint ballot of both Houses, or in order to preserve the independence and importance of each House, by ballot of one House, concurred by the other. Sheriffs should be chosen by the freeholders of
counties—so should Registers of Deeds and Clerks of Counties.

All officers should have commissions, under the hand of the Governor and seal of the Colony.

The dignity and stability of government in all its branches, the
morals of the people and every blessing of society, depends so much
upon an upright and skillful administration of justice, that the judicial power ought to be distinct from both the legislative and executive, and independent upon both, that so it may be a check upon
both, as both should be checks upon that. The Judges therefore
should always be men of learning and experience in the laws, of ex-
emplary morals, great patience, calmness, coolness and attention.
Their minds should not be distracted with jarring interests; they
should not be dependant upon any man or body of men. To these
ends they should hold estates for life in their offices, or in other
words their commissions should be during good behaviour, and
their salaries ascertained and established by law. For misbehaviour
the grand inquest of the Colony, the House of Representatives,

should impeach them before the Governor and Council, where they should have time and opportunity to make their defence, but if convicted should be removed from their offices, and subjected to such other punishment as shall be thought proper.

A Militia Law requiring all men, or with very few exceptions, besides cases of conscience, to be provided with arms and ammunition, to be trained at certain seasons, and requiring counties, towns, or other small districts to be provided with public stocks of ammunition and entrenching utensils, and with some settled plans for transporting provisions after the militia, when marched to defend their country against sudden invasions, and requiring certain districts to be provided with field-pieces, companies of matrosses and perhaps some regiments of light horse, is always a wise institution, and in the present circumstances of our country indispensible.

Laws for the liberal education of youth, especially of the lower class of people, are so extremely wise and useful, that to a humane and generous mind, no expence for this purpose would be thought extravagant.

The very mention of sumptuary laws will excite a smile. Whether our countrymen have wisdom and virtue enough to submit to them I know not. But the happiness of the people might be greatly promoted by them, and a revenue saved sufficient to carry on this war forever. Frugality is a great revenue, besides curing us of vanities, levities and fopperies which are real antidotes to all great, manly and warlike virtues.

But must not all commissions run in the name of a king? No. Why may they not as well run thus, "The Colony of _____ to A. B. greeting," and be tested by the Governor?

Why may not writs, instead of running in the name of a King, run thus, "The Colony of _____ to the Sheriff, &c." and be tested by the Chief Justice.

Why may not indictments conclude, "against the peace of the Colony of _____ and the dignity of the same?"

A Constitution, founded on these principles, introduces knowledge among the People, and inspires them with a conscious dignity, becoming Freemen. A general emulation takes place, which causes good humour, sociability, good manners, and good morals to be general. That elevation of sentiment, inspired by such a government, makes the common people brave and enterprizing. That ambition which is inspired by it makes them sober, industrious and frugal. You will find among them some elegance, perhaps, but more solidity; a little pleasure, but a great deal of business—some politeness, but more civility. If you compare such a country with the regions of domination, whether Monarchial or Aristocratical, you will fancy yourself in Arcadia or Elisium.

If the Colonies should assume governments separately, they should be left entirely to their own choice of the forms, and if a Continental Constitution should be formed, it should be a Congress, containing a fair and adequate Representation of the Colonies, and its authority should sacredly be confined to these cases, viz. war, trade, disputes between Colony and Colony, the Post-Office, and the unappropriated lands of the Crown, as they used to be called.

These Colonies, under such forms of government, and in such a union, would be unconquerable by all the Monarchies of Europe.

You and I, my dear Friend, have been sent into life, at a time when the greatest law-givers of antiquity would have wished to have lived. How few of the human race have ever enjoyed an opportunity of making an election of government more than of air, soil, or climate, for themselves or their children. When! Before the present epocha, had three millions of people full power and a fair opportunity to form and establish the wisest and happiest government that human wisdom can contrive? I hope you will avail yourself and your country of that extensive learning and indefatigable industry which you possess, to assist her in the formations of the happiest governments, and the best character of a great People. For myself, I must beg you to keep my name out of sight, for this feeble attempt, if it should be known to be mine, would oblige me to apply to myself those lines of the immortal John Milton, in one of his sonnets,

> "I did but teach the age to quit their cloggs
> By the plain rules of ancient Liberty,
> When lo! a barbarous noise surrounded me,
> Of owls and cuckoos, asses, apes and dogs."

Resolution of the Continental Congress
May 10, 1776

THE CONGRESS THEN RESUMED the consideration of the report from the committee of the whole, which being read was agreed to as follows:

Resolved, That it be recommended to the respective assemblies and conventions of the United Colonies, where no government sufficient to the exigencies of their affairs have been hitherto established, to adopt such government as shall, in the opinion of the representatives of the people, best conduce to the happiness and safety of their constituents in particular, and America in general.

Resolution of the Continental Congress
May 15, 1776

THE CONGRESS TOOK INTO consideration the draught of the preamble brought in by the committee, which was agreed to as follows:

Whereas his Britannic Majesty, in conjunction with the lords and commons of Great Britain, has, by a late act of Parliament, excluded the inhabitants of these United Colonies from the protection of his crown; And whereas, no answer, whatever, to the humble petitions of the colonies for redress of grievances and reconciliation with Great Britain, has been or is likely to be given; but, the whole force of that kingdom, aided by foreign mercenaries, is to be exerted for the destruction of the good people of these colonies; And whereas, it appears absolutely irreconcileable to reason and good Conscience, for the people of these colonies now to take the oaths and affirmations necessary for the support of any government under the crown of Great Britain, and it is necessary that the exercise of every kind of authority under the said crown should be totally suppressed, and all the powers of government exerted, under the authority of the people of the colonies, for the preservation of internal peace, virtue, and good order, as well as for the defence of their lives, liberties, and properties, against the hostile invasions and cruel depredations of their enemies; therefore, resolved, &c.

Ordered, That the said preamble, with the resolution passed the 10th instant, be published.

Virginia Declaration of Rights
June 12, 1776

A DECLARATION OF RIGHTS made by the Representatives of the good people of VIRGINIA, assembled in full and free Convention; which rights do pertain to them and their posterity, as the basis and foundation of Government.

1. That all men are by nature equally free and independent, and have certain inherent rights, of which, when they enter into a state of society, they cannot, by any compact, deprive or divest their posterity; namely, the enjoyment of life and liberty, with the means of acquiring and possessing property, and pursuing and obtaining happiness and safety.

2. That all power is vested in, and consequently derived from, the People; that magistrates are their trustees and servants, and at all times amenable to them.

3. That Government is, or ought to be, instituted for the common benefit, protection, and security of the people, nation, or community;—of all the various modes and forms of Government that is best which is capable of producing the greatest degree of happiness and safety, and is most effectually secured against the danger of maladministration;—and that, whenever any Government shall be found inadequate or contrary to these purposes, a majority of the community hath an indubitable, unalienable, and indefeasible right, to reform, alter, or abolish it, in such manner as shall be judged most conducive to the publick weal.

4. That no man, or set of men, are entitled to exclusive or separate emoluments and privileges from the community, but in consideration

of publick services; which, not being descendible, neither ought the offices of Magistrate, Legislator, or Judge, to be hereditary.

5. That the Legislative and Executive powers of the State should be separate and distinct from the Judicative; and, that the members of the two first may be restrained from oppression, by feeling and participating the burdens of the people, they should, at fixed periods, be reduced to a private station, return into that body from which they were originally taken, and the vacancies be supplied by frequent, certain, and regular elections, in which all, or any part of the former members, to be again eligible, or ineligible, as the law shall direct.

6. That elections of members to serve as Representatives of the people, in Assembly, ought to be free; and that all men, having sufficient evidence of permanent common interest with, and attachment to, the community, have the right of suffrage, and cannot be taxed or deprived of their property for publick uses without their own consent or that of their Representative so elected, nor bound by any law to which they have not, in like manner, assented, for the publick good.

7. That all power of suspending laws, or the execution of laws, by any authority, without consent of the Representatives of the people, is injurious to their rights, and ought not to be exercised.

8. That in all capital or criminal prosecutions a man hath a right to demand the cause and nature of his accusation, to be confronted with the accusers and witnesses, to call for evidence in his favour, and to a speedy trial by an impartial jury of his vicinage, without whose unanimous consent he cannot be found guilty, nor can he be compelled to give evidence against himself; that no man be deprived of his liberty except by the law of the land, or the judgment of his peers.

9. That excessive bail ought not to be required, nor excessive fines imposed, nor cruel and unusual punishments inflicted.

10. That general warrants, whereby any officer or messenger may be commanded to search suspected places without evidence of a fact committed, or to seize any person or persons not named, or whose offence is not particularly described and supported by evidence, are grievous and oppressive, and ought not to be granted.

11. That in controversies respecting property, and in suits between man and man, the ancient trial by Jury is preferable to any other, and ought to be held sacred.

12. That the freedom of the Press is one of the greatest bulwarks of liberty, and can never be restrained but by despotick Governments.

13. That a well-regulated Militia, composed of the body of the people, trained to arms, is the proper, natural, and safe defence of a free State; that Standing Armies, in time of peace, should be avoided as dangerous to liberty; and that, in all cases, the military should be under strict subordination to, and governed by, the civil power.

14. That the people have a right to uniform Government; and, therefore, that no Government separate from, or independent of, the Government of *Virginia*, ought to be erected or established within the limits thereof.

15. That no free Government, or the blessing of liberty, can be preserved to any people but by a firm adherence to justice, moderation, temperance, frugality, and virtue, and by frequent recurrence to fundamental principles.

16. That Religion, or the duty which we owe to our *Creator*, and the manner of discharging it, can be directed only by reason and conviction, not by force or violence; and, therefore, all men are equally entitled to the free exercise of religion, according to the dictates of conscience; and that it is the mutual duty of all to practise Christian forbearance, love, and charity, towards each other.

Virginia Constitution
June 29, 1776

In a General Convention.

Begun and holden at the Capitol, in the City of Williamsburg, on Monday the sixth day of May, one thousand seven hundred and seventy six, and continued, by adjournments to the _____ day of June following:

A CONSTITUTION, OR FORM OF GOVERNMENT,

agreed to and resolved upon by the Delegates and Representatives of the several Counties and Corporations of Virginia.

Whereas George the Third, King of Great Britain and Ireland, and Elector of Hanover, heretofore intrusted with the exercise of the Kingly Office in this Government, hath endeavoured to pervert the same into a detestable and insupportable Tyranny; by putting his negative on laws the most wholesome and necessary for the publick good;

by denying his Governours permission to pass Laws of immediate and pressing importance, unless suspended in their operation for his assent, and, when so suspended, neglecting to attend to them for many Years;

by refusing to pass certain other laws, unless the persons to be benefited by them would relinquish the inestimable right of representation in the legislature;

by dissolving legislative assemblies repeatedly and continually, for opposing with manly firmness his invasions of the rights of the people;

when dissolved, by refusing to call others for a long space of time, thereby leaving the political system without any legislative head;

by endeavouring to prevent the population of our Country, and, for that purpose, obstructing the laws for the naturalization of foreigners;

by keeping among us, in times of peace, standing Armies and Ships of war;

by affecting to render the Military independent of, and superiour to, the civil power;

by combining with others to subject us to a foreign Jurisdiction, giving his assent to their pretended Acts of Legislation;

for quartering large bodies of armed troops among us;

for cutting off our Trade with all parts of the World;

for imposing Taxes on us without our Consent;

for depriving us of the Benefits of Trial by Jury;

for transporting us beyond Seas, to be tried for pretended Offences;

for suspending our own Legislatures, and declaring themselves invested with power to legislate for us in all Cases whatsoever;

by plundering our Seas, ravaging our Coasts, burning our Towns, and destroying the lives of our People;

by inciting insurrections of our fellow Subjects, with the allurements of forfeiture and confiscation;

by prompting our Negroes to rise in Arms among us, those very negroes whom, by an inhuman use of his negative, he hath refused us permission to exclude by Law;

by endeavouring to bring on the inhabitants of our Frontiers the merciless Indian savages, whose known rule of Warfare is an undistinguished Destruction of all Ages, Sexes, and Conditions of Existance;

by transporting, at this time, a large Army of foreign Mercenaries, to compleat the Works of Death, desolation, and Tyranny, already begun with circumstances of Cruelty and Perfidy unworthy the head of a civilized Nation;

by answering our repeated Petitions for Redress with a Repetition of Injuries;

and finally, by abandoning the Helm of Government, and declaring us out of his Allegiance and Protection;

By which several Acts of Misrule, the Government of this Country, as formerly exercised under the Crown of Great Britain, is totally dissolved; We therefore, the Delegates and Representatives of the good People of Virginia, having maturely considered the Premises, and viewing with great concern the deplorable condition to which this once happy Country must be reduced, unless some regular adequate Mode of civil Polity is speedily adopted, and in Compliance with a Recommendation of the General Congress, do ordain and declare the future Form of Government of Virginia to be as followeth:

The legislative, executive, and judiciary departments, shall be separate and distinct, so that neither exercise the Powers properly belonging to the other; nor shall any person exercise the powers of more than one of them at the same time, except that the Justices of the County Courts shall be eligible to either House of Assembly.

The legislative shall be formed of two distinct branches, who, together, shall be a complete Legislature. They shall meet once, or oftener, every Year, and shall be called the General Assembly of Virginia.

One of these shall be called the House of Delegates, and consist of two Representatives to be chosen for each County, and for the District of West Augusta, annually, of such Men as actually reside in and are freeholders of the same, or duly qualified according to Law, and also of one Delegate or Representative to be chosen annually for the city of Williamsburg, and one for the Borough of Norfolk, and a

Representative for each of such other Cities and Boroughs, as may hereafter be allowed particular Representation by the legislature; but when any City or Borough shall so decrease as that the number of persons having right of Suffrage therein shall have been for the space of seven Years successively less than half the number of Voters in some one County in Virginia, such City or Borough thenceforward shall cease to send a Delegate or Representative to the Assembly.

The other shall be called the Senate, and consist of twenty four Members, of whom thirteen shall constitute a House to proceed on Business for whose election the different Counties shall be divided into twenty four districts, and each County of the respective District, at the time of the election of its Delegates, shall vote for one Senator, who is actually a resident and freeholder within the District, or duly qualified according to Law, and is upwards of twenty five Years of Age; And the sheriff of each County, within five days at farthest after the last County election in the District, shall meet at some convenient place, and from the Poll so taken in their respective Counties return as a Senator to the House of Senators the Man who shall have the greatest number of Votes in the whole District. To keep up this Assembly by rotation, the Districts shall be equally divided into four Classes, and numbered by Lot. At the end of one Year after the General Election, the six Members elected by the first division shall be displaced, and the vacancies thereby occasioned supplied from such Class or division, by new Election, in the manner aforesaid. This Rotation shall be applied to each division, according to its number, and continued in due order annually.

The right of Suffrage in the Election of Members for both Houses shall remain as exercised at present, and each House shall choose its own Speaker, appoint its own Officers, settle its own rules of proceding, and direct Writs of Election for supplying intermediate vacancies.

All Laws shall originate in the House of Delegates, to be approved or rejected by the Senate or to be amended with the Consent of the House of Delegates; except Money Bills, which in no instance shall be altered by the Senate but wholly approved or rejected.

A Governour, or chief Magistrate, shall be chosen annually, by joint Ballot of both Houses, (to be taken in each House respectively, deposited in the Conference room, the Boxes examined jointly by a Committee of each House, and the numbers severally reported to them, that the appointments may be entered, which shall be the mode of taking the joint Ballot of both Houses in all Cases) who shall not continue in that office longer than three Years successively, nor be eligible until the expiration of four Years after he shall have been out of that office: An adequate, but moderate Salary, shall be settled on him during his Continuance in Office; and he shall, with the advice of a Council of State, exercise the Executive powers of Government according to the laws of this Commonwealth; and shall not, under any pretence, exercise any power or prerogative by virtue of any Law, statute, or Custom, of England; But he shall, with the advice of the Council of State, have the power of granting reprieves or pardons, except where the prosecution shall have been carried on by the House of Delegates, or the Law shall otherwise particularly direct; in which Cases, no reprieve or Pardon shall be granted but by resolve of the House of Delegates.

Either House of the General Assembly may adjourn themselves respectively: The Governour shall not prorogue or adjourn the Assembly during their setting, nor dissolve them at any Time; but he shall, if necessary, either by advice of the Council of State, or on application of a Majority of the House of Delegates, call them before the time to which they shall stand prorogued or adjourned.

A Privy Council, or Council of State, consisting of eight Members, shall be chosen by joint Ballot of both Houses of Assembly, either from their own Members or the People at large, to assist in the Administration of Government. They shall annually choose out of their own Members, a President, who, in case of the death, inability, or necessary absence of the Governour from the Government, shall act as lieutenant Governour. Four Members shall be sufficient to act, and their Advice and proceedings shall be entered of Record, and signed by the Members present (to any part whereof any Member may enter his dissent) to be laid before the General Assembly, when called for by them. This Council may appoint their own Clerk, who shall have a Salary settled by Law, and take an Oath of Secrecy in such matters as he shall be directed by the Board to conceal. A sum of Money appropriated to that purpose shall be divided annually among the Members, in proportion to their attendance; and they shall be incapable, during their continuance in Office, of sitting in either House of Assembly. Two Members shall be removed, by joint Ballot of both houses of Assembly at the end of every three Years, and be ineligible for the three next years. These Vacancies, as well as those occasioned by death or incapacity, shall be supplied by new Elections, in the same manner.

The Delegates for Virginia to the Continental Congress shall be chosen annually, or superseded in the mean time by joint Ballot of both Houses of Assembly.

The present Militia Officers shall be continued, and Vacancies supplied by appointment of the Governour, with the advice of the privy Council, or recommendations from the respective County Courts; but the Governour and Council shall have a power of suspending any Officer, and ordering a Court-Martial on Complaint for misbehaviour or inability, or to supply Vacancies of Officers happening when in actual Service. The Governour may embody the Militia, with the advice of the privy Council; and, when embodied, shall alone have the direction of the Militia under the laws of the Country.

The two Houses of Assembly shall, by joint Ballot, appoint judges of the supreme Court of Appeals, and General Court, Judges in Chancery, Judges of Admiralty, Secretary, and the Attorney-General, to be commissioned by the Governour, and continue in Office during good behaviour. In case of death, incapacity, or resignation, the Governour, with the advice of the privy Council, shall appoint Persons to succeed in Office, to be approved or displaced by both Houses. These Officers shall have fixed and adequate Salaries, and, together with all others holding lucrative Offices, and all Ministers of the Gospel of every Denomination, be incapable of being elected Members of either House of Assembly, or the privy Council.

The Governour, with the Advice of the privy Council, shall appoint Justices of the Peace for the Counties; and in case of Vacancies, or a necessity of increasing the number hereafter, such appointments to be made upon the recommendation of the respective County Courts. The present acting Secretary in Virginia, and Clerks of all the County Courts, shall continue in Office. In case of Vacancies, either by death, incapacity, or resignation, a Secretary shall be appointed as before directed, and the Clerks by the respective Courts. The present and future Clerks shall hold their Offices during good behaviour, to be judged of and determined in the General Court. The Sheriffs and Coroners shall be nominated by the respective Courts, approved by the Governour with the advice of the privy

Council, and commissioned by the Governour. The Justices shall appoint Constables, and all fees of the aforesaid Officers be regulated by law.

The Governour, when he is out of Office, and others offending against the State, either by Mal-administration, Corruption, or other Means, by which the safety of the State may be endangered, shall be impeachable by the House of Delegates. Such impeachment to be prosecuted by the Attorney General, or such other Person or Persons as the House may appoint in the General Court, according to the laws of the Land. If found guilty, he or they shall be either for ever disabled to hold any Office under Government, or removed from such Office *Pro tempore,* or subjected to such Pains or Penalties as the laws shall direct.

If all, or any of the Judges of the General Court, should, on good grounds (to be judged of by the House of Delegates) be accused of any of the Crimes or Offences before-mentioned, such House of Delegates may, in like manner, impeach the Judge or Judges so accused, to be prosecuted in the Court of Appeals; and he or they, if found guilty, shall be punished in the same manner as is prescribed in the preceding Clause.

Commissions and Grants shall run, *In the Name of the Common Wealth of* Virginia, and bear teste by the Governour, with the Seal of the Common wealth annexed. Writs shall run in the same manner, and bear teste by the Clerks of the several Courts. Indictments shall conclude, *Against the Peace and Dignity of the Common-Wealth.*

A Treasurer shall be appointed annually, by joint Ballot of both Houses.

All escheats, penalties, and forfeitures, heretofore going to the King, shall go to the Common Wealth, save only such, as the Legislature may abolish, or otherwise provide for.

The territories contained within the Charters erecting the Colonies of Maryland, Pennsylvania, North and South Carolina, are hereby ceded, released, and forever confirmed to the People of those Colonies respectively, with all the rights of property, jurisdiction, and Government, and all other rights whatsoever which might at any time heretofore have been claimed by Virginia, except the free Navigation and use of the Rivers Potowmack and Pohomoke, with the property of the Virginia Shores or strands bordering on either of the said Rivers, and all improvements which have been or shall be made thereon. The western and northern extent of Virginia shall in all other respects stand as fixed by the Charter of King James the first, in the Year one thousand six hundred and nine, and by the publick Treaty of Peace between the Courts of Great Britain and France in the year one thousand seven hundred and sixty three; Unless by act of this legislature, one or more Territories shall hereafter be laid off, and Governments established Westward of the *Allegheny* Mountains. And no purchases of Land shall be made of the *Indian* Natives but on behalf of the Publick, by authority of the General Assembly.

In order to introduce this Government, the Representatives of the People met in Convention shall choose a Governour and privy Council, also such other Officers directed to be chosen by both Houses as may be judged necessary to be immediately appointed. The Senate, to be first chosen by the people, to continue until the last day of March next, and the other Officers until the end of the succeeding Session of Assembly. In case of Vacancies, the Speaker of either House shall issue Writs for new Elections.

Pennsylvania Constitution
[including "A Declaration of the Rights of the Inhabitants . . . of Pennsylvania" and "Plan or Frame of Government for . . . Pennsylvania"]
September 28, 1776

Whereas all government ought to be instituted and supported for the security and protection of the community as such, and to enable the individuals who compose it to enjoy their natural rights, and the other blessings which the Author of existence has bestowed upon man; and whenever these great ends of government are not obtained, the people have a right, by common consent to change it, and take such measures as to them may appear necessary to promote their safety and happiness. AND WHEREAS the inhabitants of this commonwealth have in consideration of protection only, heretofore acknowledged allegiance to the king of Great Britain; and the said king has not only withdrawn that protection, but commenced, and still continues to carry on, with unabated vengeance, a most cruel and unjust war against them, employing therein, not only the troops of Great Britain, but foreign mercenaries, savages and slaves, for the avowed purpose of reducing them to a total and abject submission to the despotic domination of the British parliament, with many other acts of tyranny, (more fully set forth in the declaration of Congress) whereby all allegiance and fealty to the said king and his successors, are dissolved and at an end, and all power and authority derived from him ceased in these colonies. AND WHEREAS it is absolutely necessary for the welfare and safety of the inhabitants of said colonies, that they be henceforth free and independent States, and that just, permanent, and proper forms of government exist in every part of them, derived from and founded on the authority of the people only, agreeable to the directions of the honourable American Congress. We, the representatives of the freemen of Pennsylvania, in general convention met, for the express purpose of framing such a government, confessing the goodness of the great Governor of the universe (who alone knows to what degree of earthly happiness mankind may attain, by perfecting the arts of government) in permitting the people of this State, by common consent, and without violence, deliberately to form for themselves such just rules as they shall think best, for governing their future society; and being fully convinced, that it is our indispensable duty to establish such original principles of government, as will best promote the general happiness of the people of this State, and their posterity, and provide for future improvements, without partiality for, or prejudice against any particular class, sect, or denomination of men whatever, do, by virtue of the authority vested in use by our constituents, ordain, declare, and establish, the following *Declaration of Rights* and *Frame of Government,* to be the CONSTITUTION of this commonwealth, and to remain in force therein for ever, unaltered, except in such articles as shall hereafter on experience be found to require improvement, and which shall by the same authority of the people, fairly delegated as this frame of government directs, be amended or improved for the more effectual obtaining and securing the great end and design of all government, herein before mentioned.

A Declaration of the Rights of the Inhabitants of the Common-Wealth, or State of Pennsylvania

I. That all men are born equally free and independent, and have certain natural, inherent and inalienable rights, amongst which are, the enjoying and defending life and liberty, acquiring, possessing and protecting property, and pursuing and obtaining happiness and safety.

II. That all men have a natural and unalienable right to worship Almighty God according to the dictates of their own consciences and understanding: And that no man ought or of right can be compelled to attend any religious worship, or erect or support any place of worship, or maintain any ministry, contrary to, or against, his own free will and consent: Nor can any man, who acknowledges the being of a God, be justly deprived or abridged of any civil right as a citizen, on account of his religious sentiments or peculiar mode of religious worship: And that no authority can or ought to be vested in, or assumed by any power whatever, that shall in any case interfere with, or in any manner controul, the right of conscience in the free exercise of religious worship.

III. That the people of this State have the sole, exclusive and inherent right of governing and regulating the internal police of the same.

IV. That all power being originally inherent in, and consequently derived from, the people; therefore all officers of government, whether legislative or executive, are their trustees and servants, and at all times accountable to them.

V. That government is, or ought to be, instituted for the common benefit, protection and security of the people, nation or community; and not for the particular emolument or advantage of any single man, family, or sett of men, who are a part only of that community; And that the community hath an indubitable, unalienable and indefeasible right to reform, alter, or abolish government in such manner as shall be by that community judged most conducive to the public weal.

VI. That those who are employed in the legislative and executive business of the State, may be restrained from oppression, the people have a right, at such periods as they may think proper, to reduce their public officers to a private station, and supply the vacancies by certain and regular elections.

VII. That all elections ought to be free; and that all free men having a sufficient evident common interest with, and attachment to the community, have a right to elect officers, or to be elected into office.

VIII. That every member of society hath a right to be protected in the enjoyment of life, liberty and property, and therefore is bound to contribute his proportion towards the expence of that protection, and yield his personal service when necessary, or an equivalent thereto: But no part of a man's property can be justly taken from him, or applied to public uses, without his own consent, or that of his legal representatives: Nor can any man who is conscientiously scrupulous of bearing arms, be justly compelled thereto, if he will pay such equivalent, nor are the people bound by any laws, but such as they have in like manner assented to, for their common good.

IX. That in all prosecutions for criminal offences, a man hath a right to be heard by himself and his council, to demand the cause and nature of his accusation, to be confronted with the witnesses, to call for evidence in his favour, and a speedy public trial, by an impartial jury of the country, without the unanimous consent of which jury he cannot be found guilty; nor can he be compelled to give evidence against himself; nor can any man be justly deprived of his liberty except by the laws of the land, or the judgment of his peers.

X. That the people have a right to hold themselves, their houses, papers, and possessions free from search and seizure, and therefore warrants without oaths or affirmations first made, affording a sufficient foundation for them, and whereby any officer or messenger may be commanded or required to search suspected places, or to seize any person or persons, his or their property, not particularly described, are contrary to that right, and ought not to be granted.

XI. That in controversies respecting property, and in suits between man and man, the parties have a right to trial by jury, which ought to be held sacred.

XII. That the people have a right to freedom of speech, and of writing, and publishing their sentiments; therefore the freedom of the press ought not to be restrained.

XIII. That the people have a right to bear arms for the defence of themselves and the state; and as standing armies in the time of peace are dangerous to liberty, they ought not to be kept up; And that the military should be kept under strict subordination to, and governed by, the civil power.

XIV. That a frequent recurrence to fundamental principles, and a firm adherence to justice, moderation, temperance, industry, and frugality are absolutely necessary to preserve the blessings of liberty, and keep a government free: The people ought therefore to pay particular attention to these points in the choice of officers and representatives, and have a right to exact a due and constant regard to them, from their legislatures and magistrates, in the making and executing such laws as are necessary for the good government of the state.

XV. That all men have a natural inherent right to emigrate from one state to another that will receive them, or to form a new state in vacant countries, or in such countries as they can purchase, whenever they think that thereby they may promote their own happiness.

XVI. That the people have a right to assemble together, to consult for their common good, to instruct their representatives, and to apply to the legislature for redress of grievances, by address, petition, or remonstrance.

PLAN OR FRAME OF GOVERNMENT FOR THE COMMONWEALTH OR STATE OF PENNSYLVANIA

SECTION 1. The commonwealth or state of Pennsylvania shall be governed hereafter by an assembly of the representatives of the freemen of the same, and a president and council, in manner and form following—

SECT. 2. The supreme legislative power shall be vested in a house of representatives of the freemen of the commonwealth or state of Pennsylvania.

SECT. 3. The supreme executive power shall be vested in a president and council.

SECT. 4. Courts of justice shall be established in the city of Philadelphia, and in every county of this state.

SECT. 5. The freemen of this commonwealth and their sons shall be trained and armed for its defence under such regulations, restrictions, and exceptions as the general assembly shall by law direct, preserving always to the people the right of choosing their colonels and all commissioned officers under that rank, in such manner and as often as by the said laws shall be directed.

SECT. 6. Every freemen of the full age of twenty-one years, having resided in this state for the space of one whole year next before the day of election for representatives, and paid public taxes during that time, shall enjoy the right of an elector: Provided always, that sons of freeholders of the age of twenty-one years shall be intitled to vote although they have not paid taxes.

SECT. 7. The house of representatives of the freemen of this commonwealth shall consist of persons most noted for wisdom and virtue, to be chosen by the freemen of every city and county of this commonwealth respectively. And no person shall be elected unless he has resided in the city or county for which he shall be chosen two years immediately before the said election; nor shall any member, while he continues such, hold any other office, except in the militia.

SECT. 8. No person shall be capable of being elected a member to serve in the house of representatives of the freemen of this commonwealth more than four years in seven.

SECT. 9. The members of the house of representatives shall be chosen annually by ballot, by the freemen of the commonwealth, on the second Tuesday in October forever, (except this present year,) and shall meet on the fourth Monday of the same month, and shall be stiled, *The general assembly of the representatives of the freemen of Pennsylvania,* and shall have power to choose their speaker, the treasurer of the state, and their other officers; sit on their own adjournments; prepare bills and enact them into laws; judge of the elections and qualifications of their own members; they may expel a member, but not a second time for the same cause; they may administer oaths or affirmations on examination of witnesses; redress grievances; impeach state criminals; grant charters of incorporation; constitute towns, boroughs, cities, and counties; and shall have all other powers necessary for the legislature of a free state or commonwealth: But they shall have no power to add to, alter, abolish, or infringe any part of this constitution.

SECT. 10. A quorum of the house of representatives shall consist of two-thirds of the whole number of members elected; and having met and chosen their speaker, shall each of them before they proceed to business take and subscribe, as well the oath or affirmation of fidelity and allegiance hereinafter directed, as the following oath or affirmation, viz:

I _____ do swear (or affirm) that as a member of this assembly, I will not propose or assent to any bill, vote, or resolution, which shall appear to me injurious to the people; nor do or consent to any act or thing whatever, that shall have a tendency to lessen or abridge their rights and privileges, as declared in the constitution of this state; but will in all things conduct myself as a faithful honest representative and guardian of the people, according to the best of my judgment and abilities.

And each member, before he takes his seat, shall make and subscribe the following declaration, viz:

I do believe in one God, the creator and governor of the universe, the rewarder of the good and the punisher of the wicked. And I do acknowledge the Scriptures of the Old and New Testament to be given by Divine inspiration.

And no further or other religious test shall ever hereafter be required of any civil officer or magistrate in this State.

SECT. 11. Delegates to represent this state in congress shall be chosen by ballot by the future general assembly at their first meeting, and annually forever afterwards, as long as such representation shall be necessary. Any delegate may be superseded at any time, by the general assembly appointing another in his stead. No man shall sit in congress longer than two years successively, nor be capable of reëlection for three years afterwards: and no person who holds any office in the gift of the congress shall hereafter be elected to represent this commonwealth in congress.

SECT. 12. If any city or cities, county or counties shall neglect or refuse to elect and send representatives to the general assembly, two-thirds of the members from the cities or counties that do elect and send representatives, provided they be a majority of the cities and counties of the whole state, when met, shall have all the powers of the general assembly, as fully and amply as if the whole were present.

SECT. 13. The doors of the house in which the representatives of the freemen of this state shall sit in general assembly, shall be and remain open for the admission of all persons who behave decently, except only when the welfare of this state may require the doors to be shut.

SECT. 14. The votes and proceedings of the general assembly shall be printed weekly during their sitting, with the yeas and nays, on any question, vote or resolution, where any two members require it, except when the vote is taken by ballot; and when the yeas and nays are so taken every member shall have a right to insert the reasons of his vote upon the minutes, if he desires it.

SECT. 15. To the end that laws before they are enacted may be more maturely considered, and the inconvenience of hasty determinations as much as possible prevented, all bills of public nature shall be printed for the consideration of the people, before they are read in general assembly the last time for debate and amendment; and, except on occasions of sudden necessity, shall not be passed into laws until the next session of assembly; and for the more perfect satisfaction of the public, the reasons and motives for making such laws shall be fully and clearly expressed in the preambles.

SECT. 16. The stile of the laws of this commonwealth shall be, "Be it enacted, and it is hereby enacted by the representatives of the freemen of the commonwealth of Pennsylvania in general assembly met, and by the authority of the same." And the general assembly shall affix their seal to every bill, as soon as it is enacted into a law, which seal shall be kept by the assembly, and shall be called, *The seal of the laws of Pennsylvania,* and shall not be used for any other purpose.

SECT. 17. The city of Philadelphia and each county of this commonwealth respectively, shall on the first Tuesday of November in this present year, and on the second Tuesday of October annually for the two next succeeding years, *viz.* the year one thousand seven hundred and seventy-seven, and the year one thousand seven hundred and seventy-eight, choose six persons to represent them in general assembly. But as representation in proportion to the number of taxable inhabitants is the only principle which can at all times secure liberty, and make the voice of a majority of the people the law of the land; therefore the general assembly shall cause complete lists of the taxable inhabitants in the city and each county in the commonwealth respectively, to be taken and returned to them, on or before the last meeting of the assembly elected in the year one thousand seven hundred and seventy-eight, who shall appoint a representation to each, in proportion to the number of taxables in such returns; which representation shall continue for the next seven years afterwards at the end of which, a new return of the taxable inhabitants shall be made, and a representation agreeable thereto appointed by the said assembly, and so on septennially forever. The wages of the representatives in general assembly, and all other state charges shall be paid out of the state treasury.

SECT. 18. In order that the freemen of this commonwealth may enjoy the benefit of election as equally as may be until the representation shall commence, as directed in the foregoing section, each county at its own choice may be divided into districts, hold elections therein, and elect their representatives in the county, and their other elective officers, as shall be hereafter regulated by the general assembly of this state. And no inhabitant of this state shall have more than one annual vote at the general election for representatives in assembly.

SECT. 19. For the present the supreme executive council of this state shall consist of twelve persons chosen in the following manner: The freemen of the city of Philadelphia, and of the counties of Philadelphia, Chester, and Bucks, respectively, shall choose by ballot one person for the city, and one for each county aforesaid, to serve for three years and no longer, at the time and place for electing representatives in general assembly. The freemen of the counties of Lancaster, York, Cumberland, and Berks, shall, in like manner elect one person for each county respectively, to serve as counsellors for two years and no longer. And the counties of Northampton, Bedford, Northumberland and Westmoreland, respectively, shall, in like manner, elect one person for each county, to serve as counsellors for one year, and no longer. And at the expiration of the time for which each counsellor was chosen to serve, the freemen of the city of Philadelphia, and of the several counties in this state, respectively, shall elect one person to serve as counsellor for three years and no longer; and so on every third year forever. By this mode of election and continual rotation, more men will be trained to public business, there will in every subsequent year be found in the council a number of persons acquainted with the proceedings of the foregoing years, whereby the business will be more consistently conducted, and moreover the danger of establishing an inconvenient aristocracy will be effectually prevented. All vacancies in the council that may happen by death, resignation, or otherwise, shall be filled at the next general election for representatives in general assembly, unless a particular election for that purpose shall be sooner appointed by the president and council. No member of the general assembly or delegate in congress, shall be chosen a member of the council. The president and vice-president shall be chosen annually by the joint ballot of the general assembly and council, of the members of the council. Any person having served as a counsellor for three successive years, shall be incapable of holding that office for four years afterwards. Every member of the council shall be a justice of the peace for the whole commonwealth, by virtue of his office.

In case new additional counties shall hereafter be erected in this state, such county or counties shall elect a counsellor, and such county or counties shall be annexed to the next neighbouring counties, and shall take rotation with such counties.

The council shall meet annually, at the same time and place with the general assembly.

The treasurer of the state, trustees of the loan office, naval officers, collectors of customs or excise, judge of the admirality, attornies general, sheriffs, and prothonotaries, shall not be capable of a seat in the general assembly, executive council, or continental congress.

SECT. 20. The president, and in his absence the vice-president, with the council, five of whom shall be a quorum, shall have power to appoint and commissionate judges, naval officers, judge of the admiralty, attorney general and all other officers, civil and military, except such as are chosen by the general assembly or the people, agreeable to this frame of government, and the laws that may be made hereafter; and shall supply every vacancy in any office, occasioned by death, resignation, removal or disqualification, until the office can be filled in the time and manner directed by law or this constitution. They are to correspond with other states, and transact business with the officers of government, civil and military; and to prepare such business as may appear to them necessary to lay before the general assembly. They shall sit as judges, to hear and determine on impeachments, taking to their assistance for advice only, the justices of the supreme court. And shall have power to grant pardons, and remit fines, in all cases whatsoever, except in cases of impeachment; and in cases of treason and murder, shall have power to grant reprieves, but not to pardon, until the end of the next sessions of assembly; but there shall be no remission or mitigation of punishments on impeachments, except by act of the legislature; they are also to take care that the laws be faithfully executed; they are to expedite the execution of such measures as may be resolved upon by the general assembly; and they may draw upon the treasury for such sums as shall be appropriated by the house: They may also lay embargoes, or prohibit the exportation of any commodity, for any time, not exceeding thirty days, in the recess of the house only: They may grant such licences, as shall be directed by law, and shall have power to call together the general assembly when necessary, before the day to which they shall stand adjourned. The president shall be commander in chief of the forces of the state, but shall not command in person, except advised thereto by the council, and then only so long as they shall approve thereof. The president and council shall have a secretary, and keep fair books of their proceedings, wherein any counsellor may enter his dissent, with his reasons in support of it.

SECT. 21. All commissions shall be in the name, and by the authority of the freemen of the commonwealth of Pennsylvania, sealed with the state seal, signed by the president or vice-president, and attested by the secretary; which seal shall be kept by the council.

SECT. 22. Every officer of state, whether judicial or executive, shall be liable to be impeached by the general assembly, either when in office, or after his resignation or removal for mal-administration: All impeachments shall be before the president or vice-president and council, who shall hear and determine the same.

SECT. 23. The judges of the supreme court of judicature shall have fixed salaries, be commissioned for seven years only, though capable of re-appointment at the end of that term, but removable for misbehaviour at any time by the general assembly; they shall not be allowed to sit as members in the continental congress, executive council, or general assembly, nor to hold any other office civil or military, nor to take or receive fees or perquisites of any kind.

SECT. 24. The supreme court, and the several courts of common pleas of this commonwealth, shall, besides the powers usually exercised by such courts, have the powers of a court of chancery, so far as relates to the perpetuating testimony, obtaining evidence from places not within this state, and the care of the persons and estates of those who are *non compotes mentis,* and such other powers as may be found necessary by future general assemblies, not inconsistent with this constitution.

SECT. 25. Trials shall be by jury as heretofore: And it is recommended to the legislature of this state, to provide by law against every corruption or partiality in the choice, return, or appointment of juries.

Sect. 26. Courts of sessions, common pleas, and orphans courts shall be held quarterly in each city and county; and the legislature shall have power to establish all such other courts as they may judge for the good of the inhabitants of the state. All courts shall be open, and justice shall be impartially administered without corruption or unnecessary delay: All their officers shall be paid an adequate but moderate compensation for their services: And if any officer shall take greater or other fees than the law allows him, either directly or indirectly, it shall ever after disqualify him from holding any office in this state.

Sect. 27. All prosecutions shall commence in the name and by the authority of the freemen of the commonwealth of Pennsylvania; and all indictments shall conclude with these words, *"Against the peace and dignity of the same."* The style of all process hereafter in this state shall be, *The commonwealth of Pennsylvania.*

Sect. 28. The person of a debtor, where there is not a strong presumption of fraud, shall not be continued in prison, after delivering up, *bona fide,* all his estate real and personal, for the use of his creditors, in such manner as shall be hereafter regulated by law. All prisoners shall be bailable by sufficient sureties, unless for capital offences, when the proof is evident, or presumption great.

Sect. 29. Excessive bail shall not be exacted for bailable offences: And all fines shall be moderate.

Sect. 30. Justices of the peace shall be elected by the freeholders of each city and county respectively, that is to say, two or more persons may be chosen for each ward, township, or district, as the law shall hereafter direct: And their names shall be returned to the president in council, who shall commissionate one or more of them for each ward, township, or district so returning, for seven years, removable for misconduct by the general assembly. But if any city or county, ward, township, or district in this commonwealth, shall hereafter incline to change the manner of appointing their justices of the peace as settled in this article, the general assembly may make laws to regulate the same, agreeable to the desire of a majority of the freeholders of the city or county, ward, township, or district so applying. No justice of the peace shall sit in the general assembly unless he first resigns his commission; nor shall he be allowed to take any fees, nor any salary or allowance, except such as the future legislature may grant.

SECT. 31. Sheriffs and coroners shall be elected annually in each city and county, by the freemen; that is to say, two persons for each office, one of whom for each, is to be commissioned by the president in council. No person shall continue in the office of sheriff more than three successive years, or be capable of being again elected during four years afterwards. The election shall be held at the same time and place appointed for the election of representatives: And the commissioners and assessors, and other officers chosen by the people, shall also be then and there elected, as has been usual heretofore, until altered or otherwise regulated by the future legislature of this state.

SECT. 32. All elections, whether by the people or in general assembly, shall be by ballot, free and voluntary: And any elector, who shall receive any gift or reward for his vote, in meat, drink, monies, or otherwise, shall forfeit his right to elect for that time, and suffer such other penalties as future laws shall direct. And any person who shall directly or indirectly give, promise, or bestow any such rewards to be elected, shall be thereby rendered incapable to serve for the ensuing year.

SECT. 33. All fees, licence money, fines and forfeitures heretofore granted, or paid to the governor, or his deputies for the support of government, shall hereafter be paid into the public treasury, unless altered or abolished by the future legislature.

SECT. 34. A register's office for the probate of wills and granting letters of administration, and an office for the recording of deeds, shall be kept in each city and county: The officers to be appointed by the general assembly, removable at their pleasure, and to be commissioned by the president in council.

SECT. 35. The printing presses shall be free to every person who undertakes to examine the proceedings of the legislature, or any part of government.

SECT. 36. As every freeman to preserve his independence, (if without a sufficient estate) ought to have some profession, calling, trade or farm, whereby he may honestly subsist, there can be no necessity for, nor use in establishing offices of profit, the usual effects of which are dependence and servility unbecoming freemen, in the possessors and expectants; faction, contention, corruption, and disorder among the people. But if any man is called into public service, to the prejudice of his private affairs, he has a right to a reasonable compensation: And whenever an office, through increase of fees or otherwise, becomes so profitable as to occasion many to apply for it, the profits ought to be lessened by the legislature.

Sect. 37. The future legislature of this state, shall regulate intails in such a manner as to prevent perpetuities.

Sect. 38. The penal laws as heretofore used shall be reformed by the legislature of this state, as soon as may be, and punishments made in some cases less sanguinary, and in general more proportionate to the crimes.

Sect. 39. To deter more effectually from the commission of crimes, by continued visible punishments of long duration, and to make sanguinary punishments less necessary; houses ought to be provided for punishing by hard labour, those who shall be convicted of crimes not capital; wherein the criminals shall be imployed for the benefit of the public, or for reparation of injuries done to private persons: And all persons at proper times shall be admitted to see the prisoners at their labour.

Sect. 40. Every officer, whether judicial, executive or military, in authority under this commonwealth, shall take the following oath or affirmation of allegiance, and general oath of office before he enters on the execution of his office.

THE OATH OR AFFIRMATION OF ALLEGIANCE

I _____ do swear (or affirm) that I will be true and faithful to the commonwealth of Pennsylvania: And that I will not directly or indirectly do any act or thing prejudicial or injurious to the constitution or government thereof, as established by the convention.

THE OATH OR AFFIRMATION OF OFFICE

I _____ do swear (or affirm) that I will faithfully execute the office of _____ for the _____ of _____ and will do equal right and justice to all men, to the best of my judgment and abilities, according to law.

Sect. 41. No public tax, custom or contribution shall be imposed upon, or paid by the people of this state, except by a law for that purpose: And before any law be made for raising it, the purpose for which any tax is to be raised ought to appear clearly to the legislature to be of more service to the community than the money would be, if not collected; which being well observed, taxes can never be burthens.

SECT. 42. Every foreigner of good character who comes to settle in this state, having first taken an oath or affirmation of allegiance to the same, may purchase, or by other just means acquire, hold, and transfer land or other real estate; and after one year's residence, shall be deemed a free denizen thereof, and entitled to all the rights of a natural born subject of this state, except that he shall not be capable of being elected a representative until after two years residence.

SECT. 43. The inhabitants of this state shall have liberty to fowl and hunt in seasonable times on the lands they hold, and on all other lands therein not inclosed; and in like manner to fish in all boatable waters, and others not private property.

SECT. 44. A school or schools shall be established in each county by the legislature, for the convenient instruction of youth, with such salaries to the masters paid by the public, as may enable them to instruct youth at low prices: And all useful learning shall be duly encouraged and promoted in one or more universities.

SECT. 45. Laws for the encouragement of virtue, and prevention of vice and immorality, shall be made and constantly kept in force, and provision shall be made for their due execution: And all religious societies or bodies of men heretofore united or incorporated for the advancement of religion or learning, or for other pious and charitable purposes, shall be encouraged and protected in the enjoyment of the privileges, immunities and estates which they were accustomed to enjoy, or could of right have enjoyed, under the laws and former constitution of this state.

SECT. 46. The declaration of rights is hereby declared to be a part of the constitution of this commonwealth, and ought never to be violated on any pretence whatever.

SECT. 47. In order that the freedom of the commonwealth may be preserved inviolate forever, there shall be chosen by ballot by the freemen in each city and county respectively, on the second Tuesday in October, in the year one thousand seven hundred and eighty-three, and on the second Tuesday in October, in every seventh year thereafter, two persons in each city and county of this state, to be called the COUNCIL OF CENSORS; who shall meet together on the second Monday of November next ensuing their election; the majority of whom shall be a quorum in every case, except as to calling a convention, in which two-thirds of the whole number elected shall agree: And whose duty it shall be to enquire whether the constitution has been preserved inviolate in every part; and whether the legislative and executive branches of government have performed their duty as guardians of the people, or assumed to themselves, or exercised other or greater powers than they are intitled to by the constitution: They are also to enquire whether the public taxes have been justly laid and collected in all parts of this commonwealth, in what manner the public monies have been disposed of, and whether the laws have been duly executed. For these purposes they shall have power to send for persons, papers, and records; they shall have authority to pass public censures, to order impeachments, and to recommend to the legislature the repealing such laws as appear to them to have been enacted contrary to the principles of the constitution. These powers they shall continue to have, for and during the space of one year from the day of their election and no longer: The said council of censors shall also have power to call a convention, to meet within two years after their sitting, if there appear to them an absolute necessity of amending any article of the constitution which may be defective, explaining such as may be thought not clearly expressed, and of adding such as are necessary for the preservation of the rights and happiness of the people: But the articles to be amended, and the amendments proposed, and such articles as are proposed to be added or abolished, shall be promulgated at least six months before the day appointed for the election of such convention, for the previous consideration of the people, that they may have an opportunity of instructing their delegates on the subject.

Passed in Convention the 28th day of September, 1776, and signed by their order.

BENJ. FRANKLIN, *Prest.*

Concord Town Meeting Resolutions
October 21, 1776

AT A MEETING OF the Inhabitents of the Town of Concord being free and twenty one years of age and upward, met by adjournment on the twenty first Day of October 1776 to take into Consideration a Resolve of the Honorable House of Representatives of this State on the 17th of September Last, the Town Resolved as followes____

Resolve 1st. That this State being at Present destitute of a Properly established form of Goverment, it is absolutly necesary that one should be emmediatly formed and established____

Resolved 2 That the Supreme Legislative, either in their Proper Capacity, or in Joint Committee, are by no means a Body proper to form and Establish a Constitution, or form of Government; for Reasons following.

first Because we Conceive that a Constitution in its Proper Idea intends a System of Principles Established to Secure the Subject in the Possession and enjoyment of their Rights and Priviliges, against any Encroachments of the Governing Part____

2d Because the Same Body that forms a Constitution have of Consequence a power to alter it. 3d—Because a Constitution alterable by the Supreme Legislative is no Security at all to the Subject against any Encroachment of the Governing part on any, or on all of their Rights and priviliges.

Resolve 3d. That it appears to this Town highly necesary and Expedient that a Convention, or Congress be immediately Chosen, to form and establish a Constitution, by the Inhabitents of the Respective Towns in this State, being free and of twenty one years of age, and upwards, in Proportion as the Representatives of this State formerly ware Chosen; the Convention or Congress not to Consist of a greater number then the House of assembly of this State heretofore might Consist of, Except that each Town and District shall have Liberty to Send one Representative or otherwise as Shall appear meet to the Inhabitents of this State in General

Resolve 4th. that when the Convention, or Congress have formed a Constitution they adjourn for a Short time, and Publish their Proposed Constitution for the Inspection and Remarks of the Inhabitents of this State.

Resolved 5ly. That the Honorable House of assembly of this State be Desired to Recommend it to the Inhabitants of the State to Proceed to Chuse a Convention or Congress for the Purpas abovesaid as soon as Possable.

INDEPENDENCE

WHEN AMERICANS SPOKE OF independence in 1774 and 1775, they usually meant that the colonies should be legally independent of Parliament, not of the British Empire. In theory, the colonists remained committed to a reconciliation based on preserving the authority of a Crown that would treat the separate American legislatures as virtual equivalents of Parliament. After January 1776, however, the word "independence" took on its broader meaning of a total separation from all imperial authority, royal and parliamentary. The publication on January 10, 1776, of Thomas Paine's sensational pamphlet *Common Sense* marked a critical step in this movement. Before Paine wrote, Americans were reluctant to discuss independence. After *Common Sense* appeared, they debated it everywhere.

Still, well into the spring of 1776 many American moderates continued to hope that the British government would come to its senses and send commissioners empowered to negotiate in good faith. Only in April and May did this hope finally begin to fade. Numerous communities began approving resolutions calling for a declaration of independence, and soon the provincial conventions followed suit. Acting on instructions from the Virginia provincial convention, Richard Henry Lee presented Congress with resolutions calling for the appointment of separate committees to draft a declaration of independence, articles of confederation, and a plan for negotiating treaties with potential foreign allies.

The best summary of these debates within Congress was compiled by Thomas Jefferson, the young Virginian with the quick pen who found himself tasked with being the principal author of the Declaration of Independence. If he'd had his druthers, Jefferson would have been back in Virginia, working on the state constitution. Instead, his fellow committeemen—John Adams, Benjamin Franklin, Robert Livingston, and John Jay—decided he was the best man to draft the Declaration. Like any author, he was disappointed with the changes Congress made in his text. But many commentators believe these changes were for the better.

The critical decision that Congress faced, however, involved the simple fact of independence, not the wording of the Declaration. That was why John Adams, perhaps the leading advocate of independence within Congress, thought July 2 (when Congress approved independence in principle) would be remembered as the great day. Down to the end, a few delegates continued to believe that the formal decision could wait. The leading opponent of independence was John Dickinson. Since 1775, he had been the most important moderate in Congress, and though never wavering in his support of American rights, he remained committed to the idea of reconciliation. Thus even while Dickinson chaired the committee drafting articles of confederation, he hoped to persuade Congress to defer a decision. Failing to do so, he left Congress, sacrificing much of the reputation he had earned as a leading advocate of American rights since the 1760s.

INDEPENDENCE

—Thomas Jefferson—
NOTES OF PROCEEDINGS IN CONGRESS
JUNE 7–28, 1776

IN CONGRESS. [JUNE 7–28, 1776]

FRIDAY JUNE 7. 1776. The Delegates from Virginia moved in obedience to instructions from their constituents that the Congress should declare that these United colonies are & of right ought to be free & independant states, that they are absolved from all allegiance to the British crown, and that all political connection between them and the state of Great Britain is & ought to be totally dissolved; that measures should be immediately taken for procuring the assistance of foreign powers, and a Confederation be formed to bind the colonies more closely together.

The house being obliged to attend at that time to some other business, the proposition was referred to the next day when the members were ordered to attend punctually at ten o'clock.

Saturday June 8. They proceeded to take it into consideration and referred it to a committee of the whole, into which they immediately resolved themselves, and passed that day & Monday the 10th in debating on the subject.

It was argued by Wilson, Robert R. Livingston, E. Rutlege, Dickinson and others

That tho' they were friends to the measures themselves, and saw the impossibility that we should ever again be united with Gr. Britain, yet they were against adopting them at this time:

That the conduct we had formerly observed was wise & proper now, of deferring to take any capital step till the voice of the people drove us into it:

That they were our power, & without them our declarations could not be carried into effect:

That the people of the middle colonies (Maryland, Delaware, Pennsylva., the Jersies & N. York) were not yet ripe for bidding adieu to British connection but that they were fast ripening & in a short time would join in the general voice of America:

That the resolution entered into by this house on the 15th of May for suppressing the exercise of all powers derived from the crown, had shewn, by the ferment into which it had thrown these middle colonies, that they had not yet accomodated their minds to a separation from the mother country:

That some of them had expressly forbidden their delegates to consent to such a declaration, and others had given no instructions, & consequently no powers to give such consent:

That if the delegates of any particular colony had no power to declare such colony independant, certain they were the others could not declare it for them; the colonies being as yet perfectly independant of each other:

That the assembly of Pennsylvania was now sitting above stairs, their convention would sit within a few days, the convention of New York was now sitting, & those of the Jersies & Delaware counties would meet on the Monday following & it was probable these bodies would take up the question of Independance & would declare to their delegates the voice of their state:

That if such a declaration should now be agreed to, these delegates must now retire & possibly their colonies might secede from the Union:

That such a secession would weaken us more than could be compensated by any foreign alliance:

That in the event of such a division, foreign powers would either refuse to join themselves to our fortunes, or having us so much in their power as that desperate declaration would place us, they would insist on terms proportionably more hard & prejudicial:

That we had little reason to expect an alliance with those to whom alone as yet we had cast our eyes:

That France & Spain had reason to be jealous of that rising power which would one day certainly strip them of all their American possessions:

That it was more likely they should form a connection with the British court, who, if they should find themselves unable otherwise to extricate themselves from their difficulties, would agree to a partition of our territories, restoring Canada to France, & the Floridas to Spain, to accomplish for themselves a recovery of these colonies:

That it would not be long before we should receive certain information of the disposition of the French court, from the agent whom we had sent to Paris for that purpose:

That if this disposition should be favourable, by waiting the event of the present campaign, which we all hoped would be succesful, we should have reason to expect an alliance on better terms:

That this would in fact work no delay of any effectual aid from such ally, as, from the advance of the season & distance of our situation, it was impossible we could receive any assistance during this campaign:

That it was prudent to fix among ourselves the terms on which we would form alliance, before we declared we would form one at all events:

And that if these were agreed on & our Declaration of Independance ready by the time our Ambassadour should be prepared to sail, it would be as well, as to go into that Declaration at this day.

On the other side it was urged by J. Adams, Lee, Wythe and others

That no gentleman had argued against the policy or the right of separation from Britain, nor had supposed it possible we should ever renew our connection: that they had only opposed it's being now declared:

That the question was not whether, by a declaration of independance, we should make ourselves what we are not; but whether we should declare a fact which already exists:

That as to the people or parliament of England, we had alwais been independant of them, their restraints on our trade deriving efficacy from our acquiescence only & not from any rights they possessed of imposing them, & that so far our connection had been federal only, & was now dissolved by the commencement of hostilities:

That as to the king, we had been bound to him by allegiance, but that this bond was now dissolved by his assent to the late act of parliament, by which he declares us out of his protection, and by his levying war on us, a fact which had long ago proved us out of his protection; it being a certain position in law that allegiance & protection are reciprocal, the one ceasing when the other is withdrawn:

That James the IId never declared the people of England out of his protection yet his actions proved it & the parliament declared it:

No delegates then can be denied, or ever want, a power of declaring an existent truth:

That the delegates from the Delaware counties having declared their constituents ready to join, there are only two colonies Pennsylvania & Maryland whose delegates are absolutely tied up, and that these had by their instructions only reserved a right of confirming or rejecting the measure:

That the instructions from Pennsylvania might be accounted for from the times in which they were drawn, near a twelvemonth ago, since which the face of affairs has totally changed:

That within that time it had become apparent that Britain was determined to accept nothing less than a carte blanche, and that the king's answer to the Lord Mayor, Aldermen & common council of London, which had come to hand four days ago, must have satisfied every one of this point:

That the people wait for us to lead the way ~~in this step~~:

That *they* are in favour of the measure, tho' the instructions given by some of their *representatives* are not:

That the voice of the representatives is not alwais consonant with the voice of the people, and that this is remarkeably the case in these middle colonies:

That the effect of the resolution of the 15th of May has proved this, which, raising the murmurs of some in the colonies of Pennsylvania & Maryland, called forth the opposing voice of the freer part of the people, & proved them to be the majority, even in these colonies:

That the backwardness of these two colonies might be ascribed partly to the influence of proprietary power & connections, & partly to their having not yet been attacked by the enemy:

That these causes were not likely to be soon removed, as there seemed no probability that the enemy would make either of these the seat of this summer's war:

That it would be vain to wait either weeks or months for perfect unanimity, since it was impossible that all men should ever become of one sentiment on any question:

That the conduct of some colonies from the beginning of this contest, had given reason to suspect it was their settled policy to keep in the rear of the confederacy, that their particular prospect might be better even in the worst event:

That therefore it was necessary for those colonies who had thrown themselves forward & hazarded all from the beginning, to come forward now also, and put all again to their own hazard:

That the history of the Dutch revolution, of whom three states only confederated at first proved that a secession of some colonies would not be so dangerous as some apprehended:

That a declaration of Independance alone could render it consistent with European delicacy for European powers to treat with us, or even to receive an Ambassador from us:

That till this they would not receive our vessels into their ports, nor acknowlege the adjudications of our courts of Admiralty to be legitimate, in cases of capture of British vessels:

That tho' France & Spain may be jealous of our rising power, they must think it will be much more formidable with the addition of Great Britain; and will therefore see it their interest to prevent a coalition; but should they refuse, we shall be but where we are; whereas without trying we shall never know whether they will aid us or not:

That the present campaign may be unsuccessful, & therefore we had better propose an alliance while our affairs wear a hopeful aspect:

That to wait the event of this campaign will certainly work delay, because during this summer France may assist us effectually by cutting off those supplies of provisions from England & Ireland on which the enemy's armies here are to depend; or by setting in motion the great power they have collected in the West Indies, & calling our enemy to the defence of the possessions they have there:

That it would be idle to lose time in settling the terms of alliance, till we had first determined we would enter into alliance:

That it is necessary to lose no time in opening a trade for our people, who will want clothes, and will want money too for the paiment of taxes:

And that the only misfortune is that we did not enter into alliance with France six months sooner, as besides opening their ports for the vent of our last year's produce, they might have marched an army into Germany and prevented the petty princes there from selling their unhappy subjects to subdue us.

It appearing in the course of these debates that the colonies of N. York, New Jersey, Pennsylvania, Delaware, Maryland & South Carolina were not yet matured for falling from the parent stem, but that they were fast advancing to that state, it was thought most prudent to wait a while for them, and to postpone the final decision to July 1. but that this might occasion as little delay as possible, a committee was appointed to prepare a declaration of independance. the Commee. were J. Adams, Dr. Franklin, Roger Sherman, Robert R. Livingston & myself. committees were also appointed at the same time to prepare a plan of confederation for the colonies, and to state the terms proper to be proposed for foreign alliance. the committee for drawing the Declaration of Independance desired me to do it. I did so it was accordingly done and being approved by them, I reported it to the house on Friday the 28th of June when it was read and ordered to lie on the table.

—*Thomas Jefferson*—
Notes of Proceedings in Congress
[including Jefferson's draft of the Declaration of Independence with deletions and additions indicated]
July 1–4, 1776

[July 1–4, 1776]

On monday the 1st of July the house resolved itself into a commee. of the whole & resumed the consideration of the original motion made by the delegates of Virginia, which being again debated through the day, was carried in the affirmative by the votes of N. Hampshire, Connecticut, Massachusets, Rhode island, N. Jersey, Maryland, Virginia, N. Carolina, & Georgia. S. Carolina and Pennsylvania voted against it. Delaware having but two members present, they were divided: the delegates for New York declared they were for it themselves, & were assured their constituents were for it, but that their instructions having been drawn near a twelve-month before, when reconciliation was still the general object, they were enjoined by them to do nothing which should impede that object. They therefore thought themselves not justifiable in voting on either side, and asked leave to withdraw from the question, which was given them. The Commee. rose & reported their resolution to the house. Mr. Rutlege of S. Carolina then requested the determination might be put off to the next day, as he believed his collegues, tho' they disapproved of the resolution, would then join in it for the sake of unanimity. The ultimate question whether the house would agree to the resolution of the committee was accordingly postponed to the next day, when it was again moved and S. Carolina concurred in voting for it. In the mean time a third member had come post from the Delaware counties and turned the vote of that colony in favour of the resolution. Members of a different sentiment attending that morning from Pennsylvania also, their vote was changed, so that the whole 12 colonies, who were authorized to vote at all, gave their voices for it; and within a few days the convention of N. York approved of it and thus supplied the void occasioned by the withdrawing of their delegates from the vote.

Congress proceeded the same day to consider the declaration of Independance, which had been reported & laid on the table the Friday preceding, and on Monday referred to a commee. of the whole. The pusillanimous idea that we had friends in England worth keeping terms with, still haunted the minds of many. For this reason those passages which conveyed censures on the people of England were struck out, lest they should give them offence. The clause too, reprobating the enslaving the inhabitants of Africa, was struck out in complaisance to South Carolina & Georgia, who had never attempted to restrain the importation of slaves, and who on the contrary still wished to continue it. Our Northern brethren also I believe felt a little tender under those censures; for tho' their people have very few slaves themselves yet they had been pretty considerable carriers of them to others. The debates having taken up the greater parts of the 2d 3d & 4th days of July were, in the evening of the last closed. The declaration was reported by the commee., agreed to by the house, and signed by every member present except Mr. Dickinson. As the sentiments of men are known not only by what they receive, but what they reject also, I will state the form of the declaration as originally reported. The parts struck out by Congress shall be distinguished by a black line drawn under them; & those inserted by them shall be placed in the margin or in a concurrent column.

A Declaration by the representatives of the United States of America, in ~~General~~* Congress assembled

When in the course of human events it becomes necessary for one people to dissolve the political bands which have connected them with another, and to assume among the powers of the earth the separate & equal station to which the laws of nature and of nature's god entitle them, a decent respect to the opinions of mankind requires that they should declare the causes which impel them to the separation.

We hold these truths to be self evident: that all men are created equal; that they are endowed by their creator with [certain]† ~~inherent and~~ inalienable rights; that among these are life, liberty & the pursuit of happiness: that to secure these rights, governments are instituted among men, deriving their just powers from the consent of the governed; that whenever any form of government becomes destructive of these ends, it is the right of the people to alter or to abolish it, & to institute new government, laying it's foundation on such principles, & organising it's powers in such form, as to them shall seem most likely to effect their safety & happiness. Prudence indeed will dictate that governments long established should not be changed for light & transient causes; and accordingly all experience hath shewn that mankind are more disposed to suffer while evils are sufferable than to right themselves by abolishing the forms to which they are accustomed. But when a long train of abuses & usurpations ~~begun at a distinguished period and~~ pursuing invariably the same object, evinces a design to reduce them under absolute despotism it is their right, it is their duty to throw off such government, & to provide new guards for their future security. Such has been the patient sufferance of these colonies; & such is now the necessity which constrains them to [alter] ~~expunge~~ their former systems of government. the history of the present king of Great Britain is a history of [repeated] ~~unremitting~~ injuries & usurpations, ~~among which appears no solitary fact to contradict the uniform tenor of the rest but all have~~ [all having] in direct object the establishment of an absolute tyranny over these states. to prove this let facts be submitted to a candid

---

*Words crossed out here and below were written by Jefferson but later removed from the document by Congress.

†Words in brackets here and below were written in the margin by Jefferson and approved by Congress for inclusion in the finished document.

world <u>for the truth of which we pledge a faith yet unsullied by</u> <u>falsehood</u>.

He has refused his assent to laws the most wholsome & necessary for the public good.

He has forbidden his governors to pass laws of immediate & pressing importance, unless suspended in their operation till his assent should be obtained; & when so suspended, he has utterly neglected to attend to them.

He has refused to pass other laws for the accomodation of large districts of people, unless those people would relinquish the right of representation in the legislature, a right inestimable to them, & formidable to tyrants only.

He has called together legislative bodies at places unusual, uncomfortable, and distant from the depository of their public records, for the sole purpose of fatiguing them into compliance with his measures.

He has dissolved representative houses repeatedly <u>& continually</u> for opposing with manly firmness his invasions on the rights of the people.

He has refused for a long time after such dissolutions to cause others to be elected, whereby the legislative powers, incapable of annihilation, have returned to the people at large for their exercise, the state remaining in the mean time exposed to all the dangers of invasion from without & convulsions within.

He has endeavored to prevent the population of these states; for that purpose obstructing the laws for naturalization of foreigners, refusing to pass others to encourage their migrations hither, & raising the conditions of new appropriations of lands.

He has [obstructed] <u>suffered</u> the administration of justice <u>totally</u> <u>to cease in some of these states</u> [by] refusing his assent to laws for establishing judiciary powers.

He has made *our* judges dependant on his will alone, for the tenure of their offices, & the amount & paiment of their salaries.

He has erected a multitude of new offices <u>by a self assumed power</u> and sent hither swarms of new officers to harrass our people and eat out their substance.

He has kept among us in times of peace standing armies <u>and ships</u> <u>of war</u> without the consent of our legislatures.

He has affected to render the military independant of, & superior to the civil power.

He has combined with others to subject us to a jurisdiction foreign to our constitutions & unacknoleged by our laws, giving his assent to their acts of pretended legislation for quartering large bodies of armed troops among us; for protecting them by a mock-trial from punishment for any murders which they should commit on the inhabitants of these states; for cutting off our trade with all parts of the world; for imposing taxes on us without our consent; for depriving us [in many cases] of the benefits of trial by jury; for transporting us beyond seas to be tried for pretended offences; for abolishing the free system of English laws in a neighboring province, establishing therein an arbitrary government, and enlarging it's boundaries, so as to render it at once an example and fit instrument for introducing the same absolute rule into these [colonies] states; for taking away our charters, abolishing our most valuable laws, and altering fundamentally the forms of our governments; for suspending our own legislatures, & declaring themselves invested with power to legislate for us in all cases whatsoever.

He has abdicated government here [by declaring us out of his protection & waging war against us.] ~~withdrawing his governors, and declaring us out of his allegiance & protection~~.

He has plundered our seas, ravaged our coasts, burnt our towns, & destroyed the lives of our people.

He is at this time transporting large armies of foreign mercenaries to compleat the works of death, desolation & tyranny already begun with circumstances of cruelty and perfidy [scarcely paralleled in the most barbarous ages, & totally] unworthy the head of a civilized nation.

He has constrained our fellow citizens taken captive on the high seas to bear arms against their country, to become the executioners of their friends & brethren, or to fall themselves by their hands.

He has [excited domestic insurrections amongst us, & has] endeavored to bring on the inhabitants of our frontiers the merciless Indian savages, whose known rule of warfare is an undistinguished destruction of all ages, sexes, & conditions *of* ~~existence~~.

~~He has incited treasonable insurrections of our fellow citizens, with the allurements of forfeiture & confiscation of our property.~~

~~He has waged cruel war against human nature itself, violating its most sacred rights of life and liberty in the persons of a distant people who never offended him, captivating & carrying them into slavery in~~

~~another hemisphere or to incur miserable death in their transportation thither. This piratical warfare, the opprobrium of *infidel* powers, is the warfare of the *Christian* king of Great Britain. Determined to keep open a market where *Men* should be bought & sold, he has prostituted his negative for suppressing every legislative attempt to prohibit or to restrain this execrable commerce. And that this assemblage of horrors might want no fact of distinguished die, he is now exciting those very people to rise in arms among us, and to purchase that liberty of which he has deprived them, by murdering the people on whom he also obtruded them: thus paying off former crimes committed against the *Liberties* of one people, with crimes which he urges them to commit again the *lives* of another.~~

In every stage of these oppressions we have petitioned for redress in the most humble terms: our repeated petitions have been answered only by repeated injuries. A prince whose character is thus marked by every act which may define a tyrant is unfit to be the ruler of a [free] people ~~who mean to be free. Future ages will scarcely believe that the hardiness of one man adventured, within the short compass of twelve years only, to lay a foundation so broad & so undisguised for tyranny over a people fostered & fixed in principles of freedom.~~

Nor have we been wanting in attentions to our British brethren. We have warned them from time to time of attempts by their legislature to extend [an unwarrantable] a jurisdiction over [us] ~~these our states.~~ We have reminded them of the circumstances of our emigration & settlement here, ~~no one of which could warrant so strange a pretension: that these were effected at the expence of our own blood & treasure, unassisted by the wealth or the strength of Great Britain: that in constituting indeed our several forms of government, we had adopted one common king, thereby laying a foundation for perpetual league & amity with them: but that submission to their parliament was no part of our constitution, nor ever in idea, if history may be credited: and,~~ we [have] appealed to their native justice and magnanimity [and we have conjured them by] ~~as well as to~~ the ties of our common kindred to disavow these usurpations which [would inevitably] ~~were likely to~~ interrupt our connection and correspondence. They too have been deaf to the voice of justice & of consanguinity, ~~and when occasions have been given them, by the regular course of their laws, of removing from their councils the disturbers~~

~~of our harmony, they have, by their free election, re-established~~ ~~them in power. At this very time too they are permitting their chief~~ ~~magistrate to send over not only souldiers of our common blood,~~ ~~but Scotch & foreign mercenaries to invade & destroy us.~~ These facts ~~have given the last stab to agonizing affection, and manly spirit bids~~ ~~us to renounce for ever these unfeeling brethren. We must endeavor~~ ~~to forget our former love for them, and to hold them as we hold the~~ ~~rest of mankind enemies in war, in peace friends. We might have~~ ~~been a free and a great people together; but a communication of~~ ~~grandeur & of freedom it seems is below their dignity. Be it so, since~~ ~~they will it. The road to happiness & to glory is open to us too. We~~ ~~will tread it apart from them, and~~ [we must therefore] acquiesce in the necessity which denounces our ~~eternal~~ separation [and hold them as we hold the rest of mankind, enemies in war, in peace friends]!

We therefore the representatives of the United States of America in General Congress assembled do in the name, & by the authority of the good people of these ~~states reject & renounce~~ ~~all allegiance & subjection to the~~ ~~kings of Great Britain & all oth-~~ ~~ers who may hereafter claim by,~~ ~~through or under them: we ut-~~ ~~terly dissolve all political con-~~ ~~nection which may heretofore~~ ~~have subsisted between us & the~~ ~~people or parliament of Great~~ ~~Britain: & finally we do assert &~~ ~~declare these colonies to be free &~~ ~~independant states,~~ & that as free & independant states, they have full power to levy war, conclude peace, contract alliances, establish commerce, & to do all other acts & things which independant

We therefore the representatives of the United States of America in General Congress assembled, appealing to the supreme judge of the world for the rectitude of our intentions, do in the name, & by the authority of the good people of these colonies, solemnly publish & declare that these United colonies are & of right ought to be free & independant states; that they are absolved from all allegiance to the British crown, and that all political connection between them & the state of Great Britain is, & ought to be, totally dissolved; & that as free & independant states they have full power to levy war, conclude peace, contract alliances, establish commerce & to do all other acts &

states may of right do. And for the support of this declaration we mutually pledge to each other our lives, our fortunes & our sacred honour.

things which independant states may of right do.

And for the support of this declaration, with a firm reliance on the protection of divine providence we mutually pledge to each other our lives, our fortunes & our sacred honour.

—*John Dickinson*—
NOTES FOR A SPEECH OPPOSING INDEPENDENCE
JULY 1, 1776

[JULY 1, 1776]

Arguments against the Independance of these Colonies—In Congress.

THE CONSEQUENCES INVOLVED IN the Motion now lying before You are of such Magnitude, that I tremble under the oppressive Honor of sharing in its Determination. I feel Myself unequal to the Burthen assigned Me. I believe, I had almost said, I rejoice, that the Time is approaching, when I shall be relieved from its Weight. While the Trust remains with Me, I must discharge the Duties of it, as well as I can—and I hope I shall be the more favorably heard, as I am convinced, that I shall hold such Language, as will sacrifice any private Emolument to general Interests. My Conduct, this Day, I expect will give the finishing Blow to my once too great, and my Integrity considered, now too diminish'd Popularity. It will be my Lott to [Prove?] that I had rather vote away the Enjoyment of [. . .] than the Blood and Happiness of my Countrymen—too fortunate, amidst their Calamities, if I prove a Truth known in Heaven, that I had rather they should hate Me, than that I should hurt them. I might indeed, practise an artful, an advantageous Reserve upon this Occasion. But thinking as I do on the subject of Debate, Silence would be guilt. I despise its Arts—I detest its Advantages. I must speak, tho I should lose my Life, tho I should lose the Affections of my C[oun-trymen]. Happy at present, however, I shall esteem Myself, if I can so rise to the Height of this great argument, as to offer to this Honorable Assembly in a fully clear Manner, those Reasons that have so invariably fixed my own Opinion.

It was a Custom in a wise and virtuous State, to preface Propositions in Council, with a prayer, that they might redound to the public Benefit. I beg Leave to imitate the laudable Example. And I do most humbly implore Almighty God, with whom dwells Wisdom itself, so to enlighten the Members of this House, that their Decision may be such as will best promote the Liberty, Safety and Prosperity of these Colonies—and for Myself, that his Divine Goodness may be graciously pleased to enable Me, to speak the Precepts of sound Policy on the important Question that now engages our Attention.

Sir, Gentlemen of very distinguished Abilities and Knowledge differ widely in their Sentiments upon the Point now agitated. They all agree, that the utmost Prudence is required in forming our Decision—But immediately disagree in their Notions of that Prudence, Some cautiously insisting, that We ought to obtain That previous Information which We are likely quickly to obtain, and to make those previous Establishments that are acknowledged to be necessary—Others strenously asserting, that tho regularly such Information & Establishment ought to precede the Measure proposed, yet, confiding in our Fortune more boldly than Caesar himself, We ought to brave the Storm in a Skiff made of Paper.

In all such Cases, where every Argument is adorn'd with an Eloquence that may please and yet mislead, it seems to me [the proper method of?] discovering the right Path, to enquire, which of the parties is probably the most warm'd by Passion. Other Circumstances being equal or nearly equal, that Consideration would have Influence with Me. I fear the Virtue of Americans. Resentment of the Injuries offered to their Country, may irritate them to Counsels & to Actions that may be detrimental to the Cause they would dye to advance.

What Advantages? 1. Animate People. 2. Convince foreign Powers of our Strength & Unanimity, & aid in consequence thereof.

As to 1st—Unnecessary. Life, Liberty & Property sufficient Motive. General Spirit of America.

As to 2d—foreign Powers will not rely on Words.

The Event of the Campaign will be the best Evidence. This properly the first Campaign. Who has received Intelligence that such a Proof of our Strength & daring Spirit will be agreeable to France? What must she expect from a People that begin their Empire in so high a stile, when on the Point of being invaded by the whole Power of G.B. aided by [formidable foreign?] aid—unconnected with foreign Power? She & Spain must perceive the imminent Danger of their Colonies lying at our Doors. Their Seat of Empire in another world. Masserano. Intelligence from Cadiz.

More respectful to act in Conformity to the views of France. Take advantage of their Pride, Give them Reason to believe that We confide in them, desire to act in conjunction with their Policies & Interests. Know how they will regard this ~~new Star~~ Stranger in the States of the world. People fond of what they have attained in producing. Regard it as a Child—A Cement of affection. Allow them the glory of appearing the vindicators of Liberty. It will please them.

It is treating them with Contempt to act otherwise. Especially after the application made to France which by this time has reach'd them. Bermuda 5 May. Abilities of the person sent.* What will they think, if now so quickly after without waiting for their Determination—Totally slighting their sentiments on such a prodigous [. . .] —We haughtily pursue our own Measures? May they not say to Us, Gentlemen You falsely pretended to consult Us, & disrespectfully proceeded without waiting our Resolution. You must abide the Consequences. We are not ready for a Rupture. You should have negotiated till We were. We will not be hurried by your Impetuosity. We know it is our Interest to support You. But we shall be in no haste about it. Try your own strength & Resources in which you have such Confidence. We know now you dare not look back. Reconciliation is impossible without declaring Yourselves the most rash & at the same Time the most contemptible Thrasos that ever existed on Earth. Suppose on this Event G.B. should offer Canada to France & Florida to Spain with an Extension of the old Limits. Would not France & Spain accept them? Gentlemen say the Trade of all America is more valuable to France than Canada. I grant it but suppose she may get

*Evidently a reference to Silas Deane (1737–1789), the Continental Congress's agent to France, who en route to that country reached Bermuda in early May 1776.

both. If she is politic, & none doubts that, I averr she has the easiest Game to play for attaining both, that ever presented itself to a Nation.

When We have bound ourselves to an eternal Quarrel with G.B. by a Declaration of Independence, France has nothing to do but to hold back & intimidate G.B. till Canada is put into her Hands, then to intimidate Us into a most disadvantageous Grant of our Trade. It is my firm opinion these Events will take Place—& arise naturally from our declaring Independance.

As to Aid from foreign Powers. Our Declaration can procure Us none this Campaign tho made today. It is impossible.

Now consider if all the advantages expected from foreign Powers cannot be attained in a more unexceptionable manner. Is there no way of giving Notice of a Nation's Resolutions than by proclaiming it to all the world? Let Us in the most solemn Manner inform the House of Bourbon, at least France, that we wait only for her Determination to declare an Independance. We must not talk generally of foreign Powers but of those We expect to favor Us. Let Us assure Spain that we never will give any assistance to her Colonies. Let France become Guarantee. Form arrangements of this Kind.

Besides, first Establish our governments & take the Regular Form of a State. These preventive Measures will shew Deliberation, wisdom, Caution & Unanimity.

Our Interest to keep G.B. in Opinion that We mean Reunion as long as possible. Disadvantage to administration from Opposition. Her Union from our Declaration. Wealth of London &c pour'd into Treasury. The whole Nation ardent against us. We oblige her to persevere. Her Spirit. See last petition of London. Suppose We shall ruin her. France must rise on her Ruins. Her Ambition. Her Religion. Our Danger from thence. We shall weep at our victories. Overwhelm'd with Debt. Compute that Debt 6 Millions of Pa. Money a Year.

The War will be carried on with more Severity. Burning Towns. Letting Loose Indians on our Frontiers. Not yet done. Boston might have been burnt. What advantages to be expected from a Declaration? 1. Animating our Troops. Answer, Unnecessary. 2. Union of Colonies. Answer, Also unnecessary. It may weaken that Union— when the People find themselves engaged in a [war] rendered more cruel by such a Declaration without prospect of End to their Calamities by a Continuation of the War. People changeable. In Bitterness of

Soul they may complain against our Rashness & ask why We did not apply first to foreign Powers. Why We did not settle all Differences among ourselves. Take Care to secure unsettled Lands for easing their Burthens instead of leaving them to particular Colonies. Why not wait till better prepar'd. Till We had made an Experiment of our Strength. This [probably?] the first Campaign.

3. Proof of our strength & Spirit. France & Spain may be alarm'd & provoked. Masserano. Insult to France. Not the least Evidence of her granting Us favorable Terms. Her probable Conditions. The Glory of recovering Canada. She will get that & then dictate Terms to Us.

A *Partition* of these Colonies will take Place if G.B. cant conquer Us. Destroying a House before We have got another. In Winter with a small Family. Then asking a Neighbor to take Us in. He unprepared.

4th. The Spirit of the Colonies calls for such a Declaration. Answer, not to be relied on. Not only Treaties with foreign powers but among Ourselves should precede this Declaration. We should know on what Grounds We are to stand with Regard to one another.

Declaration of Virginia about Colonies in *their Limits*.

The Committee on Confederation dispute almost every Article—some of Us totally despair of any reasonable Terms of Confederation.

We cannot look back. Men generally sell their Goods to most Advantage when they have several Chapmen. We have but two to rely on. We exclude one by this Declaration without knowing What the other will give.

G.B. after one or more unsuccessful Campaigns may be enduc'd to offer Us such a share of Commerce as would satisfy Us—to appoint Councillors during good Behaviour—to withdraw her armies—in short to redress all the Grievances complained of in our first Petition—to protect our Commerce—Establish our Militias. Let Us know, if We can get Terms from France that will be more beneficial than these. If We can, let Us declare Independence. If We cannot, let Us at least withhold that Declaration, till We obtain Terms that are tolerable.

We have many Points of the utmost moment to settle with France—Canada, Acadia, Cape Breton. What will Content her? Trade or Territory? What Conditions of Trade? Barbary Pirates.

Spain. Portugal. Will she demand an Exclusive Trade as a Compensation or grant Us protection against piratical States only for a share of our Commerce?

When our Enemies are pressing us so vigorously, When We are in so wretched a State of preparation, When the Sentiments & Designs of our expected Friends are so unknown to Us, I am alarm'd at this Declaration being so vehemently prest. A worthy Gentleman told Us, that people in this House have had different Views for more than a 12 month. Amazing after what they have so repeatedly declared in this House & private Conversations—that they meant only Reconciliation. But since they can conceal their Views so dextrously, I should be glad to read a little more in the Doomsday Book of America—Not all—that like the Book of Fate might be too dreadful. Title page—Binding. I should be glad to know whether in 20 or 30 Years this Commonwealth of Colonies may not be thought too unwieldy—& Hudson's River be a proper Boundary for a separate Commonwealth to the Northward. I have a strong Impression on my Mind that this will take place.

—*John Adams*—
LETTER TO ABIGAIL ADAMS
JULY 3, 1776

PHILADELPHIA JULY 3D. 1776

HAD A DECLARATION OF Independency been made seven Months ago, it would have been attended with many great and glorious Effects. _____ We might before this Hour, have formed Alliances with foreign States. We should have mastered Quebec and been in Possession of Canada. _____ You will perhaps wonder, how such a Declaration would have influenced our Affairs, in Canada, but if I could write with Freedom I could easily convince you, that it would, and explain to you the manner how. Many Gentlemen in high Stations and of great Influence have been duped, by the ministerial Bubble of Commissioners to treat. _____ And in real, sincere Expectation of this Event, which they so fondly wished, they have been slow and languid, in promoting Measures for the Reduction of that

Province. Others there are in the Colonies who really wished that our Enterprise in Canada would be defeated, that the Colonies might be brought into Danger and Distress between two Fires, and be thus induced to submit. Others really wished to defeat the Expedition to Canada, lest the Conquest of it, should elevate the Minds of the People too much to hearken to those Terms of Reconciliation which they believed would be offered Us. These jarring Views, Wishes and Designs, occasioned an opposition to many salutary Measures, which were proposed for the Support of that Expedition, and caused Obstructions, Embarrassments and studied Delays, which have finally, lost Us the Province.

All these Causes however in Conjunction would not have disappointed Us, if it had not been for a Misfortune, which could not be foreseen, and perhaps could not have been prevented, I mean the Prevalence of the small Pox among our Troops. _____ This fatal Pestilence compleated our Destruction. It is a Frown of Providence upon Us, which We ought to lay to heart.

But on the other Hand, the Delay of this Declaration to this Time, has many great Advantages attending it. The Hopes of Reconciliation, which were fondly entertained by Multitudes of honest and well meaning tho weak and mistaken People, have been gradually and at last totally extinguished. Time has been given for the whole People, maturely to consider the great Question of Independence and to ripen their Judgments, dissipate their Fears, and allure their Hopes, by discussing it in News Papers and Pamphletts, by debating it, in Assemblies, Conventions, Committees of Safety and Inspection, in Town and County Meetings, as well as in private Conversations, so that the whole People in every Colony of the 13, have now adopted it, as their own Act. This will cement the Union, and avoid those Heats and perhaps Convulsions which might have been occasioned, by such a Declaration Six Months ago.

But the Day is past. The Second Day of July 1776, will be the most memorable Epocha, in the History of America. I am apt to believe that it will be celebrated, by succeeding Generations, as the great anniversary Festival. It ought to be commemorated, as the Day of Deliverance by solemn Acts of Devotion to God Almighty. It ought to be solemnized with Pomp and Parade, with Shews, Games, Sports, Guns, Bells, Bonfires and Illuminations from one End of this Continent to the other from this Time forward forever more.

You will think me transported with Enthusiasm but I am not. I am well aware of the Toil and Blood and Treasure, that it will cost Us to maintain this Declaration, and support and defend these States. Yet through all the Gloom I can see the Rays of ravishing Light and Glory. I can see that the End is more than worth all the Means. And that Posterity will tryumph in that Days Transaction, even altho We should rue it, which I trust in God We shall not.

The Declaration of Independence
July 4, 1776

In Congress, July 4, 1776

The unanimous Declaration of the thirteen United States of America

When in the course of human events it becomes necessary for one people to dissolve the political bands which have connected them with another and to assume among the powers of the earth, the separate and equal station to which the Laws of Nature and of Nature's God entitle them, a decent respect to the opinions of mankind requires that they should declare the causes which impel them to the separation.

We hold these truths to be self-evident, that all men are created equal, that they are endowed by their Creator with certain un-alienable Rights, that among these are Life, Liberty and the pursuit of Happiness.—That to secure these rights, Governments are in-stituted among Men, deriving their just powers from the consent of the governed,—That whenever any Form of Government be-comes destructive of these ends, it is the Right of the People to alter or to abolish it, and to institute new Government, laying its foundation on such principles and organizing its powers in such form, as to them shall seem most likely to effect their Safety and Happiness. Prudence, indeed, will dictate that Governments long established should not be changed for light and transient causes; and accordingly all experience hath shewn that mankind are more disposed to suffer, while evils are sufferable than to right themselves by abolishing the forms to which they are accustomed. But when a long train of abuses and usurpations, pursuing invariably the same Object evinces a design to reduce them under absolute Despotism, it is their right, it is their duty, to throw off such Government, and to provide new Guards for their future security.—— Such has been the patient sufferance of these Colonies; and such is now the necessity which constrains them to alter their former Systems of Government. The history of the present King of Great Britain is a history of repeated injuries and usurpations, all having in direct object the establishment of an absolute Tyranny over these States. To prove this, let Facts be submitted to a candid world.

He has refuted his Assent to Laws, the most wholesome and necessary for the public good.

He has forbidden his Governors to pass Laws of immediate and pressing importance, unless suspended in their operation till his Assent should be obtained; and when so suspended, he has utterly neglected to attend to them.

He has refused to pass other Laws for the accommodation of large districts of people, unless those people would relinquish the right of Representation in the Legislature, a right inestimable to them and formidable to tyrants only.

He has called together legislative bodies at places unusual, uncomfortable, and distant from the depository of their Public Records, for the sole purpose of fatiguing them into compliance with his measures.

He has dissolved Representative Houses repeatedly, for opposing with manly firmness his invasions on the rights of the people.

He has refused for a long time, after such dissolutions, to cause others to be elected, whereby the Legislative Powers, incapable of Annihilation, have returned to the People at large for their exercise; the State remaining in the mean time exposed to all the dangers of invasion from without, and convulsions within.

He has endeavoured to prevent the population of these States; for that purpose obstructing the Laws for Naturalization of Foreigners; refusing to pass others to encourage their migrations hither, and raising the conditions of new Appropriations of Lands.

He has obstructed the Administration of Justice by refusing his Assent to Laws for establishing Judiciary Powers.

He has made Judges dependent on his Will alone for the tenure of their offices, and the amount and payment of their salaries.

He has erected a multitude of New Offices, and sent hither swarms of Officers to harass our people and eat out their substance.

He has kept among us, in times of peace, Standing Armies without the Consent of our legislatures.

He has affected to render the Military independent of and superior to the Civil Power.

He has combined with others to subject us to a jurisdiction foreign to our constitution, and unacknowledged by our laws; giving his Assent to their Acts of pretended Legislation:

For quartering large bodies of armed troops among us:

For protecting them, by a mock Trial from punishment for any Murders which they should commit on the Inhabitants of these States:

For cutting off our Trade with all parts of the world:

For imposing Taxes on us without our Consent:

For depriving us in many cases, of the benefit of Trial by Jury:

For transporting us beyond Seas to be tried for pretended offences:

For abolishing the free System of English Laws in a neighbouring Province, establishing therein an Arbitrary government, and enlarging its Boundaries so as to render it at once an example and fit instrument for introducing the same absolute rule into these Colonies

For taking away our Charters, abolishing our most valuable Laws and altering fundamentally the Forms of our Governments:

For suspending our own Legislatures, and declaring themselves invested with power to legislate for us in all cases whatsoever.

He has abdicated Government here, by declaring us out of his Protection and waging War against us.

He has plundered our seas, ravaged our Coasts, burnt our towns, and destroyed the lives of our people.

He is at this time transporting large Armies of foreign Mercenaries to compleat the works of death, desolation, and tyranny, already begun with circumstances of Cruelty & Perfidy scarcely paralleled in the most barbarous ages, and totally unworthy the Head of a civilized nation.

He has constrained our fellow Citizens taken Captive on the high Seas to bear Arms against their Country, to become the executioners of their friends and Brethren, or to fall themselves by their Hands.

He has excited domestic insurrections amongst us, and has endeavoured to bring on the inhabitants of our frontiers, the merciless Indian Savages whose known rule of warfare, is an undistinguished destruction of all ages, sexes and conditions.

In every stage of these Oppressions We have Petitioned for Redress in the most humble terms: Our repeated Petitions have been answered only by repeated injury. A Prince, whose character is thus marked by every act which may define a Tyrant, is unfit to be the ruler of a free people.

Nor have We been wanting in attentions to our British brethren. We have warned them from time to time of attempts by their legislature to extend an unwarrantable jurisdiction over us. We have reminded them of the circumstances of our emigration and settlement here. We have appealed to their native justice and magnanimity, and we have conjured them by the ties of our common kindred to disavow these usurpations, which would inevitably interrupt our connections and correspondence. They too have been deaf to the voice of justice and of consanguinity. We must, therefore, acquiesce in the necessity, which denounces our Separation, and hold them, as we hold the rest of mankind, Enemies in War, in Peace Friends.

We, therefore, the Representatives of the United States of America, in General Congress, Assembled, appealing to the Supreme Judge of the world for the rectitude of our intentions, do, in the Name, and by Authority of the good People of these Colonies, solemnly publish and declare, That these United Colonies are, and of Right ought to be Free and Independent States, that they are Absolved from all Allegiance to the British Crown, and that all political connection between them and the State of Great Britain, is and ought to be totally dissolved; and that as Free and Independent States, they have full Power to levy War, conclude Peace, contract Alliances, establish Commerce, and to do all other Acts and Things which Independent States may of right do.—And for the support of this Declaration, with a firm reliance on the protection of Divine Providence, we mutually pledge to each other our Lives, our Fortunes and our sacred Honor.

—John Hancock

NEW HAMPSHIRE: Josiah Bartlett, William Whipple, Matthew Thornton

MASSACHUSETTS: John Hancock, Samuel Adams, John Adams, Robert Treat Paine, Elbridge Gerry

RHODE ISLAND: Stephen Hopkins, William Ellery

CONNECTICUT: Roger Sherman, Samuel Huntington, William Williams, Oliver Wolcott

NEW YORK: William Floyd, Philip Livingston, Francis Lewis, Lewis Morris

NEW JERSEY: Richard Stockton, John Witherspoon, Francis Hopkinson, John Hart, Abraham Clark

PENNSYLVANIA: Robert Morris, Benjamin Rush, Benjamin Franklin, John Morton, George Clymer, James Smith, George Taylor, James Wilson, George Ross

DELAWARE: Caesar Rodney, George Read, Thomas McKean

MARYLAND: Samuel Chase, William Paca, Thomas Stone, Charles Carroll of Carrollton

VIRGINIA: George Wythe, Richard Henry Lee, Thomas Jefferson, Benjamin Harrison, Thomas Nelson, Jr., Francis Lightfoot Lee, Carter Braxton

NORTH CAROLINA: William Hooper, Joseph Hewes, John Penn

SOUTH CAROLINA: Edward Rutledge, Thomas Heyward, Jr., Thomas Lynch, Jr., Arthur Middleton

GEORGIA: Button Gwinnett, Lyman Hall, George Walton

DRAFTING THE ARTICLES OF CONFEDERATION

CONGRESS HAD SEVERAL PURPOSES in drafting the Articles of Confederation. One was to give formal constitutional identity to the revolutionary union of the thirteen autonomous states that were declaring their independence from British imperial rule. Since 1774 the Continental Congress had effectively conducted war and diplomacy in the name of the separate provinces of British North America. But if Americans were "to assume among the powers of the earth, the separate & equal station to which the laws of nature and of nature's god entitle them," they had to demonstrate that they were a power— that is, a nation-state—like other nations. Equally important, Congress recognized the need to clarify the boundaries between its authority and that of the states. It had to define the extent of its own authority while recognizing other powers that would remain lodged with the states. Further, it had to find ways to accommodate different interests among the states, based on their respective extent, their population, and the nature of their economies.

As Congress was readying to declare independence, the committee chaired by John Dickinson was preparing to report its draft of a confederation. Congress debated this draft extensively during July and August 1776. Three issues soon emerged as major barriers to agreement: the rule of voting in Congress; the rule for apportioning the expenses of war among the states; and the control of unsettled western lands in the interior of the continent. Disagreement on these points and the more urgent demands of the war led Congress to put the Articles aside in late August 1776.

Congress resumed debate on the confederation in the spring of 1777, only to find that the same issues remained intractable. Finally, in October 1777, in exile at York, Pennsylvania, following the British occupation of Philadelphia, Congress finally mustered the determination to complete the task. The great American victory at Saratoga gave Congress reason to hope that France would now enter the war on its side, and having a completed confederation to demonstrate that Americans could indeed form a nation would give Britain's old enemy an additional incentive to make a new alliance.

DRAFTING THE ARTICLES OF CONFEDERATION

—Thomas Jefferson—
NOTES OF PROCEEDINGS IN CONGRESS
JULY 12–AUGUST 1, 1776

[JULY 12–AUGUST, 1, 1776]

ON FRIDAY JULY 12 the Committee appointed to draw the articles of confederation reported them and on the 22d the house resolved themselves into a committee to take them into consideration. On the 30th and 31st of that month & 1st of the ensuing, those articles were debated which determined the ~~manner of voting in Congress, & that of fixing the~~ proportion or quota s of money which each state should furnish to the common treasury, and the manner of voting in Congress. The first of these articles was expressed in the original draught in these words. '*Art.* XI. All charges of war & all other expenses that shall be incurred for the common defence, or general welfare, and allowed by the United states assembled, shall be defrayed out of a common treasury, which shall be supplied by the several colonies in proportion to the number of inhabitants of every age, sex & quality, except Indians not paying taxes, in each colony, a true account of which, distinguishing the white inhabitants, shall be triennially taken & transmitted to the assembly of the United states.'

Mr. Chase* moved that the quotas should be fixed, not by the number of inhabitants of every condition, but by that of the 'white inhabitants.' He admitted that taxation should be alwais in proportion to property; that this was in theory the true rule, but that from a variety of difficulties it was a rule which could never be adopted in practice. The value of the property in every state could never be estimated justly & equally. Some other measure for the wealth of the state must therefore be devised, some ~~measure of wealth must be~~

---

*Samuel Chase (1741–1811), Maryland representative in the Continental Congress.

standard referred to which would be more simple. He considered the number of inhabitants as a tolerably good criterion of property, and that this might alwais be obtained. ~~yet numbers simply would not~~ he therefore thought it the best mode which we could adopt, with ~~some~~ one exception ~~s~~ only. He observed that negroes are property, and as such cannot be distinguished from the lands or personalties held in those states where there are few slaves. That the surplus of profit which a Northern farmer is able to lay by, he invests in ~~lands~~ cattle, horses &c. whereas a Southern farmer lays out that same surplus in slaves. There is no more reason therefore for taxing the Southern states on the farmer's head, & on his slave's head, than the Northern ones on their farmer's heads & the heads of their cattle. That the method proposed would therefore tax the Southern states according to their numbers & their wealth conjunctly, while the Northern would be taxed on numbers only: that Negroes in fact should not be considered as members of the state more than cattle & that they have no more interest in it.

Mr. John Adams observed that the numbers of people were taken by this article as an index of the wealth of the state & not as subjects of taxation. That as to this matter it was of no consequence by what name you called your people, whether by that of freemen or of slaves. That in some countries the labouring poor were called freemen, in others they were called slaves; but that the difference as to the state was imaginary only. What matters it whether a landlord employing ten labourers in his farm, gives them annually as much money as will buy them the necessaries of life, or gives them those necessaries at short hand. The ten labourers add as much wealth annually to the state, increase it's exports as much in the one case as the other. Certainly 500 freemen produce no more profits, no greater surplus for the paiment of taxes than 500 slaves. Therefore the state in which are the labourers called freemen should be taxed no more than that in which are those called slaves. Suppose by any extraordinary operation of nature or of law one half the labourers of a state could in the course of one night be transformed into slaves: would the state be made the poorer or the less able to pay taxes? That the condition of the labouring poor in most countries, that of the fishermen particularly of the Northern states is as abject as that of slaves. It is the number of labourers which produce the surplus for taxation, and numbers therefore indiscriminately are the fair index

of wealth. That it is the use of the word 'property' here, & it's application to some of the people of the state, which produces the fallacy.
How does the Southern farmer procure slaves? Either by importation or by purchase from his neighbor. If he imports a slave, he adds
one to the number of labourers in his country, and proportionably
to it's profits & abilities to pay taxes. If he buys from his neighbor, it
is only a transfer of a labourer from one farm to another, which does
not change the annual produce of the state, & therefore should not
change it's tax. That if a Northern farmer works ten labourers on his
farm, he can, it is true, invest the surplus of ten men's labour in cattle: but so may the Southern farmer working ten slaves. That a state
of 100,000 freemen can maintain no more cattle than one of 100,000
slaves. Therefore they have no more of that kind of property. That a
slave may indeed from the custom of speech be more properly called
the wealth of his master, than the free labourer might be called the
wealth of his employer: but as to the state both were equally it's
wealth, and should therefore equally add to the quota of it's tax.

Mr. Harrison* proposed a compromise, that two slaves should be
counted as one freeman. He affirmed that slaves did not do so much
work as freemen, and doubted if two effected more than one. That
this was proved by the price of labor, the hire of a labourer in the
Southern colonies being from 8 to £12, while in the Northern it was
generally £24.

Mr. Wilson† said that if this amendment should take place the
Southern colonies would have all the benefit of slaves, whilst the
Northern ones would bear the burthen. That slaves increase the profits of a state, which the Southern states mean to take to themselves;
that they also increase the burthen of defence, which would of
course fall so much the heavier on the Northern. That slaves occupy
the places of freemen and eat their food. Dismiss your slaves &
freemen will take their places. It is our duty to lay every discouragement on the importation of slaves; but this amendment would give
the *jus trium liberorum* to him who would import slaves. That other
kinds of property were pretty equally distributed thro' all the
colonies: there were as many cattle, horses, & sheep in the North as

---

*Benjamin Harrison (1726–1791), Virginia delegate to the Continental Congress.
†James Wilson (1742–1798) of Pennsylvania.

the South, & South as the North: but not so as to slaves. That experience has shewn that those colonies have been alwais able to pay most which have the most ~~males~~ inhabitants, whether they be black or white. And the practice of the Southern colonies has alwais been to make every farmer pay poll taxes upon all his labourers whether they be black or white. He acknoleges indeed that freemen work the most; but they consume the most also. They do not produce a greater surplus for taxation. The slave is neither fed nor clothed so expensively as a freeman. Again white women are exempted from labour generally, which negro women are not. In this then the Southern states have an advantage as the article now stands. It has sometimes been said that slavery is necessary because the commodities they raise would be too dear for market if cultivated by freemen; but now it is said that the labor of the slave is the dearest.

Mr. Payne* urged the original resolution of Congress, to proportion the quotas of the states to the number of souls.

Dr. Witherspoon[†] was of opinion that the value of lands & houses was the best estimate of the wealth of a nation, and that it was practicable to obtain such a valuation. This is the true barometer of wealth. The one now proposed is imperfect in itself, and unequal between the states. It has been objected that negroes eat the food of freemen & therefore should be taxed. Horses also eat the food of freemen; therefore they also should be taxed. It has been said too that in carrying slaves into the estimate of the taxes the state is to pay, we do no more than those states themselves do, who alwais take slaves into the estimate of the taxes the individual is to pay. But the cases are not parallel. In the Southern colonies slaves pervade the whole colony; but they do not pervade the whole continent. That as to the original resolution of Congress to proportion the quotas according to the souls, it was temporary only, & related to the monies heretofore emitted: whereas we are now entering into a new compact and therefore stand on original ground.

Aug. 1. The question being put the amendment proposed was rejected by the votes of N. Hampshire, Massachusets, Rhode Island,

---

*Robert Treat Paine (1731–1814) of Massachusetts.

[†]John Witherspoon (1723–1794), delegate from New Jersey, was also the president of the College of New Jersey, now Princeton University.

Connecticut, N. York, N. Jersey, & Pennsylvania, against those of Delaware, Maryland, Virginia, North & South Carolina. Georgia was divided.

The other article was in these words. 'Art. XVII. In determining questions each colony shall have one vote.'

July 30. 31. Aug. 1. Present 41 members. Mr. Chase observed that this article was the most likely to divide us of any one proposed in the draught then under consideration. That the larger colonies had threatened they would not confederate at all if their weight in congress should not be equal to the numbers of people they added to the confederacy; while the smaller ones declared against an union if they did not retain an equal vote for the protection of their rights. That it was of the utmost consequence to bring the parties together, as should we sever from each other, either no foreign power will ally with us at all, or the different states will form different alliances, and thus increase the horrors of those scenes of civil war and bloodshed which in such a state of separation & independance would render us a miserable people. That our importance, our interests, our peace required that we should confederate, and that mutual sacrifices should be made to effect a compromise of this difficult question. He was of opinion the smaller colonies would lose their rights, if they were not in some instances allowed an equal vote; and therefore that a discrimination should take place among the questions which would come before Congress. [He therefore proposed] that the smaller states should be secured in all questions concerning life or liberty & the greater ones in all respecting property. He therefore proposed that in votes relating to money, the voice of each colony should be proportioned to the number of it's inhabitants.

Dr. Franklin [seconded the proposition] thought that the votes should be so proportioned in all cases. He took notice that the Delaware counties had bound up their Delegates to disagree to this article. He thought it a very extraordinary language to be held by any state, that they would not confederate with us unless we would let them dispose of our money. Certainly if we vote equally we ought to pay equally: but the smaller states will hardly purchase the privilege at this price. That had he lived in a state where the representation, originally equal, had become unequal by time & accident he might have submitted rather than disturb government: but that we should be very wrong to set out in this practice when it is in our power to establish what is right. That at the time of the Union between England and Scotland the latter had made the objection which the smaller states now do. But experience had proved that no unfairness had ever been shewn them. That their advocates had prognosticated that it would again happen as in times of old that the whale would swallow Jonas, but he thought the prediction reversed in event and that Jonas had swallowed the whale, for the Scotch had in fact got possession of the government and gave laws to the English. He reprobated the original agreement of Congress to vote by colonies, and therefore was for their voting in all cases according to the number of taxables ~~so far going beyond Mr. Chase's proposition~~.

Dr. Witherspoon opposed every alteration of the article. All men admit that a confederacy is necessary. Should the idea get abroad that there is likely to be no union among us, it will damp the minds of the people, diminish the glory of our struggle, & lessen it's importance, because it will open to our view future prospects of war & dissension among ourselves. If an equal vote be refused, the smaller states will become vassals to the larger; & all experience has shewn that the vassals & subjects of free states are the most enslaved. He instanced the Helots of Sparta & the provinces of Rome. He observed that foreign powers discovering this blemish would make it a handle for disengaging the smaller states from so unequal a confederacy. That the colonies should in fact be considered as individuals; and that as such in all disputes they should have an equal vote. That they are now collected as individuals making a bargain with each other, & of course had a right to vote as individuals. That in the East India company they voted by persons, & not by their proportion of stock. That the Belgic confederacy voted by provinces. That in questions of war the smaller states were as much interested as the larger, & therefore should vote equally; and indeed that the larger states were more likely to bring war on the confederacy, in proportion as their frontier was more extensive. He admitted that equality of representation was an excellent principle, but then it must be of things which are co-ordinate; that is, of things similar & of the same nature: that nothing relating to individuals could ever come before Congress; nothing but what would respect colonies. He distinguished between an incorporating & a federal union. The union of England was an incorporating one; yet Scotland had suffered by that union: for that it's inhabitants were drawn from it by the hopes of places & employments. Nor was it an instance of equality of representation; because while Scotland was allowed nearly a thirteenth of representation, they were to pay only one fortieth of the land tax. He expressed his hopes that in the present enlightened state of men's minds we might expect a lasting confederacy, if it was founded on fair principles.

John Adams advocated the voting in proportion to numbers. He said that we stand here as the representatives of the people. That in some states the people are many, in others they are few; that therefore their vote here should be proportioned to the numbers from whom it comes. Reason, justice, & equity never had weight enough on the face of the earth to govern the councils of men. It is interest alone which does it, and it is interest alone which can be trusted. That therefore the interests within doors should be the mathematical representatives of the interests without doors. That the individuality of the colonies is a mere sound. Does the individuality of a colony increase it's wealth or numbers? If it does; pay equally. If it does not add weight in the scale of the confederacy, it cannot add to their rights, nor weight in arguments. A. has £50. B. £500. C. £1000 in partnership. Is it just they should equally dispose of the monies of the partnership? It has been said we are independant individuals making a bargain together. The question is not what we are now, but what we ought to be when our bargain shall be made. The confederacy is to make us one individual only; it is to form us, like separate parcels of metal, into one common mass. We shall no longer retain our separate individuality, but become a single individual as to all questions submitted to the Confederacy. Therefore all those reasons which prove the justice & expediency of equal representation in other assemblies, hold good here. It has been objected that a proportional vote will endanger the smaller states. We answer that an equal vote will endanger the larger. Virginia, Pennsylvania, & Massachusets are the three greater colonies. Consider their distance, their difference of produce, of interests, & of manners, & it is apparent they can never have an interest or inclination to combine for the oppression of the smaller. That the smaller will naturally divide on all questions with the larger. Rhode Isld. from it's relation, similarity &

intercourse will generally pursue the same objects with Massachusets; Jersey, Delaware & Maryland with Pennsylvania.

Dr. Rush* took notice that the decay of the liberties of the Dutch republic proceeded from three causes. 1. The perfect unanimity requisite on all occasions. 2. Their obligation to consult their constituents. 3. Their voting by provinces. This last destroyed the equality of representation, and the liberties of Great Britain also are sinking from the same defect. That a part of our rights is deposited in the hands of our legislatures. There it was admitted there should be an equality of representation. Another part of our rights is deposited in the hands of Congress: why is it not equally necessary there should be an equal representation there? Were it possible to collect the whole body of the people together, they would determine the questions submitted to them by their majority. Why should not the same majority decide when voting here by their representatives? The larger colonies are so providentially divided in situation as to render every fear of their combining visionary. Their interests are different, & their circumstances dissimilar. It is more probable they will become rivals & leave it in the power of the smaller states to give preponderance to any scale they please. The voting by the number of free inhabitants will have one excellent effect, that of inducing the colonies to discourage slavery & to encourage the increase of their free inhabitants.

Mr. Hopkins† observed there were 4 larger, 4 smaller & 4 middle-sized colonies. That the 4 largest would contain more than half the inhabitants of the Confederating states, & therefore would govern the others as they should please. That history affords no instance of such a thing as equal representation. The Germanic body votes by states. The Helvetic body does the same; & so does the Belgic confederacy. That too little is known of the antient confederations to say what was their practice.

Mr. Wilson thought that taxation should be in proportion to wealth, but the representation should accord with the number of freemen. That government is a collection or result of the wills of all.

---

*Benjamin Rush (1746–1813) of Pennsylvania.
†Stephen Hopkins (1707–1785), delegate from Rhode Island.

That if any government could speak the will of all it would be perfect; and that so far as it departs from this it becomes imperfect. It has been said that Congress is a representation of states; not of individuals. I say that the objects of it's care are all the individuals of the states. It is strange that annexing the name of 'State' to ten thousand men, should give them an equal right with forty thousand. This must be the effect of magic, not of reason. As to those matters which are referred to Congress, we are not so many states; we are one large state. We lay aside our individuality whenever we come here. The Germanic body is a burlesque on government: and their practice on any point is a sufficient authority & proof that it is wrong. The greatest imperfection in the constitution of the Belgic confederacy is their voting by provinces. The interest of the whole is constantly sacrificed to that of the small states. The history of the war in the reign of Q. Anne sufficiently proves this. It is asked Shall nine colonies put it into the power of four to govern them as they please? I invert the question and ask Shall two millions of people put it in the power of one million to govern them as they please? It is pretended too that the smaller colonies will be in danger from the greater. Speak in honest language & say the minority will be in danger from the majority. And is there an assembly on earth where this danger may not be equally pretended? The truth is that our proceedings will then be consentaneous with the interests of the majority, and so they ought to be. The probability is much greater that the larger states will disagree than that they will combine. I defy the wit of man to invent a possible case or to suggest any one thing on earth which shall be for the interests of Virginia, Pennsylvania & Massachusets, and which will not also be for the interest of the other states.

ARTICLES AS REVISED BY CONGRESS
AUGUST 20, 1776

Articles of Confederation and Perpetual Union, between the Colonies of

New-Hampshire,	The counties of New-Castle,
Massachusetts-Bay,	Kent and Sussex on Delaware,
Rhode-Island,	Maryland,
Connecticut,	Virginia,
New-York,	North-Carolina,
New-Jersey,	South-Carolina, and
Pennsylvania,	Georgia.

ARTICLE I. The name of this Confederacy shall be "THE UNITED STATES OF AMERICA."

ARTICLE II. The said States hereby severally enter into a firm league of friendship with each other, for their common defence, the security of their liberties, and their mutual and general welfare, binding themselves to assist each other against all force offered to or attacks made upon them or any of them, on account of religion, sovereignty, trade, or any other pretence whatever.

ARTICLE III. Each State reserves to itself the sole and exclusive regulation and government of its internal police, in all matters that shall not interfere with the articles of this Confederation.

ARTICLE IV. No State, without the consent of the United States in Congress Assembled, shall send any Embassy to or receive any embassy from, or enter into any conference, agreement, alliance or treaty with any King, Prince or State; nor shall any person holding any office of profit or trust under the United States or any [of] them, accept of any present, emolument, office, or title of any kind whatever, from any King, Prince or foreign State; nor shall the United States Assembled, or any of them, grant any title of nobility.

ARTICLE V. No two or more States shall enter into any treaty, confederation or alliance whatever between them, without the Consent of the United States in Congress Assembled, specifying accurately the purposes for which the same is to be entered into, and how long it shall continue.

ARTICLE VI. No State shall lay any imposts or duties which may interfere with any stipulations in treaties hereafter entered into by the United States Assembled with any King, Prince or State.

ARTICLE VII. No vessels of war shall be kept up in time of peace by any State, except such number only as shall be deemed necessary by the United States Assembled for the defence of such state or its trade, nor shall any body of forces be kept up by any State in time of peace, except such number only as in the judgment of the United States in Congress Assembled shall be deemed requisite to garrison the forts necessary for the defence of such State, but every State shall always keep up a well regulated and disciplined Militia, sufficiently armed and accoutred, and shall provide and constantly have ready for use in public stores a due number of field pieces and tents and a proper quantity of Ammunition and a camp equipage.

ARTICLE VIII. When land forces are raised by any State for the common defence, all officers of or under the rank of Colonel, shall be appointed by the legislatures of each State respectively, by whom such forces shall be raised, or in such manner as such State shall direct, and all vacancies shall be filled up by the State which first made the appointment.

ARTICLE IX. All charges of war and all other expences that shall be incurred for the common defence, or general welfare, and allowed by the United States Assembled, shall be defrayed out of a common treasury, which shall be supplied by the several States in proportion to the number of inhabitants of every age, sex and quality except Indians not paying taxes, in each State, a true account of which, distinguishing the white inhabitants shall be triennially taken and transmitted to the Assembly of the United States. The taxes for paying that proportion shall be laid and levied by the authority and direction of the legislatures of the several States, within the time agreed upon by the United States Assembled.

ARTICLE X. Every State shall abide by the determinations of the United States in Congress Assembled, on all questions which by this Confederation are submitted to them.

ARTICLE XI. No State shall engage in any war without the consent of the United States in Congress Assembled, unless such State be actually invaded by enemies, or shall have received certain advice of a resolution being formed by some nation of Indians to invade such State, and the danger is so imminent, as not to admit of a delay, till the other States can be consulted: Nor shall any State grant commissions to any ships or vessels of war, nor letters of marque or reprisal, except it be after a declaration of war by the United States Assembled, and then only against the Kingdom or State and the subjects thereof against which war has been so declared and under such regulations as shall be established by the United States Assembled.

ARTICLE XII. For the more convenient management of the general interests of the United States, Delegates shall be annually appointed in such manner as the legislature of each State shall direct, to meet at the city of Philadelphia, in Pennsylvania, until otherwise ordered by the United States in Congress Assembled; which meeting shall be on the first Monday in November in every year, with a power reserved to each State to recal its Delegates or any of them at any time within the year, and to send others in their stead for the remainder of the year. Each State shall support its own Delegates in a meeting of the States, and while they act as members of the Council of State, herein after mentioned.

ARTICLE XIII. In determining questions each State shall have one vote.

ARTICLE XIV. The United States Assembled shall have the sole and exclusive right and power of determining on peace and war, except in the cases mentioned in the eleventh article—Of establishing rules for deciding in all cases, what captures on land or water shall be legal—In what manner prizes taken by land or naval forces in the service of the United States shall be divided or appropriated—granting letters of marque and reprisal in times of peace—appointing Courts for the trial of piracies and felonies committed on the high seas—establishing Courts for receiving and determining finally appeals in all cases of captures—sending and recieving Ambassadors—entering into treaties and alliances—deciding all disputes and differences now subsisting, or that hereafter may arise between two or more States concerning boundaries, jurisdictions, or any other cause whatever—coining money and regulating the value thereof—fixing the standard of weights and measures throughout the United States—regulating the trade, and managing all affairs with the Indians, not members of any of the States—Establishing and regulating Post-Offices from one State to another throughout all the United States, and exacting such postage on the papers passing through the same, as may be requisite to defray the expences of said office—appointing general Officers of the land forces in the service of the United States—commissioning such other officers of the said forces as shall be appointed by virtue of the eighth article—appointing all the officers of the naval forces in the service of the United States—making rules for the government and regulation of the said land and naval forces, and directing their operations.

The United States in Congress Assembled shall have authority to appoint a Council of State, and such Committees and Civil Officers as may be necessary for managing the general affairs of the United States, under their direction while assembled, and in their recess under that of the Council of State—to appoint one of their number to preside, and a suitable person for Secretary—And to adjourn to any time within the year, and to any place within the United States—to agree upon and fix the necessary sums and expences—to borrow Money or emit bills on the credit of the United States—to build and equip a navy—to agree upon the number of land forces, and to make requisitions from each State, for its quota in proportion to the number of white inhabitants in such State, which requisitions shall be binding, and thereupon the legislature of each State shall appoint the regimental officers, raise the men, and arm and equip them in a soldier-like manner; and the officers and men so armed and equipped, shall march to the place appointed, and within the time agreed on by the United States Assembled.

But if the United States in Congress Assembled shall on consideration of circumstances judge proper, that any State or States should not raise men, or should raise a smaller number than the quota or quotas of such State or States, and that any other State or States should raise a greater number of men than the quota or quotas thereof, such extra-numbers shall be raised, officered, armed and equipped in the same Manner as the quota or quotas of such State or States, unless the the legislature of such State or States respectively, shall judge, that such extra-numbers cannot be safely spared out of the same, in which case they shall raise, officer, arm and equip as many of such extra-numbers as they judge can be safely spared; and the officers and men so armed and equipped shall march to the place appointed, and within the time agreed on by the United States Assembled.

The United States in Congress Assembled shall never engage in a war, nor grant letters of marque and reprisal in time of peace, nor enter into any treaties or alliances except for peace, nor coin money nor regulate the value thereof, nor agree upon nor fix the sums and expences necessary for the defence and welfare of the United States, or any of them, nor emit bills, nor borrow money on the credit of the United States, nor appropriate money, nor agree upon the number of vessels of war to be built or purchased, or the number of land or sea forces to be raised, nor appoint a Commander in Chief of the army or navy, unless nine States assent to the same: Nor shall a question on any other point, except for adjourning from day to day be determined, unless by the votes of a majority of the United States.

No person shall be capable of being a Delegate for more than three years in any term of six years.

No person holding any office under the United States, for which he, or another for his benefit, receives any salary, fees, or emolument of any kind, shall be capable of being a Delegate.

The Assembly of the United States to publish the Journal of their Proceedings monthly, except such parts thereof relating to treaties, alliances, or military operations, as in their judgment require secrecy, the yeas and nays of the Delegates of each State on any question to be entered on the Journal, when it is desired by any Delegate; and the Delegates of a State, or any of them, at his or their request, to be furnished with a transcript of the said Journal, except such parts as are above excepted, to lay before the legislatures of the several States.

ARTICLE XV. The Council of State shall consist of one Delegate from each State, to be a named annually by the Delegates of each State, and where they cannot agree, by the United States assembled.

This Council shall have power to receive and open all Letters directed to the United States, and to return proper Answers; but not to make any engagements that shall be binding on the United States—To correspond with the legislature of every State, and all persons acting under the authority of the United States, or of the said legislatures—To apply to such Legislatures, or to the Officers in the several States who are entrusted with the executive powers of government, for occasional aid whenever and wherever necessary—To give counsel to the Commanding Officers, and to direct military operations by sea and land, not changing any objects or expeditions determined on by the United States Assembled, unless an alteration of circumstances which shall come to the knowledge of the Council after the recess of the States, shall make such change absolutely necessary—To attend to the defence and preservation of forts and strong posts—To procure intelligence of the condition and designs of the enemy—To expedite the execution of such measures as may be resolved on by the United States Assembled, in pursuance of the powers hereby given to them—To draw upon the treasurers for such sums as may be appropriated by the United States Assembled, and for the payment of such contracts as the said Council may make in pursuance of the powers hereby given to them—To superintend and controul or suspend all Officers civil and military, acting under the authority of the United States—In case of the death or removal of any Officer within the appointment of the United States Assembled, to employ a person to fulfill the Duties of such Office until the Assembly of the States meet—To publish and disperse authentic accounts of military operations—To summon an Assembly of the States at an earlier day than that appointed for their next meeting, if any great and unexpected emergency should render it necessary for the safety or welfare of the United States or any of them—To prepare matters for the consideration of the United States, and to lay before them at their next meeting all letters and advices received by the Council, with a report of their proceedings—To appoint a proper person for their Clerk, who shall take an oath of secrecy and fidelity, before he enters on the exercise of his office—seven Members shall have power to act—In case of the death of any Member, the Council shall immediately apply to his surviving colleagues to appoint some one of themselves to be a Member thereof till the meeting of the States, and if only one survives, they shall give immediate notice, that he may take his seat as a Councillor till such meeting.

ARTICLE XVI. Canada acceding to this Confederation, and entirely joining in the measures of the United States, shall be admitted into and entitled to all the advantages of this Union: But no other Colony shall be admitted into the same, unless such admission be agreed to by nine States.

These Articles shall be proposed to the legislatures of all the United States, to be by them considered, and if approved by them, they are advised to authorize their Delegates to ratify the same in the Assembly of the United States, which being done, the Articles of this Confederation shall inviolably be observed by every State, and the Union is to be perpetual: Nor shall any alteration at any time hereafter be made in these Articles or any of them, unless such alteration be agreed to in an Assembly of the United States, and be afterwards confirmed by the Legislatures of every State.

Ordered, That eighty copies of the Articles of Confederation, as reported from the committee of the whole, be printed under the same injunctions as the former articles were printed, and delivered to the members under the like restrictions as formerly.

ARTICLES AS APPROVED
NOVEMBER 15, 1777

Articles of Confederation and Perpetual Union, between the States of

New Hampshire,	*Pennsylvania,*
Massachusetts Bay,	*Delaware,*
Rhode Island and Providence	*Maryland,*
Plantations,	*Virginia,*
Connecticut,	*North Carolina,*
New York,	*South Carolina,*
New Jersey,	*Georgia.*

ARTICLE I. The stile of this confederacy shall be "The United States of America."

ARTICLE II. Each State retains its sovereignty, freedom and independence, and every power, jurisdiction, and right, which is not by this confederation expressly delegated to the United States, in Congress assembled.

ARTICLE III. The said states hereby severally enter into a firm league of friendship with each other for their common defence, the security of their liberties and their mutual and general welfare; binding themselves to assist each other against all force offered to, or attacks made upon them, or any of them, on account of religion, sovereignty, trade, or any other pretence whatever.

ARTICLE IV. The better to secure and perpetuate mutual friendship and intercourse among the people of the different states in this union, the free inhabitants of each of these states, paupers, vagabonds, and fugitives from justice excepted, shall be entitled to all privileges and immunities of free citizens in the several states; and the people of each State shall have free ingress and regress to and from any other State, and shall enjoy therein all the privileges of trade and commerce, subject to the same duties, impositions, and restrictions, as the inhabitants thereof respectively; provided, that such restrictions shall not extend so far as to prevent the removal of property, imported into any State, to any other State of which the owner is an inhabitant; provided also, that no imposition, duties, or restriction, shall be laid by any State on the property of the United States, or either of them.

If any person guilty of, or charged with treason, felony, or other high misdemeanor in any State, shall flee from justice and be found in any of the United States, he shall, upon demand of the governor or executive power of the State from which he fled, be delivered up and removed to the State having jurisdiction of his offence.

Full faith and credit shall be given in each of these states to the records, acts, and judicial proceedings of the courts and magistrates of every other State.

ARTICLE V. For the more convenient management of the general interests of the United States, delegates shall be annually appointed, in such manner as the legislature of each State shall direct, to meet in Congress, on the 1st Monday in November in every year, with a power reserved to each State to recal its delegates, or any of them, at any time within the year, and to send others in their stead for the remainder of the year.

No State shall be represented in Congress by less than two, nor by more than seven members; and no person shall be capable of being a delegate for more than three years in any term of six years; nor shall any person, being a delegate, be capable of holding any office under the United States, for which he, or any other for his benefit, receives any salary, fees, or emolument of any kind.

Each State shall maintain its own delegates in a meeting of the states, and while they act as members of the committee of the states.

In determining questions in the United States, in Congress assembled, each State shall have one vote.

Freedom of speech and debate in Congress shall not be impeached or questioned in any court or place out of Congress: and the members of Congress shall be protected in their persons from arrests and imprisonments, during the time of their going to and from, and attendance on Congress, *except for treason*, felony, or breach of the peace.

ARTICLE VI. No State, without the consent of the United States, in Congress assembled, shall send any embassy to, or receive any embassy from, or enter into any conference, agreement, alliance, or treaty with any king, prince, or state; nor shall any person, holding any office of profit or trust under the United States, or any of them, accept of any present, emolument, office or title, of any kind whatever, from any king, prince, or foreign state; nor shall the United States, in Congress assembled, or any of them, grant any title of nobility.

No two or more states shall enter into any treaty, confederation, or alliance, whatever, between them, without the consent of the United States, in Congress assembled, specifying accurately the purposes for which the same is to be entered into, and how long it shall continue.

No state shall lay any imposts or duties which may interfere with any stipulations in treaties entered into by the United States, in Congress assembled, with any king, prince, or state, in pursuance of any treaties already proposed by Congress to the courts of France and Spain.

No vessels of war shall be kept up in time of peace by any State, except such number only as shall be deemed necessary by the United States, in Congress assembled, for the defence of such State or its trade; nor shall any body of forces be kept up by any State, in time of peace, except such number only as, in the judgment of the United

States, in Congress assembled, shall be deemed requisite to garrison the forts necessary for the defence of such State; but every State shall always keep up a well regulated and disciplined militia, sufficiently armed and accoutred, and shall provide, and constantly have ready for use, in public stores, a due number of field pieces and tents, and a proper quantity of arms, ammunition and camp equipage.

No State shall engage in any war without the consent of the United States, in Congress assembled, unless such State be actually invaded by enemies, or shall have received certain advice of a resolution being formed by some nation of Indians to invade such State, and the danger is so imminent as not to admit of a delay till the United States, in Congress assembled, can be consulted; nor shall any State grant commissions to any ships or vessels of war, nor letters of marque or reprisal, except it be after a declaration of war by the United States, in Congress assembled, and then only against the kingdom or state, and the subjects thereof, against which war has been so declared, and under such regulations as shall be established by the United States, in Congress assembled, unless such State be infested by pirates, in which case vessels of war may be fitted out for that occasion, and kept so long as the danger shall continue, or until the United States, in Congress assembled, shall determine otherwise.

ARTICLE VII. When land forces are raised by any State for the common defence, all officers of or under the rank of colonel, shall be appointed by the legislature of each State respectively, by whom such forces shall be raised, or in such manner as such State shall direct; and all vacancies shall be filled up by the State which first made the appointment.

ARTICLE VIII. All charges of war and all other expences, that shall be incurred for the common defence or general welfare, and allowed by the United States, in Congress assembled, shall be defrayed out of a common treasury, which shall be supplied by the several states, in proportion to the value of all land within each State, granted to or surveyed for any person, as such land and the buildings and improvements thereon shall be estimated according to such mode as the United States, in Congress assembled, shall, from time to time, direct and appoint.

The taxes for paying that proportion shall be laid and levied by the authority and direction of the legislatures of the several states, within the time agreed upon by the United States, in Congress assembled.

ARTICLE IX. The United States, in Congress assembled, shall have the sole and exclusive right and power of determining on peace and war, except in the cases mentioned in the 6th article; of sending and receiving ambassadors; entering into treaties and alliances, provided that no treaty of commerce shall be made, whereby the legislative power of the respective states shall be restrained from imposing such imposts and duties on foreigners as their own people are subjected to, or from prohibiting the exportation or importation of any species of goods or commodities whatsoever; of establishing rules for deciding, in all cases, what captures on land or water shall be legal, and in what manner prizes, taken by land or naval forces in the service of the United States, shall be divided or appropriated; of granting letters of marque and reprisal in times of peace; appointing courts for the trial of piracies and felonies committed on the high seas, and establishing courts for receiving and determining, finally, appeals in all cases of captures; provided, that no member of Congress shall be appointed a judge of any of the said courts.

The United States, in Congress assembled, shall also be the last resort on appeal in all disputes and differences now subsisting, or that hereafter may arise between two or more states concerning boundary, jurisdiction or any other cause whatever; which authority shall always be exercised in the manner following: whenever the legislative or executive authority, or lawful agent of any State, in controversy with another, shall present a petition to Congress, stating the matter in question, and praying for a hearing, notice thereof shall be given, by order of Congress, to the legislative or executive authority of the other State in controversy, and a day assigned for the appearance of the parties by their lawful agents, who shall then be directed to appoint, by joint consent, commissioners or judges to constitute a court for hearing and determining the matter in question; but, if they cannot agree, Congress shall name three persons out of each of the United States, and from the list of such persons each party shall alternately strike out one, the petitioners beginning, until the number shall be reduced to thirteen; and from that number not less than seven, nor more than nine names, as Congress shall direct, shall, in the presence of Congress, be drawn out by lot; and the persons whose names shall be so drawn, or any five of them, shall be commissioners or judges to hear and finally determine the controversy, so always as a major part of the judges who shall hear the cause shall agree in the determination; and if either party shall neglect to attend at the day appointed, without shewing reasons which Congress shall judge sufficient, or, being present, shall refuse to strike, the Congress shall proceed to nominate three persons out of each State, and the secretary of Congress shall strike in behalf of such party absent or refusing; and the judgment and sentence of the court to be appointed, in the manner before prescribed, shall be final and conclusive; and if any of the parties shall refuse to submit to the authority of such court, or to appear or defend their claim or cause, the court shall nevertheless proceed to pronounce sentence or judgment, which shall, in like manner, be final and decisive, the judgment or sentence and other proceedings being, in either case, transmitted to Congress, and lodged among the acts of Congress for the security of the parties concerned: provided, that every commissioner, before he sits in judgment, shall take an oath, to be administered by one of the judges of the supreme or superior court of the State where the cause shall be tried, "well and truly to hear and determine the matter in question, according to the best of his judgment, without favour, affection, or hope of reward:" provided, also, that no State shall be deprived of territory for the benefit of the United States.

All controversies concerning the private right of soil, claimed under different grants of two or more states, whose jurisdictions, as they may respect such lands and the states which passed such grants, are adjusted, the said grants, or either of them, being at the same time claimed to have originated antecedent to such settlement of jurisdiction, shall, on the petition of either party to the Congress of the United States, be finally determined, as near as may be, in the same manner as is before prescribed for deciding disputes respecting territorial jurisdiction between different states.

The United States, in Congress assembled, shall also have the sole and exclusive right and power of regulating the alloy and value of coin struck by their own authority, or by that of the respective states; fixing the standard of weights and measures throughout the United States; regulating the trade and managing all affairs with the Indians not members of any of the states; provided that the legislative right of any State within its own limits be not infringed or violated; establishing and regulating post offices from one State to another throughout all the United States, and exacting such postage on the papers passing through the same as may be requisite to defray the expences of the said office; appointing all officers of the land forces in the service of the United States, excepting regimental officers; appointing all the officers of the naval forces, and commissioning all officers whatever in the service of the United States; making rules for the government and regulation of the said land and naval forces, and directing their operations.

The United States, in Congress assembled, shall have authority to appoint a committee to sit in the recess of Congress, to be denominated "a Committee of the States," and to consist of one delegate from each State, and to appoint such other committees and civil officers as may be necessary for managing the general affairs of the United States, under their direction; to appoint one of their number to preside; provided that no person be allowed to serve in the office of president more than one year in any term of three years; to ascertain the necessary sums of money to be raised for the service of the United States, and to appropriate and apply the same for defraying the public expences; to borrow money or emit bills on the credit of the United States, transmitting, every half year, to the respective states, an account of the sums of money so borrowed or emitted; to build and equip a navy; to agree upon the number of land forces, and to make requisitions from each State for its quota, in proportion to the number of white inhabitants in such State; which requisitions shall be binding; and, thereupon, the legislature of each State shall appoint the regimental officers, raise the men, and cloathe, arm, and equip them in a soldier-like manner, at the expence of the United States; and the officers and men so cloathed, armed, and equipped, shall march to the place appointed and within the time agreed on by the United States, in Congress assembled; but if the United States, in Congress assembled, shall, on consideration of circumstances, judge proper that any State should not raise men, or should raise a smaller number than its quota, and that any other State should raise a greater number of men than the quota thereof, such extra number shall be raised, officered, cloathed, armed, and equipped in the same manner as the quota of such State, unless the legislature of such State shall judge that such extra number cannot be safely spared out of the same, in which case they shall raise, officer, cloathe, arm, and equip as many of such extra number as they judge can be safely spared. And the officers and men so cloathed, armed, and equipped, shall march to the place appointed and within the time agreed on by the United States, in Congress assembled.

The United States, in Congress assembled, shall never engage in a war, nor grant letters of marque and reprisal in time of peace, nor enter into any treaties or alliances, nor coin money, nor regulate the value thereof, nor ascertain the sums and expences necessary for the defence and welfare of the United States, or any of them: nor emit bills, nor borrow money on the credit of the United States, nor appropriate money, nor agree upon the number of vessels of war to be built or purchased, or the number of land or sea forces to be raised, nor appoint a commander in chief of the army or navy, unless nine states assent to the same; nor shall a question on any other point, except for adjourning from day to day, be determined, unless by the votes of a majority of the United States, in Congress assembled.

The Congress of the United States shall have power to adjourn to any time within the year, and to any place within the United States, so that no period of adjournment be for a longer duration than the space of six months, and shall publish the journal of their proceedings monthly, except such parts thereof, relating to treaties, alliances or military operations, as, in their judgment, require secrecy; and the yeas and nays of the delegates of each State on any question shall be entered on the journal, when it is desired by any delegate; and the delegates of a State, or any of them, at his, or their request, shall be furnished with a transcript of the said journal, except such parts as are above excepted, to lay before the legislatures of the several states.

ARTICLE X. The committee of the states, or any nine of them, shall be authorized to execute, in the recess of Congress, such of the powers of Congress as the United States, in Congress assembled, by the consent of nine states, shall, from time to time, think expedient to vest them with; provided, that no power be delegated to the said committee, for the exercise of which, by the articles of confederation, the voice of nine states, in the Congress of the United States assembled, is requisite.

Article XI. Canada acceding to this confederation, and joining in the measures of the United States, shall be admitted into and entitled to all the advantages of this union; but no other colony shall be admitted into the same, unless such admission be agreed to by nine states.

Article XII. All bills of credit emitted, monies borrowed and debts contracted by, or under the authority of Congress before the assembling of the United States, in pursuance of the present confederation, shall be deemed and considered as a charge against the United States, for payment and satisfaction whereof the said United States and the public faith are hereby solemnly pledged.

Article XIII. Every State shall abide by the determinations of the United States, in Congress assembled, on all questions which, by this confederation, are submitted to them. And the articles of this confederation shall be inviolably observed by every State, and the union shall be perpetual; nor shall any alteration at any time hereafter be made in any of them, unless such alteration be agreed to in a Congress of the United States, and be afterwards confirmed by the legislatures of every State.

These articles shall be proposed to the legislatures of all the United States, to be considered, and if approved of by them, they are advised to authorize their delegates to ratify the same in the Congress of the United States; which being done, the same shall become conclusive.

Reforming the Articles of Confederation

AFTER CONGRESS COMPLETED THE Articles in November 1777, it hoped that the thirteen state legislatures would quickly ratify the Confederation. Only eight had done so, however, by June 1778, when the first French minister to the United States arrived in Philadelphia. Nearly three years passed before Maryland, the last holdout state, gave its assent, finally allowing the Articles of Confederation to begin operation as the country's first national constitution. Maryland's opposition was based on the failure of the Articles to empower Congress to limit the extravagant land claims of states like Virginia, which relied on its original seventeenth-century charter to claim much of the territory west of Pennsylvania and north of the Ohio River.

Nevertheless, by 1780 a movement was afoot to give Congress jurisdiction over this same territory, not by amending the Articles, but through the voluntary cessions of individual states. This movement began with New York. Its own claims in the Ohio Valley rested on the dubious theory that the Six Nations of the Iroquois Confederacy were both overlords of other Indian nations further west and legally dependent on New York through previous treaties negotiated with the former colonial government as long ago as 1701. What New York leaders like Philip Schuyler and Governor George Clinton really wanted was to assert their state's jurisdiction over the area between Lake Ontario and the northern boundary of Pennsylvania. At the same time, they hoped that a cession by New York would induce other states to follow suit. By early 1781 there was good reason to think that Virginia would cede its claims as well, and this was a factor in Maryland's decision to ratify the Confederation.

Even as the Articles neared ratification, however, criticisms of their potential shortcomings were being voiced. Three years of war had exposed serious gaps between the assumptions of 1776 and 1777 and the difficulties Congress now faced. Under the Articles, Congress had no authority to raise its own revenue, but had to rely instead on the contributions of the states. It had the authority to direct the war, but lacked the resources to keep its army fully manned and provisioned. Its shortcomings were painfully evident to the officer corps of the Continental Army, including the young artillery officer Alexander Hamilton, who was serving as General Washington's aide-de-camp when he provided the New York delegate James Duane with a sweeping critique of the Articles.

As soon as the Confederation was ratified in the winter of 1781, Congress asked the states to approve its first amendment: a proposal to grant Congress a 5 percent impost (duty) on foreign imports. Opposition from Rhode Island doomed this amendment to rejection. In 1782 Superintendent of Finance Robert Morris issued a major report on public credit, which he hoped would persuade Congress to propose a new set of amendments to the Articles. But the delegates were deeply divided on Morris's plan, and instead finally adopted a compromise set of amendments over his objections. These were sent to the states in April 1783. A year later Congress proposed two further amendments, designed to give it limited authority to regulate foreign commerce. None of these proposals ever overcame the hurdle of unanimous state ratification. Congress briefly considered one last set of amendments in 1786. But by then, reformers like James Madison and Alexander Hamilton were beginning to think about a different strategy of constitutional reform.

One significant change to the Articles of Confederation did take place, however, outside the rules for its amendment. This involved the creation of a national domain, north of the Ohio River, through the voluntary cessions of states with claims to this territory. That process began with the New York cession of 1780, but the key development was the decision by the Virginia legislature in 1781 to cede its claims as well. Another three years passed before the terms of the Virginia cession were fully accepted by Congress, but when they were, the federal union was vested with the authority and responsibility to regulate the development of the trans-Appalachian West. This substantial expansion of its authority had occurred through the actions of individual states, but without the unanimous approval of the thirteen legislatures that the Articles required.

Once this national domain existed, Congress had to ask how it would be governed. Its solution to this problem was found in the Northwest Ordinance of 1787, which Congress, then sitting in New York, adopted while the constitutional convention was simultaneously meeting in Philadelphia. Rather than treat the interior of the continent as a subordinate region to be exploited and colonized by the existing seaboard states, the Northwest Ordinance envisioned the creation of new states, to be admitted to the Union with the same rights and powers as its original thirteen members.

REFORMING THE ARTICLES OF CONFEDERATION

—Philip Schuyler—
LETTER TO PIERRE VAN CORTLANDT AND EVERT BANCKER
JANUARY 29, 1780

ALBANY JANUARY 29TH 1780.

GENTLEMEN,

Concieving it my duty as a Servant of the State to advise the Legislature of any Occurrences in Congress which may immediately affect either the Honor or the Weal of the State, I beg Leave to inform the honorable Houses in which you respectively preside of some Matters which I intended to have conveyed thro' his Excellency the Governor, supposing that to be the proper Channel of Communication: but was prevented by his leaving the City, and as I humbly concieve the Subject worthy the immediate Attention of the Legislature and that Evils may possibly arise from Delay, I have taken the Liberty to address myself to you, trusting that his Excellency's Candor and that of the Legislature will excuse the Impropriety if it should be deemed one.

Deeply impressed with a Sense of the extensive Advantages which would probably result to the United States in general, and this in particular, from a perfect and permanent Reconciliation with an Enemy so formidable to a weak and extensive Frontier as fatal Experience has evinced the Indians to be, to whom Distance of Situation seems no great Obstacle to prevent or retard their Incursions; reflecting, with the most anxious Concern, on the Desolation and Variety of Distress incident on a Savage War; apprehensive that they would consider themselves without any Alternative but that of recommencing Hostilities; dreading the Effects of a consequent Desperation on their part; firmly believing that the greatly deranged State of the public Finances would render it exceedingly difficult to procure the necessary Supplies for that Army only which must keep the Enemy's Force on the Sea Board in Check; doubtful whether Detachments of sufficient Force to protect the Frontiers could be spared from our Army whilst the British retained their present position; aware of the Distresses and Expence incident on calling forth the Militia for the purpose; convinced that an Obstacle of very interesting Importance would be removed if Events should happily arise which would permit us to turn our Attention to the Reduction of Canada or the Enemies Fortresses in the interior parts of the Country; persuaded that no farther offensive Operations could be prosecuted against the Savages with any probable prospect of adequate Advantage I embraced the earliest Opportunity to advise Congress of the Overtures made by the Cayugas, and took the Liberty strongly to point at the Necessity of an Accommodation with all the Savages: but not being honored with an Answer as early as the Importance of the Object seemed to require, and wishing to improve the Advantage which the first Impulse occasioned by the Disaster the Indians had experienced would probably afford us, I hastened to Congress to sollicit their Determination which was obtained on the ____ November last, Copy whereof I have the Honor to enclose.

Whilst the Report of the Committee in the Business I have alluded to was under Consideration a Member moved in Substance "That the Commissioners for Indian Affairs in the Northern Department should require from the Indians of the six Nations, as a preliminary Article, a Cession of part of their Country, and that the Territory so to be ceded should be for the Benefit of the United States in general and grantable by Congress." A Measure so evidently injurious to this State exceedingly alarmed and chagrined those whose Duty it was to attend to its Interests. They animadverted with Severity on the unjustifiable principle held up in the Motion; the pernicious Consequence of divesting a State of its undoubted property in such an extrajudicial Manner was forcibly urged: the Apprehensions with which it would fill and affect the Minds of a people who had been as firm in the present glorious Contest; who had made more strenuous and efficacious Exertions to support it; had suffered more and still suffered as much as any were strongly painted. The Improbability that the Indians would accede to a Reconciliation when such a preliminary was insisted upon was observed by many Members and urged on a Variety of Considerations. The Gentlemen in Favor of the Motion attempted to support it on the general Ground that what was acquired or conquered at the common Expence ought to enure to the common Benefit; that the Lands in Question, altho' they might be comprehended within the Limits of the State of New York (which however was not acknowledged) was not the property of the State; that being either in the Natives or by Right of Conquest in the United States. The Motion was nevertheless after some farther desultory Debate rejected: but from what drop'd in the Debate we had Reason to apprehend that several who were opposed to the Motion founded their Opposition on the Necessity of a Reconciliation with the Indians, against which, they imagined the Spirit of the Motion would militate. And we had a few Days after a convincing proof that an Idea prevailed that this and some other States ought to be divested of part of their Territory for the Benefit of the United States, when a Member afforded us the perusal of a Resolution for which he intended to move the House purporting "that all the Lands within the Limits of any of the United States, heretofore grantable by the King of Great Britain whilst these States (then Colonies) were in the Dominion of that prince, and which had not been granted to Individuals should be considered as the joint property of the United States and disposed of by Congress for the Benefit of the whole Confederacy." The Necessity and propriety of such an Arrangement was strenuously insisted upon, in private Conversation, and even supported by Gentlemen who represented States in Circumstances seemingly similar to our's with Respect to the Object of the intended Resolution. It was observed that if such States whose Bounds were either indefinite or were pretended to extend to the South Seas would consent to a reasonable Western Limitation that it would supercede the Necessity of any Intervention by Congress other than that of permanently establishing the Bounds of each State: prevent Controversy and remove the Obstacle which prevented the Completion of the Confederation. As this State would be eminently affected by such a Measure it was deemed of Importance as fully to investigate their Intentions as could be done consistent with that Delicacy and prudence to be observed on so interesting an Occasion and a Wish was accordingly expressed, as arising from mere Curiosity, to know their Idea of a reasonable Western Limitation. This they gave by exhibiting a Map of the Country, on which they drew a Line from the North west Corner of Pennsylvania (which in that Map was laid down as in Lake Erie)* thro' the Strait that leads to Ontario and thro' that Lake and down the St. Lawrence to the forty fifth Degree of Latitude for the Bounds of this State in that Quarter. Virginia, the two Carolinas and Georgia they proposed to restrict by the Allighany Mountains, or at farthest by the Ohio to where that River enters the Missisippi and by the latter River to the South Bounds of Georgia. That all the Territory to the West of those Limits should become the property of the Confederacy. We found this Matter had been in Contemplation some Time; the Delegates from North Carolina having then already requested Instructions from their Constituents on the Subjects, and my Colleagues were in Sentiment with me that it should be humbly submitted to the Legislature, if it would not be proper to communicate their pleasure in the premises by Way of Instruction to their Servants in Congress.

I am Gentlemen with Great respect and Esteem

Your most Obedient Humble Servant

Ph: Schuyler

The Honorable Pierre Van Cortlandt and Evert Ban[c]ker Esqrs.

—*Alexander Hamilton*—

Letter to James Duane

September 3, 1780

[Liberty Pole, New Jersey, September 3, 1780]

Dr. sir

Agreeably to your request and my promise I sit down to give you my ideas of the defects of our present system, and the changes necessary to save us from ruin. They may perhaps be the reveries of a projector rather than the sober views of a politician. You will judge of them, and make what use you please of them.

---

*In the early 1780s, the northern and western boundaries of Pennsylvania had yet to be surveyed, and the exact location of Lake Erie relative to that state remained uncertain.

The fundamental defect is a want of power in Congress. It is hardly worth while to show in what this consists, as it seems to be universally acknowleged, or to point out how it has happened, as the only question is how to remedy it. It may however be said that it has originated from three causes—an excess of the spirit of liberty which has made the particular states show a jealousy of all power not in their own hands; and this jealousy has led them to exercise a right of judging in the last resort of the measures recommended by Congress, and of acting according to their own opinions of their propriety or necessity, a diffidence in Congress of their own powers, by which they have been timid and indecisive in their resolutions, constantly making concessions to the states, till they have scarcely left themselves the shadow of power; a want of sufficient means at their disposal to answer the public exigencies and of vigor to draw forth those means; which have occasioned them to depend on the states individually to fulfil their engagements with the army, and the consequence of which has been to ruin their influence and credit with the army, to establish its dependence on each state separately rather than *on them*, that is rather than on the whole collectively.

It may be pleaded, that Congress had never any definitive powers granted them and of course could exercise none—could do nothing more than recommend. The manner in which Congress was appointed would warrant, and the public good required, that they should have considered themselves as vested with full power *to preserve the republic from harm*. They have done many of the highest acts of sovereignty, which were always chearfully submitted to—the declaration of independence, the declaration of war, the levying an army, creating a navy, emitting money, making alliances with foreign powers, appointing a dictator &c. &c.—all these implications of a complete sovereignty were never disputed, and ought to have been a standard for the whole conduct of Administration. Undefined powers are discretionary powers, limited only by the object for which they were given—in the present case, the independence and freedom of America. The confederation made no difference; for as it has not been generally adopted, it had no operation. But from what I recollect of it, Congress have even descended from the authority which the spirit of that act gives them, while the particular states have no further attended to it than as it suited their pretensions and convenience. It would take too much time to enter into particular instances, each of which separately might appear inconsiderable; but united are of serious import. I only mean to remark, not to censure.

But the confederation itself is defective and requires to be altered; it is neither fit for war, nor peace. The idea of an uncontrolable sovereignty in each state, over its internal police, will defeat the other powers given to Congress, and make our union feeble and precarious. There are instances without number, where acts necessary for the general good, and which rise out of the powers given to Congress must interfere with the internal police of the states, and there are as many instances in which the particular states by arrangements of internal police can effectually though indirectly counteract the arrangements of Congress. You have already had examples of this for which I refer you to your own memory.

The confederation gives the states individually too much influence in the affairs of the army; they should have nothing to do with it. The entire formation and disposal of our military forces ought to belong to Congress. It is an essential cement of the union; and it ought to be the policy of Congress to destroy all ideas of state attachments in the army and make it look up wholly to them. For this purpose all appointments promotions and provisions whatsoever ought to be made by them. It may be apprehended that this may be dangerous to liberty. But nothing appears more evident to me, than that we run much greater risk of having a weak and disunited federal government, than one which will be able to usurp upon the rights of the people. Already some of the lines of the army would obey their states in opposition to Congress notwithstanding the pains we have taken to preserve the unity of the army—if any thing would hinder this it would be the personal influence of the General, a melancholy and mortifying consideration.

The forms of our state constitutions must always give them great weight in our affairs and will make it too difficult to bend them to the persuit of a common interest, too easy to oppose whatever they do not like and to form partial combinations subversive of the general one. There is a wide difference between our situation and that of an empire under one simple form of government, distributed into counties provinces or districts, which have no legislatures but merely magistratical bodies to execute the laws of a common sovereign. Here the danger is that the sove[re]ign will have too much power to oppress the parts of which it is composed. In our case, that of an empire composed of confederated states each with a government completely organised within itself, having all the means to draw its subjects to a close dependence on itself—the danger is directly the reverse. It is that the common sovereign will not have power sufficient to unite the different members together, and direct the common forces to the interest and happiness of the whole.

The leagues among the old Grecian republics are a proof of this. They were continually at war with each other, and for want of union fell a prey to their neighbours. They frequently held general councils, but their resolutions were no further observed than as they suited the interests and inclinations of all the parties and at length, they sunk intirely into contempt.

The Swiss-cantons are another proof of the doctrine. They have had wars with each other which would have been fatal to them, had not the different powers in their neighbourhood been too jealous of one-another and too equally matched to suffer either to take advantage of their quarrels. That they have remained so long united at all is to be attributed to their weakness, to their poverty, and to the cause just mentioned. These ties will not exist in America; a little time hence, some of the states will be powerful empires, and we are so remote from other nations that we shall have all the leisure and opportunity we can wish to cut each others throats.

The Germanic corps might also be cited as an example in favour of the position.

The United provinces may be thought to be one against it. But the family of the stadtholders* whose authority is interwoven with the whole government has been a strong link of union between them. Their physical necessities and the habits founded upon them have contributed to it. Each province is too inconsiderable by itself to undertake any thing. An analysis of their present constitutions would show that they have many ties which would not exist in ours; and that they are by no means a proper mode for us.

Our own experience should satisfy us. We have felt the difficulty of drawing out the resources of the country and inducing the states

---

*Hamilton refers to the hereditary office that had become the effective monarchy of the united provinces of the Netherlands.

to combine in equal exertions for the common cause. The ill success of our last attempt is striking. Some have done a great deal, others little or scarcely any thing. The disputes about boundaries &c. testify how flattering a prospect we have of future tranquillity, if we do not frame in time a confederacy capable of deciding the differences and compelling the obedience of the respective members.

The confederation too gives the power of the purse too intirely to the state legislatures. It should provide perpetual funds in the disposal of Congress—by a land tax, poll tax, or the like. All imposts upon commerce ought to be laid by Congress and appropriated to their use, for without certain revenues, a government can have no power; that power, which holds the purse strings absolutely, must rule. This seems to be a medium, which without making Congress altogether independent will tend to give reality to its authority.

Another defect in our system is want of method and energy in the administration. This has partly resulted from the other defect, but in a great degree from prejudice and the want of a proper executive. Congress have kept the power too much into their own hands and have meddled too much with details of every sort. Congress is properly a deliberative corps and it forgets itself when it attempts to play the executive. It is impossible such a body, numerous as it is, constantly fluctuating, can ever act with sufficient decision, or with system. Two thirds of the members, one half the time, cannot know what has gone before them or what connection the subject in hand has to what has been transacted on former occasions. The members, who have been more permanent, will only give information, that promotes the side they espouse, in the present case, and will as often mislead as enlighten. The variety of business must distract, and the proneness of every assembly to debate must at all times delay.

Lately Congress, convinced of these inconveniences, have gone into the measure of appointing boards. But this is in my opinion a bad plan. A single man, in each department of the administration, would be greatly preferable. It would give us a chance of more knowlege, more activity, more responsibility and of course more zeal and attention. Boards partake of a part of the inconveniencies of larger assemblies. Their decisions are slower their energy less their responsibility more diffused. They will not have the same abilities and knowlege as an administration by single men. Men of the first pretensions will not so readily engage them, because they will be less conspicuous, of less importance, have less opportunity of distinguishing themselves. The members of boards will take less pains to inform themselves and arrive to eminence, because they have fewer motives to do it. All these reasons conspire to give a preference to the plan of vesting the great executive departments of the state in the hands of individuals. As these men will be of course at all times under the direction of Congress, we shall blend the advantages of a monarchy and republic in our constitution.

A question has been made, whether single men could be found to undertake these offices. I think they could, because there would be then every thing to excite the ambition of candidates. But in order to this Congress by their manner of appointing them and the line of duty marked out must show that they are in earnest in making these offices, offices of real trust and importance.

I fear a little vanity has stood in the way of these arrangements, as though they would lessen the importance of Congress and leave them nothing to do. But they would have precisely the same rights and powers as heretofore, happily disencumbered of the detail. They would have to inspect the conduct of their ministers, deliberate upon their plans, originate others for the public good—only observing this rule that they ought to consult their ministers, and get all the information and advice they could from them, before they entered into any new measures or made changes in the old.

A third defect is the fluctuating constitution of our army. This has been a pregnant source of evil; all our military misfortunes, three fourths of our civil embarrassments are to be ascribed to it. The General has so fully enumerated the mischief of it in a late letter of the [20th of August] to Congress that I could only repeat what he has said, and will therefore refer you to that letter.

The imperfect and unequal provision made for the army is a fourth defect which you will find delineated in the same letter. Without a speedy change the army must dissolve; it is now a mob, rather than an army, without cloathing, without pay, without provision, without morals, without discipline. We begin to hate the country for its neglect of us; the country begins to hate us for our oppressions of them. Congress have long been jealous of us; we have now lost all confidence in them, and give the worst construction to all they do. Held together by the slenderest ties we are ripening for a dissolution.

The present mode of supplying the army—by state purchases—is not one of the least considerable defects of our system. It is too precarious a dependence, because the states will never be sufficiently impressed with our necessities. Each will make its own ease a primary object, the supply of the army a secondary one. The variety of channels through which the business is transacted will multiply the number of persons employed and the opportunities of embezzling public money. From the popular spirit on which most of the governments turn, the state agents, will be men of less character and ability, nor will there be so rigid a responsibility among them as there might easily be among those in the employ of the continent, of course not so much diligence care or economy. Very little of the money raised in the several states will go into the Continental treasury, on pretence, that it is all exhausted in providing the quotas of supplies, and the public will be without funds for the other demands of governments. The expence will be ultimately much greater and the advantages much smaller. We actually feel the insufficiency of this plan and have reason to dread under it a ruinous extremity of want.

These are the principal defects in the present system that now occur to me. There are many inferior ones in the organization of particular departments and many errors of administration which might be pointed out; but the task would be troublesome and tedious, and if we had once remedied those I have mentioned the others would not be attended with much difficulty.

I shall now propose the remedies, which appear to me applicable to our circumstances, and necessary to extricate our affairs from their present deplorable situation.

The first step must be to give Congress powers competent to the public exigencies. This may happen in two ways, one by resuming and exercising the discretionary powers I suppose to have been originally vested in them for the safety of the states and resting their conduct on the candor of their country men and the necessity of the conjuncture: the other by calling immediately a convention of all the states with full authority to conclude finally upon a general confederation, stating to them beforehand explicit the evils arising from a want of power in Congress, and the impossibility of supporting the contest on its present footing, that the delegates may come possessed of proper sentiments as well as proper authority to give to the meeting. Their commission should include a right of vesting Congress with the whole or a proportion of the unoccupied lands, to be employed for the purpose of raising a revenue, reserving the jurisdiction to the states by whom they are granted.

The first plan, I expect will be thought too bold an expedient by the generality of Congress; and indeed their practice hitherto has so rivetted the opinion of their want of power, that the success of this experiment may very well be doubted.

I see no objection to the other mode, that has any weight in competition with the reasons for it. The Convention should assemble the 1st of November next, the sooner, the better; our disorders are too violent to admit of a common or lingering remedy. The reasons for which I require them to be vested with plenipotentiary authority are that the business may suffer no delay in the execution, and may in reality come to effect. A convention may agree upon a confederation; the states individually hardly ever will. We must have one at all events, and a vigorous one if we mean to succeed in the contest and be happy hereafter. As I said before, to engage the states to comply with this mode, Congress ought to confess to them plainly and unanimously the impracticability of supporting our affairs on the present footing and without a solid coercive union. I ask that the Convention should have a power of vesting the whole or a part of the unoccupied land in Congress, because it is necessary that body should have some property as a fund for the arrangements of finance; and I know of no other kind that can be given them.

The confederation in my opinion should give Congress complete sovereignty; except as to that part of internal police, which relates to the rights of property and life among individuals and to raising money by internal taxes. It is necessary, that every thing, belonging to this, should be regulated by the state legislatures. Congress should have complete sovereignty in all that relates to war, peace, trade, finance, and to the management of foreign affairs, the right of declaring war of raising armies, officering, paying them, directing their motions in every respect, of equipping fleets and doing the same with them, of building fortifications arsenals magazines &c. &c., of making peace on such conditions as they think proper, of regulating trade, determining with what countries it shall be carried on, granting indulgencies laying prohibitions on all the articles of export or import, imposing duties granting bounties & premiums for raising exporting importing and applying to their own use the product of these duties, only giving credit to the states on whom they are raised in the general account of revenues and expences, instituting Admiralty courts &c., of coining money, establishing banks on such terms, and with such privileges as they think proper, appropriating funds and doing whatever else relates to the operations of finance, transacting every thing with foreign nations, making alliances offensive and defensive, treaties of commerce, &c. &c.

The confederation should provide certain perpetual revenues, productive and easy of collection, a land tax, poll tax or the like, which together with the duties on trade and the unlocated lands would give Congress a substantial existence, and a stable foundation for their schemes of finance. What more supplies were necessary should be occasionally demanded of the states, in the present mode of quotas.

The second step I would recommend is that Congress should instantly appoint the following great officers of state—A secretary for foreign affairs—a President of war—A President of Marine—A Financier—A President of trade; instead of this last a board of Trade may be preferable as the regulations of trade are slow and gradual and require prudence and experience (more than other qualities), for which boards are very well adapted.

Congress should choose for these offices, men of the first abilities, property and character in the continent—and such as have had the best opportunities of being acquainted with the several branches. General Schuyler* (whom you mentioned) would make an excellent President of War, General McDougall† a very good President of Marine. Mr. Robert Morris would have many things in his favour for the department of finance. He could by his own personal influence give great weight to the measures he should

---

*Philip John Schuyler (1733–1804) of Albany soon became Hamilton's father-in-law.

†Alexander McDougall (1731–1786) of New York City had been a prominent leader of the Sons of Liberty before 1776 and later served as a general in the Continental Army.

adopt. I dare say men equally capable may be found for the other departments.

I know not, if it would not be a good plan to let the Financier be President of the Board of trade; but he should only have a casting voice in determining questions there. There is a connection between trade and finance, which ought to make the director of one acquainted with the other; but the Financier should not direct the affairs of trade, because for the sake of acquiring reputation by increasing the revenues, he might adopt measures that would depress trade. In what relates to finance he should be alone.

These offices should have nearly the same powers and functions as those in France analogous to them, and each should be chief in his department, with subordinate boards composed of assistant clerks &c. to execute his orders.

In my opinion a plan of this kind would be of inconceivable utility to our affairs; its benefits would be very speedily felt. It would give new life and energy to the operations of government. Business would be conducted with dispatch method and system. A million of abuses now existing would be corrected, and judicious plans would be formed and executed for the public good.

Another step of immediate necessity is to recruit the army for the war, or at least for three years. This must be done by a mode similar to that which is practiced in Sweeden. There the inhabitants are thrown into classes of sixteen, and when the sovereign wants men each of these classes must furnish one. They raise a fixed sum of money, and if one of the class is willing to become a soldier, he receives the money and offers himself a volunteer; if none is found to do this, a draft is made and he on whom the lot falls receives the money and is obliged to serve. The minds of the people are prepared for a thing of this kind; the heavy bounties they have been obliged to pay for men to serve a few months must have disgusted them with this mode, and made them desirous of another, that will once for all answer the public purposes, and obviate a repetition of the demand. It ought by all means to be attempted, and Congress should frame a general plan and press the execution upon the states. When the confederation comes to be framed, it ought to provide for this by a fundamental law, and hereafter there would be no doubt of the success. But we cannot now wait for this; we want to replace the men whose times of service will expire the 1st of January, for then, without this, we shall have no army remaining and the enemy may do what they please. The General in his letter already quoted has assigned the most substantial reasons for paying immediate attention to this point.

Congress should endeavour, both upon their credit in Europe, and by every possible exertion in this country, to provide cloathing for their officers, and should abolish the whole system of state supplies. The making good the depreciation of the currency and all other compensations to the army should be immediately taken up by Congress, and not left to the states; if they would have the accounts of depreciation liquidated, and governmental certificates given for what is due in specie or an equivalent to specie, it would give satisfaction; appointing periodical settlements for future depreciation.

The placing the officers upon half pay during life would be a great stroke of policy, and would give Congress a stronger tie upon them, than any thing else they can do. No man, that reflects a moment, but will prefer a permanent provision of this kind to any temporary compensation, nor is it opposed to economy; the difference between this and between what has been already done will be insignificant. The benefit of it to the widows should be confined to those whose husbands die during the war. As to the survivors, not more than one half on the usual calculation of mens lives will exceed the seven years for which the half pay is already established. Besides this whatever may be the visionary speculations of some men at this time, we shall find it indispensable after the war to keep on foot a considerable body of troops; and all the officers retained for this purpose must be deducted out of the half pay list. If any one will take the pains to calculate the expence on these principles, I am persuaded he will find the addition of expence from the establishment proposed, by no means a national object.

The advantages of securing the attachment of the army to Congress, and binding them to the service by substantial ties are immense. We should then have discipline, an army in reality, as well as in name. Congress would then have a solid basis of authority and consequence, for to me it is an axiom that in our constitution an army is essential to the American union.

The providing of supplies is the pivot of every thing else (though a well constituted army would not in a small degree conduce to this, by giving consistency and weight to government). There are four ways all which must be united—a foreign loan, heavy pecuniary taxes, a tax in kind, a bank founded on public and private credit.

As to a foreign loan I dare say, Congress are doing every thing in their power to obtain it. The most effectual way will be to tell France that without it, we must make terms with great Britain. This must be done with plainness and firmness, but with respect and without petulance, not as a menace, but as a candid declaration of our circumstances. We need not fear to be deserted by France. Her interest and honor are too deeply involved in our fate; and she can make no possible compromise. She can assist us, if she is convinced it is absolutely necessary, either by lending us herself or by becoming our surety or by influencing Spain. It has been to me astonishing how any man could have doubted at any period of our affairs of the necessity of a foreign loan. It was self evident, that we had not a fund of wealth in this country, capable of affording revenues equal to the expences. We must then create artificial revenues, or borrow; the first was done, but it ought to have been foreseen, that the expedient could not last; and we should have provided in time for its failure.

Here was an error of Congress. I have good reason to believe, that measures were not taken in earnest early enough, to procure a loan abroad. I give you my honor that from our first outset, I thought as I do now and wished for a foreign loan not only because I foresaw it would be essential but because I considered it as a tie upon the nation from which it was derived and as a means to prop our cause in Europe.

Concerning the necessity of heavy pecuniary taxes I need say nothing, as it is a point in which everybody is agreed; nor is there any danger, that the product of any taxes raised in this way will over burthen the people, or exceed the wants of the public. Indeed if all the paper in circulation were drawn annually into the treasury, it would neither do one, nor the other.

As to a tax in kind, the necessity of it results from this principle— that the money in circulation is not a sufficient representative of the productions of the country, and consequently no revenues raised from it as a medium can be a competent representative of that part of the products of the country, which it is bound to contribute to the support of the public. The public therefore to obtain its due or satisfy its just demands and its wants must call for a part of those products themselves. This is done in all those countries which are not commercial, in Russia, Prussia, Denmark Sweden &c. and is peculiarly necessary in our case.

Congress in calling for specific supplies* seem to have had this in view; but their intention has not been answered. The states in general have undertaken to furnish the supplies by purchase, a mode as I have observed, attended with every inconvenience and subverting the principle on which the supplies were demanded—the insufficiency of our circulating medium as a representative for the labour and commodities of the Country. It is therefore necessary that Congress should be more explicit, should form the outlines of a plan for a tax in kind, and recommend it to the states, as a measure of absolute necessity.

The general idea I have of a plan, is that a respectable man should be appointed by the state in each county to collect the taxes and form magazines, that Congress should have in each state an officer to superintend the whole and that the state collectors should be subordinate and responsible to them. This Continental superintendent might be subject to the general direction of the Quarter Master General, or not, as might be deemed best; but if not subject to him, he should be obliged to make monthly returns to the President at War, who should instruct him what proportion to deliver to the Quarter Master General. It may be necessary that the superintendents should sometimes have power to dispose of the articles in their possession on public account; for it would happen that the contributions in places remote from the army could not be transported to the theatre of operations without too great expence, in which case it would be eligible to dispose of them and purchase with the money so raised in the countries near the immediate scene of war.

I know the objections which may be raised to this plan—its tendency to discourage industry and the like; but necessity calls for it;

---

*In 1780 the Continental Congress began asking particular states to supply specific material needs of the Continental Army.

we cannot proceed without [it], and less evils must give place to greater. It is besides practiced with success in other countries, and why not in this? It may be said, the examples cited are from nations under despotic governments and that the same would not be practicable with us; but I contend where the public good is evidently the object more may be effected in governments like ours than in any other. It has been a constant remark that free countries have ever paid the heaviest taxes. The obedience of a free people to general laws however hard they bear is ever more perfect than that of slaves to the arbitrary will of a prince. To this it may be added that Sweden was always a free government, and is so now in a great degree, notwithstanding the late revolution.

How far it may be practicable to erect a bank on the joint credit of the public and of individuals can only be certainly determined by the experiment; but it is of so much importance that the experiment ought to be fully tried. When I saw the subscriptions going on to the bank established for supplying the army, I was in hopes it was only the embryo of a more permanent and extensive establishment. But I have reason to believe I shall be disappointed. It does not seem to be at all conducted on the true principles of a bank. The directors of it are purchasing with their stock instead of bank notes as I expected; in consequence of which it must turn out to be a mere subscription of a particular sum of money for a particular purpose.

Paper credit never was long supported in any country, on a national scale, where it was not founded on the joint basis of public and private credit. An attempt to establish it on public credit alone in France under the auspices of Mr. Law* had nearly ruined the kingdom; we have seen the effects of it in America, and every successive experiment proves the futility of the attempt. Our new money is depreciating almost as fast as the old, though it has in some states as real funds as paper money ever had. The reason is, that the monied men have not an immediate interest to uphold its credit. They may even in many ways find it their interest to undermine it. The only certain manner to obtain a permanent paper credit is to engage the monied interest immediately in it by making

---

*John Law (1671–1729), Scottish economist who founded the Mississippi Company, which became one of the great speculative bubbles of the early eighteenth century.

them contribute the whole or part of the stock and giving them the whole or part of the profits.

The invention of banks on the modern principle originated in Venice. There the public and a company of monied men are mutually concerned. The Bank of England unites public authority and faith with private credit; and hence we see what a vast fabric of paper credit is raised on a visionary basis. Had it not been for this, England would never have found sufficient funds to carry on her wars; but with the help of this she has done, and is doing wonders. The bank of Amsterdam is on a similar foundation.

And why can we not have an American bank? Are our monied men less enlightened to their own interest or less enterprising in the persuit? I believe the fault is in our government which does not exert itself to engage them in such a scheme. It is true, the individuals in America are not very rich, but this would not prevent their instituting a bank; it would only prevent its being done with such ample funds as in other countries. Have they not sufficient confidence in the government and in the issue of the cause? Let the Government endeavour to inspire that confidence, by adopting the measures I have recommended or others equivalent to them. Let it exert itself to procure a solid confederation, to establish a good plan of executive administration, to form a permanent military force, to obtain at all events a foreign loan. If these things were in a train of vigorous execution, it would give a new spring to our affairs; government would recover its respectability and individuals would renounce their diffidence.

The object I should propose to myself in the first instance from a bank would be an auxiliary mode of supplies; for which purpose contracts should be made between Government and the bank on terms liberal and advantageous to the latter. Every thing should be done in the first instance to encourage the bank; after it gets well established it will take care of itself and government may make the best terms it can for itself.

The first step to establishing the bank will be to engage a number of monied men of influence to relish the project and make it a business. The subscribers to that lately established are the fittest persons that can be found; and their plan may be interwoven.

The outlines of my plan would be to open subscriptions in all the states for the stock, which we will suppose to be one million of pounds. Real property of every kind, as well as specie should be deemed good stock, but at least a fourth part of the subscription should be in specie or plate. There should be one great company in three divisions in Virginia, Philadelphia, and at Boston or two at Philadelphia and Boston. The bank should have a right to issue bank notes bearing two per Cent interest for the whole of their stock; but not to exceed it. These notes may be payable every three months or oftener, and the faith of government must be pledged for the support of the bank. It must therefore have a right from time to time to inspect its operations, and must appoint inspectors for the purpose.

The advantages of the bank may consist in this, in the profits of the contracts made with government, which should bear interest to be annually paid in specie, in the loan of money at interest say six per Cent, in purchasing lives by annuities as practiced in England &c. The benefit resulting to the company is evident from the consideration, that they may employ in circulation a great deal more money than they have specie in stock, on the credit of the real property which they will have in other use; this money will be employed either in fulfilling their contracts with the public by which also they will gain a profit, or in loans at an advantageous interest or in annuities.

The bank may be allowed to purchase plate and bullion and coin money allowing government a part of the profit. I make the bank notes bear interest to obtain a readie currency and to induce the holders to prefer them to specie to prevent too great a run upon the bank at any time beyond its ability to pay.

If Government can obtain a foreign loan it should lend to the bank on easy terms to extend its influence and facilitate a compliance with its engagements. If government could engage the states to raise a sum of money in specie to be deposited in bank in the same manner, it would be of the greatest consequence. If government could prevail on the enthusiasm of the people to make a contribution in plate for the same purpose it would be a master stroke. Things of this kind sometimes succeed in popular contests; and if undertaken with address; I should not despair of its success; but I should not be sanguine.

The bank may be instituted for a term of years by way of trial and the particular privilege of coining money be for a term still shorter. A temporary transfer of it to a particular company can have no inconvenience as the government are in no condition to improve this resource nor could it in our circumstances be an object to them, though with the industry of a knot of individuals it might be.

A bank of this kind even in its commencement would answer the most valuable purposes to government and to the proprietors; in its progress the advantages will exceed calculation. It will promote commerce by furnishing a more extensive medium which we greatly want in our circumstances. I mean a more extensive valuable medium. We have an enormous nominal one at this time; but it is only a name.

In the present unsettled state of things in this country, we can hardly draw inferences from what has happened in others, otherwise I should be certain of the success of this scheme; but I think it has enough in its favour to be worthy of trial.

I have only skimmed the surface of the different subjects I have introduced. Should the plans recommended come into contemplation in earnest and you desire my further thoughts, I will endeavour to give them more form and particularity. I am persuaded a solid confederation a permanent army a reasonable prospect of subsisting it would give us treble consideration in Europe and produce a peace this winter.

If a Convention is called the minds of all the states and the people ought to be prepared to receive its determinations by sensible and popular writings, which should conform to the views of Congress. There are epochs in human affairs, when *novelty* even is useful. If a general opinion prevails that the old way is bad, whether true or false, and this obstructs or relaxes the operation of the public service, a change is necessary if it be but for the sake of change. This is exactly the case now. 'Tis an universal sentiment that our present system is a bad one, and that things do not go right on this account. The measure of a Convention would revive the hopes of the people and give a new direction to their passions, which may be improved in carrying points of substantial utility. The Eastern states have already pointed out this mode to Congress; they ought to take the hint and anticipate the others.

And, in future, My Dear Sir, two things let me recommend, as fundamental rules for the conduct of Congress—to attach the army to them by every motive, to maintain an air of authority (not domineering) in all their measures with the states. The manner in which a thing is done has more influence than is commonly imagined. Men are governed by opinion; this opinion is as much influenced by appearances as by realities; if a Government appears to be confident of its own powers, it is the surest way to inspire the same confidence in others; if it is diffident, it may be certain, there will be a still greater diffidence in others, and that its authority will not only be distrusted, controverted, but contemned.

I wish too Congress would always consider that a kindness consists as much in the manner as in the thing: the best things done hesitatingly and with an ill grace lose their effect, and produce disgust rather than satisfaction or gratitude. In what Congress have at any time done for the army, they have commonly been too late: They have seemed to yield to importunity rather than to sentiments of justice or to a regard to the accomodation of their troops. An attention to this idea is of more importance than it may be thought. I who have seen all the workings and progress of the present discontents, am convinced, that a want of this has not been among the most inconsiderable causes.

You will perceive My Dear Sir this letter is hastily written and with a confidential freedom, not as to a member of Congress, whose feelings may be sore at the prevailing clamours; but as to a friend who is in a situation to remedy public disorders, who wishes for nothing so much as truth, and who is desirous of information, even from those less capable of judging than himself. I have not even time to correct and copy and only enough to add that I am very truly and affectionately D Sir   Your most Obed ser

A. HAMILTON

LIBERTY POLE
SEPT. 3D 1780

Impost Amendment Proposed by Congress to the States

February 3, 1781

The report from the Committee of the Whole, being amended, was agreed to as follows:

Resolved, That it be recommended to the several states, as indispensably necessary, that they vest a power in Congress, to levy for the use of the United States, a duty of five per cent. *ad valorem,* at the time and place of importation, upon all goods, wares and merchandises of foreign growth and manufactures, which may be imported into any of the said states from any foreign port, island or plantation, after the first day of May, 1781; except arms, ammunition, cloathing and other articles imported on account of the United States, or any of them; and except wool-cards and cotton-cards, and wire for making them; and also, except salt, during the war:

Also, a like duty of five per cent. on all prizes and prize goods condemned in the court of admiralty of any of these states as lawful prize:

That the monies arising from the said duties be appropriated to the discharge of the principal and interest of the debts already contracted, or which may be contracted, on the faith of the United States, for supporting the present war:

That the said duties be continued until the said debts shall be fully and finally discharged.

—*Robert Morris*—
Report on Public Credit

July 29, 1782

Office of Finance July 29th. 1782

Sir

The reference which congress were pleased to make, of a Remonstrance and Petition from Blair McClenaghan and others, has induced me to pray their Indulgence while I go somewhat at large into the Subject of that Remonstrance. The Propriety and Utility of public Loans, have been Subjects of much Controversy. Those who find themselves saddled with the Debts of a preceding Generation, naturally exclaim against Loans; and it must be confessed that when such Debts are accumulated by Negligence, Folly or Profusion, the Complaint is well founded. But it would be equally so against Taxes, when wasted in the same Way. The Difference is, that the Weight of Taxes being more sensible, the Waste occasions greater Clamor, and is therefore more speedily remedied; but it will appear that the eventual Evils which Posterity must Sustain from heavy Taxes, are greater than from Loans. Hence may be deduced this Conclusion, that in Governments liable to a vicious Administration it would be better to raise the current Expence by Taxes, but where an honest and wise Appropriation of Money prevails, it is highly advantageous to take the Benefit of Loans. Taxation to a certain Point is not only proper but useful, because by stimulating the Industry of Individuals, it increases the Wealth of the Community. But when Taxes go so far as to intrench on the Subsistence of the People, they become burthensome and oppressive. The Expenditure of Money ought in such Case to be (if possible) avoided; and if unavoidable, it will be most wise to have Recourse to Loans.

Loans may be of two Kinds, either domestic or foreign. The relative Advantages and Disadvantages of each, as well as those which are common to both, will deserve Attention. Reasonings of this Kind, (as they depend on Rules of Arithmetic), are best understood by numerical Positions. For the Purposes of Elucidation, therefore, it may be supposed, that the annual Tax of any particular Husbandman were fifteen Pounds, during a ten Year's War, and that his net Revenue were but fifteen Pounds, so that (the whole being regularly consumed in Payment of Taxes) he would be no richer at the End of the War, than he was at the Beginning. It is at the same Time notorious that the Profits made by Husbandmen, on Funds which they borrowed, were very considerable. In many Instances their Plantations, as well as the Cattle and farming Utensils, have been purchased on Credit, and the Bonds given for both have shortly been paid by Sales of Produce. It is therefore no Exageration to state the Profits at twelve per Cent. The enormous Usury which People in Trade have been induced to pay, and which will presently be noticed, demonstrates that the Profits made by other Professions are equal to those of the Husbandman. The Instance therefore taken from that, which is the most numerous Class of Citizens, will form no improper Standard for the whole. Let it then be farther supposed in the Case already stated, that the Party should annually borrow the Sum of ten Pounds, to pay Part of his Tax of fifteen Pounds, at six per Cent. On this Sum then he would make a Profit of twenty four Shillings, and have to pay an Interest of twelve shillings. The enclosed Calculation will shew that in ten years he would be indebted one hundred Pounds, but his additional Improvements would be worth: near one hundred and fifty, and his net Revenue be increased near twelve after deducting the Interest of his Debt; whereas if he had not borrowed, his Revenue would have continued the same, as has already been observed. This Mode of Reasoning might be pursued farther, but what has been said is sufficient to shew that he would have made a considerable Advantage from the yearly Loan. If it be supposed that every Person in the Community made such [a] Loan, a similar Advantage would arise to the Community. And lastly if it be supposed that the Government were to make a Loan, and ask so much less in Taxes, the same Advantage would be derived. Hence also may be deduced this Position, that in a Society where the Average Profits of Stock are double to the Interest at which Money can be obtained, every public Loan, for necessary Expenditures, provides a Fund in the Agregate of national Wealth equal to the Discharge of it's own Interest. Were it possible that a Society should exist in which every Member would, of his own accord, industriously pursue the Increase of national Property, without Waste or extravagance, the public Wealth would be impaired by every species of Taxation. But there never was, and unless human Nature should change, there never will be such a Society. In any given Number of men there will always be some who are Idle, and some who are extravagant. In every Society also, there must be some Taxes, because the Necessity of Supporting Government and defending the State always exist. To do these on the cheapest Terms is wise. And when it is considered how much Men are disposed to Indolence and Profusion, It will appear that (even if these Demands did not require the whole of what could be raised) still it would be wise to carry Taxation to a certain Amount, and expend what should remain after providing for the Support of Government and the national Defence, in works of public utility, such as the Opening of Roads and Navigations. For Taxes Operate two Ways towards the increase of national Wealth. First they Stimulate Industry to provide the Means of Payment. Secondly, they encourage Oeconomy so far as to avoid the Purchase of unnecessary Things, and keep Money in Readiness for the Tax Gatherer. Experience Shews that those Exertions of Industry and Oeconomy grow by Degrees into Habit. But in Order that Taxation may have these good Effects, the Sum which every Man is to pay, and the Period of Payment, should be certain and unavoidable.

This Digression opens the way to a comparison between foreign and domestic Loans. If the Loan be domestic, Money must be diverted from those Channels in which it would otherwise have flowed, and therefore, either the Public must give better Terms than Individuals, or there must be Money enough to supply the Wants of both. In the latter Case, if the Public did not borrow, the Quantity of Money would exceed the Demand, and the Interest would be lowered; borrowing by the Public, therefore, would keep up the Rate of Interest, which brings the latter Case within the Reason of the former. If the Public outbid Individuals, those Individuals are deprived of the Means of extending their Industry. So that no Case of a domestic Loan can well be supposed, where some public Loss will not arise to counterballance the public Gain; except when the Creditor spares from his Consumption to lend to the Government, which Operates a national Oeconomy. It is however an Advantage peculiar to domestic Loans, that they give Stability to Government, by combining together the Interests of moneyed Men for it's Support; and consequently, in this Country, a domestic Debt would greatly contribute to that Union, which seems not to have been sufficiently attended to, or provided for, in forming the national Compact. Domestic Loans are also useful from the farther Consideration that as Taxes fall heavy on the lower Orders of a Community, the Releif obtained for them by such Loans, more than counterballances the Loss sustained by those who would have borrowed Money to extend their Commerce or Tillage. Neither is it a refinement to observe, that since a Plenty of Money and consequent Ease of obtaining it, induce Men to engage in Speculations which are often unprofitable, the Check which these receive is not injurious, while the Releif obtained for the Poor is highly beneficial.

By making foreign Loans, the Community (as such) receive the same extensive Benefits which one Individual does in borrowing of another. This Country was always in the Practice of making such Loans. The Merchants in Europe trusted those of America. The American Merchants trusted the Country Storekeepers; and they the People at large. This advance of Credit may be Stated at not less than twenty Million of Dollars. And the Want of that Credit is one principle Reason of those Usurious Contracts mentioned above. These have been checked by the Institution of the Bank, but the Funds of that Corporation, not permitting those extensive Advances which the Views of different People require, the Price given for particular Accommodations of Money continues to be enormous; and that again Shews, that to make domestic Loans would be difficult if not impracticable. The Merchants not having now that extensive Credit in Europe which they formerly had, the obtaining such Credit by the Government, becomes in some Sort necessary. But there remains an Objection with many against foreign Loans, which (tho it arises from a superficial View of the Subject) has no little Influence. This is, that the Interest will form a Balance of Trade against us, and drain the Country of Specie; which is only saying in other Words, that it would be more convenient to receive Money as a Present, than as a Loan. For the Advantages derived by the Loan exist, notwithstanding the Payment of Interest. To shew this more clearly, a Case may be Stated which in this City is very familiar. An Island in the Delaware overflowed at high Water has, for a given Sum, suppose a thousand Pounds, been banked in, drained and made to produce by the Hay sold from it at Philadelphia a considerable Sum annually, for Instance two hundred Pounds. If the owner of such an Island had borrowed (in Philadelphia) the thousand Pounds to improve it, and given six per Cent Interest, he would have gained a net Revenue of one hundred and forty Pounds. This certainly would not be a Balance of Trade against his Island, nor the draining it of Specie. He would gain considerably, and the City of Philadelphia also would gain, by bringing to Market an increased Quantity of a necessary Article. In like manner, Money lent by the City of Amsterdam to clear the Forests of America, would be beneficial to both. Draining Marshes and bringing Forests under Culture are beneficial to the whole human Race, but most so to the Proprietor. But at any Rate, in a Country and in a situation like ours, to lighten the Weight of present Burthens (by Loans) must be good Policy. For as the Governments acquire more Stability, and the People more wealth, the former will be able to raise, and the latter to pay much greater Sums than can at present be expected.

What has been said on the general nature and Benefit of public Loans, as well as their particular Utility to this Country, contains more of Detail than is necessary for the United States in Congress, tho perhaps not enough for many of those to whose consideration this Subject must be Submitted. It may seem Superfluous to add that Credit is necessary to the obtaining of Loans. But among the many extraordinary Conceptions which have been produced, during the Present Revolution, it is neither the least prevalent, nor the least pernicious, that Foreigners will trust us with Millions, while our own Citizens will not trust us with a Shilling. Such an opinion must be unfounded and will appear to be false at the first Glance; Yet Men are (on some Occasions) so willing to deceive themselves, that the most flattering Expectations will be formed from the Acknowledgement of American Independance by the States General. But surely no reasonable Hope can be raised on that Circumstance, unless something more be done by ourselves. The Loans made to us hitherto, have either been by the Court of France, or on their Credit. The Government of the United Netherlands are so far from being able to lend, that they must borrow for themselves. The most therefore which can be asked from them, is to become Security for America to their own Subjects, but it cannot be expected that they will do this, untill they are assured, and convinced, that we will punctually pay. This follows necessarily from the Nature of their Government, and must be clearly seen by the Several States, as well as by Congress, if they only consider what Conduct they would pursue on a similar Occasion. Certainly Congress would not put themselves in a situation which might oblige them to call on the several States for Money to pay the Debts of a foreign Power. Since then no Aid is to be looked for from the Dutch Government, without giving them Sufficient Evidence of a Disposition and Ability to pay both the Principal and Interest of what we borrow; and since the same Evidence which would convince the Government, must convince the Individuals who compose it; Asking the Aid of Government must either be unnecessary or ineffectual. Ineffectual before the Measures taken to establish our Credit, and unnecessary afterwards.

We are therefore brought back to the Necessity of establishing public Credit. And this must be done at Home, before it can be extended abroad. The only Question which can remain, is with Respect to the Means. And here it must be remembered that a free Government whose natural offspring is public Credit, cannot have sustained a Loss of that Credit unless from particular Causes; and therefore those Causes must be investigated and removed, before the Effects will cease. When the continental Money was issued, a greater Confidence was shewn by America, than any other People ever exhibited. The general Promise of a Body not formed into, nor claiming to be a Government, was accepted as current coin, and it was not until long after an Excess of quantity had forced on Depreciation, that the Validity of these Promises was questioned. Even then the public Credit still existed in a Degree, nor was it finally lost untill March 1780, when an Idea was intertained that Government had committed Injustice. It is useless to enter into the Reasons for and against the Resolutions of that Period. They were adopted, and are now to be considered only in Relation to their Effects. These will not be altered by saying that the Resolutions were misunderstood; for in those Things which depend on public Opinion it is no matter (so far as consequences are concerned) how that opinion is influenced. Under present circumstances therefore, it may be considered as an uncontrovertible Proposition, that all paper Money ought to be absorped by Taxation (or otherwise) and destroyed before we can Expect our public Credit to be fully reestablished. For so long as there be any in Existence, the Holder will view it as a monument of national Perfidy.

But this alone would be taking only a Small Step in the important Business of establishing national Credit. There are a great Number of Individuals in the United States, who trusted the Public in the Hour of Distress, and who are impoverished, and even ruined by the Confidence they reposed. There are others, whose Property has been wrested from them by Force to Support the War, and to whom Certificates have been given in lieu of it which are entirely useless. It needed not Inspiration to shew, that Justice establisheth a Nation, neither are the Principles of Religion necessary to evince, that political Injustice will receive political Chastizement. Religious Men will cherish these Maxims in proportion to the additional Force they derive from divine Revelation. But our own Experience will Shew, that from a Defect of Justice this Nation is not established; and that her Want of Honesty is severely punished by the Want of Credit. To this Want of Credit must be attributed the Weight of Taxation for Support of the War, and the Continuance of that Weight by Continuance of the War. It is therefore with the greatest Propriety your Petitioners already mentioned have stated in their Memorial, that both Policy and Justice require a solid Provision for funding the public Debts. It is with Pleasure Sir that I see this numerous, meritorious and oppressed Body of Men, who are Creditors of the public, beginning to exert themselves for the obtaining of Justice. I hope they may succeed, not only because I wish well to a righteous Pursuit, but because this Success will be the great Ground work of a Credit which will carry us safely thro the present just, important and necessary War, which will combine us closely together on the Conclusion of a Peace, which will always give to the Supreme Representative of America a Means of acting for the general Defence on Sudden Emergencies, and which will, of consequence, procure the Third of those great Objects for which we contend, *Peace, Liberty, and Safety.*

Such Sir are the cogent Principles by which we are called on to provide solid Funds for the national Debt. Already Congress have adopted a Plan for liquidating all past Accounts; and if the States shall make the necessary Grants of Revenue, what remains will be a simple executive Operation which will presently be explained. But however powerful the Reasons in favor of such Grants, over and above those Principles of moral Justice which none, however exalted, can part from with Impunity, still there are Men who (influenced by penurious selfishness) will grumble at the Expence, and who will assert the impossibility of sustaining it. On this Occasion the Sensations with Respect to borrowing are reversed. All would be content to relieve themselves, by Loan, from the Weight of Taxes, but many are unwilling to take up, as they ought, the Weight of Debt. Yet this must be done, before the other can happen, and it is not so great but that we Should find immediate Releif by assuming it, *even if it were a foreign Debt.* I say if it were a *foreign* Debt, because I shall attempt to shew, first that being *a domestic Debt,* to fund it will cost the Community Nothing and secondly that it will produce (on the Contrary) a considerable Advantage. And as to the first Point, one

Observation will Suffice. The Expenditure has been made, and *a Part* of the Community have sustained it. If the Debt were to be paid, by a single Effort of Taxation; it could only create a Transfer of Property from one Individual to another, and the agregate Wealth of the Whole Community would be precisely the same. But since Nothing more is attempted than merely to fund the Debt by providing for the Interest (at six per Cent) The Question of Ability is resolved to this single Point, whether it is easier for *a Part of the people* to pay one hundred Dollars, than for the *whole People* to pay six Dollars. It is equally clear, tho' not equally evident, that a considerable Advantage would be produced, by funding our Debts, over and above what has been already mentioned, as the Consequence of National Credit. This Advantage is threefold. First, many Persons by being Creditors of the Public, are deprived of those Funds which are necessary to the full Exercise of their Skill and Industry. Consequently the Community are deprived of the Benefits which would result from that Exercise, whereas if these Debts which are in a manner dead, were brought back to existence, monied men would purchase them up (tho perhaps at a considerable Discount) and thereby restore to the Public many useful Members who are now entirely lost; and extend the Operations of many more to considerable Advantage. For altho not one additional Shilling would be, by this Means, brought in; yet by distributing Property into those Hands which could render it most productive, the Revenue would be increased, while the original Stock continued the Same. Secondly, many Foreigners who make Speculations to this Country would, instead of ordering back Remittances, direct much of the Proceeds of their Cargoes to be invested in our public Funds; which, according to Principles already established, would produce a clear Advantage, with this Addition (from peculiar Circumstances) that it would Supply the Want of Credit to the mercantile Part of Society. The last, but not least, Advantage is, that in restoring Ease, Harmony and Confidence, not only the Government (being more respectable) would be more respected, and consequently better obeyed; but the mutual Dealings among Men, on private Credit, would be facilitated. The Horrors which agitate People's Minds, from an Apprehension of depreciating Paper, would be done away. The secret Hoards would be unlocked. In the same Moment, the Necessity of Money would be lessened, and the Quantity increased. By these Means the Collection of Taxes would be facilitated, and thus, instead of being Obliged to give valuable Produce for useless Minerals, that Produce would purchase the Things we stand in need of, and we should obtain a sufficient circulating Medium, by giving the People what they have always a Right to Demand, solid Assurance in the Integrity of their Rulers.

The next Consideration which Offers, is the Amount of the public Debt, and every good American must lament that Confusion in public Affairs, which renders an accurate State of it unattainable. But it must continue to be so, until all accounts both at Home and abroad be finally adjusted. The enclosed is an Estimate furnished by the Comptroller of the Treasury, from which it appears that there is already an acknowledged Debt, bearing Interest, to the Amount of more than twelve Million of Dollars. On Part of this also there is a large arrearage of Interest, and there is a very considerable Debt unsetled, the Evidence whereof exists in various Certificates given for Property applied to the public Service. This (including Pay due to the army previous to the present Year) cannot be estimated at less than between seven and eight Millions. Our Debt to his most Christian Majesty is above five Millions. The nearest Guess therefore, which can be made at the Sum total, is from twenty five to twenty seven million of Dollars, and if to this we add what it may be necessary to borrow for the Year 1783 the Amount will be (with Interest) by the Time proper Revenues are obtained, considerably above thirty Millions. Of course the Interest will be between eighteen hundred Thousand and two Million Dollars. And here, previous to the Consideration of proper Revenues for that Amount, it may not be amiss to make a few general Observations. The first of which is, that it would be injurious to the United States to obtain Money on Loan without providing before hand the necessary Funds. For if those who are now so deeply engaged to Support the War, will not grant such Funds to procure immediate Relief, certainly those who come after them will not do it, to pay a former Debt. Remote Objects, dependent on abstract Reasoning, never influence the Mind like immediate Sensibility. It is therefore the Province of Wisdom to direct towards proper Objects that Sensibility which is the only Motive to Action among the Mass of Mankind. Should we be able to get Money from the Dutch, without first providing Funds, which is more than doubtful; and should the several States neglect, afterwards, making

Provision to perform the Engagements of Congress, which is more than probable; the Credit of the United States, abroad, would be ruined for ever. Very Serious Discussions also might be raised among foreign Powers, our Creditors might have Recourse to arms, and we might dishonorably be compelled to do, what dishonestly we had left undone. Secondly, the Idea which many entertain of soliciting Loans abroad to pay the Interest of ~~our~~ domestic Debts, is a Measure pregnant with it's own Destruction. If the States were to grant Revenues sufficient only to pay the Interest of present Debts, we might perhaps obtain new Credit, upon a general Opinion of our Justice, tho' that is far from certain. But when we omit paying, by Taxes, the Interest of Debts already contracted, and ask to borrow for the Purpose, making the same Promises to obtain the new Loans which had been already made to obtain the Old, we shall surely be disappointed. Thirdly, it will be necessary, not only that Revenues be granted, but that those Revenues be amply sufficient for the Purpose, because (as will presently appear) a Deficiency would be highly pernicious, while an Excess would be not only unprejudicial but very advantageous. To perceive this with all necessary Clearness, it must be remembered that the Revenues asked for on this Occasion must be appropriated to the Purposes for which they are asked, and in like Manner the Sums required for current Expenditure, must be appropriated to the current Service. If then the former be deficient, the latter cannot be brought in to Supply the Deficiencys and, of course, the public Credit would be impaired; but should there be an Excess of Revenue, it could be applied in Payment of a Part of the Debt immediately, and in such Case if the Credits should have depreciated, they would be raised to Par, and if already at Par, the Offer of Payment would induce Creditors to lower the Interest. Thus in either Case, the Means of making new Loans on good Terms would be extended, and the Necessity of asking more Revenues obviated. Lastly, these Revenues ought to be of such a Nature as naturally and necessarily to increase; for Creditors will have a greater Confidence when they have a clear Prospect of being repaid, and the People will always be desirious to see a like Prospect of Releif from the Taxes. Besides which, it will be necessary to incur some considerable Expence after the War in making necessary Establishments for a permanent naval Force, and it will always be least objectionable to borrow, for that Purpose, on Funds already established.

The Requisition of a five per Cent Impost, made on the third Day of February 1781, has not yet been complied with by the State of Rhode Island; but as there is Reason to beleive that their Compliance is not far off, this Revenue may be considered as being already granted. It will however be very inadequate to the Purposes intended. If Goods be imported and Prizes introduced to the Amount of twelve Millions annually, the five per Cent would be six hundred thousand, from which at least one sixth must be deducted, as well for the Cost of Collection, as for the various Defalcations which will necessarily happen, and which it is unnecessary to enumerate. It is not safe therefore to estimate this Revenue at more than half a Million of Dollars, for tho it may produce more, yet probably it will not produce so much. It was in Consequence of this that, on the twenty seventh Day of February last, I took the Liberty to Submit the Propriety of asking the States for a Land Tax of one Dollar for every hundred Acres of Land, a Poll Tax of one Dollar on all freemen, and all male Slaves between sixteen and sixty (excepting such as are in the federal Army, and such as are by Wounds or otherwise rendered unfit for Service) and an Excise of one eighth of [a] Dollar, per Gallon, on all distilled Spirituous Liquors. Each of these may be estimated at half a Million, and should the Product be equal to the estimation, the Sum total of Revenues for funding the public Debts, would be equal to two Millions. What has been the Fate of these Propositions I know not, but I will beg leave, on this Occasion, not only to renew them but also to state some Reasons in their favor, and answer some Objections against them.

And first, as to a Land Tax. The Advantages of it are, that it can be reduced to a Certainty as to the Amount and Time. That no extraordinary Means are necessary to ascertain it. And that Land, being the ultimate Object of human Avarice, and that particular Species of permanent Property which so peculiarly belongs to a Country as neither to be removed nor concealed, it stands foremost for the Object of Taxation; and ought most particularly to be burthened with those Debts which have been incurred by defending the Freedom of its Inhabitants. But besides these general Reasons, there are some which are in a Manner peculiar to this Country. The Land of America may, as to the Proprietors, be divided into two Kinds, that which belongs to the great Landholders and that which is owned and occupied by the industrious Cultivator. This latter Class of Citizens is, generally speaking, the most numerous and most valuable part of a Community. The Artisan may, under any Government minister to the Luxuries of the Rich, and the Rich may, under any Government, obtain the Luxuries they covet. But the free Husbandman is the natural Guardian of his Country's Freedom. A Land Tax will probably, at the first mention, startle this Order of Men, but it can only be from the Want of Reflection, or the Delusion must be kept up by the Artifice of others. To him who cultivates from one to five hundred Acres, a Dollar per hundred is a trifling Object; but to him who owns an hundred Thousand it is important. Yet a large Proportion of America is the Property of great Landholders, they monopolize it without Cultivation; they are (for the most Part) at no Expence either of Money or personal Service to defend it; and, keeping the Price higher by Monopoly than otherwise it would be, they impede the Settlement and Culture of the Country. A Land Tax, therefore, would have the salutary Operation of an Agrarian Law, without the Iniquity. It would relieve the Indigent, and aggrandize the State, by bringing Property into the Hands of those who would use it for the Benefit of Society. The Objections against such a Tax are twofold, first that it is unequal, and secondly that it is too high. To obviate the Inequality, some have proposed an Estimate of the Value of different Kinds of Lands. But this would be improper, because first it would be attended with great Delay, Expence and Inconvenience. Secondly it would be uncertain, and therefore Improper, particularly when considered as a Fund for public Debts. Thirdly, there is no reason to beleive that any Estimate would be just; and even if it were, it must be annually varied or else come within the Force of the Objection as strongly as ever; the former would cost more than the Tax, and the latter would not afford the Remedy asked for. Lastly, such Valuations would operate as a Tax upon Industry, and promote that Land Monopoly which every wise Government will study to repress. But further, the true Remedy for any Inequality will be obtained in the Apportioning other Taxes, of which there will always be enough to equalize this. Besides, the Tax being permanent and fixed, it is considered in the Price of Land on every Transfer of Property, and that produces a Degree of Equality which no Valuation could possibly arrive at. In a word, if exact numerical Proportion be sought after in Taxes, there would be no End to the Search. Not only might a Poll Tax be objected to as too heavy on the Poor and too light on the rich, but when that Objection was obviated, the phisical Differences in the human Frame would alone be as endless a Source of Contention, as the different Qualities of Land. The second Objection that the Tax is too high, is equally futile with the former. Land which is so little worth that the Owner will not pay annually one Penny per Acre for the Defence of it, ought to belong to the Society by whom the Expence of defending it is defrayed. But the Truth is that this Objection arises from, and is enforced by, those Men who can very well bear the Expence, but who wish to shift it from themselves to others. I shall close this Subject by adding, that as such a Tax would, besides the Benefits to be derived from the Object of it, have the farther Advantage of encouraging Settlements and Population, This would redound, not only to the national Good, but even to the particular Good of the Land holders themselves.

With Respect to the Poll-Tax there are many Objections against it, but in some of the States a more considerable Poll Tax already exists, without Inconvenience. The Objections are principally drawn from Europe, by Men who do not consider that a Difference of Circumstances makes a very material Difference in the Nature of political Operations. In some Parts of Europe, where nine tenths of the People are exhausted by continual Labor to procure bad cloathing and worse Food, this Tax would be extremely oppressive. But in America, where three Days of labor produce Sustenance for a week, it is not unreasonable to ask two Days out of a year as a Contribution to the Payment of public Debts. Such a Tax will, on the Rich, be next to Nothing, on the midling Ranks it will be of little consequence, and it cannot affect the Poor, because such of them as are unable to labor will fall within the Exception proposed. In fact, the Situation of America differs so widely from that of Europe, as to the matter now under Consideration, that hardly any Maxim which applies to one will be alike applicable to the other. Labor is in such Demand among us, that the Tax will fall on the Consumer. An able bodied Man who demands one hundred Dollars Bounty to go into military Service, for three Years, cannot be oppressed by the annual Payment of one Dollar, while not in that Service. This Tax also will have the good Effect of placing before the Eyes of Congress the Number of Men in the Several States; an Information always important to Government.

The Excise proposed is liable to no other Objection than what may be made against the Mode of Collection; but it is conceived that this may be such as can produce no ill Consequences. Excise Laws exist, and have long existed, in the several States. Of all Taxes those on the Consumption of Articles are most agreeable; because, being mingled with the price, they are less sensible to the People. And without entering into a Discussion with which Speculative Men have amused themselves, on the Advantages and Disadvantages of this Species of Taxation, it may be boldly affirmed that no Inconvenience can arise from laying a heavy Tax on the Use of ardent Spirits. These have always been equally prejudicial to the Constitutions and Morals of the People. The Tax will be a Means of compelling Vice to support the Cause of Virtue; and, like the Poll Tax, will draw from the Idle and Dissolute that Contribution to the public Service, which they will not otherwise make.

Having said thus much on the Propriety of these Taxes, I shall pray leave to assure you of my ready Acquiescence in the Choice of any others which may be more agreeable to the United States in Congress; praying them nevertheless to consider, that as the Situation of the respective States is widely different, it will be wise to adopt a Variety of Taxes, because by that Means the Consent of all will be more readily obtained, than if such are chosen as will fall heavy only on particular States. The next Object is the Collection, which for the most obvious Reasons ought to be by Authority derived from the United States. The collecting of a Land Tax, as has been observed above, will be very simple. That of the Poll Tax may be equally so, because Certificates of the Payment may annually be issued to the Collectors, and they be bound to return the Certificates or the Money, and empowered to compel a Payment by every Man not possessed of a Certificate. If, in addition to this, those who travel from one State to another be obliged to take out and pay for a new Certificate in each State, that would operate an useful Regulation of Police; and a slight Distinction between those and the common Certificates, would still preserve their Utility in numbering the People. It is not necessary to dwell on the Mode of collecting these Branches of Revenue, because (in Reason) a Determin[ation] on the Propriety of the Taxes should precede it. I will only take the Liberty to drop one Idea with Respect to the Impost already required. It is conceived that Laws should be so formed, as to leave little, or nothing, to the Discretion of those by whom they are executed. That Revenue Laws in particular should be guarded in this Respect from odium, being (as they are) sufficiently odious in themselves. And, therefore, that it would have been well to have stipulated the precise Sum payable on different Species of Commodities. The Objection is, that the List (to be accurate) must be numerous. But this accuracy is unnecessary, the Description ought to be very Short and General, so as to comprize many Commodities under one Head; and the Duty ought to be fixed according to their average Value. The Objection against this Regulation is, that the Tax on fine Commodities would be trivial, and on coarse Commodities great. This indeed is true, but it is desirable for two Reasons. First, that coarse and bulky Commodities *could* not be smuggled to evade the *heavy* Duty; and that fine Commodities *would* not be smuggled to evade the *light* Duty. Secondly, that coarse Commodities (generally speaking) minister to the Demands of Necessity or Convenience, and fine Commodities to those of Luxury. The heavy Duty on the former would operate an Encouragement to produce them at Home, and by that Means a Stoppage of our Commerce in Time of War would be most felt by the Wealthy, who have always the most abundant Means of procuring Relief.

I shall now Sir take the Liberty to Suppose, that the Revenues I have mentioned, or some others to the Amount of at least two Millions net annual Produce, were asked for and obtained, as a Pledge to the public Creditors; to continue untill the Principal and Interest of the Debts contracted, or to be contracted, should be finally paid. This Supposition is made that I may have an Opportunity (thus early) to express my Sentiments on the Mode of Appropriation. It would be as follows. Any one of the Revenues, being estimated, a Loan should be opened on the Credit of it, by Subscription, to a certain Amount and public Debts of a particular Description (or Specie) be received in Payment of the Subscriptions. This funded Debt should be transferable, under particular Forms, calculated for the Prevention of fraudulent, and facilitating of honest Negotiations. In like Manner on each of these Revenues should Subscriptions be opened, proceeding by Degrees so as to prevent any sudden

Revolutions in Money Matters; such Revolutions being always more or less injurious. I should farther propose, that the Surplus of each of these Revenues (and Care should be taken that there would be a Surplus) should be carried to a Sinking Fund, on the Credit of which, and of the general Promises of Government new Loans should be opened, when necessary. The Interest should be paid half yearly; which would be convenient to the Creditors and to the Government, as well as useful to the People at large: because by this Means, if four different Loans were opened at different Times, the Interest would be payable eight Times in the Year, and thus the Money would be paid out of the Treasury as fast as it came in, which would require fewer Officers to manage the Business, keep them in more constant and regular Employment, dispense the Interest so as to command the Confidence and facilitate the Views of the Creditors, and return speedily the Wealth obtained by Taxes into the Common Stock. I know it will be objected, that such a Mode of Administration would enable Speculators to perform their Operations. A general Answer to this would be, that any other Mode would be more favorable to them. But farther, I conceive, first, that it is much beneath the Dignity of Government to intermeddle in such Considerations. Secondly, that Speculators always do least Mischief where they are left most at Liberty. Thirdly, that it is not in human Prudence to counteract their Operations by Laws; whereas when left alone they invariably counteract each other. And fourthly, that even if it were possible to prevent Speculation, it is precisely the Thing which ought not to be prevented; because he who wants Money to commence, pursue or extend his Business, is more benefited by selling Stock of any Kind (even at a considerable Discount) than he could be by the Rise of it at a future Period; Every Man being able to judge better of his own Business and Situation, than the Government can for him. So much would not, perhaps, have been said on the Head of this Objection, if it did not naturally lead to a Position which has been ruinous and might prove fatal. There are many Men (and some of them honest Men) whose Zeal against Speculation leads them to be sometimes unmindful, not only of sound Policy, but even of Moral Justice. It is not uncommon to hear, that those who have bought the public Debts for small Sums, ought only to be paid their purchase Money. The Reasons given are, that they have taken Advantage of the distressed Creditor, and shewn a Diffidence in the public Faith. As to the first, it must be remembered that in giving the Creditor Money for his Debt, they have at least afforded him some Relief, which he could not obtain elsewhere; and if they are deprived of the expected Benefit, they never will afford such Relief again. As to the Second, those who buy up the public Debts shew at least as much Confidence, in the public faith, as those who sell them; but allowing (for Argument's sake) that they have exhibited the Diffidence complained of, it would certainly be wiser to remove than to Justify it. The one Mode tends to create, establish and secure public Credit; and the other to sap, overturn and destroy it. Policy is therefore on this (as I believe it to be on every other occasion) upon the same Side of the Question with Honesty. Honesty tells us, that the Duty of the Public to pay is like the same Duty in an Individual. Having benefited by the Advances, they are bound to replace them to the Party, or to his Representatives. The Debt is a Species of Property, and whether disposed of for the whole nominal Value, or the half, for something or for Nothing, is totally immaterial. The Right of receiving, and the Duty of paying, must always continue the same. In a word, that Government which can (thro' the Intervention of its Courts) compel Payment of private Debts, and Performance of private Contracts, on Principles of distributive Justice, but refuse to be guided by those Principles, as to their own Contracts and Debts, merely because they are not amenable to human Laws, shews a flagitious Contempt of moral Obligations, which must necessarily weaken, as it ought to do, their Authority over the People.

Before I conclude this long Letter, it would be unpardonable not to mention a Fund which has long since been suggested, and dwells still in the Minds of many. You Doubtless Sir anticipate my naming of what are called the back Lands. The question as to the Property of those Lands, I confess myself utterly incompetent to decide, and shall not, for that Reason, presume to enter on it. But it is my Duty to mention, that the offer of a Pledge the Right to which is contested, would have ill Consequences, and could have no Good ones. It could not strengthen our Credit because no one would rely on such a Pledge, and the Recurrence to it would give unfavorable Impressions of our political Sagacity. But admitting that the Right of Congress is clear, we must remember also, that it is disputed by some considerable Members of the Confederacy. Dissentions might arise from hasty Decissions on this Subject, and a Government torne by intestine

Commotions, is not likely to acquire or maintain Credit, at Home or abroad. I am not however the less clear in my Opinion, that it would be alike useful to the whole Nation, and to those very constituent Parts of it, that the entire Disposition of these Lands should be in Congress. Without entering therefore into the litigated Points, I am induced to beleive, and for that Reason to suggest the proposing this Matter to the States as an amicable Arrangement. I hope to be pardoned when I add, that considering the Situation of South Carolina and Georgia, it might be proper to ask their Consent to Matters of the clearest Right. But that, supposing the Right to be doubtful, urging a Decision in the present Moment might have a harsh and ungenerous Appearance. But if we suppose this matter to be arranged, either in the one Mode or in the Other, so that the Right of Congress be rendered indisputable (for that is a previous Point of indispensible Necessity) the remaining Question will be as to the Appropriation of that Fund. And I confess it does not appear to me, that the Benefits resulting from it are such as many are led to beleive. When the Imagination is heated in Pursuit of an Object, it is generally overrated. If these Lands were now in the Hands of Congress, and they were willing to mortgage them to their present Creditors, unless this were accompanied with a due Provision for the Interest, it would bring no Relief. If these Lands were to be sold for the public Debts, they would go off for almost nothing. Those who want Money could not afford to buy Land. Their Certificates would be bought up for a Trifle. Very few moneyed Men would become possessed of them, because very little money would be invested in so remote a Speculation. The small Number of Purchasers would easily and readily combine. Of Consequence they would acquire the Lands for almost Nothing, and effectually defeat the Intentions of Government, leaving it still under the Necessity of making farther Provision; after having needlessly squandered an immense Property. This Reasoning is not new. It has been advanced on similar Occasions before, and the Experience which all America has had of the Sales of confiscated Estates, and the like, will now shew that it was well founded. The back Lands, then, will not answer our Purpose without the necessary Revenues. But those Revenues will alone produce the desired effect. The back Lands may afterwards be formed into a Fund, for opening new Loans in Europe on a low Interest, redeemable within a future Period (for Instance twenty Years) with a right reserved to the Creditors of taking Portions of those Lands, on the Non Payment of their Debts, at the Expiration of that Term. Two Modes would offer for Liquidation of those Debts. First to tender Payment during the Term, to those who would not consent to alter the Nature of the Debt; which (if our Credit be well established) would place it on the general Footing of national Faith. And Secondly, to sell Portions of the Land (during the Term) sufficient to discharge the Mortgage. I perswade myself that the Consent of the reluctant States might be obtained, and that this Fund might hereafter be converted to useful Purposes. But I hope that, in a Moment when the Joint Effort of all is indispensible, no Causes of Altercation may be mingled, unnecessarily, in a question of such infinite Magnitude as the Restoration of public Credit. Let me add, Sir, that unless the Money of Foreigners be brought in for the Purpose, Sales of public Land would only absorp that Surplus Wealth, which might have been exhaled by Taxes, so that in Fact no new Resource is produced. And that, while (as at present) the Demand for Money is so great as to raise Interest to five per Cent per Month, public Lands must sell extremely low were the Title ever so clear; what then can be expected when the Validity of that Title, is one Object of the War? I have the Honor to be with great Respect your Excellency's most obedient Servant

Robt Morris

His Excellency The President of Congress

REVENUE AMENDMENTS PROPOSED
BY CONGRESS TO THE STATES
APRIL 18, 1783

RESOLVED, BY NINE STATES, That it be recommended to the several states, as indispensably necessary to the restoration of public credit, and to the punctual and honorable discharge of the public debts, to invest the United States in Congress assembled with a power to levy for the use of the United States the following duties upon goods imported into the said states from any foreign port, island or plantation:

Upon all rum of Jamaica proof per gallon, - - - - - -dols. 4–90	Upon brown sugar per pound, - - - - $\frac{1}{2}$–90
Upon all other spirituous liquors, - - - 3–90	Upon loaf sugar per pound, - - - - 2–90
Upon Madeira wine, - 12–90	Upon all other sugars, 1–90
Upon all other wines, - 6–90	Upon molasses per gallon, - - - - - 1–90
Upon common bohea tea per lb. - - - 6–90	Upon cocoa and coffee per pound, - - - 1–90
Upon all other teas, - 24–90	Upon all other goods, a duty of five per cent. ad valorem at the time and place of importation.
Upon pepper per pound, - - - - 3–90	

Provided, that none of the said duties shall be applied to any other purpose than the discharge of the interest or principal of the debts contracted on the faith of the United States, for supporting the war, agreeably to the resolution of the 16 day of December last, nor be continued for a longer term than twenty-five years: and provided, that the collectors of the said duties shall be appointed by the states, within which their offices are to be respectively exercised, but when so appointed, shall be amenable to, and removable by the United States in Congress assembled, alone; and in case any State shall not make such appointment within one month after notice given for that purpose, the appointment may be made by the United States in Congress assembled:

That it be further recommended to the several states, to establish for a term limited to twenty-five years, and to appropriate to the discharge of the interest and principal of the debts contracted on the faith of the United States for supporting the war, substantial and effectual revenues of such nature as they may judge most convenient, for supplying their respective proportions of one million five hundred thousand dollars annually, exclusive of the aforementioned duties, which proportion shall be fixed and equalized, from time to time, according to the rule which is or may be prescribed by the Articles of Confederation; and in case the revenues established by any State shall at any time yield a sum exceeding its actual proportion, the excess shall be refunded to it; and in case the revenues of any State shall be found to be deficient, the immediate deficiency shall be made up by such State with as little delay as possible, and a future deficiency guarded against by an enlargement of the revenues established: provided that until the rule of the Confederation can be carried into practice, the proportions of the said 1,500,000 dollars shall be as follows, viz.

New Hampshire, - -	52,708	Maryland, - - - -	141,517
Massachusetts, - -	224,427	Virginia, - - - -	256,487
Rhode Island, - - -	32,318	North Carolina, - -	109,006
Connecticut, - - -	132,091	South Carolina, - -	96,183
New York, - - - -	128,243	Georgia, - - - -	16,030
New Jersey, - - -	83,358		
Pensylvania, - - -	205,189		1,500,000
Delaware, - - - -	22,443		

The said last mentioned revenues to be collected by persons appointed as aforesaid, but to be carried to the seperate credit of the states within which they shall be collected.

That an annual account of the proceeds and application of all the aforementioned revenues, shall be made out and transmitted to the several states, distinguishing the proceeds of each of the specified articles, and the amount of the whole revenue received from each State, together with the allowances made to the several officers employed in the collection of the said revenues.

That none of the preceding resolutions shall take effect until all of them shall be acceded to by every State, after which unanimous accession, however, they shall be considered as forming a mutual compact among all the states, and shall be irrevocable by any one or more of them without the concurrence of the whole, or of a majority of the United States in Congress assembled.

That as a further mean, as well of hastening the extinguishment of the debts as of establishing the harmony of the United States, it be recommended to the states which have passed no acts towards complying with the resolutions of Congress of the 6th of September and 10th of October, 1780, relative to the cession of territorial claims, to make the liberal cessions therein recommended, and to the states which may have passed acts complying with the said resolutions in part only, to revise and complete such compliance.

That as a more convenient and certain rule of ascertaining the proportions to be supplied by the states respectively to the common treasury, the following alteration in the Articles of Confederation and perpetual union, between these states be, and the same is hereby agreed to in Congress; and the several states are advised to authorise their respective delegates to subscribe and ratify the same as part of the said instrument of union, in the words following, to wit:

So much of the 8th of the Articles of Confederation and perpetual union, between the thirteen states of America, as is contained in the words following, to wit:

"All charges of war and all other expences that shall be incurred for the common defence or general welfare, and allowed by the United States in Congress assembled, shall be defrayed out of a common treasury, which shall be supplied by the several states in proportion to the value of all land within each State granted to or surveyed for any person, as such land and the buildings and improvements thereon shall be estimated according to such mode as the United States in Congress assembled shall, from time to time, direct and appoint," is hereby revoked and made void; and in place thereof it is declared and concluded, the same having been agreed to in a Congress of the United States, that "all charges of war and all other expences that have been or shall be incurred for the common defence or general welfare, and allowed by the United States in Congress assembled, except so far as shall be otherwise provided for, shall be defrayed out of a common treasury, which shall be supplied by the several states in proportion to the whole number of white and other free citizens and inhabitants, of every age, sex and condition, including those bound to servitude for a term of years, and three-fifths of all other persons not comprehended in the foregoing description, except Indians, not paying taxes, in each State; which number shall be triennially taken and transmitted to the United States in Congress assembled, in such mode as they shall direct and appoint."

COMMERCIAL AMENDMENTS PROPOSED BY CONGRESS TO THE STATES

APRIL 30, 1784

THE REPORT BEING AMENDED was agreed to as follows:

The trust reposed in Congress, renders it their duty to be attentive to the conduct of foreign nations, and to prevent or restrain, as far as may be, all such proceedings as might prove injurious to the United States. The situation of Commerce at this time claims the attention of the several states, and few objects of greater importance can present themselves to their notice. The fortune of every citizen is interested in the success thereof; for it is the constant source of wealth and incentive to industry; and the value of our produce and our land must ever rise or fall in proportion to the prosperous or adverse state of trade.

Already has Great Britain adopted regulations destructive of our commerce with her West India islands. There was reason to expect that measures so unequal and so little calculated to promote mercantile intercourse, would not be persevered in by an enlightened nation. But these measures are growing into system. It would be the duty of Congress, as it is their wish, to meet the attempts of Great Britain with similar restrictions on her commerce; but their powers on this head are not explicit, and the propositions made by the legislatures of the several states, render it necessary to take the general sense of the Union on this subject.

Unless the United States in Congress assembled shall be vested with powers competent to the protection of commerce, they can never command reciprocal advantages in trade; and without these, our foreign commerce must decline, and eventually be annihilated. Hence it is necessary that the states should be explicit, and fix on some effectual mode by which foreign commerce, not founded on principles of equality, may be restrained.

That the United States may be enabled to secure such terms, they have

Resolved, That it be, and it hereby is recommended to the legislatures of the several states, to vest the United States in Congress assembled, for the term of fifteen years, with power to prohibit any goods, wares or merchandize from being imported into or exported from any of the states, in vessels belonging to or navigated by the subjects of any power with whom these states shall not have formed treaties of Commerce.

Resolved, That it be, and it hereby is recommended to the legislatures of the several states, to vest the United States in Congress assembled, for the term of fifteen years, with the power of prohibiting the subjects of any foreign state, kingdom or empire, unless authorised by treaty, from importing into the United States any goods, wares or merchandise, which are not the produce or manufacture of the dominions of the sovereign whose subjects they are.

Provided, That to all acts of the United States in Congress assembled, in pursuance of the above powers, the assent of nine states shall be necessary.

AMENDMENTS CONSIDERED BY CONGRESS
AUGUST 7, 1786

THE GRAND COMMITTEE CONSISTING of M.ʳ [Samuel] Livermore, M.ʳ [Nathan] Dane, M.ʳ [James] Manning, M.ʳ [William Samuel] Johnson, M.ʳ [Melancton] Smith, M.ʳ [John Cleves] Symmes, M.ʳ [Charles] Pettit, M.ʳ [William] Henry, M.ʳ [Henry] Lee, M.ʳ [Timothy] Blood-worth, M.ʳ [Charles] Pinckney and M.ʳ [William] Houstoun appointed to report such amendments to the confederation, and such resolutions as it may be necessary to recommend to the several states for the purpose of obtaining from them such powers as will render the federal government adequate to the ends for which it was instituted.

Beg leave to submit the following Report to the consideration of Congress:

Resolved, That it be recommended to the Legislatures of the several States to adopt the following Articles as Articles of the Confederation, and to authorise their Delegates in Congress to sign and ratify the same severally as they shall be adopted, to wit:

ART. 14. The United States in Congress Assembled shall have the sole and exclusive power of regulating the trade of the States as well with foreign Nations as with each other and of laying such prohibitions and such Imposts and duties upon imports and exports as may be Necessary for the purpose; provided the Citizens of the States shall in no instance be subjected to pay higher duties and Imposts that those imposed on the subjects of foreign powers, provided also, that all such duties as may be imposed shall be collected under such regulations as the united States in Congress Assembled shall establish consistent with the Constitutions of the States Respectively and to accrue to the use of the State in which the same shall be payable; provided also, that the Legislative power of the several States shall not be restrained from laying embargoes in time of Scarcity and provided lastly that every Act of Congress for the above purpose shall have the assent of Nine States in Congress Assembled, and in that proportion when there shall be more than thirteen in the Union.

ART. 15. That the respective States may be induced to perform the several duties mutually and solemnly agreed to be performed by their federal Compact, and to prevent unreasonable delays in any State in furnishing her just proportion of the common Charges of the Union when called upon, and those essential evils which have heretofore often arisen to the Confederacy from such delays, it is agreed that whenever a requisition shall be made by Congress upon the several States on the principles of the Confederation for their quotas of the common charges or land forces of the Union Congress shall fix the proper periods when the States shall pass Legislative Acts complying therewith and give full and compleat effect to the same and if any State shall neglect, seasonably to pass such Acts such State shall be charged with an additional sum to her quota called for from the time she may be required to pay or furnish the same, which additional sum or charge shall be at the rate of ten per Cent pr. annum on her said Quota, and if the requisition shall be for Land forces, and any State shall neglect to furnish her quota in time the average expence of such quota shall be ascertained by Congress, and such State shall be charged therewith, or with the average expence of what she may be deficient and in addition thereto from the time her forces were required to be ready to act in the field with a farther sum which sum shall be at the rate of twelve per Cent per Annum on the amount of such expences.

ART. 16. And that the resources of any State which may be negligent in furnishing her just proportion of the Common expence of the Union may in a reasonable time be applied, it is further agreed that if any State shall so Neglect as aforesaid to pass laws in compliance with the said Requisition and to adopt measures to give the same full effect for the space of Ten months, and it shall then or afterwards be found that a Majority of the States have passed such laws and adopted such measures the United States in Congress Assembled shall have full power and authority to levy, assess, and collect all sums and duties with which any such state so neglecting to comply with the requisition may stand charged on the same by the Laws and Rules by which the last State tax next preceeding such requisition in such State was levied, assessed and Collected, to apportion the sum so required on the Towns or Counties in such State to order the sums so apportioned to be assessed by the assessors of such last State tax and the said assessments to be committed to the Collector of the same last State tax to collect and to make returns of such assessments and Commitments to the Treasurer of the United States who by himself or his deputy, when directed by Congress shall have power to recover the monies of such Collectors for the use of the United States in the same manner and under the same penalties as State taxes are recovered and collected by the Treasurers of the respective States and the several Towns or Counties respectively shall be responsible for the conduct of said Assessors and Collectors and in case there shall be any vacancy in any of said Offices of Assessors or Collectors by death, removal, refusal to serve, resignation or otherwise, then other fit persons shall be chosen to fill such Vacancies in the usual manner in such Town or County within Twenty days after Notice of the assessment, and in case any Towns or Counties, any assessor, Collectors or Sheriffs shall Neglect or refuse to do their duty Congress shall have the same rights and powers to compel them that the State may have in assessing and collecting State Taxes.

And if any state by any Legislative Act shall prevent or delay the due Collection of said sums as aforesaid, Congress shall have full power and authority to appoint assessors and Collectors thereof and Sheriffs to enforce the Collections under the warrants of distress issued by the Treasurer of the United States, and if any further opposition shall be made to such Collections by the State or the Citizens thereof, and their conduct not disapproved of by the State, such conduct on the part of the State shall be considered as an open Violation of the federal compact.

ART. 17. And any State which from time to time shall be found in her payments on any Requisition in advance on an average of the payments made by the State shall be allowed an interest of ~~six~~ _____ per Cent pr. annum on her said advanced sums or expences and the State which from time to time shall be found in arrear on the principles aforesaid shall be charged with an Interest of ~~six~~ _____ per Cent pr. annum on the sums in which she may be so in arrear.

ART. 18. In case it shall hereafter be found Necessary by Congress to establish any new Systems of Revenue and to make any new regulations in the finances of the U. S. for a limited term not exceeding fifteen years in their operation for supplying the common Treasury with monies for defraying all charges of war, and all other expences that shall be incurred for the common defence or general welfare, and such new Systems or regulations shall be agreed to and adopted by the United States in Congress Assembled and afterwards be confirmed by the Legislatures of eleven States and in that proportion when there shall be more than thirteen States in the Union, the same shall become binding on all the States, as fully as if the Legislatures of all the States should confirm the same.

ART. 19. The United States in Congress Assembled shall have the sole and exclusive power of declaring what offences against the United States shall be deemed treason, and what Offences against the same Mis-prison of treason, and what Offences shall be deemed piracy or felony on the high Seas and to annex suitable punishments to all the Offences aforesaid respectively, and power to institute a federal Judicial Court for trying and punishing all officers appointed by Congress for all crimes, offences, and misbehaviour in their Offices and to which Court an Appeal shall be allowed from the Judicial Courts of the several States in all Causes wherein questions shall arise on the meaning and construction of Treaties entered into by the United States with any foreign power, or on the Law of Nations, or wherein any question shall arise respecting any regulations that may hereafter be made by Congress relative to trade and Commerce, or the Collection of federal Revenues pursuant to powers that shall be vested in that body or wherein questions of importance may arise and the United States shall be a party—provided that the trial of the fact by Jury shall ever be held sacred, and also the benefits of the writ of *Habeas Corpus;* provided also that no member of Congress or officer holding any other office under the United States shall be a Judge of said Court, and the said Court shall consist of Seven Judges, to be appointed from the different parts of the Union to wit, one from New Hampshire, Rhode Island, and Connecticut, one from Massachusetts, one from New York and New Jersey, one from Pennsylvania, one from Delaware and Maryland, one from Virginia, and one from North Carolina, South Carolina and Georgia, and four of whom shall be a quorum to do business.

Art. 20. That due attention may be given to the affairs of the Union early in the federal year, and the sessions of Congress made as short as conveniently may be each State shall elect her Delegates annually before the first of July and make it their duty to give an Answer before the first of September in every year, whether they accept their appointments or not, and make effectual provision for filling the places of those who may decline, before the first of October yearly, and to transmit to Congress by the tenth of the same month, the names of the Delegates who shall be appointed and accept their appointments, and it shall be the indispensable duty of Delegates to make a representation of their State in Congress on the first Monday in November annually, and if any Delegate or Delegates, when required by Congress to attend so far as may be Necessary to keep up a Representation of each State in Congress, or having taken his or their Seat, shall with-draw without leave of Congress, unless recalled by the State, he or they shall be proceeded against as Congress shall direct, provided no punishment shall be further extended than to disqualifications any longer to be members of Congress, or to hold any Office of trust or profit under the United States or any individual State, and the several States shall adopt regulations effectual to the attainment of the ends of this Article.

THE NORTHWEST ORDINANCE
JULY 13, 1787

An Ordinance for the government of the Territory of the United States northwest of the River Ohio.

SECTION 1. *BE IT ORDAINED by the United States in Congress assembled,* That the said territory, for the purposes of temporary government, be one district, subject, however, to be divided into two districts, as future circumstances may, in the opinion of Congress, make it expedient.

Sec 2. *Be it ordained by the authority aforesaid,* That the estates, both of resident and nonresident proprietors in the said territory, dying intestate, shall descent to, and be distributed among their children, and the descendants of a deceased child, in equal parts; the descendants of a deceased child or grandchild to take the share of their deceased parent in equal parts among them: And where there shall be no children or descendants, then in equal parts to the next of kin in equal degree; and among collaterals, the children of a deceased brother or sister of the intestate shall have, in equal parts among them, their deceased parents' share; and there shall in no case be a distinction between kindred of the whole and half blood; saving, in all cases, to the widow of the intestate her third part of the real estate for life, and one third part of the personal estate; and this law relative to descents and dower, shall remain in full force until altered by the legislature of the district. And until the governor and judges shall adopt laws as hereinafter mentioned, estates in the said territory may be devised or bequeathed by wills in writing, signed and sealed by him or her in whom the estate may be (being of full age), and attested by three witnesses; and real estates may be conveyed by lease and release, or bargain and sale, signed, sealed and delivered by the person being of full age, in whom the estate may be, and attested by two witnesses, provided such wills be duly proved, and such conveyances be acknowledged, or the execution thereof duly proved, and be recorded within one year after proper magistrates, courts, and registers shall be appointed for that purpose; and personal property may be transferred by delivery; saving, however to the French and Canadian inhabitants, and other settlers of the Kaskaskies, St. Vincents and the neighboring villages who have heretofore professed themselves citizens of Virginia, their laws and customs now in force among them, relative to the descent and conveyance, of property.

Sec. 3. *Be it ordained by the authority aforesaid,* That there shall be appointed from time to time by Congress, a governor, whose commission shall continue in force for the term of three years, unless sooner revoked by Congress; he shall reside in the district, and have a freehold estate therein in 1,000 acres of land, while in the exercise of his office.

Sec. 4. There shall be appointed from time to time by Congress, a secretary, whose commission shall continue in force for four years unless sooner revoked; he shall reside in the district, and have a freehold estate therein in 500 acres of land, while in the exercise of his office. It shall be his duty to keep and preserve the acts and laws passed by the legislature, and the public records of the district, and the proceedings of the governor in his executive department, and transmit authentic copies of such acts and proceedings, every six months, to the Secretary of Congress: There shall also be appointed a court to consist of three judges, any two of whom to form a court, who shall have a common law jurisdiction, and reside in the district, and have each therein a freehold estate in 500 acres of land while in the exercise of their offices; and their commissions shall continue in force during good behavior.

Sec. 5. The governor and judges, or a majority of them, shall adopt and publish in the district such laws of the original States, criminal and civil, as may be necessary and best suited to the circumstances of the district, and report them to Congress from time to time: which laws shall be in force in the district until the organization of the General Assembly therein, unless disapproved of by Congress; but afterwards the Legislature shall have authority to alter them as they shall think fit.

Sec. 6. The governor, for the time being, shall be commander in chief of the militia, appoint and commission all officers in the same below the rank of general officers; all general officers shall be appointed and commissioned by Congress.

Sec. 7. Previous to the organization of the general assembly, the governor shall appoint such magistrates and other civil officers in each county or township, as he shall find necessary for the preservation of the peace and good order in the same: After the general assembly shall be organized, the powers and duties of the magistrates and other civil officers shall be regulated and defined by the said assembly; but all magistrates and other civil officers not herein otherwise directed, shall during the continuance of this temporary government, be appointed by the governor.

Sec. 8. For the prevention of crimes and injuries, the laws to be adopted or made shall have force in all parts of the district, and for the execution of process, criminal and civil, the governor shall make proper divisions thereof; and he shall proceed from time to time as circumstances may require, to lay out the parts of the district in which the Indian titles shall have been extinguished, into counties and townships, subject, however, to such alterations as may thereafter be made by the legislature.

Sec. 9. So soon as there shall be five thousand free male inhabitants of full age in the district, upon giving proof thereof to the governor, they shall receive authority, with time and place, to elect a representative from their counties or townships to represent them in the general assembly: Provided, That, for every five hundred free male inhabitants, there shall be one representative, and so on progressively with the number of free male inhabitants shall the right of representation increase, until the number of representatives shall amount to twenty five; after which, the number and proportion of representatives shall be regulated by the legislature: Provided, That no person be eligible or qualified to act as a representative unless he shall have been a citizen of one of the United States three years, and be a resident in the district, or unless he shall have resided in the district three years; and, in either case, shall likewise hold in his own right, in fee simple, two hundred acres of land within the same; Provided, also, That a freehold in fifty acres of land in the district, having been a citizen of one of the states, and being resident in the district, or the like freehold and two years residence in the district, shall be necessary to qualify a man as an elector of a representative.

Sec. 10. The representatives thus elected, shall serve for the term of two years; and, in case of the death of a representative, or removal from office, the governor shall issue a writ to the county or township for which he was a member, to elect another in his stead, to serve for the residue of the term.

Sec. 11. The general assembly or legislature shall consist of the governor, legislative council, and a house of representatives. The Legislative Council shall consist of five members, to continue in office five years, unless sooner removed by Congress; any three of whom to be a quorum: and the members of the Council shall be nominated and appointed in the following manner, to wit: As soon as representatives shall be elected, the Governor shall appoint a time and place for them to meet together; and, when met, they shall nominate ten persons, residents in the district, and each possessed of a freehold in five hundred acres of land, and return their names to Congress; five of whom Congress shall appoint and commission to serve as aforesaid; and, whenever a vacancy shall happen in the council, by death or removal from office, the house of representatives shall nominate two persons, qualified as aforesaid, for each vacancy, and return their names to Congress; one of whom congress shall appoint and commission for the residue of the term. And every five years, four months at least before the expiration of the time of service of the members of council, the said house shall nominate ten persons, qualified as aforesaid, and return their names to Congress; five of whom Congress shall appoint and commission to serve as members of the council five years, unless sooner removed. And the governor, legislative council, and house of representatives, shall have authority to make laws in all cases, for the good government of the district, not repugnant to the principles and articles in this ordinance established and declared. And all bills, having passed by a majority in the house, and by a majority in the council, shall be referred to the governor for his assent; but no bill, or legislative act whatever, shall be of any force without his assent. The governor shall have power to convene, prorogue, and dissolve the general assembly, when, in his opinion, it shall be expedient.

Sec. 12. The governor, judges, legislative council, secretary, and such other officers as Congress shall appoint in the district, shall take an oath or affirmation of fidelity and of office; the governor before the president of congress, and all other officers before the Governor. As soon as a legislature shall be formed in the district, the council and house assembled in one room, shall have authority, by joint ballot, to elect a delegate to Congress, who shall have a seat in Congress, with a right of debating but not voting during this temporary government.

Sec. 13. And, for extending the fundamental principles of civil and religious liberty, which form the basis whereon these republics, their laws and constitutions are erected; to fix and establish those principles as the basis of all laws, constitutions, and governments, which forever hereafter shall be formed in the said territory: to provide also for the establishment of States, and permanent government therein, and for their admission to a share in the federal councils on an equal footing with the original States, at as early periods as may be consistent with the general interest:

Sec. 14. It is hereby ordained and declared by the authority aforesaid, That the following articles shall be considered as articles of compact between the original States and the people and States in the said territory and forever remain unalterable, unless by common consent, to wit:

Article 1. No person, demeaning himself in a peaceable and orderly manner, shall ever be molested on account of his mode of worship or religious sentiments, in the said territory.

Art. 2. The inhabitants of the said territory shall always be entitled to the benefits of the writ of habeas corpus, and of the trial by jury; of a proportionate representation of the people in the legislature; and of judicial proceedings according to the course of the common law. All persons shall be bailable, unless for capital offenses, where the proof shall be evident or the presumption great. All fines shall be moderate; and no cruel or unusual punishments shall be inflicted. No man shall be deprived of his liberty or property, but by the judgment of his peers or the law of the land; and, should the public exigencies make it necessary, for the common preservation, to take any person's property, or to demand his particular services, full compensation shall be made for the same. And, in the just preservation of rights and property, it is understood and declared, that no law ought ever to be made, or have force in the said territory, that shall, in any manner whatever, interfere with or affect private contracts or engagements, bona fide, and without fraud, previously formed.

Art. 3. Religion, morality, and knowledge, being necessary to good government and the happiness of mankind, schools and the means of education shall forever be encouraged. The utmost good faith shall always be observed towards the Indians; their lands and property shall never be taken from them without their consent; and, in their property, rights, and liberty, they shall never be invaded or disturbed, unless in just and lawful wars authorized by Congress; but laws founded in justice and humanity, shall from time to time be made for preventing wrongs being done to them, and for preserving peace and friendship with them.

Art. 4. The said territory, and the States which may be formed therein, shall forever remain a part of this Confederacy of the United States of America, subject to the Articles of Confederation, and to such alterations therein as shall be constitutionally made; and to all the acts and ordinances of the United States in Congress assembled, conformable thereto. The inhabitants and settlers in the said territory shall be subject to pay a part of the federal debts contracted or to be contracted, and a proportional part of the expenses of government, to be apportioned on them by Congress according to the same common rule and measure by which apportionments thereof shall be made on the other States; and the taxes for paying their proportion shall be laid and levied by the authority and direction of the legislatures of the district or districts, or new States, as in the original States, within the time agreed upon by the United States in Congress assembled. The legislatures of those districts or new States, shall never interfere with the primary disposal of the soil by the United States in Congress assembled, nor with any regulations Congress may find necessary for securing the title in such soil to the *bona fide* purchasers. No tax shall be imposed on lands the property of the United States; and, in no case, shall nonresident proprietors be taxed higher than residents. The navigable waters leading into the Mississippi and St. Lawrence, and the carrying places between the same, shall be common highways and forever free, as well to the inhabitants of the said territory as to the citizens of the United States, and those of any other States that may be admitted into the confederacy, without any tax, impost, or duty therefor.

Art. 5. There shall be formed in the said territory, not less than three nor more than five States; and the boundaries of the States, as soon as Virginia shall alter her act of cession, and consent to the same, shall become fixed and established as follows, to wit: The western State in the said territory, shall be bounded by the Mississippi, the Ohio, and Wabash Rivers; a direct line drawn from the Wabash and Post Vincents, due North, to the territorial line between the United States and Canada; and, by the said territorial line, to the Lake of the Woods and Mississippi. The middle State shall be bounded by the said direct line, the Wabash from Post Vincents to the Ohio, by the Ohio, by a direct line, drawn due north from the mouth of the Great Miami, to the said territorial line, and by the said territorial line. The eastern State shall be bounded by the last mentioned direct line, the Ohio, Pennsylvania, and the said territorial line: *Provided, however,* and it is further understood and declared, that the boundaries of these three States shall be subject so far to be altered, that, if Congress shall hereafter find it expedient, they shall have authority to form one or two States in that part of the said territory which lies north of an east and west line drawn through the southerly bend or extreme of Lake Michigan. And, whenever any of the said States shall have sixty thousand free inhabitants therein, such State shall be admitted, by its delegates, into the Congress of the United States, on an equal footing with the original States in all respects whatever, and shall be at liberty to form a permanent constitution and State government: *Provided,* the constitution and government so to be formed, shall be republican, and in conformity to the principles contained in these articles; and, so far as it can be consistent with the general interest of the confederacy, such admission shall be allowed at an earlier period, and when there may be a less number of free inhabitants in the State than sixty thousand.

Art. 6. There shall be neither slavery nor involuntary servitude in the said territory, otherwise than in the punishment of crimes whereof the party shall have been duly convicted: *Provided, always,* That any person escaping into the same, from whom labor or service is lawfully claimed in any one of the original States, such fugitive may be lawfully reclaimed and conveyed to the person claiming his or her labor or service as aforesaid.

Be it ordained by the authority aforesaid, That the resolutions of the 23rd of April, 1784, relative to the subject of this ordinance, be, and the same are hereby repealed and declared null and void.

Done by the United States, in Congress assembled, the 13th day of July, in the year of our Lord 1787, and of their sovereignty and independence the twelfth.

George Washington

EVEN BEFORE HIS DECISIVE victory at Yorktown in October 1781, George Washington had become the leading symbol—or the more-than-symbolic leader—of the American Revolution. By 1783 he was also becoming the most prominent and fervent advocate of American nationalism. Washington's eight years as commander-in-chief of the Continental Army seemed to embody the collective sacrifices and commitments required for victory. But Washington's vision of the American nation transcended the mere securing of independence from Britain. It was also deeply tied to the development of the interior and the generous territorial settlement that the American peace commissioners (John Jay, John Adams, and Benjamin Franklin) had secured with the Treaty of Paris. Washington had been interested in these lands since his youth, and with the arrival of peace in 1783 he looked forward to resigning his command and returning to the active management of his Mount Vernon plantation and other lands he owned.

Washington again demonstrated his commitment to republican principles during the spring of 1783. Many of his subordinates within the officer corps were angry at Congress over issues of pay and pensions, and their discontent seemed to be verging toward mutiny when Washington appeared at a general meeting called to discuss their grievances. With a single gesture and a well-delivered speech, Washington defused the officers' anger, reminding them that they had a higher calling than the fulfillment of their own ambitions.

As he prepared to retire from the army, Washington also took a role in urging the states to support the broad purposes of the Union. One of those purposes included the settlement of the national domain created by state cessions of territory above the Ohio River. Here Washington took an active role by giving Congress his ideas about the policy it should now follow toward Native Americans. Shortly afterward, he took his farewell from the army, leaving the soldiers with a final testament to their service and duty.

GEORGE WASHINGTON

—*George Washington*—
SPEECH TO THE OFFICERS OF THE ARMY
MARCH 15, 1783

HEAD QUARTERS, NEWBURGH, MARCH 15, 1783.

GENTLEMEN: BY AN ANONYMOUS summons, an attempt has been made to convene you together; how inconsistent with the rules of propriety! how unmilitary! and how subversive of all order and discipline, let the good sense of the Army decide.

In the moment of this Summons, another anonymous production was sent into circulation, addressed more to the feelings and passions, than to the reason and judgment of the Army. The author of the piece, is entitled to much credit for the goodness of his Pen and I could wish he had as much credit for the rectitude of his Heart, for, as Men see thro' different Optics, and are induced by the reflecting faculties of the Mind, to use different means, to attain the same end, the Author of the Address, should have had more charity, than to mark for Suspicion, the Man who should recommend moderation and longer forbearance, or, in other words, who should not think as he thinks, and act as he advises. But he had another plan in view, in which candor and liberality of Sentiment, regard to justice, and love of Country, have no part; and he was right, to insinuate the darkest suspicion, to effect the blackest designs.

That the Address is drawn with great Art, and is designed to answer the most insidious purposes. That it is calculated to impress the Mind, with an idea of premeditated injustice in the Sovereign power of the United States, and rouse all those resentments which must unavoidably flow from such a belief. That the secret mover of this Scheme (whoever he may be) intended to take advantage of the passions, while they were warmed by the recollection of past distresses, without giving time for cool, deliberative thinking, and that composure of Mind which is so necessary to give dignity and stability to measures is rendered too obvious, by the mode of conducting the business, to need other proof than a reference to the proceeding.

Thus much, Gentlemen, I have thought it incumbent on me to observe to you, to shew upon what principles I opposed the irregular and hasty meeting which was proposed to have been held on Tuesday last: and not because I wanted a disposition to give you every oppertunity consistent with your own honor, and the dignity of the Army, to make known your grievances. If my conduct heretofore, has not evinced to you, that I have been a faithful friend to the Army, my declaration of it at this time wd. be equally unavailing and improper. But as I was among the first who embarked in the cause of our common Country. As I have never left your side one moment, but when called from you on public duty. As I have been the constant companion and witness of your Distresses, and not among the last to feel, and acknowledge your Merits. As I have ever considered my own Military reputation as inseperably connected with that of the Army. As my Heart has ever expanded with joy, when I have heard its praises, and my indignation has arisen, when the mouth of detraction has been opened against it, it can *scarcely be supposed,* at this late stage of the War, that I am indifferent to its interests. But, how are they to be promoted? The way is plain, says the anonymous Addresser. If War continues, remove into the unsettled Country; there establish yourselves, and leave an ungrateful Country to defend itself. But who are they to defend? Our Wives, our Children, our Farms, and other property which we leave behind us. or, in this state of hostile seperation, are we to take the two first (the latter cannot be removed), to perish in a Wilderness, with hunger, cold and nakedness? If Peace takes place, never sheath your Swords Says he untill you have obtained full and ample justice; this dreadful alternative, of either deserting our Country in the extremest hour of her distress, or turning our Arms against it, (which is the apparent object, unless Congress can be compelled into instant compliance) has something so shocking in it, that humanity revolts at the idea. My God! what can this writer have in view, by recommending such measures? Can he be a friend to the Army? Can he be a friend to this Country? Rather, is he not an insidious Foe? Some Emissary, perhaps, from New York, plotting the ruin of both, by sowing the seeds of discord and seperation between the Civil and Military powers of the Continent? And what a Compliment does he pay to our Understandings, when he recommends measures in either alternative, impracticable in their Nature?

But here, Gentlemen, I will drop the curtain, because it wd. be as imprudent in me to assign my reasons for this opinion, as it would be insulting to your conception, to suppose you stood in need of them. A moment's reflection will convince every dispassionate Mind of the physical impossibility of carrying either proposal into execution.

There might, Gentlemen, be an impropriety in my taking notice, in this Address to you, of an anonymous production, but the manner in which that performance has been introduced to the Army, the effect it was intended to have, together with some other circumstances, will amply justify my observations on the tendency of that Writing. With respect to the advice given by the Author, to suspect the Man, who shall recommend moderate measures and longer forbearance, I spurn it, as every Man, who regards that liberty, and reveres that justice for which we contend, undoubtedly must; for if Men are to be precluded from offering their Sentiments on a matter, which may involve the most serious and alarming consequences, that can invite the consideration of Mankind, reason is of no use to us; the freedom of Speech may be taken away, and, dumb and silent we may be led, like sheep, to the Slaughter.

I cannot, in justice to my own belief, and what I have great reason to conceive is the intention of Congress, conclude this Address, without giving it as my decided opinion, that that Honble Body, entertain exalted sentiments of the Services of the Army; and, from a full conviction of its merits and sufferings, will do it compleat justice. That their endeavors, to discover and establish funds for this purpose, have been unwearied, and will not cease, till they have succeeded, I have not a doubt. But, like all other large Bodies, where there is a variety of different Interests to reconcile, their deliberations are slow. Why then should we distrust them? and, in consequence of that distrust, adopt measures, which may cast a shade over that glory which, has been so justly acquired; and tarnish the reputation of an Army which is celebrated thro' all Europe, for its fortitude and Patriotism? and for what is this done? to bring the object we seek nearer? No! most certainly, in my opinion, it will cast it at a greater distance.

For myself (and I take no merit in giving the assurance, being induced to it from principles of gratitude, veracity and justice), a grateful sence of the confidence you have ever placed in me, a recollection of the chearful assistance, and prompt obedience I have experienced from you, under every vicissitude of Fortune, and the sincere affection I feel for an Army, I have so long had the honor to Command, will oblige me to declare, in this public and solemn manner, that, in the attainment of compleat justice for all your toils and dangers, and in the gratification of every wish, so far as may be done consistently with the great duty I owe my Country, and those powers we are bound to respect, you may freely command my Services to the utmost of my abilities.

While I give you these assurances, and pledge myself in the most unequivocal manner, to exert whatever ability I am possessed of, in your favor, let me entreat you, Gentlemen, on your part, not to take any measures, which, viewed in the calm light of reason, will lessen the dignity, and sully the glory you have hitherto maintained; let me request you to rely on the plighted faith of your Country, and place a full confidence in the purity of the intentions of Congress; that, previous to your dissolution as an Army they will cause all your Accts. to be fairly liquidated, as directed in their resolutions, which were published to you two days ago, and that they will adopt the most effectual measures in their power, to render ample justice to you, for your faithful and meritorious Services. And let me conjure you, in the name of our common Country, as you value your own sacred honor, as you respect the rights of humanity, and as you regard the Military and National character of America, to express your utmost horror and detestation of the Man who wishes, under any specious pretences, to overturn the liberties of our Country, and who wickedly attempts to open the flood Gates of Civil discord, and deluge our rising Empire in Blood. By thus determining, and thus acting, you will pursue the plain and direct road to the attainment of your wishes. You will defeat the insidious designs of our Enemies, who are compelled to resort from open force to secret Artifice. You will give one more distinguished proof of unexampled patriotism and patient virtue, rising superior to the pressure of the most complicated sufferings; And you will, by the dignity of your Conduct, afford occasion for Posterity to say, when speaking of the glorious example you have exhibited to Mankind, "had this day been wanting, the World had never seen the last stage of perfection to which human nature is capable of attaining."

These will give you a pretty good idea of our proceedings; and that you may not want any information on the subject, I shall take the liberty of adding a few particulars, by way of narrative.

The accumulated hardships under which the army had so long labored made their situation intolerable, and called aloud for immediate redress. An application to the supreme authority of America was thought a salutary measure, and the improbability of obtaining relief from the States individually, after the treatment the Massachusetts line had experienced from their State, rendered it absolutely indispensable.

With this view, a delegation from the several regiments composing the Massachusetts line, having conferred together, came to a determination of taking the sense of the army at large; and on the 16th of November appointed a committee of seven, who should assemble on the 24th of the same month, and, in conjunction with the delegates from those lines who might see fit to send any, agree and determine upon such measures as should be found best calculated to promote the desirable purposes for which the convention was called.

Agreeably to this proposal there was a full representation of the whole army, when "it was unanimously agreed that Major-General Knox, Brigadier-General Huntington, Colonel Crane, Colonel Courtlandt, and Doctor Eustis, be a committee to draft an address and petition to Congress, in behalf of the army, and lay the same before this assembly for consideration at their meeting on the 1st of December."

At the meeting on the 1st of December, "the draft of the address and petition to Congress was read, and voted to be laid before the several lines of the army for consideration," and it was determined, "that the army at large choose a general officer, and each line send a field-officer, any two of whom, as a majority of them should agree, should, in conjunction with the said general officer, form a committee to wait on Congress and execute the business of said address." Instructions were also directed to be prepared for the conduct of said committee, and the necessary sum of money raised for their expenses.

On opening the ballots the 5th of December, Major-General McDougall, Colonel Ogden, and Colonel Brooks were chosen to proceed to Congress with the address and petition, which was signed on the 7th, and delivered to the committee,—after which the meeting adjourned without delay.

The delegation from the army to Congress set out on their mission the 21st of December. On the address and petition being read in Congress, a grand committee, consisting of a member from each State, was chosen to confer with our commissioners. The result of this conference was certain resolves of Congress, passed on the 25th of January, the purport whereof was, that the army should receive one month's pay, and that their accounts should be settled as soon as possible, for discharging the balances of which Congress would endeavour to provide adequate funds. The matter respecting a commutation of the half-pay was recommitted. These resolutions at large were transmitted by our commissioners, in a letter of the 8th of February, to General Knox, which was immediately communicated to the respective lines of the army.

This report, though far from being satisfactory, joined to the certainty that we were on the eve of a general peace, kept the army quiet. In this state of patient expectation, the anonymous address to the officers made its appearance. Immediately on this, the Commander-in-chief, by an order of the 11th of March, directed the officers to assemble on the 15th, which produced the second anonymous address.

The meeting of the officers was in itself exceedingly respectable, the matters they were called to deliberate upon were of the most serious nature, and the unexpected attendance of the Commander-in-chief heightened the solemnity of the scene. Every eye was fixed upon the illustrious man, and attention to their beloved General held the assembly mute. He opened the meeting by apologizing for his appearance there, which was by no means his intention when he published the order which directed them to assemble. But the diligence used in circulating the anonymous pieces rendered it necessary that he should give his sentiments to the army on the nature and tendency of them, and determined him to avail himself of the present opportunity; and, in order to do it with greater perspicuity, he had committed his thoughts to writing, which, with the indulgence of his brother officers, he would take the liberty of reading to them. It is needless for me to say any thing of this production; *it speaks for itself.* After he had concluded his address, he said, that, as a corroborating testimony of the good disposition in Congress towards the army, he would communicate to them a letter received from a worthy member of that body, and one who on all occasions had ever approved himself their fast friend. This was an exceedingly sensible letter; and, while it pointed out the difficulties and embarrassments of Congress, it held up very forcibly the idea that the army should, at all events, be generously dealt with. One circumstance in reading this letter must not be omitted. His Excellency, after reading the first paragraph, made a short pause, took out his spectacles, and begged the indulgence of his audience while he put them on, observing at the same time, that he had grown gray in their service, and now found himself growing blind. There was something so natural, so unaffected, in this appeal, as rendered it superior to the most studied oratory; it forced its way to the heart, and you might see sensibility moisten every eye. The General, having finished, took leave of the assembly, and the business of the day was conducted in the manner which is related in the account of the proceedings.

I cannot dismiss this subject without observing, that it is happy for America that she has a *patriot army,* and equally so that a *Washington* is its leader. I rejoice in the opportunities I have had of seeing this great man in a variety of situations;—calm and intrepid where the battle raged, patient and persevering under the pressure of misfortune, moderate and possessing himself in the full career of victory. Great as these qualifications deservedly render him, he never appeared to me more truly so, than at the assembly we have been speaking of. On other occasions he has been supported by the exertions of an army and the countenance of his friends; but in this he stood single and alone. There was no saying where the passions of an army, which were not a little inflamed, might lead; but it was generally allowed that longer forbearance was dangerous, and moderation had ceased to be a virtue. Under these circumstances he appeared, not at the head of his troops, but as it were in opposition to them; and for a dreadful moment the interests of the army and its General seemed to be in competition! He spoke,—every doubt was dispelled, and the tide of patriotism rolled again in its wonted course. Illustrious man! what he says of the army may with equal justice be applied to his own character. "Had this day been wanting, the world had never seen the last stage of perfection to which human nature is capable of attaining."

—George Washington—
CIRCULAR TO THE STATE GOVERNMENTS
JUNE 8, 1783

HEAD QUARTERS, NEWBURGH, JUNE 8, 1783.

SIR: THE GREAT OBJECT for which I had the honor to hold an appointment in the Service of my Country, being accomplished, I am now preparing to resign it into the hands of Congress, and to return to that domestic retirement, which, it is well known, I left with the greatest reluctance, a Retirement, for which I have never ceased to sigh through a long and painful absence, and in which (remote from the noise and trouble of the World) I meditate to pass the remainder of life in a state of undisturbed repose; But before I carry this resolution into effect, I think it a duty incumbent on me, to make this my last official communication, to congratulate you on the glorious events which Heaven has been pleased to produce in our favor, to offer my sentiments respecting some important subjects, which appear to me, to be intimately connected with the tranquility of the United States, to take my leave of your Excellency as a public Character, and to give my final blessing to that Country, in whose service I have spent the prime of my life, for whose sake I have consumed so many anxious days and watchfull nights, and whose happiness being extremely dear to me, will always constitute no inconsiderable part of my own.

Impressed with the liveliest sensibility on this pleasing occasion, I will claim the indulgence of dilating the more copiously on the subjects of our mutual felicitation. When we consider the magnitude of the prize we contended for, the doubtful nature of the contest, and the favorable manner in which it has terminated, we shall find the greatest possible reason for gratitude and rejoicing; this is a theme that will afford infinite delight to every benevolent and liberal mind, whether the event in contemplation, be considered as the source of present enjoyment or the parent of future happiness; and we shall have equal occasion to felicitate ourselves on the lot which Providence has assigned us, whether we view it in a natural, a political or moral point of light.

The Citizens of America, placed in the most enviable condition, as the sole Lords and Proprietors of a vast Tract of Continent, comprehending all the various soils and climates of the World, and abounding with all the necessaries and conveniencies of life, are now by the late satisfactory pacification, acknowledged to be possessed of absolute freedom and Independency; They are, from this period, to be considered as the Actors on a most conspicuous Theatre, which seems to be peculiarly designated by Providence for the display of human greatness and felicity; Here, they are not only surrounded with every thing which can contribute to the completion of private and domestic enjoyment, but Heaven has crowned all its other blessings, by giving a fairer oppertunity for political happiness, than any other Nation has ever been favored with. Nothing can illustrate these observations more forcibly, than a recollection of the happy conjuncture of times and circumstances, under which our Republic assumed its rank among the Nations; The foundation of our Empire was not laid in the gloomy age of Ignorance and Superstition, but at an Epocha when the rights of mankind were better understood and more clearly defined, than at any former period, the researches of the human mind, after social happiness, have been carried to a great extent, the Treasures of knowledge, acquired by the labours of Philosophers, Sages and Legislatures, through a long succession of years, are laid open for our use, and their collected wisdom may be happily applied in the Establishment of our forms of Government; the free cultivation of Letters, the unbounded extension of Commerce, the progressive refinement of Manners, the growing liberality of sentiment, and above all, the pure and benign light of Revelation, have had a meliorating influence on mankind and increased the blessings of Society. At this auspicious period, the United States came into existence as a Nation, and if their Citizens should not be completely free and happy, the fault will be intirely their own.

Such is our situation, and such are our prospects: but notwithstanding the cup of blessing is thus reached out to us, notwithstanding happiness is ours, if we have a disposition to seize the occasion and make it our own; yet, it appears to me there is an option still left to the United States of America, that it is in their choice, and depends upon their conduct, whether they will be respectable and prosperous, or contemptable and miserable as a Nation; This is the time of their political probation, this is the moment when the eyes of the whole World are turned upon them, this is the moment to establish or ruin their national Character forever, this is the favorable moment to give such a tone to our Federal Government, as will enable it to answer the ends of its institution, or this may be the ill-fated moment for relaxing the powers of the Union, annihilating the cement of the Confederation, and exposing us to become the sport of European politics, which may play one State against another to prevent their growing importance, and to serve their own interested purposes. For, according to the system of Policy the States shall adopt at this moment, they will stand or fall, and by their confirmation or lapse, it is yet to be decided, whether the Revolution must ultimately be considered as a blessing or a curse: a blessing or a curse, not to the present age alone, for with our fate will the destiny of unborn Millions be involved.

With this conviction of the importance of the present Crisis, silence in me would be a crime; I will therefore speak to your Excellency, the language of freedom and of sincerity, without disguise; I am aware, however, that those who differ from me in political sentiment, may perhaps remark, I am stepping out of the proper line of my duty, and they may possibly ascribe to arrogance or ostentation, what I know is alone the result of the purest intention, but the rectitude of my own heart, which disdains such unworthy motives, the part I have hitherto acted in life, the determination I have formed, of not taking any share in public business hereafter, the ardent desire I feel, and shall continue to manifest, of quietly enjoying in private life, after all the toils of War, the benefits of a wise and liberal Government, will, I flatter myself, sooner or later convince my Countrymen, that I could have no sinister views in delivering with so little reserve, the opinions contained in this Address.

There are four things, which I humbly conceive, are essential to the well being, I may even venture to say, to the existence of the United States as an Independent Power:

1st. An indissoluble Union of the States under one Federal Head.

2dly. A Sacred regard to Public Justice.

3dly. The adoption of a proper Peace Establishment, and

4thly. The prevalence of that pacific and friendly Disposition, among the People of the United States, which will induce them to forget their local prejudices and policies, to make those mutual concessions which are requisite to the general prosperity, and in some instances, to sacrifice their individual advantages to the interest of the Community.

These are the Pillars on which the glorious Fabrick of our Independency and National Character must be supported; Liberty is the Basis, and whoever would dare to sap the foundation, or overturn the Structure, under whatever specious pretexts he may attempt it, will merit the bitterest execration, and the severest punishment which can be inflicted by his injured Country.

On the three first Articles I will make a few observations, leaving the last to the good sense and serious consideration of those immediately concerned.

Under the first head, altho' it may not be necessary or proper for me in this place to enter into a particular disquisition of the principles of the Union, and to take up the great question which has been frequently agitated, whether it be expedient and requisite for the States to delegate a larger proportion of Power to Congress, or not, Yet it will be a part of my duty, and that of every true Patriot, to assert without reserve, and to insist upon the following positions, That unless the States will suffer Congress to exercise those prerogatives, they are undoubtedly invested with by the Constitution, every thing must very rapidly tend to Anarchy and confusion, That it is indispensable to the happiness of the individual States, that there should be lodged somewhere, a Supreme Power to regulate and govern the general concerns of the Confederated Republic, without which the Union cannot be of long duration. That there must be a faithfull and pointed compliance on the part of every State, with the late proposals and demands of Congress, or the most fatal consequences will ensue, That whatever measures have a tendency to dissolve the

Union, or contribute to violate or lessen the Sovereign Authority, ought to be considered as hostile to the Liberty and Independency of America, and the Authors of them treated accordingly, and lastly, that unless we can be enabled by the concurrence of the States, to participate of the fruits of the Revolution, and enjoy the essential benefits of Civil Society, under a form of Government so free and uncorrupted, so happily guarded against the danger of oppression, as has been devised and adopted by the Articles of Confederation, it will be a subject of regret, that so much blood and treasure have been lavished for no purpose, that so many sufferings have been encountered without a compensation, and that so many sacrifices have been made in vain. Many other considerations might here be adduced to prove, that without an entire conformity to the Spirit of the Union, we cannot exist as an Independent Power; it will be sufficient for my purpose to mention but one or two which seem to me of the greatest importance. It is only in our united Character as an Empire, that our Independence is acknowledged, that our power can be regarded, or our Credit supported among Foreign Nations. The Treaties of the European Powers with the United States of America, will have no validity on a dissolution of the Union. We shall be left nearly in a state of Nature, or we may find by our own unhappy experience, that there is a natural and necessary progression, from the extreme of anarchy to the extreme of Tyranny; and that arbitrary power is most easily established on the ruins of Liberty abused to licentiousness.

As to the second Article, which respects the performance of Public Justice, Congress have, in their late Address to the United States, almost exhausted the subject, they have explained their Ideas so fully, and have enforced the obligations the States are under, to render compleat justice to all the Public Creditors, with so much dignity and energy, that in my opinion, no real friend to the honor and Independency of America, can hesitate a single moment respecting the propriety of complying with the just and honorable measures proposed; if their Arguments do not produce conviction, I know of nothing that will have greater influence; especially when we recollect that the System referred to, being the result of the collected Wisdom of the Continent, must be esteemed, if not perfect, certainly the least objectionable of any that could be devised; and that if it shall not be carried into immediate execution, a National Bankruptcy, with all its deplorable consequences will take place, before any different Plan can possibly be proposed and adopted; So pressing are the present circumstances! and such is the alternative now offered to the States!

The ability of the Country to discharge the debts which have been incurred in its defence, is not to be doubted, an inclination, I flatter myself, will not be wanting, the path of our duty is plain before us, honesty will be found on every experiment, to be the best and only true policy, let us then as a Nation be just, let us fulfil the public Contracts, which Congress had undoubtedly a right to make for the purpose of carrying on the War, with the same good faith we suppose ourselves bound to perform our private engagements; in the mean time, let an attention to the chearfull performance of their proper business, as Individuals, and as members of Society, be earnestly inculcated on the Citizens of America, that will they strengthen the hands of Government, and be happy under its protection: every one will reap the fruit of his labours, every one will enjoy his own acquisitions without molestation and without danger.

In this state of absolute freedom and perfect security, who will grudge to yield a very little of his property to support the common interest of Society, and insure the protection of Government? Who does not remember, the frequent declarations, at the commencement of the War, that we should be compleatly satisfied, if at the expence of one half, we could defend the remainder of our possessions? Where is the Man to be found, who wishes to remain indebted, for the defence of his own person and property, to the exertions, the bravery, and the blood of others, without making one generous effort to repay the debt of honor and of gratitude? In what part of the Continent shall we find any Man, or body of Men, who would not blush to stand up and propose measures, purposely calculated to rob the Soldier of his Stipend, and the Public Creditor of his due? and were it possible that such a flagrant instance of Injustice could ever happen, would it not excite the general indignation, and tend to bring down, upon the Authors of such measures, the aggravated vengeance of Heaven? If after all, a spirit of disunion or a temper of obstinacy and perverseness, should manifest itself in any of the States, if such an ungracious disposition should attempt to frustrate all the happy effects that might be expected to flow from the Union, if there should be a refusal to comply with the requisitions for Funds to discharge the annual interest of the public debts, and if that refusal should revive again all those jealousies and produce all those evils, which are now happily removed, Congress, who have in all their Transaction shewn a great degree of magnanimity and justice, will stand justified in the sight of God and Man, and the State alone which puts itself in opposition to the aggregate Wisdom of the Continent, and follows such mistaken and pernicious Councils, will be responsible for all the consequences.

For my own part, conscious of having acted while a Servant of the Public, in the manner I conceived best suited to promote the real interests of my Country; having in consequence of my fixed belief in some measure pledged myself to the Army, that their Country would finally do them compleat and ample Justice; and not wishing to conceal any instance of my official conduct from the eyes of the World, I have thought proper to transmit to your Excellency the inclosed collection of Papers, relative to the half pay and commutation granted by Congress to the Officers of the Army; From these communications, my decided sentiment will be clearly comprehended, together with the conclusive reasons which induced me, at an early period, to recommend the adoption of the measure, in the most earnest and serious manner. As the proceedings of Congress, the Army, and myself are open to all, and contain in my opinion, sufficient information to remove the prejudices and errors which may have been entertained by any; I think it unnecessary to say any thing more, than just to observe, that the Resolutions of Congress, now alluded to, are undoubtedly as absolutely binding upon the United States, as the most solemn Acts of Confederation or Legislation. As to the Idea, which I am informed has in some instances prevailed, that the half pay and commutation are to be regarded merely in the odious light of a Pension, it ought to be exploded forever; that Provision, should be viewed as it really was, a reasonable compensation offered by Congress, at a time when they had nothing else to give, to the Officers of the Army, for services then to be performed. It was the only means to prevent a total dereliction of the Service, It was a part of their hire, I may be allowed to say, it was the price of their blood and of your Independency, it is therefore more than a common debt, it is a debt of honour, it can never be considered as a Pension or gratuity, nor be cancelled until it is fairly discharged.

With regard to a distinction between Officers and Soldiers, it is sufficient that the uniform experience of every Nation of the World, combined with our own, proves the utility and propriety of the discrimination. Rewards in proportion to the aids the public derives from them, are unquestionably due to all its Servants; In some Lines, the Soldiers have perhaps generally had as ample a compensation for their Services, by the large Bounties which have been paid to them, as their Officers will receive in the proposed Commutation, in others, if besides the donation of Lands, the payment of Arrearages of Cloathing and Wages (in which Articles all the component parts of the Army must be put upon the same footing) we take into the estimate, the Bounties many of the Soldiers have received and the gratuity of one Year's full pay, which is promised to all, possibly their situation (every circumstance being duly considered) will not be deemed less eligible than that of the Officers. Should a farther reward, however, be judged equitable, I will venture to assert, no one will enjoy greater satisfaction than myself, on seeing an exemption from Taxes for a limited time, (which has been petitioned for in some instances) or any other adequate immunity or compensation, granted to the brave defenders of their Country's Cause; but neither the adoption or rejection of this proposition will in any manner affect, much less militate against, the Act of Congress, by which they have offered five years full pay, in lieu of the half pay for life, which had been before promised to the Officers of the Army.

Before I conclude the subject of public justice, I cannot omit to mention the obligations this Country is under, to that meritorious Class of veteran Non-commissioned Officers and Privates, who have been discharged for inability, in consequence of the Resolution of Congress of the 23d of April 1782, on an annual pension for life, their peculiar sufferings, their singular merits and claims to that provision need only be known, to interest all the feelings of humanity in their behalf: nothing but a punctual payment of their annual allowance can rescue them from the most complicated misery, and nothing could be a more melancholy and distressing sight, than to behold those who have shed their blood or lost their limbs in the service of their Country, without a shelter, without a friend, and without the means of obtaining any of the necessaries or comforts of Life; compelled to beg their daily bread from door to door! suffer me to recommend those of this discription, belonging to your State, to the warmest patronage of your Excellency and your Legislature.

It is necessary to say but a few words on the third topic which was proposed, and which regards particularly the defence of the Republic, As there can be little doubt but Congress will recommend a proper Peace Establishment for the United States, in which a due attention will be paid to the importance of placing the Militia of the Union upon a regular and respectable footing; If this should be the case, I would beg leave to urge the great advantage of it in the strongest terms. The Militia of this Country must be considered as the Palladium of our security, and the first effectual resort in case of hostility; It is essential therefore, that the same system should pervade the whole; that the formation and discipline of the Militia of the Continent should be absolutely uniform, and that the same species of Arms, Accoutrements and Military Apparatus, should be introduced in every part of the United States; No one, (who has not learned it from experience) can conceive the difficulty, expence, and confusion which result from a contrary system, or the vague Arrangements which have hitherto prevailed.

If in treating of political points, a greater latitude than usual has been taken in the course of this Address, the importance of the Crisis, and the magnitude of the objects in discussion, must be my apology: It is, however, neither my wish or expectation, that the preceding observations should claim any regard, except so far as they shall appear to be dictated by a good intention, consonant to the immutable rules of Justice; calculated to produce a liberal system of policy, and founded on whatever experience may have been acquired by a long and close attention to public business. Here I might speak with the more confidence from my actual observations, and, if it would not swell this Letter (already too prolix) beyond the bounds I had prescribed myself: I could demonstrate to every mind open to conviction, that in less time and with much less expence than has been incurred, the War might have been brought to the same happy conclusion, if the resourses of the Continent could have been properly drawn forth, that the distresses and disappointments which have very often occurred, have in too many instances, resulted more from a want of energy, in the Continental Government, than a deficiency of means in the particular States. That the inefficiency of measures, arising from the want of an adequate authority in the Supreme Power, from a partial compliance with the Requisitions of

Congress in some of the States, and from a failure of punctuality in others, while it tended to damp the zeal of those which were more willing to exert themselves; served also to accumulate the expences of the War, and to frustrate the best concerted Plans, and that the discouragement occasioned by the complicated difficulties and embarrassments, in which our affairs were, by this means involved, would have long ago produced the dissolution of any Army, less patient, less virtuous and less persevering, than that which I have had the honor to command. But while I mention these things, which are notorious facts, as the defects of our Federal Constitution, particularly in the prosecution of a War, I beg it may be understood, that as I have ever taken a pleasure in gratefully acknowledging the assistance and support I have derived from every Class of Citizens, so shall I always be happy to do justice to the unparalleled exertion of the individual States, on many interesting occasions.

I have thus freely disclosed what I wished to make known, before I surrendered up my Public trust to those who committed it to me, the task is now accomplished, I now bid adieu to your Excellency as the Chief Magistrate of your State, at the same time I bid a last farewell to the cares of Office, and all the imployments of public life.

It remains then to be my final and only request, that your Excellency will communicate these sentiments to your Legislature at their next meeting, and that they may be considered as the Legacy of One, who has ardently wished, on all occasions, to be useful to his Country, and who, even in the shade of Retirement, will not fail to implore the divine benediction upon it.

I now make it my earnest prayer, that God would have you, and the State over which you preside, in his holy protection, that he would incline the hearts of the Citizens to cultivate a spirit of subordination and obedience to Government, to entertain a brotherly affection and love for one another, for their fellow Citizens of the United States at large, and particularly for their brethren who have served in the Field, and finally, that he would most graciously be pleased to dispose us all, to do Justice, to love mercy, and to demean ourselves with that Charity, humility and pacific temper of mind, which were the Characteristicks of the Divine Author of our blessed Religion, and without an humble imitation of whose example in these things, we can never hope to be a happy Nation.

ROCKY HILL, SEPTEMBER 7, 1783.

SIR: I HAVE CAREFULLY perused the Papers which you put into my hands relative to Indian Affairs.

My Sentiments with respect to the proper line of Conduct to be observed towards these people coincides precisely with those delivered by Genl. Schuyler, so far as he has gone in his Letter of the 29th. July to Congress (which, with the other Papers is herewith returned), and for the reasons he has there assigned; a repetition of them therefore by me would be unnecessary. But independant of the arguments made use of by him the following considerations have no small weight in my Mind.

To suffer a wide extended Country to be over run with Land Jobbers, Speculators, and Monopolisers or even with scatter'd settlers, is, in my opinion, inconsistent with that wisdom and policy which our true interest dictates, or that an enlightened People ought to adopt and, besides, is pregnant of disputes both with the Savages, and among ourselves, the evils of which are easier, to be conceived than described; and for what? but to aggrandize a few avaricious Men to the prejudice of many, and the embarrassment of Government, for the People engaged in these pursuits without contributing in the smallest degree to the support of Government, or considering themselves as amenable to its Laws, will involve it by their unrestrained conduct, in inextricable perplexities, and more than probable in a great deal of Bloodshed.

My ideas therefore of the line of Conduct proper to be observed not only towards the Indians, but for the government of the Citizens of America, in their Settlement of the Western Country (which is intimately connected therewith) are simply these.

First and as a preliminary, that all Prisoners of whatever age or Sex, among the Indians shall be delivered up.

That the Indians should be informed, that after a Contest of eight years for the Sovereignty of this Country G: Britain has ceded all the Lands of the United States within the limits discribed by the ___ arte. of the Provisional Treaty.

That as they (the Indians) maugre all the advice and admonition which could be given them at the commencemt; and during the prosecution of the War could not be restrained from acts of Hostility, but were determined to join their Arms to those of G Britain and to share their fortune; so, consequently, with a less generous People than Americans they would be made to share the same fate; and be compelld to retire along with them beyond the Lakes. But as we prefer Peace to a state of Warfare, as we consider them as a deluded People; as we perswade ourselves that they are convinced, from experience, of their error in taking up the Hatchet against us, and that their true Interest and safety must now depend upon *our* friendship. As the Country, is large enough to contain us all; and as we are disposed to be kind to them and to partake of their Trade, we will from these considerations and from motives of Compn., draw a veil over what is past and establish a boundary line between them and us beyond which we will *endeavor* to restrain our People from Hunting or Settling, and within which they shall not come, but for the purposes of Trading, Treating, or other business unexceptionable in its nature.

In establishing this line, in the first instance, care should be taken neither to yield nor to grasp at too much. But to endeavor to impress the Indians with an idea of the generosity of our disposition to accommodate them, and with the necessity we are under, of providing for our Warriors, our Young People who are growing up, and strangers who are coming from other Countries to live among us. and if they should make a point of it, or appear dissatisfied at the line we may find it necessary to establish, compensation should be made them for their claims within it.

It is needless for me to express more explicitly because the tendency of my observns. evinces it is my opinion that if the Legislature of the State of New York should insist upon expelling the Six Nations from all the Country they Inhabited previous to the War, within their Territory (as General Schuyler seems to be apprehensive of) that it will end in another Indian War. I have every reason to believe from my enquiries, and the information I have received, that they will not suffer their Country (if it was our policy to take it before we could settle it) to be wrested from them without another struggle. That they would compromise for a part of it I have very little doubt, and that it would be the cheapest way of coming at it, I have no doubt at all. The same observations, I am perswaded, will hold good with respect to Virginia, or any other state which has powerful Tribes of Indians on their Frontiers; and the reason of my mentioning New York is because General Schuyler has expressed his opinion of the temper of its Legislature; and because I have been more in the way of learning the Sentimts. of the Six Nations, than of any other Tribes of Indians on this Subject.

The limits being sufficiently extensive (in the New Ctry.) to comply with all the engagements of Government and to admit such emigrations as may be supposed to happen within a given time not only from the several States of the Union but from Foreign Countries, and moreover of such magnitude as to form a distinct and proper Government; a Proclamation in my opinion, should issue, making it Felony (if there is power for the purpose and if not imposing some very heavy restraint) for any person to Survey or Settle beyond the Line; and the Officers Commanding the Frontier Garrison should have pointed and peremptory orders to see that the Proclamation is carried into effect.

Measures of this sort would not only obtain Peace from the Indians, but would, in my opinion, be the surest means of preserving it. It would dispose of the Land to the best advantage; People the Country progressively, and check Land Jobbing and Monopolizing (which is now going forward with great avidity) while the door would be open, and the terms known for every one to obtain what is reasonable and proper for himself upon legal and constitutional ground.

Every advantage that could be expected or even wished for would result from such a mode of proceedure: our Settlements would be compact, Government well established, and our Barrier formidable, not only for ourselves but against our Neighbours, and the Indians as has been observed in Genl Schuylers Letter will ever retreat as our Settlements advance upon them and they will be as ready to sell, as we are to buy; That it is the cheapest as well as the least distressing way of dealing with them, none who are acquainted with the Nature of Indian warfare, and has ever been at the trouble of estimating the expence of one, and comparing it with the cost of purchasing their Lands, will hesitate to acknowledge.

Unless some such measures as I have here taken the liberty of suggesting are speedily adopted one of two capital evils, in my opinion, will inevitably result, and is near at hand; either that the settling, or rather overspreading the Western Country will take place, by a parcel of Banditti, who will bid defiance to all Authority while they are skimming and disposing of the Cream of the Country at the expence of many suffering Officers and Soldiers who have fought and bled to obtain it, and are now waiting the decision of Congress to point them to the promised reward of their past dangers and toils, or a renewal of Hostilities with the Indians, brought about more than probably, by this very means.

How far agents for Indian Affrs. are indispensably necessary I shall not take upon me to decide; but if any should be appointed, their powers in my opinion should be circumscribed, accurately defined, and themselves rigidly punished for every infraction of them. A recurrence to the conduct of these People under the British Administration of Indian Affairs will manifest the propriety of this caution, as it will there be found, that self Interest was the principle by which their Agents were actuated; and to promote this by accumulating Lands and passing large quantities of Goods thro their hands, the Indians were made to speak any language they pleased by their representation; were pacific or hostile as their purposes were most likely to be promoted by the one or the other. No purchase under any pretence whatever should be made by any other authority than that of the Sovereign power, or the Legislature of the State in which such Lands may happen to be. Nor should the Agents be permitted directly or indirectly to trade; but to have a fixed, and ample Salary allowed them as a full compensation for their trouble.

Whether in practice the measure may answer as well as it appears in theory to me, I will not undertake to say; but I think, if the Indian Trade was carried on, on Government Acct., and with no greater advance than what would be necessary to defray the expence and risk, and bring in a small profit, that it would supply the Indians upon much better terms than they usually are; engross their Trade, and fix them strongly in our Interest; and would be a much better mode of treating them than that of giving presents; where a few only are benefitted by them. I confess there is a difficulty in getting a Man, or set of Men, in whose Abilities and integrity there can be a perfect reliance; without which, the scheme is liable to such abuse as to defeat the salutary ends which are proposed from it. At any rate, no person should be suffered to Trade with the Indians without first obtaining a license, and giving security to conform to such rules and regulations as shall be prescribed; as was the case before the War.

In giving my Sentiments in the Month of May last (at the request of a Committee of Congress) on a Peace Establishmt. I took the liberty of suggesting the propriety, which in my opinion there appeared, of paying particular attention to the French and other Settlers at Detroit and other parts within the limits of the Western Country; the perusal of a late Pamphlet entitled "Observations on the Commerce of the American States with Europe and the West Indies" impresses the necessity of it more forcibly than ever on my Mind. The author of that Piece* strongly recommends a liberal change in the Government of Canada, and tho' he is too sanguine in his expectations of the benefits arising from it, there can be no doubt of the good policy of the measure. It behooves us therefore to counteract them, by anticipation. These People have a disposition towards us susceptible of favorable Impressions; but as no Arts will be left unattempted by the British to withdraw them from our Interest, the prest. moment should be employed by us to fix them in it, or we may loose them forever; and with them, the advantages, or disadvantages consequent of the choice they may make. From the best information and Maps of that Country, it would appear that from the Mouth of the Great Miami River wch. empties into the Ohio to its confluence with the Mad River, thence by a Line to the Miami Fort and Village on the other Miami River wch. empties into Lake Erie, and Thence by a Line to include the Settlement of Detroit would with Lake Erie to the No. ward Pensa. to the Eastwd. and the Ohio to the Soward form a Governmt. sufficiently extensive to fulfill all the public engagements, and to receive moreover a large population by Emigrants, and to confine The Settlement of the New States within these bounds would, in my opinion, be infinitely better even supposing no disputes were to happen with the Indians and that it was not necessary to guard against those other evils which have been enumerated than to suffer the same number of People to roam over a Country of at least 500,000 Square Miles contributing nothing to

---

*John Holroyd (1735–1821), first earl of Sheffield.

the support, but much perhaps to the Embarrassment of the Federal Government.

Was it not for the purpose of comprehending the Settlement of Detroit within the Jurisdn. of the New Governmt a more compact and better shaped district for a State would be for the line to proceed from the Miami Fort and Village along the River of that name to Lake Erie. leaving In that case the Settlement of Detroit, and all the Territory No. of the Rivers Miami and St. Josephs between the Lakes Erie, St. Clair, Huron, and Michigan to form, hereafter, another State equally large compact and water bounded.

At first view, it may seem a little extraneous, when I am called upon to give an opinion upon the terms of a Peace proper to be made with the Indians, that I should go into the formation of New States; but the Settlemt. of the Western Country and making a Peace with the Indians are so analogous that there can be no definition of the one without involving considerations of the other. for I repeat it, again, and I am clear in my opinion, that policy and œconomy point very strongly to the expediency of being upon good terms with the Indians, and the propriety of purchasing their Lands in preference to attempting to drive them by force of arms out of their Country; which as we have already experienced is like driving the Wild Beasts of the Forest which will return us soon as the pursuit is at an end and fall perhaps on those that are left there; when the gradual extension of our Settlements will as certainly cause the Savage as the Wolf to retire; both being beasts of prey tho' they differ in shape. In a word there is nothing to be obtained by an Indian War but the Soil they live on and this can be had by purchase at less expence, and without that bloodshed, and those distresses which helpless Women and Children are made partakers of in all kinds of disputes with them.

If there is any thing in these thoughts (which I have fully and freely communicated) worthy attention I shall be happy and am Sir Yr. etc.

P. S. A formal Address, and memorial from the Oneida Indians when I was on the Mohawk River, setting forth their Grievances and distresses and praying relief, induced me to order a pound of Powder and 3 lbs. of Lead to be issued to each Man, from the Military Magazines in the care of Colo. Willet; this, I presume, was unknown to Genl. Schuyler at the time he recommended the like measure in his Letter to Congress.

—George Washington—

FAREWELL ADDRESS TO THE ARMIES OF THE UNITED STATES

NOVEMBER 2, 1783

ROCK HILL, NEAR PRINCETON, NOVEMBER 2, 1783.

THE UNITED STATES IN Congress assembled after giving the most honorable testimony to the merits of the fœderal Armies, and presenting them with the thanks of their Country for their long, eminent, and faithful services, having thought proper by their proclamation bearing date the 18th. day of October last. to discharge such part of the Troops as were engaged for the war, and to permit the Officers on furlough to retire from service from and after tomorrow; which proclamation having been communicated in the publick papers for the information and government of all concerned; it only remains for the Comdr in Chief to address himself once more, and that for the last time, to the Armies of the U States (however widely dispersed the individuals who compose them may be) and to bid them an affectionate, a long farewell.

But before the Comdr in Chief takes his final leave of those he holds most dear, he wishes to indulge himself a few moments in calling to mind a slight review of the past. He will then take the liberty of exploring, with his military friends, their future prospects, of advising the general line of conduct, which in his opinion, ought to be pursued, and he will conclude the Address by expressing the obligations he feels himself under for the spirited and able assistance he has experienced from them in the performance of an arduous Office.

A contemplation of the compleat attainment (at a period earlier than could have been expected) of the object for which we contended against so formidable a power cannot but inspire us with astonishment and gratitude. The disadvantageous circumstances on our part, under which the war was undertaken, can never be forgotten. The singular interpositions of Providence in our feeble condition were such, as could scarcely escape the attention of the most unobserving; while the unparalleled perseverence of the Armies of the U States, through almost every possible suffering and discouragement for the space of eight long years, was little short of a standing miracle.

It is not the meaning nor within the compass of this address to detail the hardships peculiarly incident to our service, or to describe the distresses, which in several instances have resulted from the extremes of hunger and nakedness, combined with the rigours of an inclement season; nor is it necessary to dwell on the dark side of our past affairs. Every American Officer and Soldier must now console himself for any unpleasant circumstances which may have occurred by a recollection of the uncommon scenes in which he has been called to Act no inglorious part, and the astonishing events of which he has been a witness, events which have seldom if ever before taken place on the stage of human action, nor can they probably ever happen again. For who has before seen a disciplined Army form'd at once from such raw materials? Who, that was not a witness, could imagine that the most violent local prejudices would cease so soon, and that Men who came from the different parts of the Continent, strongly disposed, by the habits of education, to despise and quarrel with each other, would instantly become but one patriotic band of Brothers, or who, that was not on the spot, can trace the steps by which such a wonderful revolution has been effected, and such a glorious period put to all our warlike toils?

It is universally acknowledged, that the enlarged prospects of happiness, opened by the confirmation of our independence and sovereignty, almost exceeds the power of description. And shall not the brave men, who have contributed so essentially to these inestimable acquisitions, retiring victorious from the field of War to the field of agriculture, participate in all the blessings which have been obtained; in such a republic, who will exclude them from the rights of Citizens and the fruits of their labour. In such a Country, so happily circumstanced, the pursuits of Commerce and the cultivation of the soil will unfold to industry the certain road to competence. To those hardy Soldiers, who are actuated by the spirit of adventure the Fisheries will afford ample and profitable employment, and the extensive and fertile regions of the West will yield a most happy asylum to those, who, fond of domestic enjoyments are seeking for personal independence. Nor is it possible to conceive, that any one of the U States will prefer a national bankruptcy and a dissolution of the union, to a compliance with the requisitions of Congress and the payment of its just debts; so that the Officers and Soldiers may expect considerable assistance in recommencing their civil occupations from the sums due to them from the public, which must and will most inevitably be paid.

In order to effect this desirable purpose and to remove the prejudices which may have taken possession of the minds of any of the good people of the States, it is earnestly recommended to all the Troops that with strong attachments to the Union, they should carry with them into civil society the most conciliating dispositions; and that they should prove themselves not less virtuous and useful as Citizens, than they have been persevering and victorious as Soldiers. What tho, there should be some envious individuals who are unwilling to pay the debt the public has contracted, or to yield the tribute due to merit; yet, let such unworthy treatment produce no invective or any instance of intemperate conduct; let it be remembered that the unbiassed voice of the free Citizens of the United States has promised the just reward, and given the merited applause; let it be known and remembered, that the reputation of the fœderal Armies is established beyond the reach of malevolence; and let a consciousness of their achievements and fame still incite the men, who composed them to honourable actions; under the persuasion that the private virtues of œconomy, prudence, and industry, will not be less amiable in civil life, than the more splendid qualities of valour, perseverance, and enterprise were in the Field. Every one may rest assured that much, very much of the future happiness of the Officers and Men will depend upon the wise and manly conduct which shall be adopted by them when they are mingled with the great body of the community. And, altho the General has so frequently given it as his opinion, in the most public and explicit manner, that, unless the principles of the federal government were properly supported and the powers of the union increased, the honour, dignity, and justice of the nation would be lost forever. Yet he cannot help repeating, on this occasion, so interesting a sentiment, and leaving it as his last injunction to every Officer and every Soldier, who may view the subject in the same serious point of light, to add his best endeavours to those of his worthy fellow Citizens towards effecting these great and valuable purposes on which our very existence as a nation so materially depends.

The Commander in chief conceives little is now wanting to enable the Soldier to change the military character into that of the Citizen, but that steady and decent tenor of behaviour which has generally distinguished, not only the Army under his immediate command, but the different detachments and seperate Armies through the course of the war. From their good sense and prudence he anticipates the happiest consequences; and while he congratulates them on the glorious occasion, which renders their services in the field no longer necessary, he wishes to express the strong obligations he feels himself under for the assistance he has received from every Class, and in every instance. He presents his thanks in the most serious and affectionate manner to the General Officers, as well for their counsel on many interesting occasions, as for their Ardor in promoting the success of the plans he had adopted. To the Commandants of Regiments and Corps, and to the other Officers for their great zeal and attention, in carrying his orders promptly into execution. To the Staff, for their alacrity and exactness in performing the Duties of their several Departments. And to the Non Commissioned Officers and private Soldiers, for their extraordinary patience in suffering, as well as their invincible fortitude in Action. To the various branches of the Army the General takes this last and solemn opportunity of professing his inviolable attachment and friendship. He wishes more than bare professions were in his power, that he were really able to be useful to them all in future life. He flatters himself however, they will do him the justice to believe, that whatever could with propriety be attempted by him has been done, and being now to conclude these his last public Orders, to take his ultimate leave in a short time of the military character, and to bid a final adieu to the Armies he has so long had the honor to Command, he can only again offer in their behalf his recommendations to their grateful country, and his prayers to the God of Armies. May ample justice be done them here, and may the choicest of heaven's favours, both here and hereafter, attend those who, under the devine auspices, have secured innumerable blessings for others; with these wishes, and this benediction, the Commander in Chief is about to retire from Service. The Curtain of seperation will soon be drawn, and the military scene to him will be closed for ever.

POLITICAL REFORMERS

After writing the Declaration of Independence, Jefferson spent
most of the Revolutionary War back in Virginia. There, at the fall
1776 session of the state legislature, he first met James Madison, eight
years his junior and equally dedicated to many of the projects for reform that Jefferson tried to incorporate in a revised code of Virginia

laws that he drafted in the late 1770s. In 1780, while Jefferson was serving as governor, Madison began an extended term as a congressional delegate. Three years later, when the term-limits provision of the Articles of Confederation sent Madison back to Virginia, the widowed Jefferson briefly served in Congress, then sailed to Europe as the new American minister to France. In Europe, Jefferson arranged for the private publication of his only book, *Notes on the State of Virginia,* which he originally began to compile as a set of answers to queries about America from a French diplomat. Meanwhile Madison was elected to the Virginia assembly, where he quickly took a leading role. Among his projects was persuading the assembly to take up the revised legislative code that Jefferson had drafted back in the 1770s.

Jefferson used his *Notes on Virginia* to discuss some of his favorite ideas and projects for reform, including the need to revise the state's hastily drafted constitution of 1776; to encourage gradual emancipation of its hundreds of thousands of African-American slaves; to promote the cause of religious freedom; and to encourage public education. Madison supported many of these projects, and in 1784 circumstances conspired to enable him to move forward on the one cause to which he and Jefferson were most deeply committed: the separation of church and state. The occasion was the introduction of a bill, supported by Patrick Henry, to provide a general public subsidy to all teachers (ministers) of the Christian religion. The measure would enable all of Virginia's churches to recover from the ravages and impoverishment of the war. But the idea of a subsidy violated not only Madison's notion of conscience, but also the beliefs of radical Protestant sects, such as the Baptists, who opposed public support for religion in general. Madison drafted his *Memorial and Remonstrance against Religious Assessments* as a petition against the general assessment bill. Along with other petitions circulated by the Baptists and others, the assembly was put on notice concerning the unpopularity of a general assessment. The bill was defeated, and in the wake of its defeat, Madison easily secured passage of Jefferson's Statute for Religious Freedom, requiring the effective disestablishment of religion in the nation's most populous province.

—Thomas Jefferson—
NOTES ON THE STATE OF VIRGINIA (EXCERPTS)
1784

Query XIII (excerpt)
The constitution of the State and its several characters?

... IT IS UNNECESSARY, HOWEVER, to glean up the several instances of injury, as scattered through American and British history, and the more especially as, by passing on to the accession of the present king, we shall find specimens of them all, aggravated, multiplied and crowded within a small compass of time, so as to evince a fixed design of considering our rights natural, conventional and chartered as mere nullities. The following is an epitome of the first sixteen years of his reign: The colonies were taxed internally and externally; their essential interests sacrificed to individuals in Great Britain; their legislatures suspended; charters annulled; trials by juries taken away; their persons subjected to transportation across the Atlantic, and to trial before foreign judicatories; their supplications for redress thought beneath answer; themselves published as cowards in the councils of their mother country and courts of Europe; armed troops sent among them to enforce submission to these violences; and actual hostilities commenced against them. No alternative was presented but resistance, or unconditional submission. Between these could be no hesitation. They closed in the appeal to arms. They declared themselves independent states. They confederated together into one great republic; thus securing to every State the benefit of an union of their whole force. In each State separately a new form of government was established. Of ours particularly the following are the outlines: The executive powers are lodged in the hands of a governor, chosen annually, and incapable of acting more then three years in seven. He is assisted by a council of eight members. The judiciary powers are divided among several courts, as will be hereafter explained. Legislation is exercised by two houses of assembly, the one called the house of Delegates, composed of two members from each county, chosen annually by the citizens, possessing an estate for life in one hundred acres of uninhabited land, or twenty-five acres with a house on it, or in a house or lot in some town: the other called the Senate, consisting of twenty-four members, chosen quadrenially by the same electors, who for this purpose are distributed into twenty-four districts. The concurrence of both houses is necesary to the passage of a law. They have the appointment of the governor and council, the judges of the superior courts, auditors, attorney-general, treasurer, register of the land office, and delegates to Congress. As the dismemberment of the State had never had its confirmation, but, on the contrary, had always been the subject of protestation and complaint, that it might never be in our own power to raise scruples on that subject, or to disturb the harmony of our new confederacy, the grants to Maryland, Pennsylvania, and the two Carolinas, were ratified.

This constitution was formed when we were new and unexperienced in the science of government. It was the first, too, which was formed in the whole United States. No wonder then that time and trial have discovered very capital defects in it.

1. The majority of the men in the State, who pay and fight for its support, are unrepresented in the legislature, the roll of freeholders entitled to vote not including generally the half of those on the roll of the militia, or of the tax-gatherers.

2. Among those who share the representation, the shares are very unequal. Thus the county of Warwick, with only one hundred fighting men, has an equal representation with the county of Loudon, which has one thousand seven hundred and forty-six. So that every man in Warwick has as much influence in the government as seventeen men in Loudon. But lest it should be thought that an equal interspersion of small among large counties, through the whole State, may prevent any danger of injury to particular parts of it, we will divide it into districts, and show the proportions of land, of fighting men, and of representation in each:

Between the sea-coast and falls of	Square miles.	Fighting men.	Delegates.	Senators.
the rivers	11,205*	19,012	71	12
Between the falls of the rivers and				
the Blue Ridge of mountains .	18,759	18,828	46	8
Between the Blue Ridge and the				
Alleghany	11,911	7,673	16	2
Between the Alleghany and Ohio	79,650†	4,458	16	2
Total	121,525	49,971	149	24

An inspection of this table will supply the place of commentaries on it. It will appear at once that nineteen thousand men, living below the falls of the rivers, possess half the senate, and want four members only of possessing a majority of the house of delegates; a want more than supplied by the vicinity of their situation to the seat of government, and of course the greater degree of convenience and punctuality with which their members may and will attend in the legislature. These nineteen thousand, therefore, living in one part of the country, give law to upwards of thirty thousand living in another, and appoint all their chief officers, executive and judiciary. From the difference of their situation and circumstances, their interests will often be very different.

3. The senate is, by its constitution, too homogenous with the house of delegates. Being chosen by the same electors, at the same time, and out of the same subjects, the choice falls of course on men of the same description. The purpose of establishing different houses of legislation is to introduce the influence of different interests or different principles. Thus in Great Britain it is said their constitution relies on the house of commons for honesty, and the lords for wisdom; which would be a rational reliance, if honesty were to be bought with money, and if wisdom were hereditary. In some of the American States, the delegates and senators are so chosen, as that the first represent the persons, and the second the property of the State. But with us, wealth and wisdom have equal chance for admission into both houses. We do not, therefore, derive from the separation of our legislature into two houses, those benefits which a proper

---

*Of these 542 are on the eastern shore [Jefferson's note].

†Of these, 22,616 are eastward of the meridian of the north of the Great Kanhaway [Jefferson's note].

complication of principles are capable of producing, and those which alone can compensate the evils which may be produced by their dissensions.

4. All the powers of government, legislative, executive, and judiciary, result to the legislative body. The concentrating these in the same hands is precisely the definition of despotic government. It will be no alleviation that these powers will be exercised by a plurality of hands, and not by a single one. One hundred and seventy-three despots would surely be as oppressive as one. Let those who doubt it turn their eyes on the republic of Venice. As little will it avail us that they are chosen by ourselves. An *elective despotism* was not the government we fought for, but one which should not only be founded on free principles, but in which the powers of government should be so divided and balanced among several bodies of magistracy, as that no one could transcend their legal limits, without being effectually checked and restrained by the others. For this reason that convention which passed the ordinance of government, laid its foundation on this basis, that the legislative, executive, and judiciary departments should be separate and distinct, so that no person should exercise the powers of more than one of them at the same time. But no barrier was provided between these several powers. The judiciary and executive members were left dependent on the legislative, for their subsistence in office, and some of them for their continuance in it. If, therefore, the legislature assumes executive and judiciary powers, no opposition is likely to be made; nor, if made, can it be effectual; because in that case they may put their proceedings into the form of an act of assembly, which will render them obligatory on the other branches. They have, accordingly, in many instances, decided rights which should have been left to judiciary controversy; and the direction of the executive, during the whole time of their session, is becoming habitual and familiar. And this is done with no ill intention. The views of the present members are perfectly upright. When they are led out of their regular province, it is by art in others, and inadvertence in themselves. And this will probably be the case for some time to come. But it will not be a very long time. Mankind soon learn to make interested uses of every right and power which they possess, or may assume. The public money and public liberty, intended to have been deposited with three branches of magistracy, but found inadvertently to be in the hands of one only, will soon be

discovered to be sources of wealth and dominion to those who hold them; distinguished, too, by this tempting circumstance, that they are the instrument, as well as the object of acquisition. With money we will get men, said Cæsar, and with men we will get money. Nor should our assembly be deluded by the integrity of their own purposes, and conclude that these unlimited powers will never be abused, because themselves are not disposed to abuse them. They should look forward to a time, and that not a distant one, when a corruption in this, as in the country from which we derive our origin, will have seized the heads of government, and be spread by them through the body of the people; when they will purchase the voices of the people, and make them pay the price. Human nature is the same on every side of the Atlantic, and will be alike influenced by the same causes. The time to guard against corruption and tyranny, is before they shall have gotten hold of us. It is better to keep the wolf out of the fold, than to trust to drawing his teeth and talons after he shall have entered. To render these considerations the more cogent, we must observe in addition:

5. That the ordinary legislature may alter the constitution itself. On the discontinuance of assemblies, it became necessary to substitute in their place some other body, competent to the ordinary business of government, and to the calling forth the powers of the State for the maintenance of our opposition to Great Britain. Conventions were therefore introduced, consisting of two delegates from each county, meeting together and forming one house, on the plan of the former house of burgesses, to whose places they succeeded. These were at first chosen anew for every particular session. But in March 1775, they recommended to the people to choose a convention, which should continue in office a year. This was done, accordingly, in April 1775, and in the July following that convention passed an ordinance for the election of delegates in the month of April annually. It is well known, that in July 1775, a separation from Great Britain and establishment of republican government, had never yet entered into any person's mind. A convention, therefore, chosen under that ordinance, cannot be said to have been chosen for the purposes which certainly did not exist in the minds of those who passed it. Under this ordinance, at the annual election in April 1776, a convention for the year was chosen. Independence, and the establishment of a new form of government, were not even yet the objects

of the people at large. One extract from the pamphlet called Common Sense had appeared in the Virginia papers in February, and copies of the pamphlet itself had got in a few hands. But the idea had not been opened to the mass of the people in April, much less can it be said that they had made up their minds in its favor.

So that the electors of April 1776, no more than the legislators of July 1775, not thinking of independence and a permanent republic, could not mean to vest in these delegates powers of establishing them, or any authorities other than those of the ordinary legislature. So far as a temporary organization of government was necessary to render our opposition energetic, so far their organization was valid. But they received in their creation no power but what were given to every legislature before and since. They could not, therefore, pass an act transcendent to the powers of other legislatures. If the present assembly pass an act, and declare it shall be irrevocable by subsequent assemblies, the declaration is merely void, and the act repealable, as other acts are. So far, and no farther authorized, they organized the government by the ordinance entitled a constitution or form of government. It pretends to no higher authority than the other ordinances of the same session; it does not say that it shall be perpetual; that it shall be unalterable by other legislatures; that it shall be transcendent above the powers of those who they knew would have equal power with themselves. Not only the silence of the instrument is a proof they thought it would be alterable, but their own practice also; for this very convention, meeting as a house of delegates in general assembly with the Senate in the autumn of that year, passed acts of assembly in contradiction to their ordinance of government; and every assembly from that time to this has done the same. I am safe, therefore, in the position that the constitution itself is alterable by the ordinary legislature. Though this opinion seems founded on the first elements of common sense, yet is the contrary maintained by some persons. 1. Because, say they, the conventions were vested with every power necessary to make effectual opposition to Great Britain. But to complete this argument, they must go on, and say further, that effectual opposition could not be made to Great Britain without establishing a form of government perpetual and unalterable by the legislature; which is not true. An opposition which at some time or other was to come to an end, could not need a perpetual institution to carry it on; and a government amendable as its defects should be discovered, was as likely to make effectual resistance, as one that should be unalterably wrong. Besides, the assemblies were as much vested with all powers requisite for resistance as the conventions were. If, therefore, these powers included that of modelling the form of government in the one case, they did so in the other. The assemblies then as well as the conventions may model the government; that is, they may alter the ordinance of government. 2. They urge, that if the convention had meant that this instrument should be alterable, as their other ordinances were, they would have called it an ordinance; but they have called it a *constitution,* which, ex vi termini, means "an act above the power of the ordinary legislature." I answer that *constitutio, constitutium, statutum, lex,* are convertible terms. "*Constitutio* dicitur jus quod a principe conditure." "*Constitutium,* quod ab imperatoribus rescriptum statutumve est." "*Statutum,* idem quod lex." Calvini Lexicon juridicum. *Constitution* and *statute* were originally terms of the* civil law, and from thence introduced by ecclesiastics into the English law. Thus in the statute 25 Hen. VIII. c. 19, §. 1, "*Constitutions* and *ordinances*" are used as synonymous. The term *constitution* has many other significations in physics and politics; but in jurisprudence, whenever it is applied to any act of the legislature, it invariably means a statute, law, or ordinance, which is the present case. No inference then of a different meaning can be drawn from the adoption of this title; on the contrary, we might conclude that, by their affixing to it a term synonymous with ordinance or statute. But of what consequence is their meaning, where their power is denied? If they meant to do more than they had power to do, did this give them power? It is not the name, but the authority that renders an act obligatory. Lord Coke says, "an article of the statute, 11 R. II. c. 5, that no person should attempt to revoke any ordinance then made, is repealed, for that such restrainst is against the jurisdiction and power of the parliament." 4. Inst. 42. And again, "though divers parliaments have attempted to restrain subsequent parliaments, yet could they never effect it; for the latter parliament hath ever power to abrogate, suspend, qualify, explain, or make void the former in the whole or in any part thereof, notwithstanding any words of restraint, prohibition, or penalty, in

---

*To bid, to set, was the ancient legislative word of the English . . . [Jefferson's note].

the former; for it is a maxim in the laws of the parliament, quod leges posteriores priores contrarias abrogant." 4. Inst. 43. To get rid of the magic supposed to be in the word *constitution,* let us translate it into its definition as given by those who think it above the power of the law; and let us suppose the convention, instead of saying, "We the ordinary legislature, establish a *constitution,*" had said, "We the ordinary legislature, establish an act *above the power of the ordinary legislature.*" Does not this expose the absurdity of the attempt? 3. But, say they, the people have acquiesced, and this has given it an authority superior to the laws. It is true that the people did not rebel against it; and was that a time for the people to rise in rebellion? Should a prudent acquiescence, at a critical time, be construed into a confirmation of every illegal thing done during that period? Besides, why should they rebel? At an annual election they had chosen delegates for the year, to exercise the ordinary powers of legislation, and to manage the great contest in which they were engaged. These delegates thought the contest would be best managed by an organized government. They therefore, among others, passed an ordinance of government. They did not presume to call it perpetual and unalterable. They well knew they had no power to make it so; that our choice of them had been for no such purpose, and at a time when we could have no such purpose in contemplation. Had an unalterable form of government been meditated, perhaps we should have chosen a different set of people. There was no cause then for the people to rise in rebellion. But to what dangerous lengths will this argument lead? Did the acquiescence of the colonies under the various acts of power exercised by Great Britain in our infant State, confirm these acts, and so far invest them with the authority of the people as to render them unalterable, and our present resistance wrong? On every unauthoritative exercise of power by the legislature must the people rise in rebellion, or their silence be construed into a surrender of that power, to them? If so, how many rebellions should we have had already? One certainly for every session of assembly. The other States in the union have been of opinion that to render a form of government unalterable by ordinary acts of assembly, the people must delegate persons with special powers. They have accordingly chosen special conventions to form and fix their governments. The individuals then who maintain the contrary opinion in this country, should have the modesty to suppose it possible that they may be wrong, and the rest of America right. But if there be only a possibility of their being wrong, if only a plausible doubt remains of the validity of the ordinance of government, is it not better to remove that doubt by placing it on a bottom which none will dispute? If they be right we shall only have the unnecessary trouble of meeting once in convention. If they be wrong, they expose us to the hazard of having no fundamental rights at all. True it is, this is no time for deliberating on forms of government. While an enemy is within our bowels, the first object is to expel him. But when this shall be done, when peace shall be established, and leisure given us for intrenching within good forms, the rights for which we have bled, let no man be found indolent enough to decline a little more trouble for placing them beyond the reach of question. If anything more be requisite to produce a conviction of the expediency of calling a convention at a proper season to fix our form of government, let it be the reflection:

6. That the assembly exercises a power of determining the quorum of their own body which may legislate for us. After the establishment of the new form they adhered to the *Lex majoris partis,* founded in common law as well as common right. It is the natural law of every assembly of men, whose numbers are not fixed by any other law. They continued for some time to require the presence of a majority of their whole number, to pass an act. But the British parliament fixes its own quorum; our former assemblies fixed their own quorum; and one precedent in favor of power is stronger than an hundred against it. The house of delegates, therefore, have* lately voted that, during the present dangerous invasion, forty members shall be a house to proceed to business. They have been moved to this by the fear of not being able to collect a house. But this danger could not authorize them to call that a house which was none; and if they may fix it at one number, they may at another, till it loses its fundamental character of being a representative body. As this vote expires with the present invasion, it is probable the former rule will be permitted to revive; because at present no ill is meant. The power, however, of fixing their own quorum has been avowed, and a precedent set. From forty it may be reduced to four, and from four to one;

---

*June 4, 1781 [Jefferson's note].

from a house to a committee, from a committee to a chairman or speaker, and thus an oligarchy or monarchy be substituted under forms supposed to be regular. "Omnia mala exempla ex bonis orta sunt; sed ubi imperium ad ignaros aut minus bonos pervenit, novum illud exemplum ab dignis et idoneis adindignos et non idoneos fertur." When, therefore, it is considered, that there is no legal obstacle to the assumption by the assembly of all the powers legislative, executive, and judiciary, and that these may come to the hands of the smallest rag of delegation, surely the people will say, and their representatives, while yet they have honest representatives, will advise them to say, that they will not acknowledge as laws any acts not considered and assented to by the major part of their delegates.

In enumerating the defects of the constitution, it would be wrong to count among them what is only the error of particular persons. In December 1776, our circumstances being much distressed, it was proposed in the house of delegates to create a *dictator,* invested with every power legislative, executive, and judiciary, civil and military, of life and of death, over our persons and over our properties; and in June 1781, again under calamity, the same proposition was repeated, and wanted a few votes only of being passed. One who entered into this contest from a pure love of liberty, and a sense of injured rights, who determined to make every sacrifice, and to meet every danger, for the re-establishment of those rights on a firm basis, who did not mean to expend his blood and substance for the wretched purpose of changing this matter for that, but to place the powers of governing him in a plurality of hands of his own choice, so that the corrupt will of no one man might in future oppress him, must stand confounded and dismayed when he is told, that a considerable portion of that plurality had mediated the surrender of them into a single hand, and, in lieu of a limited monarchy, to deliver him over to a despotic one! How must we find his efforts and sacrifices abused and baffled, if he may still, by a single vote, be laid prostrate at the feet of one man! In God's name, from whence have they derived this power? Is it from our ancient laws? None such can be produced. Is it from any principle in our new constitution expressed or implied? Every lineament expressed or implied, is in full opposition to it. Its fundamental principle is, that the State shall be governed as a commonwealth. It provides a republican organization, proscribes under the name of *prerogative* the exercise of all powers undefined by the laws; places on this basis the whole system of our laws; and by consolidating them together, chooses that they should be left to stand or fall together, never providing for any circumstances, nor admitting that such could arise, wherein either should be suspended; no, not for a moment. Our ancient laws expressly declare, that those who are but delegates themselves shall not delegate to others powers which require judgment and integrity in their exercise. Or was this proposition moved on a supposed right in the movers, of abandoning their posts in a moment of distress? The same laws forbid the abandonment of that post, even on ordinary occasions; and much more a transfer of their powers into other hands and other forms, without consulting the people. They never admit the idea that these, like sheep or cattle, may be given from hand to hand without an appeal to their own will. Was it from the necessity of the case? Necessities which dissolve a government, do not convey its authority to an oligarchy or a monarchy. They throw back, into the hands of the people, the powers they had delegated, and leave them as individuals to shift for themselves. A leader may offer, but not impose himself, nor be imposed on them. Much less can their necks be submitted to his sword, their breath to be held at his will or caprice. The necessity which should operate these tremendous effects should at least be palpable and irresistible. Yet in both instances, where it was feared, or pretended with us, it was belied by the event. It was belied, too, by the preceding experience of our sister States, several of whom had grappled through greater difficulties without abandoning their forms of government. When the proposition was first made, Massachusetts had found even the government of committees sufficient to carry them through an invasion. But we at the time of that proposition, were under no invasion. When the second was made, there had been added to this example those of Rhode Island, New York, New Jersey, and Pennsylvania, in all of which the republican form had been found equal to the task of carrying them through the severest trials. In this State alone did there exist so little virtue, that fear was to be fixed in the hearts of the people, and to become the motive of their exertions, and principle of their government? The very thought alone was treason against the people; was treason against mankind in general; as rivetting forever the chains which bow down their necks, by giving to their oppressors a proof, which they would have trumpeted through the universe, of the imbecility of republican government, in times of pressing danger, to shield them from harm. Those who assume the right of giving away the reins of government in any case, must be sure that the herd, whom they hand on to the rods and hatchet of the dictator, will lay their necks on the block when he shall nod to them. But if our assemblies supposed such a recognition in the people, I hope they mistook their character. I am of opinion, that the government, instead of being braced and invigorated for greater exertions under their difficulties, would have been thrown back upon the bungling machinery of county committees for administration, till a convention could have been called, and its wheels again set into regular motion. What a cruel moment was this for creating such an embarrassment, for putting to the proof the attachment of our countrymen to republican government! Those who meant well, of the advocates of this measure, (and most of them meant well, for I know them personally, had been their fellow-laborer in the common cause, and had often proved the purity of their principles,) had been seduced in their judgment by the example of an ancient republic, whose constitution and circumstances were fundamentally different. They had sought this precedent in the history of Rome, where alone it was to be found, and where at length, too, it had proved fatal. They had taken it from a republic rent by the most bitter factions and tumults, where the government was of a heavy-handed unfeeling aristocracy, over a people ferocious, and rendered desperate by poverty and wretchedness; tumults which could not be allayed under the most trying circumstances, but by the omnipotent hand of a single despot. Their constitution, therefore, allowed a temporary tyrant to be erected, under the name of a dictator; and that temporary tyrant, after a few examples, became perpetual. They misapplied this precedent to a people mild in their dispositions, patient under their trial, united for the public liberty, and affectionate to their leaders. But if from the constitution of the Roman government there resulted to their senate a power of submitting all their rights to the will of one man, does it follow that the assembly of Virginia have the same authority? What clause in our constitution has substituted that of Rome, by way of residuary provision, for all cases not otherwise provided for? Or if they may step *ad libitum* into any other form of government for precedents to rule us by, for what oppression may not a precedent be found in this world of the *ballum omnium in omnia*? Searching for the foundations of this proposition, I can find none which may pretend a color of right or reason, but the defect before developed, that there being no barrier between the legislative, executive, and judiciary departments, the legislature may seize the whole; that having seized it, and possessing a right to fix their own quorum, they may reduce that quorum to one, whom they may call a chairman, speaker, dictator, or by any other name they please. Our situation is indeed perilous, and I hope my countrymen will be sensible of it, and will apply, at a proper season, the proper remedy; which is a convention to fix the constitution, to amend its defects, to bind up the several branches of government by certain laws, which, when they transgress, their acts shall become nullities; to render unnecessary an appeal to the people, or in other words a rebellion, on every infraction of their rights, on the peril that their acquiescence shall be construed into an intention to surrender those rights.

Query XIV (excerpt)

The administration of justice and the description of the laws?

MANY OF THE LAWS which were in force during the monarchy being relative merely to that form of government, or inculcating principles inconsistent with republicanism, the first assembly which met after the establishment of the commonwealth appointed a committee to revise the whole code, to reduce it into proper form and volume, and report it to the assembly. This work has been executed by three gentlemen, and reported; but probably will not be taken up till a restoration of peace shall leave to the legislature leisure to go through such a work.

The plan of the revisal was this. The common law of England, by which is meant, that part of the English law which was anterior to the date of the oldest statutes extant, is made the basis of the work. It was thought dangerous to attempt to reduce it to a text; it was therefore left to be collected from the usual monuments of it. Necessary alterations in that, and so much of the whole body of the British statutes, and of acts of assembly, as were thought proper to be retained, were digested into one hundred and twenty-six new acts, in which simplicity of style was aimed at, as far as was safe. The following are the most remarkable alterations proposed:

To change the rules of descent, so as that the lands of any person dying intestate shall be divisible equally among all his children, or other representatives, in equal degree.

To make slaves distributable among the next of kin, as other movables.

To have all public expenses, whether of the general treasury, or of a parish or county, (as for the maintenance of the poor, building bridges, court-houses, &c.,) supplied by assessment on the citizens, in proportion to their property.

To hire undertakers for keeping the public roads in repair, and indemnify individuals through whose lands new roads shall be opened.

To define with precision the rules whereby aliens should become citizens, and citizens make themselves aliens.

To establish religious freedom on the broadest bottom.

To emancipate all slaves born after the passing the act. The bill reported by the revisers does not itself contain this proposition; but an amendment containing it was prepared, to be offered to the legislature whenever the bill should be taken up, and farther directing, that they should continue with their parents to a certain age, then to be brought up, at the public expense, to tillage, arts, or sciences, according to their geniuses, till the females should be eighteen, and the males twenty-one years of age, when they should be colonized to such place as the circumstances of the time should render most proper, sending them out with arms, implements of household and of the handicraft arts, seeds, pairs of the useful domestic animals, &c., to declare them a free and independent people, and extend to them our alliance and protection, till they have acquired strength; and to send vessels at the same time to other parts of the world for an equal number of white inhabitants; to induce them to migrate hither, proper encouragements were to be proposed. It will probably be asked, Why not retain and incorporate the blacks into the State, and thus save the expense of supplying by importation of white settlers, the vacancies they will leave? Deep-rooted prejudices entertained by the whites; ten thousand recollections, by the blacks, of the injuries they have sustained; new provocations; the real distinctions which nature has made; and many other circumstances, will divide us into parties, and produce convulsions, which will probably never end but in the extermination of the one or the other race. To these objections, which are political, may be added others, which are physical and moral. The first difference which strikes us is that of color.

Whether the black of the negro resides in the reticular membrane between the skin and scarf-skin, or in the scarf-skin itself; whether it proceeds from the color of the blood, the color of the bile, or from that of some other secretion, the difference is fixed in nature, and is as real as if its seat and cause were better known to us. And is this difference of no importance? Is it not the foundation of a greater or less share of beauty in the two races? Are not the fine mixtures of red and white, the expressions of every passion by greater or less suffusions of color in the one, preferable to that eternal monotony, which reigns in the countenances, that immovable veil of black which covers the emotions of the other race? Add to these, flowing hair, a more elegant symmetry of form, their own judgment in favor of the whites, declared by their preference of them, as uniformly as is the preference of the Oranootan for the black woman over those of his own species. The circumstance of superior beauty, is thought worthy attention in the propagation of our horses, dogs, and other domestic animals; why not in that of man? Besides those of color, figure, and hair, there are other physical distinctions proving a difference of race. They have less hair on the face and body. They secrete less by the kidneys, and more by the glands of the skin, which gives them a very strong and disagreeable odor. This greater degree of transpiration, renders them more tolerant of heat, and less so of cold than the whites. Perhaps, too, a difference of structure in the pulminary apparatus, which a late ingenious* experimentalist has discovered to be the principal regulator of animal heat, may have disabled them from extricating, in the act of inspiration, so much of that fluid from the outer air, or obliged them in expiration, to part with more of it. They seem to require less sleep. A black after hard labor through the day, will be induced by the slightest amusements to sit up till midnight, or later, though knowing he must be out with the first dawn of the morning. They are at least as brave, and more adventuresome. But this may perhaps proceed from a want of forethought, which prevents their seeing a danger till it be present. When present, they do not go through it with more coolness or

---

*Crawford [Jefferson's note]. Jefferson refers to the published experiments of Adair Crawford, a British physician and chemist.

steadiness than the whites. They are more ardent after their female; but love seems with them to be more an eager desire, than a tender delicate mixture of sentiment and sensation. Their griefs are transient. Those numberless afflictions, which render it doubtful whether heaven has given life to us in mercy or in wrath, are less felt, and sooner forgotten with them. In general, their existence appears to participate more of sensation than reflection. To this must be ascribed their disposition to sleep when abstracted from their diversions, and unemployed in labor. An animal whose body is at rest, and who does not reflect, must be disposed to sleep of course. Comparing them by their faculties of memory, reason, and imagination, it appears to me that in memory they are equal to the whites; in reason much inferior, as I think one could scarcely be found capable of tracing and comprehending the investigations of Euclid; and that in imagination they are dull, tasteless, and anomalous. It would be unfair to follow them to Africa for this investigation. We will consider them here, on the same stage with the whites, and where the facts are not apochryphal on which a judgment is to be formed. It will be right to make great allowances for the difference of condition, of education, of conversation, of the sphere in which they move. Many millions of them have been brought to, and born in America. Most of them, indeed, have been confined to tillage, to their own homes, and their own society; yet many have been so situated, that they might have availed themselves of the conversation of their masters; many have been brought up to the handicraft arts, and from that circumstance have always been associated with the whites. Some have been liberally educated, and all have lived in countries where the arts and sciences are cultivated to a considerable degree, and all have had before their eyes samples of the best works from abroad. The Indians, with no advantages of this kind, will often carve figures on their pipes not destitute of design and merit. They will crayon out an animal, a plant, or a country, so as to prove the existence of a germ in their minds which only wants cultivation. They astonish you with strokes of the most sublime oratory; such as prove their reason and sentiment strong, their imagination glowing and elevated. But never yet could I find that a black had uttered a thought above the level of plain narration; never saw even an elementary trait of painting or sculpture. In music they are more generally gifted than the whites with accurate ears for tune and time, and they have been found capable of imagining a small catch.* Whether they will be equal to the composition of a more extensive run of melody, or of complicated harmony, is yet to be proved. Misery is often the parent of the most affecting touches in poetry. Among the blacks is misery enough, God knows, but no poetry. Love is the peculiar œstrum of the poet. Their love is ardent, but it kindles the senses only, not the imagination. Religion, indeed, has produced a Phyllis Whately;† but it could not produce a poet. The compositions published under her name are below the dignity of criticism. The heroes of the Dunciad are to her, as Hercules to the author of that poem. Ignatius Sancho‡ has approached nearer to merit in composition; yet his letters do more honor to the heart than the head. They breathe the purest effusions of friendship and general philanthropy, and show how great a degree of the latter may be compounded with strong religious zeal. He is often happy in the turn of his compliments, and his style is easy and familiar, except when he affects a Shandean§ fabrication of words. But his imagination is wild and extravagant, escapes incessantly from every restraint of reason and taste, and, in the course of its vagaries, leaves a tract of thought as incoherent and eccentric, as is the course of a meteor through the sky. His subjects should often have led him to a process of sober reasoning; yet we find him always substituting sentiment for demonstration. Upon the whole, though we admit him to the first place among those of his own color who have presented themselves to the public judgment, yet when we compare him with the writers of the race among whom he lived and

---

*The instrument proper to them is the Banjar, which they brought hither from Africa, and which is the original of the guitar, its chords being precisely the four lower chords of the guitar [Jefferson's note].

†Poet Phillis Wheatley (c. 1753–1784), born in Africa, was captured, enslaved, and sold to a Boston family who reared her in Christianity and educated her in arts and letters.

‡Ignatius Sancho (1729–1780) was born on a slave ship, carried to England as a toddler, and given to three spinster sisters at Greenwich. He eventually gained the patronage of the Montagu family, who employed him as a butler and educated him. He became a poet, playwright, and composer.

§Jefferson refers to the main character in the novel *Tristram Shandy* (1759–1767), by Laurence Sterne, which Jefferson reputedly always carried.

particularly with the epistolary class in which he has taken his own
stand, we are compelled to enrol him at the bottom of the column.
This criticism supposes the letters published under his name to be
genuine, and to have received amendment from no other hand;
points which would not be of easy investigation. The improvement
of the blacks in body and mind, in the first instance of their mixture
with the whites, has been observed by every one, and proves that
their inferiority is not the effect merely of their condition of life. We
know that among the Romans, about the Augustan age especially,
the condition of their slaves was much more deplorable than that of
the blacks on the continent of America. The two sexes were confined
in separate apartments, because to raise a child cost the master more
than to buy one. Cato, for a very restricted indulgence to his slaves
in this particular, took from them a certain price. But in this country the slaves multiply as fast as the free inhabitants. Their situation
and manners place the commerce between the two sexes almost
without restraint. The same Cato, on a principle of economy, always
sold his sick and superannuated slaves. He gives it as a standing pre-
cept to a master visiting his farm, to sell his old oxen, old wagons,
old tools, old and diseased servants, and everything else become useless. "Vendat boves vetulos, plaustrum vetus, feramenta vetera,
servum senem, servum morbosum, et si quid aliud supersit vendat."
Cato de re rusticâ, c. 2. The American slaves cannot enumerate this
among the injuries and insults they receive. It was the common
practice to expose in the island Æsculapius, in the Tyber, diseased
slaves whose cure was like to become tedious. The emperor
Claudius, by an edict, gave freedom to such of them as should recover, and first declared that if any person chose to kill rather than
to expose them, it should not be deemed homicide. The exposing
them is a crime of which no instance has existed with us; and were
it to be followed by death, it would be punished capitally. We are told
of a certain Vedius Pollio, who, in the presence of Augustus, would
have given a slave as food to his fish, for having broken a glass. With
the Romans, the regular method of taking the evidence of their
slaves was under torture. Here it has been thought better never to resort to their evidence. When a master was murdered, all his slaves, in
the same house, or within hearing, were condemned to death. Here
punishment falls on the guilty only, and as precise proof is required
against him as against a freeman. Yet notwithstanding these and

other discouraging circumstances among the Romans, their slaves were often their rarest artists. They excelled too in science, insomuch as to be usually employed as tutors to their master's children. Epictetus, Terence, and Phædrus, were slaves. But they were of the race of whites. It is not their condition then, but nature, which has produced the distinction. Whether further observation will or will not verify the conjecture, that nature has been less bountiful to them in the endowments of the head, I believe that in those of the heart she will be found to have done them justice. That disposition to theft with which they have been branded, must be ascribed to their situation, and not to any depravity of the moral sense. The man in whose favor no laws of property exist, probably feels himself less bound to respect those made in favor of others. When arguing for ourselves, we lay it down as a fundamental, that laws, to be just, must give a reciprocation of right; that, without this, they are mere arbitrary rules of conduct, founded in force, and not in conscience; and it is a problem which I give to the master to solve, whether the religious precepts against the violation of property were not framed for him as well as his slave? And whether the slave may not as justifiably take a little from one who has taken all from him, as he may slay one who would slay him? That a change in the relations in which a man is placed should change his ideas of moral right or wrong, is neither new, nor peculiar to the color of the blacks. Homer tells us it was so two thousand six hundred years ago.

Ἥμισυ, γαζ τ' ἀρετής ἀποαίνυlαι εὐρύθττα Ζεύς
'Ανερος, εντ' ἄν μιν κατὰ δφλιον ἥμαξ ἔλησιν
Od. 17. 323.

Jove fix'd it certain, that whatever day
Makes man a slave, takes half his worth away.

But the slaves of which Homer speaks were whites. Notwithstanding these considerations which must weaken their respect for the laws of property, we find among them numerous instances of the most rigid integrity, and as many as among their better instructed masters, of benevolence, gratitude, and unshaken fidelity. The opinion that they are inferior in the faculties of reason and imagination, must be hazarded with great diffidence. To justify a general conclusion, requires many observations, even where the subject may be submit-ted to the anatomical knife, to optical glasses, to analysis by fire or by solvents. How much more then where it is a faculty, not a sub-stance, we are examining; where it eludes the research of all the senses; where the conditions of its existence are various and vari-ously combined; where the effects of those which are present or ab-sent bid defiance to calculation; let me add too, as a circumstance of great tenderness, where our conclusion would degrade a whole race of men from the rank in the scale of beings which their Creater may perhaps have given them. To our reproach it must be said, that though for a century and a half we have had under our eyes the races of black and of red men, they have never yet been viewed by us as subjects of natural history. I advance it, therefore, as a suspicion only, that the blacks, whether originally a distinct race, or made dis-tinct by time and circumstances, are inferior to the whites in the en-dowments both of body and mind. It is not against experience to suppose that different species of the same genus, or varieties of the same species, may possess different qualifications. Will not a lover of natural history then, one who views the gradations in all the races of animals with the eye of philosophy, excuse an effort to keep those in the department of man as distinct as nature has formed them? This unfortunate difference of color, and perhaps of faculty, is a powerful obstacle to the emancipation of these people. Many of their advocates, while they wish to vindicate the liberty of human nature, are anxious also to preserve its dignity and beauty. Some of these, embarrassed by the question, "What further is to be done with them?" join themselves in opposition with those who are actuated by sordid avarice only. Among the Romans emancipation required but one effort. The slave, when made free, might mix with, without staining the blood of his master. But with us a second is necessary, unknown to history. When freed, he is to be removed beyond the reach of mixture.

The revised code further proposes to proportion crimes and pun-ishments. This is attempted on the following scale:

I. Crimes whose punishment extends to LIFE.
    1. High treason.   Death by hanging.
                           Forfeiture of lands and goods to the commonwealth.
    2. Petty treason. Death by hanging. Dissection.
                           Forfeiture of half the lands and goods to the representatives of
                             the party slain.

3. Murder.   1. By poison.   Death by poison.
                                      Forfeiture of one-half, as before.

                  2. In duel.   Death by hanging. Gibbeting, if the challenger.
                                        Forfeiture of one-half as before, unless it be the party
                                              challenged, then the forfeiture is to the common-
                                              wealth.

                  3. In any other way. Death by hanging.
                                          Forfeiture of one-half as before.

4. Manslaughter.   The second offence is murder.

II. Crimes whose punishment goes to Limb.

    1. Rape. . . . . .   ⎫
                      ⎬ Dismemberment.
    2. Sodomy . . . ⎭

    3. Maiming. . . ⎫ Retaliation, and the forfeiture of half of the lands and goods to
    4. Disfiguring   ⎭   the sufferer.

III. Crimes punishable by Labor.

1. Manslaughter, 1st offence.	Labor VII. years for the public.		Forfeiture of half, as in murder.
2. Counterfeiting money.	Labor VI. years	..	Forfeiture of lands and goods to the commonwealth.
3. Arson. ⎫ 4. Asportation of vessels. ⎭	Labor V. year	..	Reparation three-fold.
5. Robbery. ⎫ 6. Burglary. ⎭	Labor IV. years	..	Reparation double.
7. House-breaking. ⎫ 8. Horse-stealing. ⎭	Labor III. years	..	Reparation.
9. Grand larceny.	Labor II. years	..	Reparation. Pillory.
10. Petty larceny.	Labor I. year	..	Reparation. Pillory.
11. Pretensions to witchcraft, &c.	Ducking.		Stripes.
12. Excusable homicide. ⎫ 13. Suicide. ⎬ To be pitied, not punished. 14. Apostasy. Heresy. ⎭			

Pardon and privilege of clergy are proposed to be abolished; but if the verdict be against the defendant, the court in their discretion may allow a new trial. No attainder to cause a corruption of blood, or forfeiture of dower. Slaves guilty of offences punishable in others by labor, to be transported to Africa, or elsewhere, as the circumstances of the time admit, there to be continued in slavery. A rigorous regimen proposed for those condemned to labor.

Another object of the revisal is, to diffuse knowledge more generally through the mass of the people. This bill proposes to lay off every county into small districts of five or six miles square, called hundreds, and in each of them to establish a school for teaching, reading, writing, and arithmetic. The tutor to be supported by the hundred, and every person in it entitled to send their children three years gratis, and as much longer as they please, paying for it. These schools to be under a visitor who is annually to choose the boy of best genius in the school, of those whose parents are too poor to give them further education, and to send him forward to one of the grammar schools, of which twenty are proposed to be erected in different parts of the country, for teaching Greek, Latin, Geography, and the higher branches of numerical arithmetic. Of the boys thus sent in one year, trial is to be made at the grammar schools one or two years, and the best genius of the whole selected, and continued six years, and the residue dismissed. By this means twenty of the best geniuses will be raked from the rubbish annually, and be instructed, at the public expense, so far as the grammar schools go. At the end of six years instruction, one half are to be discontinued (from among whom the grammar schools will probably be supplied with future masters); and the other half, who are to be chosen for the superiority of their parts and disposition, are to be sent and continued three years in the study of such sciences as they shall choose, at William and Mary college, the plan of which is proposed to be enlarged, as will be hereafter explained, and extended to all the useful sciences. The ultimate result of the whole scheme of education would be the teaching all the children of the State reading, writing, and common arithmetic; turning out ten annually, of superior genius, well taught in Greek, Latin, Geography, and the higher branches of arithmetic; turning out ten others annually, of still superior parts, who, to those branches of learning, shall have added such of the sciences as their genius shall have led them to; the furnishing to the wealthier part of the people convenient schools at which their children may be educated at their own expense. The general objects of this law are to provide an education adapted to the years, to the capacity, and the condition of every one, and directed to their freedom and happiness. Specific details were not proper for the law. These must be the business of the visitors entrusted with its execution. The first stage of this education being the schools of the hundreds, wherein the great mass of the people will receive their instruction, the principal foundations of future order will be laid here. Instead, therefore, of putting the Bible and Testament into the hands of the children at an age when their judgments are not sufficiently matured for religious inquiries, their memories may here be stored with the most useful facts from Grecian, Roman, European and American history. The first elements of morality too may be instilled into their minds; such as, when further developed as their judgments advance in strength, may teach them how to work out their own greatest happiness, by showing them that it does not depend on the condition of life in which chance has placed them, but is always the result of a good conscience, good health, occupation, and freedom in all just pursuits. Those whom either the wealth of their parents or the adoption of the State shall destine to higher degrees of learning, will go on to the grammar schools, which constitute the next stage, there to be instructed in the languages. The learning Greek and Latin, I am told, is going into disuse in Europe. I know not what their manners and occupations may call for; but it would be very ill-judged in us to follow their example in this instance. There is a certain period of life, say from eight to fifteen or sixteen years of age, when the mind like the body is not yet firm enough for laborious and close operations. If applied to such, it falls an early victim to premature exertion; exhibiting, indeed, at first, in these young and tender subjects, the flattering appearance of their being men while they are yet children, but ending in reducing them to be children when they should be men. The memory is then most susceptible and tenacious of impressions; and the learning of languages being chiefly a work of memory, it seems precisely fitted to the powers of this period, which is long enough too for acquiring the most useful languages, ancient and modern. I do not pretend that language is science. It is only an instrument for the attainment of science. But that time is not lost which is employed in providing tools for future operation; more especially as in this case the books put into the hands of the youth for this purpose may be such as will at the same time impress their minds with useful facts and good principles. If this period be suffered to pass in idleness, the mind becomes lethargic and impotent, as would the body it inhabits if unexercised during the same time. The sympathy between body and mind during their rise, progress and decline, is too strict and obvious to endanger our being missed while we reason from the one to the other. As soon as they are of sufficient age, it is supposed they will be sent on from the grammar schools to the university, which constitutes our third and last stage, there to study those sciences which may be adapted to their views. By that part of our plan which prescribes the selection of the youths of genius from among the classes of the poor, we hope to avail the State of those talents which nature has sown as liberally among the poor as the rich, but which perish without use, if not sought for and cultivated. But of the views of this law none is more important, none more legitimate, than that of rendering the people the safe, as they are the ultimate, guardians of their own liberty. For this purpose the reading in the first stage, where *they* will receive their whole education, is proposed, as has been said, to be chiefly historical. History, by apprizing them of the past, will enable them to judge of the future; it will avail them of the experience of other times and other nations; it will qualify them as judges of the actions and designs of men; it will enable them to know ambition under every disguise it may assume; and knowing it, to defeat its views. In every government on earth is some trace of human weakness, some germ of corruption and degeneracy, which cunning will discover, and wickedness insensibly open, cultivate and improve. Every government degenerates when trusted to the rulers of the people alone. The people themselves therefore are its only safe depositories. And to render even them safe, their minds must be improved to a certain degree. This indeed is not all that is necessary, though it be essentially necessary. An amendment of our constitution must here come in aid of the public education. The influence over government must be shared among all the people. If every individual which composes their mass participates of the ultimate authority, the government will be safe; because the corrupting the whole mass will exceed any private resources of wealth; and public ones cannot be provided but by levies on the people. In this case every man would have to pay his own price. The government of Great Britain has been corrupted, because but one man in ten has a right to vote for members of parliament. The sellers of the government, therefore, get nine-tenths of their price clear. It has been thought that corruption is restrained by confining the right of suffrage to a few of the wealthier of the people; but it would be more effectually restrained by an extension of that right to such numbers as would bid defiance to the means of corruption.

Query XVII

THE DIFFERENT RELIGIONS RECEIVED INTO THAT STATE?

THE FIRST SETTLERS in this country were emigrants from England, of the English Church, just at a point of time when it was flushed with complete victory over the religious of all other persuasions. Possessed, as they became, of the powers of making, administering, and executing the laws, they showed equal intolerance in this country with their Presbyterian brethren, who had emigrated to the northern government. The poor Quakers were flying from persecution in England. They cast their eyes on these new countries as asylums of civil and religious freedom; but they found them free only for the reigning sect. Several acts of the Virginia assembly of 1659, 1662, and 1693, had made it penal in parents to refuse to have their children baptized; had prohibited the unlawful assembling of Quakers; had made it penal for any master of a vessel to bring a Quaker into the State; had ordered those already here, and such as should come thereafter, to be imprisoned till they should abjure the country; provided a milder punishment for their first and second return, but death for their third; had inhibited all persons from suffering their meetings in or near their houses, entertaining them individually, or disposing of books which supported their tenets. If no execution took place here, as did in New England, it was not owing to the moderation of the church, or spirit of the legislature, as may be inferred from the law itself; but to historical circumstances which have not been handed down to us. The Anglicans retained full possession of the country about a century. Other opinions began then to creep in, and the great care of the government to support their own church, having begotten an equal degree of indolence in its clergy, two-thirds of the people had become dissenters at the commencement of the present revolution. The laws, indeed, were still oppressive on them, but the spirit of the one party had subsided into moderation, and of the other had risen to a degree of determination which commanded respect.

The present state of our laws on the subject of religion is this. The convention of May 1776, in their declaration of rights, declared it to be a truth, and a natural right, that the exercise of religion should be free; but when they proceeded to form on that declaration the ordinance of government, instead of taking up every principle declared in the bill of rights, and guarding it by legislative sanction, they passed over that which asserted our religious rights, leaving them as they found them. The same convention, however, when they met as a member of the general assembly in October, 1776, repealed all *acts of Parliament* which had rendered criminal the maintaining any opinions in matters of religion, the forbearing to repair to church, and the exercising any mode of worship; and suspended the laws giving salaries to the clergy, which suspension was made perpetual in October, 1779. Statutory oppressions in religion being thus wiped away, we remain at present under those only imposed by the common law, or by our own acts of assembly. At the common law, *heresy* was a capital offence, punishable by burning. Its definition was left to the ecclesiastical judges, before whom the conviction was, till the statute of the 1 El. c. 1 circumscribed it, by declaring, that nothing should be deemed heresy, but what had been so determined by authority of the canonical scriptures, or by one of the four first general councils, or by other council, having for the grounds of their declaration the express and plain words of the scriptures. Heresy, thus circumscribed, being an offence against the common law, our act of assembly of October 1777, c. 17, gives cognizance of it to the general court, by declaring that the jurisdiction of that court shall be general in all matters at the common law. The execution is by the writ *De hæretico comburendo.** By our own act of assembly of 1705, c. 30, if a person brought up in the Christian religion denies the being of a God, or the Trinity, or asserts there are more gods than one, or denies the Christian religion to be true, or the scriptures to be of divine authority, he is punishable on the first offence by incapacity to hold any office or employment ecclesiastical, civil, or military; on the second by disability to sue, to take any gift or legacy, to be guardian, executor, or administrator, and by three years' imprisonment without bail. A father's right to the custody of his own children being founded in law on his right of guardianship, this being taken away, they may of course be severed from him, and put by the authority of a court into more orthodox hands. This is a summary

---

*"Regarding the heretic who is to be burned" (Latin); reference to an English statute of 1401 that condemned those found in possession of an English translation of the Bible to be burned at the stake.

view of that religious slavery under which a people have been willing to remain, who have lavished their lives and fortunes for the establishment of their civil freedom. The error seems not sufficiently eradicated, that the operations of the mind, as well as the acts of the body, are subject to the coercion of the laws. But our rulers can have no authority over such natural rights, only as we have submitted to them. The rights of conscience we never submitted, we could not submit. We are answerable for them to our God. The legitimate powers of government extend to such acts only as are injurious to others. But it does me no injury for my neighbor to say there are twenty gods, or no God. It neither picks my pocket nor breaks my leg. If it be said, his testimony in a court of justice cannot be relied on, reject it then, and be the stigma on him. Constraint may make him worse by making him a hypocrite, but it will never make him a truer man. It may fix him obstinately in his errors, but will not cure them. Reason and free inquiry are the only effectual agents against error. Give a loose to them, they will support the true religion by bringing every false one to their tribunal, to the test of their investigation. They are the natural enemies of error, and of error only. Had not the Roman government permitted free inquiry, Christianity could never have been introduced. Had not free inquiry been indulged at the era of the reformation, the corruptions of Christianity could not have been purged away. If it be restrained now, the present corruptions will be protected, and new ones encouraged. Was the government to prescribe to us our medicine and diet, our bodies would be in such keeping as our souls are now. Thus in France the emetic was once forbidden as a medicine, and the potato as an article of food. Government is just as infallible, too, when it fixes systems in physics. Galileo was sent to the Inquisition for affirming that the earth was a sphere; the government had declared it to be as flat as a trencher, and Galileo was obliged to abjure his error. This error, however, at length prevailed, the earth became a globe, and Descartes declared it was whirled round its axis by a vortex. The government in which he lived was wise enough to see that this was no question of civil jurisdiction, or we should all have been involved by authority in vortices. In fact, the vortices have been exploded, and the Newtonian principle of gravitation is now more firmly established, on the basis of reason, than it would be were the government to step in, and to make it an article of necessary faith. Reason and experiment have been indulged, and error has fled before them. It is error alone which needs the support of government. Truth can stand by itself. Subject opinion to coercion: whom will you make your inquisitors? Fallible men; men governed by bad passions, by private as well as public reasons. And why subject it to coercion? To produce uniformity. But is uniformity of opinion desirable? No more than of face and stature. Introduce the bed of Procrustes then, and as there is danger that the large men may beat the small, make us all of a size, by lopping the former and stretching the latter. Difference of opinion is advantageous in religion. The several sects perform the office of a *censor morum* over such other. Is uniformity attainable? Millions of innocent men, women, and children, since the introduction of Christianity, have been burnt, tortured, fined, imprisoned; yet we have not advanced one inch towards uniformity. What has been the effect of coercion? To make one half the world fools, and the other half hypocrites. To support roguery and error all over the earth. Let us reflect that it is inhabited by a thousand millions of people. That these profess probably a thousand different systems of religion. That ours is but one of that thousand. That if there be but one right, and ours that one, we should wish to see the nine hundred and ninety-nine wandering sects gathered into the fold of truth. But against such a majority we cannot effect this by force. Reason and persuasion are the only practicable instruments. To make way for these, free inquiry must be indulged; and how can we wish others to indulge it while we refuse it ourselves. But every State, says an inquisitor, has established some religion. No two, say I, have established the same. Is this a proof of the infallibility of establishments? Our sister States of Pennsylvania and New York, however, have long subsisted without any establishment at all. The experiment was new and doubtful when they made it. It has answered beyond conception. They flourish infinitely. Religion as well supported; of various kinds, indeed, but all good enough; all sufficient to preserve peace and order; or if a sect arises, whose tenets would subvert morals, good sense has fair play, and reasons and laughs it out of doors, without suffering the State to be troubled with it. They do not hang more malefactors than we do. They are not more disturbed with religious dissensions. On the contrary, their harmony is unparalleled, and can be ascribed to nothing but their unbounded tolerance, because there is no other circumstance in which they differ from every nation on earth. They have made the happy discovery, that the way to silence religious disputes, is to take no notice of them. Let us too give this experiment fair play, and get rid, while we may, of those tyrannical laws. It is true, we are as yet secured against them by the spirit of the times. I doubt whether the people of this country would suffer an execution for heresy, or a three years' imprisonment for not comprehending the mysteries of the Trinity. But is the spirit of the people an infallible, a permanent reliance? Is it government? Is this the kind of protection we receive in return for the rights we give up? Besides, the spirit of the times may alter, will alter. Our rulers will become corrupt, our people careless. A single zealot may commence persecutor, and better men be his victims. It can never be too often repeated, that the time for fixing every essential right on a legal basis is while our rulers are honest, and ourselves united. From the conclusion of this war we shall be going down hill. It will not then be necessary to resort every moment to the people for support. They will be forgotten, therefore, and their rights disregarded. They will forget themselves, but in the sole faculty of making money, and will never think of uniting to effect a due respect for their rights. The shackles, therefore, which shall not be knocked off at the conclusion of this war, will remain on us long, will be made heavier and heavier, till our rights shall revive or expire in a convulsion.

Query XVIII

The particular customs and manners that may happen to be received in that State?

It is difficult to determine on the standard by which the manners of a nation may be tried, whether *catholic or particular.* It is more difficult for a native to bring to that standard the manners of his own nation, familiarized to him by habit. There must doubtless be an unhappy influence on the manners of our people produced by the existence of slavery among us. The whole commerce between master and slave is a perpetual exercise of the most boisterous passions, the most unremitting despotism on the one part, and degrading submissions on the other. Our children see this, and learn to imitate it; for man is an imitative animal. This quality is the germ of all education in him. From his cradle to his grave he is learning to do what he sees others do. If a parent could find no motive either in his philanthropy or his self-love, for restraining the intemperance of passion towards his slave, it should always be a sufficient one that his child is present. But generally it is not sufficient. The parent storms, the child looks on, catches the lineaments of wrath, puts on the same airs in the circle of smaller slaves, gives a loose to the worst of passions, and thus nursed, educated, and daily exercised in tyranny, cannot but be stamped by it with odious peculiarities. The man must be a prodigy who can retain his manners and morals undepraved by such circumstances. And with what execration should the statesman be loaded, who, permitting one half the citizens thus to trample on the rights of the other, transforms those into despots, and these into enemies, destroys the morals of the one part, and the *amor patriæ* of the other. For if a slave can have a country in this world, it must be any other in preference to that in which he is born to live and labor for another; in which he must lock up the faculties of his nature, contribute as far as depends on his individual endeavors to the evanishment of the human race, or entail his own miserable condition on the endless generations proceeding from him. With the morals of the people, their industry also is destroyed. For in a warm climate, no man will labor for himself who can make another labor for him. This is so true, that of the proprietors of slaves a very small proportion indeed are ever seen to labor. And can the liberties of a nation be thought secure when we have removed their only firm basis, a conviction in the minds of the people that these liberties are of the gift of God? That they are not to be violated but with his wrath? Indeed I tremble for my country when I reflect that God is just; that his justice cannot sleep forever; that considering numbers, nature and natural means only, a revolution of the wheel of fortune, an exchange of situation is among possible events; that it may become probable by supernatural interference! The Almighty has no attribute which can take side with us in such a contest. But it is impossible to be temperate and to pursue this subject through the various considerations of policy, of morals, of history natural and civil. We must be contented to hope they will force their way into every one's mind. I think a change already perceptible, since the origin of the present revolution. The spirit of the master is abating, that of the slave rising from the dust, his condition mollifying, the way I hope preparing, under the auspices of heaven, for a total emancipation, and that this is disposed, in the order of events, to be with the consent of the masters, rather than by their extirpation.

Query XIX

The present state of manufactures, commerce, interior and exterior trade?

WE NEVER HAD AN interior trade of any importance. Our exterior commerce has suffered very much from the beginning of the present contest. During this time we have manufactured within our families the most necessary articles of clothing. Those of cotton will bear some comparison with the same kinds of manufacture in Europe; but those of wool, flax and hemp are very coarse, unsightly, and unpleasant; and such is our attachment to agriculture, and such our preference for foreign manufactures, that be it wise or unwise, our people will certainly return as soon as they can, to the raising raw materials, and exchanging them for finer manufactures than they are able to execute themselves.

The political economists of Europe have established it as a principle, that every State should endeavor to manufacture for itself; and this principle, like many others, we transfer to America, without calculating the difference of circumstance which should often produce a difference of result. In Europe the lands are either cultivated, or locked up against the cultivator. Manufacture must therefore be resorted to of necessity not of choice, to support the surplus of their people. But we have an immensity of land courting the industry of the husbandman. Is it best then that all our citizens should be employed in its improvement, or that one half should be called off from that to exercise manufactures and handicraft arts for the other? Those who labor in the earth are the chosen people of God, if ever He had a chosen people, whose breasts He has made His peculiar deposit for substantial and genuine virtue. It is the focus in which he keeps alive that sacred fire, which otherwise might escape from the face of the earth. Corruption of morals in the mass of cultivators is a phenomenon of which no age nor nation has furnished an example. It is the mark set on those, who, not looking up to heaven, to their own soil and industry, as does the husbandman, for their subsistence, depend for it on casualties and caprice of customers. Dependence begets subservience and venality, suffocates the germ of virtue, and prepares fit tools for the designs of ambition. This, the natural progress and consequence of the arts, has sometimes perhaps been retarded by accidental circumstances; but, generally speaking, the proportion which the aggregate of the other classes of citizens bears in any State to that of its husbandmen, is the proportion of its unsound to its healthy parts, and is a good enough barometer whereby to measure its degree of corruption. While we have land to labor then, let us never wish to see our citizens occupied at a workbench, or twirling a distaff. Carpenters, masons, smiths, are wanting in husbandry; but, for the general operations of manufacture, let our workshops remain in Europe. It is better to carry provisions and materials to workmen there, than bring them to the provisions and materials, and with them their manners and principles. The loss by the transportation of commodities across the Atlantic will be made up in happiness and permanence of government. The mobs of great cities add just so much to the support of pure government, as sores do to the strength of the human body. It is the manners and spirit of a people which preserve a republic in vigor. A degeneracy in these is a canker which soon eats to the heart of its laws and constitution.

—James Madison—
A MEMORIAL AND REMONSTRANCE AGAINST RELIGIOUS ASSESSMENTS
JUNE 20, 1785

TO THE HONOURABLE THE GENERAL ASSEMBLY OF THE COMMONWEALTH OF VIRGINIA.

WE THE SUBSCRIBERS, CITIZENS of the said Commonwealth, having taken into serious consideration a bill, printed by order of the last session of General Assembly, entitled, "A bill establishing a provision for teachers of the Christian Religion;" and conceiving, that the same, if finally armed with the sanction of a law, will be a dangerous abuse of power; are bound, as faithful members of a free

State, to remonstrate against it, and to declare the reasons by which we are determined. We remonstrate against the said bill,

Because we hold it for a fundamental and unalienable truth, "that religion, or the duty which we owe to the Creator, and the manner of discharging it, can be directed only by reason and conviction, not by force or violence."* The religion, then, of every man, must be left to the conviction and conscience of every man; and it is the right of every man to exercise it as these may dictate. This right is, in its nature, an unalienable right. It is unalienable, because the opinions of men depending only on the evidence contemplated by their own minds, cannot follow the dictates of other men. It is unalienable, also, because what is here a right towards man, is a duty towards the Creator. It is the duty of every man to render to the Creator such homage, and such only, as he believes to be acceptable to him. This duty is precedent both in order and time, and in degree of obligation, to the claims of civil society. Before any man can be considered as a member of civil society, he must be considered as a subject of the Governor of the Universe. And if a member of civil society, who enters into any subordinate association, must always do it with a reservation of his duty to the general authority; much more must every man, who becomes a member of any particular civil society, do it with a saving of his allegiance to the Universal Sovereign. We maintain, therefore, that in matters of religion, no man's right is abridged by the institution of civil society; and that religion is wholly exempt from its cognizance. True it is, that no other rule exists, by which any question, which may divide society, can be ultimately determined, but by the will of a majority; but it is also true, that the majority may trespass on the rights of the minority.

Because if religion be exempt from the authority of the society at large, still less can it be subject to that of the legislative body. The latter are but the creatures and vicegerents of the former. Their jurisdiction is both derivative and limited. It is limited with regard to the co-ordinate departments; more necessarily, it is limited with regard to the constituents. The preservation of a free government requires, not merely that the metes and bounds which separate each

---

*Declaration of Rights, Article 16 [Madison's note].

department of power, be invariably maintained; but more especially, that neither of them be suffered to overleap the great barrier which defends the rights of the people. The rulers, who are guilty of such an encroachment, exceed the commission from which they derive their authority, and are tyrants. The people who submit to it, are governed by laws made neither by themselves, nor by an authority derived from them, and are slaves.

Because it is proper to take alarm at the first experiment on our liberties. We hold this prudent jealousy to be the first duty of citizens, and one of the noblest characteristicks of the late revolution. The freemen of America did not wait until usurped power had strengthened itself by exercise, and entangled the question in precedents. They saw all the consequences in the principle, and they avoided the consequences by denying the principle. We revere this lesson too much, soon to forget it. Who does not see that the same authority, which can establish Christianity in exclusion of all other religions, may establish, with the same case, any particular sect of Christians, in exclusion of all other sects; that this same authority, which can force a citizen to contribute three pence only of his property, for the support of any one establishment, may force him to conform to any other establishment, in all cases whatsoever?

Because the bill violates that equality which ought to be the basis of every law; and which is more indispensable, in proportion as the validity or expediency of any law is more liable to be impeached. "If all men are, by nature, equally free and independent,"* all men are to be considered as entering into society on equal conditions, as relinquishing no more, and, therefore, retaining no less, one than another, of their natural rights; above all, are they to be considered as retaining an "*equal* title to the free exercise of religion according to the dictates of conscience."† Whilst we assert for ourselves a freedom to embrace, to profess, and observe the religion which we believe to be of divine origin, we cannot deny an equal freedom to those, whose minds have not yet yielded to the evidence which has convinced us. If this freedom be abused, it is an offence against God, not

---

*Declaration of Rights, Article 1 [Madison's note].
†Ditto, Art. 16 [Madison's note].

against man. To God, therefore, and not to man, must an account of it be rendered.

As the bill violates equality, by subjecting some to peculiar burdens; so it violates the same principle, by granting to other peculiar exemptions. Are the Quakers and Menonists the only sects who think a compulsive support of their religions unnecessary and unwarrantable? Can their piety alone be entrusted with the care of publick worship? Ought their religions to be endowed, above all others, with extraordinary privileges, by which proselytes may be enticed from all others? We think too favourably of the justice and good sense of these denominations, to believe, that they either covert pre-eminences over their fellow citizens, or that they will be seduced by them from the common opposition to the measure.

Because the bill implies, either that the civil magistrate is a competent judge of religious truths, or that he may employ religion as an engine of civil policy. The first is an arrogant pretension, falsified by the extraordinary opinion of rulers, in all ages, and throughout the world; the second, an unhallowed perversion of the means of salvation.

Because the establishment proposed by the bill, is not requisite for the support of the Christian religion. To say that it is, is a contradiction to the Christian religion itself; for every page of it disavows a dependence on the power of this world; it is a contradiction to fact, for it is known that this religion both existed and flourished, not only without the support of human laws, but in spite of every opposition from them; and not only during the period of miraculous aid, but long after it had been left to its own evidence and the ordinary care of Providence: nay, it is a contradiction in terms; for religion, not invented by human policy, must have pre-existed and been supported, before it was established by human policy; it is, moreover, to weaken in those, who profess this religion, a pious confidence in its innate excellence, and the patronage of its Author; and to foster in those, who still reject it, a suspicion that its friends are too conscious of its fallacies, to trust it to its own merits.

Because experience witnesses that ecclesiastical establishments, instead of maintaining the purity and efficacy of religion, have had a contrary operation. During almost fifteen centuries has the legal establishment of Christianity been on trial. What have been its fruits? More or less in all places, pride and indolence in the clergy;

ignorance and servility in the laity; in both, superstition, bigotry, and persecution. Inquire of the teachers of Christianity for the ages in which it appeared in its greatest lustre; those of every sect point to the ages prior to its incorporation with civil policy. Propose a restoration of this primitive state, in which its teachers depended on the voluntary rewards of their flocks, many of them predict its downfall. On which side ought their testimony to have the greatest weight, when for, or when against their interest?

Because the establishment in question is not necessary for the support of civil government. If it be urged as necessary for the support of civil government, only as it is a means of supporting religion, and it be not necessary for the latter purpose, it cannot be necessary for the former. If religion be not within the cognizance of civil government, how can its legal establishment be said to be necessary to civil government? What influence, in fact, have ecclesiastical establishments had on civil society? In some instances, they have been seen to erect a spiritual tyranny on the ruins of the civil authority; in more instances, have they been seen upholding the thrones of political tyranny; in no instance have they been seen the guardians of the liberties of the people. Rulers who wished to subvert the publick liberty, may have found on established clergy convenient auxiliaries. A just government instituted to secure and perpetuate it, needs them not. Such a government will be best supported by protecting every citizen in the enjoyment of his religion, with the same equal hand which protects his person and property; by neither invading the equal rights of any sect, nor suffering any sect to invade those of another.

Because the proposed establishment is a departure from that generous policy, which, offering an asylum to the persecuted and oppressed of every nation and religion, promised a lustre to our country, and an accession to the number of its citizens. What a melancholy mark is the bill, of sudden degeneracy? Instead of holding forth an asylum to the persecuted, it is itself a signal of persecution. It degrades from the equal rank of citizens, all those whose opinions in religion do not bend to those of the legislative authority. Distant as it may be, in its present form, from the inquisition, it differs from it only in degree; the one is the first step, the other the last, in the career of intolerance. The magnanimous sufferer under the cruel scourge in foreign regions, must view the bill as a beacon on our coast, warning him to seek some other haven, where liberty and philanthropy in their due extent may offer a more certain repose for his troubles.

Because it will have a like tendency to banish our citizens. The allurements presented by other situations, are every day thinning their number. To superadd a fresh motive to emigration, by revoking the liberty which they now enjoy, would be the same species of folly, which has dishonoured and depopulated flourishing kingdoms.

Because it will destroy that moderation and harmony, which the forbearance of our laws to intermeddle with religion has produced among its several sects. Torrents of blood have been spilt in the old world, by vain attempts of the secular arm to extinguish religious discord, by proscribing all differences in religious opinion. Time has at length revealed the true remedy. Every relaxation of narrow and rigorous policy, wherever it has been tried, has been found to assuage the disease. The American theatre has exhibited proofs, that equal and complete liberty, if it does not wholly eradicate it, sufficiently destroys its malignant influence on the health and prosperity of the State. If, with the salutary effects of this system under our own eyes, we begin to contract the bounds of religious freedom, we know no name that will too severely reproach our folly. At least, let warning be taken at the first fruits of the threatened innovation. The very appearance of the bill has transformed that "Christian forbearance, love and charity,"* which of late mutually prevailed, into animosities and jealousies, which may not soon be appeased. What mischiefs may not be dreaded, should this enemy to the publick quiet be armed with the force of law?

Because the policy of the bill is adverse to the diffusion of the light of Christianity. The first wish of those, who ought to enjoy this precious gift, ought to be, that it may be imparted to the whole race of mankind. Compare the number of those, who have as yet received it, with the number stil remaining under the dominion of false religions, and how small is the former! Does the policy of the bill tend to lessen the disproportion? No; it at once discourages those who are strangers to the light of truth, from coming into the regions of it; and countenances, by example, the nations who continue in

---

*Declaration of Rights, Art. 16 [Madison's note].

darkness, in shutting out those who might convey it to them. Instead of levelling, as far as possible, every obstacle to the victorious progress of truth, the bill, with an ignoble and unchristian timidity, would circumscribe it, with a wall of defence against the encroachments of error.

Because an attempt to enforce by legal sanctions, acts, obnoxious to so great a portion of citizens, tends to enervate the laws in general, and to slacken the bands of society. If it be difficult to execute any law, which is not generally deemed necessary nor salutary, what must be the case when it is deemed invalid and dangerous? And what may be the effect of so striking an example of impotency in the government on its general authority?

Because a measure of such singular magnitude and delicacy, ought not to be imposed without the clearest evidence that it is called for by a majority of citizens; and no satisfactory method is yet proposed, by which the voice of the majority in this case may be determined, or its influence secured. "The people of the respective counties are, indeed, requested to signify their opinion, respecting the adoption of the bill, to the next session of Assembly." But the representation must be made equal, before the voice, either of the representatives, or of the counties, will be that of the people. Our hope is, that neither of the former will, after due consideration, espouse the dangerous principle of the bill. Should the event disappoint us, it will still leave us in full confidence, that a fair appeal to the latter will reverse the sentence against our liberties.

Because, finally, "the equal right of every citizen to the free exercise of his religion according to the dictates of his conscience," is held by the same tenure with all our other rights. If we recur to its origin, it is equally the gift of nature; if we weigh its importance, it cannot be less dear to us; if we consult the "Declaration of those rights which pertain to the good people of Virginia, as the basis and foundation of government," it is enumerated with equal solemnity, or rather with studied emphasis. Either then we must say that the will of the Legislature is the only measure of their authority; and that in the plenitude of this authority, they may sweep away all our fundamental rights; or, that they are bound to leave this particular right untouched and sacred; either we must say, that they may control the freedom of the press; may abolish the trial by jury; may swallow up the executive and judiciary powers of the State: nay, that they may annihilate our very right of suffrage, and erect themselves into an independent and hereditary assembly; or we must say that they have no authority to enact into a law, the bill under consideration. We the subscribers say, that the General Assembly of this Commonwealth have no such authority; and that no effort may be omitted on our part, against so dangerous an usurpation, we oppose to it this Remonstrance, earnestly praying, as we are in duty bound, that the Supreme Lawgiver of the Universe, by illuminating those to whom it is addressed, may, on the one hand, turn their councils from every act, which would affront his holy prerogative, or violate the trust committed to them; and, on the other, guide them into every measure which may be worthy of his blessing, may redound to their own praise, and may establish more firmly the liberties, the property, and the happiness of this Commonwealth.

—Thomas Jefferson—
Virginia Statute for Religious Freedom
January 16, 1786

An Act for Establishing Religious Freedom

Whereas almighty God hath created the mind free; that all attempts to influence it by temporal punishments or burthens, or by civil incapacitations, tend only to beget habits of hypocrisy and meanness, and are a departure from the plan of the Holy author of our religion, who being Lord both of body and mind, yet chose not to propagate it by coercions on either, as was in his Almighty power to do; that the impious presumption of legislators and rulers, civil as well as ecclesiastical, who being themselves but fallible and uninspired men, have assumed dominion over the faith of others, setting up their own opinions and modes of thinking as the only true and infallible, and as such endeavouring to impose them on others, hath established and maintained false religions over the greatest part of the world, and through all time; that to compel a man to furnish contributions of money for the propagation of opinions which he disbelieves, is sinful and tyrannical; that even the forcing him to support this or that teacher of his own religious persuasion, is depriving him of the comfortable liberty of giving his contributions to the particular pastor, whose morals he would make his pattern, and whose powers he feels most persuasive to righteousness, and is withdrawing from the ministry those temporary rewards, which proceeding from an approbation of their personal conduct, are an additional incitement to earnest and unremitting labours for the instruction of mankind; that our civil rights have no dependence on our religious opinions, any more than our opinions in physics or geometry; that therefore the proscribing any citizen as unworthy the public confidence by laying upon him an incapacity of being called to offices of trust and emolument, unless he profess or renounce this or that religious opinion, is depriving him injuriously of those privileges and advantages to which in common with his fellow-citizens he has a natural right; that it tends only to corrupt the principles of that religion it is meant to encourage, by bribing with a monopoly of worldly honours and emoluments, those who will externally profess and conform to it; that though indeed these are criminal who do not withstand such temptation, yet neither are those innocent who lay the bait in their way; that to suffer the civil magistrate to intrude his powers into the field of opinion, and to restrain the profession or propagation of principles on supposition of their ill tendency, is a dangerous fallacy, which at once destroys all religious liberty, because he being of course judge of that tendency will make his opinions the rule of judgment, and approve or condemn the sentiments of others only as they shall square with or differ from his own; that it is time enough for the rightful purposes of civil government, for its officers to interfere when principles break out into overt acts against peace and good order; and finally, that truth is great and will prevail if left to herself, that she is the proper and sufficient antagonist to error, and has nothing to fear from the conflict, unless by human interposition disarmed of her natural weapons, free argument and debate, errors ceasing to be dangerous when it is permitted freely to contradict them:

Be it enacted by the General Assembly, That no man shall be compelled to frequent or support any religious worship, place, or ministry whatsoever, nor shall be enforced, restrained, molested, or burthened in his body or goods, nor shall otherwise suffer on account of his religious opinions or belief; but that all men shall be free to profess, and by argument to maintain, their opinion in matters of religion, and that the same shall in no way diminish, enlarge, or affect their civil capacities.

And though we well know that this assembly elected by the people for the ordinary purposes of legislation only, have no power to restrain the acts of succeeding assemblies, constituted with powers equal to our own, and that therefore to declare this act to be irrevocable would be of no effect in law; yet we are free to declare, and do declare, that the rights hereby asserted are of the natural rights of mankind, and that if any act shall be hereafter passed to repeal the present, or to narrow its operation, such act will be an infringement of natural right.

The Road to Philadelphia

DURING HIS TERM IN Congress (1780–1783), James Madison was deeply involved in the efforts to ratify and amend the Articles of Confederation. Once he returned to Virginia, he continued to do whatever he could to persuade his fellow legislators to support Congress and the Confederation. Through his correspondence with James Monroe, who had replaced him in the Virginia delegation, he remained well informed about doings in Congress. But by early 1786 Madison was coming to the conclusion that the formal procedures for amending the Articles, which required the unanimous approval of the states, were unworkable. With some misgivings, he supported a resolution of the Virginia assembly inviting other legislatures to send deputies to a meeting to discuss the need to provide Congress with the power to regulate commerce. When the appointed time came, however, only a dozen commissioners from five states appeared at Mann's Tavern in Annapolis, too few to proceed with the business at hand.

Rather than simply adjourn without doing anything, the commissioners opted to pursue a risky gambit. Drawing upon the language of the credentials of the New Jersey deputies, the Annapolis commissioners issued a call for a second convention to meet at Philadelphia in May 1787. In the months to come, all the states but Rhode Island agreed to appoint deputies to this second convention. The cause of reform was advanced when Congress itself endorsed the convention, even though this meant approving a proceeding unknown to the Articles of Confederation.

The agenda for the convention, however, remained uncertain, and many competent observers thought either that the delegates should err on the side of caution or simply discuss possible reforms without offering any particular proposals. Madison disagreed. He no longer believed that the reform of the Confederation could wait indefinitely. If it were delayed much longer, the federal union might devolve into two or three regional confederacies. Back in New York City, where he was again attending Congress, Madison began to prepare his agenda for the convention. He first sketched his general understanding of the problems of the union in a memorandum on what he called the "vices of the political system of the United States." Then, in letters to George Washington and Governor Edmund Randolph, Madison converted these general ideas into a sketch of a new government, one that would replace the existing unicameral Congress with a bicameral legislature and constitutionally independent executive and judicial departments.

THE ROAD TO PHILADELPHIA

—*James Madison*—
LETTER TO JAMES MONROE
MARCH 19, 1786

DEAR SIR,—I am just favored with yours of the 11 & 16 of Feby. A newspaper since the date of the latter has verified to me your inauguration into the mysteries of Wedlock, of which you dropped a previous hint in the former. You will accept my sincerest congratulations on this event, with every wish for the happiness it promises. I join you cheerfully in the purchase from Taylor, as preferably to taking it wholly to myself. The only circumstance I regret is that the first payment will rest with you alone, if the conveyance should be accelerated. A few months will elapse inevitably before I shall be able to place on the spot my half of the sum but the day shall be shortened as much as possible. I accede also fully to your idea of extending the purchase in that quarter. Perhaps we may be able to go beyond the thousand acres you have taken into view. But ought we not to explore the ground before we venture too far? Proximity of situation is but presumptive evidence of the quality of soil. The value of land depends on a variety of little circumstances which can only be judged of from inspection, and a knowledge of which gives a seller an undue advantage over an uninformed buyer. Can we not about the last of May or June take a turn into that district, I am in a manner determined on it myself. It will separate you but for a moment from New York, and may give us lights of great consequence. I have a project in my head which if it hits your idea and can be effected may render such an excursion of decisive value to us. I reserve it for oral communication.

"The Question of policy," you say, "is whether it will be better to correct the vices of the Confederation by recommendation gradually as it moves along, or by a Convention. If the latter should be

determined on, the powers of the Virg^a Coms̄r̄s are inadequate." If all
on whom the correction of these vices depends were well informed
and well disposed, the mode would be of little moment. But as we
have both ignorance and iniquity to combat, we must defeat the designs of the latter by humouring the prejudices of the former. The
efforts for bringing about a correction thro the medium of Congress
have miscarried. Let a Convention then, be tried. If it succeeds in the
first instance, it can be repeated as other defects force themselves on
the public attention, and as the public mind becomes prepared for
further remedies. The Assembly here would refer nothing to Congress. They would have revolted equally against a plenipotentiary
commission to their deputies for the Convention. The option therefore lay between doing what was done and doing nothing. Whether
a right choice was made time only can prove. I am not in general an
advocate for temporizing or partial remedies. But a rigor in this respect, if pushed too far may hazard everything. If the present parox-
ysm of our affairs be totally neglected our case may become
desperate. If anything comes of the Convention it will probably be
of a permanent not a temporary nature, which I think will be a great
point. The mind feels a peculiar complacency in seeing a good thing
done when it is not subject to the trouble & uncertainty of doing it
over again. The commission is to be sure not filled to every man's
mind. The History of it may be a subject of some future tête a tête.
You will be kind enough to forward the letter to Mr Jefferson and to
be assured that I am with the sincerest affection

y.^r friend & serv.^t

—*Benjamin Rush*—
ADDRESS TO THE PEOPLE OF THE UNITED STATES
JUNE 3, 1786

THERE IS NOTHING MORE common than to confound the terms of
the American revolution with those of *the late American war.* The
American war is over: but this is far from being the case with the
American revolution. On the contrary, nothing but the first act of

the great drama is closed. It remains yet to establish and perfect our new forms of government; and to prepare the principles, morals, and manners of our citizens, for these forms of government, after they are established and brought to perfection.

The confederation, together with most of our state constitutions, were formed under very unfavourable circumstances. We had just emerged from a corrupted monarchy. Although we understood perfectly the principles of liberty, yet most of us were ignorant of the forms and combinations of power in republics. Add to this, the British army was in the heart of our country, spreading desolation wherever it went: our resentments, of course, were awakened. We detested the British name; and unfortunately refused to copy some things in the administration of justice and power, in the British government, which have made it the admiration and envy of the world. In our opposition to monarchy, we forgot that the temple of tyranny has two doors. We bolted one of them by proper restraints; but we left the other open, by neglecting to guard against the effects of our own ignorance and licentiousness.

Most of the present difficulties of this country arise from the weakness and other defects of our governments.

My business at present shall be only to suggest the defects of the confederation. These consist—1st. In the deficiency of coercive power. 2d. In a defect of exclusive power to issue paper-money, and regulate commerce. 3d. In vesting the sovereign power of the united states in a single legislature: and, 4th. In the too frequent rotation of its members.

A convention is to sit soon for the purpose of devising means of obviating part of the two first defects that have been mentioned. But I wish they may add to their recommendations to each state, to surrender up to congress their power of emitting money. In this way, a uniform currency will be produced, that will facilitate trade, and help to bind the states together. Nor will the states be deprived of large sums of money by this means when sudden emergencies require it: for they may always borrow them as they did during the war, out of the treasury of congress. Even a loan-office may be better instituted in this way in each state, than in any other.

The two last defects that have been mentioned, are not of less magnitude than the first. Indeed, the single legislature of congress will become more dangerous from an increase of power than ever.

To remedy this, let the supreme federal power be divided, like the legislatures of most of our states, into two distinct, independent branches. Let one of them be styled the council of the states, and the other the assembly of the states. Let the first consist of a single delegate—and the second, of two, three, or four delegates, chosen annually by each state. Let the president be chosen annually by the joint ballot of both houses; and let him possess certain powers in conjunction with a privy council, especially the power of appointing most of the officers of the united states. The officers will not only be better when appointed this way, but one of the principal causes of faction will be thereby removed from congress. I apprehend this division of the power of congress will become more necessary, as soon as they are invested with more ample powers of levying and expending public money.

The custom of turning men out of power or office, as soon as they are qualified for it, has been found to be as absurd in practice, as it is virtuous in speculation. It contradicts our habits and opinions in every other transaction of life. Do we dismiss a general—a physician—or even a domestic, as soon as they have acquired knowledge sufficient to be useful to us, for the sake of increasing the number of able generals—skilful physicians—and faithful servants? We do not. Government is a science; and can never be perfect in America, until we encourage men to devote not only three years, but their whole lives to it. I believe the principal reason why so many men of abilities object to serving in congress, is owing to their not thinking it worth while to spend three years in acquiring a profession which their country immediately afterwards forbids them to follow.

There are two errors or prejudices on the subject of government in America, which lead to the most dangerous consequences.

It is often said, that "the sovereign and all other power is seated *in* the people." This idea is unhappily expressed. It should be—"all power is derived *from* the people." They possess it only on the days of their elections. After this, it is the property of their rulers, nor can they exercise or resume it, unless it is abused. It is of importance to circulate this idea, as it leads to order and good government.

The people of America have mistaken the meaning of the word sovereignty: hence each state pretends to be *sovereign*. In Europe, it is applied only to those states which possess the power of making war and peace—of forming treaties, and the like. As this power belongs only to congress, they are the only *sovereign* power in the united states.

We commit a similar mistake in our ideas of the word independent. No individual state, as such, has any claim to independence. She is independent only in a union with her sister states in congress.

To conform the principles, morals, and manners of our citizens to our republican forms of government, it is absolutely necessary that knowledge of every kind, should be disseminated through every part of the united states.

For this purpose, let congress, instead of laying out half a million of dollars, in building a federal town, appropriate only a fourth of that sum, in founding a federal university. In this university, let every thing connected with government, such as history—the law of nature and nations—the civil law—the municipal laws of our country—and the principles of commerce—be taught by competent professors. Let masters be employed, likewise, to teach gunnery—fortification—and every thing connected with defensive and offensive war. Above all, let a professor, of, what is called in the European universities, œconomy, be established in this federal seminary. His business should be to unfold the principles and practice of agriculture and manufactures of all kinds: and to enable him to make his lectures more extensively useful, congress should support a travelling correspondent for him, who should visit all the nations of Europe, and transmit to him, from time to time, all the discoveries and improvements that are made in agriculture and manufactures. To this seminary, young men should be encouraged to repair, after completing their academical studies in the colleges of their respective states. The honours and offices of the united states should, after a while, be confined to persons who had imbibed federal and republican ideas in this university.

For the purpose of diffusing knowledge, as well as extending the living principle of government to every part of the united states— every state—city—county—village—and township in the union, should be tied together by means of the post-office. This is the true non-electric wire of government. It is the only means of conveying heat and light to every individual in the federal commonwealth. Sweden lost her liberties, says the abbe Raynal, because her citizens were so scattered, that they had no means of acting in concert with each other. It should be a constant injunction to the post-masters, to convey newspapers free of all charge for postage. They are not only the vehicles of knowledge and intelligence, but the centinels of the liberties of our country.

The conduct of some of those strangers who have visited our country, since the peace, and who fill the British papers with accounts of our distresses, shews as great a want of good sense, as it does of good nature. They see nothing but the foundations and walls of the temple of liberty, and yet they undertake to judge of the whole fabric.

Our own citizens act a still more absurd part, when they cry out, after the experience of three or four years, that we are not proper materials for republican government. Remember, we assumed these forms of government in a hurry, before we were prepared for them. Let every man exert himself in promoting virtue and knowledge in our country, and we shall soon become good republicans. Look at the steps by which governments have been changed, or rendered stable in Europe. Read the history of Great Britain. Her boasted government has risen out of wars, and rebellions that lasted above sixty years. The united states are travelling peaceably into order and good government. They know no strife—but what arises from the collision of opinions: and in three years they have advanced further in the road to stability and happiness, than most of the nations in Europe have done, in as many centuries.

There is but one path that can lead the united states to destruction, and that is their extent of territory. It was probably to effect this, that Great Britain ceded to us so much waste land. But even this path may be avoided. Let but one new state be exposed to sale at a time; and let the land office be shut up till every part of this new state is settled.

I am extremely sorry to find a passion for retirement so universal among the patriots and heroes of the war. They resemble skilful mariners, who, after exerting themselves to preserve a ship from sinking in a storm, in the middle of the ocean, drop asleep as soon as the waves subside, and leave the care of their lives and property, during the remainder of the voyage, to sailors, without knowledge or experience. Every man in a republic is public property. His time and talents—his youth—his manhood—his old age—nay more, life, all, belong to his country.

PATRIOTS of 1774, 1775, 1776—HEROES of 1778, 1779, 1780! come forward! your country demands your services!—Philosophers and friends to mankind, come forward! your country demands your studies and speculations! Lovers of peace and order, who declined taking part in the late war, come forward! your country forgives your timidity, and demands your influence and advice! Hear her proclaiming, in sighs and groans, in her governments, in her finances, in her trade, in her manufactures, in her morals, and in her manners, "THE REVOLUTION IS NOT OVER!"

—Alexander Hamilton—
ADDRESS OF THE ANNAPOLIS CONVENTION
1786

To the Honorable the Legislatures of Virginia, Delaware, Pennsylvania, and New York.

THE COMMISSIONERS FROM THE said States, respectively, assembled at Annapolis, humbly beg leave to report: That pursuant to their several appointments they met at Annapolis, in the State of Maryland, on the eleventh day of September, instant, and having proceeded to a communication of their powers, they found that the States of New York, Pennsylvania, and Virginia had, in substance, and nearly in the same terms, authorized their respective commissioners to meet such commissioners as were or might be appointed by the other States in the Union, at such time and place as should be agreed upon by the said commissioners, to take into consideration the trade and commerce of the United States, to consider how far a uniform system in their commercial intercourse and regulations might be necessary to their common interest and permanent harmony, and to report to the several States such an act relative to this great object as, when unanimously ratified by them, would enable the United States in Congress assembled effectually to provide for the same.

That the State of Delaware had given similar powers to their commissioners; with this difference only, that the act to be framed in virtue of these powers is required to be reported "to the United

States in Congress assembled, to be agreed to by them, and confirmed by the Legislature of every State."

That the State of New Jersey had enlarged the object of their appointment, empowering their commissioners "to consider how far a
uniform system in their commercial regulations, and *other* important matters, might be necessary to the common interest and permanent harmony of the several States; and to report such an act on
the subject as, when ratified by them, would enable the United States
in Congress assembled effectually to provide for the exigencies of
the Union."

That appointments of commissioners have also been made by the
States of New Hampshire, Massachusetts, Rhode Island, and North
Carolina, none of whom, however, have attended. But that no information has been received by your commissioners of any appointment having been made by the States of Connecticut, Maryland,
South Carolina, or Georgia. That the express terms of the powers to
your commissioners supposing a deputation from all the States, and
having for their object the trade and commerce of the United States,
your commissioners did not conceive it advisable to proceed to the
business of their mission under the circumstances of so partial and
defective a representation.

Deeply impressed, however, with the magnitude and importance
of the object confided to them on this occasion, your commissioners cannot forbear to indulge an expression of their earnest and
unanimous wish that speedy measures may be taken to effect a general meeting of the States in a future convention for the same, and
such other purposes as the situation of public affairs may be found
to require.

If in expressing this wish, or intimating any further sentiment,
your commissioners should seem to exceed the strict bounds of
their appointment, they entertain a full confidence that a conduct
dictated by an anxiety for the welfare of the United States will not
fail to receive a favorable construction. In this persuasion, your
commissioners submit an opinion that the idea of extending the
powers of their deputies to other subjects than those of commerce,
which had been adopted by the State of New Jersey, was an improvement on the original plan, and will deserve to be incorporated
into that of a future convention. They are the more naturally led to

this conclusion, as, in the course of their reflections on the subject, they have been induced to think that the power of regulating trade is of such comprehensive extent, and will enter so far into the general system of the Federal Government, that to give it efficacy, and to obviate questions and doubts concerning its precise nature and limits, may require a correspondent adjustment of other parts of the Federal system. That there are important defects in the system of the Federal Government is acknowledged by the acts of all those States which have concurred in the present meeting; that the defects upon a closer examination may be found greater and more numerous than even these acts imply, is at least so far probable, from the embarrassments which characterize the present state of our national affairs, foreign and domestic, as may reasonably be supposed to merit a deliberate and candid discussion in some mode which will unite the sentiments and councils of all the States.

In the choice of the mode, your commissioners are of the opinion that a CONVENTION of deputies from the different States for the special and sole purpose of entering into this investigation, and digesting a plan of supplying such defects as may be discovered to exist, will be entitled to a preference, from considerations which will occur without being particularized. Your commissioners decline an enumeration of those national circumstances on which their opinion respecting the propriety of a future convention with those enlarged powers is founded, as it would be an intrusion of facts and observations, most of which have been frequently the subject of public discussion, and none of which can have escaped the penetration of those to whom they would in this instance be addressed.

They are, however, of a nature so serious as, in the view of your commissioners, to render the situation of the United States delicate and critical, calling for an exertion of the united virtue and wisdom of all the members of the Confederacy. Under this impression your commissioners, with the most respectful deference, beg leave to suggest their unanimous conviction, that it may effectually tend to advance the interests of the Union, if the States by which they have been respectively delegated would concur themselves and use their endeavors to procure the concurrence of the other States in the appointment of commissioners to meet at Philadelphia on the second Monday in May next, to take into consideration the situation of the

United States, to devise such further provisions as shall appear to them necessary to render the Constitution of the Federal Government *adequate to the exigencies of the Union,* and to report such an act for that purpose to the United States in Congress assembled as, when agreed to by them and afterwards confirmed by the Legislature of every State, will effectually provide for the same.

Though your commissioners could not with propriety address these observations and sentiments to any but the States they have the honor to represent, they have nevertheless concluded, from motives of respect, to transmit copies of this report to the United States in Congress assembled, and to the Executives of the other States.

RESOLUTION OF CONGRESS
FEBRUARY 21, 1787

FEBRUARY 21ST 1787.

WHEREAS THERE IS PROVISION in the Articles of Confederation and perpetual Union for making alterations therein by the assent of a Congress of the United States and of the Legislatures of the several States; And Whereas experience hath evinced that there are defects in the present Confederation, as a mean to remedy which several of the States and particularly the State of New York by express instructions to their Delegates in Congress have suggested a Convention for the purposes expressed in the following resolution and such Convention appearing to be the most probable mean of establishing in these States a firm National Government—

Resolved That in the opinion of Congress it is expedient that on the second Monday in May next a Convention of Delegates who shall have been appointed by the several States be held at Philadelphia for the sole and express purpose of revising the Articles of Confederation and reporting to Congress and the several Legislatures such alterations and provisions therein as shall when agreed to in Congress and confirmed by the States render the federal Constitution adequate to the exigencies of Government and the preservation of the Union—

—*James Madison*—
VICES OF THE POLITICAL SYSTEM
OF THE UNITED STATES
APRIL 1787

Observations by J. M. (A copy taken by permission by Dan. Carroll & sent to Ch. Carroll of Carrollton.)

1. *FAILURE OF THE STATES to comply with the Constitutional requisitions.* This evil has been so fully experienced both during the war and since the peace, results so naturally from the number and independent authority of the States and has been so uniformly exemplified in every similar Confederacy, that it may be considered as not less radically and permanently inherent in than it is fatal to the object of the present system.

2. *Encroachments by the States on the federal authority.* Examples of this are numerous and repetitions may be foreseen in almost every case where any favorite object of a State shall present a temptation. Among these examples are the wars and treaties of Georgia with the Indians. The unlicensed compacts between Virginia and Maryland, and between Pen.ª & N. Jersey—the troops raised and to be kept up by Mass^{ts}.

3. *Violations of the law of nations and of treaties.* From the number of Legislatures, the sphere of life from which most of their members are taken, and the circumstances under which their legislative business is carried on, irregularities of this kind must frequently happen. Accordingly not a year has passed without instances of them in some one or other of the States. The Treaty of Peace—the treaty with France—the treaty with Holland have each been violated. The causes of these irregularities must necessarily produce frequent violations of the law of nations in other respects.

As yet foreign powers have not been rigorous in animadverting on us. This moderation, however cannot be mistaken for a permanent partiality to our faults, or a permanent security ag.^{st} those disputes with other nations, which being among the greatest of public calamities, it ought to be least in the power of any part of the community to bring on the whole.

4. *Trespasses of the States on the rights of each other.* These are alarming symptoms, and may be daily apprehended as we are admonished by daily experience. See the law of Virginia restricting foreign vessels to certain ports—of Maryland in favor of vessels belonging to her *own citizens*—of N. York in favor of the same—

Paper money, instalments of debts, occlusion of Courts, making property a legal tender, may likewise be deemed aggressions on the rights of other States. As the Citizens of every State aggregately taken stand more or less in the relation of Creditors or debtors, to the Citizens of every other State, Acts of the debtor State in favor of debtors, affect the Creditor State, in the same manner as they do its own citizens who are relatively creditors towards other citizens. This remark may be extended to foreign nations. If the exclusive regulation of the value and alloy of coin was properly delegated to the federal authority, the policy of it equally requires a controul on the States in the cases above mentioned. It must have been meant 1) to preserve uniformity in the circulating medium throughout the nation. 2) to prevent those frauds on the citizens of other States, and the subjects of foreign powers, which might disturb the tranquillity at home, or involve the Union in foreign contests.

The practice of many States in restricting the commercial intercourse with other States, and putting their productions and manufactures on the same footing with those of foreign nations, though not contrary to the federal articles, is certainly adverse to the spirit of the Union, and tends to beget retaliating regulations, not less expensive and vexatious in themselves than they are destructive of the general harmony.

5. *Want of concert in matters where common interest requires it.* This defect is strongly illustrated in the state of our commercial affairs. How much has the national dignity, interest, and revenue, suffered from this cause? Instances of inferior moment are the want of uniformity in the laws concerning naturalization & literary property; of provision for national seminaries, for grants of incorporation for national purposes, for canals and other works of general utility, wch may at present be defeated by the perverseness of particular States whose concurrence is necessary.

6. *Want of Guaranty to the States of their Constitutions & laws against internal violence.* The confederation is silent on this point and therefore by the second article the hands of the federal authority are tied. According to Republican Theory, Right and power being both vested in the majority, are held to be synonimous. According to fact and experience a minority may in an appeal to force, be an overmatch for the majority. 1) if the minority happen to include all such as possess the skill and habits of military life, & such as possess the great pecuniary resources, one-third only may conquer the remaining two-thirds. 2) one-third of those who participate in the choice of the rulers, may be rendered a majority by the accession of those whose poverty excludes them from a right of suffrage, and who for obvious reasons will be more likely to join the standard of sedition than that of the established Government. 3) where slavery exists the republican Theory becomes still more fallacious.

7. *Want of sanction to the laws, and of coercion in the Government of the Confederacy.* A sanction is essential to the idea of law, as coercion is to that of Government. The federal system being destitute of both, wants the great vital principles of a Political Constution. Under the form of such a constitution, it is in fact nothing more than a treaty of amity of commerce and of alliance, between independent and Sovereign States. From what cause could so fatal an omission have happened in the articles of Confederation? from a mistaken confidence that the justice, the good faith, the honor, the sound policy, of the several legislative assemblies would render superfluous any appeal to the ordinary motives by which the laws secure the obedience of individuals: a confidence which does honor to the enthusiastic virtue of the compilers, as much as the inexperience of the crisis apologizes for their errors. The time which has since elapsed has had the double effect, of increasing the light and tempering the warmth, with which the arduous work may be revised. It is no longer doubted that a unanimous and punctual obedience of 13 independent bodies, to the acts of the federal Government ought not to be calculated on. Even during the war, when external danger supplied in some degree the defect of legal & coercive sanctions, how imperfectly did the States fulfil their obligations to the Union? In time of peace, we see already what is to be expected. How indeed could it be otherwise? In the first place, Every general act of the

Union must necessarily bear unequally hard on some particular member or members of it, secondly the partiality of the members to their own interests and rights, a partiality which will be fostered by the courtiers of popularity, will naturally exaggerate the inequality where it exists, and even suspect it where it has no existence, thirdly a distrust of the voluntary compliance of each other may prevent the compliance of any, although it should be the latent disposition of all. Here are causes & pretexts which will never fail to render federal measures abortive. If the laws of the States were merely recommendatory to their citizens, or if they were to be rejudged by County authorities, what security, what probability would exist, that they would be carried into execution? Is the security or probability greater in favor of the acts of Cong.^{s} which depending for their execution on the will of the State legislatures, wch are tho' nominally authoritative, in fact recommendatory only?

8. *Want of ratification by the people of the articles of Confederation.* In some of the States the Confederation is recognized by, and forms a part of the Constitution. In others however it has received no other sanction than that of the legislative authority. From this defect two evils result: 1) Whenever a law of a State happens to be repugnant to an act of Congress, particularly when the [former] is of posterior date to the [latter], it will be at least questionable whether the [former] must not prevail; and as the question must be decided by the Tribunals of the State, they will be most likely to lean on the side of the State. 2) As far as the union of the States is to be regarded as a league of sovereign powers, and not as a political Constitution by virtue of which they are become one sovereign power, so far it seems to follow from the doctrine of compacts, that a breach of any of the articles of the Confederation by any of the parties to it, absolves the other parties from their respective Obligations, and gives them a right if they chuse to exert it, of dissolving the Union altogether.

9. *Multiplicity of laws in the several States.* In developing the evils which viciate the political system of the U S., it is proper to include those which are found within the States individually, as well as those which directly affect the States collectively, since the former class have an indirect influence on the general malady and must not be overlooked in forming a compleat remedy. Among the evils then of our situation may well be ranked the multiplicity of laws from

which no State is exempt. As far as laws are necessary to mark with precision the duties of those who are to obey them, and to take from those who are to administer them a discretion which might be abused, their number is the price of liberty. As far as laws exceed this limit, they are a nuisance; a nuisance of the most pestilent kind. Try the Codes of the several States by this test, and what a luxuriancy of legislation do they present. The short period of independency has filled as many pages as the century which preceded it. Every year, almost every session, adds a new volume. This may be the effect in part, but it can only be in part, of the situation in which the revolution has placed us. A review of the several Codes will shew that every necessary and useful part of the least voluminous of them might be compressed into one tenth of the compass, and at the same time be rendered ten fold as perspicuous.

10. *Mutability of the laws of the States.* This evil is intimately connected with the former yet deserves a distinct notice, as it emphatically denotes a vicious legislation. We daily see laws repealed or superseded, before any trial can have been made of their merits, and even before a knowledge of them can have reached the remoter districts within which they were to operate. In the regulations of trade this instability becomes a snare not only to our citizens, but to foreigners also.

11. *Injustice of the laws of the States.* If the multiplicity and mutability of laws prove a want of wisdom, their injustice betrays a defect still more alarming: more alarming not merely because it is a greater evil in itself; but because it brings more into question the fundamental principle of republican Government, that the majority who rule in such governments are the safest Guardians both of public Good and private rights. To what causes is this evil to be ascribed?

These causes lie 1) in the Representative bodies. 2) in the people themselves.

1) Representative appointments are sought from 3 motives. 1. ambition. 2. personal interest. 3. public good. Unhappily the two first are proved by experience to be most prevalent. Hence the candidates who feel them, particularly, the second, are most industrious, and most successful in pursuing their object: and forming often a majority in the legislative Councils, with interested views, contrary to the interest and views of their constituents, join in a perfidious sacrifice of the latter to the former. A succeeding election it might be

supposed, would displace the offenders, and repair the mischief. But how easily are base and selfish measures, masked by pretexts of public good and apparent expediency? How frequently will a repetition of the same arts and industry which succeeded in the first instance, again prevail on the unwary to misplace their confidence?

How frequently too will the honest but unenlightened representative be the dupe of a favorite leader, veiling his selfish views under the professions of public good, and varnishing his sophistical arguments with the glowing colours of popular eloquence?

2) A still more fatal if not more frequent cause, lies among the people themselves. All civilized societies are divided into different interests and factions, as they happen to be creditors or debtors— rich or poor—husbandmen, merchants or manufacturers—members of different religious sects—followers of different political leaders— inhabitants of different districts—owners of different kinds of property &c &c. In republican Government the majority however composed, ultimately give the law. Whenever therefore an apparent interest or common passion unites a majority what is to restrain them from unjust violations of the rights and interests of the minority, or of individuals? Three motives only 1. a prudent regard to their own good as involved in the general and permanent good of the community. This consideration although of decisive weight in itself, is found by experience to be too often unheeded. It is too often forgotten, by nations as well as by individuals, that honesty is the best policy. 2dly. respect for character. However strong this motive may be in individuals, it is considered as very insufficient to restrain them from injustice. In a multitude its efficacy is diminished in proportion to the number which is to share the praise or the blame. Besides, as it has reference to public opinion, which within a particular Society, is the opinion of the majority, the standard is fixed by those whose conduct is to be measured by it. The public opinion without the Society will be little respected by the people at large of any Country. Individuals of extended views, and of national pride, may bring the public proceedings to this standard, but the example will never be followed by the multitude. Is it to be imagined that an ordinary citizen or even Assemblyman of R. Island in estimating the policy of paper money, ever considered or cared, in what light the measure would be viewed in France or Holland; or even in Mass^{ts} or Connec^{t}? It was a sufficient temptation to both that it was

for their interest; it was a sufficient sanction to the latter that it was popular in the State; to the former, that it was so in the neighbourhood. 3.[dly] will Religion the only remaining motive be a sufficient restraint? It is not pretended to be such on men individually considered. Will its effect be greater on them considered in an aggregate view? quite the reverse. The conduct of every popular assembly acting on oath, the strongest of religious ties, proves that individuals join without remorse in acts, against which their consciences would revolt if proposed to them under the like sanction, separately in their closets. When indeed Religion is kindled into enthusiasm, its force like that of other passions, is increased by the sympathy of a multitude. But enthusiasm is only a temporary state of religion, and while it lasts will hardly be seen with pleasure at the helm of Government. Besides as religion in its coolest state is not infallible, it may become a motive to oppression as well as a restraint from injustice. Place three individuals in a situation wherein the interest of each depends on the voice of the others; and give to two of them an interest opposed to the rights of the third? Will the latter be secure? The prudence of every man would shun the danger. The rules & forms of justice suppose & guard against it. Will two thousand in a like situation be less likely to encroach on the rights of one thousand? The contrary is witnessed by the notorious factions & oppressions which take place in corporate towns limited as the opportunities are, and in little republics when uncontrouled by apprehensions of external danger. If an enlargement of the sphere is found to lessen the insecurity of private rights, it is not because the impulse of a common interest or passion is less predominant in this case with the majority; but because a common interest or passion is less apt to be felt and the requisite combinations less easy to be formed by a great than by a small number. The Society becomes broken into a greater variety of interests, of pursuits of passions, which check each other, whilst those who may feel a common sentiment have less opportunity of communication and concert. It may be inferred that the inconveniences of popular States contrary to the prevailing Theory, are in proportion not to the extent, but to the narrowness of their limits.

The great desideratum in Government is such a modification of the sovereignty as will render it sufficiently neutral between the different interests and factions, to controul one part of the society from

invading the rights of another, and at the same time sufficiently controuled itself, from setting up an interest adverse to that of the whole
Society. In absolute Monarchies the prince is sufficiently, neutral towards his subjects, but frequently sacrifices their happiness to his
ambition or his avarice. In small Republics, the sovereign will is sufficiently controuled from such a sacrifice of the entire Society, but is
not sufficiently neutral towards the parts composing it. As a limited
monarchy tempers the evils of an absolute one; so an extensive Republic meliorates the administration of a small Republic.

An auxiliary desideratum for the melioration of the Republican
form is such a process of elections as will most certainly extract from
the mass of the society the purest and noblest characters which it
contains; such as will at once feel most strongly the proper motives
to pursue the end of their appointment, and be most capable to devise the proper means of attaining it.

—*James Madison*—
LETTER TO GEORGE WASHINGTON
APRIL 16, 1787

NEW YORK APRIL 16 1787.

DEAR SIR,—I have been honored with your letter of the 31 March,
and find with much pleasure that your views of the reform which
ought to be pursued by the Convention, give a sanction to those
which I have entertained. Temporising applications will dishonor
the Councils which propose them, and may foment the internal ma-
lignity of the disease, at the same time that they produce an ostensible palliation of it. Radical attempts although unsuccessful will at
least justify the authors of them.

Having been lately led to revolve the subject which is to undergo
the discussion of the Convention, and formed *some* outlines of a
new system, I take the liberty of submitting them without apology
to your eye.

Conceiving that an individual independence of the States is utterly irreconcileable with their aggregate sovereignty, and that a

consolidation of the whole into one simple republic would be as inexpedient as it is unattainable, I have sought for middle ground, which may at once support a due supremacy of the national authority, and not exclude the local authorities wherever they can be subordinately useful.

I would propose as the ground-work that a change be made in the principle of representation. According to the present form of the Union in which the intervention of the States is in all great cases necessary to effectuate the measures of Congress, an equality of suffrage, does not destroy the inequality of importance in the several members. No one will deny that Virginia and Mass.ts have more weight and influence both within & without Congress than Delaware or Rho. Island. Under a system which would operate in many essential points without the intervention of the State Legislatures, the case would be materially altered. A vote in the national Councils from Delaware, would then have the same effect and value as one from the largest State in the Union. I am ready to believe that such a change would not be attended with much difficulty. A majority of the States, and those of greatest influence, will regard it as favorable to them. To the Northern States it will be recommended by their present populousness; to the Southern by their expected advantage in this respect. The lesser States must in every event yield to the predominant will. But the consideration which particularly urges a change in the representation is that it will obviate the principal objections of the larger States to the necessary concessions of power.

I would propose next that in addition to the present federal powers, the national Government should be armed with positive and compleat authority in all cases which require uniformity; such as the regulation of trade, including the right of taxing both exports & imports, the fixing the terms and forms of naturalization, &c &c.

Over and above this positive power, a negative *in all cases whatsoever* on the legislative acts of the States, as heretofore exercised by the Kingly prerogative, appears to me to be absolutely necessary, and to be the least possible encroachment on the State jurisdictions. Without this defensive power, every positive power that can be given on paper will be evaded & defeated. The States will continue to invade the National jurisdiction, to violate treaties and the law of nations & to harass each other with rival and spiteful measures dictated by mistaken views of interest. Another happy effect of this prerogative would be its controul on the internal vicissitudes of State policy, and the aggressions of interested majorities on the rights of minorities and of individuals. The great desideratum which has not yet been found for Republican Governments seems to be some disinterested & dispassionate umpire in disputes between different passions & interests in the State. The majority who alone have the right of decision, have frequently an interest, real or supposed in abusing it. In Monarchies the sovereign is more neutral to the interests and views of different parties; but, unfortunely he too often forms interests of his own repugnant to those of the whole. Might not the national prerogative here suggested be found sufficiently disinterested for the decision of local questions of policy, whilst it would itself be sufficiently restrained from the pursuit of interests adverse to those of the whole Society. There has not been any moment since the peace at which the representatives of the Union would have given an assent to paper money or any other measure of a kindred nature.

The national supremacy ought also to be extended as I conceive to the judiciary departments. If those who are to expound & apply the laws, are connected by their interests & their oaths with the particular States wholly, and not with the Union, the participation of the Union in the making of the laws may be possibly rendered unavailing. It seems at least necessary that the oaths of the Judges should include a fidelity to the general as well as local constitution, and that an appeal should lie to some National tribunals in all cases to which foreigners or inhabitants of other States may be parties. The admiralty jurisdiction seems to fall entirely within the purview of the national Government.

The National supremacy in the Executive departments is liable to some difficulty, unless the officers administering them could be made appointable by the supreme Government. The Militia ought certainly to be placed in some form or other under the authority which is entrusted with the general protection and defence.

A Government composed of such extensive powers should be well organized and balanced. The legislative department might be divided into two branches; one of them chosen every ___ years by the people at large, or by the Legislatures; the other to consist of fewer members, to hold their places for a longer term, and to go out in such a rotation as always to leave in office a large majority of old members. Perhaps the negative on the laws might be most conveniently exercised by this branch. As a further check, a council of revision including the great ministerial officers might be superadded.

A National Executive must also be provided. I have scarcely ventured as yet to form my own opinion either of the manner in which it ought to be constituted or of the authorities with which it ought to be cloathed.

An article should be inserted expressly guarantying the tranquillity of the States against internal as well as external dangers.

In like manner the right of coercion should be expressly declared. With the resources of Commerce in hand, the National administration might always find means of exerting it either by sea or land; But the difficulty & awkwardness of operating by force on the collective will of a State, render it particularly desirable that the necessity of it might be precluded. Perhaps the negative on the laws might create such a mutuality of dependence between the General and particular authorities, as to answer this purpose or perhaps some defined objects of taxation might be submitted along with commerce, to the general authority.

To give a new System its proper validity and energy, a ratification must be obtained from the people, and not merely from the ordinary authority of the Legislatures. This will be the more essential as inroads on the *existing Constitutions* of the States will be unavoidable.

The inclosed address to the States on the subject of the Treaty of peace has been agreed to by Congress, & forwarded to the several Executives. We foresee the irritation which it will excite in many of our Countrymen; but could not withhold our approbation of the measure. Both the resolutions and the address, passed without a dissenting voice.

Congress continue to be thin, and of course do little business of importance. The settlement of the public accounts,—the disposition of the public lands, and arrangements with Spain, are subjects which claim their particular attention. As a step towards the first, the treasury board are charged with the task of reporting a plan by which the final decision on the claims of the States will be handed over from Congress to a select sett of men bound by the oaths, and cloathed with the powers of Chancellors. As to the Second article,

Congress have it themselves under consideration. Between 6 & 700 thousand acres have been surveyed and are ready for sale. The mode of sale however will probably be a source of different opinions; as will the mode of disposing of the unsurveyed residue. The Eastern gentlemen remain attached to the scheme of townships. Many others are equally strenuous for indiscriminate locations. The States which have lands of their own for sale are *suspected* of not being hearty in bringing the federal lands to market. The business with Spain is becoming extremely delicate, and the information from the Western settlements truly alarming.

A motion was made some days ago for an adjournment of Congress for a short period, and an appointment of Philad.[a] for their reassembling. The eccentricity of this place as well with regard to E. and West as to N. & South has I find been for a considerable time a thorn in the minds of many of the Southern members. Suspicion too has charged some important votes on the weight thrown by the present position of Congress into the Eastern Scale, and predicts that the Eastern members will never concur in any substantial provision or movement for a proper permanent seat for the National Government whilst they remain so much gratified in its temporary residence. These seem to have been the operative motives with those on one side who were not locally interested in the removal. On the other side the motives are obvious. Those of real weight were drawn from the apparent caprice with which Congress might be reproached, and particularly from the peculiarity of the existing moment. I own that I think so much regard due to these considerations, that notwithstanding the powerful ones on the other side, I should have assented with great repugnance to the motion, and would even have voted against it if any probability had existed that by waiting for a proper time, a proper measure might not be lost for a very long time. The plan which I sh.[d] have judged most eligible would have been to fix on the removal whenever a vote could be obtained but so as that it should not take effect until the commencement of the ensuing federal year. And if an immediate removal had been resolved on, I had intended to propose such a change in the plan. No final question was taken in the case. Some preliminary questions shewed that six States were in favor of the motion. Rho. Island the 7.th was at first on the same side, and Mr. Varnum, one of the delegates continues so. His colleague was overcome by the solicitations of his

Eastern brethren. As neither Maryland nor South Carolina were on the floor, it seems pretty evident that N. York has a very precarious tenure of the advantages derived from the abode of Congress.

We understand that the discontents in Mass[ts], which lately produced an appeal to the sword, are now producing a trial of strength in the field of electioneering. The Governor will be displaced.* The Senate is said to be already of a popular complexion, and it is expected that the other branch will be still more so. Paper money it is surmised will be the engine to be played off ag.[ts] creditors both public and private. As the event of the elections however is not yet decided, this information must be too much blended with conjecture to be regarded as a matter of certainty.

I do not learn that the proposed Act relating to Vermont has yet gone through all the stages of legislation here; nor can I say whether it will finally pass or not. In truth, it having not been a subject of conversation for some time, I am unable to say what has been done or is likely to be done with it. With the sincerest affection & the highest esteem I have the honor to be, Dear Sir your devoted Serv.[t]

---

*At the spring 1787 elections, Governor James Bowdoin (1726–1790) was defeated for reelection, presumably for his decision to suppress Shays' Rebellion, in which farmers and the poor rebelled against high taxes.

Rival Visions of Union

ONCE THE CONVENTION MET, it followed the agenda that Madison had formed in the early spring. While waiting for other delegations to straggle into Philadelphia, the Virginia delegates drafted a plan that Governor Edmund Randolph finally introduced on May 29. From that moment on, it was evident that the convention was discussing a wholesale change of government rather than a mere revision of the Articles of Confederation. Not only did the Virginia Plan call for the creation of a full government, with independent legislative, executive, and judicial departments. It also proposed abandoning the rule of one state, one vote under which Congress had operated since 1774. The Virginia Plan proposed applying rules of proportional representation to both houses of the new national legislature. More than that, the Virginia delegates and allies from other populous states insisted that this principle had to be accepted first, before the convention could go on to ask exactly how powerful a government it wanted to create.

Delegates from the small states waited a fortnight to present their alternative. On June 15, William Paterson of New Jersey introduced the New Jersey Plan, which would have preserved the unicameral Congress with modestly augmented powers. One noteworthy response came three days later when Alexander Hamilton gave a lengthy, much admired, but finally unpersuasive speech suggesting that what the country really needed was a constitution much closer in form and substance to the government of Great Britain. The next day Madison gave a speech that restated many of his fundamental criticisms of the Articles of Confederation (which the New Jersey Plan would only enlarge, not replace).

The convention then rejected the New Jersey Plan, but the central issue remained before them: whether a principle of proportional representation should be applied to both houses of the proposed national legislature, or whether the upper house (eventually known as the Senate) should preserve the rule of an equal vote for each state. The delegates debated this question repeatedly over the next month. Then, in the critical vote of July 16, it narrowly endorsed the small states' demand, by a vote of five states to four with one state, populous Massachusetts, divided. The next morning, the dismayed delegates from the large states briefly discussed whether they could proceed on this basis, and reluctantly agreed that they should.

Our principal sources for what was said at Philadelphia are the notes of debate that Madison conscientiously kept. Madison had been frustrated by how little he had been able to learn in his own private researches into the origins of other confederacies, ancient and modern. He accordingly determined to keep an accurate record of the proceedings at Philadelphia. "Nor was I unaware," he later observed, "of the value of such a contribution to the fund of materials for the History of a Constitution on which would be staked the happiness of a young people great even in its infancy, and possibly the cause of Liberty throughout the world." Madison placed himself at the front of the chamber, immediately in front of the presiding officer, and did his best to summarize what each speaker said. He did not, of course, take verbatim transcripts, and his notes captured only a fraction of what was spoken. Yet they also convey the tone as well as substance of many speeches.

Madison's notes were published only in 1840, four years after his death. He first began editing them in the early 1790s but continued to do so during his long retirement, taking advantage of the publication of the official journal of motions and votes kept, rather sloppily, by William Jackson, the convention's secretary, and of other notes of debates kept by New York delegate Robert Yates. Following the editorial procedures used by Max Farrand in his definitive edition of *The Records of the Federal Convention of 1787*, the debates reprinted below use square brackets to indicate later insertions to Madison's notes from the journals and angled brackets to identify later additions or clarifications to the delegates' speeches.

Edmund Randolph Introduces the Virginia Plan
May 29, 1787

MR. RANDOLPH* [THEN] OPENED the main business.

He expressed his regret, that it should fall to him, rather than those, who were of longer standing in life and political experience, to open the great subject of their mission. But, as the convention had originated from Virginia, and his colleagues supposed, that some proposition was expected from them, they had imposed this task on him.

He then commented on the difficulty of the crisis, and the necessity of preventing the fulfilment of the prophecies of the American downfal.

He observed that in revising the fœderal system we ought to inquire 1. into the properties, which such a government ought to possess, 2. the defects of the confederation, 3. the danger of our situation &. 4. the remedy.

1. The character of such a governme[nt] ought to secure 1. against foreign invasion: 2. against dissentions between members of the Union, or seditions in particular states: 3. to p[ro]cure to the several States various blessings, of which an isolated situation was i[n]capable: 4. to be able to defend itself against incroachment: & 5. to be paramount to the state constitutions.

2. In speaking of the defects of the confederation he professed a high respect for its authors, and considered, them as having done all that patriots could do, in the then infancy of the science, of constitutions, & of confederacies,—when the inefficiency of requisitions was unknown—no commercial discord had arisen among any states—no rebellion had appeared as in Massts.—foreign debts had not become urgent—the havoc of paper money had not been

---

*Edmund Randolph (1753–1813), governor of Virginia.

foreseen—treaties had not been violated—and perhaps nothing better could be obtained from the jealousy of the states with regard to their sovereignty.

He then proceeded to enumerate the defects: 1. that the confederation produced no security agai[nst] foreign invasion; congress not being permitted to prevent a war nor to support it by th[eir] own authority—Of this he cited many examples; most of whi[ch] tended to shew, that they could not cause infractions of treaties or of the law of nations, to be punished: that particular states might by their conduct provoke war without controul; and that neither militia nor draughts being fit for defence on such occasions, enlistments only could be successful, and these could not be executed without money.

2. that the fœderal government could not check the quarrals between states, nor a rebellion in any not having constitutional power Nor means to interpose according to the exigency:

3. that there were many advantages, which the U. S. might acquire, which were not attainable under the confederation—such as a productive impost—counteraction of the commercial regulations of other nations—pushing of commerce ad libitum—&c &c.

4. that the fœderal government could not defend itself against the incroachments from the states:

5. that it was not even paramount to the state constitutions, ratified as it was in many of the states.

3. He next reviewed the danger of our situation appealed to the sense of the best friends of the U. S.—the prospect of anarchy from the laxity of government every where; and to other considerations.

4. He then proceeded to the remedy; the basis of which he said, must be the republican principle.

He proposed as conformable to his ideas the following resolutions, which he explained one by one.

RESOLUTIONS PROPOSED BY MR RANDOLPH IN CONVENTION.
MAY 29, 1787.

1. Resolved that the articles of Confederation ought to be so corrected & enlarged as to accomplish the objects proposed by their institution; namely. "common defence, security of liberty and general welfare."

2. Resd. therefore that the rights of suffrage in the National Legislature ought to be proportioned to the Quotas of contribution, or to the number of free inhabitants, as the one or the other rule may seem best in different cases.

3. Resd. that the National Legislature ought to consist of two branches.

4. Resd. that the members of the first branch of the National Legislature ought to be elected by the people of the several States every _____ for the term of _____; to be of the age of _____ years at least, to receive liberal stipends by which they may be compensated for the devotion of their time to public service; to be ineligible to any office established by a particular State, or under the authority of the United States, except those peculiarly belonging to the functions of the first branch, during the term of service, and for the space of _____ after its expiration; to be incapable of re-election for the space of _____ after the expiration of their term of service, and to be subject to recall.

5. Resold. that the members of the second branch of the National Legislature ought to be elected by those of the first, out of a proper number of persons nominated by the individual Legislatures, to be of the age of _____ years at least; to hold their offices for a term sufficient to ensure their independency, to receive liberal stipends, by which they may be compensated for the devotion of their time to public service, and to be ineligible to any office established by a particular State, or under the authority of the United States, except those peculiarly belonging to the functions of the second branch, during the term of service, and for the space of _____ after the expiration thereof.

6. Resolved that each branch ought to possess the right of originating Acts; that the National Legislature ought to be impowered to enjoy the Legislative Rights vested in Congress by the Confederation & moreover to legislate in all cases to which the separate States are incompetent, or in which the harmony of the United States may be interrupted by the exercise of individual Legislation; to negative all laws passed by the several States, contravening in the opinion of the National Legislature the articles of Union; and to call forth the force of the Union agst. any member of the Union failing to fulfill its duty under the articles thereof.

7. Resd. that a National Executive be instituted; to be chosen by the National Legislature for the term of _____ years, to receive

punctually at stated times, a fixed compensation for the services rendered, in which no increase or diminution shall be made so as to affect the Magistracy, existing at the time of increase or diminution, and to be ineligible a second time; and that besides a general authority to execute the National laws, it ought to enjoy the Executive rights vested in Congress by the Confederation.

8. Resd. that the Executive and a convenient number of the National Judiciary, ought to compose a council of revision with authority to examine every act of the National Legislature before it shall operate, & every act of a particular Legislature before a Negative thereon shall be final; and that the dissent of the said Council shall amount to a rejection, unless the Act of the National Legislature be again passed, or that of a particular Legislature be again negatived by _____ of the members of each branch.

9. Resd. that a National Judiciary be established to consist of one or more supreme tribunals, and of inferior tribunals to be chosen by the National Legislature, to hold their offices during good behaviour; and to receive punctually at stated times fixed compensation for their services, in which no increase or diminution shall be made so as to affect the persons actually in office at the time of such increase or diminution. that the jurisdiction of the inferior tribunals shall be to hear & determine in the first instance, and of the supreme tribunal to hear and determine in the dernier resort, all piracies & felonies on the high seas, captures from an enemy; cases in which foreigners or citizens of other States applying to such jurisdictions may be interested, or which respect the collection of the National revenue; impeachments of any National officers, and questions which may involve the national peace and harmony.

10. Resolvd. that provision ought to be made for the admission of States lawfully arising within the limits of the United States, whether from a voluntary junction of Government & Territory or otherwise, with the consent of a number of voices in the National legislature less than the whole.

11. Resd. that a Republican Government & the territory of each State, except in the instance of a voluntary junction of Government & territory, ought to be guaranteed by the United States to each State.

12. Resd. that provision ought to be made for the continuance of Congress and their authorities and privileges, until a given day after

the reform of the articles of Union shall be adopted, and for the completion of all their engagements.

13. Resd. that provision ought to be made for the amendment of the Articles of Union whensoever it shall seem necessary, and that the assent of the National Legislature ought not to be required thereto.

14. Resd. that the Legislative Executive & Judiciary powers within the several States ought to be bound by oath to support the articles of Union.

15. Resd. that the amendments which shall be offered to the Confederation, by the Convention ought at a proper time, or times, after the approbation of Congress to be submitted to an assembly or assemblies of Representatives, recommended by the several Legislatures to be expressly chosen by the people, to consider & decide thereon.

He concluded with an exhortation, not to suffer the present opportunity of establishing general peace, harmony, happiness and liberty in the U. S. to pass away unimproved.

WILLIAM PATERSON INTRODUCES THE
NEW JERSEY PLAN
JUNE 15, 1787

MR. PATTERSON,* LAID BEFORE the Convention the plan which he said several of the deputations wished to be substituted in place of that proposed by Mr. Randolp. After some little discussion of the most proper mode of giving it a fair deliberation it was agreed that it should be referred to a Committee of the Whole, and that in order to place the two plans in due comparison, the other should be recommitted. At the earnest desire of Mr. Lansing & some other gentlemen, it was also agreed that the Convention should not go into Committee of the whole on the subject till tomorrow, by which delay the friends of the plan proposed by Mr. Patterson wd. be better

---

*William Paterson (1745–1806), of the New Jersey delegation.

prepared to explain & support it, and all would have an opportuy of taking copies.*—

The propositions from N. Jersey moved by Mr. Patterson were in the words following.

1. Resd. that the articles of Confederation ought to be so revised, corrected & enlarged, as to render the federal Constitution adequate to the exigences of Government, & the preservation of the Union.

2. Resd. that in addition to the powers vested in the U. States in Congress, by the present existing articles of Confederation, they be authorized to pass acts for raising a revenue, by levying a duty or duties on all goods or merchandizes of foreign growth or manufacture, imported into any part of the U. States, by Stamps on paper, vellum or parchment, and by a postage on all letters or packages passing through the general post-Office, to be applied to such federal purposes as they shall deem proper & expedient; to make rules & regulations for the collection thereof; and the same from time to time, to alter & amend in such manner as they shall think proper: to pass Acts for the regulation of trade & commerce as well with foreign nations as with each other: provided that all punishments, fines, forfeitures & penalties to be incurred for contravening such acts rules and regulations shall be adjudged by the Common law Judiciarys of the State in which any offence contrary to the true intent & meaning of such Acts rules & regulations shall have been committed or perpetrated, with liberty of commencing in the first instance all suits & prosecutions for that purpose in the superior Common law Judiciary in such State, subject nevertheless, for the correction of all

---

*(this plan had been concerted among the deputations or members thereof, from Cont. N. Y. N. J. Del. and perhaps Mr Martin from Maryd. who made with them a common cause on different principles. Cont. and N. Y. were agst. a departure from the principle of the Confederation, wishing rather to add a few new powers to Congs. than to substitute, a National Govt. The States of N. J. and Del. were opposed to a National Govt. because its patrons considered a proportional representation of the States as the basis of it. The eagourness displayed by the Members opposed to a Natl. Govt. from these different [motives] began now to produce serious anxiety for the result of the Convention.—Mr. Dickenson said to Mr. Madison you see the consequence of pushing things too far. Some of the members from the small States wish for two branches in the General Legislature, and are friends to a good National Government; but we would sooner submit to a foreign power, than submit to be deprived of an equality of suffrage, in both branches of the legislature, and thereby be thrown under domination of the large States.) [James Madison's note]

errors, both in law & fact in rendering judgment, to an appeal to the Judiciary of the U. States.

3. Resd. that whenever requisitions shall be necessary, instead of the rule for making requisitions mentioned in the articles of Confederation, the United States in Congs. be authorized to make such requisitions in proportion to the whole number of white & other free citizens & inhabitants of every age sex and condition including those bound to servitude for a term of years & three fifths of all other persons not comprehended in the foregoing description, except Indians not paying taxes; that if such requisitions be not complied with, in the time specified therein, to direct the collection thereof in the non complying States & for that purpose to devise and pass acts directing & authorizing the same; provided that none of the powers hereby vested in the U. States in Congs. shall be exercised without the consent of at least _____ States, and in that proportion if the number of Confederated States should hereafter be increased or diminished.

4. Resd. that the U. States in Congs. be authorized to elect a federal Executive to consist of ___ persons, to continue in office for the term of ___ years, to receive punctually at stated times a fixed compensation for their services, in which no increase or diminution shall be made so as to affect the persons composing the Executive at the time of such increase or diminution, to be paid out of the federal treasury; to be incapable of holding any other office or appointment during their time of service and for ___ years thereafter; to be ineligible a second time, & removeable by Congs. on application by a majority of the Executives of the several States; that the Executives besides their general authority to execute the federal acts ought to appoint all federal officers not otherwise provided for, & to direct all military operations; provided that none of the persons composing the federal Executive shall on any occasion take command of any troops, so as personally to conduct any enterprise as General, or in other capacity.

5. Resd. that a federal Judiciary be established to consist of a supreme Tribunal the Judges of which to be appointed by the Executive, & to hold their offices during good behaviour, to receive punctually at stated times a fixed compensation for their services in which no increase or diminution shall be made, so as to affect the persons actually in office at the time of such increase or diminution; that the Judiciary so established shall have authority to hear & determine in the first instance on all impeachments of federal officers, & by way of

appeal in the dernier resort in all cases touching the rights of Ambassadors, in all cases of captures from an enemy, in all cases of piracies & felonies on the high seas, in all cases in which foreigners may be interested, in the construction of any treaty or treaties, or which may arise on any of the Acts for regulation of trade, or the collection of the federal Revenue: that none of the Judiciary shall during the time they remain in Office be capable of receiving or holding any other office or appointment during their time of service, or for _____ thereafter.

6. Resd. that all Acts of the U. States in Congs. made by virtue & in pursuance of the powers hereby & by the articles of confederation vested in them, and all Treaties made & ratified under the authority of the U. States shall be the supreme law of the respective States so far forth as those Acts or Treaties shall relate to the said States or their Citizens, and that the Judiciary of the several States shall be bound thereby in their decisions, any thing in the respective laws of the Individual States to the contrary notwithstanding; and that if any State, or any body of men in any State shall oppose or prevent ye. carrying into execution such acts or treaties, the federal Executive shall be authorized to call forth ye power of the Confederated States, or so much thereof as may be necessary to enforce and compel an obedience to such Acts, or an Observance of such Treaties.

7. Resd. that provision be made for the admission of new States into the Union.

8. Resd. the rule for naturalization ought to be the same in every State.

9. Resd. that a Citizen of one State committing an offence in another State of the Union, shall be deemed guilty of the same offence as if it had been committed by a Citizen of the State in which the Offence was committed.*

Adjourned

---

*(This copy of Mr. Patterson's propositions varies in a few clauses from that in the printed Journal furnished from the papers of Mr. Brearley a Colleague of Mr. Patterson. A confidence is felt, notwithstanding, in its accuracy. That the copy in the Journal is not entirely correct is shewn by the ensuing speech of Mr. Wilson (June 16) in which he refers to the mode of removing the Executive by impeachment & conviction as a feature in the Virga. plan forming one of its contrasts to that of Mr. Patterson, which proposed a removal on the application of a majority of the Executives of the States. In the copy printed in the Journal, the two modes are combined in the same clause; whether through inadvertence, or as a contemplated amendment does not appear.) [James Madison's note]

Monday June 18. in Committee of the whole. on the propositions of Mr. Patterson & Mr. Randolph.

⟨ON MOTION OF MR. DICKINSON to postpone the 1st. Resolution in Mr. Patterson's plan, in order to take up the following. viz: "that the articles of confederation ought to be revised and amended so as to render the Government of the U. S. adequate to the exigencies, the preservation and the prosperity of the union." the postponement was agreed to by 10 States, Pen: divided.⟩

Mr. Hamilton, had been hitherto silent on the business before the Convention, partly from respect to others whose superior abilities age & experience rendered him unwilling to bring forward ideas dissimilar to theirs, and partly from his delicate situation with respect to his own State, to whose sentiments as expressed by his Colleagues, he could by no means accede. The crisis however which now marked our affairs, was too serious to permit any scruples whatever to prevail over the duty imposed on every man to contribute his efforts for the public safety & happiness. He was obliged therefore to declare himself unfriendly to both plans. He was particularly opposed to that from N. Jersey, being fully convinced, that no amendment of the confederation, leaving the States in possession of their sovereignty could possibly answer the purpose. On the other hand he confessed he was much discouraged by the amazing extent of Country in expecting the desired blessings from any general sovereignty that could be substituted.—As to the powers of the Convention, he thought the doubts started on that subject had arisen from distinctions & reasonings too subtle. A *federal* Govt. he conceived to mean an association of independent Communities into one. Different Confederacies have different powers, and exercise them in different ways. In some instances the powers are exercised over collective bodies; in others over individuals. as in the German Diet—& among ourselves in cases of piracy. Great latitude therefore must be given to the signification of the term. The plan last proposed departs itself from the *federal* idea, as understood by some, since it is to operate eventually on individuals. He agreed moreover with the Honble. gentleman from Va. (Mr. R.) that we owed it to our Country, to do on this emergency whatever we should deem essential to its happiness. The States sent us here to provide for the exigences of the Union. To rely on & propose any plan not adequate to these exigences, merely because it was not clearly within our powers, would be to sacrifice the means to the end. It may be said that the *States* can not *ratify* a plan not within the purview of the article of Confederation providing for alterations & amendments. But may not the States themselves in which no constitutional authority equal to this purpose exists in the Legislatures, have had in view a reference to the people at large. In the Senate of N. York, a proviso was moved, that no act of the Convention should be binding untill it should be referred to the people & ratified; and the motion was lost by a single voice only, the reason assigned agst. it, being that it ⟨might possibly⟩ be found an inconvenient shackle.

The great question is what provision shall we make for the happiness of our Country? He would first make a comparative examination of the two plans—prove that there were essential defects in both—and point out such changes as might render a *national one*, efficacious.—The great & essential principles necessary for the support of Government. are 1. an active & constant interest in supporting it. This principle does not exist in the States in favor of the federal Govt. They have evidently in a high degree, the esprit de corps. They constantly pursue internal interests adverse to those of the whole. They have their particular debts—their partcular plans of finance &c. all these when opposed to, invariably prevail over the requisitions & plans of Congress. 2. the love of power, Men love power. The same remarks are applicable to this principle. The States have constantly shewn a disposition rather to regain the powers delegated by them than to part with more, or to give effect to what they had parted with. The ambition of their demagogues is known to hate the controul of the Genl. Government. It may be remarked too that the Citizens have not that anxiety to prevent a dissolution of the Genl. Govt as of the particular Govts. A dissolution of the latter would be fatal: of the former would still leave the purposes of Govt. attainable to a considerable degree. Consider what such a State as Virga. will be in a few years, a few compared with the life of nations.

How strongly will it feel its importance & self-sufficiency? 3. an habitual attachment of the people. The whole force of this tie is on the side of the State Govt. Its sovereignty is immediately before the eyes of the people: its protection is immediately enjoyed by them. From its hand distributive justice, and all those acts which familiarize & endear Govt. to a people, are dispensed to them. 4. *Force* by which may be understood a *coertion of laws* or *coertion of arms.* Congs. have not the former except in few cases. In particular States, this coercion is nearly sufficient; tho' he held it in most cases, not entirely so. A certain portion of military force is absolutely necessary in large communities. Massts. is now feeling this necessity & making provision for it. But how can this force be exerted on the States collectively. It is impossible. It amounts to a war between the parties. Foreign powers also will not be idle spectators. They will interpose, the confusion will increase, and a dissolution of the Union ensue. 5. *influence.* he did not ⟨mean⟩ corruption, but a dispensation of those regular honors & emoluments, which produce an attachment to the Govt. almost all the weight of these is on the side of the States; and must continue so as long as the States continue to exist. All the passions then we see, of avarice, ambition, interest, which govern most individuals, and all public bodies, fall into the current of the States, and do not flow in the stream of the Genl. Govt. the former therefore will generally be an overmatch for the Genl. Govt. and render any confederacy, in its very nature precarious. Theory is in this case fully confirmed by experience. The Amphyctionic Council had it would seem ample powers for general purposes. It had in particular the power of fining and using force agst. delinquent members. What was the consequence. Their decrees were mere signals of war. The Phocian war is a striking example of it. Philip at length taking advantage of their disunion, and insinuating himself into their Councils, made himself master of their fortunes. The German Confederacy affords another lesson. The authority of Charlemagne seemed to be as great as could be necessary. The great feudal chiefs however, exercising their local sovereignties, soon felt the spirit & found the means of, encroachments, which reduced the imperial authority to a nominal sovereignty. The Diet has succeeded, which tho' aided by a Prince at its head, of great authority independently of his imperial attributes, is a striking illustration of the weakness of Confederated Governments. Other examples instruct us in the same truth. The Swiss cantons have scarce any Union at all, and ⟨have been more than once at⟩ war with one another— How then are all these evils to be avoided? only by such a compleat sovereignty in the general Govermt. as will turn all the strong principles & passions above mentioned on its side. Does the scheme of N. Jersey produce this effect? does it afford any substantial remedy whatever? On the contrary it labors under great defects, and the defect of some of its provisions will destroy the efficacy of others. It gives a direct revenue to Congs. but this will not be sufficient. The balance can only be supplied by requisitions; which experience proves can not be relied on. If States are to deliberate on the mode, they will also deliberate on the object of the supplies, and will grant or not grant as they approve or disapprove of it. The delinquency of one will invite and countenance it in others. Quotas too must in the nature of things be so unequal as to produce the same evil. To what standard will you resort? Land is a fallacious one. Compare Holland with Russia: France or Engd. with other countries of Europe. Pena. with N. Carolia. will the relative pecuniary abilities in those instances, correspond with the relative value of land. Take numbers of inhabitants for the rule and make like comparison of different countries, and you will find it to be equally unjust. The different degrees of industry and improvement in different Countries render the first object a precarious measure of wealth. Much depends too on *situation*. Cont. N. Jersey & N. Carolina, not being commercial States & contributing to the wealth of the commercial ones, can never bear quotas assessed by the ordinary rules of proportion. They will & must fail [in their duty.] their example will be followed, and the Union itself be dissolved. Whence then is the national revenue to be drawn? from Commerce, even [from] exports which notwithstanding the common opinion are fit objects of moderate taxation, [from] excise, &c &c. These tho' not equal, are less unequal than quotas. Another destructive ingredient in the plan, is that equality of suffrage which is so much desired by the small States. It is not in human nature that Va. & the large States should consent to it, or if they did that they shd. long abide by it. It shocks too much the ideas of Justice, and every human feeling. Bad principles in a Govt. tho slow are sure in their operation, and will gradually destroy it. A doubt has been raised whether Congs. at present have a right to keep Ships or troops in time of peace. He leans to the negative. Mr. P.s plan provides no remedy.—If the powers proposed were adequate, the organization of Congs. is such that they could never be properly & effectually exercised. The members of Congs. being chosen by the States & subject to recall, represent all the local prejudices. Should the powers be found effectual, they will from time to time be heaped on them, till a tyrannic sway shall be established. The general power whatever be its form if it preserves itself, must swallow up the State powers. otherwise it will be swallowed up by them. It is agst. all the principles of a good Government to vest the requisite powers in such a body as Congs. Two Sovereignties can not co-exist within the same limits. Giving powers to Congs. must eventuate in a bad Govt. or in no Govt. The plan of N. Jersey therefore will not do. What then is to be done? Here he was embarrassed. The extent of the Country to be governed, discouraged him. The expence of a general Govt. was also formidable; unless there were such a diminution of expence on the side of the State Govts. as the case would admit. If they were extinguished, he was persuaded that great œconomy might be obtained by substituting a general Govt. He did not mean however to shock the public opinion by proposing such a measure. On the other [hand] he saw no *other* necessity for declining it. They are not necessary for any of the great purposes of commerce, revenue, or agriculture. Subordinate authorities he was aware would be necessary. There must be district tribunals: corporations for local purposes. But cui bono, the vast & expensive apparatus now appertaining to the States. The only difficulty of a serious nature which occurred to him, was that of drawing representatives from the extremes to the center of the Community. What inducements can be offered that will suffice? The moderate wages for the 1st. branch, would only be a bait to little demagogues. Three dollars or thereabouts he supposed would be the Utmost. The Senate he feared from a similar cause, would be filled by certain undertakers who wish for particular offices under the Govt. This view of the subject almost led him to despair that a Republican Govt. could be established over so great an extent. He was sensible at the same time that it would be unwise to propose one of any other form. In his private opinion he had no scruple in declaring, supported as he was by the opinions of so many of the wise & good, that the British Govt. was the best in the world: and that he doubted much whether any thing short of it would do in America. He hoped Gentlemen of different opinions would bear with him in this, and begged them to recollect the change of opinion on this subject which had taken place and was still going on. It was once thought that the power of Congs was amply sufficient to secure the end of their institution. The error was now seen by every one. The members most tenacious of republicanism, he observed, were as loud as any in declaiming agst. the vices of democracy. This progress of the public mind led him to anticipate the time, when others as well as himself would join in the praise bestowed by Mr. Neckar* on the British Constitution, namely, that it is the only Govt. in the world "which unites public strength with individual security."—In every community where industry is encouraged, there will be a division of it into the few & the many. Hence separate interests will arise There will be debtors & Creditors &c. Give all power to the many, they will oppress the few. Give all power to the few they will oppress the many. Both therefore ought to have power, that each may defend itself agst. the other. To the want of this check we owe our paper money—instalment laws &c To the proper adjustment of it the British owe the excellence of their Constitution. Their house of Lords is a most noble institution. Having nothing to hope for by a change, and a sufficient interest by means of their property, in being faithful to the National interest, they form a permanent barrier agst. every pernicious innovation, whether attempted on the part of the Crown or of the Commons. No temporary Senate will have firmness en'o' to answer the purpose. The Senate ⟨⟨of Maryland⟩⟩ which seems to be so much appealed to, has not yet been sufficiently tried. Had the people been unanimous & eager, in the late appeal to them on the subject of a paper emission they would would have yielded to the torrent. Their acquiescing in such an appeal is a proof of it.—Gentlemen differ in their opinions concerning the necessary checks, from the different estimates they form of the human passions. They suppose Seven years a sufficient period to give the Senate an adequate firmness, from not duly considering the amazing violence & turbulence of the democratic spirit. When a great object of Govt. is pursued, which seizes the popular passions, they spread like wild fire, and become irresistable. He appealed to the

---

*As director general of the French treasury after 1776, Jacques Necker (1732–1804) had attempted to reform the finances of the kingdom under Louis XVI.

gentlemen from the N. England States whether experience had not there verified the remark. As to the Executive, it seemed to be admitted that no good one could be established on Republican principles. Was not this giving up the merits of the question; for can there be a good Govt. without a good Executive. The English model was the only good one on this subject. The Hereditary interest of the King was so interwoven with that of the Nation, and his personal emoluments so great, that he was placed above the danger of being corrupted from abroad—and at the same time was both sufficiently independent and sufficiently controuled, to answer the purpose of the institution at home. One of the weak sides of Republics was their being liable to foreign influence & corruption. Men of little character, acquiring great power become easily the tools of intermedling neibours. Sweeden was a striking instance. The French & English had each their parties during the late Revolution which was effected by the predominant influence of the former. What is the inference from all these observations? That we ought to go as far in order to attain stability and permanency, as republican principles will admit. Let one branch of the Legislature hold their places for life or at least during good-behaviour. Let the Executive also be for life. He appealed to the feelings of the members present whether a term of seven years, would induce the sacrifices of private affairs which an acceptance of public trust would require, so so as to ensure the services of the best Citizens. On this plan we should have in the Senate a permanent will, a weighty interest, which would answer essential purposes. But is this a Republican Govt. it will be asked? Yes, if all the Magistrates are appointed, and vacancies are filled, by the people, or a process of election originating with the people. He was sensible that an Executive constituted as he proposed would have in fact but little of the power and independence that might be necessary. On the other plan of appointing him for 7 years, he thought the Executive ought to have but little power. He would be ambitious, with the means of making creatures; and as the object of his ambition wd. be to *prolong* his power, it is probable that in case of a war, he would avail himself of the emergence, to evade or refuse a degradation from his place. An Executive for life has not this motive for forgetting his fidelity, and will therefore be a safer depositary of power. It will be objected probably, that such an Executive will be an *elective Monarch*, and will give birth to the tumults which characterise that form of Govt. He wd. reply that *Monarch* is an indefinite term. It marks not either the degree or duration of power. If this Executive Magistrate wd. be a monarch for life—the other propd. by the Report from the Committee of the whole, wd. be a monarch for seven years. The circumstance of being elective was also applicable to both. It had been observed by judicious writers that elective monarchies wd. be the best if they could be guarded agst. the *tumults* excited by the ambition and intrigues of competitors. He was not sure that tumults were an inseparable evil. He rather thought this character of Elective Monarchies had been taken rather from particular cases than from general principles. The election of Roman Emperors was made by the *Army.* In *Poland* the election is made by great rival *princes* with independent power, and ample means, of raising commotions. In the German Empire, The appointment is made by the Electors & Princes, who have equal motives & means, for exciting cabals & parties. Might [not] such a mode of election be devised among ourselves as will defend the community agst. these effects in any dangerous degree? Having made these observations he would read to the Committee a sketch of a plan which he shd. prefer to either of those under consideration. He was aware that it went beyond the ideas of most members. But will such a plan be adopted out of doors? In return ⟨he would ask⟩ will the people adopt the other plan? At present they will adopt neither. But ⟨he⟩ sees the Union dissolving or already dissolved—he sees evils operating in the States which must soon cure the people of their fondness for democracies—he sees that a great progress has been already made & is still going on in the public mind. He thinks therefore that the people will in time be unshackled from their prejudices; and whenever that happens, they will themselves not be satisfied at stopping where the plan of Mr. R. wd. place them, but be ready to go as far at least as he proposes. He did not mean to offer the paper he had sketched as a proposition to the Committee. It was meant only to give a more correct view of his ideas, and to suggest the amendments which he should probably propose to the plan of Mr. R. in the proper stages of its future discussion. He reads his sketch in the words following: to wit

I. The Supreme Legislative power of the United States of America to be vested in two different bodies of men; the one to be called the Assembly, the other the Senate who together shall form the Legislature of the United States with power to pass all laws whatsoever subject to the Negative hereafter mentioned.

II. The Assembly to consist of persons elected by the people to serve for three years.

III. The Senate to consist of persons elected to serve during good behaviour; their election to be made by electors chosen for that purpose by the people: in order to this the States to be divided into election districts. On the death, removal or resignation of any Senator his place to be filled out of the district from which he came.

IV. The supreme Executive authority of the United States to be vested in a Governour to be elected to serve during good behaviour— the election to be made by Electors chosen by the people in the Election Districts aforesaid— The authorities & functions of the Executive to be as follows: to have a negative on all laws about to be passed, and the execution of all laws passed, to have the direction of war when authorized or begun; to have with the advice and approbation of the Senate the power of making all treaties; to have the sole appointment of the heads or chief officers of the departments of Finance, War and Foreign Affairs; to have the nomination of all other officers (Ambassadors to foreign Nations included) subject to the approbation or rejection of the Senate; to have the power of pardoning all offences except Treason; which he shall not pardon without the approbation of the Senate.

V. On the death resignation or removal of the Governour his authorities to be exercised by the President of the Senate till a Successor be appointed.

VI. The Senate to have the sole power of declaring war, the power of advising and approving all Treaties, the power of approving or rejecting all appointments of officers except the heads or chiefs of the departments of Finance War and foreign affairs.

VII. The Supreme Judicial authority to be vested in __ Judges to hold their offices during good behaviour with adequate and permanent salaries. This Court to have original jurisdiction in all causes of capture, and an appellative jurisdiction in all causes in which the revenues of the general Government or the citizens of foreign nations are concerned.

VIII. The Legislature of the United States to have power to institute Courts in each State for the determination of all matters of general concern.

IX. The Governour Senators and all officers of the United States to be liable to impeachment for mal—and corrupt conduct; and upon conviction to be removed from office, & disqualified for holding any place of trust or profit—all impeachments to be tried by a Court to consist of the Chief _____ or Judge of the Superior Court of Law of each State, provided such Judge shall hold his place during good behavior, and have a permanent salary.

X. All laws of the particular States contrary to the Constitution or laws of the United States to be utterly void; and the better to prevent such laws being passed, the Governour or president of each state shall be appointed by the General Government and shall have a negative upon the laws about to be passed in the State of which he is Governour or President.

XI. No State to have any forces land or Naval; and the Militia of all the States to be under the sole and exclusive direction of the United States, the officers of which to be appointed and commissioned by them.

[On these several articles he entered into explanatory observations corresponding with the principles of his introductory reasoning.

Comittee rose & the House adjourned.]

James Madison Discusses the Plans
June 19, 1787

MR. M[ADISON]. MUCH STRESS had been laid by some gentlemen on the want of power in the Convention to propose any other than a *federal* plan. To what had been answered by others, he would only add, that neither of the characteristics attached to a *federal* plan would support this objection. One characteristic, was that in a *federal* Government, the power was exercised not on the people individually; but on the people *collectively,* on the *States.* Yet in some instances as in piracies, captures &c. the existing Confederacy, and in many instances, the amendments to it ⟨proposed by Mr. Patterson⟩ must operate immediately on individuals. The other characteristic was, that a *federal* Govt. derived its appointments not immediately from the people, but from the States which they respectively composed. Here too were facts on the other side. In two of the States, Connect. and Rh. Island, the delegates to Congs. were chosen, not by the Legislatures, but by the people at large; and the plan of Mr. P. intended no change in this particular.

It had been alledged (by Mr. Patterson) that the Confederation having been formed by unanimous consent, could be dissolved by unanimous Consent only. Does this doctrine result from the nature of compacts? does it arise from any particular stipulation in the articles of Confederation? If we consider the federal union as analogous to the fundamental compact by which individuals compose one Society, and which must in its theoretic origin at least, have been the unanimous act of the component members, it cannot be said that no dissolution of the compact can be effected without unanimous consent. A breach of the fundamental principles of the compact by a part of the Society would certainly absolve the other part from their obligations to it. If the breach of *any* article by *any* of the parties, does not set the others at liberty, it is because, the contrary is *implied* in the compact itself, and particularly by that law of it, which gives an indefinite authority to the majority to bind the whole in all cases. This latter circumstance shews that we are not to consider the federal Union as analogous to the social compact of individuals: for if it were so, a Majority would have a right to bind the rest, and even to form a new Constitution for the whole, which the Gentn: from N. Jersey would be among the last to admit. If we consider the federal union as analogous not to the ⟨social⟩ compacts among individual men: but to the conventions among individual States. What is the doctrine resulting from these conventions? Clearly, according to the Expositors of the law of Nations, that a breach of any one article, by any one party, leaves all the other parties at liberty, to consider the whole convention as dissolved, unless they choose rather to compel the delinquent party to repair the breach. In some treaties indeed it is expressly stipulated that a violation of particular articles shall not have this consequence, and even that particular articles shall remain in force during war, which in general is understood to dissolve all susbsisting Treaties. But are there any exceptions of this sort to the Articles of confederation? So far from it that there is not even an express stipulation that force shall be used to compell an offending member of the Union to discharge its duty. He observed that the violations of the federal articles had been numerous & notorious. Among the most notorious was an Act of N. Jersey herself; by which she *expressly refused* to comply with a constitutional requisition of Congs.—and yielded no farther to the expostulations of their deputies, than barely to rescind her vote of refusal without passing any positive act of compliance. He did not wish to draw any rigid inferences from these observations. He thought it proper however that the true nature of the existing confederacy should be investigated, and he was not anxious to strengthen the foundations on which it now stands.

Proceeding to the consideration of Mr. Patterson's plan, he stated the object of a proper plan to be twofold. 1. to preserve the Union. 2. to provide a Governmt. that will remedy the evils felt by the States both in their united and individual capacities. Examine Mr. P.s plan, & say whether it promises satisfaction in these respects.

1. Will it prevent those violations of the law of nations & of Treaties which if not prevented must involve us in the calamities of foreign wars? The tendency of the States to these violations has been manifested in sundry instances. The files of Congs. contain complaints already, from almost every nation with which treaties have been formed. Hitherto indulgence has been shewn to us. This cannot be the permanent disposition of foreign nations. A rupture with other powers is among the greatest of national calamities. It ought therefore to be effectually provided that no part of a nation shall have it in its power to bring them on the whole. The existing confederacy does [not] sufficiently provide against this evil. The proposed amendment to it does not supply the omission. It leaves the will of the States as uncontrouled as ever.

2. Will it prevent encroachments on the federal authority? A tendency to such encroachments has been sufficiently exemplified among ourselves, as well in every other confederated republic antient and Modern. By the federal articles, transactions with the Indians appertain to Congs. Yet in several instances, the States have entered into treaties & wars with them. In like manner no two or more States can form among themselves any treaties &c without the consent of Congs. yet Virga & Maryd in one instance—Pena. & N. Jersey in another, have entered into compacts, without previous application or subsequent apology. No State again can of right raise troops in time of peace without the like consent. Of all cases of the

league, this seems to require the most scrupulous observance. Has not Massts, notwithstanding, the most powerful member of the Union, already raised a body of troops? Is she not now augmenting them, without having even deigned to apprise Congs. of Her intention? In fine Have we not seen the public land dealt out to Cont. to bribe her acquiescence in the decree constitutionally awarded agst. her claim on the territory of Pena.—? for no other possible motive can account for the policy of Congs. in that measure?—if we recur to the examples of other confederacies, we shall find in all of them the same tendency of the parts to encroach on the authority of the whole. He then reviewed the Amphyctrionic & Achæan confederacies among the antients, and the Helvetic, Germanic & Belgic among the moderns, tracing their analogy to the U. States—in the constitution and extent of their federal authorities—in the tendency of the particular members to usurp on these authorities; and to bring confusion & ruin on the whole. —He observed that the plan of Mr. Pat—son besides omitting a controul over the States as a general defence of the federal prerogatives was particularly defective in two of its provisions. 1) Its ratification was not to be by the people at large, but by the *Legislatures*. It could not therefore render the acts of Congs. in pursuance of their powers even legally *paramount* to the Acts of the States. 2) It gave ⟨to the federal tribunal⟩ an appellate jurisdiction only—even in the criminal cases enumerated, The necessity of any such provision supposed a danger of undue acquittals in the State tribunals. Of what avail wd. an appellate tribunal be, after an acquttal? Besides in most if not all of the States, the Executives have by their respective *Constitutions* the right of pardg. How could this be taken from them by a *legislative ratification* only?

3. Will it prevent trespasses of the States on each other? Of these enough has been already seen. He instanced Acts of Virga. & Maryland which give a preference to their own citizens in cases where the Citizens [of other states] are entitled to equality of privileges by the Articles of Confederation. He considered the emissions of paper money [& other kindred measures] as also aggressions. The States relatively to one an other being each of them either Debtor or Creditor; The Creditor States must suffer unjustly from every emission by the debtor States. We have seen retaliating acts on this subject which threatened danger not to the harmony only, but the tranquillity of the Union. The plan of Mr. Paterson, not giving even a negative

on the Acts of the States, left them as much at liberty as ever to exe-cute their unrighteous projects agst. each other.

4. Will it secure the internal tranquillity of the States themselves? The insurrections in Massts. admonished all the States of the danger to which they were exposed. Yet the plan of Mr. P. contained no pro-visions for supplying the defect of the Confederation on this point. According to the Republican theory indeed, Right & power being both vested in the majority, are held to be synonimous. According to fact & experience, a minority may in an appeal to force be an over-match for the majority. 1. If the minority happen to include all such as possess the skill & habits of military life, with such as possess the great pecuniary resources, one third may conquer the remaining two thirds. 2. one third of those who participate in the choice of rulers may be rendered a majority by the accession of those whose poverty disqualifies them from a suffrage, & who for obvious reasons may be more ready to join the standard of sedition than that of the estab-lished Government. 3. Where slavery exists, the Republican Theory becomes still more fallacious.

5. Will it secure a good internal legislation & administration to the particular States? In developing the evils which vitiate the politi-cal system of the U. S. it is proper to take into view those which pre-vail within the States individually as well as those which affect them collectively: Since the former indirectly affect the whole; and there is great reason to believe that the pressure of them had a full share in the motives which produced the present Convention. Under this head he enumerated and animadverted on 1. the multiplicity of the laws passed by the several States. 2. the mutability of their laws. 3. the injustice of them. 4. the impotence of them: observing that Mr. Pat-terson's plan contained no remedy for this dreadful class of evils, and could not therefore be received as an adequate provision for the exigencies of the Community.

6. Will it secure the Union agst. the influence of foreign powers over its members. He pretended not to say that any such influence had yet been tried: but it naturally to be expected that occasions would produce it. As lessons which claimed particular attention, he cited the intrigues practiced among the Amphictionic Confederates first by the Kings of Persia, and afterwards fatally by Philip of Mace-don: Among the Achæans, first by Macedon & afterwards no less fa-tally by Rome: Among the Swiss by Austria, France & the lesser

neighbouring Powers; among the members of the Germanic [Body] by France, England, Spain & Russia—: and in the Belgic Republic, by all the great neighbouring powers. The plan of Mr. Patterson, not giving to the general Councils any negative on the will of the particular States, left the door open for the like pernicious machinations among ourselves.

7. He begged the smaller States which were most attached to Mr. Pattersons plan to consider the situation in which it would leave them. In the first place they would continue to bear the whole expense of maintaining their Delegates in Congress. It ought not to be said that if they were willing to bear this burden, no others had a right to complain. As far as it led the small States to forbear keeping up a representation, by which the public business was delayed, it was evidently a matter of common concern. An examination of the minutes of Congress would satisfy every one that the public business had been frequently delayed by this cause; and that the States most frequently unrepresented in Congs. were not the larger States. He reminded the convention of another consequence of leaving on a small State the burden of Maintaining a Representation in Congs. During a considerable period of the War, one of the Representatives of Delaware, in whom alone before the signing of the Confederation the entire vote of that State and after that event one half of its vote, frequently resided, was a Citizen & Resident of Pena. and held an office in his own State incompatible with an appointment from it to Congs. During another period, the same State was represented by three delegates two of whom were citizens of Penna.—and the third a Citizen of New Jersey. These expedients must have been intended to avoid the burden of supporting delegates from their own State. But whatever might have been ye. cause, was not in effect the vote of one State doubled, and the influence of another increased by it? ⟨In the 2d. place⟩ The coercion, on which the efficacy of the plan depends, can never be exerted but on themselves. The larger States will be impregnable, the smaller only can feel the vengeance of it. He illustrated the position by the history of the Amphyctionic Confederates: and the ban of the German Empire, It was the cobweb wch. could entangle the weak, but would be the sport of the strong.

8. He begged them to consider the situation in which they would remain in case their pertinacious adherence to an inadmissable plan, should prevent the adoption of any plan. The contemplation of such

an event was painful; but it would be prudent to submit to the task of examining it at a distance, that the means of escaping it might be the more readily embraced. Let the union of the States be dissolved and one of two consequences must happen. Either the States must remain individually independent & sovereign; or two or more Confederacies must be formed among them. In the first event would the small States be more secure agst. the ambition & power of their larger neighbours, than they would be under a general Government pervading with equal energy every part of the Empire, and having an equal interest in protecting every part agst. every other part? In the second, can the smaller expect that their larger neighbours would confederate with them on the principle of the present confederacy, which gives to each member, an equal suffrage; or that they would exact less severe concessions from the smaller States, than are proposed in the scheme of Mr. Randolph?

The great difficulty lies in the affair of Representation; and if this could be adjusted, all others would be surmountable. It was admitted by both the gentlemen from N. Jersey, (Mr. Brearly and Mr. Patterson) that it would not be *just to allow Virga.* which was 16 times as large as Delaware an equal vote only. Their language was that it would not be *safe for Delaware* to allow Virga. 16 times as many votes. The expedient proposed by them was that all the States should be thrown into one mass and a new partition be made into 13 equal parts. Would such a scheme be practicable? The dissimelarities existing in the rules of property, as well as in the manners, habits and prejudices of the different States, amounted to a prohibition of the attempt. It had been found impossible for the power of one of the most absolute princes in Europe (K. of France) directed by the wisdom of one of the most enlightened and patriotic Ministers (Mr. Neckar) that any age has produced, to equalize in some points only the different usages & regulations of the different provinces. But admitting a general amalgamation and repartition of the States, to be practicable, and the danger apprehended by the smaller States from a proportional representation to be real; would not a particular and voluntary coalition of these with their neighbours, be less inconvenient to the whole community, and equally effectual for their own safety. If N. Jersey or Delaware conceive that an advantage would accrue to them from an equalization of the States, in which case they would necessaryly form a junction with their neighbors, why might not this end be attained by leaving them at liberty by the Constitution to form such a junction whenever they pleased? and why should they wish to obtrude a like arrangement on all the States, when it was, to say the least, extremely difficult, would be obnoxious to many of the States, and when neither the inconveniency, nor the benefit of the expedient to themselves, would be lessened, by confining it to themselves.—The prospect of many new States to the Westward was another consideration of importance. If they should come into the Union at all, they would come when they contained but but few inhabitants. If they shd. be entitled to vote according to their proportions of inhabitants, all would be right & safe. Let them have an equal vote, and a more objectionable minority than ever might give law to the whole.

[On a question for postponing generally the 1st. proposition of Mr. Patterson's plan, it was agreed to: N. Y. &. N. J. only being no—]

On the question [moved by Mr. King] whether the Committee should rise & Mr. Randolphs propositions be re-reported without alteration, which was in fact a question whether Mr. R's should be adhered to as preferable to those of Mr. Patterson;

Massts. ay. Cont. ay. N. Y. no. N. J. no. Pa. ay. Del. no. Md. divd. Va. ay. N. C. ay. S. C. ay. Geo. ay. [Ayes—7; noes—3; divided—1.]

Oliver Ellsworth Discusses Questions of Representation
June 29, 1787

Mr. elseworth* moved that the rule of suffrage in the 2d. branch be the same with that established by the articles of confederation. He was not sorry on the whole he said that the vote just passed, had determined against this rule in the first branch. He hoped it would become a ground of compromise with regard to the 2d. branch. We were partly national; partly federal. The proportional

---

*Oliver Ellsworth (1745–1807), representative from Connecticut; later the principal author of the Judiciary Act of 1789 and chief justice of the Supreme Court.

representation in the first branch was conformable to the national principle & would secure the large States agst. the small. An equality of voices was conformable to the federal principle and was necessary to secure the Small States agst. the large. He trusted that on this middle ground a compromise would take place. He did not see that it could on any other. And if no compromise should take place, our meeting would not only be in vain but worse than in vain. To the Eastward he was sure Massts. was the only State that would listen to a proposition for excluding the States as equal political Societies, from an equal voice in both branches. The others would risk every consequence rather than part with so dear a right. An attempt to deprive them of it, was at once cutting the body ⟨of America⟩ in two, and as he supposed would be the case, somewhere about this part of it. The large States he conceived would notwithstanding the equality of votes, have an influence that would maintain their superiority. Holland, as had been admitted (by Mr. ⟨Madison⟩) had, notwithstanding a like equality in the Dutch Confederacy, a prevailing influence in the public measures. The power of self-defence was essential to the small States. Nature had given it to the smallest insect of the creation. He could never admit that there was no danger of combinations among the large States. They will like individuals find out and avail themselves of the advantage to be gained by it. It was true the danger would be greater, if they were contiguous and had a more immediate common interest. A defensive combination of the small States was rendered more difficult by their greater number. He would mention another consideration of great weight. The existing confederation was founded on the equality of the States in the article of suffrage: was it meant to pay no regard to this antecedent plighted faith. Let a strong Executive, a Judiciary & Legislative power be created; but Let not too much be attempted; by which all may be lost. He was not in general a half-way man, yet he preferred doing half the good we could, rather than do nothing at all. The other half may be added, when the necessity shall be more fully experienced.

James Wilson, Oliver Ellsworth, and James Madison Debate

June 30, 1787

THE MOTION OF MR. ELSEWORTH resumed for allowing each State an equal vote in ye 2d branch.

Mr. Wilson* did not expect such a motion after the establishment of ye. contrary principle in the 1st. branch; and considering the reasons which would oppose it, even if an equal vote had been allowed in the 1st. branch. The Gentleman from Connecticut (Mr. Elseworth) had pronounced that if the motion should not be acceded to, of all the States North of Pena. one only would agree to any Genl. Government. He entertained more favorable hopes of Connt. and of the other Northern States. He hoped the alarms exceeded their cause, and that they would not abandon a Country to which they were bound by so many strong and endearing ties. But should the deplored event happen, it would neither stagger his sentiments nor his duty. If the minority of the people of America refuse to coalesce with the majority on just and proper principles, if a separation must take place, it could never happen on better grounds. The votes of yesterday agst. the just principle of representation, were as 22 to 90 of the people of America. Taking the opinions to be the same on this point, and he was sure if there was any room for change it could not be on the side of the majority, the question will be shall less than $\frac{1}{4}$ of the U. States withdraw themselves from the Union, or shall more than $\frac{3}{4}$ renounce the inherent, indisputable, and unalienable rights of men, in favor of the artificial systems of States. If issue must be joined, it was on this point he would chuse to join it, The gentleman from Connecticut in supposing that the prepondenancy secured to the majority in the 1st. branch had removed the objections to an equality of votes in the 2d. branch for the security of the minority narrowed the case extremely. Such an equality will enable the

---

*James Wilson (1742–1798), delegate from Pennsylvania, was later a justice of the first Supreme Court.

minority to controul in all cases whatsoever, the sentiments and interests of the majority. Seven States will controul six: seven States according to the estimates that had been used, composed $\frac{24}{90}$. of the whole people. It would be in the power then of less than $\frac{1}{3}$ to overrule $\frac{2}{3}$ whenever a question should happen to divide the States in that manner. Can we forget for whom we are forming a Government? Is it for *men,* or for the imaginary beings called States? Will our honest Constituents be satisfied with metaphysical distinctions? Will they, ought they to be satisfied with being told that the one third, compose the greater number of States. The rule of suffrage ought on every principle to be the same in the 2d. as in the 1st. branch. If the Government be not laid on this foundation, it can be neither solid nor lasting, any other principle will be local, confined & temporary. This will expand with the expansion, and grow with the growth of the U. States.—Much has been said of an imaginary combination of three States. Sometimes a danger of monarchy, sometimes of aristocracy has been charged on it. No explanation however of the danger has been vouchsafed. It would be easy to prove both from reason & history that rivalships would be more probable than coalitions; and that there are no coinciding interests that could produce the latter. No answer has yet been given to the observations of (Mr. ⟨Madison⟩)—on this subject. Should the Executive Magistrate be taken from one of the large States would not the other two be thereby thrown into the scale with the other States? Whence then the danger of monarchy? Are the people of the three large States more aristocratic than those of the small ones? Whence then the danger of aristocracy from their influence? It is all a mere illusion of names. We talk of States, till we forget what they are composed of. Is a real & fair majority, the natural hot-bed of aristocracy? It is a part of the definition of this species of Govt. or rather of tyranny, that the smaller number governs the greater. It is true that a majority of States in the 2d. branch can not carry a law agst. a majority of the people in the 1st. But this removes half only of the objection. Bad Governts. are of two sorts. 1. that which does too little. 2. that which does too much: that which fails thro' weakness; and that which destroys thro' oppression. Under which of these evils do the U. States at present groan? under the weakness and inefficiency of its Govert. To remedy this weakness we have been sent to this

Convention. If the motion should be agreed to, we shall leave the U. S. fettered precisely as heretofore; with the additional mortification of seeing the good purposes of ye fair representation of the people in the 1st. branch, defeated in 2d. Twenty four will still controul sixty six. He lamented that such a disagreement should prevail on the point of representation, as he did not foresee that it would happen on the other point most contested, the boundary between the Genl. & the local authorities. He thought the States necessary & valuable parts of a good system.

Mr. Elseworth. The capital objection of Mr. Wilson "that the minority will rule the majority" is not true. The power is given to the few to save them from being destroyed by the many. If an equality of votes had been given to them in both branches, the objection might have had weight. Is it a novel thing that the few should have a check on the many? Is it not the case in the British Constitution the wisdom of which so many gentlemen have united in applauding? Have not the House of Lords, who form so small a proportion of the nation a negative on the laws, as a necessary defence of their peculiar rights agst the encroachmts of the Commons. No instance [of a Confederacy] has existed in which an equality of voices has not been exercised by the members of it. We are running from one extreme to another. We are razing the foundations of the building. When we need only repair the roof. No salutary measure has been lost for want of *a majority of the States,* to favor it. If security be all that the great States wish for the 1st. branch secures them. The danger of combinations among them is not imaginary. Altho' no particular abuses could be foreseen by him, the possibility of them would be sufficient to alarm him. But he could easily conceive cases in which they might result from such combinations. Suppose that in pursuance of some commercial treaty or arrangement, three or four free ports & no more were to be established would not combinations be formed in favor of Boston, Philada. & & some port in Chesapeak? A like concert might be formed in the appointment of the great officers. He appealed again to the obligations of the federal pact which was still in force, and which had been entered into with so much solemnity, persuading himself that some regard would still be paid to the plighted faith under which each State small as well as great, held an equal right of suffrage in the general Councils. [His remarks

were not the result of partial or local views. The State he represented
(Connecticut) held a middle rank.]

Mr. M[adison. did justice to the able and close reasoning of
Mr. E. but must observe that it did not always accord with itself.]
On another occasion, the large States were described ⟨by him⟩ as
the Aristocratic States, ready to oppress the small. Now the small
are the House of Lords requiring a negative to defend them agst
the more numerous Commons. Mr. E. had also erred in saying that
no instance had existed in which confederated States had not retained to themselves a perfect equality of suffrage. Passing over the
German system in which the K. of Prussia has nine voices, he
reminded Mr. E. of the Lycian confederacy, in which the component members had votes proportioned to their importance, and
which Montesquieu recommends as the fittest model for that form
of Government. Had the fact been as stated by Mr. E. it would have
been of little avail to him, or rather would have strengthened the
arguments agst. him; The History & fate of the several Confederacies modern as well as Antient, demonstrating some radical vice in
their structure. In reply to the appeal of Mr. E. to the faith plighted
in the existing federal compact, he remarked that the party claiming from others an adherence to a common engagement ought at
least to be guiltless itself of a violation. Of all the States however
Connecticut was perhaps least able to urge this plea. Besides the
various omissions to perform the stipulated acts from which no
State was free, the Legislature of that State had by a pretty recent
vote *positively refused* to pass a law for complying with the Requisitions of Congs. and had transmitted a copy of the vote to Congs.
It was urged, he said, continually that an equality of votes in the
2d. branch was not only necessary to secure the small, but would
be perfectly safe to the large ones whose majority in the 1st. branch
was an effectual bulwark. But notwithstanding this apparent defence, the Majority of States might still injure the majority of people. 1. they could *obstruct* the wishes and interests of the majority.
2. they could *extort* measures, repugnant to the wishes & interest
of the majority. 3. They could *impose* measures adverse thereto; as
the 2d branch will probly exercise some great powers, in which the
1st will not participate. He admitted that every peculiar interest
whether in any class of citizens, or any description of States, ought

to be secured as far as possible. Wherever there is danger of attack there ought be given a constitutional power of defence. But he contended that the States were divided into different interests not by their difference of size, but by other circumstances; the most material of which resulted partly from climate, but principally from [the effects of] their having or not having slaves. These two causes concurred in forming the great division of interests in the U. States. It did not lie between the large & small States: it lay between the Northern & Southern. and if any defensive power were necessary, it ought to be mutually given to these two interests. He was so strongly impressed with this important truth that he had been casting about in his mind for some expedient that would answer the purpose. The one which had occurred was that instead of proportioning the votes of the States in both branches, to their respective numbers of inhabitants computing the slaves in the ratio of 5 to 3. they should be represented in one branch according to the number of free inhabitants only; and in the other according to the whole no. counting the slaves as [if] free. By this arrangement the Southern Scale would have the advantage in one House, and the Northern in the other. He had been restrained from proposing this expedient by two considerations; one was his unwillingness to urge any diversity of interests on an occasion when it is but too apt to arise of itself—the other was the inequality of powers that must be vested in the two branches, and which wd. destroy the equilibrium of interests.

Mr. Elseworth assured the House that whatever might be thought of the Representatives of Connecticut the State was entirely federal in her disposition. [He appealed to her great exertions during the War, in supplying both men & money. The muster rolls would show she had more troops in the field than Virga. If she had been delinquent, it had been from inability, and not more so than other States.]

Mr. Sherman. Mr. M[adison] had animadverted on the delinquency of the States, when his object required him to prove that the Constitution of Congs. was faulty. Congs. is not to blame for the faults of the States. Their measures have been right, and the only thing wanting has been, a further power in Congs. to render them effectual.

MR. RANDOLPH. THE VOTE OF this morning (involving an equality of suffrage in 2d. branch) had embarrassed the business extremely. All the powers given in the Report from the Come. of the whole, were founded on the supposition that a Proportional representation was to prevail in both branches of the Legislature—When he came here this morning his purpose was to have offered some propositions that might if possible have united a great majority of votes, and particularly might provide agst. the danger suspected on the part of the smaller States, by enumerating the cases in which it might lie, and allowing an equality of votes in such cases. But finding from the preceding vote that they persist in demanding an equal vote in all cases, that they have succeeded in obtaining it, and that N. York if present would probably be on the same side, he could not but think we were unprepared to discuss this subject further. It will probably be in vain to come to any final decision with a bare majority on either side. For these reasons he wished the Convention might adjourn, that the large States might consider the steps proper to be taken in the present solemn crisis of the business, and that the small States might also deliberate on the means of conciliation.

Mr. Patterson, thought with Mr. R. that it was high time for the Convention to adjourn that the rule of secrecy ought to be rescinded, and that our Constituents should be consulted. No conciliation could be admissible on the part of the smaller States on any other ground than that of an equality of votes in the 2d. branch. If Mr Randolph would reduce to form his motion for an adjournment sine die,* he would second it with all his heart.

Genl. Pinkney† wished to know of Mr R. whether he meant an adjournment sine die, or only an adjournment for the day. If the

---

*Literally, "adjournment without a day [set]" (Latin); a permanent adjournment of the Convention.

†General Charles Cotesworth Pinckney (1746–1825), a delegate from South Carolina.

former was meant, it differed much from his idea He could not think of going to S. Carolina, and returning again to this place. Besides it was chimerical to suppose that the States if consulted would ever accord separately, and beforehand.

Mr. Randolph, had never entertained an idea of an adjournment sine die; & was sorry that his meaning had been so readily & strangely misinterpreted. He had in view merely an adjournment till tomorrow in order that some conciliatory experiment might if possible be devised, and that in case the smaller States should continue to hold back, the larger might then take such measures, he would not say what, as might be necessary.

Mr. Patterson seconded the adjournment till tomorrow, as an opportunity seemed to be wished by the larger States to deliberate further on conciliatory expedients.

On the question for adjourning till tomorrow, [the States were equally divided.]

Mas. no. Cont. no. N. J. ay. Pa. ay. Del. no. Md. ay. Va. ay. N. C. ay. S. C. no. Geo. no. So it was lost. [Ayes—5; noes—5.]

Mr. Broome* thought it his duty to declare his opinion agst. an adjournment sine die, as had been urged by Mr. Patterson. Such a measure he thought would be fatal. Something must be done by the Convention tho' it should be by a bare majority.

Mr. Gerry† observed that Masts. was opposed to an adjournment, because they saw no new ground of compromise. But as it seemed to be the opinion of so many States that a trial shd be made, the State would now concur in the adjournmt.

Mr. Rutlidge‡ could see no need of an adjournt. because he could see no chance of a compromise. The little States were fixt. They had repeatedly & solemnly declared themselves to be so. All that the large States then had to do, was to decide whether they would yield or not. For his part he conceived that altho' we could not do what we thought best, in itself, we ought to do something. Had we not better keep the Govt. up a little longer, hoping that another Convention will supply our omissions, than abandon every thing to hazard. Our

---

*Jacob Broom (1752–1810) represented Delaware.

†Elbridge Gerry (1744–1814), delegate from Massachusetts and later vice president during James Madison's second administration.

‡John Rutledge (1739–1800) of South Carolina.

Constituents will be very little satisfied with us if we take the latter course.

Mr. Randolph & Mr. King* renewed the motion to adjourn till tomorrow.

On the question Mas. ay. Cont. no. N. J. ay. Pa. ay. Del. no. Md. ay. Va. ay. N. C. ay. S. C. ay. Geo. divd. [Ayes—7; noes—2; divided—1.]

Adjourned

On the morning following before the hour of the Convention a number of the members from the larger States, by common agreement met for the purpose of consulting on the proper steps to be taken in consequence of the vote in favor of an equal Representation in the 2d. branch, and the apparent inflexibility of the smaller States on that point—Several members from the latter States also attended. The time was wasted in vague conversation on the subject, without any specific proposition or agreement. It appeared indeed that the opinions of the members who disliked the equality of votes differed so much as to the importance of that point, and as to the policy of risking [a failure of] a[ny] general act of the Convention by inflexibly opposing it. Several of them supposing that no good Governnt could or would be built on that foundation, and that as a division of the Convention into two opinions was unavoidable it would be better that the side comprising the principal States, and a majority of the people of America, should propose a scheme of Govt. to the States, than that a scheme should be proposed on the other side, would have concurred in a firm opposition to the smaller States, and in a separate recommendation, if eventually necessary. Others seemed inclined to yield to the smaller States, and to concur in such an Act however imperfect & exceptionable, as might be agreed on by the Convention as a body, tho' decided by a bare majority of States and by a minority of the people of the U. States. It is probable that the result of this consultation satisfied the smaller States that they had nothing to apprehend from a Union of the larger, in any plan whatever agst. the equality of votes in the 2d. branch.

---

*Rufus King (1755–1787) of Massachusetts.

Getting Down to Details

ONCE THE KEY ISSUE of representation was solved on July 16, the delegates turned their attention to the second branch of government: the executive. They spent much of the next ten days wrestling with an array of questions relating to the election and tenure of the executive (eventually called the president). Then, after two months of deliberations, the convention recessed, instructing a committee of detail to convert the resolutions it had adopted thus far into a working constitution. Their report, delivered on August 6, set the framework for the remaining six weeks of debate.

The most significant development during this final phase was the gradual enlargement of executive power. Into early August, the future presidency remained largely a cipher. It was the Senate, for example, that was expected to make treaties and appointments to other major executive and judicial offices. But once the convention took up the report of the committee of detail, it began to augment executive power. Two debates of August 17 and 23—the first concerned with the power to initiate war, the second with the negotiation of treaties—illustrate this development.

Founding America

By early September, the exhausted delegates were prepared to complete their work. Forty-two members from twelve states were still in attendance. Three of these—George Mason and Edmund Randolph of Virginia, and Elbridge Gerry of Massachusetts—had indicated they were unwilling to sign the completed Constitution. Their objections soon provided significant inspiration for the Constitution's opponents, the Anti-Federalists. It was to overcome their scruples that the convention's and the country's great sage, Benjamin Franklin, made a characteristically witty but politically futile appeal for unanimity.

RESOLUTIONS ADOPTED BY CONVENTION
JULY 26, 1787

---

1. RESOLVED That the Government of the United States ought to consist of a Supreme Legislative, Judiciary and Executive.

2. RESOLVED That the Legislature of the United States ought to consist of two Branches.

3. RESOLVED That the Members of the first Branch of the Legislature of the United States ought to be elected by the People of the several States—for the Term of two Years—to be of the Age of twenty five Years at least—to be ineligible to and incapable of holding any Office under the Authority of the United States (except those peculiarly belonging to the Functions of the first Branch) during the Time of Service of the first Branch.

4. RESOLVED That the Members of the second Branch of the Legislature of the United States ought to be chosen by the Individual Legislatures—to be of the Age of thirty Years at least—to hold their Offices for the Term of six Years; one third to go out biennially—to receive a Compensation for the Devotion of their Time to the public Service—to be ineligible to and incapable of holding any Office under the Authority of the United States (except those peculiarly belonging to the Functions of the second Branch) during the Term for which they are elected, and for one Year thereafter.

5. RESOLVED That each Branch ought to possess the Right of originating Acts.

6. RESOLVED That the Right of Suffrage in the first Branch of the Legislature of the United States ought not to be according to the Rules established in the Articles of Confederation but according to some equitable Ratio of Representation.

7. RESOLVED That in the original Formation of the Legislature of the United States the first Branch thereof shall consist of sixty five Members of which Number New Hampshire

shall send *three*—Massachusetts *eight*—Rhode Island *one*—Connecticut *five*—New. York *six*—New-Jersey *four*—Pennsylvania *eight*—Delaware *one*—Maryland *six*—Virginia *ten*—North. Carolina *five*—South Carolina *five*—Georgia *three*.

But as the present Situation of the States may probably alter in the Number of their Inhabitants, the Legislature of the United States shall be authorised from Time to Time to apportion the Number of Representatives; and in Case any of the States shall hereafter be divided, or enlarged by Addition of Territory, or any two or more States united, or any new States created within the Limits of the United States, the Legislature of the United States shall possess Authority to regulate the Number of Representatives in any of the foregoing Cases, upon the Principle of the Number of their Inhabitants, according to the Provisions herein after mentioned namely—Provided always that Representation ought to be proportioned according to direct Taxation: And in order to ascertain the Alteration in the direct Taxation, which may be required from Time to Time, by the Changes in the relative Circumstances of the States—

Resolved—that a Census be taken, within six years from the first Meeting of the Legislature of the United States, and once within the Term of every ten Years afterwards, of all the Inhabitants of the United States in the Manner and according to the Ratio recommended by Congress in their Resolution of April 18th. 1783—And that the Legislature of the United States shall proportion the direct Taxation accordingly.

Resolved—that all Bills for raising or Appropriating Money, and for fixing the Salaries of the Officers of the Government of the United States shall originate in the first Branch of the Legislature of the United States, and shall not be altered or amended by the second Branch; and that no money shall be drawn from the public Treasury but in Pursuance of Appropriations to be originated by the first Branch.

RESOLVED that from the first Meeting of the Legislature of the United States until a Census shall be taken, all Monies for supplying the public Treasury by direct Taxation shall be raised from the several States according to the Number of their Representatives respectively in the first Branch.

8. RESOLVED That in the second Branch of the Legislature of the United States each State shall have an equal Vote.

RESOLVED   That the Legislature of the United States ought to possess the legislative Rights vested in Congress by the Confederation; and moreover to legislate in all Cases for the general Interests of the Union, and also in those Cases to which the States are separately incompetent, or in which the Harmony of the United States may be interrupted by the Exercise of individual Legislation.

RESOLVED   That the legislative Acts of the United States made by Virtue and in Pursuance of the Articles of Union, and all Treaties made and ratified under the Authority of the United States shall be the supreme Law of the respective States so far as those Acts or Treaties shall relate to the said States, or their Citizens and Inhabitants; and that the Judicatures of the several States shall be bound thereby in their Decisions, any thing in the respective Laws of the individual States to the contrary notwithstanding.

RESOLVED   That a national Executive be instituted to consist of a single Person—to be chosen for the Term of six Years—with Power to carry into Execution the national Laws—to appoint to Offices in Cases not otherwise provided for—to be removeable on Impeachment and Conviction of mal Practice or Neglect of Duty—to receive a fixed Compensation for the Devotion of his Time to public Service—to be paid out of the public Treasury.

RESOLVED   That the national Executive shall have a Right to negative any legislative Act, which shall not be afterwards passed, unless by two third Parts of each Branch of the national Legislative.

RESOLVED   That a national Judiciary be established to consist of one Supreme Tribunal—the Judges of which shall be appointed by the second Branch of the national Legislature—to hold their Offices during good Behaviour—to receive punctually at stated Times a fixed Compensation for their Services, in which no Diminution shall be made so as to affect the Persons actually in Office at the Time of such Diminution.

RESOLVED   That the Jurisdiction of the national Judiciary shall extend to Cases arising under the Laws passed by the general

Legislature, and to such other Questions as involve the national Peace and Harmony.

RESOLVED   That the national Legislature be empowered to appoint inferior Tribunals.

RESOLVED   That Provision ought to be made for the Admission of States lawfully arising within the Limits of the United States, whether from a voluntary Junction of Government and Territory, or otherwise, with the Consent of a number of Voices in the national Legislature   less than the whole.

RESOLVED   That a Republican Form of Government shall be guarantied to each State; and that each State shall be protected against foreign and domestic Violence.

RESOLVED   That Provision ought to be made for the Amendment of the Articles of Union, whensoever it shall seem necessary.

RESOLVED   That the legislative, executive and judiciary Powers, within the several States, and of the national Government, ought to be bound by Oath to support the Articles of Union.

RESOLVED   That the Amendments which shall be offered to the Confederation by the Convention ought at a proper Time or Times, after the Approbation of Congress, to be submited to an Assembly or Assemblies of Representatives, recommended by the several Legislatures, to be expressly chosen by the People to consider and decide thereon.

RESOLVED   That the Representation in the second Branch of the Legislature of the United States consist of two Members from each State, who shall vote *per capita.*

DRAFT CONSTITUTION
AUGUST 6, 1787

MR. RUTLIDGE [DELIVERED IN] the Report of the Committee of detail as follows; [a printed copy being at the same time furnished to each member.]

We the people of the States of New Hampshire, Massachusetts, Rhode-Island and Providence Plantations, Connecticut, New-York, New-Jersey, Pennsylvania, Delaware, Maryland, Virginia, North-Carolina, South-Carolina, and Georgia, do ordain, declare, and establish the following Constitution for the Government of Ourselves and our Posterity.

ARTICLE I

The stile of the [this] Government shall be. "The United States of America."

II

The Government shall consist of supreme legislative, executive, and judicial powers.

III

The legislative power shall be vested in a Congress, to consist of two separate and distinct bodies of men, a House of Representatives and a Senate; each of which shall [,] in all cases [,] have a negative on the other. The Legislature shall meet on the first Monday in December [in] every year.

IV

Sect. 1. The members of the House of Representatives shall be chosen every second year, by the people of the several States comprehended within this Union. The qualifications of the electors shall be the same, from time to time, as those of the electors in the several States, of the most numerous branch of their own legislatures.

Sect. 2. Every member of the House of Representatives shall be of the age of twenty five years at least; shall have been a citizen of [in] the United States for at least three years before his election; and shall be, at the time of his election, a resident of the State in which he shall be chosen.

Sect. 3. The House of Representatives shall, at its first formation, and until the number of citizens and inhabitants shall be taken in the manner herein after described, consist of sixty five Members, of whom three shall be chosen in New Hampshire, eight in Massachusetts, one in Rhode-Island and Providence Plantations, five in Connecticut, six in New-York, four in New-Jersey, eight in Pennsylvania, one in Delaware, six in Maryland, ten in Virginia, five in North-Carolina, five in South-Carolina, and three in Georgia.

Sect. 4. As the proportions of numbers in [the] different States will alter from time to time; as some of the States may hereafter be divided; as others may be enlarged by addition of territory; as two or more States may be united; as new States will be erected within the limits of the United States, the Legislature shall, in each of these cases, regulate the number of representatives by the number of inhabitants, according to the provisions herein after made, at the rate of one for every forty thousand.

Sect. 5. All bills for raising or appropriating money, and for fixing the salaries of the officers of the Government, shall originate in the House of Representatives, and shall not be altered or amended by the Senate. No money shall be drawn from the public Treasury, but in pursuance of appropriations that shall originate in the House of Representatives.

Sect. 6. The House of Representatives shall have the sole power of impeachment. It shall choose its Speaker and other officers.

Sect. 7. Vacancies in the House of Representatives shall be supplied by writs of election from the executive authority of the State, in the representation from which it shall happen.

V

Sect. 1. The Senate of the United States shall be chosen by the Legislatures of the several States. Each Legislature shall chuse two members. Vacancies may be supplied by the Executive until the next meeting of the Legislature. Each member shall have one vote.

Sect. 2. The Senators shall be chosen for six years; but immediately after the first election they shall be divided, by lot, into three classes, as nearly as may be, numbered one, two and three. The seats of the members of the first class shall be vacated at the expiration of the second year, of the second class at the expiration of the fourth year, of the third class at the expiration of the sixth year, so that a third part of the members may be chosen every second year.

Sect. 3. Every member of the Senate shall be of the age of thirty years at least; shall have been a citizen in the United States for at least four years before his election; and shall be, at the time of his election, a resident of the State for which he shall be chosen.

Sect. 4. The Senate shall chuse its own President and other officers.

VI

Sect. 1. The times and places and [the] manner of holding the elections of the members of each House shall be prescribed by the Legislature of each State; but their provisions concerning them may, at any time, be altered by the Legislature of the United States.

Sect. 2. The Legislature of the United States shall have authority to establish such uniform qualifications of the members of each House, with regard to property, as to the said Legislature shall seem expedient.

Sect. 3. In each House a majority of the members shall constitute a quorum to do business; but a smaller number may adjourn from day to day.

Sect. 4. Each House shall be the judge of the elections, returns and qualifications of its own members.

Sect. 5. Freedom of speech and debate in the Legislature shall not be impeached or questioned in any Court or place out of the Legislature; and the members of each House shall, in all cases, except treason [,] felony and breach of the peace, be privileged from arrest during their attendance at Congress, and in going to and returning from it.

Sect. 6. Each House may determine the rules of its proceedings; may punish its members for disorderly behaviour; and may expel a member.

Sect. 7. The House of Representatives, and the Senate, when it shall be acting in a legislative capacity, shall keep a Journal of their proceedings, and shall, from time to time, publish them: and the yeas and nays of the members of each House, on any question, shall [,] at the desire of one-fifth part of the members present, be entered on the journal.

Sect. 8. Neither House, without the consent of the other, shall adjourn for more than three days, nor to any other place than that at which the two Houses are sitting. But this regulation shall not extend to the Senate, when it shall exercise the powers mentioned in the ____ article.

Sect. 9. The members of each House shall be ineligible to, and incapable of holding any office under the authority of the United

States, during the time for which they shall respectively be elected: and the members of the Senate shall be ineligible to, and incapable of holding any such office for one year afterwards.

Sect. 10. The members of each House shall receive a compensation for their services, to be ascertained and paid by the State, in which they shall be chosen,

Sect. 11. The enacting stile of the laws of the United States shall be, "Be it enacted by the Senate and Representatives in Congress assembled".

Sect. 12. Each House shall possess the right of originating bills, except in the cases beforementioned.

Sect. 13. Every bill, which shall have passed the House of Representatives and the Senate, shall, before it become a law, be presented to the President of the United States for his revision: if, upon such revision, he approve of it, he shall signify his approbation by signing it: But if, upon such revision, it shall appear to him improper for being passed into a law, he shall return it, together with his objections against it, to that House in which it shall have originated, who shall enter the objections at large on their journal and proceed to reconsider the bill. But if after such reconsideration, two thirds of that House shall, notwithstanding the objections of the President, agree to pass it, it shall together with his objections, be sent to the other House, by which it shall likewise be reconsidered, and [,] if approved by two thirds of the other House also, it shall become a law. But in all such cases, the votes of both Houses shall be determined by yeas and nays; and the names of the persons voting for or against the bill shall be entered on the journal of each House respectively. If any bill shall not be returned by the President within seven days after it shall have been presented to him, it shall be a law, unless the legislature by their adjournment, prevent its return; in which case it shall not be a law.

VII [VI]*

Sect. 1. The Legislature of the United States shall have the power to lay and collect taxes, duties, imposts and excises;

---

*In the printed copy of the draft, the number VI was repeated in error. We have here renumbered articles VII to the end and include the original, incorrect, numbers in brackets.

To regulate commerce with foreign nations, and among the several States;

To establish an uniform rule of naturalization throughout the United States;

To coin money;

To regulate the value of foreign coin;

To fix the standard of weights and measures;

To establish Post-offices;

To borrow money, and emit bills on the credit of the United States;

To appoint a Treasurer by ballot;

To constitute tribunals inferior to the Supreme Court;

To make rules concerning captures on land and water;

To declare the law and punishment of piracies and felonies committed on the high seas, and the punishment of counterfeiting the coin of the United States, and of offences against the law of nations;

To subdue a rebellion in any State, on the application of its legislature;

To make war;

To raise armies;

To build and equip fleets;

To call forth the aid of the militia, in order to execute the laws of the Union, enforce treaties, suppress insurrections, and repel invasions;

And to make all laws that shall be necessary and proper for carrying into execution the foregoing powers, and all other powers vested, by this Constitution, in the government of the United States, or in any department or officer thereof;

Sect. 2. Treason against the United States shall consist only in levying war against the United States, or any of them; and in adhering to the enemies of the United States, or any of them. The Legislature of the United States shall have power to declare the punishment of treason. No person shall be convicted of treason, unless on the testimony of two witnesses. No attainder of treason shall work corruption of bloods nor forfeiture, except during the life of the person attainted.

Sect. 3. The proportions of direct taxation shall be regulated by the whole number of white and other free citizens and inhabitants, of every age, sex and condition, including those bound to servitude

for a term of years, and three fifths of all other persons not comprehended in the foregoing description, (except Indians not paying
taxes) which number shall, within six years after the first meeting of
the Legislature, and within the term of every ten years afterwards, be
taken in such manner as the said Legislature shall direct.

Sect. 4. No tax or duty shall be laid by the Legislature on articles
exported from any State; nor on the migration or importation of
such persons as the several States shall think proper to admit; nor
shall such migration or importation be prohibited.

Sect. 5. No capitation tax shall be laid, unless in proportion to the
Census hereinbefore directed to be taken.

Sect. 6. No navigation act shall be passed without the assent of
two thirds of the members present in each House.

Sect. 7. The United States shall not grant any title of Nobility.

VIII [VII]

The Acts of the Legislature of the United States made in pursuance of this Constitution, and all treaties made under the authority of the United States shall be the supreme law of the several States,
and of their citizens and inhabitants; and the judges in the several
States shall be bound thereby in their decisions; anything in the
Constitutions or laws of the several States to the contrary notwithstanding.

IX [VIII]

Sect. 1. The Senate of the United States shall have power to make
treaties, and to appoint Ambassadors, and Judges of the supreme
Court.

Sect. 2. In all disputes and controversies now subsisting, or that
may hereafter subsist between two or more States, respecting jurisdiction or territory, the Senate shall possess the following powers.
Whenever the Legislature, or the Executive authority, or lawful
Agent of any State, in controversy with another, shall by memorial
to the Senate, state the matter in question, and apply for a hearing;
notice of such memorial and application shall be given by order of
the Senate, to the Legislature or the Executive authority of the other
State in Controversy. The Senate shall also assign a day for the appearance of the parties, by their agents, before the House. The
Agents shall be directed to appoint, by joint consent, commissioners

or judges to constitute a Court for hearing and determining the matter in question. But if the Agents cannot agree, the Senate shall name three persons out of each of the several States; and from the list of such persons each party shall alternately strike out one, until the number shall be reduced to thirteen; and from that number not less than seven nor more than nine names, as the Senate shall direct, shall in their presence, be drawn out by lot; and the persons whose names shall be so drawn, or any five of them shall be commissioners or Judges to hear and finally determine the controversy; provided a majority of the Judges, who shall hear the cause, agree in the determination. If either party shall neglect to attend at the day assigned, without shewing sufficient reasons for not attending, or being present shall refuse to strike, the Senate shall proceed to nominate three persons out of each State, and the Clerk of the Senate shall strike in behalf of the party absent or refusing. If any of the parties shall refuse to submit to the authority of such Court; or shall not appear to prosecute or defend their claim or cause, the Court shall nevertheless proceed to pronounce judgment. The judgment shall be final and conclusive. The proceedings shall be transmitted to the President of the Senate, and shall be lodged among the public records, for the security of the parties concerned. Every Commissioner shall, before he sit in judgment, take an oath, to be administred by one of the Judges of the Supreme or Superior Court of the State where the cause shall be tried, "well and truly to hear and determine the matter in question according to the best of his judgment, without favor, affection, or hope of reward."

Sect. 3. All controversies concerning lands claimed under different grants of two or more States, whose jurisdictions, as they respect such lands shall have been decided or adjusted subsequent to such grants, or any of them, shall, on application to the Senate, be finally determined, as near as may be, in the same manner as is before prescribed for deciding controversies between different States.

X [IX]

Sect. 1. The Executive Power of the United States shall be vested in a single person. His stile shall be "The President of the United States of America;" and his title shall be, "His Excellency". He shall be elected by ballot by the Legislature. He shall hold his office during the term of seven years; but shall not be elected a second time.

Sect. 2. He shall, from time to time, give information to the Legislature, of the state of the Union: he may recommend to their consideration such measures as he shall judge necessary, and expedient: he may convene them on extraordinary occasions. In case of disagreement between the two Houses, with regard to the time of adjournment, he may adjourn them to such time as he thinks proper: he shall take care that the laws of the United States be duly and faithfully executed: he shall commission all the officers of the United States; and shall appoint officers in all cases not otherwise provided for by this Constitution. He shall receive Ambassadors, and may correspond with the supreme Executives of the several States. He shall have power to grant reprieves and pardons; but his pardon shall not be pleadable in bar of an impeachment. He shall be commander in chief of the Army and Navy of the United States, and of the Militia of the Several States. He shall, at stated times, receive for his services, a compensation, which shall neither be increased nor diminished during his continuance in office. Before he shall enter on the duties of his department, he shall take the following oath or affirmation, "I _____ solemnly swear, (or affirm) that I will faithfully execute the office of President of the United States of America." He shall be removed from his office on impeachment by the House of Representatives, and conviction in the supreme Court, of treason, bribery, or corruption. In case of his removal as aforesaid, death, resignation, or disability to discharge the powers and duties of his office, the President of the Senate shall exercise those powers and duties, until another President of the United States be chosen, or until the disability of the President be removed.

XI [X]

Sect. 1. The Judicial Power of the United States shall be vested in one Supreme Court, and in such inferior Courts as shall, when necessary, from time to time, be constituted by the Legislature of the United States.

Sect. 2. The Judges of the Supreme Court, and of the Inferior Courts, shall hold their offices during good behaviour. They shall, at stated times, receive for their services, a compensation, which shall not be diminished during their continuance in office.

Sect. 3. The Jurisdiction of the Supreme Court shall extend to all cases arising under laws passed by the Legislature of the United

States; to all cases affecting Ambassadors, other Public Ministers and Consuls; to the trial of impeachments of Officers of the United States; to all cases of Admiralty and maritime jurisdiction; to controversies between two or more States, (except such as shall regard Territory or Jurisdiction) between a State and Citizens of another State, between Citizens of different States, and between a State or the Citizens thereof and foreign States, citizens or subjects. In cases of impeachment, cases affecting Ambassadors, other Public Ministers and Consuls, and those in which a State shall be party, this jurisdiction shall be original. In all the other cases before mentioned, it shall be appellate, with such exceptions and under such regulations as the Legislature shall make. The Legislature may assign any part of the jurisdiction above mentioned (except the trial of the President of the United States) in the manner, and under the limitations which it shall think proper, to such Inferior Courts, as it shall constitute from time to time.

Sect. 4. The trial of all criminal offences (except in cases of impeachments) shall be in the State where they shall be committed; and shall be by Jury.

Sect. 5. Judgment, in cases of Impeachment, shall not extend further than to removal from Office, and disqualification to hold and enjoy any office of honour, trust or profit, under the United States. But the party convicted shall, nevertheless be liable and subject to indictment, trial, judgment and punishment according to law.

XII [XI]

No State shall coin money; nor grant letters of marque and reprisals; nor enter into any treaty, alliance, or confederation; nor grant any title of Nobility.

XIII [XII]

No State, without the consent of the Legislature of the United States, shall emit bills of credit, or make any thing but specie a tender in payment of debts; nor lay imposts or duties on imports; nor keep troops or ships of war in time of peace; nor enter into any agreement or compact with another State, or with any foreign power; nor engage in any war, unless it shall be actually invaded by enemies, or the danger of invasion be so imminent, as not to admit of delay, until the Legislature of the United States can be consulted.

XIV [XIII]

The Citizens of each State shall be entitled to all privileges and immunities of citizens in the several States.

XV [XIV]

Any person charged with treason, felony or high misdemeanor in any State, who shall flee from justice, and shall be found in any other State, shall, on demand of the Executive power of the State from which he fled, be delivered up and removed to the State having jurisdiction of the offence.

XVI [XV]

Full faith shall be given in each State to the acts of the Legislatures, and to the records and judicial proceedings of the Courts and Magistrates of every other State.

XVII [XVI]

New States lawfully constituted or established within the limits of the United States may be admitted, by the Legislature, into this Government; but to such admission the consent of two thirds of the members present in each House shall be necessary. If a new State shall arise within the limits of any of the present States, the consent of the Legislatures of such States shall be also necessary to its admission. If the admission be consented to, the new States shall be admitted on the same terms with the original States. But the Legislature may make conditions with the new States, concerning the public debt which shall be then subsisting.

XVIII [XVII]

The United States shall guaranty to each State a Republican form of Government; and shall protect each State against foreign invasions, and, on the application of its Legislature, against domestic violence.

XIX [XVIII]

On the application of the Legislatures of two thirds of the States in the Union, for an amendment of this Constitution, the Legislature of the United States shall call a Convention for that purpose.

XX [XIX]

The members of the Legislatures, and the Executive and Judicial officers of the United States, and of the several States, shall be bound by oath to support this Constitution.

XXI [XX]

The ratifications of the Conventions of ＿＿ States shall be sufficient for organizing this Constitution.

XXII [XXI]

This Constitution shall be laid before the United States in Congress assembled, for their approbation; and it is the opinion of this Convention, that it should be afterwards submitted to a Convention chosen, under the recommendation of its legislature, in order to receive the ratification of such Convention.

XXIII [XXII]

To introduce this government, it is the opinion of this Convention, that each assenting Convention should notify its assent and ratification to the United States in Congress assembled; that Congress, after receiving the assent and ratification of the Conventions of ＿＿ States, should appoint and publish a day, as early as may be, and appoint a place for commencing proceedings under this Constitution; that after such publication, the Legislatures of the several States should elect members of the Senate, and direct the election of members of the House of Representatives; and that the members of the Legislature should meet at the time and place assigned by Congress, and should, as soon as may be, after their meeting, choose the President of the United States, and proceed to execute this Constitution.

[A motion was made to adjourn till Wednesday, in order to give leisure to examine the Report; which passed in the Negative—N. H. no. Mas. no. Ct. no. Pa. ay. Md. ay. Virg. ay. N. C. no. S. C. no

The House then adjourned till tomorrow 11 OC.]

DEBATE ON WAR POWER
AUGUST 17, 1787

"To make war"

MR PINKNEY* OPPOSED THE VESTING this power in the Legislature. Its proceedings were too slow. It wd. meet but once a year. The Hs. of Reps. would be too numerous for such deliberations. The Senate would be the best depositary, being more acquainted with foreign affairs, and most capable of proper resolutions. If the States are equally represented in Senate, so as to give no advantage to large States, the power will notwithstanding be safe, as the small have their all at stake in such cases as well as the large States. It would be singular for one authority to make war, and another peace.

Mr Butler.† The Objections agst the Legislature lie in a great degree agst the Senate. He was for vesting the power in the President, who will have all the requisite qualities, and will not make war but when the Nation will support it.

Mr. M[adison]‡ and Mr Gerry moved to insert *"declare,"* striking out *"make"* war; leaving to the Executive the power to repel sudden attacks.

Mr Sharman§ thought it stood very well. The Executive shd. be able to repel and not to commence war. "Make" better than "declare" the latter narrowing the power too much.

Mr Gerry never expected to hear in a republic a motion to empower the Executive alone to declare war.

Mr. Elseworth. there is a material difference between the cases of making *war,* and making *peace.* It shd. be more easy to get out of war, than into it. War also is a simple and overt declaration. peace attended with intricate & secret negociations.

---

*Charles Pinckney (1757–1824) of South Carolina.
†Pierce Butler (1744–1842), delegate from South Carolina.
‡In this and the following document, square brackets are used to indicate later insertions to Madison's notes from the journals, and angled brackets are used to identify later additions or clarifications to the delegate's speeches.
§Roger Sherman (1721–1793) represented Connecticut.

Mr. Mason* was agst giving the power of war to the Executive, because not ⟨safely⟩ to be trusted with it; or to the Senate, because not so constructed as to be entitled to it. He was for clogging rather than facilitating war; but for facilitating peace. He preferred *"declare"* to *"make".*

On the Motion to insert *declare*—in place of *Make,* [it was agreed to.]

N. H. no. Mas. abst. Cont. no.† Pa. ay. Del. ay. Md. ay. Va. ay. N. C. ay. S. C. ay. Geo. ay. [Ayes—7; noes—2; absent—1.]

Mr. Pinkney's motion to strike out whole clause, disagd. to without call of States.

Mr Butler moved to give the Legislature power of peace, as they were to have that of war.

Mr Gerry 2ds. him. 8 Senators may possibly exercise the power if vested in that body, and 14 if all should be present; and may consequently give up part of the U. States. The Senate are more liable to be corrupted by an Enemy than the whole Legislature.

On the motion for adding "and peace" after "war"

N. H. no. Mas. no. Ct. no. Pa. no. Del. no. Md. no. Va. no. N. C. [no] S. C. no. Geo. no. [Ayes—0; noes—10.]

Adjourned

DEBATE ON TREATY POWER
AUGUST 23, 1787

ART IX. SECT. 1. BEING RESUMED, to wit "The Senate of the U. S. shall have power to make treaties, and to appoint Ambassadors, and Judges of the Supreme Court."

Mr. ⟨Madison⟩ observed that the Senate represented the States

---

*George Mason (1725–1792), representative of Virginia.

†On the remark by Mr. King that *"make"* war might be understood to "conduct" it which was an Executive function, Mr. Elseworth gave up his objection [and the vote of Cont was changed to—ay] [James Madison's note].

alone, and that for this as well as other obvious reasons it was proper that the President should be an agent in Treaties.

Mr. Govr. Morris* did not know that he should agree to refer the making of Treaties to the Senate at all, but for the present wd. move to add as an amendment to the section, after "Treaties"— "but no Treaty shall be binding on the U. S. which is not ratified by a law."

Mr Madison suggested the inconvenience of requiring a legal *ratification* of treaties of alliance for the purposes of war &c &c

Mr. Ghorum.† Many other disadvantages must be experienced if treaties of peace and all negociations are to be previously ratified—and if not prevously, the Ministers would be at a loss how to proceed— What would be the case in G. Britain if the King were to proceed in this manner? American Ministers must go abroad not instructed by the same Authority (as will be the case with other Ministers) which is to ratify their proceedings.

Mr. Govr. Morris. As to treaties of alliance, they will oblige foreign powers to send their Ministers here, the very thing we should wish for. Such treaties could not be otherwise made, if his amendment shd. succeed. In general he was not solicitous to multiply & facilitate Treaties. He wished none to be made with G. Britain, till she should be at war. Then a good bargain might be made with her. So with other foreign powers. The more difficulty in making treaties, the more value will be set on them.

Mr. Wilson. In the most important Treaties, the King of G. Britain being obliged to resort to Parliament for the execution of them, is under the same fetters as the amendment of Mr. Morris will impose on the Senate. It was refused yesterday to permit even the Legislature to lay duties on exports. Under the clause, without the amendment, the Senate alone can make a Treaty, requiring all the Rice of S. Carolina to be sent to some one particular port.

Mr. Dickinson‡ concurred in the amendment, as most safe and proper, tho' he was sensible it was unfavorable to the little States; wch would otherwise have an *equal* share in making Treaties.

---

*Gouverneur Morris (1752–1816) of Pennsylvania.

†Nathaniel Gorham (1738–1796), delegate from Massachusetts.

‡John Dickinson (1732–1808), a Delaware delegate.

Docr. Johnson* thought there was something of solecism in saying that the acts of a Minister with plenipotentiary powers from one Body, should depend for ratification on another Body. The Example of the King of G. B. was not parallel. Full & compleat power was vested in him—If the Parliament should fail to provide the necessary means of execution, the Treaty would be violated.

Mr. Ghorum in answer to Mr. Govr Morris, said that negociations on the spot were not to be desired by us, especially if the whole Legislature is to have any thing to do with Treaties. It will be generally influenced by two or three men, who will be corrupted by the Ambassadors here. In such a Government as ours, it is necessary to guard against the Government itself being seduced.

Mr. Randolph observing that almost every Speaker had made objections to the clause as it stood, moved in order to a further consideration of the subject, that the Motion of Mr. Govr. Morris should be postponed, and on this question [It was lost the States being equally divided.]

Massts. no. Cont. no. N. J—ay—Pena. ay. Del. ay. Md. ay. Va. ay—N. C. no. S. C. no—Geo. no. [Ayes—5; noes—5.]

On Mr. Govr. Morris Motion

Masts. no. Cont no. N. J. no. Pa. ay—Del. no—Md. no. Va. no. N. C. divd S. C. no. Geo—no. [Ayes—1; noes—8; divided—1.]

The several clauses of Sect: 1. art IX, were then separately postponed after inserting "and other public Ministers" next after "Ambassadors."

Mr. Madison hinted for consideration, whether a distinction might not be made between different sorts of Treaties—Allowing the President & Senate to make Treaties eventual and of Alliance for limited terms—and requiring the concurrence of the whole Legislature in other Treaties.

The 1st Sect. art IX. was finally referred nem: con: to the committee of Five, and the House then

Adjourned.

---

*William Samuel Johnson (1727–1819) of Connecticut.

Objections of Edmund Randolph, George Mason, and Elbridge Gerry
September 15, 1787

Mr. randolph animadverting on the indefinite and dangerous power given by the Constitution to Congress, expressing the pain he felt at differing from the body of the Convention, on the close of the great & awful subject of their labours, and anxiously wishing for some accommodating expedient which would relieve him from his embarrassments, made a motion importing "that amendments to the plan might be offered by the State Conventions, which should be submitted to and finally decided on by another general Convention." Should this proposition be disregarded, it would he said be impossible for him to put his name to the instrument. Whether he should oppose it afterwards he would not then decide but he would not deprive himself of the freedom to do so in his own State, if that course should be prescribed by his final judgment—

Col: Mason 2ded. & followed Mr. Randolph in animadversions on the dangerous power and structure of the Government, concluding that it would end either in monarchy, or a tyrannical aristocracy; which, he was in doubt, but one or other, he was sure. This Constitution had been formed without the knowledge or idea of the people. A second Convention will know more of the sense of the people, and be able to provide a system more consonant to it. It was improper to say to the people, take this or nothing. As the Constitution now stands, he could neither give it his support or vote in Virginia; and he could not sign here what he could not support there. With the expedient of another Convention as proposed, he could sign.

Mr. Pinkney. These declarations from members so respectable at the close of this important scene, give a peculiar solemnity to the present moment. He descanted on the consequences of calling forth the deliberations & amendments of the different States on the subject of Government at large. Nothing but confusion & contrariety could spring from the experiment. The States will never agree in their plans—And the Deputies to a second Convention coming together under the discordant impressions of their Constituents, will never agree. Conventions are serious things, and ought not to be repeated— He was not without objections as well as others to the plan. He objected to the contemptible weakness & dependence of the Executive. He objected to the power of a majority only of Congs over Commerce. But apprehending the danger of a general confusion, and an ultimate decision by the Sword, he should give the plan his support.

Mr. Gerry, stated the objections which determined him to withhold his name from the Constitution. 1. the duration and re-eligibility of the Senate. 2. the power of the House of Representatives to conceal their journals. 3. the power of Congress over the places of election. 4. the unlimited power of Congress over their own compensations. 5. Massachusetts has not a due share of Representatives allotted to her. 6. 3/5 of the Blacks are to be represented as if they were freemen 7. *Under* the power over commerce, monopolies may be established. 8. The vice president being made head of the Senate. He could however he said get over all these, if the rights of the Citizens were not rendered insecure 1. by the general power of the Legislature to make what laws they may please to call necessary and proper. 2. raise armies and money without limit. 3. to establish a tribunal without juries, which will be a Star-chamber as to Civil cases. Under such a view of the Constitution, the best that could be done he conceived was to provide for a second general Convention.

On the question on the proposition of Mr Randolph. All the States answered—no

On the question to agree to the Constitution. as amended. All the States ay.

The Constitution was then ordered to be engrossed.

And the House adjourned.

—Benjamin Franklin—
CONCLUDING APPEAL FOR UNANIMITY
SEPTEMBER 17, 1787

THE ENGROSSED CONSTITUTION BEING read,

Docr. Franklin rose with a speech in his hand, which he had reduced to writing for his own conveniency, and which Mr. Wilson read in the words following.

Mr. President

I confess that there are several parts of this constitution which I do not at present approve, but I am not sure I shall never approve them: For having lived long, I have experienced many instances of being obliged by better information or fuller consideration, to change opinions even on important subjects, which I once thought right, but found to be otherwise. It is therefore that the older I grow, the more apt I am to doubt my own judgment, and to pay more respect to the judgment of others. Most men indeed as well as most sects in Religion, think themselves in possession of all truth, and that whereever others differ from them it is so far error. Steele, a Protestant in a Dedication tells the Pope, that the only difference between our Churches in their opinions of the certainty of their doctrines is, the Church of Rome is infallible and the Church of England is never in the wrong. But though many private persons think almost as highly of their own infallibility as of that of their sect, few express it so naturally as a certain french lady, who in a dispute with her sister, said "I don't know how it happens, Sister but I meet with no body but myself, that's always in the right"—"*Il n'y a que moi qui a toujours raison.*"

In these sentiments, Sir, I agree to this Constitution with all its faults, if they are such; because I think a general Government necessary for us, and there is no form of Government but what may be a blessing to the people if well administered, and believe farther that this is likely to be well administered for a course of years, and can only end in Despotism, as other forms have done before it, when the people shall become so corrupted as to need despotic Government, being incapable of any other. I doubt too whether any other Convention we can obtain may be able to make a better Constitution. For when you assemble a number of men to have the advantage of their joint wisdom, you inevitably assemble with those men, all their prejudices, their passions, their errors of opinion, their local interests, and their selfish views. From such an Assembly can a perfect production be expected? It therefore astonishes me, Sir, to find this system approaching so near to perfection as it does; and I think it will astonish our enemies, who are waiting with confidence to hear that our councils are confounded like those of the Builders of Babel; and that our States are on the point of separation, only to meet hereafter for the purpose of cutting one another's throats. Thus I consent, Sir, to this Constitution because I expect no better, and because I am not sure, that it is not the best. The opinions I have had of its errors, I sacrifice to the public good— I have never whispered a syllable of them abroad— Within these walls they were born, and here they shall die— If every one of us in returning to our Constituents were to report the objections he has had to it, and endeavor to gain partizans in support of them, we might prevent its being generally received, and thereby lose all the salutary effects & great advantages resulting naturally in our favor among foreign Nations as well as among ourselves, from our real or apparent unanimity. Much of the strength & efficiency of any Government in procuring and securing happiness to the people, depends. on opinion, on the general opinion of the goodness of the Government, as well as of the wisdom and integrity of its Governors. I hope therefore that for our own sakes as a part of the people, and for the sake of posterity, we shall act heartily and unanimously in recommending this Constitution (if approved by Congress & confirmed by the Conventions) wherever our influence may extend, and turn our future thoughts & endeavors to the means of having it well administered.

On the whole, Sir, I cannot help expressing a wish that every member of the Convention who may still have objections to it, would with me, on this occasion doubt a little of his own infallibility—and to make manifest our unanimity, put his name to this instrument.—He then moved that the Constitution be signed by the members and offered the following as a convenient form viz. "Done in Convention, by the unanimous consent of *the States* present the 17th. of Sepr. &c—In Witness whereof we have hereunto subscribed our names."

THE CONSTITUTION

THE DELEGATES SIGNED THE completed Constitution on September 17, 1787, took a concluding dinner at the City Tavern, and then left Philadelphia. The Constitution they had drafted was the culmination not only of four and a half months of deliberation, but of the decade of constitutional experimentation that began in 1776. The states had served as effective laboratories of liberty, and the lessons the framers drew as they reconstituted the national government came primarily from the experience of the states. Two days later, the Constitution was published in a Philadelphia newspaper, and the public debate over its ratification began.

The first official step in the process of ratification was for the convention to transmit the Constitution to Congress, which was in turn expected to ask the state legislatures to call elections for separate ratification conventions. In his letter submitting the Constitution to Congress, George Washington, the convention president, struck a note that would resound throughout the ratification campaign. Forming a more perfect union did not require writing a perfect document, Washington implied; instead, Americans had to consider the range of problems and interests the convention had to solve and accommodate.

THE CONSTITUTION

THE CONSTITUTION OF THE UNITED STATES
SEPTEMBER 17, 1787

WE THE PEOPLE OF the United States, in Order to form a more perfect Union, establish Justice, insure domestic Tranquility, provide for the common defence, promote the general Welfare, and secure the Blessings of Liberty to ourselves and our Posterity, do ordain and establish this Constitution for the United States of America.

ARTICLE. I.

Section. 1. All legislative Powers herein granted shall be vested in a Congress of the United States, which shall consist of a Senate and House of Representatives.

Section. 2. The House of Representatives shall be composed of Members chosen every second Year by the People of the several States, and the Electors in each State shall have the Qualifications requisite for Electors of the most numerous Branch of the State Legislature.

No Person shall be a Representative who shall not have attained to the Age of twenty five Years, and been seven Years a Citizen of the United States, and who shall not, when elected, be an Inhabitant of that State in which he shall be chosen.

Representatives and direct Taxes shall be apportioned among the several States which may be included within this Union, according to their respective Numbers, which shall be determined by adding to the whole Number of free Persons, including those bound to Service for a Term of Years, and excluding Indians not taxed, three fifths of all other Persons. The actual Enumeration shall be made within three Years after the first Meeting of the Congress of the United States, and within every subsequent Term of ten Years, in such Manner as they shall by Law direct. The Number of Representatives shall not exceed one for every thirty Thousand, but each State shall have at Least one Representative; and until such enumeration shall be made, the State of New Hampshire shall be entitled to chuse three, Massachusetts eight, Rhode-Island and Providence Plantations one, Connecticut five, New-York six, New Jersey four, Pennsylvania eight, Delaware one, Maryland six, Virginia ten, North Carolina five, South Carolina five, and Georgia three.

When vacancies happen in the Representation from any State, the Executive Authority thereof shall issue Writs of Election to fill such Vacancies.

The House of Representatives shall chuse their Speaker and other Officers; and shall have the sole Power of Impeachment.

Section. 3. The Senate of the United States shall be composed of two Senators from each State, chosen by the Legislature thereof, for six Years; and each Senator shall have one Vote.

Immediately after they shall be assembled in Consequence of the first Election, they shall be divided as equally as may be into three Classes. The Seats of the Senators of the first Class shall be vacated at the Expiration of the second Year, of the second Class at the Expiration of the fourth Year, and of the third Class at the Expiration of the sixth Year, so that one third may be chosen every second Year; and if Vacancies happen by Resignation, or otherwise, during the Recess of the Legislature of any State, the Executive thereof may make temporary Appointments until the next Meeting of the Legislature, which shall then fill such Vacancies.

No Person shall be a Senator who shall not have attained to the Age of thirty Years, and been nine Years a Citizen of the United States, and who shall not, when elected, be an inhabitant of that State for which he shall be chosen.

The Vice President of the United States shall be President of the Senate, but shall have no Vote, unless they be equally divided.

The Senate shall chuse their other Officers, and also a President pro tempore, in the Absence of the Vice President, or when he shall exercise the Office of President of the United States.

The Senate shall have the sole Power to try all Impeachments. When sitting for that Purpose, they shall be on Oath or Affirmation. When the President of the United States is tried, the Chief Justice shall preside: And no Person shall be convicted without the Concurrence of two thirds of the Members present.

Judgment in Cases of Impeachment shall not extend further than to removal from Office, and disqualification to hold and enjoy any Office of honor, Trust or Profit under the United States: but the

Party convicted shall nevertheless be liable and subject to Indictment, Trial, Judgment and Punishment, according to Law.

Section. 4. The Times, Places and Manner of holding Elections for Senators and Representatives, shall be prescribed in each State by the Legislature thereof; but the Congress may at any time by Law make or alter such Regulations, except as to the Places of chusing Senators.

The Congress shall assemble at least once in every Year, and such Meeting shall be on the first Monday in December, unless they shall by Law appoint a different Day.

Section. 5. Each House shall be the judge of the Elections, Returns and Qualifications of its own Members, and a Majority of each shall constitute a Quorum to do Business; but a smaller Number may adjourn from day to day, and may be authorized to compel the Attendance of absent Members, in such Manner, and under such Penalties as each House may provide.

Each House may determine the Rules of its Proceedings, punish its Members for disorderly Behaviour, and, with the Concurrence of two thirds, expel a Member.

Each House shall keep a Journal of its Proceedings, and from time to time publish the same, excepting such Parts as may in their Judgment require Secrecy; and the Yeas and Nays of the Members of either House on any question shall, at the Desire of one fifth of those Present, be entered on the Journal.

Neither House, during the Session of Congress, shall, without the Consent of the other, adjourn for more than three days, nor to any other Place than that in which the two Houses shall be sitting.

Section. 6. The Senators and Representatives shall receive a Compensation for their Services, to be ascertained by Law, and paid out of the Treasury of the United States. They shall in all Cases, except Treason, Felony and Breach of the Peace, be privileged from Arrest during their Attendance at the Session of their respective Houses, and in going to and returning from the same; and for any Speech or Debate in either House, they shall not be questioned in any other Place.

No Senator or Representative shall, during the Time for which he was elected, be appointed to any civil Office under the Authority of the United States, which shall have been created, or the Emoluments whereof shall have been encreased during such time; and no Person holding any Office under the United States, shall be a Member of either House during his Continuance in Office.

Section. 7. All Bills for raising Revenue shall originate in the House of Representatives; but the Senate may propose or concur with Amendments as on other Bills.

Every Bill which shall have passed the House of Representatives and the Senate, shall, before it become a Law, be presented to the President of the United States; If he approve he shall sign it, but if not he shall return it, with his Objections to that House in which it shall have originated, who shall enter the Objections at large on their Journal, and proceed to reconsider it. If after such Reconsideration two thirds of that House shall agree to pass the Bill, it shall be sent, together with the Objections, to the other House, by which it shall likewise be reconsidered, and if approved by two thirds of that House, it shall become a Law. But in all such Cases the Votes of both Houses shall be determined by yeas and Nays, and the Names of the Persons voting for and against the Bill shall be entered on the Journal of each House respectively. If any Bill shall not be returned by the President within ten Days (Sundays excepted) after it shall have been presented to him, the Same shall be a Law, in like Manner as if he had signed it, unless the Congress by their Adjournment prevent its Return, in which Case it shall not be a Law.

Every Order, Resolution, or Vote to which the Concurrence of the Senate and House of Representatives may be necessary (except on a question of Adjournment) shall be presented to the President of the United States; and before the Same shall take Effect, shall be approved by him, or being disapproved by him, shall be repassed by two thirds of the Senate and House of Representatives, according to the Rules and Limitations prescribed in the Case of a Bill.

Section. 8. The Congress shall have Power To lay and collect Taxes, Duties, Imposts and Excises, to pay the Debts and Provide for the common Defence and general Welfare of the United States; but all Duties, Imposts and Excises shall be uniform throughout the United States;

To borrow Money on the credit of the United States;

To regulate Commerce with foreign Nations, and among the several States, and with the Indian Tribes;

To establish an uniform Rule of Naturalization, and uniform Laws on the subject of Bankruptcies throughout the United States;

To coin Money, regulate the Value thereof, and of foreign Coin, and fix the Standard of Weights and Measures;

To provide for the Punishment of counterfeiting the Securities and current Coin of the United States;

To establish Post Offices and post Roads;

To promote the Progress of Science and useful Arts, by securing for limited Time to Authors and Inventors the exclusive Right to their respective Writings and Discoveries;

To constitute Tribunals inferior to the supreme Court;

To define and punish Piracies and Felonies committed on the high Seas, and Offences against the Law of Nations;

To declare War, grant Letters of Marque and Reprisal, and make Rules concerning Captures on Land and Water;

To raise and support Armies, but no Appropriation of Money to that Use shall be for a longer Term than two Years;

To provide and maintain a Navy;

To make Rules for the Government and Regulation of the land and naval Forces;

To provide for calling forth the Militia to execute the Laws of the Union, suppress Insurrections and repel Invasions;

To provide for organizing, arming, and disciplining, the Militia, and for governing such Part of them as may be employed in the Service of the United States, reserving to the States respectively, the Appointment of the Officers, and the Authority of training the Militia according to the discipline prescribed by Congress;

To exercise exclusive Legislation in all Cases whatsoever, over such District (not exceeding ten Miles square) as may, by Cession of Particular States, and the Acceptance of Congress, become the Seat of the Government of the United States, and to exercise like Authority over all Places purchased by the Consent of the Legislature of the State in which the Same shall be, for the Erection of Forts, Magazines, Arsenals, dock-Yards, and other needful Buildings;—And

To make all Laws which shall be necessary and proper for carrying into Execution the foregoing Powers, and all other Powers vested by this Constitution in the Government of the United States, or in any Department or Officer thereof.

Section. 9. The Migration or Importation of such Persons as any of the States now existing shall think proper to admit, shall not be prohibited by the Congress prior to the Year one thousand eight hundred and eight, but a Tax or duty may be imposed on such Importation, not exceeding ten dollars for each Person.

The Privilege of the Writ of Habeas Corpus shall not be suspended, unless when in Cases of Rebellion or Invasion the public Safety may require it.

No Bill of Attainder or ex post facto Law shall be passed.

No Capitation, or other direct, Tax shall be laid, unless in Proportion to the Census or Enumeration herein before directed to be taken.

No Tax or Duty shall be laid on Articles exported from any State.

No Preference shall be given by any Regulation of Commerce or Revenue to the Ports of one State over those of another: nor shall Vessels bound to, or from, one State, be obliged to enter, clear, or pay Duties in another.

No Money shall be drawn from the Treasury, but in Consequence of Appropriations made by Law; and a regular Statement and Account of the Receipts and Expenditures of all public Money shall be published from time to time.

No Title of Nobility shall be granted by the United States: And no Person holding any Office of Profit or Trust under them, shall, without the Consent of the Congress, accept of any present, Emolument, Office, or Title, of any kind whatever, from any King, Prince, or foreign State.

Section. 10. No State shall enter into any Treaty, Alliance, or Confederation; grant Letters of Marque and Reprisal; coin Money; emit Bills of Credit; make any Thing but gold and silver Coin a Tender in Payment of Debts; pass any Bill of Attainder, ex post facto Law, or Law impairing the Obligation of Contracts, or grant any Title of Nobility.

No State shall, without the Consent of the Congress, lay any Imposts or Duties on Imports or Exports, except what may be absolutely necessary for executing it's inspection Laws: and the net Produce of all Duties and Imposts, laid by any State on Imports or Exports, shall be for the Use of the Treasury of the United States; and all such Laws shall be subject to the Revision and Controul of the Congress.

No State shall, without the Consent of Congress, lay any Duty of Tonnage, keep Troops, or Ships of War in time of Peace, enter into any Agreement or Compact with another State, or with a foreign

Power, or engage in War, unless actually invaded, or in such imminent Danger as will not admit of delay.

ARTICLE. II.

Section. 1. The executive Power shall be vested in a President of the United States of America. He shall hold his Office during the Term of four Years, and, together with the Vice President, chosen for the same Term, be elected, as follows

Each State shall appoint, in such Manner as the Legislature thereof may direct, a Number of Electors, equal to the whole Number of Senators and Representatives to which the State may be entitled in the Congress: but no Senator or Representative, or Person holding an Office of Trust or Profit under the United States, shall be appointed an Elector.

The Electors shall meet in their respective States, and vote by Ballot for two Persons, of whom one at least shall not be an Inhabitant of the same State with themselves. And they shall make a List of all the Persons voted for, and of the Number of Votes for each; which List they shall sign and certify, and transmit sealed to the Seat of the Government of the United States, directed to the President of the Senate. The President of the Senate shall, in the Presence of the Senate and House of Representatives, open all the Certificates, and the Votes shall then be counted. The Person having the greatest Number of Votes shall be the President, if such Number be a Majority of the whole Number of Electors appointed; and if there be more than one who have such Majority, and have an equal Number of Votes, then the House of Representatives shall immediately chuse by Ballot one of them for President; and if no Person have a Majority, then from the five highest on the List the said House shall in like Manner chuse the President. But in chusing the President, the Votes shall be taken by States, the Representation from each State having one Vote; A quorum for this Purpose shall consist of a Member or Members from two thirds of the States, and a Majority of all the States shall be necessary to a Choice. In every Case, after the Choice of the President, the Person having the greatest Number of Votes of the Electors shall be the Vice President. But if there should remain two or more who have equal Votes, the Senate shall chuse from them by Ballot the Vice President.

The Congress may determine the Time of chusing the Electors, and the Day on which they shall give their Votes; which Day shall be the same throughout the United States.

No Person except a natural born Citizen, or a Citizen of the United States, at the time of the Adoption of this Constitution, shall be eligible to the Office of President; neither shall any Person be eligible to that Office who shall not have attained to the Age of thirty five Years, and been fourteen Years a Resident within the United States.

In Case of the Removal of the President from Office, or of his Death, Resignation, or Inability to discharge the Powers and Duties of the said Office, the Same shall devolve on the Vice President, and the Congress may by Law provide for the Case of Removal, Death, Resignation or Inability, both of the President and Vice President, declaring what Officer shall then act as President, and such Officer shall act accordingly, until the Disability be removed, or a President shall be elected.

The President shall, at stated Times, receive for his Services, a Compensation, which shall neither be encreased nor diminished during the Period for which he shall have been elected, and he shall not receive within that Period any other Emolument from the United States, or any of them.

Before he enter on the Execution of his Office, he shall take the following Oath or Affirmation:—"I do solemnly swear (or affirm) that I will faithfully execute the Office of President of the United States, and will to the best of my Ability, preserve, protect and defend the Constitution of the United States."

Section. 2. The President shall be Commander in Chief of the Army and Navy of the United States, and of the Militia of the several States, when called into the actual Service of the United States; he may require the Opinion, in writing, of the principal Officer in each of the executive Departments, upon any Subject relating to the Duties of their respective Offices, and he shall have Power to grant Reprieves and Pardons for Offences against the United States, except in Cases of Impeachment.

He shall have Power, by and with the Advice and Consent of the Senate, to make Treaties, provided two thirds of the Senators present concur; and he shall nominate, and by and with the Advice and Consent of the Senate, shall appoint Ambassadors, other public

Ministers and Consuls, Judges of the supreme Court, and all other Officers of the United States, whose Appointments are not herein otherwise provided for, and which shall be established by Law: but the Congress may by Law vest the Appointment of such inferior Officers, as they think proper, in the President alone, in the Courts of Law, or in the Heads of Departments.

The President shall have Power to fill up all Vacancies that may happen during the Recess of the Senate, by granting Commissions which shall expire at the End of their next Session.

Section. 3. He shall from time to time give to the Congress Information of the State of the Union, and recommend to their consideration such Measures as he shall judge necessary and expedient; he may, on extraordinary Occasions, convene both Houses, or either of them, and in Case of Disagreement between them, with Respect to the Time of Adjournment, he may adjourn them to such Time as he shall think proper; he shall receive Ambassadors and other public Ministers; he shall take Care that the Laws be faithfully executed, and shall Commission all the Officers of the United States.

Section. 4. The President, Vice President and all civil Officers of the United States, shall be removed from Office on Impeachment for, and conviction of, Treason, Bribery, or other high Crimes and Misdemeanors.

Article. III.

Section. 1. The judicial Power of the United States, shall be vested in one supreme Court, and in such inferior Courts as the Congress may from time to time ordain and establish. The Judges, both of the supreme and inferior Courts, shall hold their Offices during good Behaviour, and shall, at stated Times, receive for their Services, a Compensation, which shall not be diminished during their Continuance in Office.

Section. 2. The judicial Power shall extend to all Cases, in Law and Equity, arising under this Constitution, the Laws of the United States, and Treaties made, or which shall be made, under their Authority;— to all Cases affecting Ambassadors, other public Ministers and Consuls;—to all Cases of admiralty and maritime Jurisdiction;—to Controversies to which the United States shall be a Party;—to Controversies between two or more States;—between a State and Citizens of another State;—between Citizens of different States,—between Citizens of the same State claiming Lands under Grants of different States, and between a State, or the Citizens thereof, and foreign States, Citizens or Subjects.

In all Cases affecting Ambassadors, other public Ministers and Consuls, and those in which a State shall be Party, the supreme Court shall have original Jurisdiction. In all the other Cases before mentioned, the supreme Court shall have appellate Jurisdiction, both as to Law and Fact, with such Exceptions, and under such Regulations as the Congress shall make.

The Trial of all Crimes, except in Cases of Impeachment, shall be by Jury; and such Trial shall be held in the State where the said Crimes shall have been committed; but when not committed within any State, the Trial shall be at such Place or Places as the Congress may by Law have directed.

Section. 3. Treason against the United States, shall consist only in levying War against them, or in adhering to their Enemies, giving them Aid and Comfort. No Person shall be convicted of Treason unless on the Testimony of two Witnesses to the same overt Act, or on Confession in open Court.

The Congress shall have Power to declare the Punishment of Treason, but no Attainder of Treason shall work Corruption of Blood, or Forfeiture except during the Life of the Person attainted.

Article. IV.

Section. 1. Full Faith and Credit shall be given in each State to the public Acts, Records, and judicial Proceedings of every other State. And the Congress may by general Laws prescribe the Manner in which such Acts, Records and Proceedings shall be proved, and the Effect thereof.

Section. 2. The Citizens of each State shall be entitled to all Privileges and Immunities of Citizens in the several States.

A Person charged in any State with Treason, Felony, or other Crime, who shall flee from Justice, and be found in another State, shall on Demand of the executive Authority of the State from which he fled, be delivered up, to be removed to the State having Jurisdiction of the Crime.

No Person held to Service or Labour in one State, under the Laws thereof, escaping into another, shall, in Consequence of any Law or Regulation therein, be discharged from such Service or Labour, but shall be delivered up on Claim of the Party to whom such Service or Labour may be due.

Section. 3. New States may be admitted by the Congress into this Union; but no new State shall be formed or erected within the Jurisdiction of any other State; nor any State be formed by the Junction of two or more States, or Parts of States, without the Consent of the Legislatures of the States concerned as well as of the Congress.

The Congress shall have Power to dispose of and make all needful Rules and Regulations respecting the Territory or other Property belonging to the United States; and nothing in this Constitution shall be so construed as to Prejudice any Claims of the United States, or of any particular State.

Section. 4. The United States shall guarantee to every State in this Union a Republican Form of Government, and shall protect each of them against Invasion; and on Application of the Legislature, or of the Executive (when the Legislature cannot be convened) against domestic Violence.

Article. V.

The Congress, whenever two thirds of both Houses shall deem it necessary, shall propose Amendments to this Constitution, or, on the Application of the Legislatures of two thirds of the several States, shall call a Convention for proposing Amendments, which, in either Case, shall be valid to all Intents and Purposes, as Part of this Constitution, when ratified by the Legislatures of three fourths of the several States, or by Conventions in three fourths thereof, as the one or the other Mode of Ratification may be proposed by the Congress; Provided that no Amendment which may be made prior to the Year One thousand eight hundred and eight shall in any Manner affect the first and fourth Clauses in the Ninth Section of the first Article; and that no State, without its Consent, shall be deprived of it's equal Suffrage in the Senate.

Article. VI.

All Debts contracted and Engagements entered into, before the Adoption of this Constitution, shall be as valid against the United States under this Constitution, as under the Confederation.

This Constitution, and the Laws of the United States which shall be made in Pursuance thereof; and all Treaties made, or which shall be made, under the Authority of the United States, shall be the supreme Law of the Land; and the Judges in every State shall be bound thereby, any Thing in the Constitution or Laws of any State to the Contrary notwithstanding.

The Senators and Representatives before mentioned, and the Members of the several State Legislatures, and all executive and judicial Officers, both of the United States and of the several States, shall be bound by Oath or Affirmation, to support this Constitution; but no religious Test shall ever be required as a Qualification to any Office or public Trust under the United States.

ARTICLE. VII.

The Ratification of the Conventions of nine States, shall be sufficient for the Establishment of this Constitution between the States so ratifying the Same.

Done in Convention by the Unanimous Consent of the States present the Seventeenth Day of September in the Year of our Lord one thousand seven hundred and Eighty seven and of the Independence of the United States of America the Twelfth IN WITNESS whereof We have hereunto subscribed our Names,

Attest William Jackson Secretary

Go. Washington—Presidt.
and deputy from Virginia.

New Hampshire	John Langdon
	Nicholas Gilman
Massachusetts	Nathaniel Gorham
	Rufus King
Connecticut	Wm: Saml. Johnson
	Roger Sherman
New York . .	. Alexander Hamilton
New Jersey	Wil: Livingston
	David Brearley
	Wm. Paterson
	Jona: Dayton

Pensylvania	B Franklin Thomas Mifflin Robt Morris Geo. Clymer Thos. Fitzsimons Jared Ingersoll James Wilson Gouv Morris
Delaware	Geo: Read Gunning Bedford jun John Dickinson Richard Bassett Jaco: Broom
Maryland	James McHenry Dan of St Thos. Jenifer Danl. Carroll.
Virginia	John Blair— James Madison Jr.
North Carolina	Wm. Blount Richd. Dobbs Spaight. Hu Williamson
South Carolina	J. Rutledge Charles Cotesworth Pinckney Charles Pinckney Pierce Butler.
Georgia	William Few Abr Baldwin

Concluding Resolution for Ratification
September 17, 1787

Present
The States of

New Hampshire, Massachusetts, Connecticut, Mr. Hamilton from New York, New Jersey, Pennsylvania, Delaware, Maryland, Virginia, North Carolina, South Carolina and Georgia.

Resolved,

That the preceding Constitution be laid before the United States in Congress assembled, and that it is the Opinion of this Convention, that it should afterwards be submitted to a Convention of Delegates, chosen in each State by the People thereof, under the Recommendation of its Legislature, for their Assent and Ratification; and that each Convention assenting to, and ratifying the Same, should give Notice thereof to the United States in Congress assembled.

Resolved, That it is the Opinion of this Convention, that as soon as the Conventions of nine States shall have ratified this Constitution, the United States in Congress assembled should fix a Day on which Electors should be appointed by the States which shall have ratified the same, and a Day on which the Electors should assemble to vote for the President, and the Time and place for commencing Proceedings under this Constitution. That after such Publication the Electors should be appointed, and the Senators and Representatives elected: That the Electors should meet on the Day fixed for the Election of the President, and should transmit their votes certified signed, sealed and directed, as the Constitution requires, to the Secretary of the United States in Congress assembled, that the Senators and Representatives should convene at the Time and Place asigned; that the Senators should appoint a President of the Senate, for the sole Purpose of receiving, opening and counting the Votes for President; and, that after he shall be chosen, the Congress, together with the President, should, without Delay, proceed to execute this Constitution.

By the Unanimous Order of the Convention

Go: Washington Presidt.

W. Jackson Secretary

—George Washington—
LETTER OF CONVEYANCE TO CONGRESS
SEPTEMBER 17, 1787

SIR,

We have now the honor to submit to the consideration of the United States in Congress assembled, that Constitution which has appeared to us the most adviseable.

The friends of our country have long seen and desired, that the power of making war, peace and treaties, that of levying money and regulating commerce, and the correspondent executive and judicial authorities should be fully and effectually vested in the general government of the Union: but the impropriety of delegating such extensive trust to one body of men is evident—Hence results the necessity of a different organization.

It is obviously impracticable in the fœderal government of these States, to secure all rights of independent sovereignty to each, and yet provide for the interest and safety of all—Individuals entering into society, must give up a share of liberty to preserve the rest. The magnitude of the sacrifice must depend as well on situation and circumstance, as on the object to be obtained. It is at all times difficult to draw with precision the line between those rights which must be surrendered, and those which may be reserved; and on the present occasion this difficulty was encreased by a difference among the several States as to their situation, extent, habits, and particular interests.

In all our deliberations on this subject we kept steadily in our view, that which appears to us the greatest interest of every true American, the consolidation of our Union, in which is involved our prosperity, felicity, safety, perhaps our national existence. This important consideration, seriously and deeply impressed on our minds, led each State in the Convention to be less rigid on points of inferior magnitude, than might have been otherwise expected; and thus the Constitution, which we now present, is the result of a spirit of amity, and of that mutual deference and concession which the peculiarity of our political situation rendered indispensable.

That it will meet the full and entire approbation of every State is not perhaps to be expected; but each will doubtless consider, that had her interest alone been consulted, the consequences might have been particularly disagreeable or injurious to others; that it is liable to as few exceptions as could reasonably have been expected, we hope and believe; that it may promote the lasting welfare of that country so dear to us all, and secure her freedom and happiness, is our most ardent wish.

With great respect,
We have the honor to be.
SIR,
Your EXCELLENCY's most
Obedient and humble Servants,
GEORGE WASHINGTON, PRESIDENT.
By unanimous Order of the CONVENTION.
HIS EXCELLENCY
The President of Congress.

A More Perfect Union

ONCE THE CONSTITUTION REACHED Congress, it faced an early challenge from Richard Henry Lee of Virginia. Lee felt the Constitution needed amendment, and he wanted Congress to propose appropriate changes before sending it on to the states. But Madison and other framers who had returned to Congress argued that this would make the Constitution the work of Congress, not the convention. That in turn meant that it would have to be ratified according to the rule of the Confederation requiring approval by all thirteen state legislatures. This objection prevailed, and the Constitution went out to the states as the Convention had intended.

Beyond the immediate task of securing the approval of nine states lay the greater challenge of organizing a new government and adopting the right policies. One Federalist leader who was already looking ahead was Alexander Hamilton. Well before any of the states had acted on the Constitution, he was already speculating about the additional steps that would be needed for the new government to succeed.

Meanwhile, the public debate on the Constitution got under way. At the outset, statements from two former members of the convention played a key role in framing the debate. On October 6 James Wilson, the leading Pennsylvania Federalist, gave a public speech explaining why Americans should not be troubled by the omission of a bill of rights from the Constitution. Because this speech was public, Wilson's argument was taken to be an authoritative statement of the Federalist position, and it soon became a lightning rod for Anti-Federalist criticism. George Mason's reputation as a distinguished patriot similarly gave his objections to the Constitution greater authority than they would have enjoyed had he simply published them anonymously.

—James Madison:
LETTER TO GEORGE WASHINGTON
SEPTEMBER 30, 1787

I FOUND ON MY arrival here that certain ideas unfavorable to the Act of the Convention which had created difficulties in that body, had made their way into Congress. They were patronised chiefly by Mr. R.H.L.* and Mr. Dane of Massts. It was first urged that as the new Constitution was more than an Alteration of the Articles of Confederation under which Congress acted, and even subverted these articles altogether, there was a Constitutional impropriety in their taking any positive agency in the work. The answer given was that the Resolution of Congress in Feby. had recommended the Convention as the best mean of obtaining a firm *national Government;* that as the powers of the Convention were defined by their Commissions in nearly the same terms with the powers of Congress given by the Confederation on the subject of alterations, Congress were not more restrained from acceding to the new plan, than the Convention were from proposing it. If the plan was within the powers of the Convention it was within those of Congress; if beyond those powers, the same necessity which justified the Convention would justify Congress; and a failure of Congress to Concur in what was done, would imply either that the Convention had done wrong in ~~proposing a *national* Government~~ exceeding their powers, or that the Government proposed was in itself liable to insuperable objections; that such an inference would be the more natural, as Congress had never scrupled to recommend measures foreign to their constitutional functions, whenever the public good seemed to require it; and had in several instances, particularly in the establishment of the new Western Governments, exercised assumed powers of a very high

---

*Richard Henry Lee.

& delicate nature, under motives infinitely less urgent than the present state of our affairs, if any faith were due to the representations made by Congress themselves, ecchoed by 12 States in the Union, and confirmed by the general voice of the people.—An attempt was made in the next place by R.H.L. to amend the Act of the Convention before it should go forth from Congress. He proposed a bill of Rights— provision for juries in civil cases & several other things corresponding with the ideas of Col. M—.* He was supported by Mr. Me— Smith† of this State. It was contended that Congress had an undoubted right to insert amendments, and that it was their duty to make use of it in a case where the essential guards of liberty had been omitted. On the other side the right of Congress was not denied, but the inexpediency of exerting it was urged on the following grounds. 1. that every circumstance indicated that the introduction Congress as a party to the reform, was intended by the States merely as a matter of form and respect. 2. that it was evident from the contradictory objections which had been expressed by the different members who had animadverted on the plan, that a discussion of its merits would consume much time, without producing agreement even among its adversaries. 3. that it was clearly the intention of the States that the plan to be proposed should be the ~~joint~~ act of the Convention with the assent of Congress, which could not be the case, if alterations were made, the Convention being no longer in existence to adopt them. 4. that as the Act of the Convention, when altered would instantly become the mere act of Congress, and must be proposed by them as such, and of course be addressed to the Legislatures, not conventions of the States, and require the ratification of thirteen instead of nine States, and as the unaltered act would go forth to the States directly from the Convention under the auspices of that Body—Some States might ratify one & some the other of the plans, and confusion & disappointment be the least evils that could ensue. These difficulties which at one time threatened a serious division in Congs. and popular alterations with the yeas & nays on the journals, were at length fortunately terminated by the following Resolution—"Congress having recd. the Report of the Convention lately

---

*George Mason; see note on p. 387.
†Melancton Smith, a delegate to Congress from New York.

assembled in Philada., Resold. *unanimously* that the said Report, with the Resolutions & letter accompanying the same, be transmitted to the several Legislatures, in order to be submitted to a Convention of Delegates chosen in each State by the people thereof, in conformity to the Resolves of the Convention made & provided in that case." Eleven States were present, the absent ones R.I. & Maryland. A more direct approbation would have been of advantage in this & some other States, where stress will be laid on the agency of Congress in the matter, and a handle taken by adversaries of any ambiguity on the subject. With regard to Virginia & some other States, reserve on the part of Congress will do no injury. The circumstance of unanimity must be favorable every where.

The general voice of this City seems to espouse the new Constitution. It is supposed nevertheless that the party in power is strongly opposed to it. The Country must finally decide, the sense of which is as yet wholly unknown. As far as Boston & Connecticut has been heard from, the first impression seems to be auspicious. I am waiting with anxiety for the eccho from Virginia but with very faint hopes of its corresponding with my wishes.

P.S. a small packet of the size of 2 vol. 80. addressed to you lately came to my hands with books of my own from France. Genl. Pinkney has been so good as to take charge of them. He set out yesterday for S. Carolina & means to call at Mount Vernon.

—*Alexander Hamilton*—
Conjectures About the Constitution
September 1787

THE NEW CONSTITUTION HAS in favour of its success these circumstances—a very great weight of influence of the persons who framed it, particularly in the universal popularity of General Washington,—the good will of the commercial interest throughout the states which will give all its efforts to the establishment of a ~~general~~ government capable of regulating protecting and extending the commerce of the Union—the good will of ~~all~~ most men of property in the several states who wish a government of the union able to protect them against domestic violence and the depredations which the democratic spirit is apt to make on property; and who are besides anxious for the respectability of the nation—the hopes of the Creditors of the United States that a general government possessing the means of doing it will pay the debt of the Union. a strong belief in the people at large of the insufficiency of the present confederation to preserve the existence of the Union and of the necessity of the union to their safety and prosperity; of course a strong desire of a change and a predisposition to receive well the propositions of the Convention.

Against its success is to be put, the dissent of two or three important men in the Convention; who will think their characters pleged to defeat the plan—the influence of many *inconsiderable* men in possession of considerable offices under the state governments who will fear a diminution of their consequence power and emolument by the establishment of the general government and who can hope for nothing there—the influence of some *considerable* men in office possessed of talents and popularity who partly from the same motives and partly from a desire of *playing a part* in a convulsion for their own aggrandisement will oppose the quiet adoption of the new government—(some considerable men out of office, from motives of ambition may be disposed to act the same part)—add to these causes the disinclination of the people to taxes and of course to a strong government—the opposition of all men much in debt who will not wish to see a government established one object of which is to restrain this means of cheating Creditors—the democratical jealousy of the people which may be alarmed at the appearance of institutions that may seem calculated to place the power of the community in few hands and to raise a few individuals to stations of great preeminence—and the influence of some foreign powers who from different motives will not wish to see an energetic government established throughout the states.

In this view of the subject it is difficult to form any judgment whether the plan will be adopted or rejected. It must be essentially matter of conjecture. The present appearances and all other circumstances considered the probability seems to be on the side of its adoption.

But the causes operating against its adoption are powerful and there will be nothing astonishing in the Contrary—

If it do not finally obtain, it is probable the discussion of the question will beget such struggles animosities and heats in the community that this circumstance conspiring with the *real necessity* of an essential change in our present situation will produce civil war. Should this happen, whatever parties prevail it is probable governments very different from the present in their principles will be established—A dismemberment of the Union and monarchies in different portions of it may be expected. It may however happen that no civil war will take place; but several republican confederacies be established between different combinations of particular states.

A reunion with Great Britain, from universal disgust at a state of commotion, is not impossible, though not much to be feared. The most plausible shape of such a business would be the establishment of a son of the present monarch in the supreme government of this country with a family compact.

If the government is adopted, it is probable general Washington will be the President of the United States—This will ensure a wise choice of men to administer the government and a good administration. A good administration will conciliate the confidence and affection of the people and perhaps enable the government to acquire more consistency than the proposed constitution seems to promise for so great a Country—It may then triumph altogether over the state governments and reduce them to an entire subordination, dividing the large states into smaller districts. The *organs* of the general government may also acquire additional strength.

If this should not be the case, in the course of a few years, it is probable that the contests about the boundaries of power between the particular governments and the general government and the *momentum* of the larger states in such contests will produce a dissolution of the Union. This after all seems to be the most likely result.

But it is almost arrogance in so complicated a subject, depending so entirely on the incalculable fluctuations of the human passions, to attempt even a conjecture about the event.

It will be Eight or Nine months before any certain judgment can be formed respecting the adoption of the Plan.

—*Richard Henry Lee*—
LETTER TO GEORGE MASON
OCTOBER 1, 1787

I HAVE WAITED UNTIL now to answer your favor of Septr. 18th from Philadelphia, that I might inform you how the Convention plan of Government was entertained by Congress. Your prediction of what would happen in Congress was exactly verified—It was with us, as with you, this or nothing; & this urged with a most extreme intemperance—The greatness of the powers given & the multitude of Places to be created, produces a coalition of Monarchy men, Military Men, Aristocrats, and Drones whose noise, impudence & zeal exceeds all belief—Whilst the Commercial plunder of the South stimulates the rapacious Trader. In this state of things, the Patriot voice is raised in vain for such changes and securities as Reason and Experience prove to be necessary against the encroachments of power upon the indispensable rights of human nature. Upon due consideration of the Constitution under which we now Act, some of us were clearly of opinion that the 13th article of the Confederation precluded us from giving an opinion concerning a plan subversive of the present system and eventually forming a New Confederacy of Nine instead of 13 States. The contrary doctrine was asserted with great violence in expectation of the strong majority with which they might send it forward under terms of much approbation. Having procured an opinion that Congress was qualified to consider, to amend, to approve or disapprove—the next game was to determine that tho a right to amend existed, it would be highly inexpediant to exercise that right, but merely to transmit it with respectful marks of approbation—In this state of things I availed myself of the Right to amend, & moved the Amendments copy of which I send herewith & called the ayes & nays to fix them on the journal—This greatly alarmed the Majority & vexed them extremely—for the plan is, to push the business on with great dispatch, & with as little opposition as possible; that it may be adopted before it has stood the test of Reflection & due examination—They found it most eligible at last to transmit it merely, without approving or disapproving; provided nothing but the transmission should appear on the Journal—This compromise was settled and they took the opportunity of inserting the word *Unanimously*, which applied only to simple transmission, hoping to have it mistaken for an Unanimous approbation of the thing—It states that Congress having Received the Constitution unanimously transmit it &c.—It is certain that no Approbation was given—This constitution has a great many excellent Regulations in it and if it could be reasonably amended would be a fine System—As it is, I think 'tis past doubt, that if it should be established, either a tyranny will result from it, or it will be prevented by a Civil war—I am clearly of opinion with you that it should be sent back with amendments Reasonable and Assent to it with held until such amendments are admitted—You are well acquainted with Mr. Stone & others of influence in Maryland—I think it will be a great point to get Maryld. & Virginia to join in the plan of Amendments & return it with them— If you are in correspondence with our Chancelor Pendleton it will be of much use to furnish him with the objections, and if he approves our plan, his opinion will have great weight with our Convention, and I am told that his relation to Judge Pendleton of South Carolina has decided weight in that State & that he is sensible & independent—How important will be then to procure his union with our plan, which might probably be the case, if our Chancelor was to write largely & pressingly to him on the subject; that if possible it may be amended there also. It is certainly the most rash and violent proceeding in the world to cram thus suddenly into Men a business of such infinite Moment to the happiness of Millions. One of your letter[s] will go by the Packet, and one by a Merchant Ship. My compliments if you please to Your Lady & to the young Ladies & Gentlemen.

[P.S.] Suppose when the Assembly recommended a Convention to consider this new Constitution they were to use some words like these—It is earnestly recommended to the good people of Virginia to send their most wise & honest Men to this Convention that it may undergo the most intense consideration before a plan shall be without amendments adopted that admits of abuses being practised by which the best interests of this Country may be injured and Civil Liberty greatly endanger'd.—This might perhaps give a decided Tone to the business—

Please to send my Son Ludwell a Copy of the Amendments proposed by me to the new Constitution sent herewith—

—*James Wilson*—
SPEECH ON THE CONSTITUTION
OCTOBER 6, 1787

MR. CHAIRMAN AND FELLOW CITIZENS, Having received the honor of an appointment to represent you in the late convention, it is perhaps, my duty to comply with the request of many gentlemen whose characters and judgments I sincerely respect, and who have urged, that this would be a proper occasion to lay before you any information which will serve to explain and elucidate the principles and arrangements of the constitution, that has been submitted to the consideration of the United States. I confess that I am unprepared for so extensive and so important a disquisition; but the insidious attempts which are clandestinely and industriously made to pervert and destroy the new plan, induce me the more readily to engage in its defence; and the impressions of four months constant attention to the subject, have not been so easily effaced as to leave me without an answer to the objections which have been raised.

It will be proper however, before I enter into the refutation of the charges that are alledged, to mark the leading descrimination between the state constitutions, and the constitution of the United States. When the people established the powers of legislation under their separate governments, they invested their representatives with every right and authority which they did not in explicit terms reserve; and therefore upon every question, respecting the jurisdiction of the house of assembly, if the frame of government is silent, the jurisdiction is efficient and complete. But in delegating fœderal powers, another criterion was necessarily introduced, and the congressional authority is to be collected, not from tacit implication, but from the positive grant expressed in the instrument of union. Hence it is evident, that in the former case every thing which is not reserved is given, but in the latter the reverse of the proposition prevails, and every thing which is not given, is reserved. This distinction being recognized, will furnish an answer to those who think the omission of a bill of rights, a defect in the proposed constitution: for it would have been superfluous and absurd to have stipulated with a foederal body of our own creation, that we should enjoy those privileges, of which we are not divested either by the intention or the act, that has brought that body into existence. For instance, the liberty of the press, which has been a copious source of declamation and opposition, what controul can proceed from the foederal government to shackle or destroy that sacred palladium of national freedom? If indeed, a power similar to that which has been granted for the regulation of commerce, had been granted to regulate literary publications, it would have been as necessary to stipulate that the liberty of the press should be preserved inviolate, as that the impost should be general in its operation. With respect likewise to the particular district of ten miles, which is to be made the seat of foederal government, it will undoubtedly be proper to observe this salutary precaution, as there the legislative power will be exclusively lodged in the president, senate, and house of representatives of the United States. But this could not be an object with the convention, for it must naturally depend upon a future compact, to which the citizens immediately interested will, and ought to be parties; and there is no reason to suspect that so popular a privilege will in that case be neglected. In truth then, the proposed system possesses no influence whatever upon the press, and it would have been merely nugatory to have introduced a formal declaration upon the subject—nay, that very declaration might have been construed to imply that some degree of power was given, since we undertook to define its extent.

Another objection that has been fabricated against the new constitution, is expressed in this disingenuous form—"the trial by jury is abolished in civil cases." I must be excused, my fellow citizens, if upon this point, I take advantage of my professional experience to detect the futility of the assertion. Let it be remembered then, that the business of the Foederal Convention was not local, but general; not limited to the views and establishments of a single state, but co-extensive with the continent, and comprehending the views and establishments of thirteen independent sovereignties. When therefore, this subject was in discussion, we were involved in difficulties which pressed on all sides, and no precedent could be discovered to direct our course. The cases open to a trial by jury differed in the different states, it was therefore impracticable on that ground to have made a general rule. The want of uniformity would have rendered any reference to the practice of the states idle and useless; and it could not, with any propriety, be said that "the trial by jury shall be as heretofore," since there has never existed any fœderal system of jurisprudence to which the declaration could relate. Besides, it is not in all cases that the trial by jury is adopted in civil questions, for causes depending in courts of admiralty, such as relate to maritime captures, and such as are agitated in courts of equity, do not require the intervention of that tribunal. How then, was the line of discrimination to be drawn? The convention found the task too difficult for them, and they left the business as it stands, in the fullest confidence that no danger could possibly ensue, since the proceedings of the supreme court, are to be regulated by the congress, which is a faithful representation of the people; and the oppression of government is effectually barred, by declaring that in all criminal cases the trial by jury shall be preserved.

This constitution, it has been further urged, is of a pernicious tendency, because it tolerates a standing army in the time of peace.—This has always been a topic of popular declamation; and yet, I do not know a nation in the world, which has not found it necessary and useful to maintain the appearance of strength in a season of the most profound tranquility. Nor is it a novelty with us; for under the present articles of confederation, congress certainly possesses this reprobated power, and the exercise of that power is proved at this moment by her cantonments along the banks of the Ohio. But what would be our national situation were it otherwise? Every principle of policy must be subverted, and the government must declare war, before they are prepared to carry it on. Whatever may be the provocation, however important the object in view, and however necessary dispatch and secrecy may be, still the declaration must precede the preparation, and the enemy will be informed of your intention, not only before you are equipped for an attack, but even before you are fortified for a defence. The consequence is too obvious to require any further delineation, and no man, who regards the dignity and safety of his country, can deny the necessity of a military force, under the controul and with the restrictions which the new constitution provides.

Perhaps there never was a charge made with less reasons than that which predicts the institution of a baneful aristocracy in the fœderal senate. This body branches into two characters, the one legislative, and the other executive. In its legislative character it can effect no purpose, without the co-operation of the house of representatives, and in its executive character, it can accomplish no object, without the concurrence of the president. Thus fettered, I do not know any act which the senate can of itself perform, and such dependance necessarily precludes every idea of influence and superiority. But I will confess that in the organization of this body, a compromise between contending interests is descernible; and when we reflect how various are the laws, commerce, habits, population, and extent of the confederated states, this evidence of mutual concession and accommodation ought rather to command a generous applause, than to excite jealousy and reproach. For my part, my admiration can only be equalled by my astonishment, in beholding so perfect a system, formed from such heterogeneous materials.

The next accusation I shall consider, is that which represents the fœderal constitution as not only calculated, but designedly framed, to reduce the state governments to mere corporations, and eventually to annihilate them. Those who have employed the term corporation upon this occasion, are not perhaps aware of its extent. In common parlance, indeed, it is generally applied to petty associations for the ease and conveniency of a few individuals; but in its enlarged sense, it will comprehend the government of Pennsylvania, the existing union of the states, and even this projected system is nothing more than a formal act of incorporation. But upon what pretence can it be alledged that it was designed to annihilate the state governments? For, I will undertake to prove that upon their existence, depends the existence of the fœderal plan. For this purpose, permit me to call your attention to the manner in which the president, senate, and house of representatives, are proposed to be appointed. The president is to be chosen by electors, nominated in such manner as the legislature of each state may direct; so that if there is no legislature, there can be no electors, and consequently the office of president cannot be supplied. The senate is to be composed of two senators from each state, chosen by the legislature; and therefore if there is no legislature, there can be no senate. The house of representatives, is to be composed of members chosen every second year by the people of the several states, and the electors in each state shall have the qualifications requisite for electors of the most numerous branch of the state legislature,—unless therefore, there is a state legislature, that qualification cannot be ascertained, and the popular branch of the fœderal constitution must likewise be extinct. From this view, then it is evidently absurd to suppose, that the annihilation of the separate governments will result from their union; or, that having that intention, the authors of the new system would have bound their connection with such indissoluble ties. Let me here advert to an arrangement highly advantageous, for you will perceive, without prejudice to the powers of the legislature in the election of senators, the people at large will acquire an additional privilege in returning members to the house of representatives—whereas, by the present confederation, it is the legislature alone that appoints the delegates to Congress.

The power of direct taxation has likewise been treated as an improper delegation to the fœderal government; but when we consider it as the duty of that body to provide for the national safety, to support the dignity of the union, and to discharge the debts contracted upon the collective faith of the states for their common benefit, it must be acknowledged, that those upon whom such important obligations are imposed, ought in justice and in policy to possess every means requisite for a faithful performance of their trust. But why should we be alarmed with visionary evils? I will venture to predict, that the great revenue of the United States must, and always will be raised by impost, for, being at once less obnoxious, and more productive, the interest of the government will be best promoted by the accommodation of the people. Still however, the objects of direct taxation should be within reach in all cases of emergency; and there is no more reason to apprehend oppression in the mode of collecting a revenue from this resource, than in the form of an impost, which, by universal assent, is left to the authority of the fœderal government. In either case, the force of civil institutions will be adequate to the purpose; and the dread of military violence, which has been assiduously disseminated, must eventually prove the mere effusion of a wild imagination, or a factious spirit. But the salutary consequences that must flow from thus enabling the government to receive and support the credit of the union, will afford another answer to the objections upon this ground. The State of Pennsylvania particularly, which has encumbered itself with the assumption of a great proportion of the public debt, will derive considerable relief and advantage; for, as it was the imbecility of the present confederation, which gave rise to the funding law, that law must naturally expire, when a competent and energetic fœderal system shall be substituted—the state will then be discharged from an extraordinary burthen, and the national creditor will find it to be his interest to return to his original security.

After all, my fellow citizens, it is neither extraordinary or unexpected, that the constitution offered to your consideration, should meet with opposition. It is the nature of man to pursue his own interest, in preference to the public good; and I do not mean to make any personal reflection, when I add, that it is the interest of a very numerous, powerful, and respectable body to counteract and destroy the excellent work produced by the late convention. All the offices of government, and all the appointments for the administration of justice and the collection of the public revenue, which are transferred from the individual to the aggregate sovereignty of the states, will necessarily turn the stream of influence and emolument into a new channel. Every person therefore, who either enjoys, or expects to enjoy, a place of profit under the present establishment, will object to the proposed innovation; not, in truth, because it is injurious to the liberties of his country, but because it affects his schemes of wealth and consequence. I will confess indeed, that I am not a blind admirer of this plan of government, and that there are some parts of it, which if my wish had prevailed, would certainly have been altered. But, when I reflect how widely men differ in their opinions, and that every man (and the observation applies likewise to every state) has an equal pretension to assert his own, I am satisfied that any thing nearer to perfection could not have been accomplished. If there are errors, it should be remembered, that the seeds of reformation are sown in the work itself, and the concurrence of two thirds of the congress may at any time introduce alterations and amendments. Regarding it then, in every point of view, with a candid and disinterested mind, I am bold to assert, that it is the best form of government which has ever been offered to the world.

—*George Mason*—
OBJECTIONS TO THE CONSTITUTION
OCTOBER 7, 1787

THERE IS NO DECLARATION of Rights; and the Laws of the general Government being paramount to the Laws & Constitutions of the several States, the Declarations of Rights in the separate States are no Security. Nor are the People secured even in the Enjoyment of the Benefits of the common-Law; which stands here upon no other Foundation than it's having been adopted by the respective Acts forming the Constitutions of the several States.

In the House of Representatives there is not the Substance, but the Shadow only of Representation; which can never produce proper Information in the Legislature, or inspire Confidence in the People: the Laws will therefore be generally made by Men little concern'd in, and unacquainted with their Effects & Consequences.—[a]

The Senate have the Power of altering all Money-Bills, and of originating Appropriations of Money, & the Sallerys of the Officers of their own Appointment in Conjunction with the President of the United States; altho' they are not the Representatives of the People, or amenable to them.—

These with their other great Powers (vizt. their Power in the Appointment of Ambassadors & all public Officers, in making Treaties, & in trying all Impeachments) their Influence upon & Connection with the supreme Executive from these Causes, their Duration of Office, and their being a constant existing Body almost continually sitting, join'd with their being one compleat Branch of the Legislature, will destroy any Balance in the Government, and enable them to accomplish what Usurpations they please upon the Rights & Libertys of the People.—

The Judiciary of the United States is so constructed & extended, as to absorb & destroy the Judiciarys of the several States; thereby rendering Law as tedious intricate & expensive, and Justice as unattainable, by a great Part of the Community, as in England, and enabling the Rich to oppress & ruin the Poor.—

The President of the United States has no constitutional Council (a thing unknown in any safe & regular Government) he will therefore be unsupported by proper Information & Advice; and will generally be directed by Minions & Favourites—or He will become a Tool to the Senate—or a Council of State will grow out of the principal Officers of the great Departments; the worst & most dangerous of all Ingredients for such a Council, in a free Country; for they may be induced to join in any dangerous or oppressive Measures, to shelter themselves and prevent an Inquiry into their own Misconduct in Office; whereas had a constitutional Council been formed (as was proposed) of six Members; vizt. two from the Eastern, two from the Middle, and two from the Southern States, to be appointed by Vote of the States in the House of Representatives, with the same Duration & Rotation of Office as the Senate, the Executive wou'd always have had safe & proper Information & Advice, the President of such a Council might have acted as Vice President of the United States, pro tempore, upon any Vacancy or Disability of the chief Magistrate; and long continued Sessions of the Senate wou'd in a great Measure have been prevented.

From this fatal Defect of a constitutional Council has arisen the improper Power of the Senate, in the Appointment of public Officers, and the alarming Dependance & Connection between that Branch of the Legislature, and the supreme Executive.—Hence also sprung that unnecessary & dangerous Officer the Vice President; who for want of other Employment, is made President of the Senate; thereby dangerously blending the executive & legislative Powers; besides always giving to some one of the States an unnecessary & unjust Pre-eminence over the others.—

The President of the United States has the unrestrained Power of granting Pardons for Treason; which may be sometimes excercised to screen from Punishment those whom he had secretly instigated to commit the Crime, & thereby prevent a Discovery of his own Guilt.—

By declaring all Treaties supreme Laws of the Land, the Executive & the Senate have, in many Cases, an exclusive Power of Legislation; which might have been avoided, by proper Distinctions with Respect to Treaties, and requiring the Assent of the House of Representatives, where it cou'd be done with Safety.—

By requiring only a Majority to make all Commercial & Navigation Laws, the five Southern States (whose Produce & Circumstances are totally different from that of the eight Northern & Eastern States) will be ruined; for such rigid & premature Regulations may be made as will enable the Merchants of the Northern & Eastern States not only to demand an exorbitant Freight, but to monopolize the Purchase of the Commodities at their own Price, for many Years: to the great Injury of the landed Interest, & Impoverishment of the People: and the Danger is the greater, as the Gain on one Side will be in Proportion to the Loss on the other. Whereas requiring two thirds of the Members present in both Houses wou'd have produced mutual Moderation, promoted the general Interest, and removed an insuperable Objection to the Adoption of the Government.—

Under their own Construction of the general Clause at the End of the enumerated Powers, the Congress may grant Monopolies in Trade & Commerce, constitute new Crimes, inflict unusual & severe Punishments, and extend their Power as far as they shall think proper; so that the State Legislatures have no Security for the Powers now presumed to remain to them; or the People for their Rights.—

There is no Declaration of any kind for preserving the Liberty of the Press, the Tryal by jury in civil Causes; nor against the Danger of standing Armys in time of Peace.

The State Legislatures are restrained from laying Export-Duties on their own Produce.—

The general Legislature is restrained from prohibiting the further Importation of Slaves for twenty odd Years; tho' such Importations render the United States weaker, more vulnerable, and less capable of Defence.—

Both the general Legislature & the State Legislatures are expressly prohibited making ex post facto Laws; tho' there never was or can be a Legislature but must & will make such Laws, when Necessity & the public Safety require them; which will hereafter be a Breach of all the Constitutions in the Union, and afford Precedents for other Innovations.—

This Government will commence in a moderate Aristocracy; it is at present impossible to foresee whether it will, in it's Operation, produce a Monarchy, or a corrupt oppressive Aristocracy; it will most probably vibrate some years between the two, and then terminate in the one or the other.—

(a) This Objection has been in some Degree lessened by an Amendment, often before refused, and at last made by an Erasure, after the Engrossment upon Parchment, of the word *forty,* and inserting *thirty,* in the 3d. Clause of the 2d. Section of the 1st. Article.—

THE CASE AGAINST THE CONSTITUTION

Melancton Smith, *Letters from the Federal Farmer* I–V (October 1787)   PAGE 435

ONE OF THE MOST influential and thoughtful Anti-Federalist critics of the Constitution was the New York author of *Letters from the Federal Farmer*. In all likelihood, this was Melancton Smith, a political ally of Governor George Clinton and a former delegate to Congress. Like other Anti-Federalists, the Federal Farmer believed that the Constitution was designed to produce a "consolidation" of previously autonomous states into one overarching national authority. If the state governments survived at all, Anti-Federalists repeatedly argued, they would be hollow jurisdictions at best. All the real power to govern would be concentrated at the national level. Armed with a general authority to tax and broad legislative power, and with the Constitution and federal legislation hailed as "the supreme law of the land," the national government would dominate the states.

Many Anti-Federalist writers were inclined to treat every clause of the Constitution as a potential formula for tyranny. The Federal Farmer was more moderate. Rather than shrill in tone, these essays were carefully and prudently reasoned. They could not be ridiculed in the way that many Federalists commonly heaped scorn on more enthusiastic writers. These arguments had to be answered reasonably, in ways that forced Federalist writers to go beyond simple appeals to the peace and prosperity the Constitution would miraculously bring and to explain why the government it would establish would be consistent with the principles of liberty.

THE CASE AGAINST THE CONSTITUTION

—*Melancton Smith*—
LETTERS FROM THE FEDERAL FARMER I–IV
OCTOBER 1787

I

OCTOBER 8TH, 1787.

DEAR SIR,

My letters to you last winter, on the subject of a well balanced national government for the United States, were the result of free enquiry; when I passed from that subject to enquiries relative to our commerce, revenues, past administration, etc. I anticipated the anxieties I feel, on carefully examining the plan of government proposed by the convention. It appears to be a plan retaining some federal features; but to be the first important step, and to aim strongly to one consolidated government of the United States. It leaves the powers of government, and the representation of the people, so unnaturally divided between the general and state governments, that the operations of our system must be very uncertain. My uniform federal attachments, and the interest I have in the protection of property, and a steady execution of the laws, will convince you, that, if I am under any biass at all, it is in favor of any general system which shall promise those advantages. The instability of our laws increases my wishes for firm and steady government; but then, I can consent to no government, which, in my opinion, is not calculated equally to preserve the rights of all orders of men in the community. My object has been to join with those who have endeavoured to supply the defects in the forms of our governments by a steady and proper administration of them. Though I have long apprehended that fraudalent debtors, and embarrassed men, on the one hand, and men, on the other, unfriendly to republican equality, would produce an uneasiness among the people, and prepare the way, not for cool and deliberate reforms in the governments, but for changes calculated to promote the interests of particular orders of men. Acquit me, sir, of any agency in the formation of the new system; I shall be satisfied with seeing, if it shall be adopted, a prudent administration. Indeed I am so much convinced of the truth of Pope's maxim, that "That which is best administered is best," that I am much inclined to subscribe to it from experience. I am not disposed to unreasonably contend about forms. I know our situation is critical, and it behoves us to make the best of it. A federal government of some sort is necessary. We have suffered the present to languish; and whether the confederation was capable or not originally of answering any valuable purposes, it is now but of little importance. I will pass by the men, and states, who have been particularly instrumental in preparing the way for a change, and, perhaps, for governments not very favourable to the people at large. A constitution is now presented which we may reject, or which we may accept, with or without amendments; and to which point we ought to direct our exertions, is the question. To determine this question, with propriety, we must attentively examine the system itself, and the probable consequences of either step. This I shall endeavour to do, so far as I am able, with candor and fairness; and leave you to decide upon the propriety of my opinions, the weight of my reasons, and how far my conclusions are well drawn. Whatever may be the conduct of others, on the present occasion, I do not mean, hastily and positively to decide on the merits of the constitution proposed. I shall be open to conviction, and always disposed to adopt that which, all things considered, shall appear to me to be most for the happiness of the community. It must be granted, that if men hastily and blindly adopt a system of government, they will as hastily and as blindly be led to alter or abolish it; and changes must ensue, one after another, till the peaceable and better part of the community will grow weary with changes, tumults and disorders, and be disposed to accept any government, however despotic, that shall promise stability and firmness.

The first principal question that occurs, is, Whether, considering our situation, we ought to precipitate the adoption of the proposed constitution? If we remain cool and temperate, we are in no immediate danger of any commotions; we are in a state of perfect peace, and in no danger of invasions; the state governments are in the full exercise of their powers; and our governments answer all present exigencies, except the regulation of trade, securing credit, in some cases, and providing for the interest, in some instances, of the public debts; and whether we adopt a change, three or nine months hence, can make but little odds with the private circumstances of individuals; their happiness and prosperity, after all, depend principally upon their own exertions. We are hardly recovered from a long and distressing war: The farmers, fishmen, &c. have not yet fully repaired the waste made by it. Industry and frugality are again assuming their proper station. Private debts are lessened, and public debts incurred by the war have been, by various ways, diminished; and the public lands have now become a productive source for diminishing them much more. I know uneasy men, who wish very much to precipitate, do not admit all these facts; but they are facts well known to all men who are thoroughly informed in the affairs of this country. It must, however, be admitted, that our federal system is defective, and that some of the state governments are not well administered; but, then, we impute to the defects in our governments many evils and embarrassments which are most clearly the result of the late war. We must allow men to conduct on the present occasion, as on all similar ones. They will urge a thousand pretences to answer their purposes on both sides. When we want a man to change his condition, we describe it as miserable, wretched, and despised; and draw a pleasing picture of that which we would have him assume. And when we wish the contrary, we reverse our descriptions. Whenever a clamor is raised, and idle men get to work, it is highly necessary to examine facts carefully, and without unreasonably suspecting men of falshood, to examine, and enquire attentively, under what impressions they act. It is too often the case in political concerns, that men state facts not as they are, but as they wish them to be; and almost every man, by calling to mind past scenes, will find this to be true.

Nothing but the passions of ambitious, impatient, or disorderly men, I conceive, will plunge us into commotions, if time should be taken fully to examine and consider the system proposed. Men who feel easy in their circumstances, and such as are not sanguine in their expectations relative to the consequences of the proposed change, will remain quiet under the existing governments. Many commercial and monied men, who are uneasy, not without just cause, ought

*Too much emphasis
on Free-will &
[personality] determining
success; not on
opportunities &
[chance] ?*

to be respected; and, by no means, unreasonably disappointed in their expectations and hopes; but as to those who expect employments under the new constitution; as to those weak and ardent men who always expect to be gainers by revolutions, and whose lot it generally is to get out of one difficulty into another, they are very little to be regarded: and as to those who designedly avail themselves of this weakness and ardor, they are to be despised. It is natural for men, who wish to hasten the adoption of a measure, to tell us, now is the crisis—now is the critical moment which must be seized, or all will be lost: and to shut the door against free enquiry, whenever conscious the thing presented has defects in it, which time and investigation will probably discover. This has been the custom of tyrants and their dependants in all ages. If it is true, what has been so often said, that the people of this country cannot change their condition for the worse, I presume it still behoves them to endeavour deliberately to change it for the better. The fickle and ardent, in any community, are the proper tools for establishing despotic government. But it is deliberate and thinking men, who must establish and secure governments on free principles. Before they decide on the plan proposed, they will enquire whether it will probably be a blessing or a curse to this people.

The present moment discovers a new face in our affairs. Our object has been all along, to reform our federal system, and to strengthen our governments—to establish peace, order and justice in the community—but a new object now presents. The plan of government now proposed is evidently calculated totally to change, in time, our condition as a people. Instead of being thirteen republics, under a federal head, it is clearly designed to make us one consolidated government. Of this, I think, I shall fully convince you, in my following letters on this subject. This consolidation of the states has been the object of several men in this country for some time past. Whether such a change can ever be effected in any manner; whether it can be effected without convulsions and civil wars; whether such a change will not totally destroy the liberties of this country—time only can determine.

To have a just idea of the government before us, and to shew that a consolidated one is the object in view, it is necessary not only to examine the plan, but also its history, and the politics of its particular friends.

The confederation was formed when great confidence was placed in the voluntary exertions of individuals, and of the respective states; and the framers of it, to guard against usurpation, so limited and checked the powers, that, in many respects, they are inadequate to the exigencies of the union. We find, therefore, members of congress urging alterations in the federal system almost as soon as it was adopted. It was early proposed to vest congress with powers to levy an impost, to regulate trade, etc. but such was known to be the caution of the states in parting with power, that the vestment, even of these, was proposed to be under several checks and limitations. During the war, the general confusion, and the introduction of paper money, infused in the minds of people vague ideas respecting government and credit. We expected too much from the return of peace, and of course we have been disappointed. Our governments have been new and unsettled; and several legislatures, by making tender, suspension, and paper money laws, have given just cause of uneasiness to creditors. By these and other causes, several orders of men in the community have been prepared, by degrees, for a change of government; and this very abuse of power in the legislatures, which, in some cases, has been charged upon the democratic part of the community, has furnished aristocratical men with those very weapons, and those very means, with which, in great measure, they are rapidly effecting their favourite object. And should an oppressive government be the consequence of the proposed change, posterity may reproach not only a few overbearing unprincipled men, but those parties in the states which have misused their powers.

The conduct of several legislatures, touching paper money, and tender laws, has prepared many honest men for changes in government, which otherwise they would not have thought of—when by the evils, on the one hand, and by the secret instigations of artful men, on the other, the minds of men were become sufficiently uneasy, a bold step was taken, which is usually followed by a revolution, or a civil war. A general convention for mere commercial purposes was moved for—the authors of this measure saw that the people's attention was turned solely to the amendment of the federal system; and that, had the idea of a total change been started, probably no state would have appointed members to the convention. The idea of destroying, ultimately, the state government, and forming one consolidated system, could not have been admitted—a convention, therefore, merely for vesting in congress power to regulate trade was proposed. This was pleasing to the commercial towns; and the landed people had little or no concern about it. September, 1786, a few men from the middle states met at Annapolis, and hastily proposed a convention to be held in May, 1787, for the purpose, generally, of amending the confederation—this was done before the delegates of Massachusetts, and of the other states arrived—still not a word was said about destroying the old constitution, and making a new one—The states still unsuspecting, and not aware that they were passing the Rubicon, appointed members to the new convention, for the sole and express purpose of revising and amending the confederation—and, probably, not one man in ten thousand in the United States, till within these ten or twelve days, had an idea that the old ship was to be destroyed, and he put to the alternative of embarking in the new ship presented, or of being left in danger of sinking—The States, I believe, universally supposed the convention would report alterations in the confederation, which would pass an examination in congress, and after being agreed to there, would be confirmed by all the legislatures, or be rejected. Virginia made a very respectable appointment, and placed at the head of it the first man in America: In this appointment there was a mixture of political characters; but Pennsylvania appointed principally those men who are esteemed aristocratical. Here the favourite moment for changing the government was evidently discerned by a few men, who seized it with address. Ten other states appointed, and tho' they chose men principally connected with commerce and the judicial department yet they appointed many good republican characters—had they all attended we should now see, I am persuaded a better system presented. The non-attendance of eight or nine men, who were appointed members of the convention, I shall ever consider as a very unfortunate event to the United States.—Had they attended, I am pretty clear, that the result of the convention would not have had that strong tendency to aristocracy now discernable in every part of the plan. There would not have been so great an accumulation of powers, especially as to the internal police of the country, in a few hands, as the constitution reported proposes to vest in them—the young visionary men, and the consolidating aristocracy, would have been more restrained than they have been. Eleven states met in the convention, and after four months close attention presented the new constitution, to be adopted or rejected by the people. The uneasy and fickle part of the community may be prepared to receive any form of government; but, I presume, the enlightened and substantial part will give any constitution presented for their adoption, a candid and thorough examination; and silence those designing or empty men, who weakly and rashly attempt to precipitate the adoption of a system of so much importance—We shall view the convention with proper respect—and, at the same time, that we reflect there were men of abilities and integrity in it, we must recollect how disproportionably the democratic and aristocratic parts of the community were represented—Perhaps the judicious friends and opposers of the new constitution will agree, that it is best to let it rest solely on its own merits, or be condemned for its own defects.

In the first place, I shall premise, that the plan proposed is a plan of accommodation—and that it is in this way only, and by giving up a part of our opinions, that we can ever expect to obtain a government founded in freedom and compact. This circumstance candid men will always keep in view, in the discussion of this subject.

The plan proposed appears to be partly federal, but principally however, calculated ultimately to make the states one consolidated government.

The first interesting question, therefore suggested, is, how far the states can be consolidated into one entire government on free principles. In considering this question extensive objects are to be taken into view, and important changes in the forms of government to be carefully attended to in all their consequences. The happiness of the people at large must be the great object with every honest statesman, and he will direct every movement to this point. If we are so situated as a people, as not to be able to enjoy equal happiness and advantages under one government, the consolidation of the states cannot be admitted.

There are three different forms of free government under which the United States may exist as one nation; and now is, perhaps, the time to determine to which we will direct our views. 1. Distinct republics connected under a federal head. In this case the respective state governments must be the principal guardians of the peoples rights, and exclusively regulate their internal police; in them must rest the balance of government. The congress of the states, or federal head, must consist of delegates amenable to, and removeable by the respective states: This congress must have general directing powers; powers to require men and monies of the states; to make treaties, peace and war; to direct the operations of armies, etc. Under this federal modification of government, the powers of congress would be rather advisory or recommendatory than coercive. 2. We may do away the several state governments, and form or consolidate all the states into one entire government, with one executive, one judiciary, and one legislature, consisting of senators and representatives collected from all parts of the union: In this case there would be a compleat consolidation of the states. 3. We may consolidate the states as to certain national objects, and leave them severally distinct independent republics, as to internal police generally. Let the general government consist of an executive, a judiciary, and balanced legislature, and its powers extend exclusively to all foreign concerns, causes arising on the seas to commerce, imports, armies, navies, Indian affairs, peace and war, and to a few internal concerns of the community; to the coin, post-offices, weights and measures, a general plan for the militia, to naturalization, *and, perhaps to bankruptcies,* leaving the internal police of the community, in other respects, exclusively to the state governments; as the administration of justice in all causes arising internally, the laying and collecting of internal taxes, and the forming of the militia according to a general plan prescribed. In this case there would be a compleat consolidation, *quoad* certain objects only.

Touching the first, or federal plan, I do not think much can be said in its favor: The sovereignty of the nation, without coercive and efficient powers to collect the strength of it, cannot always be depended on to answer the purposes of government; and in a congress of representatives of sovereign states, there must necessarily be an unreasonable mixture of powers in the same hands.

As to the second, or compleat consolidating plan, it deserves to be carefully considered at this time, by every American: If it be impracticable, it is a fatal error to model our governments, directing our views ultimately to it.

The third plan, or partial consolidation, is, in my opinion, the only one that can secure the freedom and happiness of this people. I once had some general ideas that the second plan was practicable, but from long attention, and the proceedings of the convention, I am fully satisfied, that this third plan is the only one we can with safety and propriety proceed upon. Making t... with candor and fairness, the parts of th... appear to be improper, is my object. The con... proposed the partial consolidation evidently w... all powers ultimately, in the United States into o... ment; and from its views in this respect, and from the... small states to have an equal vote in the senate, probab... ...d the greatest defects in the proposed plan.

Independant of the opinions of many great authors, that a free elective government cannot be extended over large territories, a few reflections must evince, that one government and general legislation alone, never can extend equal benefits to all parts of the United States: Different laws, customs, and opinions exist in the different states, which by a uniform system of laws would be unreasonably invaded. The United States contain about a million of square miles, and in half a century will, probably, contain ten millions of people; and from the center to the extremes is about 800 miles.

Before we do away the state governments, or adopt measures that will tend to abolish them, and to consolidate the states into one entire government, several principles should be considered and facts ascertained:—These, and my examination into the essential parts of the proposed plan, I shall pursue in my next.

Your's &c.
The Federal Farmer.

II

OCTOBER 9, 1787.

DEAR SIR,

The essential parts of a free and good government are a full and equal representation of the people in the legislature, and the jury trial of the vicinage in the administration of justice—a full and equal representation, is that which possesses the same interests, feelings, opinions, and views the people themselves would were they all assembled—a fair representation, therefore, should be so regulated, that every order of men in the community, according to the common course of elections, can have a share in it—in order to allow professional men, merchants, traders, farmers, mechanics, etc. to bring a just proportion of their best informed men respectively into

...re, the representation must be considerably numerous—
...ave about 200 state senators in the United States, and a less
number than that of federal representatives cannot, clearly, be a full
representation of this people, in the affairs of internal taxation and
police, were there but one legislature for the whole union. The
representation cannot be equal, or the situation of the people proper
for one government only—if the extreme parts of the society cannot
be represented as fully as the central—It is apparently impracticable
that this should be the case in this extensive country—it would be
impossible to collect a representation of the parts of the country
five, six, and seven hundred miles from the seat of government.

Under one general government alone, there could be but one judiciary, one supreme and a proper number of inferior courts. I think
it would be totally impracticable in this case to preserve a due administration of justice, and the real benefits of the jury trial of the
vicinage,—there are now supreme courts in each state in the union;
and a great number of county and other courts subordinate to each
supreme court—most of these supreme and inferior courts are itin-
erant, and hold their sessions in different parts every year of their respective states, counties and districts—with all these moving courts,
our citizens, from the vast extent of the country must travel very
considerable distances from home to find the place where justice is
administered. I am not for bringing justice so near to individuals as
to afford them any temptation to engage in law suits; though I think
it one of the greatest benefits in a good government, that each citizen should find a court of justice within a reasonable distance, perhaps, within a day's travel of his home; so that, without great
inconveniences and enormous expences, he may have the advantages of his witnesses and jury—it would be impracticable to derive
these advantages from one judiciary—the one supreme court at
most could only set in the centre of the union, and move once a year
into the centre of the eastern and southern extremes of it—and, in
this case, each citizen, on an average, would travel 150 or 200 miles
to find this court—that, however, inferior courts might be properly
placed in the different counties, and districts of the union, the appellate jurisdiction would be intolerable and expensive.

If it were possible to consolidate the states, and preserve the features of a free government, still it is evident that the middle states,
the parts of the union, about the seat of government, would enjoy

great advantages, while the remote states would experience the many inconveniences of remote provinces. Wealth, offices, and the benefits of government would collect in the centre: and the extreme states and their principal towns, become much less important.

There are other considerations which tend to prove that the idea of one consolidated whole, on free principles, is ill-founded—the laws of a free government rest on the confidence of the people, and operate gently—and never can extend their influence very far—if they are executed on free principles, about the centre, where the benefits of the government induce the people to support it voluntarily; yet they must be executed on the principles of fear and force in the extremes—This has been the case with every extensive republic of which we have any accurate account.

There are certain unalienable and fundamental rights, which in forming the social compact, ought to be explicitly ascertained and fixed—a free and enlightened people, in forming this compact, will not resign all their rights to those who govern, and they will fix limits to their legislators and rulers, which will soon be plainly seen by those who are governed, as well as by those who govern: and the latter will know they cannot be passed unperceived by the former, and without giving a general alarm—These rights should be made the basis of every constitution: and if a people be so situated, or have such different opinions that they cannot agree in ascertaining and fixing them, it is a very strong argument against their attempting to form one entire society, to live under one system of laws only.—I confess, I never thought the people of these states differed essentially in these respects; they having derived all these rights from one common source, the British systems; and having in the formation of their state constitutions, discovered that their ideas relative to these rights are very similar. However, it is now said that the states differ so essentially in these respects, and even in the important article of the trial by jury, that when assembled in convention, they can agree to no words by which to establish that trial, or by which to ascertain and establish many other of these rights, as fundamental articles in the social compact. If so, we proceed to consolidate the states on no solid basis whatever.

But I do not pay much regard to the reasons given for not bottoming the new constitution on a better bill of rights. I still believe a complete federal bill of rights to be very practicable. Nevertheless

I acknowledge the proceedings of the convention furnish my mind with many new and strong reasons, against a complete consolidation of the states. They tend to convince me, that it cannot be carried with propriety very far—that the convention have gone much farther in one respect than they found it practicable to go in another; that is, they propose to lodge in the general government very extensive powers—*powers* nearly, if not altogether, complete and unlimited, over the purse and the sword. But, in its organization, they furnish the strongest proof that the proper limbs, or parts of a government, to support and execute those powers on proper principles (or in which they can be safely lodged) cannot be formed. These powers must be lodged somewhere in every society; but then they should be lodged where the strength and guardians of the people are collected. They can be wielded, or safely used, in a free country only by an able executive and judiciary, a respectable senate, and a secure, full, and equal representation of the people. I think the principles I have premised or brought into view, are well founded—I think they will not be denied by any fair reasoner. It is in connection with these, and other solid principles, we are to examine the constitution. It is not a few democratic phrases, or a few well formed features, that will prove its merits; or a few small omissions that will produce its rejection among men of sense; they will enquire what are the essential powers in a community, and what are nominal ones; where and how the essential powers shall be lodged to secure government, and to secure true liberty.

In examining the proposed constitution carefully, we must clearly perceive an unnatural separation of these powers from the substantial representation of the people. The state governments will exist, with all their governors, senators, representatives, officers and expences; in these will be nineteen-twentieths of the representatives of the people; they will have a near connection, and their members an immediate intercourse with the people; and the probability is, that the state governments will possess the confidence of the people, and be considered generally as their immediate guardians.

The general government will consist of a new species of executive, a small senate, and a very small house of representatives. As many citizens will be more than three hundred miles from the seat of this government as will be nearer to it, its judges and officers cannot be very numerous, without making our governments very expensive. Thus will stand the state and the general governments, should the constitution be adopted without any alterations in their organization; but as to powers, the general government will possess all essential ones, at least on paper, and those of the states a mere shadow of power. And therefore, unless the people shall make some great exertions to restore to the state governments their powers in matters of internal police; as the powers to lay and collect, exclusively, internal taxes, to govern the militia, and to hold the decisions of their own judicial courts upon their own laws final, the balance cannot possibly continue long; but the state governments must be annihilated, or continue to exist for no purpose.

It is however to be observed, that many of the essential powers given the national government are not exclusively given; and the general government may have prudence enough to forbear the exercise of those which may still be exercised by the respective states. But this cannot justify the impropriety of giving powers, the exercise of which prudent men will not attempt, and imprudent men will, or probably can, exercise only in a manner destructive of free government. The general government, organized as it is, may be adequate to many valuable objects, and be able to carry its laws into execution on proper principles in several cases; but I think its warmest friends will not contend, that it can carry all the powers proposed to be lodged in it into effect, without calling to its aid a military force, which must very soon destroy all elective governments in the country, produce anarchy, or establish despotism. Though we cannot have now a complete idea of what will be the operations of the proposed system, we may, allowing things to have their common course, have a very tolerable one. The powers lodged in the general government, if exercised by it, must intimately effect the internal police of the states, as well as external concerns; and there is no reason to expect the numerous state governments, and their connections, will be very friendly to the execution of federal laws in those internal affairs, which hitherto have been under their own immediate management. There is more reason to believe, that the general government, far removed from the people, and none of its members elected oftener than once in two years, will be forgot or neglected, and its laws in many cases disregarded, unless a multitude of officers and military force be continually kept in view, and employed to enforce the execution of the laws, and to make the government feared and respected. No position can be truer than this, that in this country either neglected laws, or a military execution of them, must lead to a revolution, and to the destruction of freedom. Neglected laws must first lead to anarchy and confusion; and a military execution of laws is only a shorter way to the same point—despotic government.

Your's, &c.

The Federal Farmer.

III

OCTOBER 10TH, 1787.

DEAR SIR,

The great object of a free people must be so to form their government and laws, and so to administer them, as to create a confidence in, and respect for the laws; and thereby induce the sensible and virtuous part of the community to declare in favor of the laws, and to support them without an expensive military force. I wish, though I confess I have not much hope, that this may be the case with the laws of congress under the new constitution. I am fully convinced that we must organize the national government on different principals, and make the parts of it more efficient, and secure in it more effectually the different interests in the community; or else leave in the state governments some powers propose[d] to be lodged in it—at least till such an organization shall be found to be practicable. Not sanguine in my expectations of a good federal administration, and satisfied, as I am, of the impracticability of consolidating the states, and at the same time of preserving the rights of the people at large, I believe we ought still to leave some of those powers in the state governments, in which the people, in fact, will still be represented—to define some other powers proposed to be vested in the general government, more carefully, and to establish a few principles to secure a proper exercise of the powers given it. It is not my object to multiply objections, or to contend about inconsiderable powers or amendments; I wish the system adopted with a few alterations; but those, in my mind, are essential ones; if adopted without, every good citizen will acquiesce though I shall consider the duration of our governments, and the liberties of this people, very much dependant on the administration of the general government. A wise and honest administration, may make the people happy under any government;

but necessity only can justify even our leaving open avenues to the abuse of power, by wicked, unthinking, or ambitious men. I will examine, first, the organization of the proposed government, in order to judge; 2d, with propriety, what powers are improperly, at least prematurely lodged in it. I shall examine, 3d, the undefined powers; and 4th, those powers, the exercise of which is not secured on safe and proper ground.

First. As to the organization—the house of representatives, the democrative branch, as it is called, is to consist of 65 members: that is, about one representative for fifty thousand inhabitants, to be chosen biennially—the federal legislature may increase this number to one for each thirty thousand inhabitants, abating fractional numbers in each state.—Thirty-three representatives will make a quorum for doing business, and a majority of those present determine the sense of the house.—I have no idea that the interests, feelings, and opinions of three or four millions of people, especially touching internal taxation, can be collected in such a house.—In the nature of things, nine times in ten, men of the elevated classes in the community only can be chosen—Connecticut, for instance, will have five representatives—not one man in a hundred of those who form the democrative branch in the state legislature, will, on a fair computation, be one of the five—The people of this country, in one sense, may all be democratic; but if we make the proper distinction between the few men of wealth and abilities, and consider them, as we ought, as the natural aristocracy of the country, and the great body of the people, the middle and lower classes, as the democracy, this federal representative branch will have but very little democracy in it, even this small representation is not secured on proper principles.—The branches of the legislature are essential parts of the fundamental compact, and ought to be so fixed by the people, that the legislature cannot alter itself by modifying the elections of its own members. This, by a part of Art. 1. Sect. 4. the general legislature may do, it may evidently so regulate elections as to secure the choice of any particular description of men.—It may make the whole state one district—make the capital, or any places in the state, the place or places of election—it may declare that the five men (or whatever the number may be the state may chuse) who shall have the most votes shall be considered as chosen—In this case it is easy to perceive how the people who live scattered in the inland towns will bestow their

votes on different men—and how a few men in a city, in any order
or profession, may unite and place any five men they please highest
among those that may be voted for—and all this may be done constitutionally, and by those silent operations, which are not immediately perceived by the people in general.—I know it is urged, that the
general legislature will be disposed to regulate elections on fair and
just principles:—This may be true—good men will generally govern
well with almost any constitution: but why in laying the foundation
of the social system, need we unnecessarily leave a door open to improper regulations?—This is a very general and unguarded clause,
and many evils may flow from that part which authorises the congress to regulate elections—Were it omitted, the regulations of elections would be solely in the respective states, where the people are
substantially represented; and where the elections ought to be regulated, otherwise to secure a representation from all parts of the community, in making the constitution, we ought to provide for dividing
each state into a proper number of districts, and for confining the
electors in each district to the choice of some men, who shall have a
permanent interest and residence in it; and also for this essential object, that the representative elected shall have a majority of the votes
of those electors who shall attend and give their votes.

In considering the practicability of having a full and equal representation of the people from all parts of the union, not only distances and different opinions, customs, and views, common in
extensive tracts of country, are to be taken into view, but many differences peculiar to Eastern, Middle, and Southern states. These differences are not so perceivable among the members of congress, and
men of general information in the states, as among the men who
would properly form the democratic branch. The Eastern states are
very democratic, and composed chiefly of moderate freeholders;
they have but few rich men and no slaves; the Southern states are
composed chiefly of rich planters and slaves; they have but few moderate freeholders, and the prevailing influence, in them, is generally
a dissipated aristocracy: The Middle states partake partly of the
Eastern, and partly of the Southern character.

Perhaps, nothing could be more disjointed, unweildly and incompetent to doing business with harmony and dispatch, than a
federal house of representatives properly numerous for the great objects of taxation, et cetera collected from the several states; whether

such men would ever act in concert; whether they would not worry along a few years, and then be the means of separating the parts of the union, is very problematical?—View this system in whatever form we can, propriety brings us still to this point, a federal government possessed of general and complete powers, as to those national objects which cannot well come under the cognizance of the internal laws of the respective states, and this federal government, accordingly, consisting of branches not very numerous.

The house of representatives is on the plan of consolidation, but the senate is intirely on the federal plan; and Delaware will have as much constitutional influence in the senate, as the largest state in the union: and in this senate are lodged legislative, executive and judicial powers: Ten states in this union urge that they are small states, nine of which were present in the convention.—They were interested in collecting large powers into the hands of the senate, in which each state still will have its equal share of power. I suppose it was impracticable for the three large states, as they were called, to get the senate formed on any other principles: But this only proves, that we cannot form one general government on equal and just principles—and proves, that we ought not to lodge in it such extensive powers before we are convinced of the practicability of organizing it on just and equal principles. The senate will consist of two members from each state, chosen by the state legislatures, every sixth year. The clause referred to, respecting the elections of representatives, empowers the general legislature to regulate the elections of senators also, "except as to the places of chusing senators."—There is, therefore, but little more security in the elections than in those of representatives: Fourteen senators make a quorum for business, and a majority of the senators present give the vote of the senate, except in giving judgment upon an impeachment, or in making treaties, or in expelling a member, when two-thirds of the senators present must agree—The members of the legislature are not excluded from being elected to any military offices, or any civil offices, except those created, or the emoluments of which shall be increased by themselves: two-thirds of the members present, of either house, may expel a member at pleasure. The senate is an independant branch of the legislature, a court for trying impeachments, and also a part of the executive, having a negative in the making of all treaties, and in appointing almost all officers.

The vice president is not a very important, if not an unncessary part of the system—he may be a part of the senate at one period, and act as the supreme executive magistrate at another—The election of this officer, as well as of the president of the United States seems to be properly secured; but when we examine the powers of the president, and the forms of the executive, we shall perceive that the general government, in this part, will have a strong tendency to aristocracy, or the government of the few. The executive is, in fact, the president and senate in all transactions of any importance; the president is connected with, or tied to the senate; he may always act with the senate, but never can effectually counteract its views: The president can appoint no officer, civil or military, who shall not be agreeable to the senate; and the presumption is, that the will of so important a body will not be very easily controuled, and that it will exercise its powers with great address.

In the judicial department, powers ever kept distinct in well balanced governments, are no less improperly blended in the hands of the same men—in the judges of the supreme court is lodged, the law, the equity and the fact. It is not necessary to pursue the minute organical parts of the general government proposed.— There were various interests in the convention, to be reconciled, especially of large and small states; of carrying and non-carrying states; and of states more and states less democratic—vast labour and attention were by the convention bestowed on the organization of the parts of the constitution offered; still it is acknowledged there are many things radically wrong in the essential parts of this constitution—but it is said that these are the result of our situation: On a full examination of the subject, I believe it; but what do the laborious inquiries and determinations of the convention prove? If they prove any thing, they prove that we cannot consolidate the states on proper principles: The organization of the government presented proves, that we cannot form a general government in which all power can be safely lodged; and a little attention to the parts of the one proposed will make it appear very evident, that all the powers proposed to be lodged in it, will not be then well deposited, either for the purposes of government, or the preservation of liberty. I will suppose no abuse of powers in those cases, in which the abuse of it is not well guarded against—I will suppose the words authorising the general government to regulate the elections of its own members struck out of the plan, or free district elections, in each state, amply secured.—That the small representation provided for shall be as fair and equal as it is capable of being made—I will suppose the judicial department regulated on pure principles, by future laws, as far as it can be by the constitution, and consist[ent] with the situation of the country—still there will be an unreasonable accumulation of powers in the general government, if all be granted, enumerated in the plan proposed. The plan does not present a well balanced government. The senatorial branch of the legislative and the executive are substantially united, and the president, or the first executive magistrate, may aid the senatorial interest when weakest, but never can effectually support the democratic[,] however it may be oppressed;—the excellency, in my mind, of a well balanced government is that it consists of distinct branches, each sufficiently strong and independant to keep its own station, and to aid either of the other branches which may occasionally want aid.

The convention found that any but a small house of representatives would be expensive, and that it would be impracticable to assemble a large number of representatives. Not only the determination of the convention in this case, but the situation of the states, proves the impracticability of collecting, in any one point, a proper representation.

The formation of the senate, and the smallness of the house, being, therefore, the result of our situation, and the actual state of things, the evils which may attend the exercise of many powers in this national government may be considered as without a remedy.

All officers are impeachable before the senate only—before the men by whom they are appointed, or who are consenting to the appointment of these officers. No judgment of conviction, on an impeachment, can be given unless two thirds of the senators agree. Under these circumstances the right of impeachment, in the house, can be of but little importance; the house cannot expect often to convict the offender; and, therefore, probably, will but seldom or never exercise the right. In addition to the insecurity and inconveniences attending this organization beforementioned, it may be observed, that it is extremely difficult to secure the people against the fatal effects of corruption and influence. The power of making any law will be in the president, eight senators, and seventeen representatives, relative to the important objects enumerated in the constitution.

Where there is a small representation a sufficient number to carry any measure, may, with ease, be influenced by bribes, offices and civilities; they may easily form private juntoes, and out door meetings, agree on measures, and carry them by silent votes.

Impressed, as I am, with a sense of the difficulties there are in the way of forming the parts of a federal government on proper principles, and seeing a government so unsubstantially organized, after so arduous an attempt has been made, I am led to believe, that powers ought to be given to it with great care and caution.

In the second place it is necessary, therefore, to examine the extent, and the probable operations of some of those extensive powers proposed to be vested in this government. These powers, legislative, executive, and judicial, respect internal as well as external objects. Those respecting external objects, as all foreign concerns, commerce, imposts, all causes arising on the seas, peace and war, and Indian affairs, can be lodged no where else, with any propriety, but in this government. Many powers that respect internal objects ought clearly to be lodged in it; as those to regulate trade between the states, weights and measures, the coin or current monies, post-offices, naturalization, etc. These powers may be exercised without essentially effecting the internal police of the respective states: But powers to lay and collect internal taxes, to form the militia, to make bankrupt laws, and to decide on appeals, questions arising on the internal laws of the respective states, are of a very serious nature, and carry with them almost all other powers. These taken in connection with the others, and powers to raise armies and build navies, proposed to be lodged in this government, appear to me to comprehend all the essential powers in the community, and those which will be left to the states will be of no great importance.

A power to lay and collect taxes at discretion, is, in itself, of very great importance. By means of taxes, the government may command the whole or any part of the subject's property. Taxes may be of various kinds; but there is a strong distinction between external and internal taxes. External taxes are impost duties, which are laid on imported goods; they may usually be collected in a few seaport towns, and of a few individuals, though ultimately paid by the consumer; a few officers can collect them, and they can be carried no higher than trade will bear, or smuggling permit—that in the very nature of commerce, bounds are set to them. But internal taxes, as poll and land taxes, excises, duties on all written instruments, etc. may fix themselves on every person and species of property in the community; they may be carried to any lengths, and in proportion as they are extended, numerous officers must be employed to assess them, and to enforce the collection of them. In the United Netherlands the general government has compleat powers, as to external taxation; but as to internal taxes, it makes requisitions on the provinces. Internal taxation in this country is more important, as the country is so very extensive. As many assessors and collectors of federal taxes will be above three hundred miles from the seat of the federal government as will be less. Besides, to lay and collect internal taxes, in this extensive country, must require a great number of congressional ordinances, immediately operating upon the body of the people; these must continually interfere with the state laws, and thereby produce disorder and general dissatisfaction, till the one system of laws or the other, operating upon the same subjects, shall be abolished. These ordinances alone, to say nothing of those respecting the militia, coin, commerce, federal judiciary, etc. etc. will probably soon defeat the operations of the state laws and governments.

Should the general government think it politic, as some administrations (if not all) probably will, to look for a support in a system of influence, the government will take every occasion to multiply laws, and officers to execute them, considering these as so many necessary props for its own support. Should this system of policy be adopted, taxes more productive than the impost duties will, probably, be wanted to support the government, and to discharge foreign demands, without leaving any thing for the domestic creditors. The internal sources of taxation then must be called into operation, and internal tax laws and federal assessors and collectors spread over this immense country. All these circumstances considered, is it wise, prudent, or safe, to vest the powers of laying and collecting internal taxes in the general government, while imperfectly organized and inadequate; and to trust to amending it hereafter, and making it adequate to this purpose? It is not only unsafe but absurd to lodge power in a government before it is fitted to receive it? [*Sic.*] It is confessed that this power and representation ought to go together. Why give the power first? Why give the power to the few, who, when possessed of it, may have address enough to prevent the increase of representation? Why not keep the power, and, when necessary, amend the constitution, and add to its other parts this power, and a proper increase of representation at the same time? Then men who may want the power will be under strong inducements to let in the people, by their representatives, into the government, to hold their due proportion of this power. If a proper representation be impracticable, then we shall see this power resting in the states, where it at present ought to be, and not inconsiderately given up.

When I recollect how lately congress, conventions, legislatures, and people contended in the cause of liberty, and carefully weighed the importance of taxation, I can scarcely believe we are serious in proposing to vest the powers of laying and collecting internal taxes in a government so imperfectly organized for such purposes. Should the United States be taxed by a house of representatives of two hundred members, which would be about fifteen members for Connecticut, twenty-five for Massachusetts, etc. still the middle and lower classes of people could have no great share, in fact, in taxation. I am aware it is said, that the representation proposed by the new constitution is sufficiently numerous; it may be for many purposes; but to suppose that this branch is sufficiently numerous to guard the rights of the people in the administration of the government, in which the purse and sword is placed, seems to argue that we have forgot what the true meaning of representation is. I am sensible also, that it is said that congress will not attempt to lay and collect internal taxes; that it is necessary for them to have the power, though it cannot probably be exercised.—I admit that it is not probable that any prudent congress will attempt to lay and collect internal taxes, especially direct taxes: but this only proves, that the power would be improperly lodged in congress, and that it might be abused by imprudent and designing men.

I have heard several gentlemen, to get rid of objections to this part of the constitution, attempt to construe the powers relative to direct taxes, as those who object to it would have them; as to these, it is said, that congress will only have power to make requisitions, leaving it to the states to lay and collect them. I see but very little colour for this construction, and the attempt only proves that this part of the plan cannot be defended. By this plan there can be no doubt, but that the powers of congress will be complete as to all kinds of taxes whatever—Further, as to internal taxes, the state governments will have concurrent powers with the general government, and both may tax the same objects in the same year; and the objection that the general government may suspend a state tax, as a necessary measure for the promoting the collection of a federal tax, is not without foundation.—As the states owe large debts, and have large demands upon them individually, there clearly would be a propriety in leaving in their possession exclusively, some of the internal sources of taxation, at least until the federal representation shall be properly encreased: The power in the general government to lay and collect internal taxes, will render its powers respecting armies, navies and the militia, the more exceptionable. By the constitution it is proposed that congress shall have power "to raise and support armies, but no appropriation of money to that use shall be for a longer term than two years; to provide and maintain a navy; to provide for calling forth the militia to execute the laws of the union, suppress insurrections, and repel invasions: to provide for organizing, arming, and disciplining the militia: reserving to the states the right to appoint the officers, and to train the militia according to the discipline prescribed by congress;" congress will have unlimited power to raise armies, and to engage officers and men for any number of years; but a legislative act applying money for their support can have operation for no longer term than two years, and if a subsequent congress do not within the two years renew the appropriation, or further appropriate monies for the use of the army, the army will be left to take care of itself. When an army shall once be raised for a number of years, it is not probable that it will find much difficulty in getting congress to pass laws for applying monies to its support. I see so many men in America fond of a standing army, and especially among those who probably will have a large share in administering the federal system; it is very evident to me, that we shall have a large standing army as soon as the monies to support them can be possibly found. An army is a very agreeable place of employment for the young gentlemen of many families. A power to raise armies must be lodged some where; still this will not justify the lodging this power in a bare majority of so few men without any checks; or in the government in which the great body of the people, in the nature of things, will be only nominally represented. In the state governments the great body of the people, the yeomanry, etc. of the country, are represented: It is true they will chuse the members of congress, and may now and then chuse a man of their own way of thinking; but it is impossible for forty, or thirty thousand people in this country, one time in ten to find a man who can possess similar feelings, views, and interests with themselves: Powers to lay and collect taxes and to raise armies are of the greatest moment; for carrying them into effect, laws need not be frequently made, and the yeomanry, etc of the country ought substantially to have a check upon the passing of these laws; this check ought to be placed in the legislatures, or at least, in the few men the common people of the country, will, probably, have in congress, in the true sense of the word, "from among themselves." It is true, the yeomanry of the country possess the lands, the weight of property, possess arms, and are too strong a body of men to be openly offended—and, therefore, it is urged, they will take care of themselves, that men who shall govern will not dare pay any disrespect to their opinions. It is easily perceived, that if they have not their proper negative upon passing laws in congress, or on the passage of laws relative to taxes and armies, they may in twenty or thirty years be by means imperceptible to them, totally deprived of that boasted weight and strength: This may be done in a great measure by congress, if disposed to do it, by modelling the militia. Should one fifth, or one eighth part of the men capable of bearing arms, be made a select militia, as has been proposed, and those the young and ardent part of the community, possessed of but little or no property, and all the others put upon a plan that will render them of no importance, the former will answer all the purposes of an army, while the latter will be defenceless. The state must train the militia in such form and according to such systems and rules as congress shall prescribe: and the only actual influence the respective states will have respecting the militia will be in appointing the officers. I see no provision made for calling out the *posse commitatus* for executing the laws of the union, but provision is made for congress to call forth the militia for the execution of them—and the militia in general, or any select part of it, may be called out under military officers, instead of the sheriff to enforce an execution of federal laws, in the first instance and thereby introduce an entire military execution of the laws. I know that powers to raise taxes, to regulate the military strength of the community on some uniform plan, to provide for its defence and internal order, and for duly executing the laws, must be lodged somewhere; but still we ought not so to lodge them, as evidently to give one order of men in the community, undue advantages over others; or commit the many to the mercy, prudence, and moderation of the few. And so far as it may be necessary to lodge any of the peculiar powers in the general government, a more safe exercise of them ought to be secured, by requiring the consent of two-thirds or three-fourths of congress thereto—until the federal representation can be increased, so that the democratic members in congress may stand some tolerable chance of a reasonable negative, in behalf of the numerous, important, and democratic part of the community.

I am not sufficiently acquainted with the laws and internal police of all the states to discern fully, how general bankrupt laws, made by the union, would effect them, or promote the public good. I believe the property of debtors, in the several states, is held responsible for their debts in modes and forms very different. If uniform bankrupt laws can be made without producing real and substantial inconveniences, I wish them to be made by congress.

There are some powers proposed to be lodged in the general government in the judicial department, I think very unnecessarily, I mean powers respecting questions arising upon the internal laws of the respective states. It is proper the federal judiciary should have powers co-extensive with the federal legislature—that is, the power of deciding finally on the laws of the union. By Art. 3. Sect. 2. the powers of the federal judiciary are extended (among other things) to all cases between a state and citizens of another state—between citizens of different states—between a state or the citizens thereof, and foreign states, citizens or subjects. Actions in all these cases, except against a state government, are now brought and finally determined in the law courts of the states respectively; and as there are no words to exclude these courts of their jurisdiction in these cases, they will have concurrent jurisdiction with the inferior federal courts in them; and, therefore, if the new constitution be adopted without any amendment in this respect, all those numerous actions, now brought in the state courts between our citizens and foreigners, between citizens of different states, by state governments against foreigners, and by state governments against citizens of other states, may also be brought in the federal courts; and an appeal will lay in them from the state courts, or federal inferior courts, to the supreme judicial court of the union. In almost all these cases, either party may have the trial by jury in the state courts; excepting paper money and tender laws, which are wisely guarded against in the proposed constitution, justice may be obtained in these courts on reasonable terms; they must be more competent to proper decisions on the laws of their respective states, than the federal courts can possibly be. I do not, in any point of view, see the need of opening a new jurisdiction to these causes—of opening a new scene of expensive law suits—of suffering foreigners, and citizens of different states, to drag each other many hundred miles into the federal courts. It is true, those courts may be so organized by a wise and prudent legislature, as to make the obtaining of justice in them tolerably easy; they may in general be organized on the common law principles of the country: But this benefit is by no means secured by the constitution. The trial by jury is secured only in those few criminal cases, to which the federal laws will extend—as crimes committed on the seas, against the laws of nations, treason, and counterfeiting the federal securities and coin: But even in these cases, the jury trial of the vicinage is not secured—particularly in the large states, a citizen may be tried for a crime committed in the state, and yet tried in some states 500 miles from the place where it was committed; but the jury trial is not secured at all in civil causes. Though the convention have not established this trial, it is to be hoped that congress, in putting the new system into execution, will do it by a legislative act, in all cases in which it can be done with propriety. Whether the jury trial is not excluded [from] the supreme judicial court, is an important question. By Art. 3. Sect. 2. all cases affecting ambassadors, other public ministers, and consuls, and in those cases in which a state shall be party, the supreme court shall have jurisdiction. In all the other cases beforementioned, the supreme court shall have appellate jurisdiction, both as to *law and fact,* with such exception, and under such regulations, as the congress shall make. By court is understood a court consisting of judges; and the idea of a jury is excluded. This court, or the judges, are to have jurisdiction on appeals, in all the cases enumerated, as to law and fact; the judges are to decide the law and try the fact, and the trial of the fact being assigned to the judges by the constitution, a jury for trying the fact is excluded; however, under the exceptions and powers to make regulations, congress may, perhaps introduce the jury, to try the fact in most necessary cases.

There can be but one supreme court in which the final jurisdiction will centre in all federal causes—except in cases where appeals by law shall not be allowed: The judicial powers of the federal courts extends in law and equity to certain cases: and, therefore, the powers to determine on the law, in equity, and as to the fact, all will concentre in the supreme court:—These powers, which by this constitution are blended in the same hands, the same judges, are in Great-Britain deposited in different hands—to wit, the decision of the law in the law judges, the decision in equity in the chancellor, and the trial of the fact in the jury. It is a very dangerous thing to vest in the same judge power to decide on the law, and also general powers in equity; for if the law restrain him, he is only to step into his shoes of equity, and give what judgment his reason or opinion may dictate; we have no precedents in this country, as yet, to regulate the divisions in equity as in Great Britain; equity, therefore, in the supreme court for many years will be mere discretion. I confess in the constitution of this supreme court, as left by the constitution, I do not see a spark of freedom or a shadow of our own or the British common law.

This court is to have appellate jurisdiction in all the other cases before mentioned: Many sensible men suppose that cases before mentioned respect, as well the criminal cases as the civil ones, mentioned antecedently in the constitution, if so an appeal is allowed in criminal cases—contrary to the usual sense of law. How far it may be proper to admit a foreigner or the citizen of another state to bring actions against state governments, which have failed in performing so many promises made during the war, is doubtful: How far it may be proper so to humble a state, as to oblige it to answer to an individual in a court of law, is worthy of consideration; the states are now subject to no such actions; and this new jurisdiction will subject the states, and many defendants to actions, and processes, which were not in the contemplation of the parties, when the contract was made; all engagements existing between citizens of different states, citizens and foreigners, states and foreigners; and states and citizens of other states were made the parties contemplating the remedies then existing on the laws of the states—and the new remedy proposed to be given in the federal courts, can be founded on no principle whatever.

Your's &c.
The Federal Farmer.

IV

Dear sir,

It will not be possible to establish in the federal courts the jury trial of the vicinage so well as in the state courts.

Third. There appears to me to be not only a premature deposit of some important powers in the general government—but many of those deposited there are undefined, and may be used to good or bad purposes as honest or designing men shall prevail. By Art. 1, Sect. 2, representatives and direct taxes shall be apportioned among the several states, etc.—same art. sect. 8, the congress shall have powers to lay and collect taxes, duties, etc. for the common defence and general welfare, but all duties, imposts and excises, shall be uniform throughout the United States: By the first recited clause, direct taxes shall be apportioned on the states. This seems to favour the idea suggested by some sensible men and writers, that congress, as to direct taxes, will only have power to make requisitions, but the latter clause, power to lay and collect taxes, etc seems clearly to favour the contrary opinion and, in my mind, the true one, that congress shall have power to tax immediately individuals, without the intervention of the state legislatures[;] in fact the first clause appears to me only to provide that each state shall pay a certain portion of the tax, and the latter to provide that congress shall have power to lay and collect taxes, that is to assess upon, and to collect of the individuals in the state, the state[']s quota; but these still I consider as undefined powers, because judicious men understand them differently.

It is doubtful whether the vice president is to have any qualifications; none are mentioned; but he may serve as president, and it may be inferred, he ought to be qualified therefore as the president; but the qualifications of the president are required only of the person to be elected president. By art. the 2, sect. 2. "But the congress may by law vest the appointment of such inferior officers as they think proper in the president alone, in the courts of law, or in the heads of the departments:" Who are inferior officers? May not a congress disposed to vest the appointment of all officers in the president, under this clause, vest the appointment of almost every officer in the president alone, and destroy the check mentioned in the first part of the clause, and lodged in the senate. It is true, this check is badly lodged, but then some check upon the first magistrate in appointing officers, ought it appears by the opinion of the convention, and by the general opinion, to be established in the constitution. By art. 3, sect. 2, the supreme court shall have appellate jurisdiction as to law and facts with such exceptions, etc. to what extent is it intended the exceptions shall be carried—Congress may carry them so far as to annihilate substantially the appellate jurisdiction, and the clause be rendered of very little importance.

4th. There are certain rights which we have always held sacred in the United States, and recognized in all our constitutions, and which, by the adoption of the new constitution in its present form, will be left unsecured. By article 6, the proposed constitution, and the laws of the United States, which shall be made in pursuance thereof; and all treaties made, or which shall be made under the authority of the United States, shall be the supreme law of the land; and the judges in every state shall be bound thereby; any thing in the constitution or laws of any state to the contrary notwithstanding.

It is to be observed that when the people shall adopt the proposed constitution it will be their last and supreme act; it will be adopted not by the people of New-Hampshire, Massachusetts, etc. but by the people of the United States; and wherever this constitution, or any part of it, shall be incompatible with the ancient customs, rights, the laws or the constitutions heretofore established in the United States, it will entirely abolish them and do them away: And not only this, but the laws of the United States which shall be made in pursuance of the federal constitution will be also supreme laws, and wherever they shall be incompatible with those customs, rights, laws or constitutions heretofore established, they will also entirely abolish them and do them away.

By the article before recited, treaties also made under the authority of the United States, shall be the supreme law: It is not said that these treaties shall be made in pursuance of the constitution—nor are there any constitutional bounds set to those who shall make them: The president and two thirds of the senate will be empowered to make treaties indefinitely, and when these treaties shall be made, they will also abolish all laws and state constitutions incompatible with them. This power in the president and senate is absolute, and the judges will be bound to allow full force to whatever rule, article or thing the president and senate shall establish by treaty, whether it be practicable to set any bounds to those who make treaties, I am not able to say: if not, it proves that this power ought to be more safely lodged.

The federal constitution, the laws of congress made in pursuance of the constitution, and all treaties must have full force and effect in all parts of the United States; and all other laws, rights and constitutions which stand in their way must yield: It is proper the national laws should be supreme, and superior to state or district laws: but then the national laws ought to yield to unalienable or fundamental rights—and national laws, made by a few men, should extend only to a few national objects. This will not be the case with the laws of congress: To have any proper idea of their extent, we must carefully examine the legislative, executive and judicial powers proposed to be lodged in the general government, and consider them in connection with a general clause in art. I sect. 8, in these words (after inumerating a number of powers) "To make all laws which shall be necessary and proper for carrying into execution the foregoing powers, and all other powers vested by this constitution in the government of the United States, or in any department or officer thereof."—The powers of this government as has been observed, extend to internal as well as external objects, and to those objects to which all others are subordinate; it is almost impossible to have a just conception of these powers, or of the extent and number of the laws which may be deemed necessary and proper to carry them into effect, till we shall come to exercise those powers and make the laws. In making laws to carry those powers into effect, it is to be expected, that a wise and prudent congress will pay respect to the opinions of a free people, and bottom their laws on those principles which have been considered as essential and fundamental in the British, and in our government. But a congress of a different character will not be bound by the constitution to pay respect to those principles.

It is said, that when the people make a constitution, and delegate powers that all powers not delegated by them to those who govern is [*sic*] reserved in the people; and that the people, in the present case, have reserved in themselves, and in their state governments, every right and power not expressly given by the federal constitution to those who shall administer the national government. It is said on the other hand, that the people, when they make a constitution, yield all power not expressly reserved to themselves. The truth is, in either case, it is mere matter of opinion and men usually take either side of the argument, as will best answer their purposes: But the general presumption being, that men who govern, will, in doubtful cases, construe laws and constitutions most favourably for encreasing their own powers; all wise and prudent people, in forming constitutions, have drawn the line, and carefully described the powers parted with and the powers reserved. By the state constitutions, certain rights have been reserved in the people; or rather, they have been recognized and established in such a manner, that state legislatures are bound to respect them, and to make no laws infringing upon them. The state legislatures are obliged to take notice of the bills of rights of their respective states. The bills of rights, and the state constitutions, are fundamental compacts only between those who govern, and the people of the same state.

In the year 1788 the people of the United States make a federal constitution, which is a fundamental compact between them and their federal rulers; these rulers, in the nature of things, cannot be bound to take notice of any other compact. It would be absurd for them, in making laws, to look over thirteen, fifteen, or twenty state constitutions, to see what rights are established as fundamental, and must not be infringed upon, in making laws in the society. It is true, they would be bound to do it if the people, in their federal compact, should refer to the state constitutions, recognize all parts not inconsistent with the federal constitution, and direct their federal rulers to take notice of them accordingly; but this is not the case, as the plan stands proposed at present; and it is absurd, to suppose so unnatural an idea is intended or implied. I think my opinion is not only founded in reason, but I think it is supported by the report of the convention itself. If there are a number of rights established by the state constitutions, and which will remain sacred, and the general government is bound to take notice of them—it must take notice of one as well as another; and if unnecessary to recognize or establish one by the federal constitution, it would be unnecessary to recognize or establish another by it. If the federal constitution is to be construed so far in connection with the state constitutions, as to leave the trial by jury in civil causes, for instance, secured; on the same principles it would have left the trial by jury in criminal causes, the benefits of the writ of habeas corpus, etc. secured; they all stand on the same footing; they are the common rights of Americans, and have been recognized by the state constitutions: But the convention found it necessary to recognize or re-establish the benefits of that writ, and the jury trial in criminal cases. As to *expost facto* laws, the convention has done the same in one case, and gone further in another. It is part of the compact between the people of each state and their rulers, that no *expost facto* laws shall be made. But the convention, by Art. I Sect. 10 have put a sanction upon this part even of the state compacts. In fact, the 9th and 10th Sections in Art. I in the proposed constitution, are no more nor less, than a partial bill of rights; they establish certain principles as part of the compact upon which the federal legislators and officers can never infringe. It is here wisely stipulated, that the federal legislature shall never pass a bill of attainder, or *expost facto* law; that no tax shall be laid on articles exported, etc. The establishing of one right implies the necessity of establishing another and similar one.

On the whole, the position appears to me to be undeniable, that this bill of rights ought to be carried farther, and some other principles established, as a part of this fundamental compact between the people of the United States and their federal rulers.

It is true, we are not disposed to differ much, at present, about religion; but when we are making a constitution, it is to be hoped, for ages and millions yet unborn, why not establish the free exercise of religion, as a part of the national compact. There are other essential rights, which we have justly understood to be the rights of freemen; as freedom from hasty and unreasonable search warrants, warrants not founded on oath, and not issued with due caution, for searching and seizing men's papers, property, and persons. The trials by jury in civil causes, it is said, varies so much in the several states, that no words could be found for the uniform establishment of it. If so, the federal legislation will not be able to establish it by any general laws. I confess I am of opinion it may be established, but not in that beneficial manner in which we may enjoy it, for the reasons beforementioned. When I speak of the jury trial of the vicinage, or the trial of the fact in the neighbourhood,—I do not lay so much stress upon the circumstance of our being tried by our neighbours: in this enlightened country men may be probably impartially tried by those who do not live very near them: but the trial of facts in the neighbourhood is of great importance in other respects. Nothing can be more essential than the cross examining witnesses, and generally before the triers of the facts in question. The common people can establish facts with much more ease with oral than written evidence; when trials of facts are removed to a distance from the homes of the parties and witnesses, oral evidence becomes intolerably expensive, and the parties must depend on written evidence, which to the common people is expensive and almost useless; it must be frequently taken *ex parte*, and but very seldom leads to the proper discovery of truth.

The trial by jury is very important in another point of view. It is essential in every free country, that common people should have a part and share of influence, in the judicial as well as in the legislative department. To hold open to them the offices of senators, judges, and offices to fill which an expensive education is required, cannot answer any valuable purposes for them; they are not in a situation to be brought forward and to fill those offices; these, and most other offices of any considerable importance, will be occupied by the few. The few, the well born, etc. as Mr. Adams calls them, in judicial decisions as well as in legislation, are generally disposed, and very naturally too, to favour those of their own description.

The trial by jury in the judicial department, and the collection of the people by their representatives in the legislature, are those fortunate inventions which have procured for them, in this country, their true proportion of influence, and the wisest and most fit means of protecting themselves in the community. Their situation, as jurors and representatives, enables them to acquire information and knowledge in the affairs and government of the society; and to come forward, in turn, as the centinels and guardians of each other. I am very sorry that even a few of our countrymen should consider jurors and representatives in a different point of view, as ignorant troublesome bodies, which ought not to have any share in the concerns of government.

I confess I do not see in what cases the congress can, with any pretence of right, make a law to suppress the freedom of the press;

though I am not clear, that congress is restrained from laying any duties whatever on printing, and from laying duties particularly heavy on certain pieces printed, and perhaps congress may require large bonds for the payment of these duties. Should the printer say, the freedom of the press was secured by the constitution of the state in which he lived, congress might, and perhaps, with great propriety, answer, that the federal constitution is the only compact existing between them and the people; in this compact the people have named no others, and therefore congress, in exercising the powers assigned them, and in making laws to carry them into execution, are restrained by nothing beside the federal constitution, any more than a state legislature is restrained by a compact between the magistrates and people of a county, city, or town of which the people, in forming the state constitution, have taken no notice.

It is not my object to enumerate rights of inconsiderable importance; but there are others, no doubt, which ought to be established as a fundamental part of the national system.

It is worthy observation, that all treaties are made by foreign nations with a confederacy of thirteen states—that the western country is attached to thirteen states—thirteen states have jointly and severally engaged to pay the public debts.—Should a new government be formed of nine, ten, eleven, or twelve states, those treaties could not be considered as binding on the foreign nations who made them. However, I believe the probability to be, that if nine states adopt the constitution, the others will.

It may also be worthy our examination, how far the provision for amending this plan, when it shall be adopted, is of any importance. No measures can be taken towards amendments, unless two-thirds of the congress, or two-thirds of the legislatures of the several states shall agree.—While power is in the hands of the people, or democratic part of the community, more especially as at present, it is easy, according to the general course of human affairs, for the few influential men in the community, to obtain conventions, alterations in government, and to persuade the common people they may change for the better, and to get from them a part of the power: But when power is once transferred from the many to the few, all changes become extremely difficult; the government, in this case, being beneficial to the few, they will be exceedingly artful and adroit in preventing any measures which may lead to a change; and nothing will produce it, but great exertions and severe struggles on the part of the common people. Every man of reflection must see, that the change now proposed, is a transfer of power from the many to the few, and the probability is, the artful and ever active aristocracy, will prevent all peaceable measures for changes, unless when they shall discover some favourable moment to increase their own influence. I am sensible, thousands of men in the United States, are disposed to adopt the proposed constitution, though they perceive it to be essentially defective, under an idea that amendments of it, may be obtained when necessary. This is a pernicious idea, it argues a servility of character totally unfit for the support of free government; it is very repugnant to that perpetual jealousy respecting liberty, so absolutely necessary in all free states, spoken of by Mr. Dickinson.— However, if our countrymen are so soon changed, and the language of 1774, is become odious to them, it will be in vain to use the language of freedom, or to attempt to rouse them to free enquiries: But I shall never believe this is the case with them, whatever present appearances may be, till I shall have very strong evidence indeed of it.

Your's, &c.
The Federal Farmer.

V

OCTOBER 13TH, 1787

DEAR SIR,

Thus I have examined the federal constitution as far as a few days leisure would permit. It opens to my mind a new scene; instead of seeing powers cautiously lodged in the hands of numerous legislators, and many magistrates, we see all important powers collecting in one centre, where a few men will possess them almost at discretion. And instead of checks in the formation of the government, to secure the rights of the people against the usurpations of those they appoint to govern, we are to understand the equal division of lands among our people, and the strong arm furnished them by nature and situation, are to secure them against those usurpations. If there are advantages in the equal division of our lands, and the strong and manly habits of our people, we ought to establish governments calculated to give duration to them, and not governments which never can work naturally, till that equality of property, and those free and manly habits shall be destroyed; these evidently are not the natural basis of the proposed constitution. No man of reflection, and skilled in the science of government, can suppose these will move on harmoniously together for ages, or even for fifty years. As to the little circumstances commented upon, by some writers, with applause—as the age of a representative, of the president, etc.—they have, in my mind, no weight in the general tendency of the system.

There are, however, in my opinion, many good things in the proposed system. It is founded on elective principles, and the deposits of powers in different hands, is essentially right. The guards against those evils we have experienced in some states in legislation are valuable indeed; but the value of every feature in this system is vastly lessened for the want of that one important feature in a free government, a representation of the people. Because we have sometimes abused democracy, I am not among those men who think a democratic branch a nuisance; which branch shall be sufficiently numerous, to admit some of the best informed men of each order in the community into the administration of government.

While the radical defects in the proposed system are not so soon discovered, some temptations to each state, and to many classes of men to adopt it, are very visible. It uses the democratic language of several of the state constitutions, particularly that of Massachusetts; the eastern states will receive advantages so far as the regulation of trade, by a bare majority, is committed to it: Connecticut and New-Jersey will receive their share of a general impost: The middle states will receive the advantages surrounding the seat of government: The southern states will receive protection, and have their negroes represented in the legislature, and large back countries will soon have a majority in it. This system promises a large field of employment to military gentlemen, and gentlemen of the law; and in case the government shall be executed without convulsions, it will afford security to creditors, to the clergy, salary-men and others depending on money payments. So far as the system promises justice and reasonable advantages, in these respects, it ought to be supported by all honest men: but whenever it promises unequal and improper advantages to any particular states, or orders of men, it ought to be opposed.

I have, in the course of these letters observed, that there are many good things in the proposed constitution, and I have endeavoured to point out many important defects in it. I have admitted that we want a federal system—that we have a system presented, which, with several alterations may be made a tolerable good one—I have admitted there is a well founded uneasiness among creditors and mercantile men. In this situation of things, you ask me what I think ought to be done? My opinion in this case is only the opinion of an individual, and so far only as it corresponds with the opinions of the honest and substantial part of the community, is it entitled to consideration. Though I am fully satisfied that the state conventions ought most seriously to direct their exertions to altering and amending the system proposed before they shall adopt it—yet I have not sufficiently examined the subject, or formed an opinion, how far it will be practicable for those conventions to carry their amendments. As to the idea, that it will be in vain for those conventions to attempt amendments, it cannot be admitted; it is impossible to say whether they can or not until the attempt shall be made; and when it shall be determined, by experience, that the conventions cannot agree in amendments, it will then be an important question before the people of the United States, whether they will adopt or not the system proposed in its present form. This subject of consolidating the states is new; and because forty or fifty men have agreed in a system, to suppose the good sense of this country, an enlightened nation, must adopt it without examination, and though in a state of profound peace, without endeavouring to amend those parts they perceive are defective, dangerous to freedom, and destructive of the valuable principles of republican government—is truly humiliating. It is true there may be danger in delay; but there is danger in adopting the system in its present form; and I see the danger in either case will arise principally from the conduct and views of two very unprincipled parties in the United States—two fires, between which the honest and substantial people have long found themselves situated. One party is composed of little insurgents, men in debt, who want no law, and who want a share of the property of others; these are called levellers, Shayites, etc. The other party is composed of a few, but more dangerous men, with their servile dependents; these avariciously grasp at all power and property; you may discover in all the actions of these men, an evident dislike to free and equal government, and they will go systematically to work to change, essentially, the forms of government in this country; these are called aristocrats,

M[onarch]ites [?], etc. etc. Between these two parties is the weight of the community; the men of middling property, men not in debt on the one hand, and men, on the other, content with republican governments, and not aiming at immense fortunes, offices, and power. In 1786, the little insurgents, the levellers, came forth, invaded the rights of others, and attempted to establish governments according to their wills. Their movements evidently gave encouragement to the other party, which, in 1787, has taken the political field, and with its fashionable dependants, and the tongue and the pen, is endeavouring to establish in great haste, a politer kind of government. These two parties, which will probably be opposed or united as it may suit their interests and views, are really insignificant, compared with the solid, free, and independent part of the community. It is not my intention to suggest, that either of these parties, and the real friends of the proposed constitution, are the same men. The fact is, these aristocrats support and hasten the adoption of the proposed constitution, merely because they think it is a stepping stone to their favorite object. I think I am well founded in this idea; I think the general politics of these men support it, as well as the common observation among them, That the proffered plan is the best that can be got at present, it will do for a few years, and lead to something better. The sensible and judicious part of the community will carefully weigh all these circumstances; they will view the late convention as a respectable assembly of men—America probably never will see an assembly of men of a like number, more respectable. But the members of the convention met without knowing the sentiments of one man in ten thousand in these states, respecting the new ground taken. Their doings are but the first attempts in the most important scene ever opened. Though each individual in the state conventions will not, probably, be so respectable as each individual in the federal convention, yet as the state conventions will probably consist of fifteen hundred or two thousand men of abilities, and versed in the science of government, collected from all parts of the community and from all orders of men, it must be acknowledged that the weight of respectability will be in them—In them will be collected the solid sense and the real political character of the country. Being revisers of the subject, they will possess peculiar advantages. To say that these conventions ought not to attempt, coolly and deliberately, the revision of the system, or that they cannot amend it, is very foolish or very assuming. If these conventions, after examining the system, adopt it, I shall be perfectly satisfied, and wish to see men make the administration of the government an equal blessing to all orders of men. I believe the great body of our people to be virtuous and friendly to good government, to the protection of liberty and property; and it is the duty of all good men, especially of those who are placed as centinels to guard their rights—it is their duty to examine into the prevailing politics of parties, and to disclose them—while they avoid exciting undue suspicions, to lay facts before the people, which will enable them to form a proper judgment. Men who wish the people of this country to determine for themselves, and deliberately to fit the government to their situation, must feel some degree of indignation at those attempts to hurry the adoption of a system, and to shut the door against examination. The very attempts create suspicions, that those who make them have secret views, or see some defects in the system, which, in the hurry of affairs, they expect will escape the eye of a free people.

What can be the views of those gentlemen in Pennsylvania, who precipitated decisions on this subject? What can be the views of those gentlemen in Boston, who countenanced the Printers in shutting up the press against a fair and free investigation of this important system in the usual way. The members of the convention have done their duty—why should some of them fly to their states—almost forget a propriety of behaviour, and precipitate measures for the adoption of a system of their own making? I confess candidly, when I consider these circumstances in connection with the unguarded parts of the system I have mentioned, I feel disposed to proceed with very great caution, and to pay more attention than usual to the conduct of particular characters. If the constitution presented be a good one, it will stand the test with a well informed people: all are agreed there shall be state conventions to examine it; and we must believe it will be adopted, unless we suppose it is a bad one, or that those conventions will make false divisions respecting it. I admit improper measures are taken against the adoption of the system as well [as] for it—all who object to the plan proposed ought to point out the defects objected to, and to propose those amendments with which they can accept it, or to propose some other system of government, that the public mind may be known, and that we may be brought to agree in some system of government, to strengthen and execute the present, or to provide a substitute. I consider the field of enquiry just opened, and that we are to look to the state conventions for ultimate decisions on the subject before us; it is not to be presumed, that they will differ about small amendments, and lose a system when they shall have made it substantially good; but touching the essential amendments, it is to be presumed the several conventions will pursue the most rational measures to agree in and obtain them; and such defects as they shall discover and not remove, they will probably notice, keep them in view as the ground work of future amendments, and in the firm and manly language which every free people ought to use, will suggest to those who may hereafter administer the government, that it is their expectation, that the system will be so organized by legislative acts, and the government so administered, as to render those defects as little injurious as possible. Our countrymen are entitled to an honest and faithful government; to a government of laws and not of men; and also to one of their chusing—as a citizen of the country, I wish to see these objects secured, and licentious, assuming, and overbearing men restrained; if the constitution or social compact be vague and unguarded, then we depend wholly upon the prudence, wisdom and moderation of those who manage the affairs of government; or on what, probably, is equally uncertain and precarious, the success of the people oppressed by the abuse of government, in receiving it from the hands of those who abuse it, and placing it in the hands of those who will use it well.

In every point of view, therefore, in which I have been able, as yet, to contemplate this subject, I can discern but one rational mode of proceeding relative to it: and that is to examine it with freedom and candour, to have state conventions some months hence, which shall examine coolly every article, clause, and word in the system proposed, and to adopt it with such amendments as they shall think fit. How far the state conventions ought to pursue the mode prescribed by the federal convention of adopting or rejecting the plan in toto, I leave it to them to determine. Our examination of the subject hitherto has been rather of a general nature. The republican characters in the several states, who wish to make this plan more adequate to security of liberty and property, and to the duration of the principles of a free government, will, no doubt, collect their opinions to certain points, and accurately define those alterations and amendments they wish; if it shall be found they essentially disagree in them, the conventions will then be able to determine whether to adopt the plan as it is, or what will be proper to be done.

Under these impressions, and keeping in view the improper and unadvisable lodgment of powers in the general government, organized as it at present is, touching internal taxes, armies and militia, the elections of its own members, causes between citizens of different states, etc. and the want of a more perfect bill of rights, etc. I drop the subject for the present, and when I shall have leisure to revise and correct my ideas respecting it, and to collect into points the opinions of those who wish to make the system more secure and safe, perhaps I may proceed to point out particularly for your consideration, the amendments which ought to be ingrafted into this system, not only in conformity to my own, but the deliberate opinions of others—you will with me perceive, that the objections to the plan proposed may, by a more leisure examination be set in a stronger point of view, especially the important one, that there is no substantial representation of the people provided for in a government in which the most essential powers, even as to the internal police of the country, is proposed to be lodged.

I think the honest and substantial part of the community will wish to see this system altered, permanency and consistency given to the constitution we shall adopt; and therefore they will be anxious to apportion the powers to the features and organization of the government, and to see abuse in the exercise of power more effectually guarded against. It is suggested, that state officers, from interested motives will oppose the constitution presented—I see no reason for this, their places in general will not be effected, but new openings to offices and places of profit must evidently be made by the adoption of the constitution in its present form.

Your's &c.
The Federal Farmer.

PUBLIUS REPLIES

BY FAR THE MOST sustained defense of the Constitution were the eighty-five essays published as *The Federalist* under the pen name Publius. The project was conceived by Alexander Hamilton, with the specific purpose of making a broad case for ratification in his own state of New York, where ratification faced an uphill battle. Hamilton recruited John Jay, the secretary for foreign affairs, as a coauthor, and then turned to James Madison as well. Extensive scholarly analysis has established that Hamilton wrote by far the greatest share of the essays, fifty-one in total; Madison contributed another twenty-nine, and Jay, owing to poor health, only five. Hamilton's essays were principally devoted to the importance of establishing an effective national government, armed with substantial powers over defense and taxation, and to the construction of the executive and judiciary departments. Madison wrote primarily about the complexities of federalism, the separation of powers, and the construction of the legislature.

Though Madison wrote fewer essays, his contributions have received greater scholarly attention. One essay in particular, *Federalist* No. 10, has been subjected to repeated analysis. Here Madison challenged one of the standing assumptions of eighteenth-century political thinking: that republican governments could safely operate only in small, relatively homogeneous societies, where citizens would be united by common interests. Madison disputed this conventional wisdom in two major ways. He argued, first, that human nature and the divergent interests that any modern society would inevitably create made unanimity of political opinion impossible. Faction was an inevitable element of politics, and the real problem was to figure out how to make it safe for liberty. Here Madison offered his second major argument. Far from being a danger to the liberty that all republicans prized, a diversity of interests would be conducive to its protection. Madison repeated this argument in the final passages of *Federalist* No. 51, as he concluded a series of five essays devoted to explaining why a rigid separation of powers among the three departments of government would prove less effective at preserving the balance between them than the overlapping checks and balances the Constitution proposed. In part because it was so long-winded, *The Federalist* had little apparent impact on the ratification struggle. Its value lies elsewhere: in the fact that the two men who arguably possessed the brightest and most creative intellects among the generation who came of age with the Revolution used these essays to express some of their leading ideas about constitutional government and the challenges facing the republic. Skeptics sometimes scoff that *The Federalist* is really only so much campaign propaganda. But in fact, the division of labor between the two leading authors allowed Hamilton and Madison to address the subjects that mattered most to them individually.

PUBLIUS REPLIES

—Alexander Hamilton—
THE FEDERALIST NO. 1
OCTOBER 27, 1787

AFTER FULL EXPERIENCE OF the insufficiency of the existing federal government, you are invited to deliberate upon a New Constitution for the United States of America. The subject speaks its own importance; comprehending in its consequences, nothing less than the existence of the UNION, the safety and welfare of the parts of which it is composed, the fate of an empire, in many respects, the most interesting in the world. It has been frequently remarked, that it seems to have been reserved to the people of this country to decide, by their conduct and example, the important question, whether societies of men are really capable or not, of establishing good government from reflection and choice, or whether they are forever destined to depend, for their political constitutions, on accident and force. If there be any truth in the remark, the crisis at which we are arrived may, with propriety, be regarded as the period when that decision is to be made; and a wrong election of the part we shall act, may, in this view, deserve to be considered as the general misfortune of mankind.

This idea, by adding the inducements of philanthropy to those of patriotism, will heighten the solicitude which all considerate and good men must feel for the event. Happy will it be if our choice should be directed by a judicious estimate of our true interests, uninfluenced by considerations foreign to the public good. But this is more ardently to be wished for, than seriously to be expected. The plan offered to our deliberations, affects too many particular interests, innovates upon too many local institutions, not to involve in its discussion a variety of objects extraneous to its merits, and of views, passions and prejudices little favourable to the discovery of truth.

Among the most formidable of the obstacles which the new constitution will have to encounter, may readily be distinguished the obvious interest of a certain class of men in every state to resist all changes which may hazard a diminution of the power, emolument and consequence of the offices they hold under the state establishments . . . and the perverted ambition of another class of men, who will either hope to aggrandize themselves by the confusions of their country, or will flatter themselves with fairer prospects of elevation from the subdivision of the empire into several partial confederacies, than from its union under one government.

It is not, however, my design to dwell upon observations of this nature. I am aware that it would be disingenuous to resolve indiscriminately the opposition of any set of men into interested or ambitious views, merely because their situations might subject them to suspicion. Candour will oblige us to admit, that even such men may be actuated by upright intentions; and it cannot be doubted, that much of the opposition, which has already shown itself, or that may hereafter make its appearance, will spring from sources blameless at least, if not respectable—the honest errors of minds led astray by preconceived jealousies and fears. So numerous indeed and so powerful are the causes which serve to give a false bias to the judgement, that we, upon many occasions, see wise and good men on the wrong as well as on the right side of questions, of the first magnitude to society. This circumstance, if duly attended to, would always furnish a lesson of moderation to those, who are engaged in any controversy, however well persuaded of being in the right. And a further reason for caution, in this respect, might be drawn from the reflection, that we are not always sure, that those who advocate the truth are actuated by purer principles than their antagonists. Ambition, avarice, personal animosity, party opposition, and many other motives, not more laudable than these, are apt to operate as well upon those who support, as upon those who oppose, the right side of a question. Were there not even these inducements to moderation, nothing could be more ill judged than that intolerant spirit, which has, at all times, characterized political parties. For, in politics as in religion, it is equally absurd to aim at making proselytes by fire and sword. Heresies in either can rarely be cured by persecution.

And yet, just as these sentiments must appear to candid men, we have already sufficient indications, that it will happen in this, as in all former cases of great national discussion. A torrent of angry and malignant passions will be let loose. To judge from the conduct of the opposite parties, we shall be led to conclude, that they will mutually hope to evince the justness of their opinions, and to increase the number of their converts, by the loudness of their declamations, and by the bitterness of their invectives. An enlightened zeal for the energy and efficiency of government, will be stigmatized as the offspring of a temper fond of power, and hostile to the principles of liberty. An over scrupulous jealousy of danger to the rights of the people, which is more commonly the fault of the head than of the heart, will be represented as mere pretence and artifice, the stale bait for popularity at the expense of public good. It will be forgotten, on the one hand, that jealousy is the usual concomitant of violent love, and that the noble enthusiasm of liberty is too apt to be infected with a spirit of narrow and illiberal distrust. On the other hand, it will be equally forgotten, that the vigour of government is essential to the security of liberty; that, in the contemplation of a sound and well informed judgment, their interests can never be separated; and that a dangerous ambition more often lurks behind the specious mask of zeal for the rights of the people, than under the forbidding appearances of zeal for the firmness and efficiency of government. History will teach us, that the former has been found a much more certain road to the introduction of despotism, than the latter, and that of those men who have overturned the liberties of republics, the greatest number have begun their career, by paying an obsequious court to the people; commencing demagogues, and ending tyrants.

In the course of the preceding observations it has been my aim, fellow citizens, to put you upon your guard against all attempts, from whatever quarter, to influence your decision in a matter of the utmost moment to your welfare, by any impressions, other than those which may result from the evidence of truth. You will, no doubt, at the same time, have collected from the general scope of them, that they proceed from a source not unfriendly to the new constitution. Yes, my countrymen, I own to you, that, after having given it an attentive consideration, I am clearly of opinion, it is your interest to adopt it. I am convinced, that this is the safest course for your liberty, your dignity, and your happiness. I affect not reserves, which I do not feel. I will not amuse you with an appearance of deliberation, when I have decided. I frankly acknowledge to you my convictions, and I will freely lay before you the reasons on which they are founded. The consciousness of good intentions disdains ambiguity. I shall not however multiply professions on this head. My motives must remain in the depository of my own breast: my arguments will be open to all, and may be judged of by all. They shall at least be offered in a spirit, which will not disgrace the cause of truth.

I propose, in a series of papers, to discuss the following interesting particulars—*The utility of the UNION to your political prosperity— The insufficiency of the present confederation to preserve that Union— The necessity of a government at least equally energetic with the one proposed, to the attainment of this object—The conformity of the proposed constitution to the true principles of republican government—Its analogy to your own state constitution—*and lastly, *The additional security, which its adoption will afford to the preservation of that species of government, to liberty and to property.*

In the progress of this discussion, I shall endeavour to give a satisfactory answer to all the objections which shall have made their appearance, that may seem to have any claim to attention.

It may perhaps be thought superfluous to offer arguments to prove the utility of the UNION, a point, no doubt, deeply engraved on the hearts of the great body of the people in every state, and one which, it may be imagined, has no adversaries. But the fact is, that we already hear it whispered in the private circles of those who oppose the new constitution, that the Thirteen States are of too great extent for any general system, and that we must of necessity resort to separate confederacies of distinct portions of the whole.* This doctrine will, in all probability, be gradually propagated, till it has votaries enough to countenance its open avowal. For nothing can be more evident, to those who are able to take an enlarged view of the subject, than the alternative of an adoption of the constitution, or a dismemberment of the Union. It may, therefore, be essential to examine particularly the advantages of that Union, the certain evils, and the probable dangers, to which every state will be exposed from its dissolution. This shall accordingly be done.

PUBLIUS

---

*The same idea, tracing the arguments to their consequences, is held out in several of the late publications against the New Constitution [Hamilton's note].

—James Madison—
THE FEDERALIST NO. 10
NOVEMBER 22, 1787

AMONG THE NUMEROUS ADVANTAGES promised by a well constructed union, none deserves to be more accurately developed, than
its tendency to break and control the violence of faction. The friend
of popular governments, never finds himself so much alarmed for
their character and fate, as when he contemplates their propensity to
this dangerous vice. He will not fail, therefore, to set a due value on
any plan which, without violating the principles to which he is attached, provides a proper cure for it. The instability, injustice, and
confusion, introduced into the public councils, have, in truth, been
the mortal diseases under which popular governments have every
where perished; as they continue to be the favourite and fruitful top-
ics from which the adversaries to liberty derive their most specious
declamations. The valuable improvements made by the American
constitutions on the popular models, both ancient and modern,
cannot certainly be too much admired; but it would be an unwarrantable partiality, to contend that they have as effectually obviated
the danger on this side, as was wished and expected. Complaints are
every where heard from our most considerate and virtuous citizens,
equally the friends of public and private faith, and of public and personal liberty, that our governments are too unstable; that the public
good is disregarded in the conflicts of rival parties; and that measures are too often decided, not according to the rules of justice, and
the rights of the minor party, but by the superior force of an interested and overbearing majority. However anxiously we may wish
that these complaints had no foundation, the evidence of known
facts will not permit us to deny that they are in some degree true. It
will be found, indeed, on a candid review of our situation, that some
of the distresses under which we labour, have been erroneously
charged on the operation of our governments; but it will be found,
at the same time, that other causes will not alone account for many
of our heaviest misfortunes; and, particularly, for that prevailing and
increasing distrust of public engagements, and alarm for private

485

rights, which are echoed from one end of the continent to the other. These must be chiefly, if not wholly, effects of the unsteadiness and injustice, with which a factious spirit has tainted our public administrations.

By a faction, I understand a number of citizens, whether amounting to a majority or minority of the whole, who are united and actuated by some common impulse of passion, or of interest, adverse to the rights of other citizens, or to the permanent and aggregate interests of the community.

There are two methods of curing the mischiefs of faction: The one, by removing its causes; the other, by controling its effects.

There are again two methods of removing the causes of faction: The one, by destroying the liberty which is essential to its existence; the other, by giving to every citizen the same opinions, the same passions, and the same interests.

It could never be more truly said, than of the first remedy, that it is worse than the disease. Liberty is to faction, what air is to fire, an aliment, without which it instantly expires. But it could not be a less folly to abolish liberty, which is essential to political life, because it nourishes faction, than it would be to wish the annihilation of air, which is essential to animal life, because it imparts to fire its destructive agency.

The second expedient is as impracticable, as the first would be unwise. As long as the reason of man continues fallible, and he is at liberty to exercise it, different opinions will be formed. As long as the connection subsists between his reason and his self-love, his opinions and his passions will have a reciprocal influence on each other; and the former will be objects to which the latter will attach themselves. The diversity in the faculties of men, from which the rights of property originate, is not less an insuperable obstacle to an uniformity of interests. The protection of these faculties, is the first object of government. From the protection of different and unequal faculties of acquiring property, the possession of different degrees and kinds of property immediately results; and from the influence of these on the sentiments and views of the respective proprietors, ensues a division of the society into different interests and parties.

The latent causes of faction are thus sown in the nature of man; and we see them every where brought into different degrees of activity, according to the different circumstances of civil society. A zeal for different opinions concerning religion, concerning government, and many other points, as well of speculation as of practice; an attachment to different leaders, ambitiously contending for preeminence and power; or to persons of other descriptions, whose fortunes have been interesting to the human passions, have, in turn, divided mankind into parties, inflamed them with mutual animosity, and rendered them much more disposed to vex and oppress each other, than to co-operate for their common good. So strong is this propensity of mankind, to fall into mutual animosities, that where no substantial occasion presents itself, the most frivolous and fanciful distinctions have been sufficient to kindle their unfriendly passions, and excite their most violent conflicts. But the most common and durable source of factions, has been the various and unequal distribution of property. Those who hold, and those who are without property, have ever formed distinct interests in society. Those who are creditors, and those who are debtors, fall under a like discrimination. A landed interest, a manufacturing interest, a mercantile interest, a monied interest, with many lesser interests, grow up of necessity in civilized nations, and divide them into different classes, actuated by different sentiments and views. The regulation of these various and interfering interests, forms the principal task of modern legislation, and involves the spirit of party and faction in the necessary and ordinary operations of government.

No man is allowed to be a judge in his own cause; because his interest would certainly bias his judgment, and, not improbably, corrupt his integrity. With equal, nay, with greater reason, a body of men are unfit to be both judges and parties, at the same time; yet, what are many of the most important acts of legislation, but so many judicial determinations, not indeed concerning the rights of single persons, but concerning the rights of large bodies of citizens? and what are the different classes of legislators, but advocates and parties to the causes which they determine? Is a law proposed concerning private debts? It is a question to which the creditors are parties on one side, and the debtors on the other. Justice ought to hold the balance between them. Yet the parties are, and must be, themselves the judges; and the most numerous party, or, in other words, the most powerful faction, must be expected to prevail. Shall domestic manufactures be encouraged, and in what degree, by restrictions on foreign manufactures? are questions which would be differently decided by the landed and the manufacturing classes; and probably by neither with a sole regard to justice and the public good. The apportionment of taxes, on the various descriptions of property, is an act which seems to require the most exact impartiality; yet there is, perhaps, no legislative act in which greater opportunity and temptation are given to a predominant party, to trample on the rules of justice. Every shilling with which they over-burden the inferior number, is a shilling saved to their own pockets.

It is in vain to say, that enlightened statesmen will be able to adjust these clashing interests, and render them all subservient to the public good. Enlightened statesmen will not always be at the helm: nor, in many cases, can such an adjustment be made at all, without taking into view indirect and remote considerations, which will rarely prevail over the immediate interest which one party may find in disregarding the rights of another, or the good of the whole.

The inference to which we are brought, is, that the *causes* of faction cannot be removed; and that relief is only to be sought in the means of controlling its *effects*.

If a faction consists of less than a majority, relief is supplied by the republican principle, which enables the majority to defeat its sinister views, by regular vote. It may clog the administration, it may convulse the society; but it will be unable to execute and mask its violence under the forms of the constitution. When a majority is included in a faction, the form of popular government, on the other hand, enables it to sacrifice to its ruling passion or interest, both the public good and the rights of other citizens. To secure the public good, and private rights, against the danger of such a faction, and at the same time to preserve the spirit and the form of popular government, is then the great object to which our inquiries are directed. Let me add, that it is the great desideratum, by which alone this form of government can be rescued from the opprobrium under which it has so long laboured, and be recommended to the esteem and adoption of mankind.

By what means is this object attainable? Evidently by one of two only. Either the existence of the same passion or interest in a majority, at the same time, must be prevented; or the majority, having such co-existent passion or interest, must be rendered, by their number and local situation, unable to concert and carry into effect schemes of oppression. If the impulse and the opportunity be suffered to coincide, we well know, that neither moral nor religious motives can be relied on as an adequate control. They are not found to be such on the injustice and violence of individuals, and lose their efficacy in proportion to the number combined together; that is, in proportion as their efficacy becomes needful.

From this view of the subject, it may be concluded, that a pure democracy, by which I mean, a society consisting of a small number of citizens, who assemble and administer the government in person, can admit of no cure for the mischiefs of faction. A common passion or interest will, in almost every case, be felt by a majority of the whole; a communication and concert, results from the form of government itself; and there is nothing to check the inducements to sacrifice the weaker party, or an obnoxious individual. Hence it is, that such democracies have ever been spectacles of turbulence and contention; have ever been found incompatible with personal security, or the rights of property; and have, in general, been as short in their lives, as they have been violent in their deaths. Theoretic politicians, who have patronised this species of government, have erroneously supposed, that, by reducing mankind to a perfect equality in their political rights, they would, at the same time, be perfectly equalized and assimilated in their possessions, their opinions, and their passions.

A republic, by which I mean a government in which the scheme of representation takes place, opens a different prospect, and promises the cure for which we are seeking. Let us examine the points in which it varies from pure democracy, and we shall comprehend both the nature of the cure and the efficacy which it must derive from the union.

The two great points of difference, between a democracy and a republic, are, first, the delegation of the government, in the latter, to a small number of citizens elected by the rest; secondly, the greater number of citizens, and greater sphere of country, over which the latter may be extended.

The effect of the first difference is, on the one hand, to refine and enlarge the public views, by passing them through the medium of a chosen body of citizens, whose wisdom may best discern the true interest of their country, and whose patriotism and love of justice, will be least likely to sacrifice it to temporary or partial considerations. Under such a regulation, it may well happen, that the public voice, pronounced by the representatives of the people, will be more consonant to the public good, than if pronounced by the people themselves, convened for the purpose. On the other hand, the effect may be inverted. Men of factious tempers, of local prejudices, or of sinister designs, may by intrigue, by corruption, or by other means, first obtain the suffrages, and then betray the interests of the people. The question resulting is, whether small or extensive republics are most favourable to the election of proper guardians of the public weal; and it is clearly decided in favour of the latter by two obvious considerations.

In the first place, it is to be remarked, that however small the republic may be, the representatives must be raised to a certain number, in order to guard against the cabals of a few; and that, however large it may be, they must be limited to a certain number, in order to guard against the confusion of a multitude. Hence, the number of representatives in the two cases not being in proportion to that of the constituents, and being proportionally greatest in the small republic, it follows, that if the proportion of fit characters be not less in the large than in the small republic, the former will present a greater option, and consequently a greater probability of a fit choice.

In the next place, as each representative will be chosen by a greater number of citizens in the large than in the small republic, it will be more difficult for unworthy candidates to practise with success the vicious arts, by which elections are too often carried; and the suffrages of the people being more free, will be more likely to centre in men who possess the most attractive merit, and the most diffusive and established characters.

It must be confessed, that in this, as in most other cases, there is a mean, on both sides of which inconveniences will be found to lie. By enlarging too much the number of electors, you render the representative too little acquainted with all their local circumstances and lesser interests; as by reducing it too much, you render him unduly attached to these, and too little fit to comprehend and pursue great and national objects. The federal constitution forms a happy combination in this respect; the great and aggregate interests, being referred to the national, the local and particular to the state legislatures.

The other point of difference is, the greater number of citizens, and extent of territory, which may be brought within the compass of republican, than of democratic government; and it is this circumstance principally which renders factious combinations less to be dreaded in the former, than in the latter. The smaller the society, the fewer probably will be the distinct parties and interests composing it; the fewer the distinct parties and interests, the more frequently will a majority be found of the same party; and the smaller the number of individuals composing a majority, and the smaller the compass within which they are placed, the more easily will they concert and execute their plans of oppression. Extend the sphere, and you take in a greater variety of parties and interests; you make it less probable that a majority of the whole will have a common motive to invade the rights of other citizens; or if such a common motive exists, it will be more difficult for all who feel it to discover their own strength, and to act in unison with each other. Besides other impediments, it may be remarked, that where there is a consciousness of unjust or dishonourable purposes, communication is always checked by distrust, in proportion to the number whose concurrence is necessary.

Hence it clearly appears, that the same advantage, which a republic has over a democracy, in controling the effects of faction, is enjoyed by a large over a small republic . . . is enjoyed by the union over the states composing it. Does this advantage consist in the substitution of representatives, whose enlightened views and virtuous sentiments render them superior to local prejudices, and to schemes of injustice? It will not be denied, that the representation of the union will be most likely to possess these requisite endowments. Does it consist in the greater security afforded by a greater variety of parties, against the event of any one party being able to outnumber and oppress the rest? In an equal degree does the increased variety of parties, comprised within the union, increase this security. Does it, in fine, consist in the greater obstacles opposed to the concert and accomplishment of the secret wishes of an unjust and interested majority? Here, again, the extent of the union gives it the most palpable advantage.

The influence of factious leaders may kindle a flame within their particular states, but will be unable to spread a general conflagration through the other states: a religious sect may degenerate into a political faction in a part of the confederacy; but the variety of sects dispersed over the entire face of it, must secure the national councils against any danger from that source: a rage for paper money, for an abolition of debts, for an equal division of property, or for any other improper or wicked project, will be less apt to pervade the whole body of the union, than a particular member of it; in the same proportion as such a malady is more likely to taint a particular county or district, than an entire state.

In the extent and proper structure of the union, therefore, we behold a republican remedy for the diseases most incident to republican government. And according to the degree of pleasure and pride we feel in being republicans, ought to be our zeal in cherishing the spirit, and supporting the character of federalists.

PUBLIUS

—James Madison—
THE FEDERALIST NO. 14
NOVEMBER 30, 1787

WE HAVE SEEN THE necessity of the union, as our bulwark against foreign danger; as the conservator of peace among ourselves; as the guardian of our commerce, and other common interests; as the only substitute for those military establishments which have subverted the liberties of the old world; and as the proper antidote for the diseases of faction, which have proved fatal to other popular governments, and of which alarming symptoms have been betrayed by our own. All that remains, within this branch of our inquiries, is to take notice of an objection, that may be drawn from the great extent of country which the union embraces. A few observations, on this subject, will be the more proper, as it is perceived, that the adversaries of the new constitution are availing themselves of a prevailing prejudice, with regard to the practicable sphere of republican administration, in order to supply, by imaginary difficulties, the want of those solid objections, which they endeavour in vain to find.

The error which limits republican government to a narrow district, has been unfolded and refuted in preceding papers. I remark here only, that it seems to owe its rise and prevalence chiefly to the confounding of a republic with a democracy; and applying to the former, reasonings drawn from the nature of the latter. The true distinction between these forms, was also adverted to on a former occasion. It is, that in a democracy, the people meet and exercise the government in person: in a republic, they assemble and administer it by their representatives and agents. A democracy, consequently, must be confined to a small spot. A republic may be extended over a large region.

To this accidental source of the error, may be added the artifice of some celebrated authors, whose writings have had a great share in forming the modern standard of political opinions. Being subjects, either of an absolute, or limited monarchy, they have endeavoured to heighten the advantages, or palliate the evils, of those forms, by placing in comparison with them, the vices and defects of the republican, and by citing, as specimens of the latter, the turbulent democracies of ancient Greece, and modern Italy. Under the confusion of names, it has been an easy task to transfer to a republic, observations applicable to a democracy only; and, among others, the observation, that it can never be established but among a small number of people, living within a small compass of territory.

Such a fallacy may have been the less perceived, as most of the popular governments of antiquity were of the democratic species; and even in modern Europe, to which we owe the great principle of representation, no example is seen of a government wholly popular, and founded, at the same time, wholly on that principle. If Europe has the merit of discovering this great mechanical power in government, by the simple agency of which, the will of the largest political body may be concentered, and its force directed to any object, which the public good requires; America can claim the merit of making the discovery the basis of unmixed and extensive republics. It is only to be lamented, that any of her citizens should wish to deprive her of the additional merit of displaying its full efficacy in the establishment of the comprehensive system now under her consideration.

As the natural limit of a democracy, is that distance from the central point, which will just permit the most remote citizens to assemble as often as their public functions demand, and will include no greater number than can join in those functions: so the natural limit of a republic, is that distance from the centre, which will barely allow the representatives of the people to meet as often as may be necessary for the administration of public affairs. Can it be said, that the limits of the United States exceed this distance? It will not be said by those who recollect, that the Atlantic coast is the longest side of the union; that, during the term of thirteen years, the representatives of the states have been almost continually assembled; and that the members, from the most distant states, are not chargeable with greater intermissions of attendance, than those from the states in the neighbourhood of Congress.

That we may form a juster estimate with regard to this interesting subject, let us resort to the actual dimensions of the union. The limits, as fixed by the treaty of peace, are, on the east the Atlantic, on the south the latitude of thirty one degrees, on the west the Mississippi, and on the north an irregular line running in some instances beyond the forty-fifth degree, in others falling as low as the forty-second. The southern shore of lake Erie lies below that latitude. Computing the distance between the thirty-first and forty-fifth degrees, it amounts to nine hundred and seventy-three common miles; computing it from thirty-one to forty-two degrees, to seven hundred sixty-four miles and an half. Taking the mean for the distance, the amount will be eight hundred sixty-eight miles and three-fourths. The mean distance from the Atlantic to the Mississippi, does not probably exceed seven hundred and fifty miles. On a comparison of this extent, with that of several countries in Europe, the practicability of rendering our system commensurate to it, appears to be demonstrable. It is not a great deal larger than Germany, where a diet, representing the whole empire, is continually assembled; or than Poland before the late dismemberment, where another national diet was the depository of the supreme power. Passing by France and Spain, we find that in Great Britain, inferior as it may be in size, the representatives of the northern extremity of the island, have as far to travel to the national council, as will be required of those of the most remote parts of the union.

Favourable as this view of the subject may be, some observations remain, which will place it in a light still more satisfactory.

In the first place, it is to be remembered, that the general government is not to be charged with the whole power of making and administering laws: its jurisdiction is limited to certain enumerated objects, which concern all the members of the republic, but which are not to be attained by the separate provisions of any. The subordinate governments, which can extend their care to all those other objects, which can be separately provided for, will retain their due authority and activity. Were it proposed by the plan of the convention, to abolish the governments of the particular states, its adversaries would have some ground for their objection; though it would not be difficult to show, that if they were abolished, the general government would be compelled, by the principle of self preservation, to reinstate them in their proper jurisdiction.

A second observation to be made is, that the immediate object of the federal constitution, is to secure the union of the thirteen primitive states, which we know to be practicable; and to add to them such other states, as may arise in their own bosoms, or in their neighbourhoods, which we cannot doubt to be equally practicable. The arrangements that may be necessary for those angles and fractions of our territory, which lie on our north western frontier, must be left to those whom further discoveries and experience will render more equal to the task.

Let it be remarked, in the third place, that the intercourse throughout the union will be daily facilitated by new improvements. Roads will every where be shortened, and kept in better order; accommodations for travellers will be multiplied and meliorated; an interior navigation on our eastern side, will be opened throughout, or nearly throughout, the whole extent of the Thirteen States. The communication between the western and Atlantic districts, and between different parts of each, will be rendered more and more easy, by those numerous canals, with which the beneficence of nature has intersected our country, and which art finds it so little difficult to connect and complete.

A fourth, and still more important consideration, is, that as almost every state will, on one side or other, be a frontier, and will thus find, in a regard to its safety, an inducement to make some sacrifices for the sake of the general protection: so the states which lie at the greatest distance from the heart of the union, and which of course may partake least of the ordinary circulation of its benefits, will be at the same time immediately contiguous to foreign nations, and will consequently stand, on particular occasions, in greatest need of its strength and resources. It may be inconvenient for Georgia, or the states forming our western or north-eastern borders, to send their representatives to the seat of government; but they would find it more so to struggle alone against an invading enemy, or even to support alone the whole expense of those precautions, which may be dictated by the neighbourhood of continual danger. If they should derive less benefit therefore from the union in some respects, than the less distant states, they will derive greater benefit from it in other respects, and thus the proper equilibrium will be maintained throughout.

I submit to you, my fellow citizens, these considerations, in full confidence that the good sense which has so often marked your decisions, will allow them their due weight and effect; and that you will never suffer difficulties, however formidable in appearance, or however fashionable the error on which they may be founded, to drive you into the gloomy and perilous scenes into which the advocates for disunion would conduct you. Hearken not to the unnatural voice, which tells you that the people of America, knit together as they are by so many chords of affection, can no longer live together as members of the same family; can no longer continue the mutual guardians of their mutual happiness; can no longer be fellow citizens of one great, respectable, and flourishing empire. Hearken not to the voice, which petulantly tells you, that the form of government recommended for your adoption, is a novelty in the political world; that it has never yet had a place in the theories of the wildest projectors; that it rashly attempts what it is impossible to accomplish. No, my countrymen, shut your ears against this unhallowed language. Shut your hearts against the poison which it conveys. The kindred blood which flows in the veins of American citizens, the mingled blood which they have shed in defence of their sacred rights, consecrate their union, and excite horror at the idea of their becoming aliens, rivals, enemies. And if novelties are to be shunned, believe me, the most alarming of all novelties, the most wild of all projects, the most rash of all attempts, is that of rending us in pieces, in order to preserve our liberties, and promote our happiness. But why is the experiment of an extended republic to be rejected, merely because it may comprise what is new? Is it not the glory of the people of America, that whilst they have paid a decent regard to the opinions of former times and other nations, they have not suffered a blind veneration for antiquity, for custom, or for names, to overrule the suggestions of their own good sense, the knowledge of their own situation, and the lessons of their own experience? To this manly spirit, posterity will be indebted for the possession, and the world for the example, of the numerous innovations displayed on the American theatre, in favour of private rights and public happiness. Had no important step been taken by the leaders of the revolution, for which a precedent could not be discovered; no government established of which an exact model did not present itself, the people of the United States might, at this moment, have been numbered among the melancholy victims of misguided councils; must at best have been labouring under the weight of some of those forms which have crushed the liberties of the rest of mankind. Happily for America, happily we trust for the whole human race, they pursued a new and more noble course. They accomplished a revolution which has no parallel in the annals of human society. They reared the fabrics of governments which have no model on the face of the globe. They formed the design of a great confederacy, which it is incumbent on their successors to improve and perpetuate. If their works betray imperfections, we wonder at the fewness of them. If they erred most in the structure of the union, this was the work most difficult to be executed; this is the work which has been new modelled by the act of your convention, and it is that act on which you are now to deliberate and to decide.

PUBLIUS

—*Alexander Hamilton*—
THE FEDERALIST No. 15
DECEMBER 1, 1787

IN THE COURSE OF the preceding papers, I have endeavoured, my fellow citizens, to place before you, in a clear and convincing light, the importance of union to your political safety and happiness. I have unfolded to you a complication of dangers to which you would be exposed, should you permit that sacred knot, which binds the people of America together, to be severed or dissolved by ambition or by avarice, by jealousy or by misrepresentation. In the sequel of the inquiry, through which I propose to accompany you, the truths intended to be inculcated will receive further confirmation from facts and arguments hitherto unnoticed. If the road, over which you will still have to pass, should in some places appear to you tedious or irksome, you will recollect, that you are in quest of information on a subject the most momentous, which can engage the attention of a free people; that the field through which you have to travel is in itself spacious, and that the difficulties of the journey have been unnecessarily increased by the mazes with which sophistry has beset the way. It will be my aim to remove the obstacles to your progress, in as compendious a manner as it can be done, without sacrificing utility to despatch.

In pursuance of the plan, which I have laid down for the discussion of the subject, the point next in order to be examined, is the "insufficiency of the present confederation to the preservation of the union."

It may perhaps be asked, what need there is of reasoning or proof to illustrate a position, which is neither controverted nor doubted; to which the understandings and feelings of all classes of men assent; and which in substance is admitted by the opponents as well as by the friends of the new constitution? It must in truth be acknowledged, that however these may differ in other respects, they in general appear to harmonize in the opinion, that there are material imperfections in our national system, and that something is necessary to be done to rescue us from impending anarchy. The facts that support this opinion, are no longer objects of speculation. They have forced themselves upon the sensibility of the people at large, and have at length extorted from those, whose mistaken policy has had the principal share in precipitating the extremity at which we are arrived, a reluctant confession of the reality of many of those defects in the scheme of our federal government, which have been long pointed out and regretted by the intelligent friends of the union.

We may indeed, with propriety, be said to have reached almost the last stage of national humiliation. There is scarcely any thing that can wound the pride, or degrade the character, of an independent people, which we do not experience. Are there engagements, to the performance of which we are held by every tie respectable among men? These are the subjects of constant and unblushing violation. Do we owe debts to foreigners, and to our own citizens, contracted in a time of imminent peril, for the preservation of our political existence? These remain without any proper or satisfactory provision for their discharge. Have we valuable territories and important posts in the possession of a foreign power, which, by express stipulations, ought long since to have been surrendered? These are still retained, to the prejudice of our interests not less than of our rights. Are we in a condition to resent, or to repel the aggression? We have neither troops, nor treasury, nor government.* Are we even in a condition to remonstrate with dignity? The just imputations on our own faith, in respect to the same treaty, ought first to be removed. Are we entitled, by nature and compact, to a free participation in the navigation of the Mississippi? Spain excludes us from it. Is public credit an indispensable resource in time of public danger? We seem to have abandoned its cause as desperate and irretrievable. Is commerce of importance to national wealth? Ours is at the lowest point of declension. Is respectability in the eyes of foreign powers, a safeguard against foreign encroachments? The imbecility of our government even forbids them to treat with us: our ambassadors abroad are the mere pageants of mimic sovereignty. Is a violent and unnatural decrease in the value of land, a symptom of national distress? The price of improved land, in most parts of the country, is much lower than can be accounted for by the quantity of waste land at market, and can only be fully explained by that want of private and public confidence, which are so alarmingly prevalent among all ranks, and which have a direct tendency to depreciate property of every kind. Is private credit the friend and patron of industry? That most useful kind which relates to borrowing and lending, is reduced within the narrowest limits, and this still more from an opinion of insecurity than from a scarcity of money. To shorten an enumeration of particulars which can afford neither pleasure nor instruction, it may in general be demanded, what indication is there of national disorder, poverty, and insignificance, that could befal a community so peculiarly blessed with natural advantages as we are, which does not form a part of the dark catalogue of our public misfortunes?

This is the melancholy situation to which we have been brought by those very maxims and counsels, which would now deter us from adopting the proposed constitution; and which, not content with having conducted us to the brink of a precipice, seem resolved to plunge us into the abyss that awaits us below. Here, my countrymen,

---

*I mean for the union [Hamilton's note].

impelled by every motive that ought to influence an enlightened people, let us make a firm stand for our safety, our tranquillity, our dignity, our reputation. Let us at last break the fatal charm which has too long seduced us from the paths of felicity and prosperity.

It is true, as has been before observed, that facts too stubborn to be resisted, have produced a species of general assent to the abstract proposition, that there exist material defects in our national system; but the usefulness of the concession, on the part of the old adversaries of federal measures, is destroyed by a strenuous opposition to a remedy, upon the only principles that can give it a chance of success. While they admit that the government of the United States is destitute of energy, they contend against conferring upon it those powers which are requisite to supply that energy. They seem still to aim at things repugnant and irreconcilable; at an augmentation of federal authority, without a diminution of state authority; at sovereignty in the union, and complete independence in the members. They still, in fine, seem to cherish with blind devotion the political monster of an *imperium in imperio*. This renders a full display of the principal defects of the confederation necessary, in order to show, that the evils we experience do not proceed from minute or partial imperfections, but from fundamental errors in the structure of the building, which cannot be amended, otherwise than by an alteration in the very elements and main pillars of the fabric.

The great and radical vice, in the construction of the existing confederation, is in the principle of LEGISLATION for STATES or GOVERNMENTS, in their CORPORATE or COLLECTIVE CAPACITIES, and as contradistinguished from the INDIVIDUALS of whom they consist. Though this principle does not run through all the powers delegated to the union; yet it pervades and governs those on which the efficacy of the rest depends: except, as to the rule of apportionment, the United States have an indefinite discretion to make requisitions for men and money; but they have no authority to raise either, by regulations extending to the individual citizens of America. The consequence of this is, that, though in theory, their resolutions concerning those objects, are laws, constitutionally binding on the members of the union; yet, in practice, they are mere recommendations, which the states observe or disregard at their option.

It is a singular instance of the capriciousness of the human mind, that, after all the admonitions we have had from experience on this head, there should still be found men, who object to the new constitution, for deviating from a principle which has been found the bane of the old; and which is, in itself, evidently incompatible with the idea of a GOVERNMENT; a principle, in short, which, if it is to be executed at all, must substitute the violent and sanguinary agency of the sword, to the mild influence of the magistracy.

There is nothing absurd or impracticable, in the idea of a league or alliance between independent nations, for certain defined purposes precisely stated in a treaty; regulating all the details of time, place, circumstance, and quantity; leaving nothing to future discretion; and depending for its execution on the good faith of the parties. Compacts of this kind, exist among all civilized nations, subject to the usual vicissitudes of peace and war; of observance and non-observance, as the interests or passions of the contracting powers dictate. In the early part of the present century, there was an epidemical rage in Europe for this species of compacts; from which the politicians of the times fondly hoped for benefits which were never realized. With a view to establishing the equilibrium of power, and the peace of that part of the world, all the resources of negotiation were exhausted, and triple and quadruple alliances were formed; but they were scarcely formed before they were broken, giving an instructive, but afflicting, lesson to mankind, how little dependence is to be placed on treaties which have no other sanction than the obligations of good faith; and which oppose general considerations of peace and justice, to the impulse of any immediate interest or passion.

If the particular states in this country are disposed to stand in a similar relation to each other, and to drop the project of a general DISCRETIONARY SUPERINTENDENCE, the scheme would indeed be pernicious, and would entail upon us all the mischiefs which have been enumerated under the first head; but it would have the merit of being, at least, consistent and practicable. Abandoning all views towards a confederate government, this would bring us to a simple alliance, offensive and defensive; and would place us in a situation to be alternately friends and enemies of each other, as our mutual jealousies and rivalships, nourished by the intrigues of foreign nations, should prescribe to us.

But if we are unwilling to be placed in this perilous situation; if we still adhere to the design of a national government, or, which is the same thing, of a superintending power, under the direction of a common council, we must resolve to incorporate into our plan those ingredients, which may be considered as forming the characteristic difference between a league and a government; we must extend the authority of the union to the persons of the citizens . . . the only proper objects of government.

Government implies the power of making laws. It is essential to the idea of a law, that it be attended with a sanction; or, in other words, a penalty or punishment for disobedience. If there be no penalty annexed to disobedience, the resolutions or commands which pretend to be laws, will in fact amount to nothing more than advice or recommendation. This penalty, whatever it may be, can only be inflicted in two ways; by the agency of the courts and ministers of justice, or by military force; by the COERCION of the magistracy, or by the COERCION of arms. The first kind can evidently apply only to men: the last kind must of necessity be employed against bodies politic, or communities or states. It is evident, that there is no process of a court by which their observance of the laws can, in the last resort, be enforced. Sentences may be denounced against them for violations of their duty; but these sentences can only be carried into execution by the sword. In an association, where the general authority is confined to the collective bodies of the communities that compose it, every breach of the laws must involve a state of war, and military execution must become the only instrument of civil obedience. Such a state of things can certainly not deserve the name of government, nor would any prudent man choose to commit his happiness to it.

There was a time when we were told that breaches, by the states, of the regulations of the federal authority were not to be expected; that a sense of common interest would preside over the conduct of the respective members, and would beget a full compliance with all the constitutional requisitions of the union. This language, at the present day, would appear as wild as a great part of what we now hear from the same quarter will be thought, when we shall have received further lessons from that best oracle of wisdom, experience. It at all times betrayed an ignorance of the true springs by which human conduct is actuated, and belied the original inducements to the establishment of civil power. Why has government been instituted at all? Because the passions of men will not conform to the dictates of reason and justice, without constraint. Has it been found that bodies of men act with more rectitude or greater disinterestedness than individuals? The contrary of this has been inferred by all accurate observers of the conduct of mankind; and the inference is founded upon obvious reasons. Regard to reputation, has a less active influence, when the infamy of a bad action is to be divided among a number, than when it is to fall singly upon one. A spirit of faction, which is apt to mingle its poison in the deliberations of all bodies of men, will often hurry the persons, of whom they are composed, into improprieties and excesses, for which they would blush in a private capacity.

In addition to all this, there is, in the nature of sovereign power, an impatience of control, which disposes those who are invested with the exercise of it, to look with an evil eye upon all external attempts to restrain or direct its operations. From this spirit it happens, that in every political association which is formed upon the principle of uniting in a common interest a number of lesser sovereignties, there will be found a kind of eccentric tendency in the subordinate or inferior orbs, by the operation of which there will be a perpetual effort in each to fly off from the common centre. This tendency is not difficult to be accounted for. It has its origin in the love of power. Power controled or abridged is almost always the rival and enemy of that power by which it is controled or abridged. This simple proposition will teach us how little reason there is to expect, that the persons entrusted with the administration of the affairs of the particular members of a confederacy, will at all times be ready, with perfect good humour, and an unbiassed regard to the public weal, to execute the resolutions or decrees of the general authority. The reverse of this results from the constitution of man.

If, therefore, the measures of the confederacy cannot be executed, without the intervention of the particular administrations, there will be little prospect of their being executed at all. The rulers of the respective members, whether they have a constitutional right to do it or not, will undertake to judge of the propriety of the measures themselves. They will consider the conformity of the thing proposed or required to their immediate interests or aims; the momentary conveniences or inconveniences that would attend its adoption.

All this will be done; and in a spirit of interested and suspicious scrutiny, without that knowledge of national circumstances and reasons of state, which is essential to a right judgment, and with that strong predilection in favour of local objects, which can hardly fail to mislead the decision. The same process must be repeated in every member of which the body is constituted; and the execution of the plans, framed by the councils of the whole, will always fluctuate on the discretion of the ill-informed and prejudiced opinion of every part. Those who have been conversant in the proceedings of popular assemblies; who have seen how difficult it often is, when there is no exterior pressure of circumstances, to bring them to harmonious resolutions on important points, will readily conceive how impossible it must be to induce a number of such assemblies, deliberating at a distance from each other, at different times, and under different impressions, long to co-operate in the same views and pursuits.

In our case, the concurrence of thirteen distinct sovereign wills is requisite under the confederation, to the complete execution of every important measure, that proceeds from the union. It has happened, as was to have been foreseen. The measures of the union have not been executed; the delinquencies of the states have, step by step, matured themselves to an extreme, which has at length arrested all the wheels of the national government, and brought them to an awful stand. Congress at this time scarcely possess the means of keeping up the forms of administration, till the states can have time to agree upon a more substantial substitute for the present shadow of a federal government. Things did not come to this desperate extremity at once. The causes which have been specified, produced at first only unequal and disproportionate degrees of compliance with the requisitions of the union. The greater deficiencies of some states furnished the pretext of example, and the temptation of interest to the complying, or at least delinquent states. Why should we do more in proportion than those who are embarked with us in the same political voyage? Why should we consent to bear more than our proper share of the common burthen? These were suggestions which human selfishness could not withstand, and which even speculative men, who looked forward to remote consequences, could not without hesitation combat. Each state, yielding to the persuasive voice of immediate interest or convenience, has successively withdrawn its support, till the frail and tottering edifice seems ready to fall upon our heads, and to crush us beneath its ruins.

PUBLIUS

—*James Madison*—
THE FEDERALIST NO. 38
JANUARY 12, 1788

IT IS NOT A little remarkable, that in every case reported by ancient history, in which government has been established with deliberation and consent, the task of framing it has not been committed to an assembly of men; but has been performed by some individual citizen, of pre-eminent wisdom and approved integrity.

Minos, we learn, was the primitive founder of the government of Crete; as Zaleucus was of that of the Locrians. Theseus first, and after him Draco and Solon, instituted the government of Athens. Lycurgus was the lawgiver of Sparta. The foundation of the original government of Rome was laid by Romulus; and the work completed by two of his elective successors, Numa, and Tullus Hostilius. On the abolition of royalty, the consular administration was substituted by Brutus, who stepped forward with a project for such a reform, which he alleged had been prepared by Servius Tullius, and to which his address obtained the assent and ratification of the senate and people. This remark is applicable to confederate governments also. Amphyction, we are told, was the author of that which bore his name. The Achaean league received its first birth from Achaeus, and its second from Aratus.

What degree of agency these reputed lawgivers might have in their respective establishments, or how far they might be clothed with the legitimate authority of the people, cannot, in every instance, be ascertained. In some, however, the proceeding was strictly regular. Draco appears to have been intrusted by the people of Athens, with indefinite powers to reform its government and laws. And Solon, according to Plutarch, was in a manner compelled, by the universal suffrage of his fellow citizens, to take upon him the sole and absolute power of new modelling the constitution. The proceedings under Lycurgus were less regular: but as far as the advocates for a regular reform could prevail, they all turned their eyes towards the single efforts of that celebrated patriot and sage, instead of seeking to bring about a revolution, by the intervention of a deliberative body of citizens.

Whence could it have proceeded, that a people, jealous as the Greeks were of their liberty, should so far abandon the rules of caution, as to place their destiny in the hands of a single citizen? Whence could it have proceeded that the Athenians, a people who would not suffer an army to be commanded by fewer than ten generals, and who required no other proof of danger to their liberties than the illustrious merit of a fellow citizen, should consider one illustrious citizen as a more eligible despository of the fortunes of themselves and their posterity, than a select body of citizens, from whose common deliberations more wisdom, as well as more safety, might have been expected? These questions cannot be fully answered, without supposing that the fears of discord and disunion among a number of counsellors, exceeded the apprehension of treachery or incapacity in a single individual. History informs us likewise, of the difficulties with which these celebrated reformers had to contend; as well as of the expedients which they were obliged to employ, in order to carry their reforms into effect. Solon, who seems to have indulged a more temporizing policy, confessed that he had not given to his countrymen the government best suited to their happiness, but most tolerable to their prejudices. And Lycurgus, more true to his object, was under the necessity of mixing a portion of violence with the authority of superstition; and of securing his final success, by a voluntary renunciation, first of his country, and then of his life.

If these lessons teach us, on one hand, to admire the improvement made by America on the ancient mode of preparing and establishing regular plans of government; they serve not less on the other, to admonish us of the hazards and difficulties incident to such experiments, and of the great imprudence of unnecessarily multiplying them.

Is it an unreasonable conjecture, that the errors which may be contained in the plan of the convention, are such as have resulted, rather from the defect of antecedent experience on this complicated and difficult subject, than from a want of accuracy or care in the investigation of it; and consequently, such as will not be ascertained until an actual trial shall have pointed them out? This conjecture is rendered probable, not only by many considerations of a general nature, but by the particular case of the articles of confederation.

It is observable, that among the numerous objections and amendments suggested by the several states, when these articles were submitted for their ratification, not one is found, which alludes to the great and radical error, which on actual trial has discovered itself. And if we except the observations which New Jersey was led to make rather by her local situation, than by her peculiar foresight, it may be questioned whether a single suggestion was of sufficient moment to justify a revision of the system. There is abundant reason nevertheless to suppose, that immaterial as these objections were, they would have been adhered to with a very dangerous inflexibility in some states, had not a zeal for their opinions and supposed interests, been stifled by the more powerful sentiment of self-preservation. One state, we may remember, persisted for several years in refusing her concurrence, although the enemy remained the whole period at our gates, or rather in the very bowels of our country. Nor was her pliancy in the end effected by a less motive, than the fear of being chargeable with protracting the public calamities, and endangering the event of the contest. Every candid reader will make the proper reflections on these important facts.

A patient, who finds his disorder daily growing worse, and that an efficacious remedy can no longer be delayed without extreme danger; after coolly revolving his situation, and the characters of different physicians, selects and calls in such of them as he judges most capable of administering relief, and best entitled to his confidence. The physicians attend: the case of the patient is carefully examined . . . a consultation is held: they are unanimously agreed that the symptoms are critical; but that the case, with proper and timely relief, is so far from being desperate, that it may be made to issue in an improvement of his constitution. They are equally unanimous in prescribing the remedy by which this happy effect is to be produced. The prescription is no sooner made known, however, than a number of persons interpose, and without denying the reality or danger of the disorder, assure the patient that the prescription will be poison to his constitution, and forbid him, under pain of certain death, to make use of it. Might not the patient reasonably demand, before he ventured to follow this advice, that the authors of it should at least agree among themselves, on some other remedy to be substituted? And if he found them differing as much from one another, as from his first counsellors, would he not act prudently, in trying the experiment unanimously recommended by the latter, rather than in hearkening to those who could neither deny the necessity of a speedy remedy, nor agree in proposing one.

Such a patient, and in such a situation, is America at this moment. She has been sensible of her malady. She has obtained a regular and unanimous advice from men of her own deliberate choice. And she is warned by others against following this advice, under pain of the most fatal consequences. Do the monitors deny the reality of her danger? No. Do they deny the necessity of some speedy and powerful remedy? No. Are they agreed, are any two of them agreed, in their objections to the remedy proposed, or in the proper one to be substituted? Let them speak for themselves.

This one tells us, that the proposed constitution ought to be rejected, because it is not a confederation of the states, but a government over individuals. Another admits, that it ought to be a government over individuals, to a certain extent, but by no means to the extent proposed. A third does not object to the government over individuals, or to the extent proposed, but to the want of a bill of rights. A fourth concurs in the absolute necessity of a bill of rights, but contends that it ought to be declaratory, not of the personal rights of individuals, but of the rights reserved to the states in their political capacity. A fifth is of opinion that a bill of rights of any sort would be superfluous and misplaced, and that the plan would be unexceptionable, but for the fatal power of regulating the times and places of election. An objector in a large state, exclaims loudly against the unreasonable equality of representation in the senate. An objector in a small state, is equally loud against the dangerous inequality in the house of representatives. From this quarter, we are alarmed with the amazing expense, from the number of persons who are to administer the new government. From another quarter, and sometimes from the same quarter, on another occasion, the cry is, that the congress will be but the shadow of a representation, and that the government would be far less objectionable, if the number and the expense were doubled. A patriot in a state that does not import or export, discerns insuperable objections against the power of direct taxation. The patriotic adversary in a state of great exports and imports, is not less dissatisfied that the whole burthen of taxes may be thrown on consumption. This politician discovers in the constitution a direct and irresistible tendency to monarchy: that, is equally sure, it will end in aristocracy. Another is puzzled to say which of these shapes it will ultimately assume, but sees clearly it must be one or other of them. Whilst a fourth is not wanting, who with no less confidence affirms, that the constitution is so far from having a bias towards either of these dangers, that the weight on that side will not be sufficient to keep it upright and firm against its opposite propensities. With another class of adversaries to the constitution, the language is, that the legislative, executive, and judiciary departments, are intermixed in such a manner, as to contradict all the ideas of regular government, and all the requisite precautions in favor of liberty. Whilst this objection circulates in vague and general expressions, there are not a few who lend their sanction to it. Let each one come forward with his particular explanation, and scarcely any two are exactly agreed on the subject. In the eyes of one, the junction of the senate with the president, in the responsible function of appointing to offices, instead of vesting this executive power in the executive alone, is the vicious part of the organization. To another, the exclusion of the house of representatives, whose numbers alone could be a due security against corruption and partiality in the exercise of such a power, is equally obnoxious. With another, the admission of the president into any share of a power, which must ever be a dangerous engine in the hands of the executive magistrate, is an unpardonable violation of the maxims of republican jealousy. No part of the arrangement, according to some, is more inadmissible than the trial of impeachments by the senate, which is alternately a member both of the legislative and executive departments, when this power so evidently belonged to the judiciary department. We concur fully, reply others, in the objection to this part of the plan, but we can never agree that a reference of impeachments to the judiciary authority would be an amendment of the error: our principal dislike to the organization, arises from the extensive powers already lodged in that department. Even among the zealous patrons of a council of state, the most irreconcileable variance is discovered, concerning the mode in which it ought to be constituted. The demand of one gentleman is, that the council should consist of a small number, to be appointed by the most numerous branch of the legislature. Another would prefer a larger number, and considers it as a fundamental condition, that the appointment should be made by the president himself.

As it can give no umbrage to the writers against the plan of the federal constitution, let us suppose, that as they are the most zealous, so they are also the most sagacious, of those who think the late convention were unequal to the task assigned them, and that a wiser and better plan might and ought to be substituted. Let us further suppose, that their country should concur, both in this favourable opinion of their merits, and in their unfavourable opinion of the convention; and should accordingly proceed to form them into a second convention, with full powers, and for the express purpose, of revising and remoulding the work of the first. Were the experiment to be seriously made, though it requires some effort to view it seriously even in fiction, I leave it to be decided by the sample of opinions just exhibited, whether, with all their enmity to their predecessors, they would, in any one point, depart so widely from their example, as in the discord and ferment that would mark their own deliberations; and whether the constitution, now before the public, would not stand as fair a chance for immortality, as Lycurgus gave to that of Sparta, by making its change to depend on his own return from exile and death, if it were to be immediately adopted, and were to continue in force, not until a BETTER, but until ANOTHER should be agreed upon by this new assembly of lawgivers.

It is a matter both of wonder and regret, that those who raise so many objections against the new constitution, should never call to mind the defects of that which is to be exchanged for it. It is not necessary that the former should be perfect: it is sufficient that the latter is more imperfect. No man would refuse to give brass for silver or gold, because the latter had some alloy in it. No man would refuse to quit a shattered and tottering habitation, for a firm and commodious building, because the latter had not a porch to it; or because some of the rooms might be a little larger or smaller, or the ceiling a little higher or lower than his fancy would have planned them. But wa[i]ving illustrations of this sort, is it not manifest, that most of the capital objections urged against the new system, lie with tenfold weight against the existing confederation? Is an indefinite power to raise money, dangerous in the hands of a federal government? The present congress can make requisitions to any amount they please; and the states are constitutionally bound to furnish them. They can emit bills of credit as long as they will pay for the paper: they can borrow both abroad and at home, as long as a shilling will be lent. Is an indefinite power to raise troops dangerous? The confederation gives to congress that power also; and they have already begun to make use of it. Is it improper and unsafe to intermix the different powers of government in the same body of men? Congress, a single body of men, are the sole depository of all the federal powers. Is it particularly dangerous to give the keys of the treasury, and the command of the army, into the same hands? The confederation places them both in the hands of congress. Is a bill of rights essential to liberty? The confederation has no bill of rights. Is it an objection against the new constitution, that it empowers the senate, with the concurrence of the executive, to make treaties which are to be the laws of the land? The existing congress, without any such control, can make treaties which they themselves have declared, and most of the states have recognized, to be the supreme law of the land. Is the importation of slaves permitted by the new constitution for twenty years? By the old it is permitted for ever.

I shall be told, that however dangerous this mixture of powers may be in theory, it is rendered harmless by the dependence of congress on the states for the means of carrying them into practice; that, however large the mass of powers may be, it is in fact a lifeless mass. Then, say I, in the first place, that the confederation is chargeable with the still greater folly, of declaring certain powers in the federal government to be absolutely necessary, and at the same time rendering them absolutely nugatory; and, in the next place, that if the union is to continue, and no better government be substituted, effective powers must either be granted to, or assumed by, the existing congress; in either of which events, the contrast just stated will hold good. But this is not all. Out of this lifeless mass, has already grown an excrescent power, which tends to realize all the dangers that can be apprehended from a defective construction of the supreme government of the union. It is now no longer a point of speculation and hope, that the western territory is a mine of vast wealth to the

United States; and although it is not of such a nature as to extricate them from their present distresses, or for some time to come to yield any regular supplies for the public expenses; yet must it hereafter be able, under proper management, both to effect a gradual discharge of the domestic debt, and to furnish, for a certain period, liberal tributes to the federal treasury. A very large proportion of this fund has been already surrendered by individual states; and it may with reason be expected, that the remaining states will not persist in withholding similar proofs of their equity and generosity. We may calculate, therefore, that a rich and fertile country, of an area equal to the inhabited extent of the United States, will soon become a national stock. Congress have assumed the administration of this stock. They have begun to render it productive. Congress have undertaken to do more: . . . they have proceeded to form new states; to erect temporary governments; to appoint officers for them; and to prescribe the conditions on which such states shall be admitted into the confederacy. All this has been done; and done without the least colour of constitutional authority. Yet no blame has been whispered: no alarm has been sounded. A GREAT and INDEPENDENT fund of revenue is passing into the hands of a SINGLE BODY of men, who can RAISE TROOPS to an INDEFINITE NUMBER, and appropriate money to their support for an INDEFINITE PERIOD OF TIME. And yet there are men, who have not only been silent spectators of this prospect, but who are advocates for the system which exhibits it; and, at the same time, urge against the new system the objections which we have heard. Would they not act with more consistency, in urging the establishment of the latter, as no less necessary to guard the union against the future powers and resources of a body constructed like the existing congress, than to save it from the dangers threatened by the present impotency of that assembly?

I mean not, by any thing here said, to throw censure on the measures which have been pursued by congress. I am sensible they could not have done otherwise. The public interest, the necessity of the case, imposed upon them the task of overleaping their constitutional limits. But is not the fact an alarming proof of the danger resulting from a government, which does not possess regular powers commensurate to its objects? A dissolution, or usurpation, is the dreadful dilemma to which it is continually exposed.

PUBLIUS

RESUMING THE SUBJECT OF the last paper, I proceed to inquire, whether the federal government or the state governments, will have the advantage with regard to the predilection and support of the people.

Notwithstanding the different modes in which they are appointed, we must consider both of them as substantially dependent on the great body of the citizens of the United States. I assume this position here as it respects the first, reserving the proofs for another place. The federal and state governments are in fact but different agents and trustees of the people, instituted with different powers, and designated for different purposes. The adversaries of the constitution seem to have lost sight of the people altogether in their reasonings on this subject; and to have viewed these different establishments, not only as mutual rivals and enemies, but as uncontroled by any common superior, in their efforts to usurp the authorities of each other. These gentlemen must here be reminded of their error. They must be told, that the ultimate authority, wherever the derivative may be found, resides in the people alone; and that it will not depend merely on the comparative ambition or address of the different governments, whether either, or which of them, will be able to enlarge its sphere of jurisdiction at the expense of the other. Truth, no less than decency, requires, that the event in every case, should be supposed to depend on the sentiments and sanction of their common constituents.

Many considerations, besides those suggested on a former occasion, seem to place it beyond doubt, that the first and most natural attachment of the people, will be to the governments of their respective states. Into the administration of these, a greater number of individuals will expect to rise. From the gift of these, a greater number of offices and emoluments will flow. By the superintending care of these, all the more domestic and personal interests of the people will be regulated and provided for. With the affairs of these, the people will be more familiarly and minutely conversant: and with the members of these, will a greater proportion of the people have the ties of personal acquaintance and friendship, and of family and party attachments. On the side of these, therefore, the popular bias may well be expected most strongly to incline.

Experience speaks the same language in this case. The federal administration, though hitherto very defective, in comparison with what may be hoped under a better system, had, during the war, and particularly whilst the independent fund of paper emissions was in credit, an activity and importance as great as it can well have, in any future circumstances whatever. It was engaged too in a course of measures which had for their object the protection of every thing that was dear, and the acquisition of every thing that could be desirable to the people at large. It was, nevertheless, invariably found, after the transient enthusiasm for the early congresses was over, that the attention and attachment of the people were turned anew to their own particular governments; that the federal council was at no time the idol of popular favour; and that opposition to proposed enlargements of its powers and importance, was the side usually taken by the men, who wished to build their political consequence on the prepossessions of their fellow citizens.

If, therefore, as has been elsewhere remarked, the people should in future become more partial to the federal than to the state governments, the change can only result from such manifest and irresistible proofs of a better administration, as will overcome all their antecedent propensities. And in that case, the people ought not surely to be precluded from giving most of their confidence where they may discover it to be most due: but even in that case, the state governments could have little to apprehend, because it is only within a certain sphere, that the federal power can, in the nature of things, be advantageously administered.

The remaining points on which I propose to compare the federal and state governments, are the disposition and the faculty they may respectively possess, to resist and frustrate the measures of each other.

It has been already proved, that the members of the federal will be more dependent on the members of the state governments, than the latter will be on the former. It has appeared also, that the prepossessions of the people, on whom both will depend, will be more on the side of the state governments than of the federal government. So far as the disposition of each, towards the other, may be influenced by these causes, the state governments must clearly have the advantage. But in a distinct and very important point of view, the advantage will lie on the same side. The prepossessions which the members themselves will carry into the federal government, will generally be favourable to the states; whilst it will rarely happen, that the members of the state governments will carry into the public councils, a bias in favour of the general government. A local spirit will infallibly prevail much more in the members of the congress, than a national spirit will prevail in the legislatures of the particular states. Every one knows, that a great proportion of the errors committed by the state legislatures, proceeds from the disposition of the members to sacrifice the comprehensive and permanent interests of the state, to the particular and separate views of the counties or districts in which they reside. And if they do not sufficiently enlarge their policy, to embrace the collective welfare of their particular state, how can it be imagined, that they will make the aggregate prosperity of the union, and the dignity and respectability of its government, the objects of their affections and consultations? For the same reason, that the members of the state legislatures will be unlikely to attach themselves sufficiently to national objects, the members of the federal legislature will be likely to attach themselves too much to local objects. The states will be to the latter, what counties and towns are to the former. Measures will too often be decided according to their probable effect, not on the national prosperity and happiness, but on the prejudices, interests, and pursuits of the governments and people of the individual states. What is the spirit that has in general characterized the proceedings of congress? A perusal of their journals, as well as the candid acknowledgements of such as have had a seat in that assembly, will inform us, that the members have but too frequently displayed the character, rather of partizans of their respective states, than of impartial guardians of a common interest; that where, on one occasion, improper sacrifices have been made of local considerations to the aggrandizement of the federal government; the great interests of the nation have suffered on an hundred, from an undue attention to the local prejudices, interests, and views of the particular states. I mean not by these reflections to insinuate, that the new federal government will not embrace a more enlarged plan of policy, than the existing government may have pursued; much less, that its views will be as confined as those of the state legislatures: but only that it will partake sufficiently of the spirit of both, to be disinclined to invade the rights of the individual states, or the prerogatives of their governments. The motives on the part of the state governments, to augment their prerogatives by defalcations from the federal government, will be overruled by no reciprocal predispositions in the members.

Were it admitted, however, that the federal government may feel an equal disposition with the state governments to extend its power beyond the due limits, the latter would still have the advantage in the means of defeating such encroachments. If an act of a particular state, though unfriendly to the national government, be generally popular in that state, and should not too grossly violate the oaths of the state officers, it is executed immediately, and of course, by means on the spot, and depending on the state alone. The opposition of the federal government, or the interposition of federal officers, would but inflame the zeal of all parties on the side of the state; and the evil could not be prevented or repaired, if at all, without the employment of means which must always be resorted to with reluctance and difficulty. On the other hand, should an unwarrantable measure of the federal government be unpopular in particular states, which would seldom fail to be the case, or even a warrantable measure be so, which may sometimes be the case, the means of opposition to it are powerful and at hand. The disquietude of the people; their repugnance, and perhaps refusal, to co-operate with the officers of the union; the frowns of the executive magistracy of the state; the embarrassments created by legislative devices, which would often be added on such occasions, would oppose, in any state, difficulties not to be despised; would form, in a large state, very serious impediments; and where the sentiments of several adjoining states happened to be in unison, would present obstructions which the federal government would hardly be willing to encounter.

But ambitious encroachments of the federal government, on the authority of the state governments, would not excite the opposition of a single state, or of a few states only. They would be signals of general alarm. Every government would espouse the common cause. A correspondence would be opened. Plans of resistance would be concerted. One spirit would animate and conduct the whole. The same combination, in short, would result from an apprehension of the federal, as was produced by the dread of a foreign yoke; and unless the projected innovations should be voluntarily renounced, the same appeal to a trial of force would be made in the one case, as was made in the other. But what degree of madness could ever drive the federal government to such an extremity? In the contest with Great Britain, one part of the empire was employed against the other. The more numerous part invaded the rights of the less numerous part. The attempt was unjust and unwise; but it was not in speculation absolutely chimerical. But what would be the contest, in the case we are supposing? Who would be the parties? A few representatives of the people would be opposed to the people themselves; or rather one set of representatives would be contending against thirteen sets of representatives, with the whole body of their common constituents on the side of the latter.

The only refuge left for those who prophecy the downfall of the state governments, is the visionary supposition, that the federal government may previously accumulate a military force for the projects of ambition. The reasonings contained in these papers, must have been employed to little purpose indeed, if it could be necessary now to disprove the reality of this danger. That the people and the states should, for a sufficient period of time, elect an uninterrupted succession of men ready to betray both; that the traitors should, throughout this period, uniformly and systematically pursue some fixed plan for the extension of the military establishment; that the governments and the people of the states should silently and patiently behold the gathering storm, and continue to supply the materials, until it should be prepared to burst on their own heads, must appear to every one more like the incoherent dreams of a delirious jealousy, or the misjudged exaggerations of a counterfeit zeal, than like the sober apprehensions of genuine patriotism. Extravagant as the supposition is, let it however be made. Let a regular army, fully equal to the resources of the country, be formed; and let it be entirely at the devotion of the federal government; still it would not be going too far to say, that the state governments, with the people on their side, would be able to repel the danger. The highest number to which, according to the best computation, a standing army can be carried in any country, does not exceed one hundredth part of the whole number of souls; or one twenty-fifth part of the number able to bear arms. This proportion would not yield, in the United States, an army of more than twenty-five or thirty thousand men. To these would be opposed a militia amounting to near half a million of citizens with arms in their hands, officered by men chosen from among themselves, fighting for their common liberties, and united and conducted by governments possessing their affections and confidence. It may well be doubted, whether a militia thus circumstanced, could ever be conquered by such a proportion of regular troops. Those who are best acquainted with the late successful resistance of this country against the British arms, will be most inclined to deny the possibility of it. Besides the advantage of being armed, which the Americans possess over the people of almost every other nation, the existence of subordinate governments, to which the people are attached, and by which the militia officers are appointed, forms a barrier against the enterprises of ambition, more insurmountable than any which a simple government of any form can admit of. Notwithstanding the military establishments in the several kingdoms of Europe, which are carried as far as the public resources will bear, the governments are afraid to trust the people with arms. And it is not certain, that with this aid alone, they would not be able to shake off their yokes. But were the people to possess the additional advantages of local governments chosen by themselves, who could collect the national will, and direct the national force, and of officers appointed out of the militia, by these governments, and attached both to them and to the militia, it may be affirmed with the greatest assurance, that the throne of every tyranny in Europe would be speedily overturned in spite of the legions which surround it. Let us not insult the free and gallant citizens of America with the suspicion, that they would be less able to defend the rights of which they would be in actual possession, than the debased subjects of arbitrary power would be to rescue theirs from the hands of their oppressors. Let us rather no longer insult them with the supposition, that they can ever reduce themselves to the necessity of making the experiment, by a blind and tame submission to the long train of insidious measures which must precede and produce it.

The argument under the present head may be put into a very concise form, which appears altogether conclusive. Either the mode in which the federal government is to be constructed, will render it sufficiently dependent on the people, or it will not.

On the first supposition, it will be restrained by that dependence from forming schemes obnoxious to their constituents. On the other supposition, it will not possess the confidence of the people, and its schemes of usurpation will be easily defeated by the state governments; which will be supported by the people.

On summing up the considerations stated in this and the last paper, they seem to amount to the most convincing evidence, that the powers proposed to be lodged in the federal government, are as little formidable to those reserved to the individual states, as they are indispensably necessary to accomplish the purposes of the union; and that all those alarms which have been sounded, of a meditated and consequential annihilation of the state governments, must, on the most favourable interpretation, be ascribed to the chimerical fears of the authors of them.

PUBLIUS

—*James Madison*—
THE FEDERALIST NO. 48
FEBRUARY 1, 1788

IT WAS SHOWN IN the last paper, that the political apothegm there examined, does not require that the legislative, executive, and judiciary departments, should be wholly unconnected with each other. I shall undertake in the next place to show, that unless these departments be so far connected and blended, as to give to each a constitutional control over the others, the degree of separation which the maxim requires, as essential to a free government, can never in practice be duly maintained.

It is agreed on all sides, that the powers properly belonging to one of the departments, ought not to be directly and completely administered by either of the other departments. It is equally evident, that neither of them ought to possess, directly or indirectly, an overruling influence over the others in the administration of their respective powers. It will not be denied, that power is of an encroaching nature, and that it ought to be effectually restrained from passing the limits assigned to it. After discriminating, therefore, in theory, the several classes of power, as they may in their nature be legislative, executive, or judiciary; the next, and most difficult task, is to provide some practical security for each, against the invasion of the others. What this security ought to be, is the great problem to be solved.

Will it be sufficient to mark, with precision, the boundaries of these departments, in the constitution of the government, and to trust to these parchment barriers against the encroaching spirit of power? This is the security which appears to have been principally relied on by the compilers of most of the American constitutions. But experience assures us, that the efficacy of the provision has been greatly overrated; and that some more adequate defence is indispensably necessary for the more feeble, against the more powerful members of the government. The legislative department is every where extending the sphere of its activity, and drawing all power into its impetuous vortex.

The founders of our republics have so much merit for the wisdom which they have displayed, that no task can be less pleasing than that of pointing out the errors into which they have fallen. A respect for truth, however, obliges us to remark, that they seem never for a moment to have turned their eyes from the danger to liberty, from the overgrown and all-grasping prerogative of an hereditary magistrate, supported and fortified by an hereditary branch of the legislative authority. They seem never to have recollected the danger from legislative usurpations, which, by assembling all power in the same hands, must lead to the same tyranny as is threatened by executive usurpations.

In a government where numerous and extensive prerogatives are placed in the hands of a hereditary monarch, the executive department is very justly regarded as the source of danger, and watched with all the jealousy which a zeal for liberty ought to inspire. In a democracy, where a multitude of people exercise in person the legislative functions, and are continually exposed, by their incapacity for regular deliberation and concerted measures, to the ambitious intrigues of their executive magistrates, tyranny may well be apprehended, on some favourable emergency, to start up in the same quarter. But in a representative republic, where the executive magistracy is carefully limited, both in the extent and the duration of its power; and where the legislative power is exercised by an assembly, which is inspired by a supposed influence over the people, with an intrepid confidence in its own strength; which is sufficiently numerous to feel all the passions which actuate a multitude; yet not so numerous as to be incapable of pursuing the objects of its passions, by means which reason prescribes; it is against the enterprising ambition of this department, that the people ought to indulge all their jealousy, and exhaust all their precautions.

The legislative department derives a superiority in our governments from other circumstances. Its constitutional powers being at once more extensive, and less susceptible of precise limits, it can, with the greater facility, mask under complicated and indirect measures, the encroachments which it makes on the co-ordinate departments. It is not unfrequently a question of real nicety in legislative bodies, whether the operation of a particular measure will, or will not extend beyond the legislative sphere. On the other side, the executive power being restrained within a narrower compass, and being more simple in its nature; and the judiciary being described by land-marks, still less uncertain, projects of usurpation by either of these departments, would immediately betray and defeat themselves. Nor is this all: as the legislative department alone has access to the pockets of the people, and has in some constitutions full discretion, and in all, a prevailing influence over the pecuniary rewards of those who fill the other departments; a dependence is thus created in the latter, which gives still greater facility to encroachments of the former.

I have appealed to our own experience for the truth of what I advance on this subject. Were it necessary to verify this experience by particular proofs, they might be multiplied without end. I might collect vouchers in abundance from the records and archives of every state in the union. But as a more concise, and at the same time equally satisfactory evidence, I will refer to the example of two states, attested by two unexceptionable authorities.

The first example is that of Virginia, a state which, as we have seen, has expressly declared in its constitution, that the three great departments ought not to be intermixed. The authority in support of it is Mr. Jefferson, who, besides his other advantages for remarking the operation of the government, was himself the chief magistrate of it. In order to convey fully the ideas with which his experience had impressed him on this subject, it will be necessary to quote a passage of some length from his very interesting "Notes on the state of Virginia." "All the powers of government, legislative, executive, and judiciary, result to the legislative body. The concentrating these in the same hands, is precisely the definition of despotic government. It will be no alleviation that these powers will be exercised by a plurality of hands, and not by a single one. One hundred and seventy-three despots would surely be as oppressive as one. Let those who doubt it, turn their eyes on the republic of Venice. As little will it avail us that they are chosen by ourselves. An *elective despotism* was not the government we fought for; but one which should not only be founded on free principles, but in which the powers of government should be so divided and balanced among several bodies of magistracy, as that no one could transcend their legal limits, without being effectually checked and restrained by the others. For this reason, that convention which passed the ordinance of government, laid its foundation on this basis, that the legislative, executive, and judiciary departments, should be separate and distinct, so that no person should exercise the powers of more than one of them at the same time. *But no barrier was provided between these several powers.* The judiciary and executive members were left dependent on the legislative for their subsistence in office, and some of them for their continuance in it. If, therefore, the legislature assumes executive and judiciary powers, no opposition is likely to be made; nor if made, can be effectual; because in that case, they may put their proceeding into the form of an act of assembly, which will render them obligatory on the other branches. They have accordingly, *in many* instances, *decided rights* which should have been left to *judiciary controversy;* and *the direction of the executive, during the whole time of their session, is becoming habitual and familiar."*

The other state which I shall take for an example, is Pennsylvania; and the other authority the council of censors which assembled in the years 1783 and 1784. A part of the duty of this body, as marked out by the constitution, was "to inquire whether the constitution had been preserved inviolate in every part; and whether the legislative and executive branches of government, had performed their duty as guardians of the people, or assumed to themselves, or exercised other or greater powers than they are entitled to by the constitution." In the execution of this trust, the council were necessarily led to a comparison of both the legislative and executive proceedings, with the constitutional powers of these departments: and from the facts enumerated, and to the truth of most of which both sides in the council subscribed, it appears that the constitution had been flagrantly violated by the legislature in a variety of important instances.

A great number of laws had been passed violating, without any apparent necessity, the rule requiring that all bills of a public nature shall be previously printed for the consideration of the people; although this is one of the precautions chiefly relied on by the constitution against improper acts of the legislature.

The constitutional trial by jury had been violated; and powers assumed which had not been delegated by the constitution.

Executive powers had been usurped.

The salaries of the judges, which the constitution expressly requires to be fixed, had been occasionally varied; and cases belonging to the judiciary department, frequently drawn within legislative cognizance and determination.

Those who wish to see the several particulars falling under each of these heads, may consult the journals of the council which are in print. Some of them, it will be found, may be imputable to peculiar circumstances connected with the war: but the greater part of them may be considered as the spontaneous shoots of an ill constituted government.

It appears also, that the executive department had not been innocent of frequent breaches of the constitution. There are three observations, however, which ought to be made on this head. *First.* A great proportion of the instances, were either immediately produced by the necessities of the war, or recommended by congress or the commander in chief. *Second.* In most of the other instances, they conformed either to the declared or the known sentiments of the legislative department. *Third.* The executive department of Pennsylvania is distinguished from that of the other states, by the number of members composing it. In this respect it has as much affinity to a legislative assembly, as to an executive council. And being at once exempt from the restraint of an individual responsibility for the acts of the body, and deriving confidence from mutual example and joint influence; unauthorized measures would of course be more freely hazarded, than where the executive department is administered by a single hand, or by a few hands.

The conclusion which I am warranted in drawing from these observations is, that a mere demarkation on parchment of the constitutional limits of the several departments, is not a sufficient guard against those encroachments which lead to a tyrannical concentration of all the powers of government in the same hands.

PUBLIUS

—James Madison—
THE FEDERALIST NO. 51
FEBRUARY 6, 1788

TO WHAT EXPEDIENT THEN shall we finally resort, for maintaining in practice the necessary partition of power among the several departments, as laid down in the constitution? The only answer that can be given is, that as all these exterior provisions are found to be inadequate, the defect must be supplied, by so contriving the interior structure of the government, as that its several constituent parts may, by their mutual relations, be the means of keeping each other in their proper places. Without presuming to undertake a full development of this important idea, I will hazard a few general observations, which may perhaps place it in a clearer light, and enable us to form a more correct judgment of the principles and structure of the government planned by the convention.

In order to lay a due foundation for that separate and distinct exercise of the different powers of government, which, to a certain extent, is admitted on all hands to be essential to the preservation of liberty, it is evident that each department should have a will of its own; and consequently should be so constituted, that the members of each should have as little agency as possible in the appointment of the members of the others. Were this principle rigorously adhered to, it would require that all the appointments for the supreme executive, legislative, and judiciary magistracies, should be drawn from the same fountain of authority, the people, through channels having no communication whatever with one another. Perhaps such a plan of constructing the several departments, would be less difficult in practice, than it may in contemplation appear. Some difficulties, however, and some additional expense, would attend the execution of it. Some deviations, therefore, from the principle must be admitted. In the constitution of the judiciary department in particular, it might be inexpedient to insist rigorously on the principle; first, because peculiar qualifications being essential in the members, the primary consideration ought to be to select that mode of choice which best secures these qualifications; secondly, because the permanent tenure by which the appointments are held in that department, must soon destroy all sense of dependence on the authority conferring them.

It is equally evident, that the members of each department should be as little dependent as possible on those of the others, for the emoluments annexed to their offices. Were the executive magistrate, or the judges, not independent of the legislature in this particular, their independence in every other, would be merely nominal.

But the great security against a gradual concentration of the several powers in the same department, consists in giving to those who administer each department, the necessary constitutional means, and personal motives, to resist encroachments of the others. The provision for defence must in this, as in all other cases, be made commensurate to the danger of attack. Ambition must be made to counteract ambition. The interest of the man, must be connected with the constitutional rights of the place. It may be a reflection on human nature, that such devices should be necessary to control the abuses of government. But what is government itself, but the greatest of all reflections on human nature? If men were angels, no government would be necessary. If angels were to govern men, neither external nor internal controls on government would be necessary. In framing a government which is to be administered by men over men, the great difficulty lies in this: you must first enable the government to control the governed; and in the next place oblige it to control itself. A dependence on the people is, no doubt, the primary control on the government; but experience has taught mankind the necessity of auxiliary precautions.

This policy of supplying, by opposite and rival interests, the defect of better motives, might be traced through the whole system of human affairs, private as well as public. We see it particularly displayed in all the subordinate distributions of power; where the constant aim is, to divide and arrange the several offices in such a manner as that each may be a check on the other; that the private interest of every individual may be a centinel over the public rights. These inventions of prudence cannot be less requisite in the distribution of the supreme powers of the state.

But it is not possible to give to each department an equal power of self-defence. In republican government, the legislative authority necessarily predominates. The remedy for this inconveniency is, to divide the legislature into different branches; and to render them, by different modes of election, and different principles of action, as little connected with each other, as the nature of their common functions, and their common dependence on the society, will admit. It may even be necessary to guard against dangerous encroachments by still further precautions. As the weight of the legislative authority requires that it should be thus divided, the weakness of the executive may require, on the other hand, that it should be fortified. An absolute negative on the legislature, appears, at first view, to be the natural defence with which the executive magistrate should be armed. But perhaps it would be neither altogether safe, nor alone sufficient. On ordinary occasions, it might not be exerted with the requisite firmness; and on extraordinary occasions, it might be perfidiously abused. May not this defect of an absolute negative be supplied by some qualified connexion between this weaker department, and the weaker branch of the stronger department,* by which the latter may be led to support the constitutional rights of the former, without being too much detached from the rights of its own department?

If the principles on which these observations are founded be just, as I persuade myself they are, and they be applied as a criterion to the several state constitutions, and to the federal constitution, it will be found, that if the latter does not perfectly correspond with them, the former are infinitely less able to bear such a test.

There are moreover two considerations particularly applicable to

---

*By this Madison means the Senate, which has a "qualified connexion" with the executive through the "advise and consent" it gives in making appointments and treaties.

the federal system of America, which place that system in a very interesting point of view.

First. In a single republic, all the power surrendered by the people, is submitted to the administration of a single government; and the usurpations are guarded against, by a division of the government into distinct and separate departments. In the compound republic of America, the power surrendered by the people, is first divided between two distinct governments, and then the portion allotted to each subdivided among distinct and separate departments. Hence a double security arises to the rights of the people. The different governments will control each other; at the same time that each will be controled by itself.

Second. It is of great importance in a republic, not only to guard the society against the oppression of its rulers; but to guard one part of the society against the injustice of the other part. Different interests necessarily exist in different classes of citizens. If a majority be united by a common interest, the rights of the minority will be insecure. There are but two methods of providing against this evil: the one, by creating a will in the community independent of the majority, that is, of the society itself; the other, by comprehending in the society so many separate descriptions of citizens, as will render an unjust combination of a majority of the whole very improbable, if not impracticable. The first method prevails in all governments possessing an hereditary or self-appointed authority. This, at best, is but a precarious security; because a power independent of the society may as well espouse the unjust views of the major, as the rightful interests of the minor party, and may possibly be turned against both parties. The second method will be exemplified in the federal republic of the United States. Whilst all authority in it will be derived from, and dependent on the society, the society itself will be broken into so many parts, interests, and classes of citizens, that the rights of individuals, or of the minority, will be in little danger from interested combinations of the majority. In a free government, the security for civil rights must be the same as that for religious rights. It consists in the one case in the multiplicity of interests, and in the other, in the multiplicity of sects. The degree of security in both cases will depend on the number of interests and sects; and this may be presumed to depend on the extent of country and number of people comprehended under the same government. This view of the subject must particularly recommend a proper federal system to all the sincere and considerate friends of republican government: since it shows, that in exact proportion as the territory of the union may be formed into more circumscribed confederacies, or states, oppressive combinations of a majority will be facilitated; the best security under the republican form, for the rights of every class of citizens, will be diminished; and consequently, the stability and independence of some member of the government, the only other security, must be proportionally increased. Justice is the end of government. It is the end of civil society. It ever has been, and ever will be, pursued, until it be obtained, or until liberty be lost in the pursuit. In a society, under the forms of which the stronger faction can readily unite and oppress the weaker, anarchy may as truly be said to reign, as in a state of nature, where the weaker individual is not secured against the violence of the stronger: and as, in the latter state, even the stronger individuals are prompted, by the uncertainty of their condition, to submit to a government which may protect the weak, as well as themselves: so, in the former state, will the more powerful factions or parties be gradually induced, by a like motive, to wish for a government which will protect all parties, the weaker as well as the more powerful. It can be little doubted, that if the state of Rhode Island was separated from the confederacy, and left to itself, the insecurity of rights under the popular form of government within such narrow limits, would be displayed by such reiterated oppressions of factious majorities, that some power altogether independent of the people, would soon be called for by the voice of the very factions whose misrule had proved the necessity of it. In the extended republic of the United States, and among the great variety of interests, parties, and sects, which it embraces, a coalition of a majority of the whole society could seldom take place upon any other principles, than those of justice and the general good: whilst there being thus less danger to a minor from the will of the major party, there must be less pretext also, to provide for the security of the former, by introducing into the government a will not dependent on the latter: or, in other words, a will independent of the society itself. It is no less certain than it is important, notwithstanding the contrary opinions which have been entertained, that the larger the society, provided it lie within a practicable sphere, the more duly capable it will be of self-government. And happily for the *republican cause,* the practicable sphere may be carried to a very great extent, by a judicious modification and mixture of the *federal principle.*

PUBLIUS

—*Alexander Hamilton*—
THE FEDERALIST NO. 70
MARCH 15, 1788

THERE IS AN IDEA, which is not without its advocates, that a vigorous executive is inconsistent with the genius of republican government. The enlightened well-wishers to this species of government must at least hope, that the supposition is destitute of foundation; since they can never admit its truth, without, at the same time, admitting the condemnation of their own principles. Energy in the executive is a leading character in the definition of good government. It is essential to the protection of the community against foreign attacks: it is not less essential to the steady administration of the laws; to the protection of property against those irregular and high-handed combinations which sometimes interrupt the ordinary course of justice; to the security of liberty against the enterprises and assaults of ambition, of faction, and of anarchy. Every man, the least conversant in Roman story, knows how often that republic was obliged to take refuge in the absolute power of a single man, under the formidable title of dictator, as well against the intrigues of ambitious individuals, who aspired to the tyranny, and the seditions of whole classes of the community, whose conduct threatened the existence of all government, as against the invasions of external enemies, who menaced the conquest and destruction of Rome.

There can be no need, however, to multiply arguments or examples on this head. A feeble executive implies a feeble execution of the government. A feeble execution is but another phrase for a bad execution: and a government ill executed, whatever it may be in theory, must be, in practice, a bad government.

Taking it for granted, therefore, that all men of sense will agree in the necessity of an energetic executive, it will only remain to inquire, what are the ingredients which constitute this energy? How far can they be combined with those other ingredients, which constitute safety in the republican sense? And how far does this combination characterize the plan which has been reported by the convention?

The ingredients which constitute energy in the executive, are, unity; duration; an adequate provision for its support; competent powers.

The ingredients which constitute safety in the republican sense, are, a due dependence on the people; a due responsibility.

Those politicians and statesmen who have been the most celebrated for the soundness of their principles, and for the justness of their views, have declared in favour of a single executive, and a numerous legislature. They have, with great propriety, considered energy as the most necessary qualification of the former, and have regarded this as most applicable to power in a single hand; while they have, with equal propriety, considered the latter as best adapted to deliberation and wisdom, and best calculated to conciliate the confidence of the people, and to secure their privileges and interests.

That unity is conducive to energy, will not be disputed. Decision, activity, secrecy, and despatch, will generally characterize the proceedings of one man, in a much more eminent degree than the proceedings of any greater number; and in proportion as the number is increased, these qualities will be diminished.

This unity may be destroyed in two ways; either by vesting the power in two or more magistrates, of equal dignity and authority; or by vesting it ostensibly in one man, subject, in whole or in part, to the control and cooperation of others, in the capacity of counsellors to him. Of the first, the two consuls of Rome may serve as an example: of the last, we shall find examples in the constitutions of several of the states. New York and New Jersey, if I recollect right, are the only states which have intrusted the executive authority wholly to single men.* Both these methods of destroying the unity of the executive have their partizans; but the votaries of an executive council are the most numerous. They are both liable, if not to equal, to similar objections, and may in most lights be examined in conjunction.

---

*New York has no council except for the single purpose of appointing to offices; New Jersey has a council, whom the governor may consult. But I think, from the terms of the constitution, their resolutions do not bind him [Hamilton's note].

The experience of other nations will afford little instruction on this head. As far, however, as it teaches any thing, it teaches us not to be enamoured of plurality in the executive. We have seen that the Achaeans, on an experiment of two praetors, were induced to abolish one. The Roman history records many instances of mischiefs to the republic from the dissentions between the consuls, and between the military tribunes, who were at times substituted to the consuls. But it gives us no specimens of any peculiar advantages derived to the state, from the plurality of those magistrates. That the dissentions between them were not more frequent or more fatal, is matter of astonishment, until we advert to the singular position in which the republic was almost continually placed, and to the prudent policy pointed out by the circumstances of the state, and pursued by the consuls, of making a division of the government between them. The patricians, engaged in a perpetual struggle with the plebeians, for the preservation of their ancient authorities and dignities; the consuls, who were generally chosen out of the former body, were commonly united by the personal interest they had in the defence of the privileges of their order. In addition to this motive of union, after the arms of the republic had considerably expanded the bounds of its empire, it became an established custom with the consuls to divide the administration between themselves by lot; one of them remaining at Rome to govern the city and its environs; the other taking the command in the more distant provinces. This expedient must, no doubt, have had great influence in preventing those collisions and rivalships which might otherwise have embroiled the republic.

But quitting the dim light of historical research, and attaching ourselves purely to the dictates of reason and good sense, we shall discover much greater cause to reject, than to approve, the idea of plurality in the executive, under any modification whatever.

Wherever two or more persons are engaged in any common enterprize or pursuit, there is always danger of difference of opinion. If it be a public trust or office, in which they are clothed with equal dignity and authority, there is peculiar danger of personal emulation and even animosity. From either, and especially from all these causes, the most bitter dissentions are apt to spring. Whenever these happen, they lessen the respectability, weaken the authority, and distract the plans and operations of those whom they divide. If they should unfortunately assail the supreme executive magistracy of a country, consisting of a plurality of persons, they might impede or frustrate the most important measures of the government, in the most critical emergencies of the state. And what is still worse, they might split the community into violent and irreconcilable factions, adhering differently to the different individuals who composed the magistracy.

Men often oppose a thing, merely because they have had no agency in planning it, or because it may have been planned by those whom they dislike. But if they have been consulted, and have happened to disapprove, opposition then becomes, in their estimation, an indispensable duty of self-love. They seem to think themselves bound in honor, and by all the motives of personal infallibility, to defeat the success of what has been resolved upon, contrary to their sentiments. Men of upright and benevolent tempers have too many opportunities of remarking, with horror, to what desperate lengths this disposition is sometimes carried, and how often the great interests of society are sacrificed to the vanity, to the conceit, and to the obstinacy of individuals, who have credit enough to make their passions and their caprices interesting to mankind. Perhaps the question now before the public may, in its consequences, afford melancholy proofs of the effects of this despicable frailty, or rather detestable vice in the human character.

Upon the principles of a free government, inconveniences from the source just mentioned, must necessarily be submitted to in the formation of the legislature; but it is unnecessary, and therefore unwise, to introduce them into the constitution of the executive. It is here too, that they may be most pernicious. In the legislature, promptitude of decision is oftener an evil than a benefit. The differences of opinion, and the jarring of parties in that department of the government, though they may sometimes obstruct salutary plans, yet often promote deliberation and circumspection; and serve to check excesses in the majority. When a resolution too is once taken, the opposition must be at an end. That resolution is a law, and resistance to it punishable. But no favorable circumstances palliate, or atone for the disadvantages of dissention in the executive department. Here they are pure and unmixed. There is no point at which they cease to operate. They serve to embarrass and weaken the execution of the plan or measure to which they relate, from the first step to the final conclusion of it. They constantly counteract those qualities in the executive, which are the most necessary ingredients in its composition . . . vigour and expedition; and this without any counterbalancing good. In the conduct of war, in which the energy of the executive is the bulwark of the national security, every thing would be to be apprehended from its plurality.

It must be confessed, that these observations apply with principal weight to the first case supposed, that is, to a plurality of magistrates of equal dignity and authority; a scheme, the advocates for which are not likely to form a numerous sect: but they apply, though not with equal, yet with considerable weight, to the project of a council, whose concurrence is made constitutionally necessary to the operations of the ostensible executive. An artful cabal in that council, would be able to distract and to enervate the whole system of administration. If no such cabal should exist, the mere diversity of views and opinions would alone be sufficient to tincture the exercise of the executive authority with a spirit of habitual feebleness and dilatoriness.

But one of the weightiest objections to a plurality in the executive, and which lies as much against the last as the first plan, is, that it tends to conceal faults, and destroy responsibility. Responsibility is of two kinds, to censure and to punishment. The first is the most important of the two; especially in an elective office. Men in public trust will much oftener act in such a manner as to render them unworthy of being any longer trusted, than in such a manner as to make them obnoxious to legal punishment. But the multiplication of the executive adds to the difficulty of detection in either case. It often becomes impossible, amidst mutual accusations, to determine on whom the blame or the punishment of a pernicious measure, or series of pernicious measures, ought really to fall. It is shifted from one to another with so much dexterity, and under such plausible appearances, that the public opinion is left in suspense about the real author. The circumstances which may have led to any national miscarriage or misfortune, are sometimes so complicated, that where there are a number of actors who may have had different degrees and kinds of agency, though we may clearly see upon the whole that there has been mismanagement, yet it may be impracticable to pronounce, to whose account the evil which may have been incurred is truly chargeable.

"I was overruled by my council. The council were so divided in their opinions, that it was impossible to obtain any better resolution on the point." These and similar pretexts are constantly at hand, whether true or false. And who is there that will either take the trouble, or incur the odium, of a strict scrutiny into the secret springs of the transaction? Should there be found a citizen zealous enough to undertake the unpromising task, if there happen to be a collusion between the parties concerned, how easy is it to clothe the circumstances with so much ambiguity, as to render it uncertain what was the precise conduct of any of those parties?

In the single instance in which the governor of this state is coupled with a council, that is, in the appointment to offices, we have seen the mischiefs of it in the view now under consideration. Scandalous appointments to important offices have been made. Some cases indeed have been so flagrant, that ALL PARTIES have agreed in the impropriety of the thing. When inquiry has been made, the blame has been laid by the governor on the members of the council; who, on their part, have charged it upon his nomination: while the people remain altogether at a loss to determine by whose influence their interests have been committed to hands so manifestly improper. In tenderness to individuals, I forbear to descend to particulars.

It is evident from these considerations, that the plurality of the executive tends to deprive the people of the two greatest securities they can have for the faithful exercise of any delegated power. *First.* The restraints of public opinion, which lose their efficacy as well on account of the division of the censure attendant on bad measures among a number, as on account of the uncertainty on whom it ought to fall; and *secondly,* the opportunity of discovering with facility and clearness the misconduct of the persons they trust, in order either to their removal from office, or to their actual punishment, in cases which admit of it.

In England, the king is a perpetual magistrate; and it is a maxim which has obtained for the sake of the public peace, that he is unaccountable for his administration, and his person sacred. Nothing, therefore, can be wiser in that kingdom, than to annex to the king a constitutional council, who may be responsible to the nation for the advice they give. Without this, there would be no responsibility whatever in the executive department, an idea inadmissible in a free government. But even there, the king is not bound by the resolutions of his council, though they are answerable for the advice they give. He is the absolute master of his own conduct in the exercise of his office; and may observe or disregard the counsel given to him at his sole discretion.

But in a republic, where every magistrate ought to be personally responsible for his behaviour in office, the reason which in the British constitution dictates the propriety of a council, not only ceases to apply, but turns against the institution. In the monarchy of Great Britain, it furnishes a substitute for the prohibited responsibility of the chief magistrate; which serves in some degree as a hostage to the national justice for his good behaviour. In the American republic it would serve to destroy, or would greatly diminish the intended and necessary responsibility of the chief magistrate himself.

The idea of a council to the executive, which has so generally obtained in the state constitutions, has been derived from that maxim of republican jealousy which considers power as safer in the hands of a number of men, than of a single man. If the maxim should be admitted to be applicable to the case, I should contend, that the advantage on that side would not counterbalance the numerous disadvantages on the opposite side. But I do not think the rule at all applicable to the executive power. I clearly concur in opinion in this particular with a writer whom the celebrated Junius pronounces to be "deep, solid, and ingenious," that "the executive power is more easily confined when it is ONE:"* that it is far more safe there should be a single object for the jealousy and watchfulness of the people; in a word, that all multiplication of the executive, is rather dangerous than friendly to liberty.

A little consideration will satisfy us, that the species of security sought for in the multiplication of the executive, is unattainable. Numbers must be so great as to render combination difficult; or they are rather a source of danger than of security. The united credit

---

*De Lolme [Hamilton's note]. The reference is to political philosopher Jean Louis De Lolme (1740–1806).

and influence of several individuals, must be more formidable to liberty, than the credit and influence of either of them separately. When power, therefore, is placed in the hands of so small a number of men, as to admit of their interests and views being easily combined in a common enterprise, by an artful leader, it becomes more liable to abuse, and more dangerous when abused, than if it be lodged in the hands of one man; who, from the very circumstance of his being alone, will be more narrowly watched and more readily suspected, and who cannot unite so great a mass of influence as when he is associated with others. The decemvirs of Rome, whose name denotes their number,* were more to be dreaded in their usurpation than any ONE of them would have been. No person would think of proposing an executive much more numerous than that body; from six to a dozen have been suggested for the number of the council. The extreme of these numbers, is not too great for an easy combination; and from such a combination America would have more to fear, than from the ambition of any single individual. A council to a magistrate, who is himself responsible for what he does, are generally nothing better than a clog upon his good intentions; are often the instruments and accomplices of his bad, and are almost always a cloak to his faults.

I forbear to dwell upon the subject of expense; though it be evident that if the council should be numerous enough to answer the principal end aimed at by the institution, the salaries of the members, who must be drawn from their homes to reside at the seat of government, would form an item in the catalogue of public expenditures, too serious to be incurred for an object of equivocal utility.

I will only add, that prior to the appearance of the constitution, I rarely met with an intelligent man from any of the states, who did not admit as the result of experience, that the unity of the executive of this state was one of the best of the distinguishing features of our constitution.

PUBLIUS

---

*Ten [Hamilton's note].

—Alexander Hamilton—
THE FEDERALIST NO. 78
JUNE 14, 1788

WE PROCEED NOW TO an examination of the judiciary department of the proposed government.

In unfolding the defects of the existing confederation, the utility and necessity of a federal judicature have been clearly pointed out. It is the less necessary to recapitulate the considerations there urged, as the propriety of the institution in the abstract is not disputed: the only questions which have been raised being relative to the manner of constituting it, and to its extent. To these points, therefore, our observations shall be confined.

The manner of constituting it seems to embrace these several objects: 1st. The mode of appointing the judges. 2d. The tenure by which they are to hold their places. 3d. The partition of the judiciary authority between different courts, and their relations to each other.

First. As to the mode of appointing the judges: This is the same with that of appointing the officers of the union in general, and has been so fully discussed in the two last numbers, that nothing can be said here which would not be useless repetition.

Second. As to the tenure by which the judges are to hold their places: This chiefly concerns their duration in office; the provisions for their support; the precautions for their responsibility.

According to the plan of the convention, all the judges who may be appointed by the United States are to hold their offices *during good behaviour,* which is conformable to the most approved of the state constitutions and among the rest, to that of this state. Its propriety having been drawn into question by the adversaries of that plan, is no light symptom of the rage for objection, which disorders their imaginations and judgments. The standard of good behaviour for the continuance in office of the judicial magistracy is certainly one of the most valuable of the modern improvements in the practice of government. In a monarchy, it is an excellent barrier to the despotism of the prince: in a republic it is a no less excellent barrier to the encroachments and oppressions of the representative body. And it is the best expedient which can be devised in any government, to secure a steady, upright, and impartial administration of the laws.

Whoever attentively considers the different departments of power must perceive, that, in a government in which they are separated from each other, the judiciary, from the nature of its functions, will always be the least dangerous to the political rights of the constitution; because it will be least in a capacity to annoy or injure them. The executive not only dispenses the honours, but holds the sword of the community; the legislature not only commands the purse, but prescribes the rules by which the duties and rights of every citizen are to be regulated; the judiciary, on the contrary, has no influence over either the sword or the purse; no direction either of the strength or of the wealth of the society; and can take no active resolution whatever. It may truly be said to have neither FORCE nor WILL, but merely judgment; and must ultimately depend upon the aid of the executive arm even for the efficacy of its judgments.

This simple view of the matter suggests several important consequences. It proves incontestably that the judiciary is beyond comparison the weakest of the three departments of power;* that it can never attack with success either of the other two; and that all possible care is requisite to enable it to defend itself against their attacks. It equally proves, that though individual oppression may now and then proceed from the courts of justice, the general liberty of the people can never be endangered from that quarter: I mean, so long as the judiciary remains truly distinct from both the legislature and the executive. For I agree that "there is no liberty, if the power of judging be not separated from the legislative and executive powers."† And it proves, in the last place, that as liberty can have nothing to fear from the judiciary alone, but would have everything to fear from its union with either of the other departments; that as all the effects of such a union must ensue from a dependence of the former on the latter, notwithstanding a nominal and apparent separation;

---

*The celebrated Montesquieu, speaking of them says, "of the three powers above mentioned, the JUDICIARY is next to nothing." Spirit of Laws, vol. I, page 186 [Hamilton's note].

†Idem. page 181 [Hamilton's note].

that as from the natural feebleness of the judiciary, it is in continual jeopardy of being overpowered, awed or influenced by its coordinate branches; and that as nothing can contribute so much to its firmness and independence, as permanency in office, this quality may therefore be justly regarded as an indispensable ingredient in its constitution; and in a great measure as the citadel of the public justice and the public security.

The complete independence of the courts of justice is peculiarly essential in a limited constitution. By a limited constitution I understand one which contains certain specified exceptions to the legislative authority; such for instance as that it shall pass no bills of attainder, no *ex post facto* laws, and the like. Limitations of this kind can be preserved in practice no other way than through the medium of the courts of justice; whose duty it must be to declare all acts contrary to the manifest tenor of the constitution void. Without this, all the reservations of particular rights or privileges would amount to nothing.

Some perplexity respecting the rights of the courts to pronounce legislative acts void, because contrary to the constitution, has arisen from an imagination that the doctrine would imply a superiority of the judiciary to the legislative power. It is urged that the authority which can declare the acts of another void, must necessarily be superior to the one whose acts may be declared void. As this doctrine is of great importance in all the American constitutions, a brief discussion of the grounds on which it rests cannot be unacceptable.

There is no position which depends on clearer principles, than that every act of a delegated authority, contrary to the tenor of the commission under which it is exercised, is void. No legislative act therefore contrary to the constitution can be valid. To deny this would be to affirm that the deputy is greater than his principal; that the servant is above his master; that the representatives of the people are superior to the people themselves; that men acting by virtue of powers may do not only what their powers do not authorize, but what they forbid.

If it be said that the legislative body are themselves the constitutional judges of their own powers, and that the construction they put upon them is conclusive upon the other departments, it may be answered, that this cannot be the natural presumption, where it is not to be collected from any particular provisions in the constitution. It is not otherwise to be supposed that the constitution could intend to enable the representatives of the people to substitute their *will* to that of their constituents. It is far more rational to suppose that the courts were designed to be an intermediate body between the people and the legislature, in order, among other things, to keep the latter within the limits assigned to their authority. The interpretation of the laws is the proper and peculiar province of the courts. A constitution is in fact, and must be, regarded by the judges as a fundamental law. It therefore belongs to them to ascertain its meaning as well as the meaning of any particular act proceeding from the legislative body. If there should happen to be an irreconcilable variance between the two, that which has the superior obligation and validity ought of course to be preferred; or in other words, the constitution ought to be preferred to the statute, the intention of the people to the intention of their agents.

Nor does this conclusion by any means suppose a superiority of the judicial to the legislative power. It only supposes that the power of the people is superior to both; and that where the will of the legislature declared in its statutes, stands in opposition to that of the people declared in the constitution, the judges ought to be governed by the latter, rather than the former. They ought to regulate their decisions by the fundamental laws, rather than by those which are not fundamental.

This exercise of judicial discretion in determining between two contradictory laws, is exemplified in a familiar instance. It not uncommonly happens, that there are two statutes existing at one time, clashing in whole or in part with each other, and neither of them containing any repealing clause or expression. In such a case, it is the province of the courts to liquidate and fix their meaning and operation: So far as they can by any fair construction be reconciled to each other; reason and law conspire to dictate that this should be done. Where this is impracticable, it becomes a matter of necessity to give effect to one, in exclusion of the other. The rule which has obtained in the courts for determining their relative validity is that the last in order of time shall be preferred to the first. But this is a mere rule of construction, not derived from any positive law, but from the nature and reason of the thing. It is a rule not enjoined upon the courts by legislative provision, but adopted by themselves, as consonant to truth and propriety, for the direction of their conduct as interpreters of the law. They thought it reasonable, that between the interfering acts of an *equal* authority, that which was the last indication of its will, should have the preference.

But in regard to the interfering acts of a superior and subordinate authority, of an original and derivative power, the nature and reason of the thing indicate the converse of that rule as proper to be followed. They teach us that the prior act of a superior ought to be preferred to the subsequent act of an inferior and subordinate authority; and that, accordingly, whenever a particular statute contravenes the constitution, it will be the duty of the judicial tribunals to adhere to the latter, and disregard the former.

It can be of no weight to say, that the courts on the pretence of a repugnancy, may substitute their own pleasure to the constitutional intentions of the legislature. This might as well happen in the case of two contradictory statutes; or it might as well happen in every adjudication upon any single statute. The courts must declare the sense of the law; and if they should be disposed to exercise WILL instead of JUDGMENT, the consequence would equally be the substitution of their pleasure to that of the legislative body. The observation, if it proved anything, would prove that there ought to be no judges distinct from that body.

If then the courts of justice are to be considered as the bulwarks of a limited constitution against legislative encroachments, this consideration will afford a strong argument for the permanent tenure of judicial offices, since nothing will contribute so much as this to that independent spirit in the judges, which must be essential to the faithful performance of so arduous a duty.

This independence of the judges is equally requisite to guard the constitution and the rights of individuals from the effects of those ill humours which the arts of designing men, or the influence of particular conjunctures, sometimes disseminate among the people themselves, and which, though they speedily give place to better information and more deliberate reflection, have a tendency, in the mean time, to occasion dangerous innovations in the government, and serious oppressions of the minor party in the community. Though I trust the friends of the proposed constitution will never concur with its enemies,* in questioning that fundamental principle of republican government, which admits the right of the people to alter or abolish the established constitution whenever they find it inconsistent with their happiness; yet it is not to be inferred from this principle, that the representatives of the people, whenever a momentary inclination happens to lay hold of a majority of their constituents incompatible with the provisions in the existing constitution, would, on that account, be justifiable in a violation of those provisions; or that the courts would be under a greater obligation to connive at infractions in this shape, than when they had proceeded wholly from the cabals of the representative body. Until the people have, by some solemn and authoritative act, annulled or changed the established form, it is binding upon themselves collectively, as well as individually: and no presumption, or even knowledge of their sentiments, can warrant their representatives in a departure from it, prior to such an act. But it is easy to see, that it would require an uncommon portion of fortitude in the judges to do their duty as faithful guardians of the constitution, where legislative invasions of it had been instigated by the major voice of the community.

But it is not with a view to infractions of the constitution only, that the independence of the judges may be an essential safe-guard against the effects of occasional ill humours in the society. These sometimes extend no farther than to the injury of the private rights of particular classes of citizens, by unjust and partial laws. Here also the firmness of the judicial magistracy is of vast importance in mitigating the severity and confining the operation of such laws. It not only serves to moderate the immediate mischiefs of those which may have been passed, but it operates as a check upon the legislative body in passing them; who, perceiving that obstacles to the success of an iniquitous intention are to be expected from the scruples of the courts, are in a manner compelled, by the very motives of the injustice they meditate, to qualify their attempts. This is a circumstance calculated to have more influence upon the character of our governments, than but few may imagine. The benefits of the integrity and moderation of the judiciary have already been felt in

---

*Vide Protest of the minority of the convention of Pennsylvania, Martin's speech, &c. [Hamilton's note].

more states than one; and though they may have displeased those whose sinister expectations they may have disappointed, they must have commanded the esteem and applause of all the virtuous and disinterested. Considerate men, of every description, ought to prize whatever will tend to beget or fortify that temper in the courts; as no man can be sure that he may not be tomorrow the victim of a spirit of injustice, by which he may be a gainer to-day. And every man must now feel, that the inevitable tendency of such a spirit is to sap the foundations of public and private confidence, and to introduce in its stead universal distrust and distress.

That inflexible and uniform adherence to the rights of the constitution, and of individuals, which we perceive to be indispensable in the courts of justice, can certainly not be expected from judges who hold their offices by a temporary commission. Periodical appointments, however regulated, or by whomsoever made, would, in some way or other, be fatal to their necessary independence. If the power of making them was committed either to the executive or legislature, there would be danger of an improper complaisance to the branch which possessed it; if to both, there would be an unwillingness to hazard the displeasure of either; if to the people, or to persons chosen by them for the special purpose, there would be too great a disposition to consult popularity, to justify a reliance that nothing would be consulted but the constitution and the laws.

There is yet a further and a weighty reason for the permanency of judicial offices; which is deducible from the nature of the qualifications they require. It has been frequently remarked, with great propriety, that a voluminous code of laws is one of the inconveniences necessarily connected with the advantages of a free government. To avoid an arbitrary discretion in the courts, it is indispensable that they should be bound down by strict rules and precedents, which serve to define and point out their duty in every particular case that comes before them; and it will readily be conceived, from the variety of controversies which grow out of the folly and wickedness of mankind, that the records of those precedents must unavoidably swell to a very considerable bulk, and must demand long and laborious study to acquire a competent knowledge of them. Hence it is, that there can be but few men in the society, who will have sufficient skill in the laws to qualify them for the stations of judges. And making the proper deductions for the ordinary depravity of human nature, the number must be still smaller of those who unite the requisite integrity with the requisite knowledge. These considerations apprize us, that the government can have no great option between fit characters; and that a temporary duration in office, which would naturally discourage such characters from quitting a lucrative line of practice to accept a seat on the bench, would have a tendency to throw the administration of justice into hands less able, and less well qualified, to conduct it with utility and dignity. In the present circumstances of this country, and in those in which it is likely to be for a long time to come, the disadvantages on this score would be greater than they may at first sight appear; but it must be confessed, that they are far inferior to those which present themselves under the other aspects of the subject.

Upon the whole, there can be no room to doubt, that the convention acted wisely in copying from the models of those constitutions which have established *good behaviour* as the tenure of judicial offices, in point of duration; and that, so far from being blameable on this account, their plan would have been inexcusably defective, if it had wanted this important feature of good government. The experience of Great Britain affords an illustrious comment on the excellence of the institution.

PUBLIUS

THE PROBLEM OF DECLARING RIGHTS

SHORTLY BEFORE THE CONSTITUTIONAL Convention adjourned, James Madison sent Thomas Jefferson, then serving as American minister to France, a gloomy letter, predicting that the completed Constitution "will neither effectually answer its national object nor prevent the local mischiefs which every where excite disgusts against the state governments. The grounds of this opinion will be the subject of a future letter." Madison waited another seven weeks before fulfilling this promise. When he did, in a lengthy missive of October

24, 1787, he went to great lengths to justify the most controversial proposal he had presented at Philadelphia: to give the national government a negative (we would say, a veto) on all state laws, which it could use both to protect national laws against interference from the states and to intervene within the individual states to defend the rights of minorities.

Madison's letter was the first in a series the two men exchanged—often with great delays, due to the vagaries of the Atlantic passage—over the next year and a half. It is perhaps the single most fascinating exchange of political views in all of American history, conducted by two friends who respected and admired each other, but who sometimes reasoned very differently. Jefferson was open to the idea that the proposed Constitution could benefit from modest amendments, and he particularly favored the idea of adding articles explicitly protecting particular rights to the text the Convention had proposed. Madison worried that Anti-Federalists would exploit the idea of adding amendments protective of rights to advance other structural changes in the Constitution.

But these letters also illustrate a profound development in American thinking about rights more generally. Before the Revolution, Americans would have said that their rights were derived from multiple sources. The adoption of bills of rights like those that accompanied the early state constitutions did not *create* or *establish* the rights enumerated but merely confirmed their existence. By 1787, however, the idea that a written constitution would have the status of supreme law offered a means of resolving the ambiguities that inevitably arose by appealing to nature or custom as the source of rights. A right that was explicitly mentioned in the text of a constitution would now possess the highest legal status available. But this opened other questions. Would that relegate rights left unmentioned to an inferior, more precarious status? And would it not also require the drafters of a bill of rights to be extremely careful in their use of language?

These were some of the questions that Madison and Jefferson canvassed in these absorbing letters. But they also explored other issues. Where did the real dangers to rights arise? And who could be held most accountable for their protection?

In the summer of 1789, as the First Congress was debating the amendments Madison ultimately proposed, the correspondence took a new twist. In Paris, Jefferson was observing the opening phase of the French Revolution and consulting with those liberals, like the Marquis de Lafayette, who favored American-style solutions for their nation's constitutional problems. In the wake of these conversations, Jefferson wrote Madison a remarkable letter, posing the question "whether one generation of men has a right to bind another." In the immediate context, the question was how great a political obligation the French reformers turning into revolutionaries owed to the legal structures they had inherited, with their vast concentration of aristocratic privilege. But in Madison's thoughtful reply, this question in turn pivoted around the advantages and disadvantages of thinking of constitutions as relatively fixed and stable documents.

—James Madison—
LETTER TO THOMAS JEFFERSON (EXCERPT)
OCTOBER 24 AND NOVEMBER 1, 1787

DEAR SIR,

. . . You will herewith receive the result of the Convention, which continued its session till the 17th of September. I take the liberty of making some observations on the subject which will help to make up a letter, if they should answer no other purpose.

It appeared to be the sincere and unanimous wish of the Convention to cherish and preserve the Union of the States. No proposition was made, no suggestion was thrown out in favor of a partition of the Empire into two or more Confederacies.

It was generally agreed that the objects of the Union could not be secured by any system founded on the principle of a confederation of sovereign States. A *voluntary* observance of the federal law by all the members could never be hoped for. A *compulsive* one could evidently never be reduced to practice, and if it could, involved equal calamities to the innocent and the guilty, the necessity of a military force both obnoxious and dangerous, and in general, a scene resembling much more a civil war, than the administration of a regular Government.

Hence was embraced the alternative of a government which instead of operating, on the States, should operate without their intervention on the individuals composing them: and hence the change in the principle and proportion of representation.

This ground-work being laid, the great objects which presented themselves were 1. to unite a proper energy in the Executive and a proper stability in the Legislative departments, with the essential characters of Republican Government. 2. To draw a line of demarkation which would give to the General Government every power requisite for general purposes, and leave to the States every power which might be most beneficially administered by them. 3.

To provide for the different interests of different parts of the Union. 4. To adjust the clashing pretensions of the large and small States. Each of these objects was pregnant with difficulties. The whole of them together formed a task more difficult than can be well conceived by those who were not concerned in the execution of it. Adding to these considerations the natural diversity of human opinions on all new and complicated subjects, it is impossible to consider the degree of concord which ultimately prevailed as less than a miracle.

The first of these objects as it respects the Executive, was peculiarly embarrassing. On the question whether it should consist of a single person, or a plurality of co-ordinate members, on the mode of appointment, on the duration in office, on the degree of power, on the re-eligibility, tedious and reiterated discussions took place. The plurality of co-ordinate members had finally but few advocates. Governour Randolph was at the head of them. The modes of appointment proposed were various, as by the people at large—by electors chosen by the people—by the Executives of the States—by the Congress, some preferring a joint ballot of the two Houses—some a separate concurrent ballot allowing to each a negative on the other house—some a nomination of several canditates by one House, out of whom a choice should be made by the other. Several other modifications were started. The expedient at length adopted seemed to give pretty general satisfaction to the members. As to the duration in office, a few would have preferred a tenure during good behaviour—a considerable number would have done so in case an easy and effectual removal by impeachment could be settled. It was much agitated whether a long term, seven years for example, with a subsequent and perpetual ineligibility, or a short term with a capacity to be re-elected, should be fixed. In favor of the first opinion were urged the danger of a gradual degeneracy of re-elections from time to time, into first a life and then a hereditary tenure, and the favorable effect of an incapacity to be reappointed, on the independent exercise of the Executive authority. On the other side it was contended that the prospect of necessary degradation would discourage the most dignified characters from aspiring to the office, would take away the principal motive to the faithful discharge of its duties. The hope of being rewarded with a reappointment, would stimulate ambition to violent efforts for holding over the constitutional term, and instead of producing an independent administration, and a firmer defence of the constitutional rights of the department, would render the officer more indifferent to the importance of a place which he would soon be obliged to quit for ever, and more ready to yield to the incroachments of the Legislature of which he might again be a member.

The questions concerning the degree of power turned chiefly on the appointment to offices, and the controul on the Legislature. An *absolute* appointment to all offices—to some offices—to no offices, formed the scale of opinions on the first point. On the second, some contended for an absolute negative, as the only possible mean of reducing to practice, the theory of a free government which forbids a mixture of the Legislative and Executive powers. Others would be content with a revisionary power to be overruled by three fourths of both Houses. It was warmly urged that the judiciary department should be associated in the revision. The idea of some was that a separate revision should be given to the two departments—that if either objected two thirds; if both three fourths, should be necessary to overrule.

In forming the Senate, the great anchor of the Government, the questions as they came within the first object turned mostly on the mode of appointment, and the duration of it. The different modes proposed were, 1. by the House of Representatives, 2. by the Executive, 3. by electors chosen by the people for the purpose, 4. by the State Legislatures. On the point of duration, the propositions descended from good behavior to four years, through the intermediate terms of nine, seven, six and five years. The election of the other branch was first determined to be triennial, and afterwards reduced to biennial.

The second object, the due partition of power, between the General and local Governments, was perhaps of all, the most nice and difficult. A few contended for an entire abolition of the States; Some for indefinite power of Legislation in the Congress, with a negative on the laws of the States, some for such a power without a negative, some for a limited power of legislation, with such a negative: the majority finally for a limited power without the negative. The question with regard to the Negative underwent repeated discussions, and was finally rejected by a bare majority. As I formerly intimated to you my opinion in favor of this ingredient, I will take this occasion of explaining myself on the subject. Such a check on the States appears to me necessary 1. to prevent encroachments on the General authority, 2. to prevent instability and injustice in the legislation of the States.

1. Without such a check in the whole over the parts, our system involves the evil of *imperia in imperio*.* If a compleat supremacy some where is not necessary in every Society, a controuling power at least is so, by which the general authority may be defended against encroachments of the subordinate authorities, and by which the latter may be restrained from encroachments on each other. If the supremacy of the British Parliament is not necessary as has been contended, for the harmony of that Empire, it is evident I think that without the royal negative or some equivalent controul, the unity of the system would be destroyed. The want of some such provision seems to have been mortal to the antient Confederacies, and to be the disease of the modern. Of the Lycian Confederacy little is known. That of the Amphyctions is well known to have been rendered of little use whilst it lasted, and in the end to have been destroyed by the predominance of the local over the federal authority. The same observation may be made, on the authority of Polybius, with regard to the Achæan League. The Helvetic System scarcely amounts to a confederacy and is distinguished by too many peculiarities to be a ground of comparison. The case of the United Netherlands is in point. The authority of a Statholder, the influence of a standing army, the common interest in the conquered possessions, the pressure of surrounding danger, the guarantee of foreign powers, are not sufficient to secure the authority and interests of the generality, against the antifederal tendency of the provincial sovereignties. The German Empire is another example. A Hereditary chief with vast independent resources of wealth and power, a federal Diet, with ample parchment authority, a regular Judiciary establishment, the influence of the neighbourhood of great and formidable Nations, have been found unable either to maintain the subordination of the members, or to prevent their mutual contests and encroachments. Still more to the purpose is our own experience both during the war and since the peace. Encroachments of the States on

---

*"A state within a state" or "a government within a government" (Latin); this familiar maxim meant that two sovereign bodies could not coexist within a single polity.

the general authority, sacrifices of national to local interests, interferences of the measures of different States, form a great part of the history of our political system. It may be said that the new Constitution is founded on different principles, and will have a different operation. I admit the difference to be material. It presents the aspect rather of a feudal system of republics, if such a phrase may be used, than of a Confederacy of independent States. And what has been the progress and event of the feudal Constitutions? In all of them a continual struggle between the head and the inferior members, until a final victory has been gained in some instances by one, in others, by the other of them. In one respect indeed there is a remarkable variance between the two cases. In the feudal system the sovereign, though limited, was independent; and having no particular sympathy of interests with the great Barons, his ambition had as full play as theirs in the mutual projects of usurpation. In the American Constitution the general authority will be derived entirely from the subordinate authorities. The Senate will represent the States in their political capacity, the other House will represent the people of the States in their individual capacity. The former will be accountable to their constituents at moderate, the latter at short periods. The President also derives his appointment from the States, and is periodically accountable to them. This dependence of the General, on the local authorities seems effectually to guard the latter against any dangerous encroachments of the former: Whilst the latter within their respective limits, will be continually sensible of the abridgment of their power, and be stimulated by ambition to resume the surrendered portion of it. We find the representatives of counties and corporations in the Legislatures of the States, much more disposed to sacrifice the aggregate interest, and even authority, to the local views of their Constituents, than the latter to the former. I mean not by these remarks to insinuate that an esprit de corps will not exist in the national Government, that opportunities may not occur of extending its jurisdiction in some points. I mean only that the danger of encroachments is much greater from the other side, and that the impossibility of dividing powers of legislation, in such a manner, as to be free from different constructions by different interests, or even from ambiguity in the judgment of the impartial, requires some such expedient as I contend for. Many illustrations might be given of this impossibility. How long has it taken to fix, and how imperfectly is yet fixed the legislative power of corporations, though that power is subordinate in the most compleat manner? The line of distinction between the power of regulating trade and that of drawing revenue from it, which was once considered as the barrier of our liberties, was found on fair discussion, to be absolutely undefinable. No distinction seems to be more obvious than that between spiritual and temporal matters. Yet wherever they have been made objects of Legislation, they have clashed and contended with each other, till one or the other has gained the supremacy. Even the boundaries between the Executive, Legislative and Judiciary powers, though in general so strongly marked in themselves, consist in many instances of mere shades of difference. It may be said that the Judicial authority under our new system will keep the States within their proper limits, and supply the place of a negative on their laws. The answer is that it is more convenient to prevent the passage of a law, than to declare it void after it is passed; that this will be particularly the case where the law aggrieves individuals, who may be unable to support an appeal against a State to the supreme Judiciary, that a State which would violate the Legislative rights of the Union, would not be very ready to obey a Judicial decree in support of them, and that a recurrence to force, which in the event of disobedience would be necessary, is an evil which the new Constitution meant to exclude as far as possible.

2. A Constitutional negative on the laws of the States seems equally necessary to secure individuals against encroachments on their rights. The mutability of the laws of the States is found to be a serious evil. The injustice of them has been so frequent and so flagrant as to alarm the most stedfast friends of Republicanism. I am persuaded I do not err in saying that the evils issuing from these sources contributed more to that uneasiness which produced the Convention, and prepared the public mind for a general reform, than those which accrued to our national character and interest from the inadequacy of the Confederation to its immediate objects. A reform therefore which does not make provision for private rights, must be materially defective. The restraints against paper emissions, and violations of contracts are not sufficient. Supposing them to be effectual as far as they go, they are short of the mark. Injustice may be effected by such an infinitude of legislative expedients, that where the disposition exists it can only be controuled by

some provision which reaches all cases whatsoever. The partial provision made, supposes the disposition which will evade it. It may be asked how private rights will be more secure under the Guardianship of the General Government than under the State Governments, since they are both founded on the republican principle which refers the ultimate decision to the will of the majority, and are distinguished rather by the extent within which they will operate, than by any material difference in their structure. A full discussion of this question would, if I mistake not, unfold the true principles of Republican Government, and prove in contradiction to the concurrent opinions of theoretical writers, that this form of Government, in order to effect its purposes must operate not within a small but an extensive sphere. I will state some of the ideas which have occurred to me on this subject. Those who contend for a simple Democracy, or a pure republic, actuated by the sense of the majority, and operating within narrow limits, assume or suppose a case which is altogether fictitious. They found their reasoning on the idea, that the people composing the Society enjoy not only an equality of political rights; but that they have all precisely the same interests and the same feelings in every respect. Were this in reality the case, their reasoning would be conclusive. The interest of the majority would be that of the minority also; the decisions could only turn on mere opinion concerning the good of the whole of which the major voice would be the safest criterion; and within a small sphere, this voice could be most easily collected and the public affairs most accurately managed. We know however that no Society ever did or can consist of so homogeneous a mass of Citizens. In the savage State indeed, an approach is made towards it; but in that state little or no Government is necessary. In all civilized Societies, distinctions are various and unavoidable. A distinction of property results from that very protection which a free Government gives to unequal faculties of acquiring it. There will be rich and poor; creditors and debtors; a landed interest, a monied interest, a mercantile interest, a manufacturing interest. These classes may again be subdivided according to the different productions of different situations and soils, and according to different branches of commerce and of manufactures. In addition to these natural distinctions, artificial ones will be founded on accidental differences in political, religious and other opinions, or an attachment to the persons of leading individuals. However erroneous or ridiculous these grounds of dissention and faction may appear to the enlightened Statesman, or the benevolent philosopher, the bulk of mankind who are neither Statesmen nor Philosophers, will continue to view them in a different light. It remains then to be enquired whether a majority having any common interest, or feeling any common passion, will find sufficient motives to restrain them from oppressing the minority. An individual is never allowed to be a judge or even a witness in his own cause. If two individuals are under the biass of interest or enmity against a third, the rights of the latter could never be safely referred to the majority of the three. Will two thousand individuals be less apt to oppress one thousand, or two hundred thousand, one hundred thousand? Three motives only can restrain in such cases. 1. A prudent regard to private or partial good, as essentially involved in the general and permanent good of the whole. This ought no doubt to be sufficient of itself. Experience however shews that it has little effect on individuals, and perhaps still less on a collection of individuals, and least of all on a majority with the public authority in their hands. If the former are ready to forget that honesty is the best policy; the last do more. They often proceed on the converse of the maxim: that whatever is politic is honest. 2. Respect for character. This motive is not found sufficient to restrain individuals from injustice, and loses its efficacy in proportion to the number which is to divide the praise or the blame. Besides as it has reference to public opinion, which is that of the majority, the standard is fixed by those whose conduct is to be measured by it. 3. Religion. The inefficacy of this restraint on individuals is well known. The conduct of every popular assembly, acting on oath, the strongest of religious ties, shews that individuals join without remorse in acts against which their consciences would revolt, if proposed to them separately in their closets. When Indeed Religion is kindled into enthusiasm, its force like that of other passions is increased by the sympathy of a multitude. But enthusiasm is only a temporary state of Religion, and whilst it lasts will hardly be seen with pleasure at the helm. Even in its coolest state, it has been much oftener a motive to oppression than a restraint from it. If then there must be different interests and parties in Society; and a majority when united by a common interest or passion can not be restrained from oppressing the minority, what remedy can be found in a republican Government, where the majority must ultimately decide, but that of giving such an extent to its sphere, that no common interest or passion will be likely to unite a majority of the whole number in an unjust pursuit. In a large Society, the people are broken into so many interests and parties, that a common sentiment is less likely to be felt, and the requisite concert less likely to be formed, by a majority of the whole. The same security seems requisite for the civil as for the religious rights of individuals. If the same sect form a majority and have the power, other sects will be sure to be depressed. Divide et impera, the reprobated axiom of tyranny, is under certain qualifications, the only policy, by which a republic can be administered on just principles. It must be observed however that this doctrine can only hold within a sphere of a mean extent. As in too small a sphere oppressive combinations may be too easily formed against the weaker party; so in too extensive a one a defensive concert may be rendered too difficult against the oppression of those entrusted with the administration. The great desideratum in Government is, so to modify the sovereignty as that it may be sufficiently neutral between different parts of the Society to controul one part from invading the rights of another, and at the same time sufficiently controuled itself, from setting up an interest adverse to that of the entire Society. In absolute monarchies, the Prince may be tolerably neutral towards different classes of his subjects, but may sacrifice the happiness of all to his personal ambition or avarice. In small republics, the sovereign will is controuled from such a sacrifice of the entire Society, but it is not sufficiently neutral towards the parts composing it. In the extended Republic of the United States, the General Government would hold a pretty even balance between the parties of particular States, and be at the same time sufficiently restrained by its dependence on the community, from betraying its general interests.

Begging pardon for this immoderate digression, I return to the third object abovementioned, the adjustment of the different interests of different parts of the Continent. Some contended for an unlimited power over trade including exports as well as imports, and over slaves as well as other imports; some for such a power, provided the concurrence of two thirds of both Houses were required; some for such a qualification of the power, with an exemption of exports and slaves, others for an exemption of exports only. The result is seen in the Constitution. S. Carolina and Georgia were inflexible on the point of the slaves.

The remaining object, created more embarrassment, and a greater alarm for the issue of the Convention than all the rest put together. The little States insisted on retaining their equality in both branches, unless a compleat abolition of the State Governments should take place; and made an equality in the Senate a sine qua non. The large States on the other hand urged that as the new Government was to be drawn principally from the people immediately and was to operate directly on them, not on the States; and consequently as the States would lose that importance which is now proportioned to the importance of their voluntary compliances with the requisitions of Congress, it was necessary that the representation in both Houses should be in proportion to their size. It ended in the compromise which you will see, but very much to the dissatisfaction of several members from the large States.

It will not escape you that three names only from Virginia are subscribed to the Act. Mr. Wythe did not return after the death of his lady. Docr. MClurg left the Convention some time before the adjournment. The Governour and Col. Mason refused to be parties to it. Mr. Gerry was the only other member who refused. The objections of the Govr. turn principally on the latitude of the general powers, and on the connection established between the President and the Senate. He wished that the plan should be proposed to the States with liberty to them to suggest alterations which should all be referred to another general Convention to be incorporated into the plan as far as might be judged expedient. He was not inveterate in his opposition, and grounded his refusal to subscribe pretty much on his unwillingness to commit himself so as not to be at liberty to be governed by further lights on the subject. Col. Mason left Philada. in an exceeding ill humour indeed. A number of little circumstances arising in part from the impatience which prevailed towards the close of the business, conspired to whet his acrimony. He returned to Virginia with a fixed disposition to prevent the adoption of the plan if possible. He considers the want of a Bill of Rights as a fatal objection. His other objections are to the substitution of the Senate in place of an Executive Council and to the powers vested in that body—to the powers of the Judiciary—to the vice President being made President of the Senate—to the smallness of the number of Representatives—to the restriction on the States with regard to ex post facto laws—and most of all probably to the power of regulating trade, by a majority only of each House. He has some other lesser objections. Being now under the necessity of justifying his refusal to sign, he will of course, muster every possible one. His conduct has given great umbrage to the County of Fairfax, and particularly to the Town of Alexandria. He is already instructed to promote in the Assembly the calling a Convention, and will probably be either not deputed to the Convention, or be tied up by express instructions. He did not object in general to the powers vested in the National Government, so much as to the modification. In some respects he admitted that some further powers could have improved the system. He acknowledged in particular that a negative on the State laws, and the appointment of the State Executives ought to be ingredients; but supposed that the public mind would not now bear them and that experience would hereafter produce these amendments.

The final reception which will be given by the people at large to this proposed System can not yet be decided. The Legislature of N. Hampshire was sitting when it reached that State and was well pleased with it. As far as the sense of the people there has been expressed, it is equally favorable. Boston is warm and almost unanimous in embracing it. The impression on the country is not yet known. No symptoms of disapprobation have appeared. The Legislature of that State is now sitting, through which the sense of the people at large will soon be promulged with tolerable certainty. The paper money faction in Rh. Island is hostile. The other party zealously attached to it. Its passage through Connecticut is likely to be very smooth and easy. There seems to be less agitation in this* state than any where. The discussion of the subject seems confined to the newspapers. The principal characters are known to be friendly. The Governour's party which has hitherto been the popular and most numerous one, is supposed to be on the opposite side; but considerable reserve is practiced, of which he sets the example. N. Jersey takes the affirmative side of course. Meetings of the people are declaring their approbation, and instructing their representatives. Penna. will be divided. The City of Philada., the Republican party, the Quakers, and most of the Germans espouse the Constitution. Some of the Constitutional leaders, backed by the western Country

---

*N. York [Madison's note].

will oppose. An unlucky ferment on the subject in their assembly just before its late adjournment has irritated both sides, particularly the opposition, and by redoubling the exertions of that party may render the event doubtful. The voice of Maryland I understand from pretty good authority, is, as far as it has been declared, strongly in favor of the Constitution. Mr. Chase is an enemy, but the Town of Baltimore which he now represents, is warmly attached to it, and will shackle him as far as they can. Mr. Paca will probably be, as usually, in the politics of Chase. My information from Virginia is as yet extremely imperfect. I have a letter from Genl. Washington which speaks favorably of the impression within a circle of some extent, and another from Chancellor Pendleton which expresses his full acceptance of the plan, and the popularity of it in his district. I am told also that Innis and Marshall are patrons of it. In the opposite scale are Mr. James Mercer, Mr. R. H. Lee, Docr. Lee and their connections of course, Mr. M. Page according to Report, and most of the Judges and Bar of the general Court. The part which Mr. Henry will take is unknown here. Much will depend on it. I had taken it for granted from a variety of circumstances that he would be in the opposition, and still think that will be the case. There are reports however which favor a contrary supposition. From the States South of Virginia nothing has been heard. As the deputation from S. Carolina consisted of some of its weightiest characters, who have returned unanimously zealous in favor of the Constitution, it is probable that State will readily embrace it. It is not less probable, that N. Carolina will follow the example unless that of Virginia should counterbalance it. Upon the whole, although, the public mind will not be fully known, nor finally settled for a considerable time, appearances at present augur a more prompt, and general adoption of the plan than could have been well expected.

When the plan came before Congress for their sanction, a very serious report was made by R. H. Lee and Mr. Dane from Masts. to embarrass it. It was first contended that Congress could not properly give any positive countenance to a measure which had for its object the subversion of the Constitution under which they acted. This ground of attack failing, the former gentleman urged the expediency of sending out the plan with amendments, and proposed a number of them corresponding with the objections of Col. Mason. This experiment had still less effect. In order however to obtain unanimity it was necessary to couch the resolution in very moderate terms. . . .

—*Thomas Jefferson*—
LETTER TO JAMES MADISON (EXCERPT)
DECEMBER 20, 1787

DEAR SIR,

. . . The season admitting only of operations in the Cabinet, and these being in a great measure secret, I have little to fill a letter.* I will therefore make up the deficiency by adding a few words on the Constitution proposed by our Convention. I like much the general idea of framing a government which should go on of itself peaceably, without needing continual recurrence to the state legislatures. I like the organization of the government into Legislative, Judiciary and Executive. I like the power given the Legislature to levy taxes; and for that reason solely approve of the greater house being chosen by the people directly. For tho' I think a house chosen by them will be very illy qualified to legislate for the Union, for foreign nations etc. yet this evil does not weigh against the good of preserving inviolate the fundamental principle that the people are not to be taxed but by representatives chosen immediately by themselves. I am captivated by the compromise of the opposite claims of the great and little states, of the latter to equal, and the former to proportional influence. I am much pleased too with the substitution of the method of voting by persons, instead of that of voting by states: and I like the negative given to the Executive with a third of either house, though I should have liked it better had the Judiciary been associated for that purpose, or invested with a similar and separate power. There are other good things of less moment. I will now add what I do not

---

*As the American minister to France, Jefferson was alluding to deliberations of King Louis XVI and his advisers.

like. First the omission of a bill of rights providing clearly and without the aid of sophisms for freedom of religion, freedom of the press, protection against standing armies, restriction against monopolies, the eternal and unremitting force of the habeas corpus laws, and trials by jury in all matters of fact triable by the laws of the land and not by the law of Nations. To say, as Mr. Wilson does that a bill of rights was not necessary because all is reserved in the case of the general government which is not given, while in the particular ones all is given which is not reserved might do for the Audience to whom it was addressed, but is surely gratis dictum, opposed by strong inferences from the body of the instrument, as well as from the omission of the clause of our present confederation which had declared that in express terms. It was a hard conclusion to say because there has been no uniformity among the states as to the cases triable by jury, because some have been so incautious as to abandon this mode of trial, therefore the more prudent states shall be reduced to the same level of calamity. It would have been much more just and wise to have concluded the other way that as most of the states had judiciously preserved this palladium, those who had wandered should be brought back to it, and to have established general right instead of general wrong. Let me add that a bill of rights is what the people are entitled to against every government on earth, general or particular, and what no just government should refuse, or rest on inference. The second feature I dislike, and greatly dislike, is the abandonment in every instance of the necessity of rotation in office, and most particularly in the case of the President. Experience concurs with reason in concluding that the first magistrate will always be re-elected if the constitution permits it. He is then an officer for life. This once observed it becomes of so much consequence to certain nations to have a friend or a foe at the head of our affairs that they will interfere with money and with arms. A Galloman or an Angloman* will be supported by the nation he befriends. If once elected, and at a second or third election outvoted by one or two votes, he will pretend false votes, foul play, hold possession of the reins of government, be supported by the states voting for him, especially if

---

*Jefferson means a president partial to either France or Britain.

they are the central ones lying in a compact body themselves and separating their opponents; and they will be aided by one nation of Europe, while the majority are aided by another. The election of a President of America some years hence will be much more interesting to certain nations of Europe than ever the election of a king of Poland was. Reflect on all the instances in history antient and modern, of elective monarchies, and say if they do not give foundation for my fears, the Roman emperors, the popes, while they were of any importance, the German emperors till they became hereditary in practice, the kings of Poland, the Deys of the Ottoman dependancies. It may be said that if elections are to be attended with these disorders, the seldomer they are renewed the better. But experience shews that the only way to prevent disorder is to render them uninteresting by frequent changes. An incapacity to be elected a second time would have been the only effectual preventative. The power of removing him every fourth year by the vote of the people is a power which will not be exercised. The king of Poland is removeable every day by the Diet, yet he is never removed.

Smaller objections are the Appeal in fact as well as law, and the binding all persons Legislative, Executive and Judiciary by oath to maintain that constitution. I do not pretend to decide what would be the best method of procuring the establishment of the manifold good things in this constitution, and of getting rid of the bad. Whether by adopting it in hopes of future amendment, or, after it has been duly weighed and canvassed by the people, after seeing the parts they generally dislike, and those they generally approve, to say to them 'We see now what you wish. Send together your deputies again, let them frame a constitution for you omitting what you have condemned, and establishing the powers you approve. Even these will be a great addition to the energy of your government.'

At all events I hope you will not be discouraged from other trials, if the present one should fail of it's full effect.

I have thus told you freely what I like and dislike: merely as a matter of curiosity for I know your own judgment has been formed on all these points after having heard every thing which could be urged on them. I own I am not a friend to a very energetic government. It is always oppressive. The late rebellion in Massachusets has given more alarm than I think it should have done. Calculate that one rebellion in 13 states in the course of 11 years, is but one for each state in a century and a half. No country should be so long without one. Nor will any degree of power in the hands of government prevent insurrections. France with all it's despotism, and two or three hundred thousand men always in arms has had three insurrections in the three years I have been here in every one of which greater numbers were engaged than in Massachusets and a great deal more blood was spilt. In Turkey, which Montesquieu supposes more despotic, insurrections are the events of every day. In England, where the hand of power is lighter than here, but heavier than with us they happen every half dozen years. Compare again the ferocious depredations of their insurgents with the order, the moderation and the almost self extinguishment of ours.

After all, it is my principle that the will of the Majority should always prevail. If they approve the proposed Convention in all it's parts, I shall concur in it chearfully, in hopes that they will amend it whenever they shall find it work wrong. I think our governments will remain virtuous for many centuries; as long as they are chiefly agricultural; and this will be as long as there shall be vacant lands in any part of America. When they get piled upon one another in large cities, as in Europe, they will become corrupt as in Europe. Above all things I hope the education of the common people will be attended to; convinced that on their good sense we may rely with the most security for the preservation of a due degree of liberty. I have tired you by this time with my disquisitions and will therefore only add assurances of the sincerity of those sentiments of esteem and attachment with which I am Dear Sir your affectionate friend and servant,

TH: JEFFERSON

P.S. The instability of our laws is really an immense evil. I think it would be well to provide in our constitutions that there shall always be a twelvemonth between the ingrossing a bill and passing it: that it should then be offered to it's passage without changing a word: and that if circumstances should be thought to require a speedier passage, it should take two thirds of both houses instead of a bare majority.

VIRGINIA ORANGE APR. 22, 1788

DEAR SIR

The proposed Constitution still engrosses the public attention. The elections for the Convention here are but just over and promulged. From the returns (excluding those from Kentucky which are not yet known) it seems probable, though not absolutely certain that a majority of the members elect are friends to the Constitution. The superiority of abilities at least seems to lie on that side. The characters of most note which occur to me, are marshalled thus. For the Constitution, Pendleton, Wythe, Blair, Innis, Marshal, Doctr. W. Jones, G. Nicholas, Wilson Nicholas, Gabl. Jones, Thos. Lewis, F. Corbin, Ralph Wormley Jr. White of Frederik, Genl. Gates, Genl. A. Stephens, Archd. Stuart, Zachy. Johnson, Docr. Stuart, Parson Andrews, H. Lee Jr. Bushrod Washington considered as a young Gentleman of talents: against the Constitution, Mr. Henry, Mason, Harrison, Grayson, Tyler, M. Smith, W. Ronald, Lawson, Bland, Wm. Cabell, Dawson.

The Governor is so temperate in his opposition and goes so far with the friends of the Constitution that he cannot properly be classed with its enemies. Monroe is considered by some as an enemy, but I believe him to be a friend though a cool one. There are other individuals of weight whose opinions are unknown to me. R. H. Lee is not elected. His brother F. L. Lee is a warm friend to the Constitution, as I am told, but also is not elected. So are Jno. and Man Page.

The adversaries take very different grounds of opposition. Some are opposed to the substance of the plan; others to particular modifications only. Mr. H[enr]y is supposed to aim at disunion. Col. M[aso]n is growing every day more bitter, and outrageous in his efforts to carry his point; and will probably in the end be thrown by the violence of his passions into the politics of Mr. H[enr]y. The preliminary question will be whether previous alterations shall be insisted on or not? Should this be carried in the affirmative, either a conditional ratification, or a proposal for a new Convention will ensue. In either event, I think the Constitution and the Union will be both endangered. It is not to be expected that the States which have ratified will reconsider their determinations, and submit to the alterations prescribed by Virga. and if a second Convention should be formed, it is as little to be expected that the same spirit of compromise will prevail in it as produced an amicable result to the first. It will be easy also for those who have latent views of disunion, to carry them on under the mask of contending for alterations popular in some but inadmissible in other parts of the U. States.

The real sense of the people of this State cannot be easily ascertained. They are certainly attached and with warmth to a continuance of the Union; and I believe a large majority of the most intelligent and independent are equally so to the plan under consideration. On a geographical view of them, almost all the counties in the N. Neck have elected fœderal deputies. The Counties on the South side of James River have pretty generally elected adversaries to the Constitution. The intermediate district is much chequered in this respect. The Counties between the blue ridge and the Alleghany have chosen friends to the Constitution without a single exception. Those Westward of the latter, have as I am informed, generally though not universally pursued the same rule. Kentucky it is supposed will be divided.

Js. Madison Jr.

—*Thomas Jefferson*—
LETTER TO JAMES MADISON (EXCERPT)
JULY 31, 1788

DEAR SIR,

. . . I sincerely rejoice at the acceptance of our new constitution by nine states. It is a good canvas, on which some strokes only want retouching. What these are, I think are sufficiently manifested by the general voice from North to South, which calls for a bill of rights. It seems pretty generally understood that this should go to Juries, Habeas corpus, Standing armies, Printing, Religion and Monopolies.

I conceive there may be difficulty in finding general modification of these suited to the habits of all the states. But if such cannot be found then it is better to establish trials by jury, the right of Habeas corpus, freedom of the press and freedom of religion in all cases, and to abolish standing armies in time of peace, and Monopolies, in all cases, than not to do it in any. The few cases wherein these things may do evil, cannot be weighed against the multitude wherein the want of them will do evil. In disputes between a foreigner and a native, a trial by jury may be improper. But if this exception cannot be agreed to, the remedy will be to model the jury by giving the medietas linguae in civil as well as criminal cases. Why suspend the Hab. corp. in insurrections and rebellions? The parties who may be arrested may be charged instantly with a well defined crime. Of course the judge will remand them. If the publick safety requires that the government should have a man imprisoned on less probable testimony in those than in other emergencies; let him be taken and tried, retaken and retried, while the necessity continues, only giving him redress against the government for damages. Examine the history of England: see how few of the cases of the suspension of the Habeas corpus law have been worthy of that suspension. They have been either real treasons wherein the parties might as well have been charged at once, or sham-plots where it was shameful they should ever have been suspected. Yet for the few cases wherein the suspension of the hab. corp. has done real good, that operation is now become habitual, and the minds of the nation almost prepared to live under it's constant suspension. A declaration that the federal government will never restrain the presses from printing any thing they please, will not take away the liability of the printers for false facts printed. The declaration that religious faith shall be unpunished, does not give impunity to criminal acts dictated by religious error. The saying there shall be no monopolies lessens the incitements to ingenuity, which is spurred on by the hope of a monopoly for a limited time, as of 14. years; but the benefit even of limited monopolies is too doubtful to be opposed to that of their general suppression. If no check can be found to keep the number of standing troops within safe bounds, while they are tolerated as far as necessary, abandon them altogether, discipline well the militia, and guard the magazines with them. More than magazine-guards will be useless if few, and dangerous if many. No European nation can ever send against us such a regular army as we need fear, and it is hard if our militia are not equal to those of Canada or Florida. My idea then is, that tho' proper exceptions to these general rules are desireable and probably practicable, yet if the exceptions cannot be agreed on, the establishment of the rules in all cases will do ill in very few. I hope therefore a bill of rights will be formed to guard the people against the federal government, as they are already guarded against their state governments in most instances.

The abandoning the principle of necessary rotation in the Senate, has I see been disapproved by many; in the case of the President, by none. I readily therefore suppose my opinion wrong, when opposed by the majority as in the former instance, and the totality as in the latter. In this however I should have done it with more complete satisfaction, had we all judged from the same position. . . .

I am with very sincere esteem Dear Sir Your affectionate friend and servt.,

TH: JEFFERSON

—*James Madison*—
LETTER TO THOMAS JEFFERSON (EXCERPT)
OCTOBER 17, 1788

DEAR SIR,

. . . The States which have adopted the new Constitution are all proceeding to the arrangements for putting it into action in March next. Pennsylva. alone has as yet actually appointed deputies; and that only for the Senate. My last mentioned that these were Mr. R. Morris and a Mr. McClay. How the other elections there and elsewhere will run is matter of uncertainty. The Presidency alone unites the conjectures of the public. The vice president is not at all marked out by the general voice. As the President will be from a Southern State, it falls almost of course for the other part of the Continent to supply the next in rank. South Carolina may however think of Mr. Rutledge unless it should be previously discovered that votes will be wasted on him. The only candidates in the

Northern States brought forward with their known consent are *Hancock and Adams** and *between these it seems probable the question will lie.* Both of them *are objectionable and would I think be postponed* by the *general suffrage to several others* if they *would accept the place. Hancock* is *weak, ambitious, a courtier of popularity given to low intrigue* and *lately reunited by a factious friendship with S. Adams.*

J. Adams has made *himself obnoxious to many* particularly in the *Southern states by the political principles avowed in his book.*† Others *recolecting his cabal during the war against General Washington,* knowing *his extravagant self importance* and *considering his preference of an unprofitable dignity* to some *place of emolument* better *adapted to private fortune as a proof of his* having *an eye to the presidency conclude* that *he would not be a very cordial second to the General* and that *an impatient ambition* might *even intrigue for a premature advancement.* The *danger would be the greater if* particular *factious characters,* as may be the case, *should get into the public councils. Adams* it appears, is *not unaware of* some *of the obstacles to his wish* and *thro a letter to Smith* has *thrown out popular sentiments as to the proposed president.*

The little pamphlet herewith inclosed‡ will give you a collective view of the alterations which have been proposed for the new Constitution. Various and numerous as they appear they certainly omit many of the true grounds of opposition. The articles relating to Treaties, to paper money, and to contracts, created more enemies than all the errors in the System positive and negative put together. It is true nevertheless that not a few, particularly in Virginia have contended for the proposed alterations from the most honorable and patriotic motives; and that among the advocates for the Constitution there are some who wish for further guards to public liberty and individual rights. As far as these may consist of a constitutional declaration of the most essential rights, it is probable they will be

---

*These and all other italicized words in this letter were originally written in code.

†Madison refers to the three-volume *A Defence of the Constitutions of Government of the United States of America* (1787–1788), written while Adams was minister to Great Britain.

‡Madison refers to a recently published pamphlet reprinting all the amendments to the Constitution proposed by the various state ratification conventions.

added; though there are many who think such addition unnecessary, and not a few who think it misplaced in such a Constitution. There is scarce any point on which the party in opposition is so much divided as to its importance and its propriety. My own opinion has always been in favor of a bill of rights; provided it be so framed as not to imply powers not meant to be included in the enumeration. At the same time I have never thought the omission a material defect, nor been anxious to supply it even by *subsequent* amendment, for any other reason than that it is anxiously desired by others. I have favored it because I supposed it might be of use, and if properly executed could not be of disservice. I have not viewed it in an important light 1. Because I conceive that in a certain degree, though not in the extent argued by Mr. Wilson, the rights in question are reserved by the manner in which the federal powers are granted. 2. Because there is great reason to fear that a positive declaration of some of the most essential rights could not be obtained in the requisite latitude. I am sure that the rights of conscience in particular, if submitted to public definition would be narrowed much more than they are likely ever to be by an assumed power. One of the objections in New England was that the Constitution by prohibiting religious tests opened a door for Jews Turks and infidels. 3. Because the limited powers of the federal Government and the jealousy of the subordinate Governments, afford a security which has not existed in the case of the State Governments, and exists in no other. 4. Because experience proves the inefficacy of a bill of rights on those occasions when its controul is most needed. Repeated violations of these parchment barriers have been committed by overbearing majorities in every State. In Virginia I have seen the bill of rights violated in every instance where it has been opposed to a popular current. Notwithstanding the explicit provision contained in that instrument for the rights of Conscience it is well known that a religious establishment would have taken place in that State, if the legislative majority had found as they expected, a majority of the people in favor of the measure; and I am persuaded that if a majority of the people were now of one sect, the measure would still take place and on narrower ground than was then proposed, notwithstanding the additional obstacle which the law has since created. Wherever the real power in a Government lies, there is the danger of oppression. In our Governments the real power lies in the majority of the Community, and the invasion of private rights is *chiefly* to be apprehended, not from acts of Government contrary to the sense of its constituents, but from acts in which the Government is the mere instrument of the major number of the constituents. This is a truth of great importance, but not yet sufficiently attended to: and is probably more strongly impressed on my mind by facts, and reflections suggested by them, than on yours which has contemplated abuses of power issuing from a very different quarter.* Wherever there is an interest and power to do wrong, wrong will generally be done, and not less readily by a powerful and interested party than by a powerful and interested prince. The difference, so far as it relates to the superiority of republics over monarchies, lies in the less degree of probability that interest may prompt abuses of power in the former than in the latter; and in the security in the former against oppression of more than the smaller part of the Society, whereas in the former [latter] it may be extended in a manner to the whole. The difference so far as it relates to the point in question—the efficacy of a bill of rights in controuling abuses of power—lies in this: that in a monarchy the latent force of the nation is superior to that of the Sovereign, and a solemn charter of popular rights must have a great effect, as a standard for trying the validity of public acts, and a signal for rousing and uniting the superior force of the community; whereas in a popular Government, the political and physical power may be considered as vested in the same hands, that is in a majority of the people, and consequently the tyrannical will of the sovereign is not to be controuled by the dread of an appeal to any other force within the community. What use then it may be asked can a bill of rights serve in popular Governments? I answer the two following which though less essential than in other Governments, sufficiently recommend the precaution. 1. The political truths declared in that solemn manner acquire by degrees the character of fundamental maxims of free Government, and as they become incorporated with the national sentiment, counteract the impulses of interest and passion. 2. Altho' it be generally true as above stated that the danger of oppression lies in the interested majorities of the people rather than in usurped acts of the

---

*Madison alludes to the fact that Jefferson has been serving as the minister to France and thus observing the traditional problem of how to protect rights against the concentrated power of monarchy.

Government, yet there may be occasions on which the evil may spring from the latter sources; and on such, a bill of rights will be a good ground for an appeal to the sense of the community. Perhaps too there may be a certain degree of danger, that a succession of artful and ambitious rulers, may by gradual and well-timed advances, finally erect an independent Government on the subversion of liberty. Should this danger exist at all, it is prudent to guard against it, especially when the precaution can do no injury. At the same time I must own that I see no tendency in our governments to danger on that side. It has been remarked that there is a tendency in all Governments to an augmentation of power at the expence of liberty. But the remark as usually understood does not appear to me well founded. Power when it has attained a certain degree of energy and independence goes on generally to further degrees. But when below that degree, the direct tendency is to further degrees of relaxation, until the abuses of liberty beget a sudden transition to an undue degree of power. With this explanation the remark may be true; and in the latter sense only is it in my opinion applicable to the Governments in America. It is a melancholy reflection that liberty should be equally exposed to danger whether the Government have too much or too little power; and that the line which divides these extremes should be so inaccurately defined by experience.

Supposing a bill of rights to be proper the articles which ought to compose it, admit of much discussion. I am inclined to think that *absolute* restrictions in cases that are doubtful, or where emergencies may overrule them, ought to be avoided. The restrictions however strongly marked on paper will never be regarded when opposed to the decided sense of the public; and after repeated violations in extraordinary cases, they will lose even their ordinary efficacy. Should a Rebellion or insurrection alarm the people as well as the Government, and a suspension of the Hab. Corp. be dictated by the alarm, no written prohibitions on earth would prevent the measure. Should an army in time of peace be gradually established in our neighbourhood by Britn: or Spain, declarations on paper would have as little effect in preventing a standing force for the public safety. The best security against these evils is to remove the pretext for them. With regard to Monopolies they are justly classed among the greatest nusances in Government. But is it clear that as encouragements to literary works and ingenious discoveries, they are not too valuable to be wholly renounced? Would it not suffice to reserve in all cases a right to the public to abolish the privilege at a price to be specified in the grant of it? Is there not also infinitely less danger of this abuse in our Governments than in most others? Monopolies are sacrifices of the many to the few. Where the power is in the few it is natural for them to sacrifice the many to their own partialities and corruptions. Where the power, as with us, is in the many not in the few, the danger can not be very great that the few will be thus favored. It is much more to be dreaded that the few will be unnecessarily sacrificed to the many.

I inclose a paper containing the late proceedings in Kentucky. I wish the ensuing Convention may take no step injurious to the character of the district, and favorable to the views of those who wish ill to the U. States. One of my late letters communicated some circumstances which will not fail to occur on perusing the objects of the proposed Convention in next month. Perhaps however there may be less connection between the two cases than at first one is ready to conjecture. I am Dr. Sir with the sincerest esteem and affectn. Yours,

JS. MADISON JR

—*James Madison*—
LETTER TO THOMAS JEFFERSON (EXCERPT)
DECEMBER 8, 1788

PHILADELPHIA DEC. 8, 1788

DEAR SIR

This will be handed to you by Mr. Governeur Morris who will embark in a few days for Havre, from whence he will proceed immediately to Paris. He is already well known to you by character; and as far as there may be a defect of personal acquaintance I beg leave to supply it by this introduction.

My two last were of Ocr. 8 and 17th. They furnished a State of our affairs as they then stood. I shall here add the particulars of most consequence, which have since taken place, remembering however that many details will be most conveniently gathered from the conversation of Mr. Morris who is thoroughly possessed of American transactions.

Notwithstanding the formidable opposition made to the new federal government, first in order to prevent its adoption, and since in order to place its administration in the hands of disaffected men, there is now both a certainty of its peaceable commencement in March next, and a flattering prospect that it will be administred by men who will give it a fair trial. General Washington will certainly be called to the Executive department. Mr. Adams who is *pledged to support him** will probably be the vice president. The enemies to the Government, at the head and the most inveterate of whom, is Mr. Henry are laying a train for the election of Governour Clinton, but it cannot succeed unless the federal votes be more dispersed than can well happen. Of the seven States which have appointed their Senators, Virginia alone will have anti-federal members in that branch. Those of N. Hampshire are President Langdon and Judge Bartlett, of Massachusetts Mr. Strong and Mr. Dalton, of Connecticut Docr. Johnson and Mr. Elseworth, of N. Jersey Mr. Patterson and Mr. Elmer, of Penna. Mr. R. Morris and Mr. McClay, of Delaware Mr. Geo: Reed and Mr. Bassett, of Virginia Mr. R. H. Lee and Col. Grayson. Here is already a majority of the ratifying States on the side of the Constitution. And it is not doubted that it will be reinforced by the appointments of Maryland, S. Carolina and Georgia. As one branch of the Legislature of N. York is attached to the Constitution, it is not improbable that one of the Senators from that State also will be added to the majority.

In the House of Representatives the proportion of antifederal members will of course be greater, but can not if present appearances are to be trusted amount to a majority or even a very formidable minority. The election for this branch has taken place as yet no where except in Penna. and here the returns are not yet come in from all the Counties. It is certain however that seven out of the

---

*These and all other italicized words in this letter were originally written in code.

eight, and probable that the whole eight representatives will bear the federal stamp. Even in Virginia where the enemies to the Government form $\frac{2}{3}$ of the *legislature* it is computed that more than half the number of Representatives, who will be elected by the *people,* formed into districts for the purpose, will be of the same stamp. By some it is computed that 7 out of the 10 allotted to that State will be opposed to the politics of the present Legislature.

The questions which divide the public at present relate 1. to the extent of the amendments that ought to be made to the Constitution, 2. to the mode in which they ought to be made. The friends of the Constitution, some from an approbation of particular amendments, others from a spirit of conciliation, are generally agreed that the System should be revised. But they wish the revisal to be carried no farther than to supply additional guards for liberty, without abridging the sum of power transferred from the States to the general Government, or altering previous to trial, the particular structure of the latter and are fixed in opposition to the risk of another Convention, whilst the purpose can be as well answered, by the other mode provided for introducing amendments. Those who have opposed the Constitution, are on the other hand, zealous for a second Convention, and for a revisal which may either not be restrained at all, or extend at least as far as alterations have been proposed by any State. Some of this class are, no doubt, friends to an effective Government, and even to the substance of the particular Government in question. It is equally certain that there are others who urge a second Convention with the insidious hope of throwing all things into Confusion, and of subverting the fabric just established, if not the Union itself. If the first Congress embrace the policy which circumstances mark out, they will not fail to propose of themselves, every desireable safeguard for popular rights; and by thus separating the well meaning from the designing opponents fix on the latter their true character, and give to the Government its due popularity and stability. . . .

JS. MADISON JR.

Paris Mar. 15, 1789

Dear Sir

I wrote you last on the 12th. of Jan. since which I have received yours of Octob. 17. Dec. 8. and 12. That of Oct. 17. came to hand only Feb. 23. How it happened to be four months on the way, I cannot tell, as I never knew by what hand it came. Looking over my letter of Jan. 12th. I remark an error of the word 'probable' instead of 'improbable,' which doubtless however you had been able to correct. Your thoughts on the subject of the Declaration of rights in the letter of Oct. 17. I have weighed with great satisfaction. Some of them had not occurred to me before, but were acknoleged just in the moment they were presented to my mind. In the arguments in favor of a declaration of rights, you omit one which has great weight with me, the legal check which it puts into the hands of the judiciary. This is a body, which if rendered independent, and kept strictly to their own department merits great confidence for their learning and integrity. In fact what degree of confidence would be too much for a body composed of such men as Wythe, Blair, and Pendleton? On characters like these the 'civium ardor prava jubentium' would make no impression. I am happy to find that on the whole you are a friend to this amendment. The Declaration of rights is like all other human blessings alloyed with some inconveniences, and not accomplishing fully it's object. But the good in this instance vastly overweighs the evil. I cannot refrain from making short answers to the objections which your letter states to have been raised. 1. That the rights in question are reserved by the manner in which the federal powers are granted. Answer. A constitutive act may certainly be so formed as to need no declaration of rights. The act itself has the force of a declaration as far as it goes: and if it goes to all material points nothing more is wanting. In the draught of a constitution which I had once a thought of proposing in Virginia, and printed afterwards, I endeavored to reach all the great objects of public liberty, and did not mean to add a declaration of rights. Probably the object was imperfectly executed: but the deficiencies would have been supplied by others in the course of discussion. But in a constitutive act which leaves some precious articles unnoticed, and raises implications against others, a declaration of rights becomes necessary by way of supplement. This is the case of our new federal constitution. This instrument forms us into one state as to certain objects, and gives us a legislative and executive body for these objects. It should therefore guard us against their abuses of power within the feild submitted to them. 2. A positive declaration of some essential rights could not be obtained in the requisite latitude. Answer. Half a loaf is better than no bread. If we cannot secure all our rights, let us secure what we can. 3. The limited powers of the federal government and jealousy of the subordinate governments afford a security which exists in no other instance. Answer. The first member of this seems resolvable into the 1st. objection before stated. The jealousy of the subordinate governments is a precious reliance. But observe that those governments are only agents. They must have principles furnished them whereon to found their opposition. The declaration of rights will be the text whereby they will try all the acts of the federal government. In this view it is necessary to the federal government also: as by the same text they may try the opposition of the subordinate governments. 4. Experience proves the inefficacy of a bill of rights. True. But tho it is not absolutely efficacious under all circumstances, it is of great potency always, and rarely inefficacious. A brace the more will often keep up the building which would have fallen with that brace the less.

There is a remarkeable difference between the characters of the Inconveniencies which attend a Declaration of rights, and those which attend the want of it. The inconveniences of the Declaration are that it may cramp government in it's useful exertions. But the evil of this is shortlived, moderate, and reparable. The inconveniencies of the want of a Declaration are permanent, afflicting and irreparable: they are in constant progression from bad to worse. The executive in our governments is not the sole, it is scarcely the principal object of my jealousy. The tyranny of the legislatures is the most formidable dread at present, and will be for long years. That of the executive will come in it's turn, but it will be at a remote period. I know there are some among us who would now establish a monarchy. But they are inconsiderable in number and weight of character. The rising race are all republicans. We were educated in royalism: no wonder if some of us retain that idolatry still. Our young people are educated in republicanism. An apostacy from that to royalism is unprecedented and impossible.

I am much pleased with the prospect that a declaration of rights will be added: and hope it will be done in that way which will not endanger the whole frame of the government, or any essential part of it. . . .

TH: JEFFERSON

—*Thomas Jefferson*—
LETTER TO JAMES MADISON
SEPTEMBER 6, 1789

PARIS SEPT. 6, 1789

DEAR SIR

I sit down to write to you without knowing by what occasion I shall send my letter. I do it because a subject comes into my head which I would wish to develope a little more than is practicable in the hurry of the moment of making up general dispatches.

The question Whether one generation of men has a right to bind another, seems never to have been started [stated?] either on this or our side of the water. Yet it is a question of such consequences as not only to merit decision, but place also, among the fundamental principles of every government. The course of reflection in which we are immersed here on the elementary principles of society has presented this question to my mind; and that no such obligation can be so transmitted I think very capable of proof.

I set out on this ground, which I suppose to be self evident, '*that the earth belongs in usufruct to the living*': that the dead have neither powers nor rights over it. The portion occupied by any individual ceases to be his when himself ceases to be, and reverts to the society. If the society has formed no rules for the appropriation of it's lands in severalty, it will be taken by the first occupants. These will generally be the wife and children of the decedent. If they have formed rules of appropriation, those rules may give it to the wife and children, or to some one of them, or to the legatee of the deceased. So they may give it to his creditor. But the child, the legatee, or creditor takes it, not by any natural right, but by a law of the society of which they are members, and to which they are subject. Then no man can, by *natural right,* oblige the lands he occupied, or the persons who succeed him in that occupation, to the paiment of debts contracted by him. For if he could, he might, during his own life, eat up the usufruct of the lands for several generations to come, and then the lands would belong to the dead, and not to the living, which would be the reverse of our principle.

What is true of every member of the society individually, is true of them all collectively, since the rights of the whole can be no more than the sum of the rights of the individuals.

To keep our ideas clear when applying them to a multitude, let us suppose a whole generation of men to be born on the same day, to attain mature age on the same day, and to die on the same day, leaving a succeeding generation in the moment of attaining their mature age all together. Let the ripe age be supposed of 21. years, and their period of life 34. years more, that being the average term given by the bills of mortality to persons who have already attained 21. years of age. Each successive generation would, in this way, come on, and go off the stage at a fixed moment, as individuals do now. Then I say the earth belongs to each of these generations, during it's course, fully, and in their own right. The 2d. generation receives it clear of the debts and incumberances of the 1st. the 3d of the 2d. and so on. For if the 1st. could charge it with a debt, then the earth would belong to the dead and not the living generation. Then no generation can contract debts greater than may be paid during the course of it's own existence. At 21. years of age they may bind themselves and their lands for 34. years to come: at 22. for 33: at 23. for 32. and at 54. for one year only; because these are the terms of life which remain to them at those respective epochs.

But a material difference must be noted between the succession of an individual, and that of a whole generation. Individuals are parts only of a society, subject to the laws of the whole. These laws may appropriate the portion of land occupied by a decedent to his creditor rather than to any other, or to his child on condition he satisfies the creditor. But when a whole generation, that is, the whole society dies, as in the case we have supposed, and another generation or society succeeds, this forms a whole, and there is no superior who can give their territory to a third society, who may have lent money to their predecessors beyond their faculties of paying.

What is true of a generation all arriving to self-government on the same day, and dying all on the same day, is true of those in a constant course of decay and renewal, with this only difference. A generation coming in and going out entire, as in the first case, would have a right in the 1st. year of their self-dominion to contract a debt for 33. years, in the 10th. for 24. in the 20th. for 14. in the 30th. for 4. whereas generations, changing daily by daily deaths and births, have one constant term, beginning at the date of their contract, and ending when a majority of those of full age at that date shall be dead. The length of that term may be estimated from the tables of mortality, corrected by the circumstances of climate, occupation etc. peculiar to the country of the contractors. Take, for instance, the table of M. de Buffon wherein he states 23,994 deaths, and the ages at which they happened. Suppose a society in which 23,994 persons are born every year, and live to the ages stated in this table. The conditions of that society will be as follows. 1st. It will consist constantly of 617,703. persons of all ages. 2ly. Of those living at any one instant of time, one half will be dead in 24. years 8. months. 3dly. 10,675 will arrive every year at the age of 21. years complete. 4ly. It will constantly have 348,417 persons of all ages above 21. years. 5ly. And the half of those of 21. years and upwards living at any one instant of time will be dead in 18. years 8. months, or say 19. years as the nearest integral number. Then 19. years is the term beyond which neither the representatives of a nation, nor even the whole nation itself assembled, can validly extend a debt.

To render this conclusion palpable by example, suppose that Louis XIV. and XV. had contracted debts in the name of the French nation to the amount of 10,000 milliards of livres, and that the whole had been contracted in Genoa. The interest of this sum would be 500. milliards, which is said to be the whole rent roll or nett proceeds of the territory of France. Must the present generation of men have retired from the territory in which nature produced them, and ceded it to the Genoese creditors? No. They have the same rights over the soil on which they were produced, as the preceding generations had. They derive these rights not from their predecessors, but from nature. They then and their soil are by nature clear of the debts of their predecessors.

Again suppose Louis XV. and his cotemporary generation had said to the money-lenders of Genoa, give us money that we may eat, drink, and be merry in our day; and on condition you will demand no interest till the end of 19. years you shall then for ever after receive an annual interest of $12\frac{5}{8}$ per cent.* The money is lent on these conditions, is divided among the living, eaten, drank, and squandered. Would the present generation be obliged to apply the produce of the earth and of their labour to replace their dissipations? Not at all.

I suppose that the recieved opinion, that the public debts of one generation devolve on the next, has been suggested by our seeing habitually in private life that he who succeeds to lands is required to pay the debts of his ancestor or testator: without considering that this requisition is municipal only, not moral; flowing from the will of the society, which has found it convenient to appropriate lands, become vacant by the death of their occupant, on the condition of a paiment of his debts: but that between society and society, or generation and generation, there is no municipal obligation, no umpire but the law of nature. We seem not to have percieved that, by the law of nature, one generation is to another as one independant nation to another.

The interest of the national debt of France being in fact but a two thousandth part of it's rent roll, the paiment of it is practicable enough: and so becomes a question merely of honor, or of expediency. But with respect to future debts, would it not be wise and just for that nation to declare, in the constitution they are forming, that neither the legislature, nor the nation itself, can validly contract more debt than they may pay within their own age, or within the term of 19. years? And that all future contracts will be deemed void as to what shall remain unpaid at the end of 19. years from their date? This would put the lenders, and the borrowers also, on their guard. By

---

*100£, at a compound interest of 5. percent, makes, at the end of 19. years, an aggregate of principle and interest of £252-14, the interest of which is 12£-12s-7d which is nearly $12\frac{5}{8}$ per cent on the first capital of 100.£ [Jefferson's note].

reducing too the faculty of borrowing within it's natural limits, it would bridle the spirit of war, to which too free a course has been procured by the inattention of money-lenders to this law of nature, that succeeding generations are not responsible for the preceding.

On similar ground it may be proved that no society can make a perpetual constitution, or even a perpetual law. The earth belongs always to the living generation. They may manage it then, and what proceeds from it, as they please, during their usufruct. They are masters too of their own persons, and consequently may govern them as they please. But persons and property make the sum of the objects of government. The constitution and the laws of their predecessors extinguished then in their natural course with those who gave them being. This could preserve that being till it ceased to be itself, and no longer. Every constitution then, and every law, naturally expires at the end of 19 years. If it be enforced longer, it is an act of force, and not of right.

It may be said that the succeeding generation exercising in fact the power of repeal, this leaves them as free as if the constitution or law had been expressly limited to 19 years only. In the first place, this objection admits the right, in proposing an equivalent. But the power of repeal is not an equivalent. It might be indeed if every form of government were so perfectly contrived that the will of the majority could always be obtained fairly and without impediment. But this is true of no form. The people cannot assemble themselves. Their representation is unequal and vicious. Various checks are opposed to every legislative proposition. Factions get possession of the public councils. Bribery corrupts them. Personal interests lead them astray from the general interests of their constituents: and other impediments arise so as to prove to every practical man that a law of limited duration is much more manageable than one which needs a repeal.

This principle that the earth belongs to the living, and not to the dead, is of very extensive application and consequences, in every country, and most especially in France. It enters into the resolution of the questions Whether the nation may change the descent of lands holden in tail? Whether they may change the appropriation of lands given antiently to the church, to hospitals, colleges, orders of chivalry, and otherwise in perpetuity? Whether they may abolish the

charges and privileges attached on lands, including the whole catalogue ecclesiastical and feudal? It goes to hereditary offices, authorities and jurisdictions; to hereditary orders, distinctions and
appellations; to perpetual monopolies in commerce, the arts and
sciences; with a long train of et ceteras: and it renders the question
of reimbursement a question of generosity and not of right. In all
these cases, the legislature of the day could authorize such appropriations and establishments for their own time, but no longer; and the
present holders, even where they, or their ancestors, have purchased,
are in the case of bonâ fide purchasers of what the seller had no right
to convey.

Turn this subject in your mind, my dear Sir, and particularly as
to the power of contracting debts; and develope it with that perspicuity and cogent logic so peculiarly yours. Your station in the
councils of our country gives you an opportunity of producing it to
public consideration, of forcing it into discussion. At first blush it
may be rallied, as a theoretical speculation: but examination will
prove it to be solid and salutary. It would furnish matter for a fine
preamble to our first law for appropriating the public revenue; and
it will exclude at the threshold of our new government the conta-
gious and ruinous errors of this quarter of the globe, which have
armed despots with means, not sanctioned by nature, for binding
in chains their fellow men. We have already given in example one
effectual check to the Dog of war by transferring the power of
letting him loose from the Executive to the Legislative body, from
those who are to spend to those who are to pay. I should be pleased
to see this second obstacle held out by us also in the first instance. No
nation can make a declaration against the validity of long-contracted
debts so disinterestedly as we, since we do not owe a shilling which
may not be paid with ease, principal and interest, within the time
of our own lives.

Establish the principle also in the new law to be passed for protecting copyrights and new inventions, by securing the exclusive
right for 19. instead of 14. years. Besides familiarising us to this term,
it will be an instance the more of our taking reason for our guide, instead of English precedent, the habit of which fetters us with all the
political heresies of a nation equally remarkeable for it's early excite-
ment from some errors, and long slumbering under others.

I write you no news, because, when an occasion occurs, I shall write a separate letter for that. I am always with great and sincere esteem, dear Sir Your affectionate friend and servt,

TH: JEFFERSON

—*James Madison*—
LETTER TO THOMAS JEFFERSON
FEBRUARY 4, 1790

NEW YORK FEB. 4, 1790

DEAR SIR

Your favor of the 9th. of Jany. inclosing one of Sepr. last did not get to hand till a few days ago. The idea which the latter evolves is a great one, and suggests many interesting reflections to legislators; particularly when contracting and providing for public debts. Whether it can be received in the extent your reasonings give it, is a question which I ought to turn more in my thoughts than I have yet been able to do, before I should be justified in making up a full opinion on it. My first thoughts though coinciding with many of yours, lead me to view the doctrine as not in *all* respects compatible with the course of human affairs. I will endeavor to sketch the grounds of my skepticism.

"As the earth belongs to the living, not to the dead, a living generation can bind itself only: In every society the will of the majority binds the whole: According to the laws of mortality, a majority of those ripe at any moment for the exercise of their will do not live beyond nineteen years: To that term then is limited the validity of *every* act of the Society; Nor within that limitation, can any declaration of the public will be valid which is not *express*."

This I understand to be the outline of the argument.

The acts of a political Society may be divided into three classes.

1. The fundamental Constitution of the Government.

2. Laws involving stipulations which render them irrevocable at the will of the Legislature.

3. Laws involving no such irrevocable quality.

However applicable in Theory the doctrine may be to a Constitution, it seems liable in practice to some very powerful objections. Would not a Government so often revised become too mutable to retain those prejudices in its favor which antiquity inspires, and which are perhaps a salutary aid to the most rational Government in the most enlightened age? Would not such a periodical revision engender pernicious factions that might not otherwise come into existence? Would not, in fine, a Government depending for its existence beyond a fixed date, on some positive and authentic intervention of the Society itself, be too subject to the casualty and consequences of an actual interregnum?

In the 2d. class, exceptions at least to the doctrine seem to be *requisite* both in Theory and practice:

If the earth be the gift of nature to the living their title can extend to the earth in its natural State only. The *improvements* made by the dead form a charge against the living who take the benefit of them. This charge can no otherwise be satisfyed than by executing the will of the dead accompanying the improvements.

Debts may be incurred for purposes which interest the unborn, as well as the living: such are debts for repelling a conquest, the evils of which descend through many generations. Debts may even be incurred principally for the benefit of posterity: such perhaps is the present debt of the U. States, which far exceeds any burdens which the present generation could well apprehend for itself. The term of 19 years might not be sufficient for discharging the debts in either of these cases.

There seems then to be a foundation in the nature of things, in the relation which one generation bears to another, for the *descent* of obligations from one to another. Equity requires it. Mutual good is promoted by it. All that is indispensable in adjusting the account between the dead and the living is to see that the debits against the latter do not exceed the advances made by the former. Few of the incumbrances entailed on nations would bear a liquidation even on this principle.

The objections to the doctrine as applied to the 3d. class of acts may perhaps be merely practical. But in that view they appear to be of great force.

Unless such laws should be kept in force by new acts regularly anticipating the end of the term, all the rights depending on positive laws, that is, most of the rights of property would become absolutely defunct; and the most violent struggles be generated between those interested in reviving and those interested in new-modelling the former state of property. Nor would events of this kind be improbable. The obstacles to the passage of laws which render a power to repeal inferior to an opportunity of rejecting, as a security against oppression, would here render an opportunity of rejecting an insecure provision against anarchy. Add, that the possibility of an event so hazardous to the rights of property could not fail to depreciate its value; that the approach of the crisis would increase this effect; that the frequent return of periods superseding all the obligations depending on antecedent laws and usages, must be weak[en]ing the reverence for those obligations, co-operate with motives to licentiousness already too powerful; and that the uncertainty incident to such a state of things would on one side discourage the steady exertions of industry produced by permanent laws, and on the other, give a disproportionate advantage to the more, over the less, sagacious and interprizing part of the Society.

I find no releif from these consequences, but in the received doctrine that a tacit assent may be given to established Constitutions and laws, and that this assent may be inferred, where no positive dissent appears. It seems less impracticable to remedy, by wise plans of Government, the dangerous operation of this doctrine, than to find a remedy for the difficulties inseparable from the other.

May it not be questioned whether it be possible to exclude wholly the idea of tacit assent, without subverting the foundation of civil Society?

On what principle does the voice of the majority bind the minority? It does not result I conceive from the law of nature, but from compact founded on conveniency. A greater proportion might be required by the fundamental constitution of a Society if it were judged eligible. Prior then to the establishment of this principle, *unanimity* was necessary; and strict Theory at all times presupposes the assent of every member to the establishment of the rule itself. If this assent can not be given tacitly, or be not implied where no positive evidence forbids, persons born in Society would not on attaining ripe age be bound by acts of the Majority; and either a *unanimous* repetition of every law would be necessary on the accession of new members, or an express assent must be obtained from these to the rule by which the voice of the Majority is made the voice of the whole.

If the observations I have hazarded be not misapplied, it follows that a limitation of the validity of national acts to the computed life of a nation, is in some instances not required by Theory, and in others cannot be accomodated to practice. The observations are not meant however to impeach either the utility of the principle in some particular cases; or the general importance of it in the eye of the philosophical Legislator. On the contrary it would give me singular pleasure to see it first announced in the proceedings of the U. States, and always kept in their view, as a salutary curb on the living generation from imposing unjust or unnecessary burdens on their successors. But this is a pleasure which I have little hope of enjoying. The spirit of philosophical legislation has never reached some parts of the Union, and is by no means the fashion here, either within or without Congress. The evils suffered and feared from weakness in Government, and licentiousness in the people, have turned the attention more towards the means of strengthening the former than of narrowing its extent in the minds of the latter. Besides this, it is so much easier to espy the little difficulties immediately incident to every great plan, than to comprehend its general and remote benefits, that our hemisphere must be still more enlightened before many of the sublime truths which are seen thro' the medium of Philosophy, become visible to the naked eye of the ordinary Politician. I have nothing to add at present but that I remain always and most affectly. Yours,

Js. Madison Jr.

Proposing Amendments

IN RATIFICATION CONVENTIONS WHERE they enjoyed decided majorities, Federalists felt little inclination to placate their opponents, and insisted that the Constitution be ratified as proposed. In states where the sides were more evenly balanced, like Massachusetts, or where Anti-Federalists had potential or real majorities, like Virginia and New York, the Constitution's supporters had to act more prudently. Here they adopted a twofold strategy. On the one hand, they still insisted that the Constitution had to be ratified now, in its entirety, without prior conditions to be satisfied before a state's assent would be conclusive. But on the other hand, if those conditions were met, Federalists indicated they would acquiesce in recommending amendments for future consideration, presumably by the first Congress to meet under the new Constitution. In the three populous and critical states just mentioned, this formula became the basis for securing ratification.

Many scholars have argued that this process produced an effective promise by Federalists to make sure that articles like the eventual Bill of Rights would be added to the Constitution. The decision to recommend amendments thus became another compromise, like those that affected the rules of representation in the new Congress. Federalists, however, did not see it quite the same way. Their main goal was to make sure that the Constitution was ratified immediately and unconditionally, and that is what happened. Whether amendments would be added, and if so, what kind, were matters to be determined later.

Massachusetts Ratification Convention
February 6, 1788

COMMONWEALTH OF MASSACHUSETTS.

In Convention of the delegates of the PEOPLE of the
Commonwealth of Massachusetts February 6th. 1788.

THE CONVENTION HAVING IMPARTIALLY discussed, & fully considered The Constitution for the United States of America, reported to Congress by the Convention of Delegates from the United States of America, & submitted to us by a resolution of the General Court of the said Commonwealth, passed the twenty fifth day of October last past, & acknowledging with grateful hearts the goodness of the Supreme Ruler of the Universe in affording the People of the United States in the course of his providence an opportunity deliberately & peaceably without fraud or surprize of entering into an explicit & solemn Compact with each other by assenting to & ratifying a New Constitution in order to form a more perfect Union, establish Justice, insure Domestic tranquillity, provide for the common defence, promote the general welfare & secure the blessings of Liberty to themselves & their posterity; Do in the name & in behalf of the People of the Commonwealth of Massachusetts assent to & ratify the said Constitution for the United States of America.

And as it is the opinion of this Convention that certain amendments & alterations in the said Constitution would remove the fears & quiet the apprehensions of many of the good people of this Commonwealth & more effectually guard against an undue administration of the Federal Government, The Convention do therefore recommend that the following alterations & provisions be introduced into the said Constitution.

First, That it be explicitly declared that all Powers not expressly delegated by the aforesaid Constitution are reserved to the several States to be by them exercised.

Secondly, That there shall be one representative to every thirty thousand persons according to the Census mentioned in the Constitution until the whole number of the Representatives amounts to Two hundred.

Thirdly, That Congress do not exercise the powers vested in them by the fourth Section of the first article, but in cases when a State shall neglect or refuse to make the regulations therein mentioned or shall make regulations subversive of the rights of the People to a free & equal representation in Congress agreeably to the Constitution.

Fourthly, That Congress do not lay direct Taxes but when the Monies arising from the Impost & Excise are insufficient for the Publick exigencies nor then until Congress shall have first made a requisition upon the States to assess levy & pay their respective proportions of such Requisition agreeably to the Census fixed in the said Constitution, in such way & manner as the Legislature of the States shall think best, & in such case if any State shall neglect or refuse to pay its proportion pursuant to such requisition then Congress may assess & levy such State's proportion together with interest thereon at the rate of Six per cent per annum from the time of payment prescribed in such requisition.

Fifthly, That Congress erect no Company of Merchants with exclusive advantages of Commerce.

Sixthly, That no person shall be tried for any Crime by which he may incur an infamous punishment or loss of life until he be first indicted by a Grand Jury, except in such cases as may arise in the Government & regulation of the Land & Naval forces.

Seventhly, The Supreme Judicial Federal Court shall have no jurisdiction of Causes between Citizens of different States unless the matter in dispute whether it concerns the realty or personalty be of the value of Three thousand dollars the least nor shall the Federal Judicial Powers extend to any actions between Citizens of different States where the matter in dispute whether it concerns the Realty or Personalty is not of the value of Fifteen hundred dollars at the least.

Eighthly, In civil actions between Citizens of different States every issue of fact arising in Actions at common law shall be tried by a Jury if the parties or either of them request it.

Ninthly, Congress shall at no time consent that any Person holding an office of trust or profit under the United States shall accept of a title of Nobility or any other title or office from any King, Prince or Foreign State.

And the Convention do in the name & in behalf of the People of this Commonwealth enjoin it upon their Representatives in Congress at all times until the alterations & provisions aforesaid have been considered agreeably to the Fifth article of the said Constitution to exert all their influence & use all reasonable & legal methods to obtain a ratification of the said alterations & provisions in such manner as is provided in the said Article.

And that the United States in Congress Assembled may have due notice of the Assent & Ratification of the said Constitution by this Convention it is, Resolved, that the Assent & Ratification aforesaid be engrossed on Parchment together with the recommendation & injunction aforesaid & with this resolution & that His Excellency John Hancock Esqr. President & the Honble. William Cushing Esqr. Vice President, of this Convention transmit the same, countersigned by the Secretary of the Convention under their hands & seals to the United States in Congress Assembled.

George Richards Minot, Secretary.
John Hancock President
Wm Cushing Vice President

Pursuant to the Resolution aforesaid WE the President & Vice President abovenamed Do hereby transmit to the United States in Congress Assembled, the same Resolution with the above Assent and Ratification of the Constitution aforesaid for the United States, And the recommendation & injunction above specified.

In Witness whereof We have hereunto set our hands & seals at Boston in the Commonwealth aforesaid this Seventh day of February Anno Domini one thousand Seven Hundred & Eighty eight, and in the Twelfth year of the Independence of the United States of America.

John Hancock President
Wm Cushing Vice President

Virginia Ratification Convention

June 27, 1788

Debates

[Another engrossed form of the ratification agreed to on Wednesday last, containing the proposed Constitution of Government, as recommended by the Federal Convention on the seventeenth day of *September,* one thousand seven hundred and eighty seven, being prepared by the Secretary, was read, and signed by the President in behalf of the Con[ven]tion.]

On motion, *Ordered,* That the said ratification be deposited by the Secretary of this Convention in the archives of the General Assembly of this State.

Mr. *Wythe* reported, from the Committee appointed, such amendments to the proposed Constitution of Government for the United States, as were by them deemed necessary to be recommended to the consideration of the Congress which shall first assemble under the said Constitution, to be acted upon according to the mode prescribed in the fifth article thereof; and he read the same in his place, and afterwards delivered them in at the Clerk's table, where the same were again read, and are as followeth:

That there be a Declaration or Bill of Rights asserting and securing from encroachment the essential and unalienable rights of the people in some such manner as the following:

1st. That there are certain natural rights of which men when they form a social compact cannot deprive or divest their posterity, among which are the enjoyment of life, and liberty, with the means of acquiring, possessing and protecting property, and pursuing and obtaining happiness and safety.

2d. That all power is naturally vested in, and consequently derived from, the people; that magistrates therefore are their trustees, and agents, and at all times amenable to them.

3d. That Government ought to be instituted for the common benefit, protection and security of the people; and that the doctrine of non-resistance against arbitrary power and oppression, is absurd, slavish, and destructive to the good and happiness of mankind.

4th. That no man or set of men are entitled to exclusive or separate public emoluments or privileges from the community, but in consideration of public services; which not being descendible, neither ought the offices of magistrate, legislator or judge, or any other public office to be hereditary.

5th. That the Legislative, Executive and Judiciary powers of Government should be separate and distinct, and that the members of the two first may be restrained from oppression by feeling and participating the public burthens, they should at fixed periods be reduced to a private station, return into the mass of the people, and the vacancies be supplied by certain and regular elections; in which all or any part of the former members to be eligible or ineligible, as the rules of the Constitution of Government, and the laws shall direct.

6th. That elections of Representatives in the Legislature ought to be free and frequent, and all men having sufficient evidence of permanent common interest with, and attachment to the community, ought to have the right of suffrage: and no aid, charge, tax or fee can be set, rated, or levied upon the people without their own consent, or that of their Representatives, so elected, nor can they be bound by any law, to which they have not in like manner assented for the public good.

7th. That all power of suspending laws, or the execution of laws by any authority without the consent of the Representatives of the people in the Legislature, is injurious to their rights, and ought not to be exercised.

8th. That in all criminal and capital prosecutions, a man hath a right to demand the cause and nature of his accusation, to be confronted with the accusers and witnesses, to call for evidence and be allowed counsel in his favor, and to a fair and speedy trial by an impartial jury of his vicinage, without whose unanimous consent he cannot be found guilty (except in the government of the land and naval forces) nor can he be compelled to give evidence against himself.

9th. That no freeman ought to be taken, imprisoned, or disseized of his freehold, liberties, privileges or franchises, or outlawed, or exiled, or in any manner destroyed or deprived of his life, liberty, or property, but by the law of the land.

10th. That every freeman restrained of his liberty is entitled to a remedy to enquire into the lawfulness thereof, and to remove the same, if unlawful, and that such remedy ought not to be denied nor delayed.

11th. That in controversies respecting property, and in suits between man and man, the ancient trial by jury, is one of the greatest securities to the rights of the people, and ought to remain sacred and inviolable.

12th. That every freeman ought to find a certain remedy by recourse to the laws for all injuries and wrongs he may receive in his person, property, or character. He ought to obtain right and justice freely without sale, completely and without denial, promptly and without delay, and that all establishments or regulations, contravening these rights, are oppressive and unjust.

13th. That excessive bail ought not to be required, nor excessive fines imposed, nor cruel and unusual punishments inflicted.

14th. That every freeman has a right to be secure from all unreasonable searches and seizures of his person, his papers, and property: all warrants therefore to search suspected places, or seize any freeman, his papers or property, without information upon oath (or affirmation of a person religiously scrupulous of taking an oath) of legal and sufficient cause, are grievous and oppressive, and all general warrants to search suspected places, or to apprehend any suspected person without specially naming or describing the place or person, are dangerous and ought not to be granted.

15th. That the people have a right peaceably to assemble together to consult for the common good, or to instruct their Representatives; and that every freeman has a right to petition or apply to the Legislature for redress of grievances.

16th. That the people have a right to freedom of speech, and of writing and publishing their sentiments; that the freedom of the press is one of the greatest bulwarks of liberty, and ought not to be violated.

17th. That the people have a right to keep and bear arms: that a well regulated militia composed of the body of the people trained to arms, is the proper, natural and safe defence of a free State. That standing armies in time of peace are dangerous to liberty, and therefore ought to be avoided, as far as the circumstances and protection of the community will admit; and that in all cases, the military should be under strict subordination to and governed by the civil power.

18th. That no soldier in time of peace ought to be quartered in any house without the consent of the owner, and in time of war in such manner only as the laws direct.

19th. That any person religiously scrupulous of bearing arms ought to be exempted upon payment of an equivalent to employ another to bear arms in his stead.

20th. That religion, or the duty which we owe to our Creator, and the manner of discharging it, can be directed only by reason and conviction, not by force or violence, and therefore all men have an equal, natural and unalienable right to the free exercise of religion according to the dictates of conscience, and that no particular religious sect or society ought to favored or established by law in preference to others.

AMENDMENTS TO THE CONSTITUTION.

1st. That each State in the Union shall respectively retain every power, jurisdiction and right, which is not by this Constitution delegated to the Congress of the United States, or to the departments of the Federal Government.

2d. That there shall be one Representative for every thirty thousand, according to the enumeration or census mentioned in the Constitution, until the whole number of Representatives amounts to two hundred; after which that number shall be continued or encreased as Congress shall direct, upon the principles fixed in the Constitution, by apportioning the Representatives of each State to some greater number of people from time to time as population encreases.

3d. When the Congress shall lay direct taxes or excises, they shall immediately inform the Executive power of each State, of the quota of such State according to the census herein directed, which is proposed to be thereby raised; and if the Legislature of any State shall pass a law which shall be effectual for raising such quota at the time required by Congress, the taxes and excises laid by Congress, shall not be collected in such State.

4th. That the Members of the Senate and House of Representatives shall be ineligible to, and incapable of holding any civil office under the authority of the United States, during the time for which they shall respectively be elected.

5th. That the journals of the proceedings of the Senate and House of Representatives shall be published at least once in every year, except such parts thereof relating to treaties, alliances, or military operations, as in their judgment require secrecy.

6th. That a regular statement and account of the receipts and expenditures of all public money, shall be published at least once in every year.

7th. That no commercial treaty shall be ratified without the concurrence of two-thirds of the whole number of the Members of the Senate; and no treaty, ceding, contracting, restraining or suspending the territorial rights or claims of the United States, or any of them, or their, or any of their rights or claims to fishing in the American seas, or navigating the American rivers, shall be made, but in cases of the most urgent and extreme necessity, nor shall any such treaty be ratified without the concurrence of three fourths of the whole number of the Members of both Houses respectively.

8th. That no navigation law or law regulating commerce shall be passed without the consent of two-thirds of the Members present, in both Houses.

9th. That no standing army or regular troops shall be raised, or kept up in time of peace, without the consent of two-thirds of the Members present, in both Houses.

10th. That no soldier shall be inlisted for any longer term than four years, except in time of war, and then for no longer term than the continuance of the war.

11th. That each State respectively shall have the power to provide for organizing, arming, and disciplining its own militia, whensoever Congress shall omit or neglect to provide for the same. That the militia shall not be subject to martial law, except when in actual service in time of war, invasion or rebellion, and when not in the actual service of the United States, shall be subject only to such fines, penalties and punishments, as shall be directed or inflicted by the laws of its own State.

12th. That the exclusive power of Legislation given to Congress over the Federal Town and its adjacent district, and other places, purchased or to be purchased by Congress of any of the States, shall extend only to such regulations as respect the police and good government thereof.

13th. That no person shall be capable of being President of the United States for more than eight years in any term of sixteen years.

14th. That the Judicial power of the United States shall be vested in one Supreme Court, and in such Courts of Admiralty as Congress may from time to time ordain and establish in any of the different States: The Judicial power shall extend to all cases in law and equity arising under treaties made, or which shall be made under the authority of the United States; to all cases affecting Ambassadors, other foreign Ministers and Consuls; to all cases of Admiralty and Maritime jurisdiction; to controversies to which the United States shall be a party; to controversies between two or more States, and between parties claiming lands under the grants of different States. In all cases affecting Ambassadors, other foreign Ministers and Consuls, and those in which a State shall be a party, the Supreme Court shall have original jurisdiction; in all other cases before mentioned, the Supreme Court shall have appellate jurisdiction, as to matters of law only; except in cases of equity, and of Admiralty and Maritime jurisdiction, in which the Supreme Court shall have appellate jurisdiction both as to law and fact, with such exceptions and under such regulations as the Congress shall make: But the Judicial power of the United States shall extend to no case where the cause of action shall have originated before the ratification of this Constitution; except in disputes between States about their territory; disputes between persons claiming lands under the grants of different States, and suits for debts due to the United States.

15th. That in criminal prosecutions, no man shall be restrained in the exercise of the usual and accustomed right of challenging or excepting to the jury.

16th. That Congress shall not alter, modify, or interfere in the times, places, or manner of holding elections for Senators and Representatives, or either of them, except when the Legislature of any State shall neglect, refuse, or be disabled by invasion or rebellion to prescribe the same.

17th. That those clauses which declare that Congress shall not exercise certain powers, be not interpreted in any manner what-soever, to extend the powers of Congress; but that they be con-strued either as making exceptions to the specified powers where this shall be the case, or otherwise, as inserted merely for greater caution.

18th. That the laws ascertaining the compensation of Senators and Representatives for their services, be postponed in their opera-tion, until after the election of Representatives immediately suc-ceeding the passing thereof; that excepted, which shall first be passed on the subject.

19th. That some tribunal other than the Senate be provided for trying impeachments of Senators.

20th. That the salary of a Judge shall not be encreased or dimin-ished during his continuance in office otherwise than by general regulations of salary, which may take place on a revision of the sub-ject at stated periods of not less than seven years, to commence from the time such salaries shall be first ascertained by Congress.

AND the Convention do, in the name and behalf of the people of this Commonwealth, enjoin it upon their Representatives in Con-gress to exert all their influence and use all reasonable and legal methods to obtain a RATIFICATION of the foregoing alterations and provisions in the manner provided by the fifth article of the said Constitution; and in all Congressional laws to be passed in the mean time, to conform to the spirit of these amendments as far as the said Constitution will admit.

And so much of the said amendments as is contained in the first twenty articles, constituting the Bill of Rights, being again read;

Resolved, That this Convention doth concur therein.

New York Ratification Convention
July 26, 1788

We the delegates of the People of the State of New York, duly elected and Met in Convention, having maturely considered the Constitution for the United States of America, agreed to on the seventeenth day of September, in the year One thousand Seven hundred and Eighty seven, by the Convention then assembled at Philadelphia in the Common-wealth of Pennsylvania (a Copy whereof precedes these presents) and having also seriously and deliberately considered the present situation of the United States, Do DECLARE AND MAKE KNOWN.

That all Power is originally vested in and consequently derived from the People, and that Government is instituted by them for their common Interest Protection and Security.

That the enjoyment of Life, Liberty and the pursuit of Happiness are essential rights which every Government ought to respect and preserve.

That the powers of Government may be reassumed by the People, whensoever it shall become necessary to their Happiness; that every Power, Jurisdiction and right, which is not by the said Constitution clearly delegated to the Congress of the United States, or the departments of the Government thereof, remains to the People of the several States, or to their respective State Governments to whom they may have granted the same; And that those Clauses in the said Constitution, which declare, that Congress shall not have or exercise certain Powers, do not imply that Congress is entitled to any Powers not given by the said Constitution; but such Clauses are to be construed either as exceptions to certain specified Powers, or as inserted merely for greater Caution.

That the People have an equal, natural and unalienable right, freely and peaceably to Exercise their Religion according to the dictates of Conscience, and that no Religious Sect or Society ought to be favoured or established by Law in preference of others.

That the People have a right to keep and bear Arms; that a well regulated Militia, including the body of the People *capable of bearing Arms*, is the proper, natural and safe defence of a free State;

That the Militia should not be subject to Martial Law, except in time of War, Rebellion or Insurrection.

That standing Armies in time of Peace are dangerous to Liberty, and ought not to be kept up, except in Cases of necessity; and that at all times, the Military should be under strict Subordination to the civil Power.

That in time of Peace no Soldier ought to be quartered in any

House without the consent of the Owner, and in time of War only by the civil Magistrate in such manner as the Laws may direct.

That no Person ought to be taken imprisoned, or disseised of his freehold, or be exiled or deprived of his Privileges, Franchises, Life, Liberty or Property, but by due process of Law.

That no Person ought to be put twice in Jeopardy of Life or Limb for one and the same Offence, nor, unless in case of impeachment, be punished more than once for the same Offence.

That every Person restrained of his Liberty is entitled to an enquiry into the lawfulness of such restraint, and to a removal thereof if unlawful, and that such enquiry and removal ought not to be denied or delayed, except when on account of Public Danger the Congress shall suspend the privilege of the Writ of Habeas Corpus.

That excessive Bail ought not to be required; nor excessive Fines imposed; nor Cruel or unusual Punishments inflicted.

That (except in the Government of the Land and Naval Forces, and of the Militia when in actual Service, and in cases of Impeachment) a Presentment or Indictment by a Grand Jury ought to be observed as a necessary preliminary to the trial of all Crimes cognizable by the Judiciary of the United States, and such Trial should be speedy, public, and by an impartial Jury of the County where the Crime was committed; and that no person can be found Guilty without the unanimous consent of such Jury. But in cases of Crimes not committed within any County of any of the United States, and in Cases of Crimes committed within any County in which a general Insurrection may prevail, or which may be in the possession of a foreign Enemy, the enquiry and trial may be in such County as the Congress shall by Law direct; which County in the two Cases last mentioned should be as near as conveniently may be to that County in which the Crime may have been committed. And that in all Criminal Prosecutions, the Accused ought to be informed of the cause and nature of his Accusation, to be confronted with his accusers and the Witnesses against him, to have the means of producing his Witnesses, and the assistance of Council for his defense, and should not be compelled to give Evidence against himself.

That the trial by Jury in the extent that it obtains by the Common Law of England is one of the greatest securities to the rights of a free People, and ought to remain inviolate.

That every Freeman has a right to be secure from all unreasonable searches and seizures of his person his papers or his property, and therefore, that all Warrants to search suspected places or seize any Freeman his papers or property, without information upon Oath or Affirmation of sufficient cause, are grievous and oppressive; and that all general Warrants (or such in which the place or person suspected are not particularly designated) are dangerous and ought not to be granted.

That the People have a right peaceably to assemble together to consult for their common good, or to instruct their Representatives; and that every person has a right to Petition or apply to the Legislature for redress of Grievances.—That the Freedom of the Press ought not to be violated or restrained.

That there should be once in four years an Election of the President and Vice President, so that no Officer who may be appointed by the Congress to act as President in case of the removal, death, resignation or inability of the President and Vice President can in any case continue to act beyond the termination of the period for which the last President and Vice President were elected.

That nothing contained in the said Constitution is to be construed to prevent the Legislature of any State from passing Laws at its discretion from time to time to divide such State into convenient Districts, and to apportion its Representatives to and amongst such Districts.

That the Prohibition contained in the said Constitution against *ex post facto* Laws, extends only to Laws concerning Crimes.

That all Appeals in Causes determineable according to the course of the common Law, ought to be by Writ of Error and not otherwise.

That the Judicial Power of the United States in cases in which a State may be a party, does not extend to criminal Prosecutions, or to authorize any Suit by any Person against a State.

That the Judicial Power of the United States as to Controversies between Citizens of the same State claiming Lands under Grants of different States is not to be construed to extend to any other Controversies between them, except those which relate to such Lands, so claimed under Grants of different States.

That the Jurisdiction of the Supreme Court of the United States, or of any other Court to be instituted by the Congress, is not in any case to be encreased enlarged or extended by any Fiction Collusion or mere suggestion;—And That no Treaty is to be construed so to operate as to alter the Constitution of any State.

UNDER these impressions and declaring that the rights aforesaid cannot be abridged or violated, and that the Explanations aforesaid are consistent with the said Constitution, And in Confidence that the Amendments which shall have been proposed to the said Constitution will receive an early and mature Consideration: WE the said Delegates, in the Name and in the behalf of the People of the State of New York Do by these presents Assent to and Ratify the said Constitution. IN FULL CONFIDENCE NEVERTHELESS that until a Convention shall be called and convened for proposing Amendments to the said Constitution, the Militia of this State will not be continued in Service out of this State for a longer term than six weeks without the Consent of the Legislature thereof;—that the Congress will not make or alter any Regulation in this State respecting the times places and manner of holding Elections for Senators or Representatives unless the Legislature of this State shall neglect or refuse to make Laws or regulations for the purpose, or from any circumstance be incapable of making the same, and that in those cases such power will only be exercised until the Legislature of this State shall make provision in the Premises;—that no Excise will be imposed on any Article of the Growth production or Manufacture of the United States, or any of them within this State, Ardent Spirits excepted; And that the Congress will not lay direct Taxes within this State, but when the Monies arising from the Impost and Excise shall be insufficient for the public Exigencies, nor then, until Congress shall first have made a Requisition upon this State to assess levy and pay the Amount of such Requisition made agreably to the Census fixed in the said Constitution in such way and manner as the Legislature of this State shall judge best, but that in such case, if the State shall neglect or refuse to pay its proportion pursuant to such Requisition, then the Congress may assess and levy this States proportion together with Interest at the Rate of six per Centum per Annum from the time at which the same was required to be paid.

> DONE in Convention at Poughkeepsie in the County of Dutchess in the State of New York and twenty sixth day of July in the year of our Lord One thousand Seven hundred and Eighty eight.

By Order of the Convention.
GEO: CLINTON President

Attested

JOHN MCKESSON ⎫
AB^M B. BANCKER ⎭ Secretaries—

And the Convention do in the Name and Behalf of the People of the State of New York enjoin it upon their Representatives in the Congress, to Exert all their Influence, and use all reasonable means to Obtain a Ratification of the following Amendments to the said Constitution in the manner prescribed therein; and in all Laws to be passed by the Congress in the meantime to conform to the spirit of the said Amendments as far as the Constitution will admit.

That there shall be one Representative for every thirty thousand Inhabitants, according to the enumeration or Census mentioned in the Constitution, until the whole number of Representatives amounts to two hundred; after which that number shall be continued or encreased but not diminished, as Congress shall direct, and according to such ratio as the Congress shall fix, in conformity to the rule prescribed for the Apportionment of Representatives and direct Taxes.

That the Congress do not impose any Excise on any Article (except Ardent Spirits) of the Growth Production or Manufacture of the United States, or any of them.

That Congress do not lay direct Taxes but when the Monies arising from the Impost and Excise shall be insufficient for the Public Exigencies, nor then until Congress shall first have made a Requisition upon the States to assess levy and pay their respective proportions of such Requisition, agreably to the Census fixed in the said Constitution, in such way and manner as the Legislatures of the respective States shall judge best; and in such Case, if any State shall neglect or refuse to pay its proportion persuant to such Requisition, then Congress may assess and levy such States proportion, together with Interest at the rate of six per Centum per Annum, from the time of Payment prescribed in such Requisition.

That the Congress shall not make or alter any Regulation in any State respecting the times places and manner of holding Elections for Senators or Representatives, unless the Legislature of such State shall neglect or refuse to make Laws or Regulations for the purpose, or from any circumstance be incapable of making the same, and then only until the Legislature of such State shall make provision in the premises; provided that Congress may prescribe the time for the Election of Representatives.

That no Persons except natural born Citizens, or such as were Citizens on or before the fourth day of July one thousand seven hundred and seventy six, or such as held Commissions under the United States during the War, and have at any time since the fourth day of July one thousand seven hundred and seventy six become Citizens of one or other of the United States, and who shall be Freeholders, shall be eligible to the Places of President, Vice President, or Members of either House of the Congress of the United States.

That the Congress do not grant Monopolies or erect any Company with exclusive Advantages of Commerce.

That no standing Army or regular Troops shall be raised or kept up in time of peace, without the consent of two-thirds of the Senators and Representatives present in each House.

That no Money be borrowed on the Credit of the United States without the Assent of two-thirds of the Senators and Representatives present in each House.

That the Congress shall not declare War without the concurrence of two-thirds of the Senators and Representatives present in each House.

That the Privilege of the *Habeas Corpus* shall not by any Law be suspended for a longer term than six Months, or until twenty days after the Meeting of the Congress next following the passing of the Act for such suspension.

That the Right of the Congress to exercise exclusive Legislation over such District, not exceeding ten Miles square, as may by cession of a particular State, and the acceptance of Congress, become the Seat of the Government of the United States, shall not be so exercised, as to exempt the Inhabitants of such District from paying the like Taxes Imposts Duties and Excises, as shall be imposed on the other Inhabitants of the State in which such District may be; and that no person shall be privileged within the said Districts from Arrest for Crimes committed, or Debts contracted out of the said District.

That the Right of exclusive Legislation with respect to such places as may be purchased for the Erection of Forts, Magazines, Arsenals,

Dockyards and other needful Buildings, shall not authorize the Congress to make any Law to prevent the Laws of the States respectively in which they may be, from extending to such places in all civil and Criminal Matters, except as to such Persons as shall be in the Service of the United States; nor to them with respect to Crimes committed without such Places.

That the Compensation for the Senators and Representatives be ascertained by standing Laws; and that no alteration of the existing rate of Compensation shall operate for the Benefit of the Representatives, until after a subsequent Election shall have been had.

That the Journals of the Congress shall be published at least once a year, with the exception of such parts relating to Treaties or Military operations, as in the Judgment of either House shall require Secrecy; and that both Houses of Congress shall always keep their Doors open during their Sessions, unless the Business may in their Opinion requires Secrecy. That the yeas & nays shall be entered on the Journals whenever two Members in either House may require it.

That no Capitation Tax shall ever be laid by the Congress.

That no Person be eligible as a Senator for more than six years in any term of twelve years; and that the Legislatures of the respective States may recal their Senators or either of them, and elect others in their stead, to serve the remainder of the time for which the Senators so recalled were appointed.

That no Senator or Representative shall during the time for which he was elected be appointed to any Office under the Authority of the United States.

That the Authority given to the Executives of the States to fill the vacancies of Senators be abolished, and that such vacancies be filled by the respective Legislatures.

That the Power of Congress to pass uniform Laws concerning Bankruptcy shall only extend to Merchants and other Traders; and that the States respectively may pass Laws for the relief of other Insolvent Debtors.

That no Person shall be eligible to the Office of President of the United States a third time.

That the Executive shall not grant Pardons for Treason, unless with the Consent of the Congress; but may at his discretion grant

Reprieves to persons convicted of Treason, until their Cases, can be laid before the Congress.

That the President or person exercising his Powers for the time being, shall not command an Army in the Field in person, without the previous desire of the Congress.

That all Letters Patent, Commissions, Pardons, Writs and Process of the United States, shall run in the Name of *the People of the United States,* and be tested in the Name of the President of the United States, or the person exercising his powers for the time being, or the first Judge of the Court out of which the same shall issue, as the case may be.

That the Congress shall not constitute ordain or establish any Tribunals or Inferior Courts, with any other than Appellate Jurisdiction, except such as may be necessary for the Tryal of Causes of Admiralty and Maritime Jurisdiction, and for the Trial of Piracies and Felonies committed on the High Seas; and in all other Cases to which the Judicial Power of the United States extends, and in which the Supreme Court of the United States has not original Jurisdiction, the Causes shall be heard tried, and determined in some one of the State Courts, with the right of Appeal to the Supreme Court of the United States, or other proper Tribunal to be established for that purpose by the Congress, with such exceptions, and under such regulations as the Congress shall make.

That the Court for the Trial of Impeachments shall consist of the Senate, the Judges of the Supreme Court of the United States, and the first or Senior Judge for the time being, of the highest Court of general and ordinary common Law Jurisdiction in each State;—that the Congress shall by standing Laws designate the Courts in the respective States answering this Description, and in States having no Courts exactly answering this Description, shall designate some other Court, preferring such if any there be, whose Judge or Judges may hold their places during good Behaviour—Provided that no more than one Judge, other than Judges of the Supreme Court of the United States, shall come from one State—That the Congress be authorized to pass Laws for compensating the said Judges for such Services and for compelling their Attendance—and that a Majority at least of the said Judges shall be requisite to constitute the said Court—that no person impeached shall sit as a Member thereof.

That each Member shall previous to the entering upon any Trial take an Oath or Affirmation, honestly and impartially to hear and determine the Cause—and that a Majority of the Members present shall be necessary to a Conviction.

That persons aggrieved by any Judgment, Sentence or Decree of the Supreme Court of the United States, in any Cause in which that Court has original Jurisdiction, with such exceptions and under such Regulations as the Congress shall make concerning the same, shall upon application, have a Commission to be issued by the President of the United States, to such Men learned in the Law as he shall nominate, and by and with the Advice and consent of the Senate appoint, not less than seven, authorizing such Commissioners, or any seven or more of them, to correct the Errors in such Judgment or to review such Sentence and Decree, as the case may be, and to do Justice to the parties in the Premises.

That no Judge of the Supreme Court of the United States shall hold any other Office under the United States, or any of them.

That the Judicial Power of the United States shall extend to no Controversies respecting Land, unless it relate to Claims of Territory or Jurisdiction between States, or to Claims of Land between Individuals, or between States and Individuals under the Grants of different States.

That the Militia of any State shall not be compelled to serve without the limits of the State for a longer term than six weeks, without the Consent of the Legislature thereof.

That the words *without the Consent of the Congress* in the seventh Clause of the ninth Section of the first Article of the Constitution, be expunged.

That the Senators and Representatives and all Executive and Judicial Officers of the United States shall be bound by Oath or Affirmation not to infringe or violate the Constitutions or Rights of the respective States.

That the Legislatures of the respective States may make Provision by Law, that the Electors of the Election Districts to be by them appointed shall chuse a Citizen of the United States who shall have been an Inhabitant of such District for the Term of one year immediately preceeding the time of his Election, for one of the Representatives of such State.

Done in Convention at Poughkeepsie in the County of Dutchess in the State of New York the twenty sixth day of July in the year of our Lord One thousand seven hundred and Eighty eight.

By Order of the Convention.

Geo: Clinton President

Attested—

John McKesson
Ab^M B. Bancker   } Secretaries—

Framing the Bill of Rights

THE PRINCIPAL RESPONSIBILITY FOR assuring that amendments were adopted fell to James Madison. As his correspondence with Thomas Jefferson reveals, Madison never really came to believe that the protection of rights depended on the adoption of amendments. But during a tough election campaign against his friend James Monroe for election to the House of Representatives, he found it necessary to issue a public letter affirming his support for amendments protecting rights. Once elected, he felt obliged to honor this pledge. He had also come to believe that the adoption of a limited number of carefully tailored amendments would do much to reconcile moderate Anti-Federalists to the Constitution. Accordingly, in the early months of 1789, he reviewed all of the proposals that the various state conventions had put forward—they had been conveniently reprinted in a single pamphlet—and culled from this lengthy list a moderate number of proposals that could be safely added to the Constitution without affecting any of the critical decisions taken at Philadelphia.

Though Madison gave early notice of his intentions, not until June 8, 1789 was he able to lay his proposed amendments before the House of Representatives. Most of his colleagues were reluctant to pursue the subject. The Federalists who dominated both houses of Congress felt little obligation to honor the ostensible pledges made during the ratification campaign, while the Anti-Federalist minority realized they would never obtain the substantive changes they desired. Madison persisted, however, and eventually the House appointed a committee to consider his amendments, as well as another draft prepared by Roger Sherman of Connecticut (who had the distinction of serving at the Stamp Act Congress of 1765 as well as being a signer of the Declaration of Independence, the Articles of Confederation, and the Constitution). While the committee largely ignored his proposals, the House ultimately agreed with Sherman on one key point. Where Madison had wanted to "interweave" his amendments at those points in the Constitution where each seemed most pertinent, Sherman argued that the amendments had to be presented as separate supplemental articles. In this form, the House sent seventeen proposed amendments to the Senate on August 24. The alterations made by the Senate were then referred to a conference committee, and in late September, Congress sent a final compilation of twelve amendments on to the states.

Ten of these amendments (originally the third through twelfth) were ratified by December 1791. The original Second Amendment, relating to congressional pay raises, initially failed to obtain ratification. But in 1981 its existence was discovered by a young Texas college student, Gregory Watson, who subsequently launched a campaign to secure its ratification. In 1993, after a voyage of 203 years, Madison's proposal was brought safely to harbor as the Twenty-Seventh Amendment.

FRAMING THE BILL OF RIGHTS

—*James Madison*—
SPEECH INTRODUCING AMENDMENTS IN THE HOUSE OF REPRESENTATIVES
JUNE 8, 1789

I AM SORRY TO be accessary to the loss of a single moment of time by the House. If I had been indulged in my motion, and we had gone into a Committee of the Whole, I think we might have rose and resumed the consideration of other business before this time; that is, so far as it depended upon what I proposed to bring forward. As that mode seems not to give satisfaction, I will withdraw the motion, and move you, sir, that a select committee be appointed to consider and report such amendments as are proper for Congress to propose to the Legislatures of the several States, conformably to the fifth article of the Constitution.

I will state my reasons why I think it proper to propose amendments, and state the amendments themselves, so far as I think they ought to be proposed. If I thought I could fulfil the duty which I owe to myself and my constituents, to let the subject pass over in silence, I most certainly should not trespass upon the indulgence of this House. But I cannot do this, and am therefore compelled to beg a patient hearing to what I have to lay before you. And I do most sincerely believe, that if Congress will devote but one day to this subject, so far as to satisfy the public that we do not disregard their wishes, it will have a salutary influence on the public councils, and prepare the way for a favorable reception of our future measures. It appears to me that this House is bound by every motive of prudence, not to let the first session pass over without proposing to the State Legislatures, some things to be incorporated into the Constitution, that will render it as acceptable to the whole people of the United States, as it has been found acceptable to a majority of them. I wish, among other reasons why something should be done, that those who had been friendly to the adoption of this Constitution may have the opportunity of proving to those who were opposed to it that they were as sincerely devoted to liberty and a Republican Government, as those who charged them with wishing the adoption of this Constitution in order to lay the foundation of an aristocracy or despotism. It will be a desirable thing to extinguish from the bosom of every member of the community, any apprehensions that there are those among his countrymen who wish to deprive them of the liberty for which they valiantly fought and honorably bled. And if there are amendments desired of such a nature as will not injure the Constitution, and they can be ingrafted so as to give satisfaction to the doubting part of our fellow-citizens, the friends of the Federal Government will evince that spirit of deference and concession for which they have hitherto been distinguished.

It cannot be a secret to the gentlemen in this House, that, notwithstanding the ratification of this system of Government by eleven of the thirteen United States, in some cases unanimously, in others by large majorities; yet still there is a great number of our constituents who are dissatisfied with it, among whom are many respectable for their talents and patriotism, and respectable for the jealousy they have for their liberty, which, though mistaken in its object is laudable in its motive. There is a great body of the people falling under this description, who at present feel much inclined to join their support to the cause of Federalism, if they were satisfied on this one point. We ought not to disregard their inclination, but, on principles of amity and moderation, conform to their wishes, and expressly declare the great rights of mankind secured under this Constitution. The acquiescence which our fellow-citizens show under the Government, calls upon us for a like return of moderation. But perhaps there is a stronger motive than this for our going into a consideration of the subject. It is to provide those securities for liberty which are required by a part of the community; I allude in a particular manner to those two States that have not thought fit to throw themselves into the bosom of the Confederacy.* It is a desirable thing, on our part as well as theirs,

---

*Rhode Island and North Carolina initially rejected the Constitution.

that a re-union should take place as soon as possible. I have no doubt, if we proceed to take those steps which would be prudent and requisite at this juncture, that in a short time we should see that disposition prevailing in those States which have not come in, that we have seen prevailing in those States which have embraced the Constitution.

But I will candidly acknowledge, that, over and above all these considerations, I do conceive that the Constitution may be amended; that is to say, if all power is subject to abuse, that then it is possible the abuse of the powers of the General Government may be guarded against in a more secure manner than is now done, while no one advantage arising from the exercise of that power shall be damaged or endangered by it. We have in this way something to gain, and, if we proceed with caution, nothing to lose. And in this case it is necessary to proceed with caution; for while we feel all these inducements to go into a revisal of the Constitution, we must feel for the Constitution itself, and make that revisal a moderate one. I should be unwilling to see a door opened for a reconsideration of the whole structure the Government—for a re-consideration of the principles and the substance of the powers given; because I doubt, if such a door were opened, we should be very likely to stop at that point which would be safe to the Government itself. But I do wish to see a door opened to consider, so far as to incorporate those provisions for the security of rights, against which I believe no serious objection has been made by any class of our constituents: such as would be likely to meet with the concurrence of two-thirds of both Houses, and the approbation of three-fourths of the State Legislatures. I will not propose a single alteration which I do not wish to see take place, as intrinsically proper in itself, or proper because it is wished for by a respectable number of my fellow-citizens; and therefore I shall not propose a single alteration but is likely to meet the concurrence required by the Constitution. There have been objections of various kinds made against the Constitution. Some were levelled against its structure because the President was without a council; because the Senate, which is a legislative body, had judicial powers in trials on impeachments; and because the powers of that body were compounded in other respects, in a manner that did not correspond with a particular theory; because it grants more power than is supposed to be necessary for every good purpose, and controls the ordinary powers of the State governments. I know some respectable characters who opposed this Government on these grounds; but I believe that the great mass of the people who opposed it, disliked it because it did not contain effectual provisions against the encroachments on particular rights, and those safeguards which they have been long accustomed to have interposed between them and the magistrate who exercises the sovereign power; nor ought we to consider them safe, while a great number of our fellow-citizens think these securities necessary.

It is a fortunate thing that the objection to the Government has been made on the ground I stated; because it will be practicable, on that ground, to obviate the objection, so far as to satisfy the public mind that their liberties will be perpetual, and this without endangering any part of the Constitution, which is considered as essential to the existence of the Government by those who promoted its adoption.

The amendments which have occurred to me, proper to be recommended by Congress to the State Legislatures, are these:

First. That there be prefixed to the Constitution a declaration, that all power is originally vested in, and consequently derived from, the people.

That Government is instituted and ought to be exercised for the benefit of the people; which consists in the enjoyment of life and liberty, with the right of acquiring and using property, and generally of pursuing and obtaining happiness and safety.

That the people have an indubitable, unalienable, and indefeasible right to reform or change their Government, whenever it be found adverse or inadequate to the purposes of its institution.

Secondly. That in article 1st, section 2, clause 3, these words be struck out, to wit: "The number of Representatives shall not exceed one for every thirty thousand, but each State shall have at least one Representative, and until such enumeration shall be made;" and that in place thereof be inserted these words, to wit: "After the first actual enumeration, there shall be one Representative for every thirty thousand, until the number amounts to _____, after which the proportion shall be so regulated by Congress, that the number shall never be less than ———, nor more than ———, but each State shall, after the first enumeration, have at least two Representatives; and prior thereto."

Thirdly. That in article 1st, section 6, clause 1, there be added to the end of the first sentence, these words, to wit: "But no law varying the compensation last ascertained shall operate before the next ensuing election of Representatives."

Fourthly. That in article 1st, section 9, between clauses 3 and 4, be inserted these clauses, to wit: The civil rights of none shall be abridged on account of religious belief or worship, nor shall any national religion be established, nor shall the full and equal rights of conscience be in any manner, or on any pretext, infringed.

The people shall not be deprived or abridged of their right to speak, to write, or to publish their sentiments; and the freedom of the press, as one of the great bulwarks of liberty, shall be inviolable.

The people shall not be restrained from peaceably assembling and consulting for their common good; nor from applying to the Legislature by petitions, or remonstrances, for redress of their grievances.

The right of the people to keep and bear arms shall not be infringed; a well armed and well regulated militia being the best security of a free country: but no person religiously scrupulous of bearing arms shall be compelled to render military service in person.

No soldiers shall in time of peace be quartered in any house without the consent of the owner; nor at any time, but in a manner warranted by law.

No person shall be subject, except in cases of impeachment, to more than one punishment or one trial for the same offence; nor shall be compelled to be a witness against himself; nor be deprived of life, liberty, or property, without due process of law; nor be obliged to relinquish his property, where it may be necessary for public use, without a just compensation.

Excessive bail shall not be required, nor excessive fines imposed, nor cruel and unusual punishments inflicted.

The rights of the people to be secured in their persons, their houses, their papers, and their other property, from all unreasonable searches and seizures, shall not be violated by warrants issued without probable cause, supported by oath or affirmation, or not particularly describing the places to be searched, or the persons or things to be seized.

In all criminal prosecutions, the accused shall enjoy the right to a speedy and public trial, to be informed of the cause and nature of the accusation, to be confronted with his accusers, and the witnesses against him; to have a compulsory process for obtaining witnesses in his favor; and to have the assistance of counsel for his defence.

The exceptions here or elsewhere in the Constitution, made in favor of particular rights, shall not be so construed as to diminish the just importance of other rights retained by the people, or as to enlarge the powers delegated by the Constitution; but either as actual limitations of such powers, or as inserted merely for greater caution.

Fifthly. That in article 1st, section 10, between clauses 1 and 2, be inserted this clause, to wit:

No State shall violate the equal rights of conscience, or the freedom of the press, or the trial by jury in criminal cases.

Sixthly. That, in article 3d, section 2, be annexed to the end of clause 2d, these words, to wit:

But no appeal to such court shall be allowed where the value in controversy shall not amount to _____ dollars: nor shall any fact triable by jury, according to the course of common law, be otherwise re-examinable than may consist with the principles of common law.

Seventhly. That in article 3d, section 2, the third clause be struck out, and in its place be inserted the clauses following, to wit:

The trial of all crimes (except in cases of impeachments, and cases arising in the land or naval forces, or the militia when on actual service, in time of war or public danger) shall be by an impartial jury of freeholders of the vicinage, with the requisite of unanimity for conviction, of the right of challenge, and other accustomed requisites; and in all crimes punishable with loss of life or member, presentment or indictment by a grand jury shall be an essential preliminary, provided that in cases of crimes committed within any county which may be in possession of an enemy, or in which a general insurrection may prevail, the trial may by law be authorized in some other county of the same State, as near as may be to the seat of the offence.

In cases of crimes committed not within any county, the trial may by law be in such county as the laws shall have prescribed. In suits at common law, between man and man, the trial by jury, as one of the best securities to the rights of the people, ought to remain inviolate.

Eighthly. That immediately after article 6th, be inserted, as article 7th, the clauses following, to wit:

The powers delegated by this Constitution are appropriated to the departments to which they are respectively distributed: so that the Legislative Department shall never exercise the powers vested in the Executive or Judicial, nor the Executive exercise the powers vested in the Legislative or Judicial, nor the Judicial exercise the powers vested in the Legislative or Executive Departments.

The powers not delegated by this Constitution, nor prohibited by it to the States, are reserved to the States respectively.

Ninthly. That article 7th be numbered as article 8th.

The first of these amendments relates to what may be called a bill of rights. I will own that I never considered this provision so essential to the Federal Constitution as to make it improper to ratify it, until such an amendment was added; at the same time, I always conceived, that in a certain form, and to a certain extent, such a provision was neither improper nor altogether useless. I am aware that a great number of the most respectable friends to the Government, and champions for republican liberty, have thought such a provision not only unnecessary, but even improper; nay, I believe some have gone so far as to think it even dangerous. Some policy has been made use of, perhaps, by gentlemen on both sides of the question: I acknowledge the ingenuity of those arguments which were drawn against the Constitution, by a comparison with the policy of Great Britain, in establishing a declaration of rights; but there is too great a difference in the case to warrant the comparison: therefore, the arguments drawn from that source were in a great measure inapplicable. In the declaration of rights which that country has established, the truth is, they have gone no farther than to raise a barrier against the power of the Crown; the power of the Legislature is left altogether indefinite. Although I know whenever the great rights, the trial by jury, freedom of the press, or liberty of conscience, come in question in that body, the invasion of them is resisted by able advocates, yet their Magna Charta does not contain any one provision for the security of those rights, respecting which the people of America are most alarmed. The freedom of the press and rights of conscience, those choicest privileges of the people, are unguarded in the British Constitution.

But although the case may be widely different, and it may not be thought necessary to provide limits for the legislative power in that country, yet a different opinion prevails in the United States. The people of many States have thought it necessary to raise barriers against power in all forms and departments of Government, and I am inclined to believe, if once bills of rights are established in all the States as well as the Federal Constitution, we shall find, that, although some of them are rather unimportant, yet, upon the whole, they will have a salutary tendency. It may be said, in some instances, they do no more than state the perfect equality of mankind. This, to be sure, is an absolute truth, yet it is not absolutely necessary to be inserted at the head of a Constitution.

In some instances they assert those rights which are exercised by the people in forming and establishing a plan of Government. In other instances, they specify those rights which are retained when particular powers are given up to be exercised by the Legislature. In other instances, they specify positive rights, which may seem to result from the nature of the compact. Trial by jury cannot be considered as a natural right, but a right resulting from a social compact, which regulates the action of the community, but is as essential to secure the liberty of the people as any one of the pre-existent rights of nature. In other instances, they lay down dogmatic maxims with respect to the construction of the Government; declaring that the Legislative, Executive, and Judicial branches, shall be kept separate and distinct. Perhaps the best way of securing this in practice is, to provide such checks as will prevent the encroachment of the one upon the other.

But, whatever may be the form which the several States have adopted in making declarations in favor of particular rights, the great object in view is to limit and qualify the powers of Government, by excepting out of the grant of power those cases in which the Government ought not to act, or to act only in a particular mode. They point these exceptions sometimes against the abuse of the Executive power, sometimes against the Legislative, and, in some cases, against the community itself; or, in other words, against the majority in favor of the minority.

In our Government it is, perhaps, less necessary to guard against the abuse in the Executive Department than any other; because it is not the stronger branch of the system, but the weaker. It therefore must be levelled against the Legislative, for it is the most powerful, and most likely to be abused, because it is under the least control. Hence, so far as a declaration of rights can tend to prevent the exercise of undue power, it cannot be doubted but such declaration is proper. But I confess that I do conceive, that in a Government modified like this of the United States, the great danger lies rather in the abuse of the community than in the Legislative body. The prescriptions in favor of liberty ought to be levelled against that quarter where the greatest danger lies, namely, that which possesses the highest prerogative of power. But this is not found in either the Executive or Legislative departments of Government, but in the body of the people, operating by the majority against the minority.

It may be thought that all paper barriers against the power of the community are too weak to be worthy of attention. I am sensible they are not so strong as to satisfy gentlemen of every description who have seen and examined thoroughly the texture of such a defence; yet, as they have a tendency to impress some degree of respect for them, to establish the public opinion in their favor, and rouse the attention of the whole community, it may be one means to control the majority from those acts to which they might be otherwise inclined.

It has been said, by way of objection to a bill of rights, by many respectable gentlemen out of doors, and I find opposition on the same principles likely to be made by gentlemen on this floor, that they are unnecessary articles of a Republican Government, upon the presumption that the people have those rights in their own hands, and that is the proper place for them to rest. It would be a sufficient answer to say, that this objection lies against such provisions under the State Governments, as well as under the General Government; and there are, I believe, but few gentlemen who are inclined to push their theory so far as to say that a declaration of rights in those cases is either ineffectual or improper. It has been said, that in the Federal

Government they are unnecessary, because the powers are enumerated, and it follows, that all that are not granted by the Constitution are retained; that the Constitution is a bill of powers, the great residuum being the rights of the people; and, therefore, a bill of rights cannot be so necessary as if the residuum was thrown into the hands of the Government. I admit that these arguments are not entirely without foundation; but they are not conclusive to the extent which has been supposed. It is true, the powers of the General Government are circumscribed, they are directed to particular objects; but even if Government keeps within those limits, it has certain discretionary powers with respect to the means, which may admit of abuse to a certain extent, in the same manner as the powers of the State Governments under their constitutions may to an indefinite extent; because in the Constitution of the United States, there is a clause granting to Congress the power to make all laws which shall be necessary and proper for carrying into execution all the powers vested in the Government of the United States, or in any department or officer thereof; this enables them to fulfil every purpose for which the Government was established. Now, may not laws be considered necessary and proper by Congress, (for it is for them to judge of the necessity and propriety to accomplish those special purposes which they may have in contemplation,) which laws in themselves are neither necessary nor proper; as well as improper laws could be enacted by the State Legislatures, for fulfilling the more extended objects of those Governments? I will state an instance, which I think in point, and proves that this might be the case. The General Government has a right to pass all laws which shall be necessary to collect its revenue; the means for enforcing the collection are within the direction of the Legislature: may not general warrants be considered necessary for this purpose, as well as for some purposes which it was supposed at the framing of their constitutions the State Governments had in view? If there was reason for restraining the State Governments from exercising this power, there is like reason for restraining the Federal Government.

It may be said, indeed it has been said, that a bill of rights is not necessary, because the establishment of this Government has not repealed those declarations of rights which are added to the several State constitutions; that those rights of the people which had been established by the most solemn act, could not be annihilated by a subsequent act of that people, who meant and declared at the head of the instrument, that they ordained and established a new system, for the express purpose of securing to themselves and posterity the liberties they had gained by an arduous conflict.

I admit the force of this observation, but I do not look upon it to be conclusive. In the first place, it is too uncertain ground to leave this provision upon, if a provision is at all necessary to secure rights so important as many of those I have mentioned are conceived to be, by the public in general, as well as those in particular who opposed the adoption of this Constitution. Besides, some States have no bills of rights, there are others provided with very defective ones, and there are others whose bills of rights are not only defective, but absolutely improper; instead of securing some in the full extent which republican principles would require, they limit them too much to agree with the common ideas of liberty.

It has been objected also against a bill of rights, that, by enumerating particular exceptions to the grant of power, it would disparage those rights which were not placed in that enumeration; and it might follow by implication, that those rights which were not singled out, were intended to be assigned into the hands of the General Government, and were consequently insecure. This is one of the most plausible arguments I have ever heard urged against the admission of a bill of rights into this system; but, I conceive, that it may be guarded against. I have attempted it, as gentlemen may see by turning to the last clause of the fourth resolution.

It has been said that it is unnecessary to load the Constitution with this provision, because it was not found effectual in the constitution of the particular States. It is true, there are a few particular States in which some of the most valuable articles have not, at one time or other, been violated; but it does not follow but they may have, to a certain degree, a salutary effect against the abuse of power. If they are incorporated into the Constitution, independent tribunals of justice will consider themselves in a peculiar manner the guardians of those rights; they will be an impenetrable bulwark against every assumption of power in the Legislative or Executive; they will be naturally led to resist every encroachment upon rights expressly stipulated for in the Constitution by the declaration of rights. Besides this security, there is a great probability that such a declaration in the federal system would be enforced; because the State Legislatures will jealously and closely watch the operations of this Government, and be able to resist with more effect every assumption of power, than any other power on earth can do; and the greatest opponents to a Federal Government admit the State Legislatures to be sure guardians of the people's liberty. I conclude, from this view of the subject, that it will be proper in itself, and highly politic, for the tranquillity of the public mind, and the stability of the Government, that we should offer something, in the form I have proposed, to be incorporated in the system of Government, as a declaration of the rights of the people.

In the next place, I wish to see that part of the Constitution revised which declares that the number of Representatives shall not exceed the proportion of one for every thirty thousand persons, and allows one Representative to every State which rates below that proportion. If we attend to the discussion of this subject, which has taken place in the State conventions, and even in the opinion of the friends to the Constitution, an alteration here is proper. It is the sense of the people of America, that the number of Representatives ought to be increased, but particularly that it should not be left in the discretion of the Government to diminish them, below that proportion, which certainly is in the power of the Legislature, as the Constitution now stands; and they may, as the population of the country increases, increase the House of Representatives to a very unwieldy degree. I confess I always thought this part of the Constitution defective, though not dangerous; and that it ought to be particularly attended to whenever Congress should go into the consideration of amendments.

There are several minor cases enumerated in my proposition, in which I wish also to see some alteration take place. That article which leaves it in the power of the Legislature to ascertain its own emolument, is one to which I allude. I do not believe this is a power which, in the ordinary course of Government, is likely to be abused. Perhaps of all the powers granted, it is least likely to abuse; but there is a seeming impropriety in leaving any set of men without control to put their hand into the public coffers, to take out money to put in their pockets; there is a seeming indecorum in such power, which leads me to propose a change. We have a guide to this alteration in several of the amendments which the different conventions have proposed. I have gone, therefore, so far as to fix it, that no law varying the compensation, shall operate until there is a change in the Legislature; in which case it cannot be for the particular benefit of those who are concerned in determining the value of the service.

I wish, also, in revising the Constitution, we may throw into that section, which interdicts the abuse of certain powers in the State Legislatures, some other provisions of equal, if not greater importance than those already made. The words, "No State shall pass any bill of attainder, *ex post facto* law," &c., were wise and proper restrictions in the Constitution. I think there is more danger of those powers being abused by the State Governments than by the Government of the United States. The same may be said of other powers which they possess, if not controlled by the general principle, that laws are unconstitutional which infringe the rights of the community. I should, therefore, wish to extend this interdiction, and add, as I have stated in the 5th resolution, that no State shall violate the equal right of conscience, freedom of the press, or trial by jury in criminal cases; because it is proper that every Government should be disarmed of powers which trench upon those particular rights. I know, in some of the State constitutions, the power of the Government is controlled by such a declaration; but others are not. I cannot see any reason against obtaining even a double security on those points; and nothing can give a more sincere proof of the attachment of those who opposed this Constitution to these great and important rights, than to see them join in obtaining the security I have now proposed; because it must be admitted, on all hands, that the State Governments are as liable to attack these invaluable privileges as the General Government is, and therefore ought to be as cautiously guarded against.

I think it will be proper, with respect to the judiciary powers, to satisfy the public mind on those points which I have mentioned. Great inconvenience has been apprehended to suitors from the distance they would be dragged to obtain justice in the Supreme Court of the United States, upon an appeal on an action for a small debt. To remedy this, declare that no appeal shall be made unless the matter in controversy amounts to a particular sum; this, with the regulations respecting jury trials in criminal cases, and suits at common law, it is to be hoped, will quiet and reconcile the minds of the people to that part of the Constitution.

I find, from looking into the amendments proposed by the State conventions, that several are particularly anxious that it should be declared in the Constitution, that the powers not therein delegated should be reserved to the several States. Perhaps other words may define this more precisely than the whole of the instrument now does. I admit they may be deemed unnecessary; but there can be no harm in making such a declaration, if gentlemen will allow that the fact is as stated. I am sure I understand it so, and do therefore propose it.

These are the points on which I wish to see a revision of the Constitution take place. How far they will accord with the sense of this body, I cannot take upon me absolutely to determine; but I believe every gentleman will readily admit that nothing is in contemplation, so far as I have mentioned, that can endanger the beauty of the Government in any one important feature, even in the eyes of its most sanguine admirers. I have proposed nothing that does not appear to me as proper in itself, or eligible as patronised by a respectable number of our fellow-citizens; and if we can make the Constitution better in the opinion of those who are opposed to it, without weakening its frame, or abridging its usefulness in the judgment of those who are attached to it, we act the part of wise and liberal men to make such alterations as shall produce that effect.

Having done what I conceived was my duty, in bringing before this House the subject of amendments, and also stated such as I wish for and approve, and offered the reasons which occurred to me in their support, I shall content myself, for the present, with moving "that a committee be appointed to consider of and report such amendments as ought to be proposed by Congress to the Legislatures of the States, to become, if ratified by three-fourths thereof, part of the Constitution of the United States." By agreeing to this motion, the subject may be going on in the committee, while other important business is proceeding to a conclusion in the House. I should advocate greater despatch in the business of amendments, if I were not convinced of the absolute necessity there is of pursuing the organization of the Government; because I think we should obtain the confidence of our fellow-citizens, in proportion as we fortify the rights of the people against the encroachments of the Government.

—Roger Sherman—
Draft Amendments
July 21–28, 1789

REPORT AS THEIR OPINION, that the following articles be proposed by Congress to the legislatures of the Several States to be adopted by them as amendments of the Constitution of the united States, and when ratified by the legislatures of three fourths (at least) of the Said States in the union, to become a part of the Constitution of the United States, pursuant to the fifth Article of the Said Constitution.

1 The powers of government being derived from the people, ought to be exercised for their benefit, and they have an inherent and unalienable right, to change or amend their political constitution, when ever they judge such change will advance their interest & happiness.

2 The people have certain natural rights which are retained by them when they enter into society, Such are the rights of conscience in matters of religion; of acquiring property, and of pursuing happiness & safety; of Speaking, writing and publishing their Sentiments with decency and freedom; of peaceably Assembling to consult their common good, and of applying to Government by petition or remonstrance for redress of grievances. Of these rights therefore they Shall not be deprived by the government of the united States.

3 No person shall be tried for any crime whereby he may incur loss of life or any infamous punishment, without Indictment by a grand Jury, nor be convicted but by the unanimous verdict of a Petit Jury of good and lawful men Freeholders of the vicinage or district where the trial shall be had.

4 After a census Shall be taken, each State Shall be allowed one representative for every thirty thousand Inhabitants of the description in the Second Section of the first Article of the Constitution, until the

whole number of representatives Shall amount to _____ but never to exceed _____.

5 The Militia shall be under the government of the laws of the respective States, when not in the actual Service of the united States, but Such rules as may be prescribed by Congress for their uniform organisation & discipline shall be observed in officering and training them. but military Service Shall not be required of persons religiously Scrupulous of bearing arms.

6 No Soldier Shall be quartered in any private house, in time of Peace, nor at any time, but by authority of law.

7 Excessive bail shall not be required, nor excessive fines imposed, nor cruel & unusual punishments be inflicted in any case.

8 Congress shall not have power to grant any monopoly or exclusive advantages of Commerce to any person or Company; nor to restrain the liberty of the Press.

9 In Suits at common law in courts acting under the authority of the united States, issues of fact Shall be tried by a Jury if either party, request it.

10 No law that Shall be passed for fixing a compensation for the members of Congress except the first Shall take effect until after the next election of representatives *posterior* to the passing Such law.

11 The legislative, executive and judiciary powers vested by the Constitution in the respective branches of the government of the united States, shall be exercised according to the distribution therein made, so that neither of said branches shall assume or exercise any of the powers peculiar to either of the other branches.

And the powers not delegated to the government of the united States by the Constitution, nor prohibited by it to the particular States, are retained by the States respectively. nor Shall any the exercise of power by the government of the united States the particular instances here in enumerated by way of caution be construed to imply the contrary.

Amendments Proposed by the House of Representatives

August 24, 1789

Congress of the United States
In the *House* of *Representatives,*

Monday, 24th August, 1789,

Resolved, by the Senate and House of Representatives of the United States of America in Congress assembled, two thirds of both Houses deeming it necessary, That the following Articles be proposed to the Legislatures of the several States, as Amendments to the Constitution of the United States, all or any of which Articles, when ratified by three fourths of the said Legislatures, to be valid to all intents and purposes as part of the said Constitution—Viz.

Articles in addition to, and amendment of, the Constitution of the United States of America, proposed by Congress, and ratified by the Legislatures of the several States, pursuant to the fifth Article of the original Constitution.

Article the First.

After the first enumeration, required by the first Article of the Constitution, there shall be one Representative for every thirty thousand, until the number shall amount to one hundred, after which the proportion shall be so regulated by Congress, that there shall be not less than one hundred Representatives, nor less than one Representative for every forty thousand persons, until the number of Representatives shall amount to two hundred, after which the proportion shall be so regulated by Congress, that there shall not be less than two hundred Representatives, nor less than one Representative for every fifty thousand persons.

Article the Second.

No law varying the compensation to the members of Congress, shall take effect, until an election of Representatives shall have intervened.

Article the Third.

Congress shall make no law establishing religion or prohibiting the free exercise thereof, nor shall the rights of Conscience be infringed.

Article the Fourth.

The Freedom of Speech, and of the Press, and the right of the People peaceably to assemble, and consult for their common good, and to apply to the Government for a redress of grievances, shall not be infringed.

Article the Fifth.

A well regulated militia, composed of the body of the People, being the best security of a free State, the right of the People to keep and bear arms, shall not be infringed, but no one religiously scrupulous of bearing arms, shall be compelled to render military service in person.

Article the Sixth.

No soldier shall, in time of peace, be quartered in any house without the consent of the owner, nor in time of war, but in a manner to be prescribed by law.

Article the Seventh.

The right of the People to be secure in their persons, houses, papers and effects, against unreasonable searches and seizures, shall not be violated, and no warrants shall issue, but upon probable cause supported by oath or affirmation, and particularly describing the place to be searched, and the persons or things to be seized.

Article the Eighth.

No person shall be subject, except in case of impeachment, to more than one trial, or one punishment for the same offense, nor shall be compelled in any criminal case, to be a witness against himself, nor be deprived of life, liberty or property, without due process of law; nor shall private property be taken for public use without just compensation.

Article the Ninth.

In all criminal prosecutions, the accused shall enjoy the right to a speedy and public trial, to be informed of the nature and cause of the accusation, to be confronted with the witnesses against him, to have compulsory process for obtaining witnesses in his favor, and to have the assistance of counsel for his defence.

Article the Tenth.

The trial of all crimes (except in cases of impeachment, and in cases arising in the land or naval forces, or in the militia when in actual service in time of War or public danger) shall be by an impartial Jury of the Vicinage, with the requisite of unanimity for conviction, the right of challenge, and other accostomed requisites; and no person shall be held to answer for a capital, or otherways infamous crime, unless on a presentment or indictment by a Grand Jury; but if a crime be committed in a place in the possession of an enemy, or in which an insurrection may prevail, the indictment and trial may by law be authorised in some other place within the same State.

Article the Eleventh.

No appeal to the Supreme Court of the United States, shall be allowed, where the value in controversy shall not amount to one thousand dollars, nor shall any fact, triable by a Jury according to the course of the common law, be otherwise re-examinable, than according to the rules of common law.

Article the Twelfth.

In suits at common law, the right of trial by Jury shall be preserved.

Article the Thirteenth.

Excessive bail shall not be required, nor excessive fines imposed, nor cruel and unusual punishments inflicted.

Article the Fourteenth.

No State shall infringe the right of trial by Jury in criminal cases, nor the rights of conscience, nor the freedom of speech, or of the press.

Article the Fifteenth.

The enumeration in the Constitution of certain rights, shall not be construed to deny or disparage others retained by the people.

Article the Sixteenth.

The powers delegated by the Constitution to the government of the United States, shall be exercised as therein appropriated, so that the Legislative shall never exercise the powers vested in the Executive or Judicial; nor the Executive the powers vested in the Legislative or Judicial; nor the Judicial the powers vested in the Legislative or Executive.

Article the Seventeenth.

The powers not delegated by the Constitution, nor prohibited by it, to the States, are reserved to the States respectively.

Teste,
John Beckley, Clerk
In Senate, *August* 25, 1789

Read and ordered to be printed for the consideration of the Senate.

Attest, Samuel A. Otis, Secretary

New-York, Printed by T. Greenleaf, near the Coffee-House.

Amendments Proposed by the Senate
September 14, 1789

The Conventions of a Number of the States having, at the Time of their adopting the Constitution, expressed a Desire, in Order to prevent misconstruction or abuse of its Powers, that further declaratory and restrictive Clauses should be added: And as extending the Ground of public Confidence in the Government, will best insure the beneficent ends of its Institution—

Resolved, by the Senate and House of Representatives of the United States of America in Congress assembled, two thirds of both Houses concurring, That the following articles be proposed to the Legislatures of the several States, as amendments to the Constitution of the United States, all or any of which articles, when ratified by three fourths of the said Legislatures, to be valid to all intents and purposes, as part of the said Constitution—Viz.

Articles in addition to, and amendment of, the Constitution of the United States of America, proposed by Congress, and ratified by the Legislatures of the several States, pursuant to the fifth Article of the original Constitution.

Article the First.

After the first enumeration, required by the first article of the Constitution, there shall be one Representative for every thirty thousand, until the number shall amount to one hundred; to which number one Representative shall be added for every subsequent increase of forty thousand, until the Representatives shall amount to two hundred, to wh[ich numbe]r one Representative shall be added f[or every subsequent increase of six]ty thou[sand] persons.

Article the Second.

No law, varying the compensation for the services of the Senators and Representatives, shall take effect, until an election of Representatives shall have intervened.

Article the Third.

Congress shall make no law establishing articles of faith, or a mode of worship, or prohibiting the free exercise of religion, or abridging the freedom of speech, or of the press, or the right of the people peaceably to assemble, and to petition to the government for a redress of grievances.

Article the Fourth.

A well regulated militia, being necessary to the security of a free State, the right of the people to keep and bear arms, shall not be infringed.

ARTICLE THE FIFTH.

No soldier shall, in time of peace, be quartered in any house, without the consent of the owner, nor in time of war, but in a manner to be prescribed by law.

ARTICLE THE SIXTH.

The right of the people to be secure in their persons, houses, papers, and effects, against unreasonable searches and seizures, shall not be violated, and no warrants shall issue, but upon probable cause, supported by oath or affirmation, and particularly describing the place to be searched, and the persons or things to be seized.

ARTICLE THE SEVENTH.

No person shall be held to answer for a capital, or otherwise infamous crime, unless on a presentment or indictment of a Grand Jury, except in cases arising in the land or naval forces, or in the militia, when in actual service in time of war or public danger; nor shall any person be subject for the same offence to be twice put in jeopardy of life or limb; nor shall be compelled in any criminal case, to be a witness against himself, nor be deprived of life, liberty or property, without due process of law; nor shall private property be taken for public use without just compensation.

ARTICLE THE EIGHTH.

In all criminal prosecutions, the accused shall enjoy the right to a speedy and public trial, to be informed of the nature and cause of the accusation, to be confronted with the witnesses against him, to have compulsory process for obtaining witnesses in his favour, and to have the assistance of counsel for his defence.

ARTICLE THE NINTH.

In suits at common law, where the value in controversy shall exceed twenty dollars, the right of trial by Jury shall be preserved, and no fact, tried by a Jury, shall be otherwise re-examined in any court of the United States, than according to the rules of the common law.

ARTICLE THE TENTH.

Excessive bail shall not be required, nor excessive fines imposed, nor cruel and unusual punishments inflicted.

Article the Eleventh.

The en[umeration in the Constitution of certain] rights, shall not be construed to deny or disparage others retained by the people.

Article the Twelfth.

The powers not delegated to the United States by the Constitution, nor prohibited by it to the States, are reserved to the States respectively, or to the people.

New-York, printed by Thomas Greenleaf.

Amendments Proposed to the States
September 28, 1789

The Conventions of a number of the States, having at the time of their adopting the Constitution, expressed a desire, in order to prevent misconstruction or abuse of its powers, that further declaratory and restrictive clauses should be added: And as extending the ground of public confidence in the Government, will best ensure the benificent ends of its institution.

Resolved by the Senate and House of Representatives of the United States of America, in Congress assembled, two thirds of both Houses concurring, that the following Articles be proposed to the Legislatures of the several States, as amendments to the Constitution of the United States, all or any of which Articles, when ratified by three fourths of the said Legislatures, to be valid to all intents and purposes, as part of the said Constitution; vizt.

Articles in addition to, and amendment of the Constitution of the United States of America, proposed by Congress, and ratified by the Legislatures of the several States, pursuant to the fifth Article of the original Constitution.

Article the First.

After the first enumeration required by the first Article of the Constitution, there shall be one Representative for every thirty thousand, until the number shall amount to one hundred, after which, the proportion shall be so regulated by Congress, that there shall be not less than one hundred Representatives, nor less than one Representative for every forty thousand persons, until the number of Representatives shall amount to two hundred, after which the proportion shall be so regulated by Congress, that there shall not be less than two hundred Representatives, nor more than one Representative for every fifty thousand persons.

ARTICLE THE SECOND.

No law, varying the compensation for the services of the Senators and Representatives, shall take effect, until an election of Representatives shall have intervened.

ARTICLE THE THIRD.

Congress shall make no law respecting an establishment of religion, or prohibiting the free exercise thereof; or abridging the freedom of speech, or of the press, or the right of the people peaceably to assemble, and to petition the Government for a redress of grievances.

ARTICLE THE FOURTH.

A well regulated militia, being necessary to the security of a free State, the right of the people to keep and bear arms, shall not be infringed.

ARTICLE THE FIFTH.

No Soldier shall, in time of peace be quartered in any House, without the consent of the owner, nor in time of war, but in a manner to be prescribed by law.

ARTICLE THE SIXTH.

The right of the people to be secure in their persons, houses, papers, and effects, against unreasonable searches and seizures, shall not be violated, and no warrants shall issue, but upon probable cause, supported by oath or affirmation, and particularly describing the place to be searched and the persons or things to be seized.

ARTICLE THE SEVENTH.

No person shall be held to answer for a capital, or otherwise infamous crime, unless on a presentment or indictment of [a] Grand

Jury, except in cases arising in the land or naval forces, or in the militia, when in actual service in time of war or public danger; nor shall any person be subject for the same offence to be twice put in jeopardy of life or limb; nor shall be compelled in any criminal case to be a witness against himself, nor be deprived of life, liberty, or property, without due process of law; nor shall private property be taken for public use, without just compensation.

ARTICLE THE EIGHTH.

In all criminal prosecutions, the accused shall enjoy the right to a speedy and public trial, by an impartial jury of the State and district wherein the crime shall have been committed; which district shall have been previously ascertained by law, and to be informed of the nature and cause of the accusation; to be confronted with the witnesses against him; to have compulsory process for obtaining witnesses in his favor, and to have the assistance of counsel for his defence.

ARTICLE THE NINTH.

In suits at common law, where the value in controversy shall exceed twenty dollars, the right of trial by jury shall be preserved, and no fact tried by a jury, shall be otherwise re-examined in any Court of the United States, than according to the rules of the common law.

ARTICLE THE TENTH.

Excessive bail shall not be required, nor excessive fines imposed, nor cruel and unusual punishments inflicted.

ARTICLE THE ELEVENTH.

The enumeration in the Constitution, of certain rights, shall not be construed to deny or disparage others retained by the people.

ARTICLE THE TWELFTH.

The powers not delegated to the United States by the Constitution, nor prohibited by it to the States, are reserved to the States respectively, or to the people.

FREDERICK AUGUSTUS MUHLENBERG
Speaker of the House of Representatives

The Bill of Rights, as Ratified by the States
December 15, 1791

Amendment I

Congress shall make no law respecting an establishment of religion, or prohibiting the free exercise thereof; or abridging the freedom of speech, or of the press; or the right of the people peaceably to assemble, and to petition the government for a redress of grievances.

Amendment II

A well regulated militia, being necessary to the security of a free state, the right of the people to keep and bear arms, shall not be infringed.

Amendment III

No soldier shall, in time of peace be quartered in any house, without the consent of the owner, nor in time of war, but in a manner to be prescribed by law.

Amendment IV

The right of the people to be secure in their persons, houses, papers, and effects, against unreasonable searches and seizures, shall not be violated, and no warrants shall issue, but upon probable cause, supported by oath or affirmation, and particularly describing the place to be searched, and the persons or things to be seized.

Amendment V

No person shall be held to answer for a capital, or otherwise infamous crime, unless on a presentment or indictment of a grand jury, except in cases arising in the land or naval forces, or in the militia, when in actual service in time of war or public danger; nor shall any person be subject for the same offense to be twice put in jeopardy of life or limb; nor shall be compelled in any criminal case to be a witness against himself, nor be deprived of life, liberty, or property, without due process of law; nor shall private property be taken for public use, without just compensation.

Amendment VI

In all criminal prosecutions, the accused shall enjoy the right to a speedy and public trial, by an impartial jury of the state and district wherein the crime shall have been committed, which district shall have been previously ascertained by law, and to be informed of the nature and cause of the accusation; to be confronted with the witnesses against him; to have compulsory process for obtaining witnesses in his favor, and to have the assistance of counsel for his defense.

Amendment VII

In suits at common law, where the value in controversy shall exceed twenty dollars, the right of trial by jury shall be preserved, and no fact tried by a jury, shall be otherwise reexamined in any court of the United States, than according to the rules of the common law.

Amendment VIII

Excessive bail shall not be required, nor excessive fines imposed, nor cruel and unusual punishments inflicted.

Amendment IX

The enumeration in the Constitution, of certain rights, shall not be construed to deny or disparage others retained by the people.

Amendment X

The powers not delegated to the United States by the Constitution, nor prohibited by it to the states, are reserved to the states respectively, or to the people.

For Further Reading

Bailyn, Bernard. *The Ideological Origins of the American Revolution.* Enlarged edition. Cambridge, MA: Harvard University Press, 1992. Pulitzer Prize–winning study of the sources of American political ideas and their impact on the Revolutionary crisis.

Berkin, Carol. *A Brilliant Solution: Inventing the American Constitution.* New York: Harcourt, 1992. Snappy study of the framing and ratification of the Constitution.

Bowen, Catherine Drinker. *Miracle at Philadelphia: The Story of the Constitutional Convention, May to September 1787.* Boston: Little, Brown, 1966. The best-known narrative account of the framing of the Constitution.

Ferling, John. *A Leap in the Dark: The Struggle to Create the American Republic.* New York: Oxford University Press, 2003. Broad survey of the Revolutionary era, from the Seven Years' War until Jefferson's election as president in 1801.

Fischer, David Hackett. *Paul Revere's Ride.* New York: Oxford University Press, 1994. Sparkling narrative of the outbreak of the Revolutionary War.

Goldwin, Robert A. *From Parchment to Power: How James Madison Used the Bill of Rights to Save the Constitution.* Washington, DC: AEI Press, 1997. Traces Madison's role in making sure the Constitution was amended to satisfy Anti-Federalist arguments about a bill of rights.

Jensen, Merrill. *The New Nation: A History of the United States during the Confederation, 1781–1789.* New York: Alfred A. Knopf, 1950. Standard account of the 1780s, written from the perspective of the Progressive historians.

Maier, Pauline. *American Scripture: Making the Declaration of Independence.* New York: Alfred A. Knopf, 1997. Close study of the drafting of the Declaration in its immediate political context.

McDonald, Forrest. *Novus Ordo Seclorum: The Intellectual Origins of the Constitution.* Lawrence: University Press of Kansas, 1985.

Examines the impact of eighteenth-century ideas on the framing of the Constitution.

Middlekauff, Robert. *The Glorious Cause: The American Revolution, 1763–1789.* Revised and expanded edition. New York: Oxford University Press, 2005. Balanced interpretive survey of the Revolution, giving due attention to both its political and military aspects.

Morgan, Edmund Sears, and Helen M. Morgan. *The Stamp Act Crisis: Prologue to Revolution.* Revised edition. New York: Collier, 1963. A work that launched the modern reinterpretation of the Revolution, emphasizing the depth of the colonists' commitment to their political ideas.

Morris, Richard Brandon. *The Forging of the Union, 1781–1789.* New York: Harper and Row, 1987. Part of the famous New American Nation series.

Norton, Mary Beth. *Liberty's Daughters: The Revolutionary Experience of American Women, 1750–1800.* Second edition. Ithaca, NY: Cornell University Press, 1996. The most illuminating study of the impact of the Revolution on women's lives and place within society.

Rakove, Jack N. *Original Meanings: Politics and Ideas in the Making of the Constitution.* New York: Alfred A. Knopf, 1996. Pulitzer Prize–winning account of the adoption of the Constitution, framed to address the modern debate over interpreting it according to its "original intent."

Royster, Charles A. *A Revolutionary People at War: The Continental Army and American Character, 1775–1783.* Chapel Hill: University of North Carolina Press for the Institute of Early American History and Culture, 1979. Provocative interpretation of the meaning of the war to soldiers and civilians.

Wood, Gordon S. *The American Revolution: A History.* New York: Modern Library, 2002. Best short survey of the Revolution.

———. *The Creation of the American Republic, 1776–1787.* Chapel Hill: University of North Carolina Press for the Institute of Early American History and Culture, 1969. Brilliant path-breaking study of the constitutional innovations that began with independence and culminated in the federal Constitution.

List of Sources

Note: In compiling this volume, the editors have altered or removed many of the editorial interventions made in the sources listed below.

THE IMPERIAL DISPUTE

Page 5–Hutchinson, The Address of the Governor. Reprinted from: Reid, John P., ed. *The briefs of the American Revolution: constitutional arguments between Thomas Hutchinson, Governor of Massachusetts Bay, and James Bowdoin for the Council and John Adams for the House of Representatives.* New York: New York University Press, 1981. **Page 12**–Franklin, *Rules by Which a Great Empire May Be Reduced to a Small One.* Reprinted from: Franklin, Benjamin. *Benjamin Franklin, Writings.* Edited by J.A. Leo Lemay. New York: Library of America, 1987. **Page 20**–Jefferson, *A Summary View of the Rights of British America.* Reprinted from: Jefferson, Thomas. *The Papers of Thomas Jefferson.* Vol. 1. Edited by Julian P. Boyd et al. Princeton: Princeton University Press, 1950.

FIRST CONTINENTAL CONGRESS

Page 39–Declaration and Resolves. Reprinted from: Ford, Worthington Chauncey, ed. *Journals of the Continental Congress.* Vol. 1. Washington, D.C.: Government Printing Office, 1904. **Page 44**–Association. Reprinted from: Ford, *Journals*, vol. 1.

SECOND CONTINENTAL CONGRESS

Page 53–Declaration on Causes and Necessity of Taking Arms. Reprinted from: Ford, Worthington Chauncey, ed. *Journals of the Continental Congress.* Vol. 2. Washington, D.C.: Government Printing Office, 1905. **Page 59**–Franklin, Plan of Confederation. Reprinted from: Ford, *Journals*, vol. 2.

"REMEMBER THE LADIES"

Page 67–Adams, Abigail, Letter to John Adams. Reprinted from: Butterfield, L.H. et al., eds. *Adams Family Correspondence.* Vol. 1. Cambridge: The Belknap Press of Harvard University Press, 1963. **Page 70**–Adams, John, Letter to Abigail Adams. Reprinted from: Butterfield, *Adams*, vol. 1. **Page 72**–Adams, John, Letter to James Sullivan. Reprinted from: Adams, John. *Papers of John Adams.* Vol. 4. Edited by Robert J. Taylor et al. Cambridge: The Belknap Press of Harvard University Press, 1977.

INVENTING A REPUBLIC

Page 79–Adams, John, *Thoughts on Government.* Reprinted from: Adams, *Papers*, vol. 4. **Page 87**–Resolutions of the Continental Congress (excerpt), May 10, 1776. Reprinted from: Ford, Worthington Chauncey, ed. *Journals of the Continental Congress.* Vol. 4. Washington, D.C.: Government Printing Office, 1906. **Page 87**–Resolutions of the Continental Congress (excerpt), May 15, 1776. Reprinted from: Ford, *Journals*, vol. 4. **Page 88**–Virginia Declaration of Rights. Reprinted from: Mason, George. *The Papers of George Mason.* Vol. 1. Edited by Robert A. Rutland. Chapel Hill: University of North Carolina Press, 1970. **Page 90**–Virginia Constitution. Reprinted from: Jefferson, Thomas. *The Papers of Thomas Jefferson.* Edited by Julian P. Boyd et al. Princeton: Princeton University Press, 1950. **Page 97**–Pennsylvania Constitution. Reprinted from: Thorpe, Francis Newton, ed. *The Federal and State Constitutions.* Vol. 5. Washington: Government

Printing Office, 1909. **Page 113**–Concord Town Meeting Resolutions. Reprinted from: Handlin, Mary and Oscar Handlin, eds. *The Popular Sources of Political Authority: Documents on the Massachusetts Constitution of 1780.* Cambridge: Belknap Press of Harvard University Press, 1966.

INDEPENDENCE
Page 117–Jefferson, Notes of Proceedings in Congress, June 7–28, 1776. Reprinted from: Smith, Paul H. et al., eds. *Letters of Delegates to Congress, 1774–1789.* Vol. 4. Washington, D.C.: Library of Congress, 1979. **Page 122**–Jefferson, Notes of Proceedings in Congress, July 1–4, 1776. Reprinted from: Smith, *Letters,* vol. 4. **Page 129**–Dickinson, Notes for a Speech Opposing Independence. Reprinted from: Smith, *Letters,* vol. 4. **Page 134**–Adams, John, Letter to Abigail Adams. Reprinted from: Smith, *Letters,* vol. 4. **Page 136**–The Declaration of Independence. Reprinted from: Tansill, Charles C., ed. *Documents Illustrative of the Formation of the Union of the American States.* Washington, D.C.: Government Printing Office, 1927.

DRAFTING THE ARTICLES OF CONFEDERATION
Page 145–Jefferson, Notes of Proceedings in Congress, July 12–August 1, 1776. Reprinted from: Smith, *Letters,* vol. 4. **Page 154**–Articles as Approved, August 20, 1776. Reprinted from: Ford, Worthington Chauncey, ed. *Journals of the Continental Congress.* Vol. 5. Washington, D.C.: Government Printing Office, 1906. **Page 160**–Articles as Approved, November 15, 1777. Reprinted from: Ford, Worthington Chauncey, ed. *Journals of the Continental Congress.* Vol. 9. Washington, D.C.: Government Printing Office, 1907.

REFORMING THE ARTICLES OF CONFEDERATION
Page 173–Schuyler, Letter to Pierre Van Cortlandt and Evert Bancker. Reprinted from: Burnett, Edmund C., ed. *Letters of Members of the Continental Congress.* Vol. 5. Washington, D.C.: Carnegie Institute of Washington, 1931. **Page 176**–Hamiton, Letter to James Duane. Reprinted from: Hamilton, Alexander. *The Papers of Alexander Hamilton.* Vol. 2. Edited by Harold C. Syrett et al. New York: Columbia University Press, 1961. **Page 194**–Impost Amendment Proposed by Congress. Reprinted from: Ford, Worthington Chauncey, ed. *Journals of the Continental Congress.* Vol. 19. Washington, D.C.: Government Printing Office, 1912. **Page 194**–Morris, Report on Public Credit. Reprinted from: Morris, Robert. *The Papers of Robert Morris.* Vol. 6. Edited by John Catanzariti et al. Pittsburgh: University of Pittsburgh Press, 1984. **Page 213**–Revenue Amendments Proposed by Congress. Reprinted from: Ford, *Journals,* vol. 19. **Page 217**–Commercial Amendments Proposed by Congress. Reprinted from: Ford, Worthington Chauncey, ed. *Journals of the Continental Congress.* Vol. 26. Washington, D.C.: Government Printing Office, 1928. **Page 218**–Amendments Considered by Congress. Reprinted from: Ford, Worthington Chauncey, ed. *Journals of the Continental Congress.* Vol. 31.Washington, D.C.: Government Printing Office, 1934. **Page 223**–The Northwest Ordinance. Reprinted from: Tansill, *Documents.*

GEORGE WASHINGTON
Page 233–Washington, Speech to the Officers of the Army. Reprinted from: Washington, George. *The Writings of George Washington from the Original Manuscript Sources, 1745–1799.* Vol. 26. Edited by John C. Fitzpatrick. Washington, D.C.: Government Printing Office, 1938. **Page 237**–Shaw, Letter to the Rev. Eliot. Reprinted from: Shaw, Samuel. *The Journals of Major Samuel Shaw.* Boston: W.M. Crosby and H.P. Nichols, 1847. **Page 240**–Washington, Circular to the State Governments. Reprinted from:

Washington, *Writings*, vol. 26. **Page 250**–Washington, Letter to James Duane. Reprinted from: Washington, George. *The Writings of George Washington from the Original Manuscript Sources, 1745–1799*. Vol. 27. Edited by John C. Fitzpatrick. Washington, D.C.: Government Printing Office, 1938. **Page 256**–Washington, Farewell Address to the Armies of the United States. Reprinted from: Washington, *Writings*, vol. 27.

POLITICAL REFORMERS

Page 263–Jefferson, Excerpts from *Notes on the States of Virginia*. Reprinted from: Jefferson, Thomas. *Notes on the State of Virginia*. New York: Harper & Row, 1964. **Page 294**–Madison, *A Memorial and Remonstrance against Religious Assessments*. Reprinted from: Madison, James. *Religious Freedoms, a Memorial and Remonstrance*. Boston: Lincoln & Edmands, 1819. **Page 301**–Jefferson, Virginia Statute for Religious Freedom. Reprinted from: Peterson, Merrill D. and Robert C. Vaughan, eds. *The Virginia Statute for Religious Freedom: Its Evolution and Consequences in American History*. Cambridge: Cambridge University Press, 1988.

THE ROAD TO PHILADELPHIA

Page 307–Madison, Letter to James Monroe. Reprinted from: Madison, James. *The Writings of James Madison*. Vol. 2. Edited by Gaillard Hunt. New York: G.P. Putnam's Sons, 1901. **Page 308**–Rush, Address to the People of the United States (excerpt). Reprinted from: Kaminski, John P. et al, eds. *The Documentary History of the Ratification of the Constitution*. Vol. 13. Madison: State Historical Society of Wisconsin, 2000. **Page 313**–Hamilton, Address of the Annapolis Convention. Reprinted from: Hamilton, Alexander. *The Works of Alexander Hamilton*. Vol. 1. Edited by Henry Cabot Lodge. New York: G.P. Putnam's Sons, 1904. **Page 316**–Resolutions of Congress. Reprinted from: Kaminski, *Documentary*, vol. 13. **Page 317**–Madison, Vices of the Political System of the United States. Reprinted from: Madison, *Writings*, vol. 2. **Page 324**–Madison, Letter to George Washington. Reprinted from: Madison, *Writings*, vol. 2.

RIVAL VISIONS OF UNION

Page 335–Randolph Introduces the Virginia Plan. Reprinted from: Farrand, Max, ed. *The Records of the Federal Convention of 1787*. Vol. 1. New Haven: Yale University Press, 1911. **Page 339**–Paterson Introduces the New Jersey Plan. Reprinted from: Farrand, *Records*, vol. 1. **Page 343**–Hamilton Discusses the Two Proposed Plans. Reprinted from: Farrand, *Records*, vol. 1. **Page 352**–Madison Discusses the Plans. Reprinted from: Farrand, *Records*, vol. 1. **Page 359**–Ellsworth Discusses Questions of Representation. Reprinted from: Farrand, *Records*, vol. 1. **Page 361**–Wilson, Ellsworth, and Madison Debate. Reprinted from: Farrand, *Records*, vol. 1. **Page 366**–General Debate. Reprinted from: Farrand, Max, ed. *The Records of the Federal Convention of 1787*. Vol. 2. New Haven: Yale University Press, 1911.

GETTING DOWN TO DETAILS

Page 371–Resolutions Adapted by Convention. Reprinted from: Farrand, *Records*, vol. 2. **Page 374**–Draft Constitution. Reprinted from: Farrand, *Records*, vol. 2. **Page 386**–Debate on War Power. Reprinted from: Farrand, *Records*, vol. 2. **Page 387**–Debate on Treaty Power. Reprinted from: Farrand, *Records*, vol. 2. **Page 390**–Objections of Randolph, Mason, and Gerry. Reprinted from: Farrand, *Records*, vol. 2. **Page 392**–Franklin, Concluding Appeal for Unanimity. Reprinted from: Farrand, *Records*, vol. 2.

THE CONSTITUTION

Page 397–Constitution of the United States. Reprinted from: Farrand, *Records*, vol. 2.

Page 410–Concluding Resolution for Ratification. Reprinted from: Farrand, *Records*, vol. 2. **Page 411**–Washington, Letter of Conveyance to Congress. Reprinted from: Farrand, *Records*, vol. 2.

A More Perfect Union

Page 415–Madison, Letter to George Washington. Reprinted from: Kaminski, *Documentary*, vol. 13. **Page 417**–Hamilton, Conjectures About the Constitution. Reprinted from: Kaminski, *Documentary*, vol. 13. **Page 420**–Lee, Letter to George Mason. Reprinted from: Kaminski, *Documentary*, vol. 13. **Page 422**–Wilson, Speech on the Constitution. Reprinted from: Kaminski, *Documentary*, vol. 13. **Page 428**–Mason, Objections to the Constitution. Reprinted from: Kaminski, *Documentary*, vol. 13.

The Case Against the Constitution

Page 435–Smith, *Letters from the Federal Farmer* I–V. Reprinted from: Storing, Herbert J., ed. *The Complete Anti-Federalist*. Vol. 2. Chicago: University of Chicago Press, 1981.

Publius Replies

Pages 481, 485, 492, 497, 505, 513, 519, 524, 529, 537–Hamilton and Madison *The Federalist*. All selections reprinted from: Hamilton, Alexander, James Madison, and John Jay. *The Federalist*. Edited by George W. Carey and James McClellan. Indianapolis: Liberty Fund, 2001.

The Problem of Declaring Rights

Page 549, 561, 565, 566, 568, 573, 576, 578, 584–Letters between Thomas Jefferson and James Madison. All selections reprinted from: Jefferson, Thomas and James Madison. *The Republic of Letters: The Correspondence between Thomas Jefferson and James Madison 1776–1826*. Edited by James Morton Smith. New York: W.W. Norton & Company, 1995.

Proposing Amendments

Page 591–Massachusetts Ratification Convention. Reprinted from: Kaminski, John P. et al., eds. *The Documentary History of the Ratification of the Constitution*. Vol. 6. Madison: State Historical Society of Wisconsin, 2000. **Page 594**–Virginia Ratification Convention. Reprinted from: Kaminski, John P. et al., eds. *The Documentary History of the Ratification of the Constitution*. Vol. 10. Madison: State Historical Society of Wisconsin, 2000. **Page 600**–New York Ratification Convention. Reprinted from: De Pauw, Linda Grant. *The Eleventh Pillar*. Ithaca: Cornell Univeristy Press, 1966.

Framing the Bill of Rights

Page 613–Madison, Speech Introducing Amendments in the House of Representatives. Reprinted from: Madison, James. *The Writings of James Madison*. Vol. 5. Edited by Gaillard Hunt. New York: G.P. Putnam's Sons, 1904. **Page 627**–Sherman, Draft Amendments. Reprinted from: Veit, Helen E. et al., eds. *Creating the Bill of Rights*. Baltimore: The Johns Hopkins University Press, 1991. **Page 629**–Amendments Proposed by the House of Representatives. Reprinted from: Veit et al., *Creating*. **Page 632**–Amendments Proposed by the Senate. Reprinted from: Veit et al., *Creating*. **Page 635**–Amendments Proposed to the States. Reprinted from: Veit et al., *Creating*. **Page 638**–The Bill of Rights, as Ratified by the States. Reprinted from: Tansill, *Documents*.